W9-CZH-553

PENGUIN BOOKS

THE PORTABLE OSCAR WILDE

Each volume in The Viking Portable Library either presents a representative selection from the works of a single outstanding writer or offers a comprehensive anthology on a special subject. Averaging 700 pages in length and designed for compactness and readability, these books fill a need not met by other compilations. All are edited by distinguished authorities, who have written introductory essays and included much other helpful material.

"The Viking Portables have done more for good reading and good writers than anything that has come along since I can remember."   —Arthur Mizener

Born in 1892, Richard Aldington was one of the most outstanding of the London Imagist poets in the years before and during the First World War. His poems began to appear in 1909, and in 1913 he married Hilda Doolittle (H.D.) and became assistant editor of the Imagist magazine the *Egoist*. His first book, *Images Old and New,* was published in 1915; but his literary career was interrupted by military service on the Continent—an experience that left him in a state of shell-shock and severe neurosis. While regaining his health he worked as a translator and journalist, then turned to writing such powerful anti-war novels as *Death of a Hero* (1929) and *The Colonel's Daughter* (1931). After World War II, when he had emigrated to the United States, he published acclaimed, though controversial, biographies, among them, *Wellington* (1946); *Portrait of a Genius, But . . .* (1950), about D.H. Lawrence; and *Lawrence of Arabia* (1955). He died in 1962.

The Portable

Oscar Wilde

Selected and Edited
by
Richard Aldington

PENGUIN BOOKS

Penguin Books Ltd, Harmondsworth,
Middlesex, England
Penguin Books, 625 Madison Avenue,
New York, New York 10022, U.S.A.
Penguin Books Australia Ltd, Ringwood,
Victoria, Australia
Penguin Books Canada Limited, 2801 John Street,
Markham, Ontario, Canada L3R 1B4
Penguin Books (N.Z.) Ltd, 182–190 Wairau Road,
Auckland 10, New Zealand

First published in the United States of America
by The Viking Press 1946
Paperbound edition published 1955
Reprinted 1957, 1959, 1960, 1962, 1963, 1965, 1966, 1967,
1969 (twice), 1971 (twice), 1972, 1973, 1974, 1975, 1976
Published in Penguin Books 1977
Reprinted 1978 (twice), 1979

LIBRARY OF CONGRESS CATALOGING IN PUBLICATION DATA
Wilde, Oscar, 1854–1900.
The portable Oscar Wilde.
Reprint of the 1946 ed. published by The Viking Press,
New York, in series: The Viking portable library.
I. Aldington, Richard, 1892–1962. II. Title.
PR5811.A4 1977   828'.8'09   77–1710
ISBN 0 14 015.016 1

Printed in the United States of America
by Kingsport Press, Inc., Kingsport, Tennessee
Set in Linotype Caledonia

Contents

▼

CONTENTS

Introduction

By Richard Aldington

I

ALMOST everything that could be said about Oscar Wilde has been said already (*"tout a été dit"*), including much that had better have been left unsaid. But, as is the way with us human beings and our "points of view," this mass of printed material is more remarkable for diversity than lucidity. Opinions of Wilde as human being run from the savage contempt of Mr. Justice Wills (sentencing him to virtual death) to the hero-worship of Sherard and Ross; and the estimates of his writings occupy many varying positions between the one extreme, that he was a ridiculous plagiarist and poseur, and the other extreme, that he was the greatest English (pardon! Irish) writer of the nineteenth century.

So far as I recollect, the personal reminiscences of Wilde agree that his personality was more important than his talents, and his conversation more fascinating than his writings. This is not a hopeful thought for posterity, which cannot have the privilege of listening to "dear Oscar's" talk which, according to Mr. E.F. Benson, was "like to the play of a sunlit fountain." Even Mr. G.B. Shaw, who writes about Wilde with prejudice (which is not surprising) and obtuseness (which is most surprising) admits the brilliance of

Wilde's talk. But that is about as far as agreement goes; and seldom has the old tag about so many men, so many opinions, been so fully justified as it is by the various witnesses to Wilde's life and character.

At this date and distance we have always to keep in mind that for the contemporary world of newspaper readers Wilde began by being ridiculous as Bunthorne (in Gilbert's *Patience*) and ended up by being execrated as a kind of fatuously impudent would-be Nero who had sprawled full length in the gutter, where the amiable "world" took good care he should remain. So extreme was the violently disproportionate storm of "morality" against the unfortunate Wilde that only the courageous dared, for some years, to say anything decent about him. So far as the "normal" men are concerned the attitude may be not too unfairly summarised as: "Of course, I never took Wilde seriously, and for heaven's sake don't think I was that way myself, but he was rather amusing and some of his work isn't bad." As the reader will find from the little collection of anecdotes at the end of this volume, these witnesses have contributed to the Wilde tradition, not to say legend.

The most voluminous memoirs of Wilde naturally come from those who to a greater or less extent shared his inter-sexual or bi-sexual nature. It is not surprising that they should try to make a hero of the man, a persecuted martyr, a great genius destroyed by heterosexual brutality. If the evidence were no more complicated than that, it would not be difficult to discount the heroics and to arrive at a coherent if not perfectly accurate idea of the man. What confounds the inquirer is the discovery that these fugelmen (as Frank Harris rather aptly names them) could not remain loyal to their hero or refrain from bickering among themselves, during the course of which they constantly change their ground and unsay what they have solemnly said. They could not refrain from joining in the bitterly useless debate of Oscar versus "Bosie" (Lord Alfred Douglas) —which of the two was to blame for Oscar's downfall? —as if both had not behaved with folly and insolence!

To top this off the reader must know that the present text of *De Profundis* (the letter written by Wilde in Reading Gaol) is only part of the original, cleverly selected by Robert Ross to show Wilde in the best light possible. The suppressed portions of *De Profundis* (which I have been permitted to read, but which cannot be publicly printed until 1960) are not scandalous, but consist almost entirely of a bitter review of Wilde's relations with Douglas up to and including the trial. From this (if Wilde is to be believed) it emerges that Wilde was fascinated by Douglas and utterly swayed by his influence (as a lover is by the beloved), an influence which was entirely disastrous. Douglas is shown as selfish and heartless, sponging on Wilde to pay for his extravagances, wasting Wilde's time so that he was unable to work, degrading him from an intellectual to a sensual life of eating, drinking, and sloth. Finally Douglas, in his hatred of his father (he actually threatened the life of Lord Queensberry), urged Wilde into taking the legal action which resulted in his own conviction. "Bosie," in fact, tried to put his father in prison, and landed Oscar there instead.

The production of some parts of the suppressed *De Profundis* in court lost Douglas a libel action he had brought against Arthur Ransome. This seems to have goaded Douglas to one of the insensate furies described by Wilde, and in rebuttal he wrote a venomously bitter diatribe called *Oscar Wilde and Myself,* which is so excessive that it makes one think that on the whole Wilde was telling the truth.

Still, this is not the whole confusion. Frank Harris arrived with his *Oscar Wilde, His Life and Confessions.* Now we all know about Frank Harris, a gifted and bumptious person who lived by what he called "white-mailing," for whom Truth was something he had heard about but seldom met, and who at the time he published this book privately in New York was a passionate pro-German and anxious to do anything to discredit the British. Of course, Harris had a perfect right to his point of view about the War of 1914-18 (unfortunate as it turned out for him), but it can hardly be claimed as impartial. The fact is that what is new in Harris's *Life* is seldom true, and that the alleged "confessions" are largely bogus.

Let me add that many if not most of Wilde's letters seem to have been destroyed by the terrified recipients in 1895. Most of those which have been published relate to the post-prison epoch, but these have never been collected in one volume, and there are still others which have never been published.

When Arthur Ransome published his critical study in 1912 he spoke of "Wilde's vice." That apparently was still the accepted view among men of letters, even those who admired Wilde's wit and writings, though it had long been abandoned by the pioneer psychologists of sex. Nothing better illustrates the change that has taken place in these matters in the past thirty years, the growing tolerance, than the fact that most writers would feel ridiculous if they used the word "vice." Unfortunately Science has not yet made up its mind on the subject. The bio-chemists and geneticists stress "deficiency of hormones"; the psychologists insist on "early influences." May not both be partly right? Unlucky influences acting on a predisposed nature cause a deviation from what we "others" somewhat too smugly call the "norm," whatever that may be. At all events, public opinion nowadays would think the only too deplorably notorious "Wilde case" a subject for psychiatrists and medical specialists and not for the British Criminal Law and the average stony British judge.

I am anxious to get away from this topic, but I brought it up in the beginning of this notice for two reasons. In the first place, if Wilde had not been a sort of martyr of homosexuality he would not have attained his immense notoriety—hideous as the burden of it was to him in the wretched fag-end of life after Reading Gaol. It is of course quite impossible to estimate what proportion of Wilde's reputation during the greater part of the past half-century was due to this fact and what was due to his undoubted literary talents, his sparkling wit, and charming personality. In the second place, the merest outline of Wilde's life is completely falsified unless we realize that he was always the homosexual type, always potentially liable to succumb to overt practices, though Ransome (I assume) had some private information leading him to fix the date so confidently at 1886.

It is a fact (which I suppose we can only deplore) that the male homosexual type always annoys and irritates the average heterosexual male even when the latter (as frequently happens) is ignorant of what it is that annoys him. (The popular word "sissie" indicates what I mean.) It was just this which made Wilde unpopular in spite of all his wit and charm, which, however, were more fully revealed to the more intelligent people he met, who were less likely to be prejudiced.

The traits in Wilde's character which were stressed to his detriment by his sexual make-up might be not unfairly described as affectation, vanity, folly, and a curious lack of judgment almost approximating a failure to correlate the actual world with his own private world of wish and fantasy. I am not going to venture on so hazardous a piece of psychology as "the homosexual character" (what is "the heterosexual character"?) but I do think these traits are often observable in men of this type. In the origin these traits are probably harmless enough, but are envenomed by a hostile, ignorant environment, which in turn reacts more violently, and so on until there is intense bitterness or a catastrophe. If we say of Wilde that he brought his fate on himself by inconceivable insolence and lack of judgment, what on earth are we to say of a society which behaved in the utterly savage and unpardonable manner it did in 1895 and after? Nor was this confined to England, even if England was the worst culprit. As Vincent O'Sullivan (an Irishman) has pointed out, the most brutal attacks on Wilde came from America, and the moment the ex-convict landed in France he was warned by the sub-prefect that he would be instantly expelled if he caused any scandal.

In the height of his fame Wilde was "the brilliant Irishman." After 1895 he became the *Anglais,* the Englander, the Britisher. I note with pleasure that once more he has become the brilliant Irishman. "I have made my name a low byword among low people," wrote Wilde of himself bitterly but truly. If he has been redeemed from that degrading situation it is not because of the hero-worshipping homosexuals or tales of "marvellous conversation" which has left practically no trace, but because of the merit of his writings and the general change in outlook.

II

Oscar Wilde was twenty when he went up to Oxford in 1874, and he already had a small but deserved reputation as a young classical scholar of great promise. Indeed, his whole academic career was a series of successes, which could only come from hard work and certain gifts which, as always in the young, might or might not develop into something notable. Wilde had spent three years at Trinity College, Dublin, where he had been a Queen's Scholar and a University Scholar, and had come out high in classics "Honours." He had won a gold medal with an essay on the extant fragments of Greek Comic Dramatists. And he was a favourite pupil of Mahaffy, who acknowledged Wilde's assistance in the preface to his *Social Life in Greece*. It is perhaps necessary to explain to a generation which knows not Zion that Mahaffy was provost of Trinity and president of the Royal Irish Academy, that he was perhaps the best classical scholar of his time in Ireland, and that several of his books on Greece remained in print for nearly half a century.

The "Greek sympathy," as Peacock calls the freemasonry of classical scholars, would naturally mean that the Magdalen dons watched the progress of the clever young Irishman discreetly but with interest. Would he keep up his intellectual life or would he waste his time in any of the half hundred ways evolved by undergraduates to frustrate all efforts to educate them? Wilde's first answer to that was to win a "demyship" worth £95 a year for five years.

In those days Jowett was professor of Greek and Master of Balliol; Matthew Arnold had only recently ceased to lecture as professor of Poetry; Ruskin, as

Slade professor, was exerting all his eloquence and knowledge of medieval art to civilize the young barbarians, though rapidly approaching the nervous and mental breakdown of 1878. These were powerful influences, but more delightful—because less official or entirely unofficial—were the English Romantic poets, the still living Pre-Raphaelite poets and painters, that amusing and gifted Mr. Whistler, and the retiring Brazenose don who had published some fascinating essays on the Italian Renaissance which Jowett had frowned upon—Walter Pater. All this was "very heaven" to a sensitive, intelligent boy in the city of dreaming spires, and old grey colleges, and brilliant green lawns, with one of those pretty little brooks the English call a river. Moreover chance had given Oscar Wilde the best undergraduate's rooms in Magdalen, which he furnished with blue china and engravings of female nudes, expressing the pious hope that he might live up to the blue china.

Of course, he was "ragged" by the "hearties." He was an æsthete and a poet. It was said that at Oxford he read nothing but the English poets—if so, Mahaffy had grounded him wonderfully, for he took a First in Moderations, and then spent his vacations travelling with Mahaffy in Italy and Greece, where he saw the German archæologists recover the Hermes of Praxiteles. His Hellenic zeal made him late in coming up next term, and the dons fined him heavily; but returned the money later when Wilde finished his Oxford career in a blaze of academic triumph, winning a First Class in Literae Humaniores and the Newdigate Prize with his poem "Ravenna."

When Oscar Wilde went down from Oxford for the last time, he had spent eight of his most impressionable years at universities. For good and for ill these years left their permanent mark on him. For one thing, his series of academic triumphs had made success necessary to him. In a world which is at best indifferent to and frequently hostile to the intellectual and æsthetic way of life, Wilde expected to be surrounded by admiring sympathizers; and as he was gifted with uncommon impudence and wit he made an enemy with every *mot*. He wanted life always to be as it had been at Oxford, when his father paid the bills, and the university protected him from the world, and poured out for him the knowledge and beauty salvaged from the ages, and he was free to choose always what was lovely and refined and exquisite, and to reject all that was sordid and harsh and vile. He wanted to eat of all the fruits in the garden of life, he told a friend as they strolled along Magdalen Walk, but only those in the sunny side of the garden. He had taken too literally and was to apply too sensually, too coarsely, too selfishly Pater's wonderful words:

"The service of philosophy, or speculative culture, towards the human spirit is to rouse, to startle it into sharp and eager observation. Every moment some form grows perfect in hand or face; some tone on the hills or the sea is choicer than the rest; some mood of passion or insight or intellectual excitement is irresistibly real and attractive for us,—for that moment only. Not the fruit of experience, but experience itself, is the end. A counted number of pulses only is given to us of a variegated, dramatic life. How may we see in them all that is to be seen in them by the finest senses? How shall we pass most swiftly from point to point, and be present always at the focus where the greatest number of vital forces unite in their purest energy?"

It was Wilde's error to want always to enjoy the ecstasy without paying the price beforehand in labour, in self-discipline, in restraint. He paid the immensely accumulated price afterwards.

Yet when Oscar Wilde extravagantly took a first-class ticket from Oxford to London and treated himself to an armful of new books and periodicals to beguile that brief journey, he had already received warnings if he had not been too self-absorbed to notice them. After a life of lavish expenditure Sir William Wilde had suddenly died, leaving only £7000 to his widow and a small income to Oscar. The natural thing in such circumstances would have been for the Magdalen fellows to elect so brilliant a young graduate to a probationary fellowship, with the chance of a life income so long as he behaved himself and remained unmarried. The Magdalen dons ominously did nothing. With Wilde's academic record, this was a significant snub. Perhaps he had offended the dons; more likely, in their quiet way, they saw already the type he was and did not want him.

Young Wilde had "immeasurable ambitions"—at least, he said he had. What he actually achieved when he had at last earned enough money to cut a figure in the great world, we shall see. He had been trained for no profession, and if he had been trained he would not have practised successfully—like his fellow-countryman, Tom Moore, he was a born social entertainer and also a born writer. Indeed it is the greatest mistake to rate Wilde too low as a writer. If he had not been an excellent writer he would now be as nearly forgotten as those heroes of resounding British scandals, Charles Parnell and Charles Dilke.

At this time Wilde had little enough to offer a publisher. He had his "Rise of Historical Criticism," which would probably have won him another Oxford prize if the dons hadn't thought he had too many already. He had begun to write (with unconscious prescience) a play about Russian revolutionaries. And he was completing a volume of poems.

For a good many years now it has been the custom to treat Wilde's poems with contempt—he was a plagiarist, a *précieux*, and he had not read Paul Eluard. Let it be remembered that much criticism of poetry is only a long grinding of intellectual axes, a strenuous form of competition for an almost non-existent market. Of course Wilde's poems have faults! I even believe I could myself point out a few which have been overlooked by swift-eyed censors. For example, in "The Burden of Itys," which is a kind of expanded "Ode to a Nightingale" loaded with æsthetic images, we suddenly trip over a prosaic almost eighteenth-century line:

"The harmless rabbit gambols with its young . . ." Yet the poem is filled with beautiful allusions and suggestions, some of which belong to the author. It must be remembered that Wilde came at the end of the last great period of English poetry. Within less than a century there had been Blake, Burns, Wordsworth, Scott, Coleridge, Byron, Shelley, Keats, Tennyson, Browning, Arnold, Meredith, Rossetti, William Morris, Swinburne, and hosts of minor poets. It was impossible for a young man, loving poetry as Wilde did, to write poems without reproducing what he had admired so intensely. When, in maturity, he wrote the "Ballad of Reading Gaol" out of the bitter intensity of his own experience, he had all the originality of the *fait divers* in his lines.

In spite of their heavy debts to Milton, Keats, Tennyson, Rossetti, and Arnold (not to mention others), these early poems have vitality and charm. You can take every one of them to pieces, and show their derivations, yet they are readable in a way which more approved specimens of the art are not. They make the Romantic poetry of England accessible to young readers who are not yet competent to appreciate the greater men. They represent the moment when Romanticism became classical—like the Parnassians in France—but a classicism of joyous reminiscence, not of plodding obedience to rule and precept. They should be taken in the spirit of the Latin poetry of the Renaissance, when the subtle flavours of innumerable reminiscences of earlier writers were deliberately enjoyed, when every line and phrase was drenched in older poetry, yet there was something new about it all, some expression of the writer's own personality. What an interesting kinship there is between Wilde's methods and those of Poliziano in such a poem as that on violets, which begins:

> *Molles o violae, veneris munuscula nostrae,*
> *Dulce quibus tanti pignus amoris inest,*
> *Quae vos quae genuit tellus? quo nectare odoras*
> *Sparserunt zephyri mollis et aura comas?* *

and the exquisite Italian *Stanze* which clearly inspired Botticelli. Both poets work for and achieve similar effects.

The most ambitious of Wilde's æsthetic poems are those nominally on Hellenic themes ("The Garden of Eros," "The Burden of Itys," "Charmides," "Panthea," "Humanitad,") and all suffer from a curiously inæsthetic stanza, made up of a quatrain of alternately rhymed pentameters followed by a pentameter rhyming with a "fourteener." It is clumsy, and the extra syllables are nearly always either a *"cheville"* (a bit of padding)

---

* O soft violets, the little gift of my beloved, in which is the sweet pledge of so much love—what earth brought you forth? with what perfume do the western breezes and the air sprinkle your leaves?

or compel an awkward run-over to the next stanza. An amusing fact is that this young man, who was soon to repudiate poor Nature with such witty insolence, shows in these poems a considerable knowledge and love of picturesque Nature—not indeed of the Greece which is his theme but of the lush Thames Valley. His observation was, however, not that of Wordsworth, still less of Richard Jeffries, for he makes the tench (a bottom-feeding pond fish) "leap at the dragon-fly," an insect no fish would attempt. Wilde's love of flowers was often laughed at and probably still is:

> Soon will the musk carnation break and swell,
> Soon shall we have gold-dusted snapdragon,
> Sweet-William with his homely cottage-smell,
> And stocks in fragrant blow;
> Roses that down the alleys shine afar . . .

That piece of æstheticism, however, is not by Wilde, but by one of his Masters, the austere Matthew Arnold.

Later, after Wilde went to live in France, he added to his verse something from Gautier and the Verlaine of *Eaux-Fortes*. "The Sphinx," which some people prefer because it is un-Hellenic and un-English, comes straight out of Flaubert's *Tentation de Saint Antoine*, suggested by the marvellous dialogue of the Sphinx and the Chimæra. Wilde may have got later suggestions for this poem from Huysmans's *A Rebours* (1884), but he knew French well enough to go direct to Flaubert, and indeed the technique of strange erudition made poetic is entirely Flaubertian. His last work in verse, the "Ballad," is a repudiation of his whole artistic creed —it is contemporary, realistic, and sordid in theme, and is full of philanthropic propaganda. The butterfly had certainly been broken on the treadmill.

Although in 1878-80 Wilde could show only a few publications in periodicals, his personality was already attracting attention, and was extremely welcome to the little satirists of *Punch* longing to curry favour with the middle classes by holding art up to ridicule. They hadn't much success with such recluses and haters of newspaper notoriety as Burne-Jones, Rossetti, Morris, Pater, and indeed all the older generation of artists and poets. (Tennyson had a horror of publicity, and Arnold a genuine contempt for it.) But Wilde was just what the satirists were looking for—a seemingly obvious æsthetic charlatan. Gilbert's Bunthorne, originally meant for Pater, was transferred hastily to Wilde.

Even before the newspapers got hold of him, the reputation made by Wilde's personality and æsthetic talk was in excess of his achievements. It is said that an ardent female disciple holding forth about him was interrupted by a sweet old lady with: "But what has Mr. Wilde done, dear? Is he a soldier?" Perhaps the old lady wasn't such a fool as the indignant disciple assumed. It is usually taken for granted that Wilde's æsthetic costume, his lilies and languors, his blue china ("them flymy little bits o' blue"), and all the rest of it were taken from the hard-working, publicity-hating pre-Raphaelites. No doubt he stole his gilded rags from them, but his real master in the art of getting talked about was someone quite different, one of the most astute and attractive adventurers who ever worked himself from nothing to sway the fortunes of a great empire—Benjamin Disraeli.

Disraeli, like Wilde, had set out to conquer society by his wits, and had done anything and everything to get himself talked about and to push his way—a Julien Sorel who succeeded. At the age of twenty-one Disraeli had written in an absurd novel of genius, "To enter into high society a man must either have blood,

a million, or a genius." Neither Disraeli nor Wilde had a
million or "blood." It was Disraeli who had strained
every faculty to dominate the most brilliant of his contemporaries by his *mots* and unflagging talk, and they
honestly agreed that "the cleverest fellow in the party
was the young Jew in the green velvet trousers."
Moreover, the young Dizzy used æstheticism and fancy
dress to advertise himself, bursting upon the world in
"the black velvet dress-coat lined with white satin, the
gorgeous gold flowers on a splendidly embroidered
waistcoat, the jewelled rings worn outside the white
gloves, the evening cane of ivory inlaid with gold
and adorned with a tassel of black silk."

Young Disraeli's hero was not Brummell, as is supposed, but Byron, who also in his day wore astonishing
clothes and dazzled the world with sartorial fame.
Wilde took Disraeli and Disraeli's novels as his guide
to worldly success with the English aristocracy. Just as
Dizzy dropped his dandyism like a hot potato when he
began to succeed in Parliament, so Wilde changed into
the clothes of a gentleman when he left America. But,
in taking Disraeli as a model, Wilde overlooked certain important factors. Disraeli's early novels are exaggerated, they are intentional caricatures of Disraeli's
arrivisme; moreover, the dandy posings and strained
bons mots did him harm—lots of people thought Dizzy
a mountebank until the magnificent speech introducing
his first budget; and then Wilde lacked much that
Disraeli had—the concentrated ambition, the unflagging energy and determination, the tireless patience,
the character of granite. We know now what success
was scored by master and pupil, and can estimate their
respective abilities in the conduct of life. It is odd that
Wilde never noticed that Disraeli had once remarked

of a character—"the only way to keep him out of the House of Correction was to get him into the House of Commons."

Wilde's poems were published and went into several editions—of two hundred copies each. His sayings were repeated. He 'was constantly caricatured in *Punch*. But he remained poor and extravagant. Nobody was paying to see this puny Alcibiades cut the tail off the pre-Raphaelite movement. The blot on Wilde's career as an "artist" is not Reading Gaol but the lecture tour in America. There is no particular turpitude in lecturing, even when the lecturer can be heard, and of course lecturing in America is just like lecturing anywhere else. Dickens made an immense success of his readings in America, but then Dickens had something of his own to offer which all English-speaking people were eager to hear. Wilde had nothing of his own to give; he could only betray his masters by peddling them to audiences who were not prepared to accept them.

It has been said, but never proved, that Wilde was entrapped into making this tour by the impresario of Gilbert and Sullivan, who thought it necessary to show Americans just what was being parodied in Bunthorne. If true, the discredit falls not on Wilde, but on the perpetrators of a somewhat dirty deal. The turpitude of the thing lies in Wilde's willingness to cheapen for the sake of a little money and a lot of worthless notoriety two generations of poets, painters, and critics who had never asked for a penny of money and who hated noisy publicity. They had worked, as artists should work, silently and to do the best that was in them, living poorly when they were poor, mostly on small private incomes and the purchases of a few patrons, disregarding the screams and squibs and "serious" critics, and only asking the public to take or leave their work as it chose. After leaving it for a long time, but with plenty of mud-throwing, the public at last began to take it. Furthermore, these poets and painters had never cared what other countries said about them—they left the spite and envy and denigration as unheeded and unanswered as the even more destructive "serious criticism," which is the most malicious form of impotence. And then Wilde made the whole movement ridiculous, opening the breach by which the Philistine attack could be made. Having done all the lecturing mischief possible both in England and America, Mr. Wilde collected his dollars, dropped his mountebank's clothes into the Atlantic, and turned up in Paris as an English gentleman, where he started to clear himself by writing "The Sphinx."

The money derived from the æsthetic lectures in costume was easily spent, and Wilde was soon back in London, generously giving help and shelter to a penniless poet, and earning a little money by lecturing in the English provinces. In a moment of mental lassitude Wilde made the blunder (imagine Disraeli doing anything of equivalent folly!) of asking Whistler's help in composing a lecture on painting; for Whistler, at once the most generous and meanest of men, was certain to make public the obligation, to exaggerate it, and to twit his "friend" without urbanity:

"What has Oscar in common with Art? except that he dines at our tables and picks from our platters the plums for the pudding he peddles in the provinces. Oscar—the amiable, irresponsible, esurient Oscar. . . ." ("The Gentle Art of Making Enemies.")

The most revealing item in that rather strained attempt at satire is the curious use of the word "amiable" as a term of abuse. It is true enough—Oscar *was* amiable, but who except the "Butterfly" would have thought of it as a demerit?

Poetry, costume, and lecturing having all failed to conquer society, Wilde seems to have become desperate, and plunged recklessly into reviewing and marriage. His wife was a sweetly pretty young woman with the significant attraction of a considerable dowry, which enabled the couple to set up at 16 Tite Street, Chelsea. This marriage, which inevitably could only turn out unhappily, took place on May 29, 1884; and there were two children. The problem of Wilde's ambiguous sexual nature is certainly complicated by the fact that at an earlier time he had been in love (genuinely or as a pose?) with the beautiful Lily Langtry, while more than one personal friend at the time asserts that Mr. and Mrs. Wilde seemed very much in love, and that Oscar, especially, appeared very happy. It is not true to say, as is often said, that Wilde, immediately after marriage, accepted the editorship of the *Woman's World* to support his wife. He did not do that until June 1887, after the birth of his two sons.

It was as a reviewer—in fact in the role of a journalist, which Wilde so snobbishly affected to despise—that he began to find himself as a prose writer, though, it is true, he seldom again matched the grace and cadence of the end of "L'Envoi," which was written in America. Considering that nearly all reviews are hastily written it is not surprising that so many are too slovenly and dull for republication. Wilde's reviews stand up well, especially those written for the comparatively free mental atmosphere of the *Pall Mall Gazette*. Some of them are very witty, and only the long editorials for the *Woman's World* ("Literary and Other Notes") are so toned down to their audience as to be insipid. Quite a number of afterwards famous *mots* and passages for *Intentions* first appeared in these *Pall Mall Gazette* reviews. Unfortunately, these pieces only appear (so far as I know) in the Collected Editions; and, still more unfortunately, the American Collected Edition volume of criticisms and reviews includes a lot of the tamer articles, and leaves out much of what is amusing and brilliant. I have given in this volume a few snippets from the *Pall Mall* reviews, and wish space had enabled me to give many more.

It was an ironic twist of circumstances which for two years compelled Wilde, as editor of the *Woman's World,* to write flattering chronicles of a sex in which he daily became less interested. But the eighties were the period of Wilde's development and of his real work. Though still bitterly pursued by *Punch* (which having once found a joke is reluctant to drop it in case of never hitting on another), Oscar Wilde was socially successful, and was welcomed at many a luncheon and dinner table for the pleasure guests took in his talk. He now visited Paris, not as an unknown æsthete retreating from America, but as a social figure who was written up in the French press by his friend, Robert Sherard. He met Moréas and Verlaine, Mallarmé, Gourmont, and Gide—perhaps also Huysmans, whom he greatly admired. I do not know what Yeats means by saying that Wilde talked "with a manner and music that he had learnt from Pater *or Flaubert*," for though Wilde certainly "fluted" like Pater, he never met Flaubert (who died in 1880), and if he had tried any of his æsthetic blarney on the irritable sage of Croisset would have received as ferocious a snub as Henry James when he made the unlucky remark in Flaubert's presence that the Duc de Saint-Simon is a bad writer. From this distance of time it looks as if Wilde's Paris acquaintances were chiefly among the upper Bohemia—the kind of people who are aristocrats to artists, or artists to aristocrats.

With his customary good nature Wilde never complained of the hack-work he had to do for the *Woman's World* (the only writing of his which is comparatively lifeless and uninteresting) or of his reviewing, which I suspect he rather enjoyed within limits. But work is a habit like everything else, and it was during the last half of the eighties that Wilde did much of the work which brought him genuine fame in the nineties. Once more he looked about for some form of writing which would enable him to express the charm of his personality, to employ effectively his talents and accomplishments. He tried the fairy tale, the short story, the Platonic dialogue, and the novel. In every one of these he obtained brilliant results, except perhaps in the short story as soon as it ceased to be either a parable or a prose poem.

The publication in book form of *The Happy Prince and Other Tales* in 1888 brought a letter of commendation from Walter Pater, and at last furnished an answer to catty old ladies who wanted to know what Mr. Wilde had *done*, and was he a soldier? "The Canterville Ghost"—somewhat too obviously aimed at the American public—was published in a periodical in 1887. Two years later Wilde issued serially "Pen, Pencil, and Poison"; "The Portrait of Mr. W. H."; and "The Decay of Lying." We can see from the diversity of his attempts at this time how anxiously he was looking for a form which would please a bigger audience. "The Sphinx Without a Secret" and the "Model Millionaire" are magazine stories and best passed over in silence. "The Canterville Ghost" is much better, an attempt at supernatural farce—a somewhat distant tribute perhaps to Edgar Poe. "Pen, Pencil, and Poison" is a biographical sketch of Wainewright, author and æsthete, forger and probably poisoner. Egotists seldom make good biographers, tending as they must to exhibit themselves rather than their nominal subjects; so the chief interest of this study is extraneous, the melancholy coincidence that Wainewright too was a man of culture and talents who stood his trial, and was sentenced to transportation for life.

"The Portrait of Mr. W. H." is more original, ingenious and entertaining, for, by a clever manipulation of extracts from Shakespeare's *Sonnets* Wilde makes out a seemingly excellent case to a benevolent reader for believing that the sonnets were written to a Mr. W. H., or Willie Hughes, a handsome boy actor who played women's parts on the Elizabethan stage. I say "benevolent," because apart from the serious obstacle that no such person as Willie Hughes is known to have existed, a study of the sonnets alongside Wilde's fictionalized essay shows at once how much he has solicited the text. Still, the idea so fascinated him that he persuaded Ricketts to paint him a portrait of Mr. W. H. in the style of Clouet. It was not very wise to write this essay; but in the state of public opinion at that day publication was madness. Apart from other dangerous implications, there is particular emphasis on the cult of "Alexis" by certain minor Elizabethan poets; and, as everyone knows, "Alexis" names the second eclogue of Vergil, *"Formosum pastor Corydon ardebat Alexin, Delicias domini"* . . . an exquisitely beautiful poem but flagrantly homosexual. To anyone who had read Vergil—and at that time most upper-class Englishmen had—"The Portrait of Mr. W. H." was an unequivocal declaration and an insolent defiance. Prudent men began to drop Mr. Wilde's acquaintance.

Nevertheless, so pleasant and charming was Wilde in

company, that many people—in spite of this evidence which to us looks so obvious—refused to believe anything against him. The late Wilfrid Scawen Blunt used to give an annual dinner at Crabbet Park to a small group of distinguished friends he called the Crabbet Club—members were automatically expelled when they became prime ministers or proconsuls. It was the custom that each new member should be charged after dinner with any and all misdoings alleged against him by public gossip, and from this he had to defend himself. I once spent a week-end with Mr. Blunt, and he told me that when Wilde was the new member of the Club he was attacked rather savagely by George Wyndham (an uncle of Lord Alfred Douglas, who was also related to Blunt) and that Wilde got up and made so witty and laughable a speech, humorously admitting everything of which he was afterwards convicted but excusing it on the ground of its being necessary to his art, that Mr. Blunt at any rate was wholly convinced of his innocence. (Douglas gives a very different version of this episode; I relate it as nearly as I can remember Mr. Blunt's telling it.) People then thought that homosexuality was a mere affectation with Wilde, like sunflowers and æsthetic clothes. The flowers and clothes had been discarded for conventional garb, so, when the full advertising value had been derived from this very dangerous "pose," Mr. Wilde would subside into respectability with a bevy of chorus girls.

Wilde found himself as a writer, and easily excelled all he had hitherto published, with "The Decay of Lying"; followed in 1890 by two even finer Platonic dialogues which appeared in *The Nineteenth Century* while *The Picture of Dorian Gray* was coming out serially in *Lippincott's Magazine*. The form of the dialogue has often been used by English writers who hoped to give a light tone to their reflections and ideas, from Dryden's *Of Dramatick Poesie* and Bishop Berkeley's *Three Dialogues between Hylas and Philonous in Opposition to Sceptics and Atheists* down to Flecker's *The Grecians* and Sturge Moore's *Hark to These Three Talk about Art*; but none has produced dialogues so readable, so witty, so coloured, so eloquent, so solidly constructed and full of thought and good sense.

Certainly, in these dialogues there are faults of affectation, of paradox not more than half true, of exuberance—but surely we may forgive the paradoxes for their wit, the exuberances for their beauty, and even the affectations for their harmlessness. "The Decay of Lying" was a plea for imagination and the *beau idéal* as against the then rising school of realists, unfortunately still with us, who "find life crude and leave it raw." Pater, breathing the remoter air of Oxford, held that "all art aspires to the condition of music"; but Wilde seems to have had a momentary prescience of the horror that was coming, when all art would aspire to the condition of journalism.

I shall not dwell upon the learning of these three dialogues, learning which is used so lightly and so appreciatively, to give the reader pleasure, to stimulate appreciation, to communicate enthusiasm. It is one of the misfortunes of our times that under the stress of our apparently infinite public calamities we have forgotten how to admire, that we who have much to learn or relearn from our predecessors in the arts think it becoming to treat them with the contempt of ignorance. Like his masters in criticism, Ruskin, Pater, and J. A. Symonds, Wilde believed that criticism exists to help people to enjoy art, not to disgust them by wearisome superiorities and browbeating.

For an excellent and sympathetically intelligent analysis of *Intentions* (the collective title of these dialogues,) I refer the reader to pages 104-129 of Arthur Ransome's *Oscar Wilde*. Mr. Ransome seems to me to have described admirably the secret of this book's vitality and charm in the sentence where he speaks of "the fresh and debonair personality that keeps the book alive, tossing thoughts like roses, and playing with them in happiness of heart."

In his unaccountable endorsement of Frank Harris's work on Wilde, Mr. Bernard Shaw makes the astonishing statement that Wilde knew nothing about music or painting, while he (Mr. Shaw) had listened to his family practising concertos for public performance and had studied the pictures at the Dublin Art Gallery. Now, Wilde never claimed to be a critic of music, and only refers to musicians *en passant;* and it is a notorious fact that many poets have been unappreciative of music. Wilde has been sneered at for speaking (rather affectedly, it is true) of Dvorak's "mad scarlet thing" as if he imagined Dvorak was a painter; but Wilde was probably thinking of Rimbaud's sonnet on the colour of sounds or the elaborate (not to say ridiculous) colour-sound theories of René Ghil.

Chesterton and Mr. Shaw are Wilde's two most distinguished imitators, taking up the manner of his witty paradox and using it for propaganda purposes— the one for Catholicism, the other for communism. Mr. Shaw is about the greatest pamphleteer in English, and has written admirable talkies for the stage, but he is unjust to Wilde's knowledge of painting. It is true that only a dozen or fifteen painters are mentioned in *In-*

tentions and those rather obvious ones, but from Wilde's more fugitive writings (which Mr. Shaw doubtless overlooked) I have collected references to thirty-two painters, including such precise recollections as "Guido's Saint Sebastian in Genoa," "Perugino's Ganymede in Perugia," "Corregio's lily-bearer in the Cathedral at Parma," and so on. He may of course have taken these from Symonds or Ruskin (whose knowledge of medieval and Renaissance painting respectively has rarely been equalled), but it looks as if they were genuine. At any rate Wilde also cites painters so diverse as Angelico and Boucher, Blake and Giorgione, Mantegna and Van Huysum. I am not claiming that he was a "serious critic" of painting. All I claim is that he had seen more pictures than those in the Dublin Art Gallery, and cared about them as a source of artistic pleasure.

Wilde's latent dramatic talent must surely be counted among the most potent reasons for the success of his dialogues. Wilde loved the stage, and by 1890-91 had already made more than one unsuccessful attempt at tragedy. Now that he was "getting warm," as children say, and coming near his true vocation of comedy, he was diverted by Lippincott's offer for him to write a novel, which resulted in *The Picture of Dorian Gray*. One of the striking facts about this book has nothing whatever to do with its merits or demerits as a novel. It is that the character of Dorian Gray and his relationship to Lord Henry Wotton (Wilde) were imagined and written down before Wilde met Lord Alfred Douglas. The subsequent reality seemed to give some substance to the hoary paradox about Life imitating Art; and when Robert Hichens wrote his cruelly witty *The Green Carnation* from a personal study of

Wilde and Douglas in Egypt he often seemed to be parodying the conversations in *The Picture of Dorian Gray*. Take this, for instance:

"Oh! he has not changed," said Mr. Amarinth [Wilde]. "That is so wonderful. He never develops at all. He alone understands the beauty of rigidity, the exquisite serenity of the statuesque nature. Men always fall into the absurdity of endeavouring to develop the mind, to push it violently forward in this direction or in that. The mind should be receptive, a harp waiting to catch the winds, a pool ready to be ruffled, not a bustling busybody, forever trotting about on the pavement looking for a new bun shop. . . ."

The parody is so close to exact imitation that it scarcely gives itself away until the end of the last sentence. *The Green Carnation* is in fact so like Wilde that it is the best thing Hichens ever wrote.

The Picture of Dorian Gray is a very literary novel, an exposition of Wilde's exaggerated hedonism, and, like his other writings, so dominated by the author's personality that all other characters are reduced to shadows. Several books have been suggested as the basis of this novel—Balzac's *La Peau de Chagrin* (1831), J. K. Huysman's *A Rebours* (1884), R. L. Stevenson's *The Strange Case of Dr. Jekyll and Mr. Hyde* (1886). I see a little of Balzac's novel and a good deal of Stevenson's in *Dorian Gray*. Some critics go so far as to hint that the whole thing was lifted from Huysmans. I can scarcely believe that they can have read *A Rebours*. It is true that *A Rebours* must be the French novel which "fascinated" Dorian Gray, and that its hero Des Esseintes is an æsthete who delights in the perverse and artificial. Beyond that the resemblance ceases. Wilde's chapter on jewels can hardly be derived from *A Rebours* (which hasn't much about precious stones except for the episode of the tortoise encased in gold and gems), and the chapter on tapestries and embroidery comes from Ernest Lefébure's *Embroidery and Lace*, the English translation of which Wilde had reviewed. Des Esseintes is a misanthropic, dyspeptic, prematurely impotent, neurotic Parisian who retires from Paris to complete isolation, sleeping by day and living by night, occasionally enlivened by some ghastly sexual nightmare, and trying to whip up his jaded senses by such witty devices as collecting flowers which look as if they were made of zinc, admiring the last sterile drippings of the imitators of the generation of 1830, reading Latin poets of the Dark Ages (taken by Huysmans not from the originals but from Ebert's *Allgemeine Geschichte der Literatur des Mittelalters*), enjoying an imaginary trip to England by smelling a tarry rope, reading Dickens and Baedeker, and drinking port in a bodega, and so on. The intense *taedium vitae* which drove Huysmans eventually into the Church finds full expression in this work. But what a contrast is *The Picture of Dorian Gray!* In comparison the bloom of health is on its cheek. Wilde's fault was not a sterile *taedium vitae*, but rather "too much love of (good) living"; and few more amiably sociable men ever existed. Wilde's book is full of amusing if over-studied talk and witticisms; whereas Des Esseintes rarely gets beyond such eloquence as "'Sapristi!' dit-il enthousiasmé!" *A Rebours* is all sulky monologue and self-pity, where *Dorian Gray*, for all its affected "sins" and tragical ending, is full of the enjoyment of life and of sunny talk. *The Picture of Dorian Gray* owes little to *A Rebours*, but *Salomé* may owe a good deal.

Perhaps the weakest scenes in *Dorian Gray* occur in chapters XVII and XVIII, when Wilde was growing weary of his imposed task and tried to brighten his last pages with a snappy Duchess. Unluckily indeed, instead of making her talk like Wilde, he tried to make her talk like the characters in a Meredith novel—and the result is dreadful, though it certainly was a sincere flattery of the author of *The Egoist*. But to find the plain factual origin of the magic picture idea (which is, after all, the central part of the novel's plot, just as the talk and "philosophy" are its real excuse), we must go back to a book which appeared in 1826.

Wilde christened his first novel *Dorian Gray* and his second son Vivian; and Benjamin Disraeli called his first novel, *Vivian Grey*. It is a remarkable though very unequal performance, full of insolence and naïveté, with excellent thumb-nail sketches of character and a heap of epigrams lost in a frantic purposeless plot and floods of would-be German romanticism. Far more than any of Browning's books it deserves Wilde's description,—"chaos illuminated by flashes of lightning." I suppose (though I don't know) that Wilde read this as a boy in his mother's library, and found in it the theme of *The Picture of Dorian Gray*, as he had found hints and inspiration for his advertising career in the life of Disraeli. Since to the best of my knowledge this source has never been pointed out before, I may perhaps be forgiven for quoting this curious piece of Disraeli juvenilia:

"Max Rodenstein was the glory of his house. A being so beautiful in body and in soul you cannot imagine, and I will not attempt to describe . . . The only wish of Baroness Rodenstein, which never could be accomplished, was the possession of a portrait of her youngest son, for no consideration could induce Max to allow his likeness to be taken. His old nurse had always told him that the moment his portrait was taken he would die. The condition upon which such a beautiful thing was allowed to remain in the world was, she always said, that his beauty should not be imitated. About three months before the battle of Leipsic, Max was absent at the University, which was nearly four hundred miles from Roden-

stein Castle, there arrived one morning a large case directed
to the Baroness. On opening it it was found to contain a picture, the portrait of her son. The colouring was so vivid, the
general execution so miraculous, that for some moments they
forgot to wonder at the incident in their admiration of the
work of art. In one corner of the picture, in small characters
yet fresh, was an inscription which on examining they found
consisted of these words: "Painted last night. Now, lady, thou
hast thy wish." My aunt sank into the Baron's arms . . .

The next day they received letters from Max. He was quite
well, but mentioned nothing of the mysterious painting.

Three months afterwards, as a lady was sitting alone in
the Baroness's room, and gazing on the portrait of him she
loved right dearly, she suddenly started from her seat, and
would have shrieked, had not an indefinable sensation prevented her. The eyes of the portrait moved. The lady stood
leaning on a chair, pale and trembling like an aspen, but
gazing steadfastly on the animated portrait. It was no illusion
of a heated fancy; again the eyelids trembled, there was a
melancholy smile, and then they closed. The clock of Rodenstein Castle struck three . . . Three days afterwards came
the news of the battle of Leipsic, and at the very moment that
the eyes of the portrait closed **Max Rodenstein had been
pierced by a Polish Lancer!"**

A little further on, apropos other things, is the
sentence: "I fancy that in this mysterious foreigner, I
have met a kind of double of myself"; and a page or
two beyond Disraeli speaks of "an intellectual Don Juan,
reckless of human minds, as he was of human bodies, a
spiritual libertine." Put these together with Dr. Jekyll
and Mr. Hyde, and you have the basis for *The Picture of
Dorian Gray*. Of course Disraeli picked up his fantasy
from German Romantics, but Wilde's truly amazing
feat is the bringing up to date and breathing life into
such obsolete fustian.

At this point I should like to pause a moment and to
ask the reader to consider more particularly Wilde's
method of building a piece of writing. Absolute originality in art is of course a delusion. Not only are we all

the sons of somebody in whatever art we attempt, but
the "higher" our aims the greater the number of predecessors to whom we are indebted. Willed originality
is false originality. The only true originality is unconscious or at least unplotted—a fresh way of looking at
the world, a new personality. All writers borrow from
others, consciously or unconsciously. The successful—
I mean artistically successful—do it consciously, and
justify themselves by claiming that they improve their
thefts. Writers who try to avoid these obligations and
labour to appear wholly original are inevitably either
dull or preposterous.

As a poet, as a critic, as a novelist, and later as a
dramatist, Wilde openly took materials from many
sources and put them together in the confident belief
that he was making a new synthesis, that his unique
personality would transform them into something fresh
and attractive. I have touched on a few of the sources
of Wilde's poems, his dialogues, and *The Picture of
Dorian Gray;* and the reader's degree of esteem for
Wilde as a writer will depend on how far he thinks
Wilde did succeed in remaking these inherited materials
into something fascinating and new. Those who accuse
Wilde of plagiarism are in a sense right; but the borrow-
ing is too open for it to be considered as anything but
deliberate. For instance, in the very first paragraph of
"The Decay of Lying" there is a sentence about the
mist on the hills looking like the bloom on a ripe plum;
and this was taken from a contemporary poet whose
work Wilde had reviewed, picking out this very image
for praise. A little further on he amusingly takes up
Whistler's phrase about "having the courage of the
opinions of others" (a phrase Whistler had used to
try to squelch Wilde), and prints it without any
acknowledgment. To those who· are still doubtful of

the value of such work, I would say: "Very well, show me art criticism which has the quality and charm and wit of Wilde's dialogues, bring me a novel like *Dorian Gray*, or even poems with that 'something' Wilde added to his innumerable poetic borrowings."

Returning for a moment to *The Picture of Dorian Gray*—it seems reasonable to suppose that Wilde did not care very much for the idea of this supernatural portrait he borrowed from Disraeli's forgotten first novel. It pleased the commercial publisher, helped to create the effect of an æsthetic novel, provided a facile "moral" (for which Wilde did not care tuppence, but which the public demanded), and provided, so to speak, a rough framework of sticks on which the modeller could build his group.

Actually there is only one character in the book—Oscar Wilde. The notion of dual personality was much in vogue at the time, as shown by the enormous success of Dr. Jekyll and Mr. Hyde. In himself Wilde had a genuine case to display. Lord Henry Wotton is Wilde as he hoped to remain, Dorian Gray as he feared he might become. It almost seems as if Wilde were warning himself throughout the book that as long as he kept his aesthetic theories (i.e. his homosexuality) to the realm of pure Platonism and idealistic art, he was safe; but that as soon as he transferred them to the sphere of action he was courting disaster. Many of his contemporaries noted with surprise the vein of shrewd common sense in Wilde. It comes out in Henry Wotton when Dorian Gray hints to him that he has murdered Basil Hallward—Lord Henry shrugs it off and says, "My dear fellow, one should never do anything one can't talk about after dinner."

The novel then is a projection into life of Pater's phrase about "the dialogue of the soul with itself."

What conclusion Wilde came to is hard to say, for he was constricted on all sides by prejudices and commercial obligations, so that the end of the book is melodramatic and dull. Perhaps its real ending comes when Dorian decides to renounce Hetty, and finds he has only added hypocrisy to his other crimes. A man cannot escape the consequences of his temperament, Wilde implies; when he tries to do the conventional "right thing" he merely blunders. And then, after all, what is it the "world" punishes? Not crime, but the error of being found out; not squalid meanness, cheating, oppression, and infinite humbug, but distinction, beauty, genius, culture, all that is above the average:

"There is a fatality about all physical and intellectual distinction, the sort of fatality that seems to dog through history the faltering steps of kings. It is better not to be different from one's fellows. The ugly and the stupid have the best of it in this world. They can sit at their ease and gape at the play. . . ."

How true that is! It is not the whole tragedy of Man, but it is one of his tragedies. But how odd it seems that Wilde, knowing all this, should have acted as he did, that even as he wrote these and other paragraphs of worldly—and world—wisdom, he was digging the grave of his own career and all he cared for with frenzied folly. And now in 1891 he was on the verge of that financial success which was to add "hybris" to his other errors—hybris, that insolent excess against which his masters of Greek drama and Greek philosophy had warned him. In the person of Alfred Douglas he met the pinchbeck Antinous with whom he was to play the part of a fatuous and feeble Hadrian.

Wilde had for years been trying to write a successful play. In 1883 he returned to America for the production of *Vera*; and the *Duchess of Padua* was produced in 1891 at the Broadway Theater, New York. But his first success was with *Lady Windermere's Fan* (February 20, 1892) in London; shortly after which license was refused for *Salomé*. The earlier and minor plays may be fairly safely neglected, which reduces those to be considered to three comedy-dramas, one comedy-farce, and a tragedy. By general consent *Salomé* and *The Importance of Being Earnest* are placed at the head of Wilde's stage writings; and, for once, general consent is quite right, though the other three are by no means the negligible imitations they are sometimes said to be.

Wilde had two distinct styles of writing, though he sometimes mixed them (as in the dialogues) with the happiest results. One of these was the æsthetic or symbolist style, gorgeous and poetic, full of allusion and reminiscence and jewelled words (the purple patch, as it is so aptly called); and the other light, worldly, cynical, paradoxical, full of laughter. In his plays he mostly kept them apart, and on the few occasions when he does attempt the purple patch in his comedy-dramas, the result is failure. It was grotesque to make drawing-room characters suddenly talk the speech of *Salammbô* and the *Tentation*, but it was appropriate enough for Salomé.

The tale of Salomé dancing before the Tetrarch Herod, and demanding as her reward "the head of John the Baptist on a charger" is of course a world story, and belongs to any artist or writer who thinks himself strong enough to re-handle it. It appears first, at no more than anecdote length, in the fourteenth chapter of the Gospel of St. Matthew and the seventh of St. Mark. The name "Salomé" is not mentioned in the Gospels, but she is the "daughter of Herodias." The theme was often handled by the old masters of painting. Rubens painted a Salomé for example, and a picture of her by a Venetian master used to hang in the London National Gallery.

The theme came up again in France in the late seventies and early eighties. Gustave Moreau, a painter who did not rest content with "visual experiences" of two oranges and a banana, produced a number of imaginative and detailed visions of ideal beauty between 1850 and his death. He painted two pictures of the Salomé legend, one before the dance, and the other, "L'Apparition," showing with great power and gorgeous decoration Salomé's hallucinated vision of the decapitated saint after she has gained her terrible reward. The picture was one of the most discussed at the Salon of 1876.

Did Flaubert see these pictures? I think he probably did, and that they suggested his marvellously imagined story of Herodias—first mentioned in his correspondence, apparently as a new idea for a story, in an undated letter to Madame des Genettes, placed by Madame Commanville in May 1876—the month of the spring salon. On this story Flaubert concentrated his erudition, his personal knowledge of the Near East, and the limitless resources of his prose. He developed the story far beyond the mere outline of the New Testament, created and motivated the characters, constructed the setting, and made the seemingly purposeless murder entirely credible. As often with Flaubert, the end is severely toned-down and matter of fact. The disciples flee with John's head—"As it was very heavy they carried it alternately."

Then came Huysmans with the *A Rebours* we have already dipped into apropos *The Picture of Dorian Gray*. Several over-written pages are devoted to a very interesting interpretation of Moreau's pictures (Flaubert is not mentioned) and, as the critics put it, "the note of perversity and sadism was added." This was in 1884, and not long afterwards Wilde began talking about a play on Salomé, telling people his version of it, and changing his mind about the treatment of Salomé's character. "Plagiarism!" cry the censorious. But whose? Surely Wilde had as much right to make use of the work of his predecessors as Huysmans, as much right to dramatize Flaubert, Moreau, and Huysmans as Shakespeare had to take a play from a new novel by Robert Greene or a short story by Giraldi Cinthio or the historical legends of Holinshed. As to Wilde having taken the method of *Salomé* from Maeterlinck, it seems from what Sherard says that he must have been at work on it before Maeterlinck's first play was published. Very soon after, anyway.

Wilde has been successful in reconstituting this grotesque old tragedy, and in supplying some very dramatic motivations avoided by his predecessors. Flaubert kept to the ancient narrative, and made Salomé the more or less innocent tool of her mother Herodias, while he supplied the description of the famous dance (which has since inspired so many poets and dancers) from his recollections of the performance given by an Arab harlot he knew in Egypt. Wilde brings Salomé into the foreground at once, and keeps her there. He takes up Huysmans's hint of the predatory lust of Woman, and makes Salomé fall in love with the chaste saint, who of course ungallantly rebuffs her with a good deal of scriptural insult. Seeing her stepfather, the Tetrarch, is plainly hankering after her, Salomé dances for him (against the strenuous opposition of her mother) after having made him promise a reward, "even to half my kingdom." The end is original and dramatic. As Salomé in a frenzy of remorse and sinister blood-lust kisses the lips of the severed head, Herod in a spasm of jealousy orders his soldiers: "Kill that woman!"

Here again we see Wilde's habitual method of openly taking material from sources everyone knew and recombining them into something of his own, colouring and dominating them by his personality. I incline to believe him when he says that he used the repetitions in *Salomé* (which Max Nordau in his *Degeneration* solemnly proclaimed to be an infallible sign of cretinism!)—that he used these repetitions to give the effect of the refrain in an old ballad. This would give him priority over Maeterlinck—not that it matters, but after all Wilde was writing *Symboliste* poems years before the *Symboliste* movement began. Of course, he was aided in writing the French by Pierre Loüys and Marcel Schwob, but their help did not go beyond making verbal corrections. Writing it in French has been censured as an affectation, as if half the poets of England from Chaucer and Gower to Swinburne had not written in other languages! The practice has only disappeared with the vogue of the uneducated author. There were sound artistic reasons for writing *Salomé* in French. Effects are possible with French which cannot be obtained by English; and then the Salomé legend Wilde treated was so much the creation of French artists that it was not only a proper homage to them to write the play in French, but the whole feeling and atmosphere of the story demanded it. Anyway, the play as it stands is much better in French than in Douglas's translation, although Wilde revised and corrected it.

I am at a disadvantage in discussing the three comedy-dramas, which, the dramatic critics tell us, are once more the typical Wilde re-working of known

material—in this case the plays of Augier and Dumas
fils, with elements from Scribe and Sardou. I have long
felt that life is too short and too pleasant to spend any
of it in reading the boulevard plays of the Second
Empire. However, anyone who has been to the theatre
can recognize in these plays stock situations, stock characters, stock morals, and stock accessories—in fact, that
stock view of life which for some quaint reason is known
as "realism" in the theatre. There are the wronged
woman and the wicked lover, the good woman who
seems to trip and the bad woman who saves her, the successful politician with a skeleton in his bank account and
the female blackmailer from Vienna, the compromising
letter, the all-important fan, bracelet, glove, *"tirade à
faire, nous aurons des larmes, etcétera, etcétera."* . . .
What is original in these three pieces is the dominating
Wilde personality. Except when they are being moral
to please the stalls or melodramatic to please the gallery,
all the characters talk like Oscar Wilde; and it is just
this witty amusing talk with its mixture of nonsense,
affectation, and shrewd wisdom which keeps these plays
from oblivion.

A Woman of No Importance is the worst of the
three. The fact that the first act consists almost entirely
of talk is not unwelcome to a reader, though the audience (one surmises) must have fidgetted a good deal.
Is this witty froth meant to warn the discerning that
Mr. Wilde is plotting with his tongue in his cheek? At
any rate he must have known that in real life his
penny-tract morality would have been completely dis-
regarded. After twenty years of poverty the wronged
woman would have been only too delighted to see
her nameless boy rescued from a bank clerk's stool to
become private secretary to his illegitimate father,
now wealthy, powerful, and feared as Lord Illingworth.

She herself would have jumped at the chance of marrying Illingworth, even though it was only a marriage in name—but it would have given her wealth, position, leisure, and the frequent company of her son in his new career. As to the Puritan maiden (fished out of *The Courtship of Miles Standish*, one surmises) who denounces Society as a leper smeared with gold, she is a grotesque, a parody of self-righteous cant. However, the 1890 theatre audiences swallowed it all and applauded—this was what they had been taught to believe and what they came to hear. The one sensible person in the play, who says a number of good things, is the villain, Lord Illingworth, who was probably hissed and cat-called by the boxes as he left the stage for his dressing-room, to remove his wig and grease paint and reveal the smiling and well-known features of Mr. Oscar Wilde.

Lady Windermere's Fan and *An Ideal Husband* are better. Lady Windermere is an aggressively chaste woman who has a disreputable mother without knowing it—they must have been giants for keeping secrets in those days. The mother turns up as Mrs. Erlynn (from Vienna? I believe so), and Lord Windermere foolishly gives her money and tries even to arrange a social come-back without telling his wife. (In fact the real moral of the play is: Never do a silly thing without first telling your wife.) Lady Windermere suspects her husband of a love affair with Mrs. Erlynn, and as an intelligent contribution to the situation compromises herself (the fan!) with Lord Darlington, but is nobly saved—you have guessed it!—by her unknown mother. In doing so Mrs. Erlynn has hopelessly compromised herself, thereby of course confirming everybody's prurient suspicions; but the author is merciful and al-

lows her to marry her Tubby (Lord Augustus Some-
thing-or-Other) who, very oddly, talks like the Scarlet
Pimpernel years before that superman was invented.

An Ideal Husband is a little more emancipated,
but. . . . It is the blackmail play. Sir Robert Chiltern,
a successful politician on the verge of cabinet rank,
has a Secret in his life. Mrs. Cheveley (did I mention
that she was from Vienna?) attempts to profit by it in no
uncertain terms, but is happily defeated by a bracelet
and Lord Goring.

On the whole it may be said that one moral of
these three dramas is that really "good" women cause
a great deal more trouble than they are worth; though
of course such was not the intention of the author (at
least, explicitly) nor the understanding of his delighted
audience. *The Importance of Being Earnest* has no
moral, and is a very happy transfer of literary allegiance
from the fustily "moral" dramatic school of nineteenth-
century France to the happier days of Wycherley
and Congreve. *The Importance of Being Earnest* is a
comedy-farce without a moral, and it is a masterpiece.
Mr. Bernard Shaw (for one astounding moment ap-
pearing in the guise of Mrs. Grundy) denounces it as
a "thoroughly heartless play," (in which he is supported
by that unspotted Galahad, Frank Harris), which is
sheer nonsense. *The Importance of Being Earnest* is
not heartless; it is delightfully and amusingly light-
hearted. For a masterly stroke of visual comedy there
is nothing better than the appearance of Jack Worthing in deepest mourning for the death of his fictitious
brother, Earnest, when the audience knows that Algy
Moncrieff masquerading successfully as that brother is
enjoying a delightful meal inside the house with pretty
Cecily Cardew. This grotesque figure of gloom among

the roses and the sunshine is no bad figure of sombre Victorian morality, and it was very nice of Wilde to make the Victorians laugh at it.

With three artistically immoral plays and one masterpiece Wilde had earned the money he thought he needed to realize his "immeasurable ambition," for which he had worked perhaps harder than is usually supposed. His income in the nineties is said to have been about £8000 a year. These were gold pounds, in a day when income tax was negligible and goods and services much cheaper than today. Goodness knows what astronomical figure in supertaxed paper dollars a man would have to earn today to enjoy its real equivalent. But when Wilde had at last got his opportunity what did his "immeasurable ambition" lead him to achieve? The post of Prime Minister, like his unacknowledged master, Disraeli? No, he merely footed the bill for the ridiculous extravagancies of the younger son of a Scotch marquess, who repaid him by getting him sentenced to two years' penal servitude. In allowing this to happen, Wilde not only ruined himself and his family, but completely betrayed the "Art" he had so often and so ostentatiously proclaimed to be the dearest thing in the world to him. He gave the British Philistine his most resounding triumph, and at a stroke undid the patient work of two generations. The hatred of art, which is one of the few genuine emotions of the English-speaking peoples, was immensely fortified. It may be said of him that he helped unintentionally to prolong the barbarism of nations.

But I cannot leave Wilde on this note of condemnation, just though I believe it to be. The savagery of his sentence and punishment (scientifically worked out to break body and spirit of a ruthless and physically tough criminal) and the horrible public persecution to which he was subjected, are really topics for the psychologist of sadism, lynching, and mob terrorism. For the victim one can only feel indignation and pity. Nobody was made a whit the happier or more "moral" by this brutality; there was simply an increase of hypocrisy and cant, and posterity was deprived of the mature work of a very distinguished writer. It is impossible not to feel that so violent a reaction on the part of society and its legal representatives showed that there was something as wrong with that society as with its prisoner.

III

Some Unpublished Wilde Letters

By the kindness of Dr. Lawrence Powell, the Librarian, and the William Andrews Clark Memorial Library of the University of California, Los Angeles, I am permitted to include twelve unpublished letters from the Wilde manuscripts acquired by Mr. Clark in his lifetime. The prison and post-prison letters preserved in this great collection are to be dealt with by Dr. Rolfe. I am limited to the period before 1895, but many of the more interesting prison and post-prison letters have already been published (I reproduce a couple of these) while, as already indicated, so many of the pre-prison letters have been destroyed that to come on as many as twelve is a real piece of luck.

The first letter, to Lady Wilde, is a travelogue about his first brief trip to Italy, intended for home consumption only. My first feeling on reading it was one of indignation with Mahaffy for showing the boy so little. Imagine going to Venice without seeing the

Tintorettos at the Scuola di San Rocco, to Padua without seeing Mantegna and the Donatello equestrian bronze, to Verona without seeing San Zeno! But perhaps Mahaffy was right to show him a few obvious things and to leave it to him to come back at leisure when the spirit moved him and the bank account permitted. What a pity it seems that when Wilde at last did earn money and the freedom money gives he did not spend some of the money in making a closer acquaintance with the arts of Italy (which he did genuinely love) instead of wasting it in senseless gorgings with Douglas. Still, this long letter to his mother shows genuine enjoyment and a pleasant boyish personality. The little beg for a "genial five pounds" is very nice, and is that touch of money trouble which makes all boys kin.

A. S. Benson, to whom the second letter is addressed, must have been a relative, perhaps a brother, of Frank Benson, the Shakespearean actor and producer. Mr. Wilde, just down from Oxford, is now the professor of art and æsthetics, and rather more sensible than one would have imagined. The criticism of Morris wall papers is very just, though I fear the distemper was caught from Mr. Whistler. But the letter is characteristic. In Wilde's art criticism there is often a touch of the interior decorator—now known in Hollywood as an "environment delineator," which is better than "mortician" and nearly as good as "statesman." Wilde's postscript about Morris's *Earthly Paradise* is also very just—whoever dreamed of reading those charmingly pretty Chaucerian verse tales for their socialism? Only socialists, I should imagine, and how disappointed they must be.

Mrs. Alfred Hunt was the wife of "Watercolour Hunt." Going over these letters to her it occurs to me that they were really intended for her daughter, Violet, whom it would not have been proper then for a young man to address by mail. (In a brief note I have not used, Wilde speaks of Violet Hunt as "the sweetest Violet in all England, only you must not tell her I say so," of course meaning he wanted her told.) Violet Hunt when I knew her was a vivacious, still handsome woman of fifty, with a frightfully indiscreet tongue. Poor Mrs. Hunt was hidden permanently upstairs in a state of senile decay. At the foot of the stairway of South Lodge (the I Tor Villas of Wilde's letters) hung a Rossetti portrait of Violet, who must have been really lovely as a girl. I don't wonder Oscar was attracted to her in 1880, as Ford Madox Ford was in 1912. However, Oscar doesn't seem to have done anything about it, and Violet, who was fond of bragging of her conquest of Andrew Lang and other eminent personages, never mentioned him in my hearing. Perhaps the "wonderful radicalism" of Mrs. Hunt's "wonderful husband" put Oscar off. When I knew the house Mr. Hunt had carried his wonderful radicalism to the next world, where presumably he wouldn't need it.

The joke about Russell Lowell in the Hunt letter of February 17, 1881, is best ignored. The Sir Charles Dilke, mentioned as the other "lion," was a successful Liberal politician, whose career was abruptly smashed by the scandalous divorce suit brought against him by his wife. In its day it made almost as much newspaper noise as the Wilde case, but I imagine has never been heard of by most people today. In the letter to Violet Hunt I am not sure whether the poem referred to as "The Burden of Styx" is "The Burden of Itys" or "Charmides." Certainly the burden of sticks was not a very happy title for a Serious Attempt at Beauty. I don't know who the "Thanes" may be, but it is interesting to know that Wilde was on sufficiently good

terms with Burne-Jones to go calling with him in 1882.
It would be even more interesting to know if this
acquaintanceship survived the American lecture tour.
Burne-Jones had letters from Wilde, for Ross specifically
mentions him as one who destroyed them in 1895.

Colonel Morse was Oscar's lecture manager in
America. The Colonel's recollections of Wilde as published in the Gabriel Wells Collected Edition are very
good-natured and sensible. The letter written from
St. Louis gives a detailed order for more æsthetic
costume. Evidently Wilde realized that he was expected
to dress the part, and made up his mind not to disappoint his audience.

The letter about the new baby is addressed to
"Norman" who, I deduce, was Norman Forbes, afterwards Forbes-Robertson. Wilde in the part of an ex-
ultant young father urging his friend to get married
"at once!" is pleasantly unexpected, as is the undated
letter to Oscar Browning putting off a trip to Cambridge
because one of the babies was ill.

The idea that Ellen Terry should be asked to give
a reading of "The Happy Prince" was obviously David
Nutt's, and, as Wilde says, "charming"—while it lasted.
The remainder of the letter shows Wilde, like all other
authors, fretting himself and his publisher with useless
little publicity devices for selling his book. Nothing
ever sells a book except a fit of collective insanity on
the part of the public.

Mrs. Bernard-Beere was an actress to whom Wilde
wrote a very amusing letter from Kansas City (published before, and reproduced here). The reference to
a play called Once Upon a Time would date it, but I
haven't attempted this piece of important research.
From the rather unpleasantly insincere tone I should
put the letter as late as the early nineties. Perhaps the

most disappointing part of these letters is that they have little of the "wit and sparkle" which poor Reggie Turner (who was with Wilde when he died) used to tell me his generation had and mine hadn't. Wilde needed the immediate applause of a dinner table or a theatre audience in order to be in the right mood to throw off his sparkling jests. . . .

A jester! Yes, in a sense Oscar Wilde was the Court Jester of his age. Alas, poor Yorick!

Hollywood, 1945

SOME DATES

IN THE LIFE OF OSCAR WILDE

1854. October 16. Birth of Oscar Fingall O'Flahertie Wills Wilde, second son of Dr. William (afterwards Sir William) Wilde and his wife, Jane Francesca Elgee, who wrote under the pen name of "Speranza." The Wilde family then lived at 21 Westland Row, Dublin, Ireland.

1864. O.W. at Portora Royal School, Enniskillen, Ireland. Travelled in France.

1867. February 23. Death of O. W.'s sister, Isola, later commemorated in poem "Requiescat."

1871. Matriculated at Trinity College, Dublin, passed scholarship examination and elected a "Queen's Scholar."

1872. Won the Michaelmas Prize at Trinity; third in Classics "Honours" examination.

1873. Elected to a University Scholarship at Trinity.

1874. Won Berkeley Gold Medal for Greek. Professor Mahaffy acknowledged O.W.'s aid in writing his *Social Life in Greece*. O.W. matriculated at Magdalen College, Oxford, for which he won a scholarship.

1875. Visited Italy. First poem (a translation from the Greek) published in Dublin.

1876. Death of Sir W.W. O.W. took a First Class in Classical Moderations at Oxford.

1877. Visited Italy and Greece with Professor Mahaffy.

1878. Won the Newdigate Prize with "Ravenna." Took a First First Class in Literae Humaniores.

1881. *Poems.* Several "editions" sold, but they were bogus, only 200 copies each. American edition of poems in Boston.

1882. January 2. Wilde reached New York, spent the year lecturing; sailed for England December 27.

1883. In Paris with Robert Sherard; lectured in England; returned to America for production of *Vera* written the year before.

1884. May 29. Married Constance Lloyd in London; to Paris for honeymoon. Home at Tite Street, No. 16, Chelsea.

1885. February 20. Review of "Mr. Whistler's Ten o'Clock."

1886. "He began that course of conduct which was to lead to his downfall in 1895." (Ransome.)

1887. *The Canterville Ghost.* In June became editor of *The Woman's World.*

1888. *The Happy Prince and Other Tales;* praised by Walter Pater.

1889. "Pen, Pencil, and Poison." "The Decay of Lying." "Portrait of Mr. W.H." (In periodicals.)

1890. *The Picture of Dorian Gray* (in *Lippincott's Magazine*). "The Critic as Artist" (*Nineteenth Century*).

1891. *The Duchess of Padua* produced (under another title and anonymously) at Broadway Theatre, New York. "The Soul of Man under Socialism" (*Fortnightly*). *Dorian Gray* in book form, April 24. *Intentions,* May 2. *Lord Arthur Savile's Crime and Other Stories,* July. Met Lord Alfred Douglas about June-August through Lionel Johnson. *The House of Pomegranates,* November.

1892. February 20. *Lady Windermere's Fan.* June, *Salomé* in rehearsal—licence refused by Lord Chamberlain's Office.

1893. *Salomé* published in Paris. April 19, *A Woman of No Importance,* produced by Beerbohm Tree at the Haymarket, London.

1894. April 2. Lord Alfred Douglas sends insulting telegram to his father, the Marquess of Queensberry, who (in June) goes to Tite Street, insults O.W., is thrown out. June 11, *The Sphinx.* September 15, Robert Hichens's *The Green Carnation,* an amusing satire of O.W. and Douglas.

1895. January 3. *An Ideal Husband,* produced by Lewis Waller, Royal Theatre, London. February 14, *The Importance of Being Earnest,* produced by George Alexander, St. James's Theatre, London. February 18, Queensberry left an insulting card for O.W. at the Albemarle Club. March 2, Lord Queensberry arrested on O.W.'s complaint for criminal libel. March 12, *An Ideal Husband* at Lyceum Theater, New York. April 3-5, trial of Queensberry, collapse of prosecution, Q. acquitted. April 5, O.W. arrested on charge of "committing acts of gross indecency with other male persons." Wilde on bail. First trial of O.W., April 26-May 1. Jury disagreed. Second trial of O.W., May 22-25. Jury found O.W. guilty on all counts, and Mr. Justice Wills sentenced him to the maximum penalty, two years with hard labour.

1895. August 26. Robert Sherard visited O.W. at Wandsworth Gaol. September 21, Mrs. Wilde visited O.W. Wilde made bankrupt, and moved to Reading Gaol. October, Ward, Lock & Co. republished *Dorian Gray*.

1896. February 3. Death of Lady Wilde. February 11, *Salomé* produced in Paris by Lugné-Poë.

1897. O.W. allowed to write in prison, produced *De Profundis*. May 19, released from prison, went to Dieppe, then to Berneval-sur-Mer. August 24, *Ballad of Reading Gaol* completed. September 5, rejoined Lord Alfred Douglas; separated 1898.

1898. February 13. *Ballad of Reading Gaol* published by L. Smithers, London. April 7, death of Mrs. Wilde.

1899. February. O.W. visited his wife's grave. L. Smithers published *The Importance of Being Earnest*. March, death of O.W.'s brother, William. June, 7th edition of *Reading Gaol*. L. Smithers published *An Ideal Husband*. O.W. travelled in Switzerland, Italy, France.

1900. August. O.W. returned to Paris. October 10, an operation. November 29, O.W. received into Catholic Church. November 30, Wilde died, watched over by Robert Ross and Reginald Turner. Dec. 3, Wilde buried in Cemetery of Bagneux, Paris. The mourners were Dr. Tucker, Robert Ross, Alfred Douglas, Reginald Turner, Maurice Gilbert, the hotel keeper, two servants, and three others not identified.

1905. Feb. 23. Robert Ross published portions of O.W.'s letter from prison under title *De Profundis*. An edition of 15 copies of suppressed parts published in U. S. by Ross to prevent Douglas issuing his copy. Two of these are in the Library of Congress, one in the Clark Memorial Library, Los Angeles. There have been a small pirated edition and a German edition, but the whole work cannot be published until 1960.

Art should never try to be popular; the public should try to make itself artistic.
　　　　　　　　　　　　　—Oscar Wilde
　　　　　　　The Soul of Man under Socialism

The Critic as Artist

Part I

A Dialogue. With Some Remarks Upon the Importance of Discussing Everything.

Persons: GILBERT and ERNEST.
Scene: The library of a house in Piccadilly, overlooking the Green Park.

GILBERT (*at the piano*). My dear Ernest, what are you laughing at?

ERNEST (*looking up*). At a capital story that I have just come across in this volume of Reminiscences that I have found on your table.

GILBERT. What is the book? Ah! I see. I have not read it yet. Is it good?

ERNEST. Well, while you have been playing, I have been turning over the pages with some amusement, though, as a rule, I dislike modern memoirs. They are generally written by people who have either entirely lost their memories, or have never done anything worth remembering; which, however, is, no doubt, the true explanation of their popularity, as the English public always feels perfectly at its ease when a mediocrity is talking to it.

GILBERT. Yes: the public is wonderfully tolerant. It forgives everything except genius. But I must confess that I like all memoirs. I like them for their form, just as much as for their matter. In literature mere egotism is delightful. It is what fascinates us in the letters of personalities so different as Cicero and Balzac, Flaubert and Berlioz, Byron and Madame de Sévigné. Whenever we come across it, and, strangely enough, it is rather rare, we cannot but welcome it, and do not easily forget it. Humanity will always love Rousseau for having confessed his sins, not to a priest, but to the world, and the couchant nymphs that Cellini wrought in bronze for the castle of King Francis, the green and gold Perseus, even, that in the open Loggia at Florence shows the moon the dead terror that once turned life to stone, have not given it more pleasure than has that autobiography in which the supreme scoundrel of the Renaissance relates the story of his splendour and his shame. The opinions, the character, the achievements of the man, matter very little. He may be a sceptic like the gentle Sieur de Montaigne, or a saint like the bitter son of Monica, but when he tells us his own secrets he can always charm our ears to listening and our lips to silence. The mode of thought that Cardinal Newman represented—if that can be called a mode of thought which seeks to solve intellectual problems by a denial of the supremacy of the intellect—may not, cannot, I think, survive. But the world will never weary of watching that troubled soul in its progress from darkness to darkness. The lonely church at Littlemore, where "the breath of the morning is damp, and worshippers are few," will always be dear to it, and whenever men see the yellow snapdragon blossoming on the wall of Trinity they will think of that gracious undergraduate who saw in the flower's sure recurrence a prophecy that he would abide for ever with the Benign Mother of his days—a prophecy that Faith, in her wisdom or her folly, suffered not to be fulfilled.

Yes, autobiography is irresistible. Poor, silly, conceited Mr. Secretary Pepys has chattered away into the circle of the Immortals, and, conscious that indiscretion is the better part of valour, bustles about among them in that "shaggy purple gown with gold buttons and looped lace" which he is so fond of describing to us, perfectly at his ease, and prattling, to his own and our infinite pleasure, of the Indian blue petticoat that he bought for his wife, of the "good hog's harslet," and the "pleasant French fricassee of veal" that he loved to eat, of his game of bowls with Will Joyce, and his "gadding after beauties," and his reciting of *Hamlet* on a Sunday, and his playing of the viol on weekdays, and other wicked or trivial things. Even in actual life egotism is not without its attractions. When people talk to us about others they are usually dull. When they talk to us about themselves they are nearly always interesting, and if one could shut them up, when they become wearisome, as easily as one can shut up a book of which one has grown wearied, they would be perfect absolutely.

ERNEST. There is much virtue in that If, as Touchstone would say. But do you seriously propose that every man should become his own Boswell? What would become of our industrious compilers of Lives and Recollections in that case?

GILBERT. What has become of them? They are the pest of the age, nothing more and nothing less. Every great man nowadays has his disciples, and it is always Judas who writes the biography.

ERNEST. My dear fellow!

GILBERT. I am afraid it is true. Formerly we used to canonize our heroes. The modern method is to vulgarize them. Cheap editions of great books may be delightful, but cheap editions of great men are absolutely detestable.

ERNEST. May I ask, Gilbert, to whom you allude?

GILBERT. Oh! to all our second-rate littérateurs. We are overrun by a set of people who, when poet or painter passes away, arrive at the house along with the undertaker, and forget that their one duty is to behave as mutes. But we won't talk about them. They are the body-snatchers of literature. The dust is given to one, and the ashes to another, and the soul is out of their reach. And now, let me play Chopin to you, or Dvorak? Shall I play you a fantasy by Dvorak? He writes passionate, curiously coloured things.

ERNEST. No; I don't want music just at present. It is far too indefinite. Besides, I took the Baroness Bernstein down to dinner last night, and, though absolutely charming in every other respect, she insisted on discussing music as if it were actually written in the German language. Now, whatever music sounds like, I am glad to say that it does not sound in the smallest degree like German. There are forms of patriotism that are really quite degrading. No, Gilbert, don't play any more. Turn round and talk to me. Talk to me till the white-horned day comes into the room. There is something in your voice that is wonderful.

GILBERT (rising from the piano). I am not in a mood for talking tonight. How horrid of you to smile! I really am not. Where are the cigarettes? Thanks. How exquisite these single daffodils are. They seem to be made of amber and cool ivory. They are like Greek things of the best period. What was the story in the confessions of the remorseful Academician that made you laugh? Tell it to me. After playing Chopin, I feel as if I had been weeping over sins that I had never committed, and mourning over tragedies that were not my own. Music always seems to me to produce that effect. It creates for one a past of which one has been ignorant, and fills one with a sense of sorrows that have been hidden from one's tears. I can fancy a man who had led a perfectly commonplace life, hearing by chance some curious piece of music, and suddenly discovering that his soul, without his being conscious of it, had passed through terrible experiences, and known fearful joys, or wild romantic loves, or great renunciations. And so, tell me this story, Ernest. I want to be amused.

ERNEST. Oh! I don't know that it is of any importance. But I thought it a really admirable illustration of the true value of ordinary art criticism. It seems that a lady once gravely asked the remorseful Academician, as you call him, if his celebrated picture of *A Spring-Day at Whiteley's*, or *Waiting for the Last Omnibus*, or some subject of that kind, was all painted by hand.

GILBERT. And was it?

ERNEST. You are quite incorrigible. But, seriously speaking, what is the use of art criticism? Why cannot the artist be left alone, to create a new world if he wishes it, or, if not, to shadow forth the world which we already know, and of which, I fancy, we would each one of us be wearied if Art, with her fine spirit of choice and delicate instinct of selection, did not, as it were, purify it for us, and give to it a momentary perfection. It seems to me that the imagination spreads, or should spread, a solitude around it, and works best in silence and isolation. Why should the artist be troubled by the shrill clamour of criticism? Why should those who cannot create take upon themselves to estimate the value of creative work? What can they know about it? If a man's work is easy to understand, an explanation is unnecessary.

GILBERT. And if his work is incomprehensible, an explanation is wicked.

ERNEST. I did not say that.

GILBERT. Ah! but you should have. Nowadays, we have so few mysteries left to us that we cannot afford to part with one of them. The members of the Browning Society, like the theologians of the Broad Church Party, or the authors of Mr. Walter Scott's Great Writers Series, seem to me to spend their time in trying to explain their divinity away. Where one had hoped that Browning was a mystic, they have sought to show that he was simply inarticulate. Where one had fancied that he had something to conceal, they have proved that he had but little to reveal. But I speak merely of his incoherent work. Taken as a whole, the man was great. He did not belong to the Olympians, and had all the incompleteness of the Titan. He did not survey, and it was but rarely that he could sing. His work is marred by struggle, violence, and effort, and he passed not from emotion to form, but from thought to chaos. Still, he was great. He has been called a thinker, and was certainly a man who was always thinking, and always thinking aloud; but it was not thought that fascinated him, but rather the processes by which thought moves. It was the machine he loved, not what the machine makes. The method by which the fool arrives at his folly was as dear to him as the ultimate wisdom of the wise. So much, indeed, did the subtle mechanism of mind fascinate him that he despised language, or looked upon it as an incomplete instrument of expression. Rhyme, that exquisite echo which in the Muse's hollow hill creates and answers its own voice; rhyme, which in the hands of the real artist becomes not merely a material element of metrical beauty, but a spiritual element of thought and passion also, waking a new mood, it may be, or stirring a fresh train of ideas, or opening by mere sweetness and suggestion of sound some golden door at which the Imagination itself had knocked in vain; rhyme, which can turn man's utterance to the speech of gods; rhyme, the one chord we have added to the Greek lyre, became in Robert Browning's hands a grotesque, misshapen thing, which at times made him masquerade in poetry as a low comedian, and ride Pegasus too often with his tongue in his cheek. There are moments when he wounds us by monstrous music. Nay, if he can only get his music by breaking the strings of his lute, he breaks them, and they snap in discord, and no Athenian tettix, making melody from tremulous wings, lights on the ivory horn to make the movement perfect, or the interval less harsh. Yet, he was great: and though he turned language into ignoble clay, he made from it men and women that live. He is the most Shakespearian creature since Shakespeare. If Shakespeare could sing with myriad lips, Browning could stammer through a thousand mouths. Even now, as I am speaking, and speaking not against him but for him, there glides through the room the pageant of his persons. There, creeps Fra Lippo Lippi with his cheeks still burning from some girl's hot kiss. There, stands dread Saul with the lordly male-sapphires gleaming in his turban. Mildred Tresham is there, and the Spanish monk, yellow with hatred, and Blougram, and Ben Ezra, and the Bishop of St. Praxed's. The spawn of Setebos gibbers in the corner, and Sebald, hearing Pippa pass by, looks on Ottima's haggard face, and loathes her and his own sin, and himself. Pale as the white satin of his doublet, the melancholy king watches with dreamy treacherous eyes too loyal Strafford pass forth to his doom, and Andrea shudders as he hears the cousins whistle in the garden, and bids his perfect wife go down. Yes, Browning was great. And as what will he be remembered? As a poet? Ah, not as a poet! He

will be remembered as a writer of fiction, as the most
supreme writer of fiction, it may be, that we have ever
had. His sense of dramatic situation was unrivalled, and,
if he could not answer his own problems, he could at
least put problems forth, and what more should an artist
do? Considered from the point of view of a creator of
character he ranks next to him who made Hamlet. Had
he been articulate, he might have sat beside him. The
only man who can touch the hem of his garment is
George Meredith. Meredith is a prose Browning, and
so is Browning. He used poetry as a medium for writing
in prose.

ERNEST. There is something in what you say, but
there is not everything in what you say. In many points
you are unjust.

GILBERT. It is difficult not to be unjust to what
one loves. But let us return to the particular point at
issue. What was it that you said?

ERNEST. Simply this: that in the best days of art
there were no art critics.

GILBERT. I seem to have heard that observation before, Ernest. It has all the vitality of error and all the
tediousness of an old friend.

ERNEST. It is true. Yes: there is no use your tossing
your head in that petulant manner. It is quite true. In
the best days of art there were no art critics. The
sculptor hewed from the marble block the great white-
limbed Hermes that slept within it. The waxers and
gilders of images gave tone and texture to the statue,
and the world, when it saw it, worshipped and was
dumb. He poured the glowing bronze into the mould of
sand, and the river of red metal cooled into noble
curves and took the impress of the body of a god.
With enamel or polished jewels he gave sight to the
sightless eyes. The hyacinth-like curls grew crisp be-

neath his graver. And when, in some dim frescoed fane, or pillared sunlit portico, the child of Leto stood upon his pedestal, those who passed by, ἁβρῶς βαίνοντες διὰ λαμπροτάτου αἰθέρος, became conscious of a new influence that had come across their lives, and dreamily, or with a sense of strange and quickening joy, went to their homes or daily labour, or wandered, it may be, through the city gates to that nymph-haunted meadow where young Phædrus bathed his feet, and, lying there on the soft grass, beneath the tall wind-whispering planes and flowering *agnus castus*, began to think of the wonder of beauty, and grew silent with unaccustomed awe. In those days the artist was free. From the river valley he took the fine clay in his fingers, and with a little tool of wood or bone, fashioned it into forms so exquisite that the people gave them to the dead as their playthings, and we find them still in the dusty tombs on the yellow hillside by Tanagra, with the faint gold and the fading crimson still lingering about hair and lips and raiment. On a wall of fresh plaster, stained with bright sandyx or mixed with milk and saffron, he pictured one who trod with tired feet the purple white-starred fields of asphodel, one "in whose eyelids lay the whole of the Trojan War," Polyxena, the daughter of Priam; or figured Odysseus, the wise and cunning, bound by tight cords to the mast-step, that he might listen without hurt to the singing of the Sirens, or wandering by the clear river of Acheron, where the ghosts of fishes flitted over the pebbly bed; or showed the Persian in trews or mitre flying before the Greek at Marathon, or the galleys clashing their beaks of brass in the little Salaminian bay. He drew with silver-point and charcoal upon parchment and prepared cedar. Upon ivory and rose-coloured terra-cotta he painted with wax, making the wax fluid with juice of

olives, and with heated irons making it firm. Panel and
marble and linen canvas became wonderful as his
brush swept across them; and life, seeing her own
image, was still, and dared not speak. All life, indeed,
was his, from the merchants seated in the market-place
to the cloaked shepherd lying on the hill; from the
nymph hidden in the laurels and the faun that pipes at
noon, to the king whom, in long green-curtained litter,
slaves bore upon oil-bright shoulders, and fanned with
peacock fans. Men and women, with pleasure or sorrow
in their faces, passed before him. He watched them,
and their secret became his. Through form and colour
he re-created a world.

All subtle arts belonged to him also. He held the
gem against the revolving disk, and the amethyst became the purple couch for Adonis, and across the veined
sardonyx sped Artemis with her hounds. He beat out
the gold into roses, and strung them together for neck-
lace or armlet. He beat out the gold into wreaths for
the conqueror's helmet, or into palmates for the Tyrian
robe, or into masks for the royal dead. On the back of
the silver mirror he graved Thetis borne by her Nereids,
or love-sick Phædra with her nurse, or Persephone,
weary of memory, putting poppies in her hair. The
potter sat in his shed, and, flowerlike from the silent
wheel, the vase rose up beneath his hands. He
decorated the base and stem and ears with pattern of
dainty olive-leaf, or foliated acanthus, or curved and
crested wave. Then in black or red he painted lads
wrestling, or in the race: knights in full armour, with
strange heraldic shields and curious visors, leaning from
shell-shaped chariot over rearing steeds: the gods
seated at the feast or working their miracles: the heroes
in their victory or in their pain. Sometimes he would
etch in thin vermilion lines upon a ground of white the

languid bridegroom and his bride, with Eros hovering round them—an Eros like one of Donatello's angels, a little laughing thing with gilded or with azure wings. On the curved side he would write the name of his friend. ΚΑΛΟΣ ΑΛΚΙΒΙΑΔΗΣ or ΚΑΛΟΣ ΧΑΡΜΙ-ΔΗΣ tells us the story of his days. Again, on the rim of the wide flat cup he would draw the stag browsing, or the lion at rest, as his fancy willed it. From the tiny perfume bottle laughed Aphrodite at her toilet, and, with bare-limbed Mænads in his train, Dionysius danced round the wine jar on naked must-stained feet, while, satyr-like, the old Silenus sprawled upon the bloated skins, or shook that magic spear which was tipped with a fretted fir cone, and wreathed with dark ivy. And no one came to trouble the artist at his work. No irresponsible chatter disturbed him. He was not worried by opinions. By the Ilyssus, says Arnold somewhere, there was no Higginbotham. By the Ilyssus, my dear Gilbert, there were no silly art congresses, bringing provincialism to the provinces and teaching the mediocrity how to mouth. By the Ilyssus there were no tedious magazines about art, in which the industrious prattle of what they do not understand. On the reed-grown banks of that little stream strutted no ridiculous journalism monopolizing the seat of judgment when it should be apologizing in the dock. The Greeks had no art critics.

GILBERT. Ernest, you are quite delightful, but your views are terribly unsound. I am afraid that you have been listening to the conversation of someone older than yourself. That is always a dangerous thing to do, and if you allow it to degenerate into a habit, you will find it absolutely fatal to any intellectual development. As for modern journalism, it is not my business to defend it. It justifies its own existence by the great Darwinian principle of the survival of the vulgarest. I have merely to do with literature.

ERNEST. But what is the difference between literature and journalism?

GILBERT. Oh! journalism is unreadable, and literature is not read. That is all. But with regard to your statement that the Greeks had no art critics, I assure you that is quite absurd. It would be more just to say that the Greeks were a nation of art critics.

ERNEST. Really?

GILBERT. Yes, a nation of art critics. But I don't wish to destroy the delightfully unreal picture that you have drawn of the relation of the Hellenic artist to the intellectual spirit of his age. To give an accurate description of what has never occurred is not merely the proper occupation of the historian, but the inalienable privilege of any man of parts and culture. Still less do I desire to talk learnedly. Learned conversation is either the affectation of the ignorant or the profession of the mentally unemployed. And, as for what is called improving conversation, that is merely the foolish method by which the still more foolish philanthropist feebly tries to disarm the just rancour of the criminal classes. No: let me play to you some mad scarlet thing by Dvorak. The pallid figures on the tapestry are smiling at us, and the heavy eyelids of my bronze Narcissus are folded in sleep. Don't let us discuss anything solemnly. I am but too conscious of the fact that we are born in an age when only the dull are treated seriously, and I live in terror of not being misunderstood. Don't degrade me into the position of giving you useful information. Education is an admirable thing, but it is well to remember from time to time that nothing that is worth knowing can be taught. Through the parted curtains of the window I see the moon like a clipped piece of silver. Like gilded bees the stars cluster round her. The sky is a hard hollow sapphire. Let us go out into the night. Thought is wonderful, but adventure is more wonderful still. Who knows but we may meet Prince Florizel of Bohemia, and hear the fair Cuban tell us that she is not what she seems?

ERNEST. You are horribly wilful. I insist on your discussing the matter with me. You have said that the Greeks were a nation of art critics. What art criticism have they left us?

GILBERT. My dear Ernest, even if not a single fragment of art criticism had come down to us from Hellenic or Hellenistic days, it would be none the less true that the Greeks were a nation of art critics, and that they invented the criticism of art just as they invented the criticism of everything else. For, after all, what is our primary debt to the Greeks? Simply the critical spirit. And, this spirit, which they exercised on questions of religion and science, of ethics and metaphysics, of politics and education, they exercised on questions of art also, and, indeed, of the two supreme and highest arts, they have left us the most flawless system of criticism that the world has ever seen.

ERNEST. But what are the two supreme and highest arts?

GILBERT. Life and literature, life and the perfect expression of life. The principles of the former, as laid down by the Greeks, we may not realize in an age so marred by false ideals as our own. The principles of the latter, as they laid them down, are, in many cases, so subtle that we can hardly understand them. Recognizing that the most perfect art is that which most fully mirrors man in all his infinite variety, they elaborated the criticism of language, considered in the light of the mere material of that art, to a point to which we, with our accentual system of reasonable or emotional emphasis, can barely if at all attain; studying, for instance, the metrical movements of a prose as scientifically as a modern musician studies harmony and counterpoint, and, I need hardly say, with much keener æsthetic instinct. In this they were right, as they were right in all things. Since the introduction of printing, and the fatal development of the habit of reading amongst the middle and lower classes of this country, there has been a tendency in literature to appeal more and more to the eye, and less and less to the ear, which is really the sense which, from the standpoint of pure art, it should seek to please, and by whose canons of pleasure it should abide always. Even the work of Mr. Pater, who is, on the whole, the most perfect master of English prose now creating amongst us, is often far more like a piece of mosaic than a passage in music, and seems, here and there, to lack the true rhythmical life of words and the fine freedom and richness of effect that such rhythmical life produces. We, in fact, have made writing a definite mode of composition, and have treated it as a form of elaborate design. The Greeks, upon the other hand, regarded writing simply as a method of chronicling. Their test was always the spoken word in its musical and metrical relations. The voice was the medium, and the ear the critic. I have sometimes thought that the story of Homer's blindness might be really an artistic myth, created in critical days, and serving to remind us, not merely that the great poet is always a seer, seeing less with the eyes of the body than he does with the eyes of the soul, but that he is a true singer also, building his song out of music, repeating each line over and over again to himself till he has caught the secret of its melody, chanting in darkness the words that are winged with light. Certainly,

whether this be so or not, it was to his blindness, as
an occasion if not as a cause, that England's great poet
owed much of the majestic movement and sonorous
splendour of his later verse. When Milton could no
longer write, he began to sing. Who would match the
measures of *Comus* with the measures of *Samson
Agonistes*, or of *Paradise Lost* or *Regained*? When
Milton became blind he composed, as everyone should
compose, with the voice purely, and so the pipe or reed
of earlier days became that mighty, many-stopped organ
whose rich, reverberant music has all the stateliness
of Homeric verse, if it seeks not to have its swiftness,
and is the one imperishable inheritance of English
literature, sweeping through all the ages, because
above them, and abiding with us ever, being immortal
in its form. Yes: writing has done much harm to writers.
We must return to the voice. That must be our test,
and perhaps then we shall be able to appreciate some
of the subtleties of Greek art criticism.

As it is, we cannot do so. Sometimes, when I have
written a piece of prose that I have been modest
enough to consider absolutely free from fault, a dreadful thought comes over me that I may have been guilty
of the immoral effeminacy of using trochaic and
tribrachic movements, a crime for which a learned critic
of the Augustan age censures with most just severity
the brilliant if somewhat paradoxical Hegesias. I grow
cold when I think of it, and wonder to myself if the
admirable ethical effect of the prose of that charming
writer, who once, in a spirit of reckless generosity towards the uncultivated portion of our community, proclaimed the monstrous doctrine that conduct is three-
fourths of life, will not some day be entirely annihilated
by the discovery that the pæons have been wrongly
placed.

ERNEST. Ah! now you are flippant.

GILBERT. Who would not be flippant when he is
gravely told that the Greeks had no art critics? I can
understand it being said that the constructive genius of
the Greeks lost itself in criticism, but not that the race
to whom we owe the critical spirit did not criticize.
You will not ask me to give you a survey of Greek art
criticism from Plato to Plotinus. The night is too lovely
for that, and the moon, if she heard us, would put more
ashes on her face than are there already. But think
merely of one perfect little work of æsthetic criticism,
Aristotle's *Treatise on Poetry*. It is not perfect in form,
for it is badly written, consisting perhaps of notes jotted
down for an art lecture, or of isolated fragments
destined for some larger book, but in temper and
treatment it is perfect absolutely. The ethical effect of
art, its importance to culture, and its place in the
formation of character, had been done once for all by
Plato; but here we have art treated, not from the moral,
but from the purely æsthetic point of view. Plato had,
of course, dealt with many definitely artistic subjects,
such as the importance of unity in a work of art, the
necessity for tone and harmony, the æsthetic value of
appearances, the relation of the visible arts to the
external world, and the relation of fiction to fact. He
first perhaps stirred in the soul of man that desire which
we have not yet satisfied, the desire to know the connexion between beauty and truth, and the place of
beauty in the moral and intellectual order of the
cosmos. The problems of idealism and realism, as he
sets them forth may seem to many to be somewhat
barren of result in the metaphysical sphere of abstract
being in which he places them, but transfer them to the
sphere of art, and you will find that they are still vital
and full of meaning. It may be that it is as a critic of

beauty that Plato is destined to live, and that by alter-
ing the name of the sphere of his speculation we shall
find a new philosophy. But Aristotle, like Goethe, deals
with art primarily in its concrete manifestations, taking
tragedy, for instance, and investigating the material
it uses, which is language, its subject matter, which is
life, the method by which it works, which is action, the
conditions under which it reveals itself, which are
those of theatric presentation, its logical structure,
which is plot, and its final æsthetic appeal, which is to
the sense of beauty realized through the passions of
pity and awe. That purification and spiritualizing of
the nature which he calls κάθαρσις is, as Goethe saw,
essentially æsthetic, and is not moral, as Lessing
fancied. Concerning himself primarily with the impression that the work of art produces, Aristotle sets himself to analyse that impression, to investigate its source,
to see how it is engendered. As a physiologist and
psychologist, he knows that the health of a function resides in energy. To have a capacity for passion and not
to realize it, is to make oneself incomplete and limited.
The mimic spectacle of life that tragedy affords
cleanses the bosom of much "perilous stuff," and by
presenting high and worthy objects for the exercise of
the emotions, purifies and spiritualizes the man; nay,
not merely does it spiritualize him, but it initiates him
also into noble feelings of which he might else have
known nothing, the word κάθαρσις having, it has
sometimes seemed to me, a definite allusion to the rite
of initiation, if indeed that be not, as I am occasionally
tempted to fancy, its true and only meaning here. This
is, of course, a mere outline of the book. But you see
what a perfect piece of æsthetic criticism it is. Who,
indeed, but a Greek could have analysed art so well?
After reading it, one does not wonder any longer that

Alexandria devoted itself so largely to art criticism, and that we find the artistic temperaments of the day investigating every question of style and manner, discussing the great Academic schools of painting, for instance, such as the school of Sicyon, that sought to preserve the dignified traditions of the antique mode, or the realistic and impressionist schools, that aimed at reproducing actual life, or the elements of ideality in portraiture, or the artistic value of the epic form in an age so modern as theirs, or the proper subject matter for the artist. Indeed, I fear that the inartistic temperaments of the day busied themselves also in matters of literature and art, for the accusations of plagiarism were endless, and such accusations proceed either from the thin, colourless lips of impotence, or from the grotesque mouths of those who, possessing nothing of their own, fancy that they can gain a reputation for wealth by crying out that they have been robbed. And I assure you, my dear Ernest, that the Greeks chattered about painters quite as much as people do nowadays, and had their private views, and shilling exhibitions, and Arts and Crafts guilds, and pre-Raphaelite movements, and movements towards realism, and lectured about art, and wrote essays on art, and produced their art historians, and their archæologists, and all the rest of it. Why, even the theatrical managers of travelling companies brought their dramatic critics with them when they went on tour, and paid them very handsome salaries for writing laudatory notices. Whatever, in fact, is modern in our life we owe to the Greeks. Whatever is an anachronism is due to mediævalism. It is the Greeks who have given us the whole system of art criticism, and how fine their critical instinct was, may be seen from the fact that the material they criticized with most care was, as I have already said, language. For the material that painter or sculptor uses is meagre in comparison with that of words. Words have not merely music as sweet as that of viol and lute, colour as rich and vivid as any that makes lovely for us the canvas of the Venetian or the Spaniard, and plastic form no less sure and certain than that which reveals itself in marble or in bronze, but thought and passion and spirituality are theirs also, are theirs, indeed, alone. If the Greeks had criticized nothing but language they would still have been the great art critics of the world. To know the principles of the highest art is to know the principles of all the arts.

But I see that the moon is hiding behind a sulphur-coloured cloud. Out of a tawny mane of drift she gleams like a lion's eye. She is afraid that I will talk to you of Lucian and Longinus, of Quintilian and Dionysius, of Pliny and Fronto and Pausanias, of all those who in the antique world wrote or lectured upon art matters. She need not be afraid. I am tired of my expedition into the dim, dull abyss of facts. There is nothing left for me now but the divine μονόχρονος ἡδονή of another cigarette. Cigarettes have at least the charm of leaving one unsatisfied.

ERNEST. Try one of mine. They are rather good. I get them direct from Cairo. The only use of our attachés is that they supply their friends with excellent tobacco. And as the moon has hidden herself, let us talk a little longer. I am quite ready to admit that I was wrong in what I said about the Greeks. They were, as you have pointed out, a nation of art critics. I acknowledge it, and I feel a little sorry for them. For the creative faculty is higher than the critical. There is really no comparison between them.

GILBERT. The antithesis between them is entirely

arbitrary. Without the critical faculty, there is no artistic creation at all worthy of the name. You spoke a little while ago of that fine spirit of choice and delicate instinct of selection by which the artist realizes life for us, and gives to it a momentary perfection. Well, that spirit of choice, that subtle tact of omission, is really the critical faculty in one of its most characteristic moods, and no one who does not possess this critical faculty can create anything at all in art. Arnold's definition of literature as a criticism of life, was not very felicitous in form, but it showed how keenly he recognized the importance of the critical element in all creative work.

ERNEST. I should have said that great artists worked unconsciously, that they were "wiser than they knew," as, I think, Emerson remarks somewhere.

GILBERT. It is really not so, Ernest. All fine imaginative work is self-conscious and deliberate. No poet sings because he must sing. At least, no great poet does. A great poet sings because he chooses to sing. It is so now, and it has always been so. We are sometimes apt to think that the voices that sounded at the dawn of poetry were simpler, fresher, and more natural than ours, and that the world which the early poets looked at, and through which they walked, had a kind of poetical quality of its own, and almost without changing could pass into song. The snow lies thick now upon Olympus, and its steep, scarped sides are bleak and barren, but once, we fancy, the white feet of the Muses brushed the dew from the anemones in the morning, and at evening came Apollo to sing to the shepherds in the vale. But in this we are merely lending to other ages what we desire, or think we desire, for our own. Our historical sense is at fault. Every century that produces poetry is, so far, an artificial century, and the work that seems to us to be the most natural and simple product of its time is always the result of the most self-conscious effort. Believe me, Ernest, there is no fine art without self-consciousness, and self-consciousness and the critical spirit are one.

ERNEST. I see what you mean, and there is much in it. But surely you would admit that the great poems of the early world, the primitive, anonymous collective poems, were the result of the imagination of races, rather than of the imagination of individuals?

GILBERT. Not when they became poetry. Not when they received a beautiful form. For there is no art where there is no style, and no style where there is no unity, and unity is of the individual. No doubt Homer had old ballads and stories to deal with, as Shakespeare had chronicles and plays and novels from which to work, but they were merely his rough material. He took them and shaped them into song. They became his, because he made them lovely. They were built out of music,

> And so not built at all,
> And therefore built for ever.

The longer one studies life and literature, the more strongly one feels that behind everything that is wonderful stands the individual, and that it is not the moment that makes the man, but the man who creates the age. Indeed, I am inclined to think that each myth and legend that seems to us to spring out of the wonder, or terror, or fancy of tribe and nation, was in its origin the invention of one single mind. The curiously limited number of the myths seems to me to point to this conclusion. But we must not go off into questions of comparative mythology. We must keep to criticism. And what I want to point out is this. An age that has no criticism is either an age in which art is immobile, hieratic, and confined to the reproduction of formal types, or an age that possesses no art at all. There have been critical ages that have not been creative, in the ordinary sense of the word, ages in which the spirit of man has sought to set in order the treasures of his treasure-house, to separate the gold from the silver, and the silver from the lead, to count over the jewels, and to give names to the pearls. But there has never been a creative age that has not been critical also. For it is the critical faculty that invents fresh forms. The tendency of creation is to repeat itself. It is to the critical instinct that we owe each new school that springs up, each new mould that art finds ready to its hand. There is really not a single form that art now uses that does not come to us from the critical spirit of Alexandria, where these forms were either stereotyped, or invented, or made perfect. I say Alexandria, not merely because it was there that the Greek spirit became most self-conscious, and indeed ultimately expired in scepticism and theology, but because it was to that city, and not to Athens, that Rome turned for her models, and it was through the survival, such as it was, of the Latin language that culture lived at all. When, at the Renaissance, Greek literature dawned upon Europe, the soil had been in some measure prepared for it. But to get rid of the details of history, which are always wearisome, and usually inaccurate, let us say generally that the forms of art have been due to the Greek critical spirit. To it we owe the epic, the lyric, the entire drama in everyone of its developments, including burlesque, the idyll, the romantic novel, the novel of adventure, the essay, the dialogue, the oration, the lecture, for which perhaps we should not forgive them, and the epigram, in all the wide meaning of that word. In fact, we owe it everything, except the sonnet, to which, however, some curious parallels of thought movement may be traced in the Anthology, American journalism, to which no parallel can be found anywhere, and the ballad in sham Scotch dialect, which one of our most industrious writers has recently proposed should be made the basis for a final and unanimous effort on the part of our second-rate poets to make themselves really romantic. Each new school, as it appears, cries out against criticism, but it is to the critical faculty in man that it owes its origin. The mere creative instinct does not innovate, but reproduces.

ERNEST. You have been talking of criticism as an essential part of the creative spirit, and I now fully accept your theory. But what of criticism outside creation? I have a foolish habit of reading periodicals, and it seems to me that most modern criticism is perfectly valueless.

GILBERT. So is most modern creative work, also. Mediocrity weighing mediocrity in the balance, and incompetence applauding its brother—that is the spectacle which the artistic activity of England affords us from time to time. And yet, I feel I am a little unfair in this matter. As a rule, the critics—I speak, of course, of the higher class, of those, in fact, who write for the sixpenny papers—are far more cultured than the people whose work they are called upon to review. This is, indeed, only what one would expect, for criticism demands infinitely more cultivation than creation does.

ERNEST. Really?

GILBERT. Certainly. Anybody can write a three-volumed novel. It merely requires a complete ignorance of both life and literature. The difficulty that I should fancy the reviewer feels is the difficulty of sustaining any standard. Where there is no style a standard must be impossible. The poor reviewers are apparently reduced to be the reporters of the police court of literature, the chroniclers of the doings of the habitual criminals of art. It is sometimes said of them that they do not read all through the works they are called upon to criticize. They do not. Or at least they should not. If they did so, they would become confirmed misanthropes; or, if I may borrow a phrase from one of the pretty Newnham graduates, confirmed womanthropes for the rest of their lives. Nor is it necessary. To know the vintage and quality of a wine one need not drink the whole cask. It must be perfectly easy in half an hour to say whether a book is worth anything or worth nothing. Ten minutes are really sufficient, if one has the instinct for form. Who wants to wade through a dull volume? One tastes it, and that is quite enough—more than enough, I should imagine. I am aware that there are many honest workers in painting as well as in literature who object to criticism entirely. They are quite right. Their work stands in no intellectual relation to their age. It brings us no new element of pleasure. It suggests no fresh departure of thought, or passion, or beauty. It should not be spoken of. It should be left to the oblivion that it deserves.

ERNEST. But, my dear fellow—excuse me for interrupting you—you seem to me to be allowing your passion for criticism to lead you a great deal too far. For, after all, even you must admit that it is much more difficult to do a thing than to talk about it.

GILBERT. More difficult to do a thing than to talk about it? Not at all. That is a gross popular error. It is very much more difficult to talk about a thing than to do it. In the sphere of actual life that is, of course, obvious. Anybody can make history. Only a great man can write it. There is no mode of action, no form of emotion, that we do not share with the lower animals. It is only by language that we rise above them, or above each other

—by language, which is the parent, and not the child, of thought. Action, indeed, is always easy, and when presented to us in its most aggravated, because most continuous form, which I take to be that of real industry, becomes simply the refuge of people who have nothing whatsoever to do. No, Ernest, don't talk about action. It is a blind thing, dependent on external influences, and moved by an impulse of whose nature it is unconscious. It is a thing incomplete in its essence, because limited by accident, and ignorant of its direction, being always at variance with its aim. Its basis is the lack of imagination. It is the last resource of those who know not how to dream.

ERNEST. Gilbert, you treat the world as if it were a crystal ball. You hold it in your hand, and reverse it to please a wilful fancy. You do nothing but rewrite history.

GILBERT. The one duty we owe to history is to rewrite it. That is not the least of the tasks in store for the critical spirit. When we have fully discovered the scientific laws that govern life we shall realize that the one person who has more illusions than the dreamer is the man of action. He, indeed, knows neither the origin of his deeds nor their results. From the field in which he thought that he had sown thorns we have gathered our vintage, and the fig tree that he planted for our pleasure is as barren as the thistle, and more bitter. It is because Humanity has never known where it was going that it has been able to find its way.

ERNEST. You think, then, that in the sphere of action a conscious aim is a delusion?

GILBERT. It is worse than a delusion. If we lived long enough to see the results of our actions, it may be that those who call themselves good would be sickened with a dull remorse, and those whom the world calls

evil stirred by a noble joy. Each little thing that we do
passes into the great machine of life, which may grind
our virtues to powder and make them worthless, or
transform our sins into elements of a new civilization,
more marvellous and more splendid than any that has
gone before. But men are the slaves of words. They
rage against materialism, as they call it, forgetting
that there has been no material improvement that has
not spiritualized the world, and that there have been
few, if any, spiritual awakenings that have not wasted
the world's faculties in barren hopes, and fruitless
aspirations, and empty or trammelling creeds. What is
termed Sin is an essential element of progress. Without
it the world would stagnate, or grow old, or become
colourless. By its curiosity, Sin increases the experience
of the race. Through its intensified assertion of individualism it saves us from monotony of type. In its
rejection of the current notions about morality, it is one
with the higher ethics. And as for the virtues! What
are the virtues? Nature, M. Renan tells us, cares little
about chastity, and it may be that it is to the shame of
the Magdalen, and not to their own purity, that the
Lucretias of modern life owe their freedom from
stain. Charity, as even those of whose religion it makes
a formal part have been compelled to acknowledge,
creates a multitude of evils. The mere existence of
conscience, that faculty of which people prate so much
nowadays, and are so ignorantly proud, is a sign of our
imperfect development. It must be merged in instinct
before we become fine. Self-denial is simply a method
by which man arrests his progress, and self-sacrifice a
survival of the mutilation of the savage, part of that
old worship of pain which is so terrible a factor in the
history of the world, and which even now makes its
victims day by day, and has its altars in the land.

Virtues! Who knows what the virtues are? Not you. Not I. Not anyone. It is well for our vanity that we slay the criminal, for if we suffered him to live he might show us what we had gained by his crime. It is well for his peace that the saint goes to his martyrdom. He is spared the sight of the horror of his harvest.

ERNEST. Gilbert, you sound too harsh a note. Let us go back to the more gracious fields of literature. What was it you said? That it was more difficult to talk about a thing than to do it?

GILBERT (*after a pause*). Yes, I believe I ventured upon that simple truth. Surely you see now that I am right? When man acts, he is a puppet. When he describes, he is a poet. The whole secret lies in that. It was easy enough on the sandy plains by windy Ilion to send the notched arrow from the painted bow, to hurl against the shield of hide and flame-like brass the long, ash-handled spear. It was easy for the adulterous queen to spread the Tyrian carpets for her lord, and then, as he lay couched in the marble bath, to throw over his head the purple net, and call to her smooth-faced lover to stab through the meshes at the heart that should have broken at Aulis. For Antigone even, with Death waiting for her as her bridegroom, it was easy to pass through the tainted air at noon, and climb the hill, and strew with kindly earth the wretched naked corse that had no tomb. But what of those who wrote about these things? What of those who gave them reality, and made them live for ever? Are they not greater than the men and women they sing of? "Hector, that sweet knight, is dead," and Lucian tells us how in the dim underworld Menippus saw the bleaching skull of Helen, and marvelled that it was for so grim a favour that all those horned ships were launched, those beautiful mailed men laid low, those towered cities brought to dust. Yet every day the swan-like daughter of Leda comes out on the battlements, and looks down at the tide of war. The greybeards wonder at her loveliness, and she stands by the side of the king. In his chamber of stained ivory lies her leman. He is polishing his dainty armour, and combing the scarlet plume. With squire and page, her husband passes from tent to tent. She can see his bright hair, and hears, or fancies that she hears, that clear, cold voice. In the courtyard below, the son of Priam is buckling on his brazen cuirass. The white arms of Andromache are around his neck. He sets his helmet on the ground, lest their babe should be frightened. Behind the embroidered curtains of his pavilion sits Achilles, in perfumed raiment, while in harness of gilt and silver the friend of his soul arrays himself to go forth to the fight. From a curiously carven chest that his mother Thetis had brought to his shipside, the Lord of the Myrmidons takes out that mystic chalice that the lip of man had never touched, and cleanses it with brimstone, and with fresh water cools it, and, having washed his hands, fills with black wine its burnished hollow, and spills the thick grape-blood upon the ground in honour of Him whom at Dodona barefooted prophets worshipped, and prays to Him, and knows not that he prays in vain, and that by the hands of two knights from Troy, Panthous' son, Euphorbus, whose love-locks were looped with gold, and the Priamid, the lion-hearted, Patroklus, the comrade of comrades, must meet his doom. Phantoms, are they? Heroes of mist and mountain? Shadows in a song? No, they are real. Action! What is action? It dies at the moment of its energy. It is a base concession to fact. The world is made by the singer for the dreamer.

ERNEST. While you talk it seems to me to be so.

GILBERT. It is so in truth. On the mouldering citadel

of Troy lies the lizard like a thing of green bronze. The owl has built her nest in the palace of Priam. Over the empty plain wander shepherd and goatherd with their flocks, and where, on the wine-surfaced, oily sea οἶνοψ πόντος, as Homer calls it, copper-prowed and streaked with vermilion, the great galleys of the Danaoi came in their gleaming crescent, the lonely tunny-fisher sits in his little boat and watches the bobbing corks of his net. Yet, every morning the doors of the city are thrown open, and on foot, or in horse-drawn chariot, the warriors go forth to battle and mock their enemies from behind their iron masks. All day long the fight rages, and, when night comes, the torches gleam by the tents and the cresset burns in the hall. Those who live in marble or on painted panel know of life but a single exquisite instant, eternal indeed in its beauty, but limited to one note of passion or one mood of calm. Those whom the poet makes live have their myriad emotions of joy and terror, of courage and despair, of pleasure and of suffering. The seasons come and go in glad or saddening pageant, and with winged or leaden feet the years pass by before them. They have their youth and their manhood, they are children, and they grow old. It is always dawn for St. Helena, as Veronese saw her at the window. Through the still morning air the angels bring her the symbol of God's pain. The cool breezes of the morning lift the gilt threads from her brow. On that little hill by the city of Florence, where the lovers of Giorgione are lying, it is always the solstice of noon, of noon made so languorous by summer suns that hardly can the slim, naked girl dip into the marble tank the round bubble of clear glass, and the long fingers of the lute-player rest idly upon the chords. It is twilight always for the dancing nymphs whom Corot set free among the silver poplars of France.

In eternal twilight they move, those frail, diaphanous
figures, whose tremulous white feet seem not to touch
the dew-drenched grass they tread on. But those who
walk in epos, drama, or romance, see through the labouring months the young moons wax and wane, and
watch the night from evening unto morning star, and
from sunrise unto sunsetting can note the shifting day
with all its gold and shadow. For them, as for us, the
flowers bloom and wither, and "the Earth, that Green-
tressed Goddess," as Coleridge calls her, alters her
raiment for their pleasure. The statue is concentrated to
one moment of perfection. The image stained upon the
canvas possesses no spiritual element of growth or
change. If they know nothing of death, it is because
they know little of life, for the secrets of life and death
belong to those, and those only, whom the sequence of
time affects, and who possess not merely the present
but the future, and can rise or fall from a past of glory
or of shame. Movement, that problem of the visible
arts, can be truly realized by literature alone. It is
literature that shows us the body in its swiftness and
the soul in its unrest.

ERNEST. Yes; I see now what you mean. But, surely,
the higher you place the creative artist, the lower must
the critic rank.

GILBERT. Why so?

ERNEST. Because the best that he can give us will be
but an echo of rich music, a dim shadow of clear-
outlined form. It may, indeed, be that life is chaos, as
you tell me that it is; that its martyrdoms are mean and
its heroisms ignoble; and that it is the function of
literature to create, from the rough material of actual
existence, a new world that will be more marvellous,
more enduring, and more true than the world that
common eyes look upon, and through which common

natures seek to realize their perfection. But surely, if this new world has been made by the spirit and touch of a great artist, it will be a thing so complete and perfect that there will be nothing left for the critic to do. I quite understand now, and indeed admit most readily, that it is far more difficult to talk about a thing than to do it. But it seems to me that this sound and sensible maxim, which is really extremely soothing to one's feelings, and should be adopted as its motto by every Academy of Literature all over the world, applies only to the relations that exist between art and life, and not to any relations that there may be between art and criticism.

GILBERT. But, surely, criticism is itself an art. And just as artistic creation implies the working of the critical faculty, and, indeed, without it cannot be said to exist at all, so criticism is really creative in the highest sense of the word. Criticism is, in fact, both creative and independent.

ERNEST. Independent?

GILBERT. Yes; independent. Criticism is no more to be judged by any low standard of imitation or resemblance than is the work of poet or sculptor. The critic occupies the same relation to the work of art that he criticizes as the artist does to the visible world of form and colour, or the unseen world of passion and of thought. He does not even require for the perfection of his art the finest materials. Anything will serve his purpose. And just as out of the sordid and sentimental amours of the silly wife of a small country doctor in the squalid village of Yonville-l'Abbaye, near Rouen, Gustave Flaubert was able to create a classic, and make a masterpiece of style, so from subjects of little or of no importance, such as the pictures in this year's Royal Academy, or in any year's Royal Academy, for that matter, Mr. Lewis Morris's poems, M. Ohnet's novels, or the plays of Mr. Henry Arthur Jones, the true critic can, if it be his pleasure so to direct or waste his faculty of contemplation, produce work that will be flawless in beauty and instinct with intellectual subtlety. Why not? Dullness is always an irresistible temptation for brilliancy, and stupidity is the permanent *Bestia Trionfans* that calls wisdom from its cave. To an artist so creative as the critic, what does subject matter signify? No more and no less than it does to the novelist and the painter. Like them, he can find his motives everywhere. Treatment is the test. There is nothing that has not in it suggestion or challenge.

ERNEST. But is criticism really a creative art?

GILBERT. Why should it not be? It works with materials, and puts them into a form that is at once new and delightful. What more can one say of poetry? Indeed, I would call criticism a creation within a creation. For just as the great artists, from Homer and Æschylus, down to Shakespeare and Keats, did not go directly to life for their subject matter, but sought for it in myth, and legend, and ancient tale, so the critic deals with materials that others have, as it were, purified for him, and to which imaginative form and colour have been already added. Nay, more, I would say that the highest criticism, being the purest form of personal impression, is, in its way, more creative than creation, as it has least reference to any standard external to itself, and is, in fact, its own reason for existing, and, as the Greeks would put it, in itself, and to itself, an end. Certainly, it is never trammelled by any shackles of verisimilitude. No ignoble considerations of probability, that cowardly concession to the tedious repetitions of domestic or public life, affect it ever.

One may appeal from fiction unto fact. But from the soul there is no appeal.

ERNEST. From the soul?

GILBERT. Yes, from the soul. That is what the highest criticism really is, the record of one's own soul. It is more fascinating than history, as it is concerned simply with oneself. It is more delightful than philosophy, as its subject is concrete and not abstract, real and not vague. It is the only civilized form of autobiography, as it deals not with the events, but with the thoughts of one's life; not with life's physical accidents of deed or circumstance, but with the spiritual moods and imaginative passions of the mind. I am always amused by the silly vanity of those writers and artists of our day who seem to imagine that the primary function of the critic is to chatter about their second-rate work. The best that one can say of most modern creative art is that it is just a little less vulgar than reality, and so the critic, with his fine sense of distinction and sure instinct of delicate refinement, will prefer to look into the silver mirror or through the woven veil, and will turn his eyes away from the chaos and clamour of actual existence, though the mirror be tarnished and the veil be torn. His sole aim is to chronicle his own impressions. It is for him that pictures are painted, books written, and marble hewn into form.

ERNEST. I seem to have heard another theory of criticism.

GILBERT. Yes, it has been said by one whose gracious memory we all revere, and the music of whose pipe once lured Proserpina from her Sicilian fields, and made those white feet stir, and not in vain, the Cumnor cowslips, that the proper aim of criticism is to see the object as in itself it really is. But this is a very serious error, and takes no cognizance of criticism's most perfect form, which is in its essence purely subjective, and seeks to reveal its own secret and not the secret of another. For the highest criticism deals with art not as expressive, but as impressive, purely.

ERNEST. But is that really so?

GILBERT. Of course it is. Who cares whether Mr. Ruskin's views on Turner are sound or not? What does it matter? That mighty and majestic prose of his, so fervid and so fiery-coloured in its noble eloquence, so rich in its elaborate, symphonic music, so sure and certain, at its best, in subtle choice of word and epithet, is at least as great a work of art as any of those wonderful sunsets that bleach or rot on their corrupted canvases in England's Gallery; greater, indeed, one is apt to think at times, not merely because its equal beauty is more enduring, but on account of the fuller variety of its appeal, soul speaking to soul in those long-cadenced lines, not through form and colour alone, though through these, indeed, completely and without loss, but with intellectual and emotional utterance, with lofty passion and with loftier thought, with imaginative insight, and with poetic aim; greater, I always think, even as Literature is the greater art. Who, again, cares whether Mr. Pater has put into the portrait of Mona Lisa something that Leonardo never dreamed of? The painter may have been merely the slave of an archaic smile, as some have fancied, but whenever I pass into the cool galleries of the Palace of the Louvre, and stand before that strange figure "set in its marble chair in that cirque of fantastic rocks, as in some faint light under sea," I murmur to myself, "She is older than the rocks among which she sits; like the vampire, she has been dead many times, and learned the secrets of the grave; and has been a diver in deep seas, and keeps their fallen day about her; and trafficked for strange webs with Eastern merchants; and, as Leda, was the mother of Helen of Troy, and, as St. Anne, the mother of Mary; and all this has been to her but as the sound of lyres and flutes, and lives only in the delicacy with which it has moulded the changing lineaments, and tinged the eyelids and the hands." And I say to my friend, "The presence that thus so strangely rose beside the waters is expressive of what in the ways of a thousand years man had come to desire"; and he answers me, "Hers is the head upon which all 'the ends of the world are come,' and the eyelids are a little weary."

And so the picture becomes more wonderful to us than it really is, and reveals to us a secret of which, in truth, it knows nothing, and the music of the mystical prose is as sweet in our ears as was that flute-player's music that lent to the lips of La Gioconda those subtle and poisonous curves. Do you ask me what Leonardo would have said had anyone told him of this picture that "all the thoughts and experience of the world had etched and moulded there in that which they had of power to refine and make expressive the outward form, the animalism of Greece, the lust of Rome, the reverie of the Middle Age with its spiritual ambition and imaginative loves, the return of the Pagan world, the sins of the Borgias?" He would probably have answered that he had contemplated none of these things, but had concerned himself simply with certain arrangements of lines and masses, and with new and curious colour-harmonies of blue and green. And it is for this very reason that the criticism which I have quoted is criticism of the highest kind. It treats the work of art simply as a starting-point for a new creation. It does not confine itself—let us at least suppose so for the moment—to discovering the real intention of the artist and accepting

that as final. And in this it is right, for the meaning of
any beautiful created thing is, at least, as much in the
soul of him who looks at it as it was in his soul who
wrought it. Nay, it is rather the beholder who lends to
the beautiful thing its myriad meanings, and makes it
marvellous for us, and sets it in some new relation to
the age, so that it becomes a vital portion of our lives,
and a symbol of what we pray for, or perhaps of what,
having prayed for, we fear that we may receive. The
longer I study, Ernest, the more clearly I see that the
beauty of the visible arts is, as the beauty of music,
impressive primarily, and that it may be marred, and
indeed often is so, by any excess of intellectual intention
on the part of the artist. For when the work is finished
it has, as it were, an independent life of its own, and
may deliver a message far other than that which was
put into its lips to say. Sometimes, when I listen to the
overture of *Tannhäuser*, I seem indeed to see that
comely knight treading delicately on the flower-strewn
grass, and to hear the voice of Venus calling to him
from the caverned hill. But at other times it speaks to
me of a thousand different things, of myself, it may be,
and my own life, or of the lives of others whom one has
loved and grown weary of loving, or of the passions
that man has known, or of the passions that man has
not known, and so has sought for. Tonight it may fill
one with that ΕΡΩΣ ΤΩΝ ΑΔΥΝΑΤΩΝ, that *Amour
de l'Impossible,* which falls like a madness on many
who think they live securely and out of reach of harm,
so that they sicken suddenly with the poison of unlimited desire, and, in the infinite pursuit of what they
may not obtain, grow faint and swoon or stumble. Tomorrow, like the music of which Aristotle and Plato tell
us, the noble Dorian music of the Greek, it may perform
the office of a physician, and give us an anodyne against

pain, and heal the spirit that is wounded, and "bring the soul into harmony with all right things." And what is true about music is true about all the arts. Beauty has as many meanings as man has moods. Beauty is the symbol of symbols. Beauty reveals everything, because it expresses nothing. When it shows us itself it shows us the whole fiery-coloured world.

ERNEST. But is such work as you have talked about really criticism?

GILBERT. It is the highest criticism, for it criticizes not merely the individual work of art, but beauty itself, and fills with wonder a form which the artist may have left void, or not understood, or understood incompletely.

ERNEST. The highest criticism, then, is more creative than creation, and the primary aim of the critic is to see the object as in itself it really is not; that is your theory, I believe?

GILBERT. Yes, that is my theory. To the critic the work of art is simply a suggestion for a new work of his own, that need not necessarily bear any obvious resemblance to the thing it criticizes. The one characteristic of a beautiful form is that one can put into it whatever one wishes, and see in it whatever one chooses to see; and the beauty, that gives to creation its universal and æsthetic element, makes the critic a creator in his turn, and whispers of a thousand different things which were not present in the mind of him who carved the statue or painted the panel or graved the gem.

It is sometimes said by those who understand neither the nature of the highest criticism nor the charm of the highest art, that the pictures that the critic loves most to write about are those that belong to the anecdotage of painting, and that deal with scenes taken out of literature or history. But this is not so. Indeed, pictures of this kind are far too intelligible. As a class, they rank with illustrations, and, even considered from this point of view, are failures, as they do not stir the imagination, but set definite bounds to it. For the domain of the painter is, as I suggested before, widely different from that of the poet. To the latter belongs life in its full and absolute entirety; not merely the beauty that men look at, but the beauty that men listen to also; not merely the momentary grace of form or the transient gladness of colour, but the whole sphere of feeling, the perfect cycle of thought. The painter is so far limited that it is only through the mask of the body that he can show us the mystery of the soul; only through conventional images that he can handle ideas; only through its physical equivalents that he can deal with psychology. And how inadequately does he do it then, asking us to accept the torn turban of the Moor for the noble rage of Othello, or a dotard in a storm for the wild madness of Lear! Yet it seems as if nothing could stop him. Most of our elderly English painters spend their wicked and wasted lives in poaching upon the domain of the poets, marring their motives by clumsy treatment, and striving to render, by visible form or colour, the marvel of what is invisible, the splendour of what is not seen. Their pictures are, as a natural consequence, insufferably tedious. They have degraded the visible arts into the obvious arts, and the one thing not worth looking at is the obvious. I do not say that poet and painter may not treat of the same subject. They have always done so, and will always do so. But while the poet can be pictorial or not, as he chooses, the painter must be pictorial always. For a painter is limited, not to what he sees in nature, but to what upon canvas may be seen.

And so, my dear Ernest, pictures of this kind will not really fascinate the critic. He will turn from them to such works as make him brood and dream and fancy, to works that possess the subtle quality of suggestion, and seem to tell one that even from them there is an escape into a wider world. It is sometimes said that the tragedy of an artist's life is that he cannot realize his ideal. But the true tragedy that dogs the steps of most artists is that they realize their ideal too absolutely. For, when the ideal is realized, it is robbed of its wonder and its mystery, and becomes simply a new starting point for an ideal that is other than itself. This is the reason why music is the perfect type of art. Music can never reveal its ultimate secret. This, also, is the explanation of the value of limitations in art. The sculptor gladly surrenders imitative colour, and the painter the actual dimensions of form, because by such renunciations they are able to avoid too definite a presentation of the real, which would be mere imitation, and too definite a realization of the ideal, which would be too purely intellectual. It is through its very incompleteness that art becomes complete in beauty, and so addresses itself, not to the faculty of recognition nor to the faculty of reason, but to the æsthetic sense alone, which, while accepting both reason and recognition as stages of apprehension, subordinates them both to a pure synthetic impression of the work of art as a whole, and, taking whatever alien emotional elements the work may possess, uses their very complexity as a means by which a richer unity may be added to the ultimate impression itself. You see, then, how it is that the æsthetic critic rejects those obvious modes of art that have but one message to deliver, and having delivered it becomes dumb and sterile, and seeks rather for such modes as suggest reverie and mood, and by their imaginative beauty make all interpretations true and no interpretation final. Some resemblance, no doubt, the creative work of the critic will have to the work that has stirred him to creation, but it will be such resemblance as exists, not between nature and the mirror that the painter of landscape or figure may be supposed to hold up to her, but between nature and the work of the decorative artist. Just as on the flowerless carpets of Persia, tulip and rose blossom indeed, and are lovely to look on, though they are not reproduced in visible shape or line; just as the pearl and purple of the seashell is echoed in the church of St. Mark at Venice; just as the vaulted ceiling of the wondrous chapel of Ravenna is made gorgeous by the gold and green and sapphire of the peacock's tail, though the birds of Juno fly not across it; so the critic reproduces the work that he criticizes in a mode that is never imitative, and part of whose charm may really consist in the rejection of resemblance, and shows us in this way not merely the meaning but also the mystery of beauty, and, by transforming each art into literature, solves once for all the problem of art's unity.

But I see it is time for supper. After we have discussed some Chambertin and a few ortolans, we will pass on to the question of the critic considered in the light of the interpreter.

ERNEST. Ah! you admit, then, that the critic may occasionally be allowed to see the object as in itself it really is?

GILBERT. I am not quite sure. Perhaps I may admit it after supper. There is a subtle influence in supper.

THE CRITIC AS ARTIST

Part II

A Dialogue. With Some Remarks Upon the Importance of Doing Nothing.

Persons and *Scene:* The same.

ERNEST. The ortolans were delightful, and the Chambertin perfect. And now let us return to the point at issue.

GILBERT. Ah! don't let us do that. Conversation should touch everything, but should concentrate itself on nothing. Let us talk about *Moral Indignation, Its Cause and Cure,* a subject on which I think of writing: or about *The Survival of Thersites,* as shown by the English comic papers; or about any topic that may turn up.

ERNEST. No: I want to discuss the critic and criticism. You have told me that the highest criticism deals with art, not as expressive, but as impressive purely, and is, consequently, both creative and independent; is, in fact, an art by itself, occupying the same relation to creative work that creative work does to the visible world of form and colour, or the unseen world of passion and of thought. Well, now tell me, will not the critic be sometimes a real interpreter?

GILBERT. Yes; the critic will be an interpreter, if he chooses. He can pass from his sympathetic impression of the work of art as a whole, to an analysis or exposition of the work itself, and in this lower sphere, as I hold it to be, there are many delightful things to be said and done. Yet his object will not always be to explain the work of art. He may seek rather to deepen its mystery, to raise round it, and round its maker, that mist of wonder which is dear to both gods and worshippers alike. Ordinary people are "terribly at ease in Zion." They propose to walk arm-in-arm with the poets, and have a glib, ignorant way of saying, "Why should we read what is written about Shakespeare and Milton? We can read the plays and the poems. That is enough." But an appreciation of Milton is, as the late Rector of Lincoln remarked once, the reward of consummate scholarship. And he who desires to understand Shakespeare truly must understand the relations in which Shakespeare stood to the Renaissance and the Reformation, to the age of Elizabeth and the age of James; he must be familiar with the history of the struggle for supremacy between the old classical forms and the new spirit of romance, between the school of Sidney, and Daniel, and Jonson, and the school of Marlowe and Marlowe's greater son; he must know the materials that were at Shakespeare's disposal, and the method in which he used them, and the conditions of theatric presentation in the sixteenth and seventeenth centuries, their limitations and their opportunities for freedom, and the literary criticism of Shakespeare's day, its aims and modes and canons; he must study the English language in its progress, and blank or rhymed verse in its various developments; he must study the Greek drama, and the connection between the art of the creator of the *Agamemnon* and the art of the creator of *Macbeth;* in a word, he must be able to bind Elizabethan London to the Athens of Pericles, and to learn Shakespeare's true position in the history of European drama and the drama of the world. The critic will certainly be an interpreter, but he will not treat art as a riddling Sphinx, whose shallow secret may be guessed and revealed by one whose feet are wounded and who knows not his name. Rather, he will look upon art as a goddess whose mystery it is his province to intensify, and whose majesty his privilege to make more marvellous in the eyes of men.

And here, Ernest, this strange thing happens. The critic will, indeed, be an interpreter, but he will not be an interpreter in the sense of one who simply repeats in another form a message that has been put into his lips to say. For, just as it is only by contact with the art of foreign nations that the art of a country gains that individual and separate life that we call nationality, so, by curious inversion, it is only by intensifying his own personality that the critic can interpret the personality and work of others, and the more strongly this personality enters into the interpretation the more real the interpretation becomes, the more satisfying, the more convincing, and the more true.

ERNEST. I would have said that personality would have been a disturbing element.

GILBERT. No; it is an element of revelation. If you wish to understand others you must intensify your own individualism.

ERNEST. What, then, is the result?

GILBERT. I will tell you, and perhaps I can tell you best by definite example. It seems to me that, while the literary critic stands, of course, first, as having the wider range, and larger vision, and nobler material, each of the arts has a critic, as it were, assigned to it. The actor is a critic of the drama. He shows the poet's work under new conditions, and by a method special to himself. He takes the written word, and action, gesture, and voice become the media of revelation. The singer, or the player on lute and viol, is the critic of music.

The etcher of a picture robs the painting of its fair colours, but shows us by the use of a new material its true colour-quality, its tones and values, and the relations of its masses, and so is, in his way, a critic of it, for the critic is he who exhibits to us a work of art in a form different from that of the work itself, and the employment of a new material is a critical as well as a creative element. Sculpture, too, has its critic, who may be either the carver of a gem, as he was in Greek days, or some painter like Mantegna, who sought to reproduce on canvas the beauty of plastic line and the symphonic dignity of processional bas-relief. And in the case of all these creative critics of art it is evident that personality is an absolute essential for any real interpretation. When Rubinstein plays to us the *Sonata Appassionata* of Beethoven, he gives us not merely Beethoven, but also himself, and so gives us Beethoven absolutely—Beethoven re-interpreted through a rich artistic nature, and made vivid and wonderful to us by a new and intense personality. When a great actor plays Shakespeare we have the same experience. His own individuality becomes a vital part of the interpretation. People sometimes say that actors give us their own Hamlets, and not Shakespeare's; and this fallacy— for it is a fallacy—is, I regret to say, repeated by that charming and graceful writer who has lately deserted the turmoil of literature for the peace of the House of Commons—I mean the author of *Obiter Dicta*. In point of fact, there is no such thing as Shakespeare's Hamlet. If Hamlet has something of the definiteness of a work of art, he has also all the obscurity that belongs to life. There are as many Hamlets as there are melancholies.

ERNEST. As many Hamlets as there are melancholies?

GILBERT. Yes, and as art springs from personality,

so it is only to personality that it can be revealed, and from the meeting of the two comes right interpretative criticism.

ERNEST. The critic, then, considered as the interpreter, will give no less than he receives, and lend as much as he borrows?

GILBERT. He will be always showing us the work of art in some new relation to our age. He will always be reminding us that great works of art are living things —are, in fact, the only things that live. So much, indeed, will he feel this, that I am certain that, as civilization progresses and we become more highly organized, the elect spirits of each age, the critical and cultured spirits, will grow less and less interested in actual life, and *will seek to gain their impressions almost entirely from what art has touched.* For life is terribly deficient in form. Its catastrophes happen in the wrong way and to the wrong people. There is a grotesque horror about its comedies, and its tragedies seem to culminate in farce. One is always wounded when one approaches it. Things last either too long, or not long enough.

ERNEST. Poor life! Poor human life! Are you not even touched by the tears that the Roman poet tells us are part of its essence?

GILBERT. Too quickly touched by them, I fear. For when one looks back upon the life that was so vivid in its emotional intensity, and filled with such fervent moments of ecstasy or of joy, it all seems to be a dream and an illusion. What are the unreal things, but the passions that once burned one like fire? What are the incredible things, but the things that one has faithfully believed? What are the improbable things? The things that one has done oneself. No, Ernest! life cheats us with shadows, like a puppet-master. We ask it for pleasure. It gives it to us, with bitterness and disappointment in its train. We come across some noble grief that we think will lend the purple dignity of tragedy to our days, but it passes away from us, and things less noble take its place, and on some grey, windy dawn, or odorous eve of silence and of silver, we find ourselves looking with callous wonder, or dull heart of stone, at the tress of gold-flecked hair that we had once so wildly worshipped and so madly kissed.

ERNEST. Life, then, is a failure?

GILBERT. From the artistic point of view, certainly. And the chief thing that makes life a failure from this artistic point of view is the thing that lends to life its sordid security, the fact that one can never repeat exactly the same emotion. How different it is in the world of art! On a shelf of the bookcase behind you stands the *Divine Comedy,* and I know that, if I open it at a certain place, I shall be filled with a fierce hatred of someone who has never wronged me, or stirred by a great love for someone whom I shall never see. There is no mood or passion that art cannot give us, and those of us who have discovered her secret can settle beforehand what our experiences are going to be. We can choose our day and select our hour. We can say to ourselves, "Tomorrow, at dawn, we shall walk with grave Virgil through the valley of the shadow of death," and lo! the dawn finds us in the obscure wood, and the Mantuan stands by our side. We pass through the gate of the legend fatal to hope, and with pity or with joy behold the horror of another world. The hypocrites go by, with their painted faces and their cowls of gilded lead. Out of the ceaseless winds that drive them, the carnal look at us, and we watch the heretic rending his flesh, and the glutton lashed by the rain. We break the withered branches from the tree in the grove of the Harpies, and each dull-hued, poisonous twig bleeds with red blood before us, and cries aloud with bitter cries. Out of a horn of fire Odysseus speaks to us, and when from his sepulchre of flame the great Ghibelline rises, the pride that triumphs over the torture of that bed becomes ours for a moment. Through the dim purple air fly those who have stained the world with the beauty of their sin, and in the pit of loathsome disease, dropsy-stricken and swollen of body into the semblance of a monstrous lute, lies Adamo di Brescia, the coiner of false coin. He bids us listen to his misery; we stop, and with dry and gaping lips he tells us how he dreams day and night of the brooks of clear water that in cool, dewy channels gush down the green Casentine hills. Sinon, the false Greek of Troy, mocks at him. He smites him in the face, and they wrangle. We are fascinated by their shame, and loiter, till Virgil chides us and leads us away to that city turreted by giants, where great Nimrod blows his horn. Terrible things are in store for us, and we go to meet them in Dante's raiment and with Dante's heart. We traverse the marshes of the Styx, and Argenti swims to the boat through the slimy waves. He calls to us, and we reject him. When we hear the voice of his agony we are glad, and Virgil praises us for the bitterness of our scorn. We tread upon the cold crystal of Cocytus, in which traitors stick like straws in glass. Our foot strikes against the head of Bocca. He will not tell us his name, and we tear the hair in handfuls from the screaming skull. Alberigo prays us to break the ice upon his face that he may weep a little. We pledge our word to him, and when he has uttered his dolorous tale we deny the word that we have spoken, and pass from him; such cruelty being courtesy indeed, for who more base than he who has mercy for the condemned of God? In the jaws of Lucifer we see the man who sold Christ, and in the jaws of Lucifer the man who slew Cæsar. We tremble, and come forth to re-behold the stars.

In the land of Purgation the air is freer, and the holy mountain rises into the pure light of day. There is peace for us, and for those who for a season abide in it there is some peace also, though, pale from the poison of the Maremma, Madonna Pia passes before us, and Ismene, with the sorrow of earth still lingering about her, is there. Soul after soul makes us share in some repentance or some joy. He whom the mourning of his widow taught to drink the sweet wormwood of pain, tells us of Nella praying in her lonely bed, and we learn from the mouth of Buonconte how a single tear may save a dying sinner from the fiend. Sordello, that noble and disdainful Lombard, eyes us from afar like a couchant lion. When he learns that Virgil is one of Mantua's citizens he falls upon his neck, and when he learns that he is the singer of Rome he falls before his feet. In that valley whose grass and flowers are fairer than cleft emerald and Indian wood, and brighter than scarlet and silver, they are singing who in the world were kings; but the lips of Rudolph of Hapsburg do not move to the music of the others, and Philip of France beats his breast, and Henry of England sits alone. On and on we go, climbing the marvellous stair, and the stars become larger than their wont, and the song of the kings grows faint, and at length we reach the seven trees of gold and the garden of the Earthly Paradise. In a griffin-drawn chariot appears one whose brows are bound with olive, who is veiled in white, and mantled in green, and robed in a vesture that is coloured like live fire. The ancient flame wakes within us. Our blood quickens through terrible pulses. We recognize her. It is Beatrice, the woman we have worshipped. The ice congealed about our hearts melts. Wild tears of anguish break from us, and we bow our forehead to the ground, for we know that we have sinned. When we have done penance, and are purified, and have drunk of the fountain of Lethe, and bathed in the fountain of Eunoe, the mistress of our soul raises us to the Paradise of Heaven. Out of that eternal pearl, the moon, the face of Piccarda Donati leans to us. Her beauty troubles us for a moment, and when, like a thing that falls through water, she passes away, we gaze after her with wistful eyes. The sweet planet of Venus is full of lovers. Cunizza, the sister of Ezzelin, the lady of Sordello's heart, is there, and Folco, the passionate singer of Provence, who in sorrow for Azalais forsook the world, and the Canaanitish harlot whose soul was the first that Christ redeemed. Joachim of Flora stands in the sun, and, in the sun, Aquinas recounts the story of St. Francis and Bonaventure the story of St. Dominic. Through the burning rubies of Mars, Cacciaguida approaches. He tells us of the arrow that is shot from the bow of exile, and how salt tastes the bread of another, and how steep are the stairs in the house of a stranger. In Saturn the souls sing not, and even she who guides us dare not smile. On a ladder of gold the flames rise and fall. At last, we see the pageant of the Mystical Rose. Beatrice fixes her eyes upon the face of God, to turn them not again. The beatific vision is granted to us; we know the Love that moves the sun and all the stars.

Yes, we can put the earth back six hundred courses and make ourselves one with the great Florentine, kneel at the same altar with him, and share his rapture and his scorn. And if we grow tired of an antique time, and desire to realize our own age in all its weariness and sin, are there not books that can make us live more in one single hour than life can make us live in a score of shameful years? Close to your hand lies a little volume, bound in some Nile-green skin that has been powdered with gilded nenuphars and smoothed with hard ivory. It is the book that Gautier loved, it is Baudelaire's masterpiece. Open it at that sad madrigal that begins

Que m'importe que tu sois sage?
Sois belle! et sois triste!

and you will find yourself worshipping sorrow as you have never worshipped joy. Pass on to the poem on the man who tortures himself, let its subtle music steal into your brain and colour your thoughts, and you will become for a moment what he was who wrote it; nay, not for a moment only, but for many barren moonlit nights and sunless sterile days will a despair that is not your own make its dwelling within you, and the misery of another gnaw your heart away. Read the whole book, suffer it to tell even one of its secrets to your soul, and your soul will grow eager to know more, and will feed upon poisonous honey, and seek to repent of strange crimes of which it is guiltless, and to make atonement for terrible pleasures that it has never known. And then, when you are tired of these flowers of evil, turn to the flowers that grow in the garden of Perdita, and in their dew-drenched chalices cool your fevered brow, and let their loveliness heal and restore your soul; or wake from his forgotten tomb the sweet Syrian, Meleager, and bid the lover of Heliodore make you music, for he, too, has flowers in his song, red pomegranate blossoms, and irises that smell of myrrh, ringed daffodils and dark blue hyacinths, and marjoram and crinkled ox-eyes. Dear to him was the perfume of the bean-field at evening, and dear to him the odorous eared-spikenard that grew on the Syrian hills, and the fresh, green thyme, the wine-cup's charm. The feet of his love, as she walked in the garden, were like lilies set upon lilies. Softer than sleep-laden poppy petals were her lips, softer than violets and as scented. The flame-like crocus sprang from the grass to look at her. For her the slim narcissus stored the cool rain; and for her the anemones forgot the Sicilian winds that wooed them. And neither crocus, nor anemone, nor narcissus was as fair as she was.

It is a strange thing, this transference of emotion. We sicken with the same maladies as the poets, and the singer lends us his pain. Dead lips have their message for us, and hearts that have fallen to dust can communicate their joy. We run to kiss the bleeding mouth of Fantine, and we follow Manon Lescaut over the whole world. Ours is the love-madness of the Tyrian, and the terror of Orestes is ours also. There is no passion that we cannot feel, no pleasure that we may not gratify, and we can choose the time of our initiation and the time of our freedom, also. Life! Life! Don't let us go to life for our fulfilment or our experience. It is a thing narrowed by circumstances, incoherent in its utterance, and without that fine correspondence of form and spirit which is the only thing that can satisfy the artistic and critical temperament. It makes us pay too high a price for its wares, and we purchase the meanest of its secrets at a cost that is monstrous and infinite.

ERNEST. Must we go, then, to art for everything?

GILBERT. For everything. Because art does not hurt us. The tears that we shed at a play are a type of the exquisite sterile emotions that it is the function of art to awaken. We weep, but we are not wounded. We grieve, but our grief is not bitter. In the actual life of man, sorrow, as Spinoza says somewhere, is a passage to a lesser perfection. But the sorrow with which art fills us both purifies and initiates, if I may quote once more from the great art critic of the Greeks. It is through art, and through art only, that we can realize our perfection; through art, and through art only, that we can shield ourselves from the sordid perils of actual existence. This results not merely from the fact that nothing that one can imagine is worth doing, and that one can imagine everything, but from the subtle law that emotional forces, like the forces of the physical sphere, are limited in extent and energy. One can feel so much, and no more. And how can it matter with what pleasure life tries to tempt one, or with what pain it seeks to maim and mar one's soul, if in the spectacle of the lives of those who have never existed one has found the true secret of joy, and wept away one's tears over their deaths who, like Cordelia and the daughter of Brabantio, can never die?

ERNEST. Stop a moment. It seems to me that in everything that you have said there is something radically immoral.

GILBERT. All art is immoral.

ERNEST. All art?

GILBERT. Yes. For emotion for the sake of emotion is the aim of art, and emotion for the sake of action is the aim of life, and of that practical organization of life that we call society. Society, which is the beginning and basis of morals, exists simply for the concentration of human energy, and in order to ensure its own continuance and healthy stability it demands, and no doubt rightly demands, of each of its citizens that he should contribute some form of productive labour to the common weal, and toil and travail that the day's work may be done. Society often forgives the criminal; it never forgives the dreamer. The beautiful sterile emotions that art excites in us are hateful in its eyes, and so completely are people dominated by the tyranny of this dreadful social ideal that they are always coming shamelessly up to one at Private Views and other places that are open to the general public, and saying in a loud, stentorian voice, "What are you doing?" whereas "What are you thinking?" is the only question that any single civilized being should ever be allowed to whisper to another. They mean well, no doubt, these honest, beaming folk. Perhaps that is the reason why they are so excessively tedious. But someone should teach them that while, in the opinion of society, contemplation is the gravest sin of which any citizen can be guilty, in the opinion of the highest culture it is the proper occupation of man.

ERNEST. Contemplation?

GILBERT. Contemplation. I said to you some time ago that it was far more difficult to talk about a thing than to do it. Let me say to you now that to do nothing at all is the most difficult thing in the world, the most difficult and the most intellectual. To Plato, with his passion for wisdom, this was the noblest form of energy. To Aristotle, with his passion for knowledge, this was the noblest form of energy, also. It was to this that the passion for holiness led the saint and the mystic of mediæval days.

ERNEST. We exist, then, to do nothing?

GILBERT. It is to do nothing that the elect exist. Action is limited and relative. Unlimited and absolute is the vision of him who sits at ease and watches, who walks in loneliness and dreams. But we who are born at the close of this wonderful age, are at once too cultured and too critical, too intellectually subtle and too curious of exquisite pleasures, to accept any speculations about life in exchange for life itself. To us the *citta divina* is colourless, and the *fruitio Dei* without meaning. Metaphysics do not satisfy our temperaments, and religious ecstasy is out of date. The world through which the Academic philosopher becomes "the spectator of all time and of all existence" is not really an ideal world, but simply a world of abstract ideas. When we enter it, we starve amidst the chill mathematics of thought. The courts of the city of God are not open to us now. Its gates are guarded by ignorance, and to pass them we have to surrender all that in our nature is most divine. It is enough that our fathers believed. They have exhausted the faith-faculty of the species. Their legacy to us is the scepticism of which they were afraid. Had they put it into words, it might not live within us as thought. No, Ernest, no. We cannot go back to the saint. There is far more to be learned from the sinner. We cannot go back to the philosopher, and the mystic leads us astray. Who, as Mr. Pater suggests somewhere, would exchange the curve of a single rose-leaf for that formless, intangible Being which Plato rates so high? What to us is the Illumination of Philo, the Abyss of Eckhart, the Vision of Böhme, the monstrous Heaven itself that was revealed to Swedenborg's blinded eyes? Such things are less than the yellow trumpet of one daffodil of the field, far less than the meanest of the visible arts; for, just as Nature is matter struggling into mind, so Art is mind expressing itself under the conditions of matter, and thus, even in the lowliest of her manifestations, she speaks to both sense and soul alike. To the æsthetic temperament the vague is always repellent. The Greeks were a nation of artists, because they were spared the sense of the infinite. Like Aristotle, like Goethe after he had read Kant, we desire the concrete, and nothing but the concrete can satisfy us.

ERNEST. What, then, do you propose?

GILBERT. It seems to me that with the development of the critical spirit we shall be able to realize, not merely our own lives, but the collective life of the race, and so to make ourselves absolutely modern, in the true meaning of the word modernity. For he to whom the present is the only thing that is present, knows nothing of the age in which he lives. To realize the nineteenth century, one must realize every century that has preceded it and that has contributed to its making. To know anything about oneself, one must know all about others. There must be no mood with which one cannot sympathize, no dead mode of life that one cannot make alive. Is this impossible? I think not. By revealing to us the absolute mechanism of all action, and so freeing us from the self-imposed and trammelling burden of moral responsibility, the scientific principle of heredity has become, as it were, the warrant for the contemplative life. It has shown us that we are never less free than when we try to act. It has hemmed us round with the nets of the hunter, and written upon the wall the prophecy of our doom. We may not watch it, for it is within us. We may not see it, save in a mirror that mirrors the soul. It is Nemesis without her mask. It is the last of the Fates, and the most terrible. It is the only one of the gods whose real name we know.

And yet, while in the sphere of practical and external life it has robbed energy of its freedom and activity of its choice, in the subjective sphere, where the soul is at work, it comes to us, this terrible shadow, with many gifts in its hands, gifts of strange temperaments and subtle susceptibilities, gifts of wild ardours and chill moods of indifference, complex multiform gifts of thoughts that are at variance with each other, and passions that war against themselves. And so, it is not our own life that we live, but the lives of the dead, and the soul that dwells within us is no single spiritual entity, making us personal and individual, created for our service, and entering into us for our joy. It is something that has dwelt in fearful places, and in ancient sepulchres has made its abode. It is sick with many maladies, and has memories of curious sins. It is wiser than we are, and its wisdom is bitter. It fills us with impossible desires, and makes us follow what we know we cannot gain. One thing, however, Ernest, it can do for us. It can lead us away from surroundings whose beauty is dimmed to us by the mist of familiarity, or whose ignoble ugliness and sordid claims are marring the perfection of our development. It can help us to leave the age in which we were born, and to pass into other ages, and find ourselves not exiled from their air. It can teach us how to escape from our experience, and to realize the experiences of those who are greater than we are. The pain of Leopardi crying out against life becomes our pain. Theocritus blows on his pipe, and we laugh with the lips of nymph and shepherd. In the wolfskin of Pierre Vidal we flee before the hounds, and in the armour of Lancelot we ride from the bower of the Queen. We have whispered the secret of our love beneath the cowl of Abelard, and in the stained raiment of Villon have put our shame into song. We can see the dawn through Shelley's eyes, and when we wander with Endymion the Moon grows amorous of our youth. Ours is the anguish of Atys, and ours the weak rage and noble sorrows of the Dane. Do you think that it is the imagination that enables us to live these countless lives? Yes, it is the imagination; and the imagination is the result of heredity. It is simply concentrated race-experience.

ERNEST. But where in this is the function of the critical spirit?

GILBERT. The culture that this transmission of racial experiences makes possible can be made perfect by the critical spirit alone, and indeed may be said to be one with it. For who is the true critic but he who bears within himself the dreams, and ideas, and feelings of myriad generations, and to whom no form of thought is alien, no emotional impulse obscure? And who the true man of culture, if not he who by fine scholarship and fastidious rejection has made instinct self-conscious and intelligent, and can separate the work that has distinction from the work that has it not, and so by contact and comparison makes himself master of the secrets of style and school, and understands their meanings, and listens to their voices, and develops that spirit of disinterested curiosity which is the real root, as it is the real flower, of the intellectual life, and thus attains to intellectual clarity; and, having learned "the best that is known and thought in the world," lives—it is not fanciful to say so—with those who are the Immortals?

Yes, Ernest: the contemplative life, the life that has for its aim not *doing* but *being*, and not *being* merely, but *becoming*—that is what the critical spirit can give us. The gods live thus: either brooding over their own perfection, as Aristotle tells us, or, as Epicurus fancied, watching with the calm eyes of the spectator the tragi-comedy of the world that they have made. We, too, might live like them, and set ourselves to witness with appropriate emotions the varied scenes that man and nature afford. We might make ourselves spiritual by detaching ourselves from action, and become perfect by the rejection of energy. It has often seemed to me that Browning felt something of this. Shakespeare hurls Hamlet into active life, and makes him realize his mission by effort. Browning might have given us a Hamlet who would have realized his mission by thought. Incident and event were to him unreal or un-meaning. He made the soul the protagonist of life's tragedy, and looked on action as the one undramatic element of a play. To us, at any rate, the ΒΙΟΣ ΘΕΩΡΗΤΙΚΟΣ is the true ideal. From the high tower of thought we can look out at the world. Calm, and self-centred, and complete, the æsthetic critic con-templates life, and no arrow drawn at a venture can pierce between the joints of his harness. He at least is safe. He has discovered how to live.

Is such a mode of life immoral? Yes, all the arts are immoral, except those baser forms of sensual or didactic art that seek to excite to action of evil or of good. For action of every kind belongs to the sphere of ethics. The aim of art is simply to create a mood. Is such a mode of life unpractical? Ah! it is not so easy to be unpractical as the ignorant Philistine imagines. It were well for England if it were so. There is no country in the world so much in need of unpractical people as this country of ours. With us, thought is degraded by its constant association with practice. Who that moves in the stress and turmoil of actual existence, noisy politician, or brawling social reformer, or poor, narrow-minded priest, blinded by the sufferings of that unim-portant section of the community among whom he has cast his lot, can seriously claim to be able to form a disinterested intellectual judgment about any one thing? Each of the professions means a prejudice. The necessity for a career forces everyone to take sides. We live in the age of the overworked, and the under-educated; the age in which people are so industrious that they become absolutely stupid. And, harsh though it may sound, I cannot help saying that such people deserve their doom. The sure way of knowing nothing about life is to try to make oneself useful.

ERNEST. A charming doctrine, Gilbert.

GILBERT. I am not sure about that, but it has at least the minor merit of being true. That the desire to do good to others produces a plentiful crop of prigs is the least of the evils of which it is the cause. The prig is a very interesting psychological study, and though of all poses a moral pose is the most offensive, still to have a pose at all is something. It is a formal recognition of the importance of treating life from a definite and reasoned standpoint. That humanitarian sympathy wars against Nature, by securing the survival of the failure, may make the man of science loathe its facile virtues. The political economist may cry out against it for putting the improvident on the same level as the provident, and so robbing life of the strongest, because most sordid, incentive to industry. But, in the eyes of the thinker, the real harm that emotional sympathy does is that it limits knowledge, and so prevents us from solving any single social problem. We are trying at present to stave off the coming crisis, the coming revolution, as my friends the Fabianists call it, by means of doles and alms. Well, when the revolution or crisis arrives, we shall be powerless because we shall know nothing. And so, Ernest, let us not be deceived. England will never be civilized until she has added Utopia to her dominions. There is more than one of her colonies that she might with advantage surrender for so fair a land. What we want are unpractical people who see beyond the moment, and think beyond the day. Those who try to lead the people can only do so by following the mob. It is through the voice of one crying in the wilderness that the ways of the gods must be prepared.

But perhaps you think that in beholding for the mere joy of beholding, and contemplating for the sake of contemplation, there is something that is egotistic. If you think so, do not say so. It takes a thoroughly selfish age, like our own, to deify self-sacrifice. It takes a thoroughly grasping age, such as that in which we live, to set above the fine intellectual virtues those shallow and emotional virtues that are an immediate practical benefit to itself. They miss their aim, too, these philanthropists and sentimentalists of our day, who are always chattering to one about one's duty to one's neighbour. For the development of the race depends on the development of the individual, and where self-culture has ceased to be the ideal the intellectual standard is instantly lowered, and, often, ultimately lost. If you meet at dinner a man who has spent his life in educating himself—a rare type in our time, I admit, but still one occasionally to be met with—you rise from table richer, and conscious that a high ideal has for a moment touched and sanctified your days. But oh! my dear Ernest, to sit next to a man who has spent his life in trying to educate others! What a dreadful experience that is! How appalling is that ignorance which is the inevitable result of the fatal habit of imparting opinions! How limited in range the creature's mind proves to be! How it wearies us, and must weary himself, with its endless repetitions and sickly reiteration! How lacking it is in any element of intellectual growth! In what a vicious circle it always moves!

ERNEST. You speak with strange feeling, Gilbert. Have you had this dreadful experience, as you call it, lately?

GILBERT. Few of us escape it. People say that the schoolmaster is abroad. I wish to goodness he were. But the type of which, after all, he is only one, and certainly the least important, of the representatives, seems to me to be really dominating our lives; and just as the philanthropist is the nuisance of the ethical sphere, so the nuisance of the intellectual sphere is the man who is so occupied in trying to educate others that he has never had any time to educate himself. No, Ernest, self-culture is the true ideal of man. Goethe saw it, and the immediate debt that we owe to Goethe is greater than the debt we owe to any man since Greek days. The Greeks saw it, and have left us, as their legacy to modern thought, the conception of the contemplative life as well as the critical method by which alone can that life be truly realized. It was the one thing that made the Renaissance great, and gave us Humanism. It is the one thing that could make our own age great also; for the real weakness of England lies, not in incomplete armaments or unfortified coasts, not in the poverty that creeps through sunless lanes, or the drunkenness that brawls in loathsome courts, but simply in the fact that her ideals are emotional and not intellectual.

I do not deny that the intellectual ideal is difficult of attainment, still less that it is, and perhaps will be for years to come, unpopular with the crowd. It is so easy for people to have sympathy with suffering. It is so difficult for them to have sympathy with thought. Indeed, so little do ordinary people understand what thought really is, that they seem to imagine that, when they have said that a theory is dangerous, they have pronounced its condemnation, whereas it is only such theories that have any true intellectual value. An idea that is not dangerous is unworthy of being called an idea at all.

ERNEST. Gilbert, you bewilder me. You have told me that all art is, in its essence, immoral. Are you going to tell me now that all thought is, in its essence, dangerous?

GILBERT. Yes, in the practical sphere it is so. The security of society lies in custom and unconscious instinct, and the basis of the stability of society, as a healthy organism, is the complete absence of any intelligence amongst its members. The great majority of people being fully aware of this, rank themselves naturally on the side of that splendid system that elevates them to the dignity of machines, and rage so wildly against the intrusion of the intellectual faculty into any question that concerns life, that one is tempted to define man as a rational animal who always loses his temper when he is called upon to act in accordance with the dictates of reason. But let us turn from the practical sphere, and say no more about the wicked philanthropists, who, indeed, may well be left to the mercy of the almond-eyed sage of the Yellow River, Chuang Tsŭ the wise, who has proved that such well-meaning and offensive busybodies have destroyed the simple and spontaneous virtue that there is in man. They are a wearisome topic, and I am anxious to get back to the sphere in which criticism is free.

ERNEST. The sphere of the intellect?

GILBERT. Yes. You remember that I spoke of the critic as being in his own way as creative as the artist, whose work, indeed, may be merely of value in so far as it gives to the critic a suggestion for some new mood of thought and feeling which he can realize with equal or perhaps greater distinction of form, and, through the use of a fresh medium of expression, make differently beautiful and more perfect. Well, you seemed to me to be a little sceptical about the theory. But perhaps I wronged you?

ERNEST. I am not really sceptical about it, but I must admit that I feel very strongly that such work as you describe the critic producing—and creative such work must undoubtedly be admitted to be—is, of necessity, purely subjective, whereas the greatest work is objective always, objective and impersonal.

GILBERT. The difference between objective and subjective work is one of external form merely. It is accidental, not essential. All artistic creation is absolutely subjective. The very landscape that Corot looked at was, as he said himself, but a mood of his own mind; and those great figures of Greek or English drama that seem to us to possess an actual existence of their own, apart from the poets who shaped and fashioned them, are, in their ultimate analysis, simply the poets themselves, not as they thought they were, but as they thought they were not; and by such thinking came in strange manner, though but for a moment, really so to be. For out of ourselves we can never pass, nor can there be in creation what in the creator was not. Nay, I would say that the more objective a creation appears to be, the more subjective it really is. Shakespeare might have met Rosencrantz and Guildenstern in the white streets of London, or seen the serving-men of rival houses bite their thumbs at each other in the open square; but Hamlet came out of his soul, and Romeo out of his passion. They were elements of his nature to which he gave visible form, impulses that stirred so strongly within him that he had, as it were, perforce, to suffer them to realize their energy, not on the lower plane of actual life, where they would have been trammelled and constrained and so made imperfect, but on that imaginative plane of art where love can indeed find in death its rich fulfilment, where one can stab the eavesdropper behind the arras, and wrestle in a new-made grave, and make a guilty king drink his own hurt, and see one's father's spirit, beneath the glimpses of the moon, stalking in complete steel from misty wall to wall. Action, being limited, would have left Shakespeare unsatisfied and unexpressed; and, just as it is because he did nothing that he has been able to achieve everything, so it is because he never speaks to us of himself in his plays that his plays reveal him to us absolutely, and show us his true nature and temperament far more completely than do those strange and exquisite sonnets, even, in which he bares to crystal eyes the secret closet of his heart. Yes, the objective form is the most subjective in matter. Man is least himself when he talks in his own person. Give him a mask, and he will tell you the truth.

ERNEST. The critic, then, being limited to the subjective form, will necessarily be less able to fully express himself than the artist, who has always at his disposal the forms that are impersonal and objective.

GILBERT. Not necessarily, and certainly not at all if he recognizes that each mode of criticism is, in its highest development, simply a mood, and that we are never more true to ourselves than when we are inconsistent. The æsthetic critic, constant only to the principle of beauty in all things, will ever be looking for fresh impressions, winning from the various schools the secret of their charm, bowing, it may be, before foreign altars, or smiling, if it be his fancy, at strange, new gods. What other people call one's past has, no doubt, everything to do with them, but has absolutely nothing to do with oneself. The man who regards his past is a man who deserves to have no future to look forward to. When one has found expression for a mood, one has done with it. You laugh; but, believe me, it is so. Yesterday it was realism that charmed one. One gained from it that *nouveau frisson* which it was its aim to produce. One analysed it, explained it, and wearied of it. At sunset came the *Luministe* in painting, and the

Symboliste in poetry, and the spirit of mediævalism, that spirit which belongs not to time but to temperament, woke suddenly in wounded Russia, and stirred us for a moment by the terrible fascination of pain. To-day the cry is for romance, and already the leaves are tremulous in the valley, and on the purple hill-tops walks Beauty with slim, gilded feet. The old modes of creation linger, of course. The artists reproduce either themselves or each other, with wearisome iteration. But criticism is always moving on, and the critic is always developing.

Nor, again, is the critic really limited to the subjective form of expression. The method of the drama is his, as well as the method of the epos. He may use dialogue, as he did who set Milton talking to Marvel on the nature of comedy and tragedy, and made Sidney and Lord Brooke discourse on letters beneath the Penshurst oaks; or adopt narration, as Mr. Pater is fond of doing, each of whose *Imaginary Portraits*—is not that the title of the book?—presents to us, under the fanciful guise of fiction, some fine and exquisite piece of criticism, one on the painter Watteau, another on the philosophy of Spinoza, a third on the pagan elements of the early Renaissance, and the last, and in some respects the most suggestive, on the source of that *Aufklärung*, that enlightening which dawned on Germany in the last century, and to which our own culture owes so great a debt. Dialogue, certainly, that wonderful literary form which, from Plato to Lucian, and from Lucian to Giordano Bruno, and from Bruno to that grand old Pagan in whom Carlyle took such delight, the creative critics of the world have always employed, can never lose for the thinker its attraction as a mode of expression. By its means he can both reveal and conceal himself, and give form to every fancy, and reality to every mood. By its means he can exhibit the object from each point of view, and show it to us in the round, as a sculptor shows us things, gaining in this manner all the richness and reality of effect that comes from those side issues that are suddenly suggested by the central idea in its progress, and really illumine the idea more completely, or from those felicitous afterthoughts that give a fuller completeness to the central scheme, and yet convey something of the delicate charm of chance.

ERNEST. By its means, too, he can invent an imaginary antagonist, and convert him when he chooses by some absurdly sophistical argument.

GILBERT. Ah! it is so easy to convert others. It is so difficult to convert oneself. To arrive at what one really believes, one must speak through lips different from one's own. To know the truth one must imagine myriads of falsehoods. For what is truth? In matters of religion it is simply the opinion that has survived. In matters of science it is the ultimate sensation. In matters of art it is one's last mood. And you see now, Ernest, that the critic has at his disposal as many objective forms of expression as the artist has. Ruskin put his criticism into imaginative prose, and is superb in his changes and contradictions; and Browning put his into blank verse, and made painter and poet yield us their secret; and M. Renan uses dialogue, and Mr. Pater fiction, and Rossetti translated into sonnet-music the colour of Giorgione and the design of Ingres, and his own design and colour also, feeling, with the instinct of one who had many modes of utterance, that the ultimate art is literature, and the finest and fullest medium that of words.

ERNEST. Well, now that you have settled that the critic has at his disposal all objective forms, I wish you would tell me what are the qualities that should characterize the true critic.

GILBERT. What would you say they were?

ERNEST. Well, I should say that a critic should, above all things, be fair.

GILBERT. Ah! not fair. A critic cannot be fair in the ordinary sense of the word. It is only about things that do not interest one that one can give a really unbiased opinion, which is, no doubt, the reason why an unbiased opinion is always absolutely valueless. The man who sees both sides of a question is a man who sees absolutely nothing at all. Art is a passion, and, in matters of art, thought is inevitably coloured by emotion, and so is fluid rather than fixed, and, depending upon fine moods and exquisite moments, cannot be narrowed into the rigidity of a scientific formula, or a theological dogma. It is to the soul that art speaks, and the soul may be made the prisoner of the mind as well as of the body. One should, of course, have no prejudices; but, as a great Frenchman remarked a hundred years ago, it is one's business in such matters to have preferences, and when one has preferences one ceases to be fair. It is only an auctioneer who can equally and impartially admire all schools of art. No, fairness is not one of the qualities of the true critic. It is not even a condition of criticism. Each form of art with which we come in contact dominates us for the moment to the exclusion of every other form. We must surrender ourselves absolutely to the work in question, whatever it may be, if we wish to gain its secret. For the time, we must think of nothing else, can think of nothing else, indeed.

ERNEST. The true critic will be rational, at any rate, will he not?

GILBERT. Rational? There are two ways of disliking art, Ernest. One is to dislike it. The other, to like it rationally. For art, as Plato saw, and not without regret, creates in listener and spectator a form of divine madness. It does not spring from inspiration, but it makes others inspired. Reason is not the faculty to which it appeals. If one loves art at all, one must love it beyond all other things in the world, and against such love, the reason, if one listened to it, would cry out. There is nothing sane about the worship of beauty. It is too splendid to be sane. Those of whose lives it forms the dominant note will always seem to the world to be pure visionaries.

ERNEST. Well, at least the critic will be sincere.

GILBERT. A little sincerity is a dangerous thing, and a great deal of it is absolutely fatal. The true critic will, indeed, always be sincere in his devotion to the principle of beauty, but he will seek for beauty in every age and in each school, and will never suffer himself to be limited to any settled custom of thought, or stereotyped mode of looking at things. He will realize himself in many forms, and by a thousand different ways, and will ever be curious of new sensations and fresh points of view. Through constant change, and through constant change alone, he will find his true unity. He will not consent to be the slave of his own opinions. For what is mind but motion in the intellectual sphere? The essence of thought, as the essence of life, is growth. You must not be frightened by words, Ernest. What people call insincerity is simply a method by which we can multiply our personalities.

ERNEST. I am afraid I have not been fortunate in my suggestions.

GILBERT. Of the three qualifications you mentioned, two, sincerity and fairness, were, if not actually moral, at least on the border-land of morals, and the first condition of criticism is that the critic should be able to recognize that the sphere of art and the sphere of ethics are absolutely distinct and separate. When they are confused, chaos has come again. They are too often confused in England now, and though our modern Puritans cannot destroy a beautiful thing, yet, by means of their extraordinary prurience they can almost taint beauty for a moment. It is chiefly, I regret to say, through journalism that such people find expression. I regret it because there is much to be said in favour of modern journalism. By giving us the opinions of the uneducated, it keeps us in touch with the ignorance of the community. By carefully chronicling the current events of contemporary life, it shows us of what very little importance such events really are. By invariably discussing the unnecessary, it makes us understand what things are requisite for culture, and what are not. But it should not allow poor Tartuffe to write articles upon modern art. When it does this it stultifies itself. And yet Tartuffe's articles, and Chadband's notes, do this good, at least: They serve to show how extremely limited is the area over which ethics, and ethical considerations, can claim to exercise influence. Science is out of the reach of morals, for her eyes are fixed upon eternal truths. Art is out of the reach of morals, for her eyes are fixed upon things beautiful and immortal and ever-changing. To morals belong the lower and less intellectual spheres. However, let these mouthing Puritans pass; they have their comic side. Who can help laughing when an ordinary journalist seriously proposes to limit the subject matter at the disposal of the artist? Some limitation might well, and will soon, I hope, be placed upon some of our newspapers and newspaper writers. For they give us the bald, sordid, disgusting facts of life. They chronicle, with degrading avidity, the sins of the second-rate, and with the conscientiousness of the illiterate give us accurate and prosaic details of the doings of people of absolutely no interest whatsoever. But the artist, who accepts the facts of life, and yet transforms them into shapes of beauty, and makes them vehicles of pity or of awe, and shows their colour element, and their wonder, and their true ethical import also, and builds out of them a world more real than reality itself, and of loftier and more noble import— who shall set limits to him? Not the apostles of that new journalism which is but the old vulgarity "writ large." Not the apostles of that new Puritanism, which is but the whine of the hypocrite, and is both writ and spoken badly. The mere suggestion is ridiculous. Let us leave these wicked people, and proceed to the discussion of the artistic qualifications necessary for the true critic.

ERNEST. And what are they? Tell me yourself.

GILBERT. Temperament is the primary requisite for the critic—a temperament exquisitely susceptible to beauty, and to the various impressions that beauty gives us. Under what conditions, and by what means, this temperament is engendered in race or individual, we will not discuss at present. It is sufficient to note that it exists, and that there is in us a beauty sense, separate from the other senses and above them; separate from the reason, and of nobler import; separate from the soul, and of equal value—a sense that leads some to create, and others, the finer spirits, as I think, to contemplate merely. But to be purified and made perfect, this sense requires some form of exquisite environment. Without this it starves, or is dulled. You remember that lovely passage in which Plato describes how a young Greek should be educated, and with what insistence he dwells upon the importance of surroundings, telling us how the lad is to be brought up in the midst of fair sights and sounds, so that the beauty of material things may prepare his soul for the reception of the beauty that is spiritual. Insensibly, and without knowing the reason why, he is to develop that real love of beauty which, as Plato is never weary of reminding us, is the true aim of education. By slow degrees there is to be engendered in him such a temperament as will lead him naturally and simply to choose the good in preference to the bad, and, rejecting what is vulgar and discordant, to follow by fine instinctive taste all that possesses grace and charm and loveliness. Ultimately, in its due course, this taste is to become critical and self-conscious, but at first it is to exist purely as a cultivated instinct, and "he who has received this true culture of the inner man will, with clear and certain vision, perceive the omissions and faults in art or nature, and with a taste that cannot err, while he praises, and finds his pleasure in what is good, and receives it into his soul, and so becomes good and noble, he will rightly blame and hate the bad, now in the days of his youth, even before he is able to know the reason why": and so, when, later on, the critical and self-conscious spirit develops in him, he "will recognize and salute it as a friend with whom his education has made him long familiar." I need hardly say, Ernest, how far we in England have fallen short of this ideal, and I can imagine the smile that would illuminate the glossy face of the Philistine if one ventured to suggest to him that the true aim of education was the love of beauty, and that the methods by which education should work were the development of temperament, the cultivation of taste, and the creation of the critical spirit.

Yet, even for us, there is left some loveliness of environment, and the dullness of tutors and professors matters very little when one can loiter in the grey cloisters at Magdalen, and listen to some flute-like voice singing in Waynfleete's chapel, or lie in the green meadow, among the strange snake-spotted fritillaries, and watch the sunburnt noon smite to a finer gold the tower's gilded vanes, or wander up the Christ Church staircase beneath the vaulted ceiling's shadowy fans, or pass through the sculptured gateway of Laud's building in the College of St. John. Nor is it merely at Oxford, or Cambridge, that the sense of beauty can be formed and trained and perfected. All over England there is a renaissance of the decorative arts. Ugliness has had its day. Even in the houses of the rich there is taste, and the houses of those who are not rich have been made gracious and comely and sweet to live in. Caliban, poor, noisy Caliban, thinks that when he has ceased to make mows at a thing, the thing ceases to exist. But if he mocks no longer, it is because he has been met with mockery, swifter and keener than his own, and for a moment has been bitterly schooled into that silence which should seal for ever his uncouth, distorted lips. What has been done up to now, has been chiefly in the clearing of the way. It is always more difficult to destroy than it is to create, and when what one has to destroy is vulgarity and stupidity, the task of destruction needs not merely courage but also contempt. Yet it seems to me to have been, in a measure, done. We have got rid of what was bad. We have now to make what is beautiful. And though the mission of the æsthetic movement is to lure people to contemplate, not to lead them to create, yet as the creative instinct is strong in the Celt, and it is the Celt who leads in art, there is no reason why in future years this strange renaissance should not become almost as mighty in its way as was that new birth of art that woke many centuries ago in the cities of Italy.

Certainly, for the cultivation of temperament, we must turn to the decorative arts: to the arts that touch us, not to the arts that teach us. Modern pictures are, no doubt, delightful to look at. At least, some of them are. But they are quite impossible to live with; they are too clever, too assertive, too intellectual. Their meaning is too obvious, and their method too clearly defined. One exhausts what they have to say in a very short time, and then they become as tedious as one's relations. I am very fond of the work of many of the Impressionist painters of Paris and London. Subtlety and distinction have not yet left the school. Some of their arrangements and harmonies serve to remind one of the unapproachable beauty of Gautier's immortal *Symphonie en blanc majeur*, that flawless masterpiece of colour and music which may have suggested the type as well as the titles of many of their best pictures. For a class that welcomes the incompetent with sympathetic eagerness, and that confuses the bizarre with the beautiful, and vulgarity with truth, they are extremely accomplished. They can do etchings that have the brilliancy of epigrams, pastels that are as fascinating as paradoxes, and as for their portraits, whatever the commonplace may say against them, no one can deny that they possess that unique and wonderful charm which belongs to works of pure fiction. But even the Impressionists, earnest and industrious as they are, will not do. I like them. Their white keynote, with its variations in lilac, was an era in colour. Though the moment does not make the man, the moment certainly makes the Impressionist, and for the moment in art, and the "moment's monument," as Rossetti phrased it, what may not be said? They are suggestive, also. If they have not opened the eyes of the blind, they have at least given great encouragement to the short-sighted; and while their leaders may have all the inexperience of old age, their young men are far too wise to be ever sensible. Yet they will insist on treating painting as if it were a mode of autobiography invented for the use of the illiterate, and are always prating to us on their coarse, gritty canvases of their unnecessary selves and their unnecessary opinions, and spoiling by a vulgar overemphasis that fine contempt of nature which is the best and only modest thing about them. One tires, at the end, of the work of individuals whose individuality is always noisy, and generally uninteresting. There is far more to be said in favour of that newer school at Paris, the *Archaicistes*, as they call themselves, who, refusing to leave the artist entirely at the mercy of the weather, do not find the ideal of art in mere atmospheric effect, but seek rather for the imaginative beauty of design and the loveliness of fair colour, and rejecting the tedious realism of those who merely paint what they see, try to see something worth seeing, and to see it not merely with actual and physical vision, but with that nobler vision of the soul which is as far wider in spiritual scope as it is far more splendid in artistic purpose. They, at any rate, work under those decorative conditions that each art requires for its perfection, and have sufficient æsthetic instinct to regret those sordid and stupid limitations of absolute modernity of form which have proved the ruin of so many of the Impressionists. Still, the art that is frankly decorative is the art to live with. It is, of all our visible arts, the one art that creates in us both mood and temperament. Mere colour, unspoiled by meaning, and unallied with definite form, can speak to the soul in a thousand different ways. The harmony that resides in the delicate proportions of lines and masses becomes mirrored in the mind. The repetitions of pattern give us rest. The marvels of design stir the imagination. In the mere loveliness of the materials employed there are latent elements of culture. Nor is this all. By its deliberate rejection of Nature as the ideal of beauty, as well as of the imitative method of the ordinary painter, decorative art not merely prepares the soul for the reception of true imaginative work, but develops in it that sense of form which is the basis of creative no less than of critical achievement. For the real artist is he who proceeds, not from feeling to form, but from form to thought and passion. He does not first conceive an idea, and then say to himself, "I will put my idea into a complex metre of fourteen lines," but, realizing the beauty of the sonnet-scheme, he conceives certain modes of music and methods of rhyme, and the mere form suggests what is to fill it and make it intellectually and emotionally complete. From time to time the world cries out against some charming artistic poet, because, to use its hackneyed and silly phrase, he has "nothing to say." But if he had something to say he would probably say it, and the result would be tedious. It is just because he has no new message that he can do beautiful work. He gains his inspiration from form, and from form purely, as an artist should. A real passion would ruin him. Whatever actually occurs is spoiled for art. All bad poetry springs from genuine feeling. To be natural is to be obvious, and to be obvious is to be inartistic.

ERNEST. I wonder do you really believe what you say.

GILBERT. Why should you wonder? It is not merely in art that the body is the soul. In every sphere of life form is the beginning of things. The rhythmic, harmonious gestures of dancing convey, Plato tells us, both rhythm and harmony into the mind. Forms are the food of faith, cried Newman in one of those great moments of sincerity that made us admire and know the man. He was right, though he may not have known how terribly right he was. The Creeds are believed, not because they are rational, but because they are repeated. Yes, form is everything. It is the secret of life. Find expression for a sorrow, and it will become dear to you. Find expression for a joy, and you intensify its ecstasy. Do you wish to love? Use Love's Litany, and the words will create the yearning from which the world fancies that they spring. Have you a grief that corrodes your heart? Steep yourself in the language of grief, learn its utterance from Prince Hamlet and Queen Constance, and you will find that mere expression is a mode of consolation, and that form, which is the birth of passion, is also the death of pain. And so, to return to the sphere of art, it is form that creates not merely the critical temperament, but also the æsthetic instinct, that unerring instinct that reveals to one all things under their conditions of beauty. Start with the worship of form, and there is no secret in art that will not be revealed to you, and remember that in criticism, as in creation, temperament is everything, and that it is, not by the time of their production, but by the temperaments to which they appeal, that the schools of art should be historically grouped.

ERNEST. Your theory of education is delightful. But what influence will your critic, brought up in these exquisite surroundings, possess? Do you really think that any artist is ever affected by criticism?

GILBERT. The influence of the critic will be the mere fact of his own existence. He will represent the flawless type. In him the culture of the century will see itself realized. You must not ask of him to have any aim other than the perfecting of himself. The demand of the intellect, as has been well said, is simply to feel itself alive. The critic may, indeed, desire to exercise influence; but, if so, he will concern himself not with the individual, but with the age, which he will seek to wake into consciousness, and to make responsive, creating in it new desires and appetites, and lending it his larger vision and his nobler moods. The actual art of today will occupy him less than the art of tomorrow, far less than the art of yesterday, and as for this or that person at present toiling away, what do the industrious matter? They do their best, no doubt, and consequently we get the worst from them. It is always with the best intentions that the worst work is done. And besides, my dear Ernest, when a man reaches the age of forty, or becomes a Royal Academician, or is elected a member of the Athenæum Club, or is recognized as a popular novelist, whose books are in great demand at suburban railway stations, one may have the amusement of exposing him, but one cannot have the pleasure of reforming him. And this is, I dare say, very fortunate for him; for I have no doubt that reformation is a much more painful process than punishment, is indeed punishment in its most aggravated and moral form—a fact which accounts for our entire failure as a community to reclaim that interesting phenomenon who is called the confirmed criminal.

ERNEST. But may it not be that the poet is the best judge of poetry, and the painter of painting? Each art must appeal primarily to the artist who works in it. His judgment will surely be the most valuable?

GILBERT. The appeal of all art is simply to the artistic temperament. Art does not address herself to the specialist. Her claim is that she is universal, and that in all her manifestations she is one. Indeed, so far from its being true that the artist is the best judge of art, a really great artist can never judge of other people's work at all, and can hardly, in fact, judge of his own. That very concentration of vision that makes a man an artist limits by its sheer intensity his faculty of fine appreciation. The energy of creation hurries him blindly on to his own goal. The wheels of his chariot raise the dust as a cloud around him. The gods are hidden from each other. They can recognize their worshippers. That is all.

ERNEST. You say that a great artist cannot recognize the beauty of work different from his own.

GILBERT. It is impossible for him to do so. Wordsworth saw in *Endymion* merely a pretty piece of paganism, and Shelley, with his dislike of actuality, was deaf to Wordsworth's message, being repelled by its form; and Byron, that great, passionate, human, incomplete creature, could appreciate neither the poet of the cloud nor the poet of the lake, and the wonder of Keats was hidden from him. The realism of Euripides was hateful to Sophocles. Those droppings of warm tears had no music for him. Milton, with his sense of the grand style, could not understand the method of Shakespeare, any more than could Sir Joshua the method of Gainsborough. Bad artists always admire each other's work. They call it being large-minded and free from prejudice. But a truly great artist cannot conceive of life being shown, or beauty fashioned, under any conditions other than those that he has selected. Creation employs all its critical faculty within its own sphere. It may not use it in the sphere that belongs to others. It is exactly because a man cannot do a thing that he is the proper judge of it.

ERNEST. Do you really mean it?

GILBERT. Yes, for creation limits, while contemplation widens, the vision.

ERNEST. But what about technique? Surely, each art has its separate technique?

GILBERT. Certainly: each art has its grammar and its materials. There is no mystery about either, and the incompetent can always be correct. But, while the laws upon which art rests may be fixed and certain, to find their true realization they must be touched by the imagination into such beauty that they will seem an exception, each one of them. Technique is really personality. That is the reason why the artist cannot teach it, why the pupil cannot learn it, and why the æsthetic critic can understand it. To the great poet there is only one method of music—his own. To the great painter there is only one manner of painting—that which he himself employs. The æsthetic critic, and the æsthetic critic alone, can appreciate all forms and modes. It is to him that Art makes her appeal.

ERNEST. Well, I think I have put all my questions to you. And now I must admit—

GILBERT. Ah! don't say that you agree with me. When people agree with me I always feel that I must be wrong.

ERNEST. In that case I certainly won't tell you whether I agree with you or not. But I will put another question. You have explained to me that criticism is a creative art. What future has it?

GILBERT. It is to criticism that the future belongs. The subject matter at the disposal of creation becomes every day more limited in extent and variety. Providence and Mr. Walter Besant have exhausted the obvious. If creation is to last at all, it can only do so on the condition of becoming far more critical than it is at present. The old roads and dusty highways have been traversed too often. Their charm has been worn away by plodding feet, and they have lost that element of novelty or surprise which is so essential for romance. He who would stir us now by fiction must either give us an entirely new background, or reveal to us the soul of man in its innermost workings. The first is for the moment being done for us by Mr. Rudyard Kipling. As one turns over the pages of his *Plain Tales from the*

Hills, one feels as if one were seated under a palm tree, reading life by superb flashes of vulgarity. The bright colours of the bazaars dazzle one's eyes. The jaded, second-rate Anglo-Indians are in exquisite incongruity with their surroundings. The mere lack of style in the story teller gives an odd journalistic realism to what he tells us. From the point of view of literature Mr. Kipling is a genius who drops his aspirates. From the point of view of life, he is a reporter who knows vulgarity better than anyone has ever known it. Dickens knew its clothes and its comedy. Mr. Kipling knows its essence and its seriousness. He is our first authority on the second-rate, and has seen marvellous things through keyholes, and his backgrounds are real works of art. As for the second condition, we have had Browning, and Meredith is with us. But there is still much to be done in the sphere of introspection. People sometimes say that fiction is getting too morbid. As far as psychology is concerned, it has never been morbid enough. We have merely touched the surface of the soul, that is all. In one single ivory cell of the brain there are stored away things more marvellous and more terrible than even they have dreamed of who, like the author of *Le rouge et le noir,* have sought to track the soul into its most secret places, and to make life confess its dearest sins. Still, there is a limit even to the number of untried backgrounds, and it is possible that a further development of the habit of introspection may prove fatal to that creative faculty to which it seeks to supply fresh material. I myself am inclined to think that creation is doomed. It springs from too primitive, too natural an impulse. However this may be, it is certain that the subject matter at the disposal of creation is always diminishing, while the subject matter of criticism increases daily. There are always new attitudes for the mind, and new points of view. The duty of imposing form upon chaos does not grow less as the world advances. There was never a time when criticism was more needed than it is now. It is only by its means that humanity can become conscious of the point at which it has arrived.

Hours ago, Ernest, you asked me the use of criticism. You might just as well have asked me the use of thought. It is criticism, as Arnold points out, that creates the intellectual atmosphere of the age. It is criticism, as I hope to point out myself some day, that makes the mind a fine instrument. We, in our educational system, have burdened the memory with a load of unconnected facts, and laboriously striven to impart our laboriously acquired knowledge. We teach people how to remember, we never teach them how to grow. It has never occurred to us to try and develop in the mind a more subtle quality of apprehension and discernment. The Greeks did this, and when we come in contact with the Greek critical intellect we cannot but be conscious that, while our subject matter is in every respect larger and more varied than theirs, theirs is the only method by which this subject matter can be interpreted. England has done one thing; it has invented and established public opinion, which is an attempt to organize the ignorance of the community and to elevate it to the dignity of physical force. But wisdom has always been hidden from it. Considered as an instrument of thought the English mind is coarse and undeveloped. The only thing that can purify it is the growth of the critical instinct.

It is criticism, again, that, by concentration, makes culture possible. It takes the cumbersome mass of creative work, and distils it into a finer essence. Who that desires to retain any sense of form could struggle through the monstrous multitudinous books that the

world has produced, books in which thought stammers
or ignorance brawls? The thread that is to guide us
across the wearisome labyrinth is in the hands of criticism. Nay, more, where there is no record, and history
is either lost or was never written, criticism can re-create
the past for us from the very smallest fragment of language or art, just as surely as the man of science can,
from some tiny bone, or the mere impress of a foot upon
a rock, re-create for us the winged dragon or Titan
lizard that once made the earth shake beneath its
tread, can call Behemoth out of his cave, and make
Leviathan swim once more across the startled sea. Pre-
historic history belongs to the philological and archæo-
logical critic. It is to him that the origins of things are
revealed. The self-conscious deposits of an age are
nearly always misleading. Through philological criticism alone we know more of the centuries of which no
actual record has been preserved, than we do of the
centuries that have left us their scrolls. It can do for us
what can be done neither by physics nor metaphysics.
It can give us the exact science of mind in the process
of becoming. It can do for us what history cannot do.
It can tell us what man thought before he learned how
to write. You have asked me about the influence of
criticism. I think I have answered that question already;
but there is this also to be said. It is criticism that
makes us cosmopolitan. The Manchester school tried to
make men realize the brotherhood of humanity, by
pointing out the commercial advantages of peace. It
sought to degrade the wonderful world into a common
market place for the buyer and the seller. It addressed
itself to the lowest instincts, and it failed. War followed upon war, and the tradesman's creed did not
prevent France and Germany from clashing together in
blood-stained battle. There are others of our own day

who seek to appeal to mere emotional sympathies, or to the shallow dogmas of some vague system of abstract ethics. They have their Peace Societies, so dear to the sentimentalists, and their proposals for unarmed international arbitration, so popular among those who have never read history. But mere emotional sympathy will not do. It is too variable, and too closely connected with the passions; and a board of arbitrators who, for the general welfare of the race, are to be deprived of the power of putting their decisions into execution, will not be of much avail. There is only one thing worse than injustice, and that is justice without her sword in her hand. When right is not might, it is evil.

No, the emotions will not make us cosmopolitan, any more than the greed for gain could do so. It is only by the cultivation of the habit of intellectual criticism that we shall be able to rise superior to race prejudices. Goethe—you will not misunderstand what I say—was a German of the Germans. He loved his country—no man more so. Its people were dear to him; and he led them. Yet, when the iron hoof of Napoleon trampled upon vineyard and cornfield, his lips were silent. "How can one write songs of hatred without hating?" he said to Eckerman, "and how could I, to whom culture and barbarism are alone of importance, hate a nation which is among the most cultivated of the earth, and to which I owe so great a part of my own cultivation?" This note, sounded in the modern world by Goethe first, will become, I think, the starting point for the cosmopolitanism of the future. Criticism will annihilate race prejudices by insisting upon the unity of the human mind in the variety of its forms. If we are tempted to make war upon another nation, we shall remember that we are seeking to destroy an element of our own culture, and possibly its most important element. As long as war is regarded

as wicked it will always have its fascination. When it is
looked upon as vulgar, it will cease to be popular. The
change will, of course, be slow, and people will not be
conscious of it. They will not say "We will not war
against France because her prose is perfect," but because the prose of France is perfect they will not hate
the land. Intellectual criticism will bind Europe together in bonds far closer than those that can be
forged by shopman or sentimentalist. It will give us the
peace that springs from understanding.

Nor is this all. It is criticism that, recognizing no position as final, and refusing to bind itself by the shallow
shibboleths of any sect or school, creates that serene
philosophic temper which loves truth for its own sake,
and loves it not the less because it knows it to be unat-
tainable. How little we have of this temper in England,
and how much we need it! The English mind is always
in a rage. The intellect of the race is wasted in the
sordid and stupid quarrels of second-rate politicians or
third-rate theologians. It was reserved for a man of
science to show us the supreme example of that "sweet
reasonableness" of which Arnold spoke so wisely, and,
alas! to so little effect. The author of the *Origin of
Species* had, at any rate, the philosophic temper. If one
contemplates the ordinary pulpits and platforms of England, one can but feel the contempt of Julian, or the
indifference of Montaigne. We are dominated by the
fanatic, whose worst vice is his sincerity. Anything approaching to the free play of the mind is practically
unknown amongst us. People cry out against the sinner,
yet it is not the sinful, but the stupid, who are our
shame. There is no sin except stupidity.

ERNEST. Ah! what an antinomian you are!

GILBERT. The artistic critic, like the mystic, is an

antinomian always. To be good, according to the vulgar standard of goodness, is obviously quite easy. It merely requires a certain amount of sordid terror, a certain lack of imaginative thought, and a certain low passion for middle-class respectability. Æsthetics are higher than ethics. They belong to a more spiritual sphere. To discern the beauty of a thing is the finest point to which we can arrive. Even a colour sense is more important, in the development of the individual, than a sense of right and wrong. Æsthetics, in fact, are to ethics, in the sphere of conscious civilization, what, in the sphere of the external world, sexual is to natural selection. Ethics, like natural selection, make existence possible. Æsthetics, like sexual selection, make life lovely and wonderful, fill it with new forms, and give it progress, and variety, and change. And when we reach the true culture that is our aim, we attain to that perfection of which the saints have dreamed, the perfection of those to whom sin is impossible, not because they make the renunciations of the ascetic, but because they can do everything they wish without hurt to the soul, and can wish for nothing that can do the soul harm, the soul being an entity so divine that it is able to transform into elements of a richer experience, or a finer suscepti- bility, or a newer mode of thought, acts or passions that with the common would be commonplace, or with the uneducated ignoble, or with the shameful vile. Is this dangerous? Yes, it is dangerous—all ideas, as I told you, are so. But the night wearies, and the light flickers in the lamp. One more thing I cannot help saying to you. You have spoken against criticism as being a sterile thing. The nineteenth century is a turning-point in his- tory simply on account of the work of two men, Darwin and Renan, the one the critic of the Book of Nature, the other the critic of the Books of God. Not to recognize this is to miss the meaning of one of the most important eras in the progress of the world. Creation is always behind the age. It is criticism that leads us. The critical spirit and the world spirit are one.

ERNEST. And he who is in possession of this spirit, or whom this spirit possesses, will, I suppose, do nothing?

GILBERT. Like the Persephone of whom Landor tells us, the sweet, pensive Persephone around whose white feet the asphodel and amaranth are blooming, he will sit contented "in that deep, motionless quiet which mortals pity, and which the gods enjoy." He will look out upon the world and know its secret. By contact with divine things he will become divine. His will be the perfect life, and his only.

ERNEST. You have told me many strange things to-night, Gilbert. You have told me that it is more difficult to talk about a thing than to do it, and that to do nothing at all is the most difficult thing in the world; you have told me that all art is immoral, and all thought dangerous; that criticism is more creative than creation, and that the highest criticism is that which reveals in the work of art what the artist had not put there; that it is exactly because a man cannot do a thing that he is the proper judge of it; and that the true critic is unfair, insincere, and not rational. My friend, you are a dreamer.

GILBERT. Yes: I am a dreamer. For a dreamer is one who can only find his way by moonlight, and his punishment is that he sees the dawn before the rest of the world.

ERNEST. His punishment?

GILBERT. And his reward. But see, it is dawn already. Draw back the curtains and open the windows wide. How cool the morning air is! Piccadilly lies at our feet like a long riband of silver. A faint purple mist hangs over the Park, and the shadows of the white houses are purple. It is too late to sleep. Let us go down to Covent Garden and look at the roses. Come! I am tired of thought.

The Picture of Dorian Gray

PREFACE

The artist is the creator of beautiful things.

To reveal art and conceal the artist is art's aim.

The critic is he who can translate into another manner or a new material his impression of beautiful things.

The highest as the lowest form of criticism is a mode of autobiography.

Those who find ugly meanings in beautiful things are corrupt without being charming. This is a fault.

Those who find beautiful meanings in beautiful things are the cultivated. For these there is hope.

They are the elect to whom beautiful things mean only beauty.

There is no such thing as a moral or an immoral book. Books are well written, or badly written. That is all.

The nineteenth-century dislike of realism is the rage of Caliban seeing his own face in a glass.

The nineteenth-century dislike of romanticism is the rage of Caliban not seeing his own face in a glass.

The moral life of man forms part of the subject matter of the artist, but the morality of art consists in the perfect use of an imperfect medium.

No artist desires to prove anything. Even things that are true can be proved.

No artist has ethical sympathies. An ethical sympathy in an artist is an unpardonable mannerism of style.

No artist is ever morbid. The artist can express everything.

Thought and language are to the artist instruments of an art.

Vice and virtue are to the artist materials for an art.

From the point of view of form, the type of all the arts is the art of the musician. From the point of view of feeling, the actor's craft is the type.

All art is at once surface and symbol.

Those who go beneath the surface do so at their peril.

Those who read the symbol do so at their peril.

It is the spectator, and not life, that art really mirrors.

Diversity of opinion about a work of art shows that the work is new, complex, and vital.

When critics disagree the artist is in accord with himself.

We can forgive a man for making a useful thing as long as he does not admire it. The only excuse for making a useless thing is that one admires it intensely.

All art is quite useless.

I

THE studio was filled with the rich odour of roses, and when the light summer wind stirred amidst the trees of the garden there came through the open door the heavy scent of the lilac, or the more delicate perfume of the pink-flowering thorn.

From the corner of the divan of Persian saddle-bags on which he was lying, smoking, as was his custom, innumerable cigarettes, Lord Henry Wotton could just catch the gleam of the honey-sweet and honey-coloured blossoms of a laburnum, whose tremulous branches seemed hardly able to bear the burden of a beauty so flame-like as theirs; and now and then the fantastic shadows of birds in flight flitted across the long tussore-silk curtains that were stretched in front of the huge window, producing a kind of momentary Japanese effect, and making him think of those pallid jade-faced painters of Tokyo who, through the medium of an art that is necessarily immobile, seek to convey the sense of swiftness and motion. The sullen murmur of the bees shouldering their way through the long unmown grass, or circling with monotonous insistence round the dusty gilt horns of the straggling woodbine, seemed to make the stillness more oppressive. The dim roar of London was like the bourdon note of a distant organ.

In the centre of the room, clamped to an upright easel, stood the full-length portrait of a young man of extraordinary personal beauty, and in front of it, some little distance away, was sitting the artist himself, Basil Hallward, whose sudden disappearance some years ago caused, at the time, such public excitement, and gave rise to so many strange conjectures.

As the painter looked at the gracious and comely form he had so skilfully mirrored in his art, a smile of pleasure passed across his face, and seemed about to linger there. But he suddenly started up, and, closing his eyes, placed his fingers upon the lids, as though he sought to imprison within his brain some curious dream from which he feared he might awake.

"It is your best work, Basil, the best thing you have ever done," said Lord Henry, languidly. "You must certainly send it next year to the Grosvenor. The Academy is too large and too vulgar. Whenever I have gone there, there have been either so many people that I have not been able to see the pictures, which was dreadful, or so many pictures that I have not been able to see the people, which was worse. The Grosvenor is really the only place."

"I don't think I shall send it anywhere," he answered, tossing his head back in that odd way that used to make his friends laugh at him at Oxford. "No, I won't send it anywhere."

Lord Henry elevated his eyebrows, and looked at him in amazement through the thin blue wreaths of smoke that curled up in such fanciful whorls from his heavy opium-tainted cigarette.

"Not send it anywhere? My dear fellow, why? Have you any reason? What odd chaps you painters are! You do anything in the world to gain a reputation. As soon as you have one, you seem to want to throw it away. It is silly of you, for there is only one thing in the world worse than being talked about, and that is not being talked about. A portrait like this would set you far above all the young men in England, and make the old men quite jealous, if old men are ever capable of any emotion."

"I know you will laugh at me," he replied, "but I really can't exhibit it. I have put too much of myself into it."

Lord Henry stretched himself out on the divan and laughed.

"Yes, I knew you would; but it is quite true, all the same."

"Too much of yourself in it! Upon my word, Basil, I didn't know you were so vain; and I really can't see any resemblance between you, with your rugged strong face and your coal-black hair, and this young Adonis, who looks as if he was made out of ivory and rose-leaves. Why, my dear Basil, he is a Narcissus, and you—well, of course you have an intellectual expression, and all that. But beauty, real beauty, ends where an intellectual expression begins. Intellect is in itself a mode of exaggeration, and destroys the harmony of any face. The moment one sits down to think, one becomes all nose, or all forehead, or something horrid. Look at the successful men in any of the learned professions. How perfectly hideous they are! Except, of course, in the Church. But then in the Church they don't think. A bishop keeps on saying at the age of eighty what he was told to say when he was a boy of eighteen, and as a natural consequence he always looks absolutely delightful. Your mysterious young friend, whose name you have never told me, but whose picture really fascinates me, never thinks. I feel quite sure of that. He is some brainless, beautiful creature, who should be always here in winter when we have no flowers to look at, and always here in summer when we want something to chill our intelligence. Don't flatter yourself, Basil, you are not in the least like him."

"You don't understand me, Harry," answered the artist. "Of course I am not like him. I know that perfectly well. Indeed, I should be sorry to look like him. You shrug your shoulders? I am telling you the truth. There is a fatality about all physical and intellectual distinction, the sort of fatality that seems to dog through history the faltering steps of kings. It is better not to be different from one's fellows. The ugly and the stupid have the best of it in this world. They can sit at their ease and gape at the play. If they know nothing of victory, they are at least spared the knowledge of defeat. They live as we all should live, undisturbed, indifferent, and without disquiet. They neither bring ruin upon others, nor ever receive it, from alien hands. Your rank and wealth, Harry; my brains, such as they are—my art, whatever it may be worth; Dorian Gray's good looks—we shall all suffer for what the gods have given us, suffer terribly."

"Dorian Gray? Is that his name?" asked Lord Henry, walking across the studio towards Basil Hallward.

"Yes, that is his name. I didn't intend to tell it to you."

"But why not?"

"Oh, I can't explain. When I like people immensely I never tell their names to anyone. It is like surrendering a part of them. I have grown to love secrecy. It seems to be the one thing that can make modern life mysterious or marvellous to us. The commonest thing is delightful if one only hides it. When I leave town now I never tell my people where I am going. If I did, I would lose all my pleasure. It is a silly habit, I dare say, but somehow it seems to bring a great deal of romance into one's life. I suppose you think me awfully foolish about it?"

"Not at all," answered Lord Henry, "not at all, my dear Basil. You seem to forget that I am married, and the one charm of marriage is that it makes a life of deception absolutely necessary for both parties. I never know where my wife is, and my wife never knows what I am doing. When we meet—we do meet occasionally, when we dine out together, or go down to the Duke's —we tell each other the most absurd stories with the most serious faces. My wife is very good at it—much better, in fact, than I am. She never gets confused over her dates, and I always do. But when she does find me out, she makes no row at all. I sometimes wish she would; but she merely laughs at me."

"I hate the way you talk about your married life, Harry," said Basil Hallward, strolling towards the door that led into the garden. "I believe that you are really a very good husband, but that you are thoroughly ashamed of your own virtues. You are an extraordinary fellow. You never say a moral thing, and you never do a wrong thing. Your cynicism is simply a pose."

"Being natural is simply a pose, and the most irritating pose I know," cried Lord Henry, laughing; and the two young men went out into the garden together, and ensconced themselves on a long bamboo seat that stood in the shade of a tall laurel bush. The sunlight slipped over the polished leaves. In the grass, white daisies were tremulous.

After a pause, Lord Henry pulled out his watch. "I am afraid I must be going, Basil," he murmured, "and before I go, I insist on your answering a question I put to you some time ago."

"What is that?" said the painter, keeping his eyes fixed on the ground.

"You know quite well."

"I do not, Harry."

"Well, I will tell you what it is. I want you to explain to me why you won't exhibit Dorian Gray's picture. I want the real reason."

"I told you the real reason."

"No, you did not. You said it was because there was too much of yourself in it. Now, that is childish."

"Harry," said Basil Hallward, looking him straight in the face, "every portrait that is painted with feeling is a portrait of the artist, not of the sitter. The sitter is merely the accident, the occasion. It is not he who is revealed by the painter; it is rather the painter who, on the coloured canvas, reveals himself. The reason I will not exhibit this picture is that I am afraid that I have shown in it the secret of my own soul."

Lord Henry laughed. "And what is that?" he asked.

"I will tell you," said Hallward; but an expression of perplexity came over his face.

"I am all expectation, Basil," continued his companion, glancing at him.

"Oh, there is really very little to tell, Harry," answered the painter; "and I am afraid you will hardly understand it. Perhaps you will hardly believe it."

Lord Henry smiled, and, leaning down, plucked a pink-petalled daisy from the grass, and examined it. "I am quite sure I shall understand it," he replied, gazing intently at the little golden white-feathered disk, "and as for believing things, I can believe anything, provided that it is quite incredible."

The wind shook some blossoms from the trees, and the heavy lilac-blooms, with their clustering stars, moved to and fro in the languid air. A grasshopper began to chirrup by the wall, and like a blue thread a long thin dragon-fly floated past on its brown gauze wings. Lord Henry felt as if he could hear Basil Hallward's heart beating, and wondered what was coming.

"The story is simply this," said the painter after some time. "Two months ago I went to a crush at Lady Brandon's. You know we poor artists have to show ourselves in society from time to time, just to remind the public that we are not savages. With an evening coat and a white tie, as you told me once, anybody, even a stock-broker, can gain a reputation for being civilized. Well, after I had been in the room about ten minutes, talking to huge overdressed dowagers and tedious Academicians, I suddenly became conscious that some-one was looking at me. I turned half-way round, and saw Dorian Gray for the first time. When our eyes met, I felt that I was growing pale. A curious sensation of terror came over me. I knew that I had come face to face with someone whose mere personality was so fascinating that, if I allowed it to do so, it would absorb my whole nature, my whole soul, my very art itself. I did not want any external influence in my life. You know yourself, Harry, how independent I am by nature. I have always been my own master; had at least always been so, till I met Dorian Gray. Then—but I don't know how to explain it to you. Something seemed to tell me that I was on the verge of a terrible crisis in my life. I had a strange feeling that Fate had in store for me exquisite joys and exquisite sorrows. I grew afraid, and turned to quit the room. It was not conscience that made me do it: it was a sort of cowardice. I take no credit to myself for trying to escape."

"Conscience and cowardice are really the same things, Basil. Conscience is the trade-name of the firm. That is all."

"I don't believe that, Harry, and I don't believe you do either. However, whatever was my motive—and it may have been pride, for I used to be very proud—I certainly struggled to the door. There, of course, I stumbled against Lady Brandon. 'You are not going to run away so soon, Mr. Hallward?' she screamed out. You know her curiously shrill voice?"

"Yes; she is a peacock in everything but beauty," said Lord Henry, pulling the daisy to bits with his long, nervous fingers.

"I could not get rid of her. She brought me up to Royalties, and people with Stars and Garters, and elderly ladies with gigantic tiaras and parrot noses. She spoke of me as her dearest friend. I had only met her once before, but she took it into her head to lionize me. I believe some picture of mine had made a great success at that time, at least had been chattered about in the penny newspapers, which is the nineteenth-century standard of immortality. Suddenly I found myself face to face with the young man whose personality had so strangely stirred me. We were quite close, almost touching. Our eyes met again. It was reckless of me, but I asked Lady Brandon to introduce me to him. Perhaps it was not so reckless, after all. It was simply inevitable. We would have spoken to each other without any introduction. I am sure of that. Dorian told me so afterwards. He, too, felt that we were destined to know each other."

"And how did Lady Brandon describe this wonderful young man?" asked his companion. "I know she goes in for giving a rapid précis of all her guests. I remember her bringing me up to a truculent and red-faced old gentleman covered all over with orders and ribbons, and hissing into my ear, in a tragic whisper which must have been perfectly audible to everybody in the room, the most astounding details. I simply fled. I like to find out people for myself. But Lady Brandon treats her guests exactly as an auctioneer treats his goods. She either explains them entirely away, or tells one everything about them except what one wants to know."

"Poor Lady Brandon! You are hard on her, Harry!" said Hallward, listlessly.

"My dear fellow, she tried to found a *salon,* and only succeeded in opening a restaurant. How could I admire her? But tell me, what did she say about Mr. Dorian Gray?"

"Oh, something like 'Charming boy—poor dear mother and I absolutely inseparable. Quite forget what he does—afraid he—doesn't do anything—oh, yes, plays the piano—or is it the violin, dear Mr. Gray?" Neither of us could help laughing, and we became friends at once."

"Laughter is not at all a bad beginning for a friendship, and it is far the best ending for one," said the young lord, plucking another daisy.

Hallward shook his head. "You don't understand what friendship is, Harry," he murmured—"or what enmity is, for that matter. You like everyone; that is to say, you are indifferent to everyone."

"How horribly unjust of you!" cried Lord Henry, tilting his hat back, and looking up at the little clouds that, like ravelled skeins of glossy white silk, were drifting across the hollowed turquoise of the summer sky. "Yes, horribly unjust of you. I make a great difference between people. I choose my friends for their good looks, my acquaintances for their good characters, and my enemies for their good intellects. A man cannot be too careful in the choice of his enemies. I have not got one who is a fool, they are all men of some intellectual power, and consequently they all appreciate me. Is that very vain of me? I think it is rather vain."

"I should think it was, Harry. But according to your category I must be merely an acquaintance."

"My dear old Basil, you are much more than an acquaintance."

"And much less than a friend. A sort of brother, I suppose?"

"Oh, brothers! I don't care for brothers. My elder brother won't die, and my younger brothers seem never to do anything else."

"Harry!" exclaimed Hallward, frowning.

"My dear fellow, I am not quite serious. But I can't help detesting my relations. I suppose it comes from the fact that none of us can stand other people having the same faults as ourselves. I quite sympathize with the rage of the English democracy against what they call the vices of the upper orders. The masses feel that drunkenness, stupidity, and immorality should be their own special property, and that if anyone of us makes an ass of himself he is poaching on their preserves. When poor Southwark got into the Divorce Court, their indignation was quite magnificent. And yet I don't suppose that ten per cent of the proletariat live correctly."

"I don't agree with a single word that you have said, and, what is more, Harry, I feel sure you don't either."

Lord Henry stroked his pointed brown beard, and tapped the toe of his patent-leather boot with a tasselled ebony cane. "How English you are, Basil! That is the second time you have made that observation. If one puts forward an idea to a true Englishman— always a rash thing to do—he never dreams of considering whether the idea is right or wrong. The only thing he considers of any importance is whether one believes it oneself. Now, the value of an idea has nothing whatsoever to do with the sincerity of the man who expresses it. Indeed, the probabilities are that the more insincere the man is, the more purely intellectual will the idea be, as in that case it will not be coloured by either his wants, his desires, or his prejudices. However, I don't propose to discuss politics, sociology, or metaphysics with you. I like persons better than principles, and I like persons with no principles better than anything else in the world. Tell me more about Mr. Dorian Gray. How often do you see him?"

"Every day. I couldn't be happy if I didn't see him every day. He is absolutely necessary to me."

"How extraordinary! I thought you would never care for anything but your art."

"He is all my art to me now," said the painter, gravely. "I sometimes think, Harry, that there are only two eras of any importance in the world's history. The first is the appearance of a new medium for art, and the second is the appearance of a new personality for art also. What the invention of oil-painting was to the Venetians, the face of Antinoüs was to late Greek sculpture, and the face of Dorian Gray will some day be to me. It is not merely that I paint from him, draw from him, sketch from him. Of course I have done all that. But he is much more to me than a model or a sitter. I won't tell you that I am dissatisfied with what I have done of him, or that his beauty is such that art cannot express it. There is nothing that art cannot express, and I know that the work I have done, since I met Dorian Gray, is good work, is the best work of my life. But in some curious way—I wonder will you understand me? —his personality has suggested to me an entirely new manner in art, an entirely new mode of style. I see things differently, I think of them differently. I can now re-create life in a way that was hidden from me before. 'A dream of form in days of thought':—who is it who says that? I forget; but it is what Dorian Gray has been to me. The merely visible presence of this lad— for he seems to me little more than a lad, though he is really over twenty—his merely visible presence—ah! I wonder can you realize all that that means? Unconsciously he defines for me the lines of a fresh school, a school that is to have in it all the passion of the romantic spirit, all the perfection of the spirit that is Greek. The harmony of soul and body—how much that is! We in our madness have separated the two, and have invented a realism that is vulgar, an ideality that is void. Harry!

if you only knew what Dorian Gray is to me! You remember that landscape of mine, for which Agnew offered me such a huge price, but which I would not part with? It is one of the best things I have ever done. And why is it so? Because, while I was painting it, Dorian Gray sat beside me. Some subtle influence passed from him to me, and for the first time in my life I saw in the plain woodland the wonder I had always looked for, and always missed."

"Basil, this is extraordinary! I must see Dorian Gray."

Hallward got up from his seat, and walked up and down the garden. After some time he came back. "Harry," he said, "Dorian Gray is to me simply a motive in art. You might see nothing in him. I see everything in him. He is never more present in my work than when no image of him is there. He is a suggestion, as I have said, of a new manner. I find him in the curves of certain lines, in the loveliness and subtleties of certain colours. That is all."

"Then why won't you exhibit his portrait?" asked Lord Henry.

"Because, without intending it, I have put into it some expression of all this curious artistic idolatry, of which, of course, I have never cared to speak to him. He knows nothing about it. He shall never know anything about it. But the world might guess it; and I will not bare my soul to their shallow, prying eyes. My heart shall never be put under their microscope. There is too much of myself in the thing, Harry—too much of myself!"

"Poets are not so scrupulous as you are. They know how useful passion is for publication. Nowadays a broken heart will run to many editions."

"I hate them for it," cried Hallward. "An artist should create beautiful things, but should put nothing of his own life into them. We live in an age when men treat art as if it were meant to be a form of autobiography. We have lost the abstract sense of beauty. Some day I will show the world what it is; and for that reason the world shall never see my portrait of Dorian Gray."

"I think you are wrong, Basil, but I won't argue with you. It is only the intellectually lost who ever argue. Tell me, is Dorian Gray very fond of you?"

The painter considered for a few moments. "He likes me," he answered, after a pause; "I know he likes me. Of course I flatter him dreadfully. I find a strange pleasure in saying things to him that I know I shall be sorry for having said. As a rule, he is charming to me, and we sit in the studio and talk of a thousand things. Now and then, however, he is horribly thoughtless, and seems to take a real delight in giving me pain. Then I feel, Harry, that I have given away my whole soul to someone who treats it as if it were a flower to put in his coat, a bit of decoration to charm his vanity, an ornament for a summer's day."

"Days in summer, Basil, are apt to linger," murmured Lord Henry. "Perhaps you will tire sooner than he will. It is a sad thing to think of, but there is no doubt that genius lasts longer than beauty. That accounts for the fact that we all take such pains to overeducate ourselves. In the wild struggle for existence, we want to have something that endures, and so we fill our minds with rubbish and facts, in the silly hope of keeping our place. The thoroughly well-informed man—that is the modern ideal. And the mind of the thoroughly well-informed man is a dreadful thing. It is like a bric-à-brac shop, all monsters and dust, with everything priced above its proper value. I think you will tire first, all the same. Some day you will look at your friend and he will seem to you to be a little out of drawing, or you won't like his tone of colour, or something. You will bitterly reproach him in your own heart, and seriously think that he has behaved very badly to you. The next time he calls, you will be perfectly cold and indifferent. It will be a great pity, for it will alter you. What you have told me is quite a romance, a romance of art one might call it, and the worst of having a romance of any kind is that it leaves one so unromantic."

"Harry, don't talk like that. As long as I live, the personality of Dorian Gray will dominate me. You can't feel what I feel. You change too often."

"Ah, my dear Basil, that is exactly why I can feel it. Those who are faithful know only the trivial side of love: it is the faithless who know love's tragedies." And Lord Henry struck a light on a dainty silver case, and began to smoke a cigarette with a self-conscious and satisfied air, as if he had summed up the world in a phrase. There was a rustle of chirruping sparrows in the green lacquer leaves of the ivy, and the blue cloud-shadows chased themselves across the grass like swallows. How pleasant it was in the garden! And how delightful other people's emotions were!—much more delightful than their ideas, it seemed to him. One's own soul, and the passions of one's friends—those were the fascinating things in life. He pictured to himself with silent amusement the tedious luncheon that he had missed by staying so long with Basil Hallward. Had he gone to his aunt's, he would have been sure to have met Lord Goodbody there, and the whole conversation would have been about the feeding of the poor, and the necessity for model lodging-houses. Each class would have preached the importance of those virtues, for whose exercise there was no necessity in their own lives. The rich would have spoken on the value of thrift, and the idle grown eloquent over the dignity of labour. It was charming to have escaped all that! As he thought of his aunt, an idea seemed to strike him. He turned to Hallward, and said, "My dear fellow, I have just remembered."

"Remembered what, Harry?"

"Where I heard the name of Dorian Gray."

"Where was it?" asked Hallward, with a slight frown.

"Don't look so angry, Basil. It was at my aunt, Lady Agatha's. She told me she had discovered a wonderful young man, who was going to help her in the East End, and that his name was Dorian Gray. I am bound to state that she never told me he was good-looking. Women have no appreciation of good looks; at least, good women have not. She said that he was very earnest, and had a beautiful nature. I at once pictured to myself a creature with spectacles and lank hair, horribly freckled, and tramping about on huge feet. I wish I had known it was your friend."

"I am very glad you didn't, Harry."

"Why?"

"I don't want you to meet him."

"You don't want me to meet him?"

"No."

"Mr. Dorian Gray is in the studio, sir," said the butler, coming into the garden.

"You must introduce me now," cried Lord Henry, laughing.

The painter turned to his servant, who stood blinking in the sunlight. "Ask Mr. Gray to wait, Parker: I shall be in in a few moments." The man bowed, and went up the walk.

Then he looked at Lord Henry. "Dorian Gray is my dearest friend," he said. "He has a simple and a beautiful nature. Your aunt was quite right in what she said of him. Don't spoil him. Don't try to influence him. Your influence would be bad. The world is wide, and has many marvellous people in it. Don't take away from me the one person who gives to my art whatever charm it possesses; my life as an artist depends on him. Mind, Harry, I trust you." He spoke very slowly, and the words seemed wrung out of him almost against his will.

"What nonsense you talk!" said Lord Henry, smiling, and, taking Hallward by the arm, he almost led him into the house.

II

AS THEY entered they saw Dorian Gray. He was seated at the piano, with his back to them, turning over the pages of a volume of Schumann's *Forest Scenes*. "You must lend me these, Basil," he cried. "I want to learn them. They are perfectly charming."

"That entirely depends on how you sit today, Dorian."

"Oh, I am tired of sitting, and I don't want a life-sized portrait of myself," answered the lad, swinging round on the music-stool, in a wilful, petulant manner. When he caught sight of Lord Henry, a faint blush coloured his cheeks for a moment, and he started up. "I beg your pardon, Basil, but I didn't know you had anyone with you."

"This is Lord Henry Wotton, Dorian, an old Oxford friend of mine. I have just been telling him what a capital sitter you were, and now you have spoiled everything."

"You have not spoiled my pleasure in meeting you,

Mr. Gray," said Lord Henry, stepping forward and extending his hand. "My aunt has often spoken to me about you. You are one of her favourites, and, I am afraid, one of her victims, also."

"I am in Lady Agatha's black books at present," answered Dorian, with a funny look of penitence. "I promised to go to a club in Whitechapel with her last Tuesday, and I really forgot all about it. We were to have played a duet together—three duets, I believe. I don't know what she will say to me. I am far too frightened to call."

"Oh, I will make your peace with my aunt. She is quite devoted to you. And I don't think it really matters about your not being there. The audience probably thought it was a duet. When Aunt Agatha sits down to the piano she makes quite enough noise for two people."

"That is very horrid to her, and not very nice to me," answered Dorian, laughing.

Lord Henry looked at him. Yes, he was certainly wonderfully handsome, with his finely-curved scarlet lips, his frank blue eyes, his crisp gold hair. There was something in his face that made one trust him at once. All the candour of youth was there, as well as all youth's passionate purity. One felt that he had kept himself unspotted from the world. No wonder Basil Hallward worshipped him.

"You are too charming to go in for philanthropy, Mr. Gray—far too charming." And Lord Henry flung himself down on the divan, and opened his cigarette-case.

The painter had been busy mixing his colours and getting his brushes ready. He was looking worried, and when he heard Lord Henry's last remark he glanced at him, hesitated for a moment, and then said, "Harry, I want to finish this picture today. Would you think it awfully rude of me if I asked you to go away?"

Lord Henry smiled, and looked at Dorian Gray. "Am I to go, Mr. Gray?" he asked.

"Oh, please don't, Lord Henry. I see that Basil is in one of his sulky moods; and I can't bear him when he sulks. Besides, I want you to tell me why I should not go in for philanthropy."

"I don't know that I shall tell you that, Mr. Gray. It is so tedious a subject that one would have to talk seriously about it. But I certainly shall not run away, now that you have asked me to stop. You don't really mind, Basil, do you? You have often told me that you liked your sitters to have someone to chat to."

Hallward bit his lip. "If Dorian wishes it, of course you must stay. Dorian's whims are laws to everybody, except himself."

Lord Henry took up his hat and gloves. "You are very pressing, Basil, but I am afraid I must go. I have promised to meet a man at the Orleans. Good-bye, Mr. Gray. Come and see me some afternoon in Curzon Street. I am nearly always at home at five o'clock. Write to me when you are coming. I should be sorry to miss you."

"Basil," cried Dorian Gray, "if Lord Henry Wotton goes I shall go too. You never open your lips while you are painting, and it is horribly dull standing on a platform and trying to look pleasant. Ask him to stay. I insist upon it."

"Stay, Harry, to oblige Dorian, and to oblige me," said Hallward, gazing intently at his picture. "It is quite true, I never talk when I am working, and never listen either, and it must be dreadfully tedious for my unfortunate sitters. I beg you to stay."

"But what about my man at the Orleans?"

The painter laughed. "I don't think there will be any difficulty about that. Sit down again, Harry. And now, Dorian, get up on the platform, and don't move about too much, or pay any attention to what Lord Henry says. He has a very bad influence over all his friends, with the single exception of myself."

Dorian Gray stepped up on the dais, with the air of a young Greek martyr, and made a little *moue* of discontent to Lord Henry, to whom he had rather taken a fancy. He was so unlike Basil. They made a delightful contrast. And he had such a beautiful voice. After a few moments he said to him, "Have you really a very bad influence, Lord Henry? As bad as Basil says?"

"There is no such thing as a good influence, Mr. Gray. All influence is immoral—immoral from the scientific point of view."

"Why?"

"Because to influence a person is to give him one's own soul. He does not think his natural thoughts, or burn with his natural passions. His virtues are not real to him. His sins, if there are such things as sins, are borrowed. He becomes an echo of someone else's music, an actor of a part that has not been written for him. The aim of life is self-development. To realize one's nature perfectly—that is what each of us is here for. People are afraid of themselves, nowadays. They have forgotten the highest of all duties, the duty that one owes to oneself. Of course they are charitable. They feed the hungry, and clothe the beggar. But their own souls starve, and are naked. Courage has gone out of our race. Perhaps we never really had it. The terror of society, which is the basis of morals, the terror of God, which is the secret of religion—these are the two things that govern us. And yet—"

"Just turn your head a little more to the right, Dorian, like a good boy," said the painter, deep in his work, and conscious only that a look had come into the lad's face that he had never seen there before.

"And yet," continued Lord Henry, in his low, musical voice, and with that graceful wave of the hand that was always so characteristic of him, and that he had even in his Eton days, "I believe that if one man were to live out his life fully and completely, were to give form to every feeling, expression to every thought, reality to every dream—I believe that the world would gain such a fresh impulse of joy that we would forget all the maladies of mediævalism, and return to the Hellenic ideal—to something finer, richer, than the Hellenic ideal, it may be. But the bravest man amongst us is afraid of himself. The mutilation of the savage has its tragic survival in the self-denial that mars our lives. We are punished for our refusals. Every impulse that we strive to strangle broods in the mind, and poisons us. The body sins once, and has done with its sin, for action is a mode of purification. Nothing remains then but the recollection of a pleasure, or the luxury of a regret. The only way to get rid of a temptation is to yield to it. Resist it, and your soul grows sick with longing for the things it has forbidden to itself, with desire for what its monstrous laws have made monstrous and unlawful. It has been said that the great events of the world take place in the brain. It is in the brain, and the brain only, that the great sins of the world take place also. You, Mr. Gray, you yourself, with your rose-red youth and your rose-white boyhood, you have had passions that have made you afraid, thoughts that have filled you with terror, day-dreams and sleeping dreams whose mere memory might stain your cheek with shame—"

"Stop!" faltered Dorian Gray, "stop! you bewilder me. I don't know what to say. There is some answer to you, but I cannot find it. Don't speak. Let me think. Or, rather, let me try not to think."

For nearly ten minutes he stood there, motionless, with parted lips, and eyes strangely bright. He was dimly conscious that entirely fresh influences were at work within him. Yet they seemed to him to have come really from himself. The few words that Basil's friend had said to him—words spoken by chance, no doubt, and with wilful paradox in them—had touched some secret chord that had never been touched before, but that he felt was now vibrating and throbbing to curious pulses.

Music had stirred him like that. Music had troubled him many times. But music was not articulate. It was not a new world, but rather another chaos, that it created in us. Words! Mere words! How terrible they were! How clear, and vivid, and cruel. One could not escape from them. And yet what a subtle magic there was in them! They seemed to be able to give a plastic form to formless things, and to have a music of their own as sweet as that of viol or of lute. Mere words! Was there anything so real as words?

Yes, there had been things in his boyhood that he had not understood. He understood them now. Life suddenly became fiery-coloured to him. It seemed to him that he had been walking in fire. Why had he not known it?

With his subtle smile, Lord Henry watched him. He knew the precise psychological moment when to say nothing. He felt intensely interested. He was amazed at the sudden impression that his words had produced, and, remembering a book that he had read when he was sixteen, a book which had revealed to him much that he had not known before, he wondered whether Dorian Gray was passing through a similar experience. He had merely shot an arrow into the air. Had it hit the mark? How fascinating the lad was!

Hallward painted away with that marvellous bold touch of his, that had the true refinement and perfect delicacy that in art, at any rate, comes only from strength. He was unconscious of the silence.

"Basil, I am tired of standing," cried Dorian Gray, suddenly. "I must go out and sit in the garden. The air is stifling here."

"My dear fellow, I am so sorry. When I am painting, I can't think of anything else. But you never sat better. You were perfectly still. And I have caught the effect I wanted—the half-parted lips and the bright look in the eyes. I don't know what Harry has been saying to you, but he has certainly made you have the most wonderful expression. I suppose he has been paying you compliments. You mustn't believe a word that he says."

"He has certainly not been paying me compliments. Perhaps that is the reason that I don't believe anything he has told me."

"You know you believe it all," said Lord Henry, looking at him with his dreamy, languorous eyes. "I will go out to the garden with you. It is horribly hot in the studio. Basil, let us have something iced to drink, something with strawberries in it."

"Certainly, Harry. Just touch the bell, and when Parker comes I will tell him what you want. I have got to work up this background, so I will join you later on. Don't keep Dorian too long. I have never been in better form for painting than I am today. This is going to be my masterpiece. It is my masterpiece as it stands."

Lord Henry went out to the garden, and found Dorian Gray burying his face in the great cool lilac blossoms, feverishly drinking in their perfume as if it had been wine. He came close to him, and put his hand upon his shoulder. "You are quite right to do that," he murmured. "Nothing can cure the soul but the senses, just as nothing can cure the senses but the soul."

The lad started and drew back. He was bare-headed, and the leaves had tossed his rebellious curls and tangled all their gilded threads. There was a look of fear in his eyes, such as people have when they are suddenly awakened. His finely-chiselled nostrils quivered, and some hidden nerve shook the scarlet of his lips and left them trembling.

"Yes," continued Lord Henry, "that is one of the great secrets of life—to cure the soul by means of the senses, and the senses by means of the soul. You are a wonderful creation. You know more than you think you know, just as you know less than you want to know."

Dorian Gray frowned and turned his head away. He could not help liking the tall, graceful young man who was standing by him. His romantic olive-coloured face and worn expression interested him. There was something in his low, languid voice that was absolutely fascinating. His cool, white, flower-like hands, even, had a curious charm. They moved, as he spoke, like music, and seemed to have a language of their own. But he felt afraid of him, and ashamed of being afraid. Why had it been left for a stranger to reveal him to himself? He had known Basil Hallward for months, but the friendship between them had never altered him. Suddenly there had come someone across his life who seemed to have disclosed to him life's mystery. And, yet, what was there to be afraid of? He was not a schoolboy or a girl. It was absurd to be frightened.

"Let us go and sit in the shade," said Lord Henry. "Parker has brought out the drinks, and if you stay any longer in this glare you will be quite spoiled, and Basil will never paint you again. You really must not allow yourself to become sunburnt. It would be unbecoming."

"What can it matter?" cried Dorian Gray, laughing, as he sat down on the seat at the end of the garden.

"It should matter everything to you, Mr. Gray."

"Why?"

"Because you have the most marvellous youth, and youth is the one thing worth having."

"I don't feel that, Lord Henry."

"No, you don't feel it now. Some day, when you are old and wrinkled and ugly, when thought has seared your forehead with its lines, and passion branded your lips with its hideous fires, you will feel it, you will feel it terribly. Now, wherever you go, you charm the world. Will it always be so? . . . You have a wonderfully beautiful face, Mr. Gray. Don't frown. You have. And beauty is a form of genius—is higher, indeed, than genius, as it needs no explanation. It is of the great facts of the world, like sunlight, or springtime, or the reflection in dark waters of that silver shell we call the moon. It cannot be questioned. It has its divine right of sovereignty. It makes princes of those who have it. You smile? Ah! when you have lost it you won't smile. . . . People say sometimes that beauty is only superficial. That may be so. But at least it is not so superficial as thought is. To me, beauty is the wonder of wonders. It is only shallow people who do not judge by appearances. The true mystery of the world is the visible, not the invisible. . . . Yes, Mr. Gray, the gods have been good to you. But what the gods give they quickly take away. You have only a few years in which to live really, perfectly, and fully. When your youth goes, your beauty will go with it, and then you will suddenly discover that there are no triumphs left for you, or have to content yourself with those mean triumphs that the memory of your past will make more bitter than defeats. Every month as it wanes brings you nearer to something dreadful. Time is jealous of you, and wars against your lilies and your roses. You will become sallow, and hollow-cheeked, and dull-eyed. You will suffer horribly. . . . Ah! realize your youth while you have it. Don't squander the gold of your days, listening to the tedious, trying to improve the hopeless failure, or giving away your life to the ignorant, the common, and the vulgar. These are the sickly aims, the false ideals, of our age. Live! Live the wonderful life that is in you! Let nothing be lost upon you. Be always searching for new sensations. Be afraid of nothing. . . . A new Hedonism—that is what our century wants. You might be its visible symbol. With your personality there is nothing you could not do. The world belongs to you for a season. . . . The moment I met you I saw that you were quite unconscious of what you really are, of what you really might be. There was so much in you that charmed me that I felt I must tell you something about yourself. I thought how tragic it would be if you were wasted. For there is such a little time that your youth will last—such a little time. The common hill-flowers wither, but they blossom again. The laburnum will be as yellow next June as it is now. In a month there will be purple stars on the clematis, and year after year the green night of its leaves will hold its purple stars. But we never get back our youth. The pulse of joy that beats in us at twenty, becomes sluggish. Our limbs fail, our senses rot. We degenerate into hideous puppets, haunted by the memory of the passions of which we were too much afraid, and the exquisite temptations that we had not the courage to yield to. Youth! Youth! There is absolutely nothing in the world but youth!"

Dorian Gray listened, open-eyed and wondering. The spray of lilac fell from his hand upon the gravel. A furry bee came and buzzed round it for a moment. Then it began to scramble all over the oval stellated globe of the tiny blossoms. He watched it with that strange interest in trivial things that we try to develop when things of high import make us afraid, or when we are stirred by some new emotion for which we cannot find expression, or when some thought that terrifies us lays sudden siege to the brain and calls on us to yield. After a time the bee flew away. He saw it creeping into the stained trumpet of a Tyrian convolvulus. The flower seemed to quiver, and then swayed gently to and fro.

Suddenly the painter appeared at the door of the studio, and made staccato signs for them to come in. They turned to each other, and smiled.

"I am waiting," he cried. "Do come in. The light is quite perfect, and you can bring your drinks."

They rose up, and sauntered down the walk together. Two green-and-white butterflies fluttered past them, and in the pear tree at the corner of the garden a thrush began to sing.

"You are glad you have met me, Mr. Gray," said Lord Harry, looking at him.

"Yes, I am glad now. I wonder shall I always be glad?"

"Always! That is a dreadful word. It makes me shudder when I hear it. Women are so fond of using it. They spoil every romance by trying to make it last for ever. It is a meaningless word, too. The only difference between a caprice and a life-long passion is that the caprice lasts a little longer."

As they entered the studio, Dorian Gray put his hand upon Lord Henry's arm. "In that case, let our friendship be a caprice," he murmured, flushing at his own boldness, then stepped up on the platform and resumed his pose.

Lord Henry flung himself into a large wicker armchair, and watched him. The sweep and dash of the brush on the canvas made the only sound that broke the stillness, except when, now and then, Hallward stepped back to look at his work from a distance. In the slanting beams that streamed through the open doorway the dust danced and was golden. The heavy scent of the roses seemed to brood over everything.

After about a quarter of an hour Hallward stopped painting, looked for a long time at Dorian Gray, and then for a long time at the picture, biting the end of one of his huge brushes, and frowning. "It is quite finished," he cried at last, and stooping down he wrote his name in long vermilion letters on the left-hand corner of the canvas.

Lord Henry came over and examined the picture. It was certainly a wonderful work of art, and a wonderful likeness as well.

"My dear fellow, I congratulate you most warmly," he said. "It is the finest portrait of modern times. Mr. Gray, come over and look at yourself."

The lad started, as if awakened from some dream. "Is it really finished?" he murmured, stepping down from the platform.

"Quite finished," said the painter. "And you have sat splendidly today. I am awfully obliged to you."

"That is entirely due to me," broke in Lord Henry. "Isn't it, Mr. Gray?"

Dorian made no answer, but passed listlessly in front of his picture and turned towards it. When he saw it he drew back, and his cheeks flushed for a moment with pleasure. A look of joy came into his eyes, as if he had recognized himself for the first time. He stood there motionless and in wonder, dimly conscious that Hallward was speaking to him, but not catching the meaning of his words. The sense of his own beauty came on him like a revelation. He had never felt it before. Basil Hallward's compliments had seemed to him to be merely the charming exaggerations of friendship. He had listened to them, laughed at them, forgotten them. They had not influenced his nature. Then had come Lord Henry Wotton with his strange panegyric on youth, his terrible warning of its brevity. That had stirred him at the time, and now, as he stood gazing at the shadow of his own loveliness, the full reality of the description flashed across him. Yes, there would be a day when his face would be wrinkled and wizen, his eyes dim and colourless, the grace of his figure broken and deformed. The scarlet would pass away from his lips, and the gold steal from his hair. The life that was to make his soul would mar his body. He would become dreadful, hideous, and uncouth.

As he thought of it, a sharp pang of pain struck through him like a knife, and made each delicate fibre of his nature quiver. His eyes deepened into amethyst, and across them came a mist of tears. He felt as if a hand of ice had been laid upon his heart.

"Don't you like it?" cried Hallward at last, stung a little by the lad's silence, not understanding what it meant.

"Of course he likes it," said Lord Henry. "Who wouldn't like it? It is one of the greatest things in modern art. I will give you anything you like to ask for it. I must have it."

"It is not my property, Harry."

"Whose property is it?"

"Dorian's, of course," answered the painter.

"He is a very lucky fellow."

"How sad it is!" murmured Dorian Gray, with his eyes still fixed upon his own portrait. "How sad it is! I shall grow old, and horrible, and dreadful. But this picture will remain always young. It will never be older than this particular day of June. . . . If it were only the other way! If it were I who was to be always young, and the picture that was to grow old! For that —for that—I would give everything! Yes, there is nothing in the whole world I would not give! I would give my soul for that!"

"You would hardly care for such an arrangement, Basil," cried Lord Henry, laughing. "It would be rather hard lines on your work."

"I should object very strongly, Harry," said Hallward.

Dorian Gray turned and looked at him. "I believe you would, Basil. You like your art better than your friends. I am no more to you than a green bronze figure. Hardly as much, I dare say."

The painter stared in amazement. It was so unlike Dorian to speak like that. What had happened? He seemed quite angry. His face was flushed and his cheeks burning.

"Yes," he continued, "I am less to you than your ivory Hermes or your silver Faun. You will like them always. How long will you like me? Till I have my first wrinkle, I suppose. I know, now, that when one loses one's good looks, whatever they may be, one loses everything. Your picture has taught me that. Lord Henry Wotton is perfectly right. Youth is the only thing worth having. When I find that I am growing old, I shall kill myself."

Hallward turned pale, and caught his hand. "Dorian! Dorian!" he cried, "don't talk like that. I have never had such a friend as you, and I shall never have such another. You are not jealous of material things, are you?—you who are finer than any of them!"

"I am jealous of everything whose beauty does not die. I am jealous of the portrait you have painted of me. Why should it keep what I must lose? Every moment that passes takes something from me, and gives something to it. Oh, if it were only the other way! If the picture could change, and I could be always what I am now! Why did you paint it? It will mock me some day—mock me horribly!" The hot tears welled into his eyes; he tore his hand away, and, flinging himself on the divan, he buried his face in the cushions, as though he was praying.

"This is your doing, Harry," said the painter, bitterly.

Lord Henry shrugged his shoulders. "It is the real Dorian Gray—that is all."

"It is not."

"If it is not, what have I to do with it?"

"You should have gone away when I asked you," he muttered.

"I stayed when you asked me," was Lord Henry's answer.

"Harry, I can't quarrel with my two best friends at once, but between you both you have made me hate the finest piece of work I have ever done, and I will destroy it. What is it but canvas and colour? I will not let it come across our three lives and mar them."

Dorian Gray lifted his golden head from the pillow, and with pallid face and tear-stained eyes looked at him, as he walked over to the deal painting-table that was set beneath the high curtained window. What was he doing there? His fingers were straying about among the litter of tin tubes and dry brushes, seeking for something. Yes, it was for the long palette knife, with its thin blade of lithe steel. He had found it at last. He was going to rip up the canvas.

With a stifled sob the lad leaped from the couch, and, rushing over to Hallward, tore the knife out of his hand, and flung it to the end of the studio. "Don't, Basil, don't!" he cried. "It would be murder!"

"I am glad you appreciate my work at last, Dorian," said the painter, coldly, when he had recovered from his surprise. "I never thought you would."

"Appreciate it? I am in love with it, Basil. It is part of myself. I feel that."

"Well, as soon as you are dry, you shall be varnished, and framed, and sent home. Then you can do what you like with yourself." And he walked across the room and rang the bell for tea. "You will have tea, of course, Dorian? And so will you, Harry? Or do you object to such simple pleasures?"

"I adore simple pleasures," said Lord Henry. "They are the last refuge of the complex. But I don't like scenes, except on the stage. What absurd fellows you are, both of you! I wonder who it was defined man as a rational animal. It was the most premature definition ever given. Man is many things, but he is not rational. I am glad he is not, after all: though I wish you chaps would not squabble over the picture. You had much better let me have it, Basil. This silly boy doesn't really want it, and I really do."

"If you let anyone have it but me, Basil, I shall

never forgive you!" cried Dorian Gray; "and I don't allow people to call me a silly boy."

"You know the picture is yours, Dorian. I gave it to you before it existed."

"And you know you have been a little silly, Mr. Gray, and that you don't really object to being reminded that you are extremely young."

"I should have objected very strongly this morning, Lord Henry."

"Ah! this morning! You have lived since then."

There came a knock at the door, and the butler entered with a laden tea tray and set it down upon a small Japanese table. There was a rattle of cups and saucers and the hissing of a fluted Georgian urn. Two globe-shaped china dishes were brought in by a page. Dorian Gray went over and poured out the tea. The two men sauntered languidly to the table, and examined what was under the covers.

"Let us go to the theatre tonight," said Lord Henry. "There is sure to be something on, somewhere. I have promised to dine at White's, but it is only with an old friend, so I can send him a wire to say that I am ill, or that I am prevented from coming in consequence of a subsequent engagement. I think that would be a rather nice excuse: it would have all the surprise of candour."

"It is such a bore putting on one's dress-clothes," muttered Hallward. "And, when one has them on, they are so horrid."

"Yes," answered Lord Henry, dreamily, "the costume of the nineteenth century is detestable. It is so sombre, so depressing. Sin is the only real colour element left in modern life."

"You really must not say things like that before Dorian, Harry."

"Before which Dorian? The one who is pouring out tea for us, or the one in the picture?"

"Before either."

"I should like to come to the theatre with you, Lord Henry," said the lad.

"Then you shall come; and you will come too, Basil, won't you?"

"I can't, really. I would sooner not. I have a lot of work to do."

"Well, then, you and I will go, Mr. Gray."

"I should like that awfully."

The painter bit his lip and walked over, cup in hand, to the picture. "I shall stay with the real Dorian," he said, sadly.

"Is it the real Dorian?" cried the original of the portrait, strolling across to him. "Am I really like that?"

"Yes; you are just like that."

"How wonderful, Basil!"

"At least you are like it in appearance. But it will never alter," sighed Hallward. "That is something."

"What a fuss people make about fidelity!" exclaimed Lord Henry. "Why, even in love it is purely a question for physiology. It has nothing to do with our own will. Young men want to be faithful, and are not; old men want to be faithless, and cannot: that is all one can say."

"Don't go to the theatre tonight, Dorian," said Hallward. "Stop and dine with me."

"I can't, Basil."

"Why?"

"Because I have promised Lord Henry Wotton to go with him."

"He won't like you the better for keeping your promises. He always breaks his own. I beg you not to go."

Dorian Gray laughed and shook his head.

"I entreat you."

The lad hesitated, and looked over at Lord Henry, who was watching them from the tea table with an amused smile.

"I must go, Basil," he answered.

"Very well," said Hallward; and he went over and laid down his cup on the tray. "It is rather late, and, as you have to dress, you had better lose no time. Good-bye, Harry. Good-bye, Dorian. Come and see me soon. Come tomorrow."

"Certainly."

"You won't forget?"

"No, of course not," cried Dorian.

"And . . . Harry!"

"Yes, Basil?"

"Remember what I asked you, when we were in the garden this morning."

"I have forgotten it."

"I trust you."

"I wish I could trust myself," said Lord Henry, laughing. "Come, Mr. Gray, my hansom is outside, and I can drop you at your own place. Good-bye, Basil. It has been a most interesting afternoon."

As the door closed behind them, the painter flung himself down on a sofa, and a look of pain came into his face.

III

AT HALF-PAST twelve next day Lord Henry Wotton strolled from Curzon Street over to the Albany to call on his uncle, Lord Fermor, a genial if somewhat rough-mannered old bachelor, whom the outside world called selfish because it derived no particular benefit from him, but who was considered generous by Society as he fed the people who amused him. His father had been our ambassador at Madrid when Isabella was young, and Prim unthought of, but had retired from the Diplomatic Service in a capricious moment of annoyance on not being offered the Embassy at Paris, a post to which he considered that he was fully entitled by reason of his birth, his indolence, the good English of his despatches, and his inordinate passion for pleasure. The son, who had been his father's secretary, had resigned along with his chief, somewhat foolishly as was thought at the time, and on succeeding some months later to the title, had set himself to the serious study of the great aristocratic art of doing absolutely nothing. He had two large town houses, but preferred to live in chambers as it was less trouble, and took most of his meals at his club. He paid some attention to the management of his collieries in the Midland counties, excusing himself for this taint of industry on the ground that the one advantage of having coal was that it enabled a gentleman to afford the decency of burning wood on his own hearth. In politics he was a Tory, except when the Tories were in office, during which period he roundly abused them for being a pack of Radicals. He was a hero to his valet, who bullied him, and a terror to most of his relations, whom he bullied in turn. Only England could have produced him, and he always said that the country was going to the dogs. His principles were out of date, but there was a good deal to be said for his prejudices.

When Lord Henry entered the room, he found his uncle sitting in a rough shooting coat, smoking a cheroot and grumbling over *The Times*. "Well, Harry," said the old gentleman, "what brings you out so early? I thought you dandies never got up until two, and were not visible till five."

"Pure family affection, I assure you, Uncle George. I want to get something out of you."

"Money, I suppose," said Lord Fermor, making a wry face. "Well, sit down and tell me all about it. Young people, nowadays, imagine that money is everything."

"Yes," murmured Lord Henry, settling his buttonhole in his coat; "and when they grow older they know it. But I don't want money. It is only people who pay their bills who want that, Uncle George, and I never pay mine. Credit is the capital of a younger son, and one lives charmingly upon it. Besides, I always deal with Dartmoor's tradesmen, and consequently they never bother me. What I want is information; not useful information, of course; useless information."

"Well, I can tell you anything that is in an English Blue book, Harry, although those fellows nowadays write a lot of nonsense. When I was in the Diplomatic, things were much better. But I hear they let them in now by examination. What can you expect? Examinations, sir, are pure humbug from beginning to end. If a man is a gentleman, he knows quite enough, and if he is not a gentleman, whatever he knows is bad for him."

"Mr. Dorian Gray does not belong to Blue books, Uncle George," said Lord Henry, languidly.

"Mr. Dorian Gray? Who is he?" asked Lord Fermor, knitting his bushy white eyebrows.

"That is what I have come to learn, Uncle George. Or rather, I know who he is. He is the last Lord Kelso's grandson. His mother was a Devereux, Lady Margaret Devereux. I want you to tell me about his mother. What was she like? Whom did she marry? You have known nearly everybody in your time, so you might have known her. I am very much interested in Mr. Gray at present. I have only just met him."

"Kelso's grandson!" echoed the old gentleman— "Kelso's grandson! . . . Of course. . . . I knew his mother intimately. I believe I was at her christening. She was an extraordinarily beautiful girl, Margaret Devereux, and made all the men frantic by running away with a penniless young fellow, a mere nobody, sir, a subaltern in a foot regiment, or something of that kind. Certainly. I remember the whole thing as if it happened yesterday. The poor chap was killed in a duel at Spa a few months after the marriage. There was an ugly story about it. They said Kelso got some rascally adventurer, some Belgian brute, to insult his son-in-law in public, paid him, sir, to do it, paid him, and that the fellow spitted his man as if he had been a pigeon. The thing was hushed up, but, egad, Kelso ate his chop alone at the club for some time afterwards. He brought his daughter back with him, I was told, and she never spoke to him again. Oh, yes; it was a bad business. The girl died too, died within a year. So she left a son, did she? I had forgotten that. What sort of boy is he? If he is like his mother he must be a good-looking chap."

"He is very good-looking," assented Lord Henry.

"I hope he will fall into proper hands," continued the old man. "He should have a pot of money waiting for him if Kelso did the right thing by him. His mother had money too. All the Selby property came to her, through her grandfather. Her grandfather hated Kelso, thought him a mean dog. He was, too. Came to Madrid once when I was there. Egad, I was ashamed of him. The Queen used to ask me about the English noble who was always quarrelling with the cabmen about their fares. They made quite a story of it. I didn't dare show my face at Court for a month. I hope he treated his grandson better than he did the jarvies."

"I don't know," answered Lord Henry. "I fancy that the boy will be well off. He is not of age yet. He has Selby, I know. He told me so. And . . . his mother was very beautiful?"

"Margaret Devereux was one of the loveliest creatures I ever saw, Harry. What on earth induced her to behave as she did, I never could understand. She could have married anybody she chose. Carlington was mad after her. She was romantic, though. All the women of that family were. The men were a poor lot, but, egad! the women were wonderful. Carlington went on his knees to her. Told me so himself. She laughed at him, and there wasn't a girl in London at the time who wasn't after him. And by the way, Harry, talking about silly marriages, what is this humbug your father tells me about Dartmoor wanting to marry an American? Ain't English girls good enough for him?"

"It is rather fashionable to marry Americans just now, Uncle George."

"I'll back English women against the world, Harry," said Lord Fermor, striking the table with his fist.

"The betting is on the Americans."

"They don't last, I am told," muttered his uncle.

"A long engagement exhausts them, but they are capital at a steeplechase. They take things flying. I don't think Dartmoor has a chance."

"Who are her people?" grumbled the old gentleman. "Has she got any?"

Lord Henry shook his head. "American girls are as clever at concealing their parents, as English women are at concealing their past," he said, rising to go.

"They are pork-packers, I suppose?"

"I hope so, Uncle George, for Dartmoor's sake. I am

told that pork-packing is the most lucrative profession in America, after politics."

"Is she pretty?"

"She behaves as if she was beautiful. Most American women do. It is the secret of their charm."

"Why can't these American women stay in their own country? They are always telling us that it is the Paradise for women."

"It is. That is the reason why, like Eve, they are so excessively anxious to get out of it," said Lord Henry. "Good-bye, Uncle George. I shall be late for lunch, if I stop any longer. Thanks for giving me the information I wanted. I always like to know everything about my new friends, and nothing about my old ones."

"Where are you lunching, Harry?"

"At Aunt Agatha's. I have asked myself and Mr. Gray. He is her latest protégé."

"Humph! Tell your Aunt Agatha, Harry, not to bother me any more with her charity appeals. I am sick of them. Why, the good woman thinks that I have nothing to do but to write cheques for her silly fads."

"All right, Uncle George, I'll tell her, but it won't have any effect. Philanthropic people lose all sense of humanity. It is their distinguishing characteristic."

The old gentleman growled approvingly, and rang the bell for his servant. Lord Henry passed up the low arcade into Burlington Street, and turned his steps in the direction of Berkeley Square.

So that was the story of Dorian Gray's parentage. Crudely as it had been told to him, it had yet stirred him by its suggestion of a strange, almost modern romance. A beautiful woman risking everything for a mad passion. A few wild weeks of happiness cut short by a hideous, treacherous crime. Months of voiceless agony, and then a child born in pain. The mother snatched away by death, the boy left to solitude and the tyranny of an old and loveless man. Yes; it was an interesting background. It posed the lad, made him more perfect as it were. Behind every exquisite thing that existed, there was something tragic. Worlds had to be in travail, that the meanest flower might blow. . . . And how charming he had been at dinner the night before, as with startled eyes and lips parted in frightened pleasure he had sat opposite to him at the club, the red candle-shades staining to a richer rose the wakening wonder of his face. Talking to him was like playing upon an exquisite violin. He answered to every touch and thrill of the bow. . . . There was something terribly enthralling in the exercise of influence. No other activity was like it. To project one's soul into some gracious form, and let it tarry there for a moment; to hear one's own intellectual views echoed back to one with all the added music of passion and youth; to convey one's temperament into another as though it were a subtle fluid or a strange perfume: there was a real joy in that—perhaps the most satisfying joy left to us in an age so limited and vulgar as our own, an age grossly carnal in its pleasures, and grossly common in its aims. . . . He was a marvellous type, too, this lad, whom by so curious a chance he had met in Basil's studio, or could be fashioned into a marvellous type, at any rate. Grace was his, and the white purity of boyhood, and beauty such as old Greek marbles kept for us. There was nothing that one could not do with him. He could be made a Titan or a toy. What a pity it was that such beauty was destined to fade! . . . And Basil? From a psychological point of view, how interesting he was! The new manner in art, the fresh mode of looking at life, suggested so strangely by the merely visible presence of one who was unconscious of it all; the silent spirit that dwelt in dim woodland, and walked unseen in open field, suddenly showing herself, dryad-like and not afraid, because in his soul who sought for her there had been wakened that wonderful vision to which alone are wonderful things revealed; the mere shapes and patterns of things becoming, as it were, refined, and gaining a kind of symbolical value, as though they were themselves patterns of some other and more perfect form whose shadow they made real: how strange it all was! He remembered something like it in history. Was it not Plato, that artist in thought, who had first analysed it? Was it not Buonaroti who had carved it in the coloured marbles of a sonnet sequence? But in our own country it was strange. . . . Yes; he would try to be to Dorian Gray what, without knowing it, the lad was to the painter who had fashioned the wonderful portrait. He would seek to dominate him— had already, indeed, half done so. He would make that wonderful spirit his own. There was something fascinating in this son of love and death.

Suddenly he stopped, and glanced up at the houses. He found that he had passed his aunt's some distance, and, smiling to himself, turned back. When he entered the somewhat sombre hall the butler told him that they had gone in to lunch. He gave one of the footmen his hat and stick and passed into the dining-room.

"Late as usual, Harry," cried his aunt, shaking her head at him.

He invented a facile excuse, and having taken the vacant seat next to her, looked round to see who was there. Dorian bowed to him shyly from the end of the table, a flush of pleasure stealing into his cheek. Opposite was the Duchess of Harley, a lady of admirable good nature and good temper, much liked by everyone who knew her, and of those ample architectural proportions that in women who are not Duchesses are described by contemporary historians as stoutness. Next to her sat, on her right, Sir Thomas Burdon, a Radical member of Parliament, who followed his leader in public life and in private life followed the best cooks, dining with the Tories, and thinking with the Liberals, in accordance with a wise and well-known rule. The post on her left was occupied by Mr. Erskine of Treadley, an old gentleman of considerable charm and culture, who had fallen, however, into bad habits of silence, having, as he explained once to Lady Agatha, said everything that he had to say before he was thirty. His own neighbour was Mrs. Vandeleur, one of his aunt's oldest friends, a perfect saint amongst women, but so dreadfully dowdy that she reminded one of a badly bound hymn-book. Fortunately for him she had on the other side Lord Faudel, a most intelligent middle-aged mediocrity, as bald as a Ministerial statement in the House of Commons, with whom she was conversing in that intensely earnest manner which is the one unpardonable error, as he remarked once himself, that all really good people fall into, and from which none of them ever quite escape.

"We are talking about poor Dartmoor, Lord Henry," cried the Duchess, nodding pleasantly to him across the table. "Do you think he will really marry this fascinating young person?"

"I believe she has made up her mind to propose to him, Duchess."

"How dreadful!" exclaimed Lady Agatha. "Really, someone should interfere."

"I am told, on excellent authority, that her father keeps an American dry-goods store," said Sir Thomas Burdon, looking supercilious.

"My uncle has already suggested pork-packing, Sir Thomas."

"Dry-goods! What are American dry-goods?" asked the Duchess, raising her large hands in wonder, and accentuating the verb.

"American novels," answered Lord Henry, helping himself to some quail.

The Duchess looked puzzled.

"Don't mind him, my dear," whispered Lady Agatha. "He never means anything that he says."

"When America was discovered," said the Radical member, and he began to give some wearisome facts. Like all people who try to exhaust a subject, he exhausted his listeners. The Duchess sighed, and exercised her privilege of interruption. "I wish to goodness it never had been discovered at all!" she exclaimed. "Really, our girls have no chance nowadays. It is most unfair."

"Perhaps, after all, America never has been discovered," said Mr. Erskine; "I myself would say that it had merely been detected."

"Oh! but I have seen specimens of the inhabitants," answered the Duchess, vaguely. "I must confess that most of them are extremely pretty. And they dress well, too. They get all their dresses in Paris. I wish I could afford to do the same."

"They say that when good Americans die they go to Paris," chuckled Sir Thomas, who had a large wardrobe of Humour's cast-off clothes.

"Really! And where do bad Americans go to when they die?" inquired the Duchess.

"They go to America," murmured Lord Henry.

Sir Thomas frowned. "I am afraid that your nephew is prejudiced against that great country," he said to Lady Agatha. "I have travelled all over it, in cars provided by the directors, who, in such matters, are extremely civil. I assure you that it is an education to visit it."

"But must we really see Chicago in order to be educated?" asked Mr. Erskine, plaintively. "I don't feel up to the journey."

Sir Thomas waved his hand. "Mr. Erskine of Treadley has the world on his shelves. We practical men like to see things, not to read about them. The Americans are an extremely interesting people. They are absolutely reasonable. I think that is their distinguishing characteristic. Yes, Mr. Erskine, an absolutely reasonable people. I assure you there is no nonsense about the Americans."

"How dreadful!" cried Lord Henry. "I can stand brute force, but brute reason is quite unbearable. There is something unfair about its use. It is hitting below the intellect."

"I do not understand you," said Sir Thomas, growing rather red.

"I do, Lord Henry," murmured Mr. Erskine, with a smile.

"Paradoxes are all very well in their way . . . " rejoined the Baronet.

"Was that a paradox?" asked Mr. Erskine. "I did not think so. Perhaps it was. Well, the way of paradoxes is the way of truth. To test reality we must see it on the tight-rope. When the verities become acrobats we can judge them."

"Dear me!" said Lady Agatha, "how you men argue! I am sure I never can make out what you are talking about. Oh! Harry, I am quite vexed with you. Why do you try to persuade our nice Mr. Dorian Gray to give up the East End? I assure you he would be quite invaluable. They would love his playing."

"I want him to play to me," cried Lord Henry, smiling, and he looked down the table and caught a bright answering glance.

"But they are so unhappy in Whitechapel," continued Lady Agatha.

"I can sympathize with everything, except suffering," said Lord Henry, shrugging his shoulders. "I cannot sympathize with that. It is too ugly, too horrible, too distressing. There is something terribly morbid in the modern sympathy with pain. One should sympathize with the colour, the beauty, the joy of life. The less said about life's sores the better."

"Still, the East End is a very important problem," remarked Sir Thomas, with a grave shake of the head.

"Quite so," answered the young lord. "It is the problem of slavery, and we try to solve it by amusing the slaves."

The politician looked at him keenly. "What change do you propose, then?" he asked.

Lord Henry laughed. "I don't desire to change anything in England except the weather," he answered. "I am quite content with philosophic contemplation. But, as the nineteenth century has gone bankrupt through an overexpenditure of sympathy, I would suggest that we should appeal to science to put us straight. The advantage of the emotions is that they lead us astray, and the advantage of science is that it is not emotional."

"But we have such grave responsibilities," ventured Mrs. Vandeleur, timidly.

"Terribly grave," echoed Lady Agatha.

Lord Henry looked over at Mr. Erskine. "Humanity takes itself too seriously. It is the world's original sin. If the caveman had known how to laugh, history would have been different."

"You are really very comforting," warbled the Duchess. "I have always felt rather guilty when I came to see your dear aunt, for I take no interest at all in the East End. For the future I shall be able to look her in the face without a blush."

"A blush is very becoming, Duchess," remarked Lord Henry.

"Only when one is young," she answered. "When an old woman like myself blushes, it is a very bad sign. Ah! Lord Henry, I wish you would tell me how to become young again."

He thought for a moment. "Can you remember any great error that you committed in your early days, Duchess?" he asked, looking at her across the table.

"A great many, I fear," she cried.

"Then commit them over again," he said, gravely. "To get back one's youth, one has merely to repeat one's follies."

"A delightful theory!" she exclaimed. "I must put it into practice."

"A dangerous theory," came from Sir Thomas's tight lips. Lady Agatha shook her head, but could not help being amused. Mr. Erskine listened.

"Yes," he continued, "that is one of the great secrets of life. Nowadays most people die of a sort of creeping common sense, and discover when it is too late that the only things one never regrets are one's mistakes."

A laugh ran round the table.

He played with the idea, and grew wilful; tossed it into the air and transformed it; let it escape and recaptured it; made it iridescent with fancy, and winged it with paradox. The praise of folly, as he went on, soared into a philosophy, and Philosophy herself became young, and catching the mad music of Pleasure, wearing, one might fancy, her wine-stained robe and wreath of ivy, danced like a bacchante over the hills of life, and mocked the slow Silenus for being sober. Facts fled before her like frightened forest things. Her white feet trod the huge press at which wise Omar sits, till the seething grape-juice rose round her bare limbs in waves of purple bubbles, or crawled in red foam over the vat's black, dripping, sloping sides. It was an extraordinary improvisation. He felt that the eyes of Dorian Gray were fixed on him, and the consciousness that amongst his audience there was one whose temperament he wished to fascinate, seemed to give his wit keenness, and to lend colour to his imagination. He was brilliant, fantastic, irresponsible. He charmed his listeners out of themselves, and they followed his pipe laughing. Dorian Gray never took his gaze off him, but sat like one under a spell, smiles chasing each other over his lips, and wonder growing grave in his darkening eyes.

At last, liveried in the costume of the age, reality entered the room in the shape of a servant to tell the Duchess that her carriage was waiting. She wrung her hands in mock despair. "How annoying!" she cried. "I must go. I have to call for my husband at the club, to take him to some absurd meeting at Willis's Rooms, where he is going to be in the chair. If I am late he is sure to be furious, and I couldn't have a scene in this bonnet. It is far too fragile. A harsh word would ruin it. No, I must go, dear Agatha. Good-bye, Lord Henry, you are quite delightful, and dreadfully demoralizing. I am sure I don't know what to say about your views.

You must come and dine with us some night. Tuesday? Are you disengaged Tuesday?"

"For you I would throw over anybody, Duchess," said Lord Henry, with a bow.

"Ah! that is very nice, and very wrong of you," she cried; "so mind you come;" and she swept out of the room, followed by Lady Agatha and the other ladies.

When Lord Henry had sat down again, Mr. Erskine moved round, and taking a chair close to him, placed his hand upon his arm.

"You talk books away," he said; "why don't you write one?"

"I am too fond of reading books to care to write them, Mr. Erskine. I should like to write a novel certainly, a novel that would be as lovely as a Persian carpet and as unreal. But there is no literary public in England for anything except newspapers, primers, and encyclopædias. Of all people in the world the English have the least sense of the beauty of literature."

"I fear you are right," answered Mr. Erskine. "I myself used to have literary ambitions, but I gave them up long ago. And now, my dear young friend, if you will allow me to call you so, may I ask if you really meant all that you said to us at lunch?"

"I quite forget what I said," smiled Lord Henry. "Was it all very bad?"

"Very bad indeed. In fact I consider you extremely dangerous, and if anything happens to our good Duchess we shall all look on you as being primarily responsible. But I should like to talk to you about life. The generation into which I was born was tedious. Some day, when you are tired of London, come down to Treadley, and expound to me your philosophy of pleasure over some admirable Burgundy I am fortunate enough to possess."

"I shall be charmed. A visit to Treadley would be a great privilege. It has a perfect host, and a perfect library."

"You will complete it," answered the old gentleman, with a courteous bow. "And now I must bid good-bye to your excellent aunt. I am due at the Athenæum. It is the hour when we sleep there."

"All of you, Mr. Erskine?"

"Forty of us, in forty arm-chairs. We are practising for an English Academy of Letters."

Lord Henry laughed, and rose. "I am going to the Park," he cried.

As he was passing out of the door Dorian Gray touched him on the arm. "Let me come with you," he murmured.

"But I thought you had promised Basil Hallward to go and see him," answered Lord Henry.

"I would sooner come with you; yes, I feel I must come with you. Do let me. And you will promise to talk to me all the time? No one talks so wonderfully as you do."

"Ah! I have talked quite enough for today," said Lord Henry, smiling. "All I want now is to look at life. You may come and look at it with me, if you care to."

IV

ONE afternoon, a month later, Dorian Gray was reclining in a luxurious arm-chair, in the little library of Lord Henry's house in Mayfair. It was, in its way, a very charming room, with its high panelled wainscoting of olive-stained oak, its cream-coloured frieze and ceiling of raised plaster-work, and its brick-dust felt carpet strewn with silk long-fringed Persian rugs. On a tiny satinwood table stood a statuette by Clodion, and beside it lay a copy of *Les Cent Nouvelles*, bound for Margaret of Valois by Clovis Eve, and powdered with the gilt daisies that Queen had selected for her device. Some large blue china jars and parrot-tulips were ranged on the mantelshelf, and through the small leaded panes of the window streamed the apricot-coloured light of a summer day in London.

Lord Henry had not yet come in. He was always late on principle, his principle being that punctuality is the thief of time. So the lad was looking rather sulky, as with listless fingers he turned over the pages of an elaborately illustrated edition of *Manon Lescaut* that he had found in one of the bookcases. The formal monotonous ticking of the Louis Quatorze clock annoyed him. Once or twice he thought of going away.

At last he heard a step outside, and the door opened. "How late you are, Harry!" he murmured.

"I am afraid it is not Harry, Mr. Gray," answered a shrill voice.

He glanced quickly round, and rose to his feet. "I beg your pardon. I thought—"

"You thought it was my husband. It is only his wife. You must let me introduce myself. I know you quite well by your photographs. I think my husband has got seventeen of them."

"Not seventeen, Lady Henry?"

"Well, eighteen, then. And I saw you with him the other night at the Opera." She laughed nervously as she spoke, and watched him with her vague forget-me-not eyes. She was a curious woman, whose dresses always looked as if they had been designed in a rage and put on in a tempest. She was usually in love with somebody, and, as her passion was never returned, she had kept all her illusions. She tried to look picturesque, but only succeeded in being untidy. Her name was Victoria, and she had a perfect mania for going to church.

"That was at *Lohengrin*, Lady Henry, I think?"

"Yes; it was at dear *Lohengrin*. I like Wagner's music better than anybody's. It is so loud that one can talk the whole time without other people hearing what one says. That is a great advantage: don't you think so, Mr. Gray?"

The same nervous staccato laugh broke from her thin lips, and her fingers began to play with a long tortoise-shell paper-knife.

Dorian smiled, and shook his head: "I am afraid I don't think so, Lady Henry. I never talk during music —at least, during good music. If one hears bad music, it is one's duty to drown it in conversation."

"Ah! that is one of Harry's views, isn't it, Mr. Gray? I always hear Harry's views from his friends. It is the only way I get to know of them. But you must not think I don't like good music. I adore it, but I am afraid of it. It makes me too romantic. I have simply wor-shipped pianists—two at a time, sometimes, Harry tells me. I don't know what it is about them. Perhaps it is that they are foreigners. They all are, ain't they? Even those that are born in England become foreigners after a time, don't they? It is so clever of them, and such a compliment to art. Makes it quite cosmopolitan, doesn't it? You have never been to any of my parties, have you, Mr. Gray? You must come. I can't afford orchids, but I spare no expense in foreigners. They make one's rooms look so picturesque. But here is Harry!—Harry, I came in to look for you, to ask you something—I forget what it was—and I found Mr. Gray here. We have had such a pleasant chat about music. We have quite the same ideas. No; I think our ideas are quite different. But he has been most pleasant. I am so glad I've seen him."

"I am charmed, my love, quite charmed," said Lord Henry, elevating his dark crescent-shaped eyebrows and looking at them both with an amused smile. "So sorry I am late, Dorian. I went to look after a piece of old brocade in Wardour Street, and had to bargain for hours for it. Nowadays people know the price of everything, and the value of nothing."

"I am afraid I must be going," exclaimed Lady Henry, breaking an awkward silence with her silly sudden laugh. "I have promised to drive with the Duchess. Good-bye, Mr. Gray. Good-bye, Harry. You are dining out, I suppose? So am I. Perhaps I shall see you at Lady Thornbury's."

"I dare say, my dear," said Lord Henry, shutting the door behind her, as, looking like a bird of paradise that had been out all night in the rain, she flitted out of the room, leaving a faint odour of frangipanni. Then he lit a cigarette, and flung himself down on the sofa.

"Never marry a woman with straw-coloured hair, Dorian," he said, after a few puffs.

"Why, Harry?"

"Because they are so sentimental."

"But I like sentimental people."

"Never marry at all, Dorian. Men marry because they are tired; women, because they are curious: both are disappointed."

"I don't think I am likely to marry, Harry. I am too much in love. That is one of your aphorisms. I am putting it into practice, as I do everything that you say."

"Who are you in love with?" asked Lord Henry, after a pause.

"With an actress," said Dorian Gray, blushing.

Lord Henry shrugged his shoulders. "That is a rather commonplace début."

"You would not say so if you saw her, Harry."

"Who is she?"

"Her name is Sibyl Vane."

"Never heard of her."

"No one has. People will some day, however. She is a genius."

"My dear boy, no woman is a genius. Women are a decorative sex. They never have anything to say, but they say it charmingly. Women represent the triumph of matter over mind, just as men represent the triumph of mind over morals."

"Harry, how can you?"

"My dear Dorian, it is quite true. I am analysing women at present, so I ought to know. The subject is not so abstruse as I thought it was. I find that, ultimately, there are only two kinds of women, the plain and the coloured. The plain women are very useful. If you want to gain a reputation for respectability, you have merely to take them down to supper. The other women are very charming. They commit one mistake, however. They paint in order to try and look young. Our grandmothers painted in order to try and talk brilliantly. *Rouge* and *esprit* used to go together. That is all over now. As long as a woman can look ten years younger than her own daughter, she is perfectly satisfied. As for conversation, there are only five women in London worth talking to and two of these can't be admitted into decent society. However, tell me about your genius. How long have you known her?"

"Ah! Harry, your views terrify me."

"Never mind that. How long have you known her?"

"About three weeks."

"And where did you come across her?"

"I will tell you, Harry; but you mustn't be unsympathetic about it. After all, it never would have happened if I had not met you. You filled me with a wild desire to know everything about life. For days after I met you, something seemed to throb in my veins. As I lounged in the Park, or strolled down Piccadilly, I used to look at everyone who passed me, and wonder, with a mad curiosity, what sort of lives they led. Some of them fascinated me. Others filled me with terror. There was an exquisite poison in the air. I had a passion for sensations. . . . Well, one evening about seven o'clock, I determined to go out in search of some adventure. I felt that this grey, monstrous London of ours, with its myriads of people, its sordid sinners, and its splendid sins, as you once phrased it, must have something in store for me. I fancied a thousand things. The mere danger gave me a sense of delight. I remembered what you had said to me on that wonderful evening when we first dined together, about the search for beauty being the real secret of life. I don't know what I expected, but I went out and wandered eastward, soon losing my way in a labyrinth of grimy streets and black, grassless squares. About half-past eight I passed by an absurd little theatre, with great flaring gas-jets and gaudy play-bills. A hideous Jew, in the most amazing waistcoat I ever beheld in my life, was standing at the entrance, smoking a vile cigar. He had greasy ringlets, and an enormous diamond blazed in the centre of a soiled shirt. 'Have a box, my Lord?' he said, when he saw me, and he took off his hat with an air of gorgeous servility. There was something about him, Harry, that amused me. He was such a monster. You will laugh at me, I know, but I really went in and paid a whole guinea for the stage-box. To the present day I can't make out why I did so; and yet if I hadn't—my dear Harry, if I hadn't, I should have missed the greatest romance of my life. I see you are laughing. It is horrid of you!"

"I am not laughing, Dorian; at least I am not laughing at you. But you should not say the greatest romance of your life. You should say the first romance of your life. You will always be loved, and you will always be in love with love. A *grande passion* is the privilege of people who have nothing to do. That is the one use of the idle classes of a country. Don't be afraid. There are exquisite things in store for you. This is merely the beginning."

"Do you think my nature so shallow?" cried Dorian Gray, angrily.

"No; I think your nature so deep."

"How do you mean?"

"My dear boy, the people who love only once in their lives are really the shallow people. What they call their loyalty, and their fidelity, I call either the lethargy of custom or their lack of imagination. Faithfulness is to the emotional life what consistency is to the life of the intellect—simply a confession of failure. Faithfulness! I must analyse it some day. The passion for property is in it. There are many things that we would throw away if we were not afraid that others might pick them up. But I don't want to interrupt you. Go on with your story."

"Well, I found myself seated in a horrid little private box, with a vulgar drop-scene staring me in the face. I looked out from behind the curtain, and surveyed the house. It was a tawdry affair, all Cupids and cornucopias, like a third-rate wedding-cake. The gallery and pit were fairly full, but the two rows of dingy stalls were quite empty, and there was hardly a person in what I suppose they called the dress-circle. Women went about with oranges and ginger-beer, and there was a terrible consumption of nuts going on."

"It must have been just like the palmy days of the British Drama."

"Just like, I should fancy, and very depressing. I began to wonder what on earth I should do, when I caught sight of the play-bill. What do you think the play was, Harry?"

"I should think 'The Idiot Boy, or Dumb but Innocent.' Our fathers used to like that sort of piece, I believe. The longer I live, Dorian, the more keenly I feel that whatever was good enough for our fathers is not good enough for us. In art, as in politics, *les grandpères ont toujours tort.*"

"This play was good enough for us, Harry. It was *Romeo and Juliet.* I must admit that I was rather annoyed at the idea of seeing Shakespeare done in such a wretched hole of a place. Still, I felt interested, in a sort of way. At any rate, I determined to wait for the first act. There was a dreadful orchestra, presided over by a young Hebrew who sat at a cracked piano, that nearly drove me away, but at last the drop-scene was drawn up, and the play began. Romeo was a stout elderly gentleman, with corked eyebrows, a husky tragedy voice, and a figure like a beer-barrel. Mercutio was almost as bad. He was played by the low-comedian, who had introduced gags of his own and was on most friendly terms with the pit. They were both as grotesque as the scenery, and that looked as if it had come out of a country-booth. But, Juliet! Harry, imagine a girl, hardly seventeen years of age, with a little flower-like face, a small Greek head with plaited coils of dark-brown hair, eyes that were violet wells of passion, lips that were like the petals of a rose. She was the loveliest thing I had ever seen in my life. You said to me once that pathos left you unmoved, but that beauty, mere beauty, could fill your eyes with tears. I tell you, Harry, I could hardly see this girl for the mist of tears that came across me. And her voice—I never heard such a voice. It was very low at first, with deep mellow notes, that seemed to fall singly upon one's ear. Then it became a little louder, and sounded like a flute or a distant hautbois. In the garden scene it had all the tremulous ecstasy that one hears just before dawn when nightingales are singing. There were moments, later on, when it had the wild passion of violins. You know how a voice can stir one. Your voice and the voice of Sibyl Vane are two things that I shall never forget. When I close my eyes, I hear them, and each of them says something different. I don't know which to follow. Why should I not love her? Harry, I do love her. She is everything to me in life. Night after night I go to see her play. One evening she is Rosalind, and the next evening she is Imogen. I have seen her die in the gloom of an Italian tomb, sucking the poison from her lover's lips. I have watched her wandering through the forest of Arden, disguised as a pretty boy in hose and doublet and dainty cap. She has been mad, and has come into the presence of a guilty king, and given him rue to wear, and bitter herbs to taste of. She has been innocent, and the black hands of jealousy have crushed her reed-like throat. I have seen her in every age and in every costume. Ordinary women never appeal to one's imagination. They are limited to their century. No glamour ever transfigures them. One knows their minds as easily as one knows their bonnets. One can always find them. There is no mystery in any of them: They ride in the Park in the morning, and chatter at tea parties in the afternoon. They have their stereotyped

smile, and their fashionable manner. They are quite obvious. But an actress! How different an actress is! Harry!
why didn't you tell me that the only thing worth loving
is an actress?"

"Because I have loved so many of them, Dorian."

"Oh, yes, horrid people with dyed hair and painted
faces."

"Don't run down dyed hair and painted faces. There
is an extraordinary charm in them, sometimes," said
Lord Henry.

"I wish now I had not told you about Sibyl Vane."

"You could not have helped telling me, Dorian. All
through your life you will tell me everything you do."

"Yes, Harry, I believe that is true. I cannot help
telling you things. You have a curious influence over me.
If I ever did a crime, I would come and confess it to
you. You would understand me."

"People like you—the wilful sunbeams of life—
don't commit crimes, Dorian. But I am much obliged
for the compliment, all the same. And now tell me—
reach me the matches, like a good boy: thanks:—what
are your actual relations with Sibyl Vane?"

Dorian Gray leaped to his feet, with flushed cheeks
and burning eyes. "Harry! Sibyl Vane is sacred!"

"It is only the sacred things that are worth touching,
Dorian," said Lord Henry, with a strange touch of
pathos in his voice. "But why should you be annoyed?
I suppose she will belong to you some day. When one is
in love, one always begins by deceiving oneself, and
one always ends by deceiving others. That is what the
world calls a romance. You know her, at any rate, I
suppose?"

"Of course I know her. On the first night I was at the
theatre, the horrid old Jew came round to the box after
the performance was over, and offered to take me be-

hind the scenes and introduce me to her. I was furious with him, and told him that Juliet had been dead for hundreds of years, and that her body was lying in a marble tomb in Verona. I think, from his blank look of amazement, that he was under the impression that I had taken too much champagne, or something."

"I am not surprised."

"Then he asked me if I wrote for any of the newspapers. I told him I never even read them. He seemed terribly disappointed at that, and confided to me that all the dramatic critics were in a conspiracy against him, and that they were everyone of them to be bought."

"I should not wonder if he was quite right there. But, on the other hand, judging from their appearance, most of them cannot be at all expensive."

"Well, he seemed to think they were beyond his means," laughed Dorian. "By this time, however, the lights were being put out in the theatre, and I had to go. He wanted me to try some cigars that he strongly recommended. I declined. The next night, of course, I arrived at the place again. When he saw me he made me a low bow, and assured me that I was a munificent patron of art. He was a most offensive brute, though he had an extraordinary passion for Shakespeare. He told me once, with an air of pride, that his five bankruptcies were entirely due to 'The Bard,' as he insisted on calling him. He seemed to think it a distinction."

"It was a distinction, my dear Dorian—a great distinction. Most people become bankrupt through having invested too heavily in the prose of life. To have ruined oneself over poetry is an honour. But when did you first speak to Miss Sibyl Vane?"

"The third night. She had been playing Rosalind. I could not help going round. I had thrown her some flowers, and she had looked at me; at least I fancied that she had. The old Jew was persistent. He seemed determined to take me behind, so I consented. It was curious my not wanting to know her, wasn't it?"

"No; I don't think so."

"My dear Harry, why?"

"I will tell you some other time. Now I want to know about the girl."

"Sibyl? Oh, she was so shy, and so gentle. There is something of a child about her. Her eyes opened wide in exquisite wonder when I told her what I thought of her performance, and she seemed quite unconscious of her power. I think we were both rather nervous. The old Jew stood grinning at the doorway of the dusty greenroom, making elaborate speeches about us both, while we stood looking at each other like children. He would insist on calling me 'My Lord,' so I had to assure Sibyl that I was not anything of the kind. She said quite simply to me, 'You look more like a prince. I must call you Prince Charming.'"

"Upon my word, Dorian, Miss Sibyl knows how to pay compliments."

"You don't understand her, Harry. She regarded me merely as a person in a play. She knows nothing of life. She lives with her mother, a faded tired woman who played Lady Capulet in a sort of magenta dressing-wrapper on the first night, and looks as if she had seen better days."

"I know that look. It depresses me," murmured Lord Henry, examining his rings.

"The Jew wanted to tell me her history, but I said it did not interest me."

"You were quite right. There is always something infinitely mean about other people's tragedies."

"Sibyl is the only thing I care about. What is it to me where she came from? From her little head to her little feet, she is absolutely and entirely divine. Every night of my life I go to see her act, and every night she is more marvellous."

"That is the reason, I suppose, that you never dine with me now. I thought you must have some curious romance on hand. You have; but it is not quite what I expected."

"My dear Harry, we either lunch or sup together every day, and I have been to the Opera with you several times," said Dorian, opening his blue eyes in wonder.

"You always come dreadfully late."

"Well, I can't help going to see Sibyl play," he cried, "even if it is only for a single act. I get hungry for her presence; and when I think of the wonderful soul that is hidden away in that little ivory body, I am filled with awe."

"You can dine with me tonight, Dorian, can't you?"

He shook his head. "Tonight she is Imogen," he answered, "and tomorrow night she will be Juliet."

"When is she Sibyl Vane?"

"Never."

"I congratulate you."

"How horrid you are! She is all the great heroines of the world in one. She is more than an individual. You laugh, but I tell you she has genius. I love her, and I must make her love me. You, who know all the secrets of life, tell me how to charm Sibyl Vane to love me! I want to make Romeo jealous. I want the dead lovers of the world to hear our laughter, and grow sad. I want a breath of our passion to stir their dust into consciousness, to wake their ashes into pain. My God, Harry, how I worship her!" He was walking up and down the room as he spoke. Hectic spots of red burned on his cheeks. He was terribly excited.

Lord Henry watched him with a subtle sense of pleasure. How different he was now from the shy, frightened boy he had met in Basil Hallward's studio! His nature had developed like a flower, had borne blossoms of scarlet flame. Out of its secret hiding-place had crept his soul, and desire had come to meet it on the way.

"And what do you propose to do?" said Lord Henry, at last.

"I want you and Basil to come with me some night and see her act. I have not the slightest fear of the result. You are certain to acknowledge her genius. Then we must get her out of the Jew's hands. She is bound to him for three years—at least for two years and eight months—from the present time. I shall have to pay him something, of course. When all that is settled, I shall take a West End theatre and bring her out properly. She will make the world as mad as she has made me."

"That would be impossible, my dear boy."

"Yes, she will. She has not merely art, consummate art instinct, in her, but she has personality also; and you have often told me that it is personalities, not principles, that move the age."

"Well, what night shall we go?"

"Let me see. Today is Tuesday. Let us fix tomorrow. She plays Juliet tomorrow."

"All right. The Bristol at eight o'clock; and I will get Basil."

"Not eight, Harry, please. Half-past six. We must be there before the curtain rises. You must see her in the first act, where she meets Romeo."

"Half-past six! What an hour! It will be like having a meat-tea, or reading an English novel. It must be seven. No gentleman dines before seven. Shall you see Basil between this and then? Or shall I write to him?"

"Dear Basil! I have not laid eyes on him for a week. It is rather horrid of me, as he has sent me my portrait in the most wonderful frame, specially designed by himself, and, though I am a little jealous of the picture for being a whole month younger than I am, I must admit that I delight in it. Perhaps you had better write to him. I don't want to see him alone. He says things that annoy me. He gives me good advice."

Lord Henry smiled. "People are very fond of giving away what they need most themselves. It is what I call the depth of generosity."

"Oh, Basil is the best of fellows, but he seems to me to be just a bit of a Philistine. Since I have known you, Harry, I have discovered that."

"Basil, my dear boy, puts everything that is charming in him into his work. The consequence is that he has nothing left for life but his prejudices, his principles, and his common sense. The only artists I have ever known, who are personally delightful, are bad artists. Good artists exist simply in what they make, and consequently are perfectly uninteresting in what they are. A great poet, a really great poet, is the most unpoetical of all creatures. But inferior poets are absolutely fascinating. The worse their rhymes are, the more picturesque they look. The mere fact of having published a book of second-rate sonnets makes a man quite irresistible. He lives the poetry that he cannot write. The others write the poetry that they dare not realize."

"I wonder is that really so, Harry?" said Dorian Gray, putting some perfume on his handkerchief out of a large gold-topped bottle that stood on the table. "It must be, if you say it. And now I am off. Imogen is waiting for me. Don't forget about tomorrow. Good-bye."

As he left the room Lord Henry's heavy eyelids

drooped, and he began to think. Certainly few people had ever interested him so much as Dorian Gray, and yet the lad's mad adoration of someone else caused him not the slightest pang of annoyance or jealousy. He was pleased by it. It made him a more interesting study. He had been always enthralled by the methods of natural science, but the ordinary subject matter of that science had seemed to him trivial and of no import. And so he had begun by vivisecting himself, as he had ended by vivisecting others. Human life— that appeared to him the one thing worth investigating. Compared to it there was nothing else of any value. It was true that as one watched life in its curious crucible of pain and pleasure, one could not wear over one's face a mask of glass, nor keep the sulphurous fumes from troubling the brain and making the imagination turbid with monstrous fancies and misshapen dreams. There were poisons so subtle that to know their properties one had to sicken of them. There were maladies so strange that one had to pass through them if one sought to understand their nature. And, yet, what a great reward one received! How wonderful the whole world became to one! To note the curious hard logic of passion, and the emotional coloured life of the intellect—to observe where they met, and where they separated, at what point they were in unison, and at what point they were at discord—there was a delight in that! What matter what the cost was? One could never pay too high a price for any sensation.

He was conscious—and the thought brought a gleam of pleasure into his brown agate eyes—that it was through certain words of his, musical words said with musical utterance, that Dorian Gray's soul had turned to this white girl and bowed in worship before her. To a large extent the lad was his own creation. He had made him premature. That was something. Ordinary people waited till life disclosed to them its secrets, but to the few, to the elect, the mysteries of life were revealed before the veil was drawn away. Sometimes this was the effect of art, and chiefly of the art of literature, which dealt immediately with the passions and the intellect. But now and then a complex personality took the place and assumed the office of art, was indeed, in its way, a real work of art, Life having its elaborate masterpieces, just as poetry has, or sculpture, or painting.

Yes, the lad was premature. He was gathering his harvest while it was yet spring. The pulse and passion of youth were in him, but he was becoming self-conscious. It was delightful to watch him. With his beautiful face, and his beautiful soul, he was a thing to wonder at. It was no matter how it all ended, or was destined to end. He was like one of those gracious figures in a pageant or a play, whose joys seem to be remote from one, but whose sorrows stir one's sense of beauty, and whose wounds are like red roses.

Soul and body, body and soul—how mysterious they were! There was animalism in the soul, and the body had its moments of spirituality. The senses could refine, and the intellect could degrade. Who could say where the fleshly impulse ceased, or the psychical impulse began? How shallow were the arbitrary definitions of ordinary psychologists! And yet how difficult to decide between the claims of the various schools! Was the soul a shadow seated in the house of sin? Or was the body really in the soul, as Giordano Bruno thought? The separation of spirit from matter was a mystery, and the union of spirit with matter was a mystery also.

He began to wonder whether we could ever make

psychology so absolute a science that each little spring of life would be revealed to us. As it was, we always misunderstood ourselves, and rarely understood others. Experience was of no ethical value. It was merely the name men gave to their mistakes. Moralists had, as a rule, regarded it as a mode of warning, had claimed for it a certain ethical efficacy in the formation of character, had praised it as something that taught us what to follow and showed us what to avoid. But there was no motive power in experience. It was as little of an active cause as conscience itself. All that it really demonstrated was that our future would be the same as our past, and that the sin we had done once, and with loathing, we would do many times, and with joy.

It was clear to him that the experimental method was the only method by which one could arrive at any scientific analysis of the passions; and certainly Dorian Gray was a subject made to his hand, and seemed to promise rich and fruitful results. His sudden mad love for Sibyl Vane was a psychological phenomenon of no small interest. There was no doubt that curiosity had much to do with it, curiosity and the desire for new experiences; yet it was not a simple but rather a very complex passion. What there was in it of the purely sensuous instinct of boyhood had been transformed by the workings of the imagination, changed into something that seemed to the lad himself to be remote from sense, and was for that very reason all the more dangerous. It was the passions about whose origin we deceived ourselves that tyrannized most strongly over us. Our weakest motives were those of whose nature we were conscious. It often happened that when we thought we were experimenting on others we were really experimenting on ourselves.

While Lord Henry sat dreaming on these things, a knock came to the door, and his valet entered, and reminded him it was time to dress for dinner. He got up and looked out into the street. The sunset had smitten into scarlet gold the upper windows of the houses opposite. The panes glowed like plates of heated metal. The sky above was like a faded rose. He thought of his friend's young fiery-coloured life, and wondered how it was all going to end.

When he arrived home, about half-past twelve o'clock, he saw a telegram lying on the hall table. He opened it, and found it was from Dorian Gray. It was to tell him that he was engaged to be married to Sibyl Vane.

V

"MOTHER, Mother, I am so happy!" whispered the girl, burying her face in the lap of the faded, tired-looking woman who, with back turned to the shrill intrusive light, was sitting in the one armchair that their dingy sitting-room contained. "I am so happy!" she repeated, "and you must be happy too!"

Mrs. Vane winced, and put her thin bismuth-whitened hands on her daughter's head. "Happy!" she echoed, "I am only happy, Sibyl, when I see you act. You must not think of anything but your acting. Mr. Isaacs has been very good to us, and we owe him money."

The girl looked up and pouted. "Money, Mother?" she cried, "what does money matter? Love is more than money."

"Mr. Isaacs has advanced us fifty pounds to pay off

our debts, and to get a proper outfit for James. You must not forget that, Sibyl. Fifty pounds is a very large sum. Mr. Isaacs has been most considerate."

"He is not a gentleman, Mother, and I hate the way he talks to me," said the girl, rising to her feet, and going over to the window.

"I don't know how we could manage without him," answered the elder woman, querulously.

Sibyl Vane tossed her head and laughed. "We don't want him any more, Mother. Prince Charming rules life for us now." Then she paused. A rose shook in her blood, and shadowed her cheeks. Quick breath parted the petals of her lips. They trembled. Some southern wind of passion swept over her, and stirred the dainty folds of her dress. "I love him," she said, simply.

"Foolish child! foolish child!" was the parrot-phrase flung in answer. The waving of crooked, false-jewelled fingers gave grotesqueness to the words.

The girl laughed again. The joy of a caged bird was in her voice. Her eyes caught the melody, and echoed it in radiance: then closed for a moment, as though to hide their secret. When they opened, the mist of a dream had passed across them.

Thin-lipped wisdom spoke at her from the worn chair, hinted at prudence, quoted from that book of cowardice whose author apes the name of common sense. She did not listen. She was free in her prison of passion. Her prince, Prince Charming, was with her. She had called on memory to remake him. She had sent her soul to search for him, and it had brought him back. His kiss burned again upon her mouth. Her eyelids were warm with his breath.

Then wisdom altered its method and spoke of espial and discovery. This young man might be rich. If so, marriage should be thought of. Against the shell of her ear broke the waves of worldly cunning. The arrows of craft shot by her. She saw the thin lips moving, and smiled.

Suddenly she felt the need to speak. The wordy silence troubled her. "Mother, Mother," she cried, "why does he love me so much? I know why I love him. I love him because he is like what Love himself should be. But what does he see in me? I am not worthy of him. And yet—why, I cannot tell—though I feel so much beneath him, I don't feel humble. I feel proud, terribly proud. Mother, did you love my father as I love Prince Charming?"

The elder woman grew pale beneath the coarse powder that daubed her cheeks, and her dry lips twitched with a spasm of pain. Sibyl rushed to her, flung her arms round her neck, and kissed her. "Forgive me, Mother. I know it pains you to talk about our father. But it only pains you because you loved him so much. Don't look so sad. I am as happy today as you were twenty years ago. Ah! let me be happy for ever!"

"My child, you are far too young to think of falling in love. Besides, what do you know of this young man? You don't even know his name. The whole thing is most inconvenient, and really, when James is going away to Australia, and I have so much to think of, I must say that you should have shown more consideration. However, as I said before, if he is rich. . . ."

"Ah! Mother, Mother, let me be happy!"

Mrs. Vane glanced at her, and with one of those false theatrical gestures that so often become a mode of second nature to a stage-player, clasped her in her arms. At this moment the door opened, and a young lad with rough brown hair came into the room. He was thick-set of figure, and his hands and feet were large, and somewhat clumsy in movement. He was not so finely bred as his sister. One would hardly have guessed the close relationship that existed between them. Mrs. Vane fixed her eyes on him, and intensified her smile. She mentally elevated her son to the dignity of an audience. She felt sure that the *tableau* was interesting.

"You might keep some of your kisses for me, Sibyl, I think," said the lad, with a good-natured grumble.

"Ah! but you don't like being kissed, Jim," she cried. "You are a dreadful old bear." And she ran across the room and hugged him.

James Vane looked into his sister's face with tenderness. "I want you to come out with me for a walk, Sibyl. I don't suppose I shall ever see this horrid London again. I am sure I don't want to."

"My son, don't say such dreadful things," murmured Mrs. Vane, taking up a tawdry theatrical dress, with a sigh, and beginning to patch it. She felt a little disappointed that he had not joined the group. It would have increased the theatrical picturesqueness of the situation.

"Why not, Mother? I mean it."

"You pain me, my son. I trust you will return from Australia in a position of affluence. I believe there is no society of any kind in the Colonies, nothing that I would call society; so when you have made your fortune you must come back and assert yourself in London."

"Society!" muttered the lad. "I don't want to know anything about that. I should like to make some money to take you and Sibyl off the stage. I hate it."

"Oh, Jim!" said Sibyl, laughing, "how unkind of you! But are you really going for a walk with me? That will be nice! I was afraid you were going to say good-bye to some of your friends—to Tom Hardy, who gave you that hideous pipe, or Ned Langton, who makes fun of you for smoking it. It is very sweet of you to let me have your last afternoon. Where shall we go? Let us go to the Park."

"I am too shabby," he answered, frowning. "Only swell people go to the Park."

"Nonsense, Jim," she whispered, stroking the sleeve of his coat.

He hesitated for a moment. "Very well," he said at last, "but don't be too long dressing." She danced out of the door. One could hear her singing as she ran upstairs. Her little feet pattered overhead.

He walked up and down the room two or three times. Then he turned to the still figure in the chair. "Mother, are my things ready?" he asked.

"Quite ready, James," she answered, keeping her eyes on her work. For some months past she had felt ill at ease when she was alone with this rough, stern son of hers. Her shallow secret nature was troubled when their eyes met. She used to wonder if he suspected anything. The silence, for he made no other observation, became intolerable to her. She began to complain. Women defend themselves by attacking, just as they attack by sudden and strange surrenders. "I hope you will be contented, James, with your sea-faring life," she said. "You must remember that it is your own choice. You might have entered a solicitor's office. Solicitors are a very respectable class, and in the country often dine with the best families."

"I hate offices, and I hate clerks," he replied. "But you are quite right. I have chosen my own life. All I say is, watch over Sibyl. Don't let her come to any harm. Mother, you must watch over her."

"James, you really talk very strangely. Of course I watch over Sibyl."

"I hear a gentleman comes every night to the theatre,

and goes behind to talk to her. Is that right? What about that?"

"You are speaking about things you don't understand, James. In the profession we are accustomed to receive a great deal of most gratifying attention. I myself used to receive many bouquets at one time. That was when acting was really understood. As for Sibyl, I do not know at present whether her attachment is serious or not. But there is no doubt that the young man in question is a perfect gentleman. He is always most polite to me. Besides, he has the appearance of being rich, and the flowers he sends are lovely."

"You don't know his name, though," said the lad, harshly.

"No," answered his mother, with a placid expression in her face. "He has not yet revealed his real name. I think it is quite romantic of him. He is probably a member of the aristocracy."

James Vane bit his lip. "Watch over Sibyl, Mother," he cried, "watch over her."

"My son, you distress me very much. Sibyl is always under my special care. Of course, if this gentleman is wealthy, there is no reason why she should not contract an alliance with him. I trust he is one of the aristocracy. He has all the appearance of it, I must say. It might be a most brilliant marriage for Sibyl. They would make a charming couple. His good looks are really quite remarkable; everybody notices them."

The lad muttered something to himself, and drummed on the windowpane with his coarse fingers. He had just turned round to say something, when the door opened, and Sibyl ran in.

"How serious you both are!" she cried. "What is the matter?"

"Nothing," he answered. "I suppose one must be

serious sometimes. Good-bye, Mother; I will have my dinner at five o'clock. Everything is packed, except my shirts, so you need not trouble."

"Good-bye, my son," she answered, with a bow of strained stateliness.

She was extremely annoyed at the tone he had adopted with her, and there was something in his look that had made her feel afraid.

"Kiss me, Mother," said the girl. Her flower-like lips touched the withered cheek, and warmed its frost.

"My child! my child!" cried Mrs. Vane, looking up to the ceiling in search of an imaginary gallery.

"Come, Sibyl," said her brother, impatiently. He hated his mother's affectations.

They went out into the flickering wind-blown sunlight, and strolled down the dreary Euston Road. The passers-by glanced in wonder at the sullen, heavy youth, who, in coarse, ill-fitting clothes, was in the company of such a graceful, refined-looking girl. He was like a common gardener walking with a rose.

Jim frowned from time to time when he caught the inquisitive glance of some stranger. He had that dislike of being stared at which comes on geniuses late in life, and never leaves the commonplace. Sibyl, however, was quite unconscious of the effect she was producing. Her love was trembling in laughter on her lips. She was thinking of Prince Charming, and, that she might think of him all the more, she did not talk of him, but prattled on about the ship in which Jim was going to sail, about the gold he was certain to find, about the wonderful heiress whose life he was to save from the wicked, red-shirted bushrangers. For he was not to remain a sailor, or a super-cargo, or whatever he was going to be. Oh, no! A sailor's existence was dreadful. Fancy being cooped up in a horrid ship, with the hoarse, humpbacked waves trying to get in, and a black wind blowing the masts down, and tearing the sails into long screaming ribands! He was to leave the vessel at Melbourne, bid a polite good-bye to the captain, and go off at once to the goldfields. Before a week was over he was to come across a large nugget of pure gold, the largest nugget that had ever been discovered, and bring it down to the coast in a waggon guarded by six mounted policemen. The bushrangers were to attack them three times, and be defeated with immense slaughter. Or, no. He was not to go to the goldfields at all. They were horrid places, where men got intoxicated, and shot each other in barrooms, and used bad language. He was to be a nice sheep-farmer, and one evening, as he was riding home, he was to see the beautiful heiress being carried off by a robber on a black horse, and give chase, and rescue her. Of course she would fall in love with him, and he with her, and they would get married, and come home, and live in an immense house in London. Yes, there were delightful things in store for him. But he must be very good, and not lose his temper, or spend his money foolishly. She was only a year older than he was, but she knew so much more of life. He must be sure, also, to write to her by every mail, and to say his prayers each night before he went to sleep. God was very good, and would watch over him. She would pray for him, too, and in a few years he would come back quite rich and happy.

The lad listened sulkily to her, and made no answer. He was heart-sick at leaving home.

Yet it was not this alone that made him gloomy and morose. Inexperienced though he was, he had still a strong sense of the danger of Sibyl's position. This young dandy who was making love to her could mean her no good. He was a gentleman, and he hated him for that, hated him through some curious race instinct for which he could not account, and which for that reason was all the more dominant within him. He was conscious also of the shallowness and vanity of his mother's nature, and in that saw infinite peril for Sibyl and Sibyl's happiness. Children begin by loving their parents; as they grow older they judge them; sometimes they forgive them.

His mother! He had something on his mind to ask of her, something that he had brooded on for many months of silence. A chance phrase that he had heard at the theatre, a whispered sneer that had reached his ears one night as he waited at the stage door, had set loose a train of horrible thoughts. He remembered it as if it had been the lash of a hunting crop across his face. His brows knit together into a wedge-like furrow, and with a twitch of pain he bit his under-lip.

"You are not listening to a word I am saying, Jim," cried Sibyl, "and I am making the most delightful plans for your future. Do say something."

"What do you want me to say?"

"Oh! that you will be a good boy, and not forget us," she answered, smiling at him.

He shrugged his shoulders. "You are more likely to forget me, than I am to forget you, Sibyl."

She flushed. "What do you mean, Jim?" she asked.

"You have a new friend, I hear. Who is he? Why have you not told me about him? He means you no good."

"Stop, Jim!" she exclaimed. "You must not say anything against him. I love him."

"Why, you don't even know his name," answered the lad. "Who is he? I have a right to know."

"He is called Prince Charming. Don't you like the name? Oh! you silly boy! you should never forget it. If you only saw him, you would think him the most wonderful person in the world. Some day you will meet him: when you come back from Australia. You will like him so much. Everybody likes him, and I . . . love him. I wish you could come to the theatre tonight. He is going to be there, and I am to play Juliet. Oh! how I shall play it! Fancy, Jim, to be in love and play Juliet! To have him sitting there! To play for his delight! I am afraid I may frighten the company, frighten or enthrall them. To be in love is to surpass one's self. Poor dreadful Mr. Isaacs will be shouting 'genius' to his loafers at the bar. He has preached me as a dogma; tonight he will announce me as a revelation. I feel it. And it is all his, his only, Prince Charming, my wonderful lover, my god of graces. But I am poor beside him. Poor? What does that matter? When poverty creeps in at the door, love flies in through the window. Our proverbs want rewriting. They were made in winter, and it is summer now; springtime for me, I think, a very dance of blossoms in blue skies."

"He is a gentleman," said the lad, sullenly.

"A prince!" she cried, musically. "What more do you want?"

"He wants to enslave you."

"I shudder at the thought of being free."

"I want you to beware of him."

"To see him is to worship him, to know him is to trust him."

"Sibyl, you are mad about him."

She laughed, and took his arm. "You dear old Jim, you talk as if you were a hundred. Some day you will be in love yourself. Then you will know what it is. Don't look so sulky. Surely you should be glad to think that, though you are going away, you leave me happier than I have ever been before. Life has been hard for us both, terribly hard and difficult. But it will be different now.

You are going to a new world, and I have found one. Here are two chairs; let us sit down and see the smart people go by."

They took their seats amidst a crowd of watchers. The tulip beds across the road flamed like throbbing rings of fire. A white dust, tremulous cloud of orris-root it seemed, hung in the panting air. The brightly coloured parasols danced and dipped like monstrous butterflies.

She made her brother talk of himself, his hopes, his prospects. He spoke slowly and with effort. They passed words to each other as players at a game pass counters. Sibyl felt oppressed. She could not communicate her joy. A faint smile curving that sullen mouth was all the echo she could win. After some time she became silent. Suddenly she caught a glimpse of golden hair and laughing lips, and in an open carriage with two ladies Dorian Gray drove past.

She started to her feet. "There he is!" she cried.

"Who?" said Jim Vane.

"Prince Charming," she answered, looking after the victoria.

He jumped up, and seized her roughly by the arm. "Show him to me. Which is he? Point him out. I must see him!" he exclaimed; but at that moment the Duke of Berwick's four-in-hand came between, and when it had left the space clear, the carriage had swept out of the Park.

"He is gone," murmured Sibyl, sadly. "I wish you had seen him."

"I wish I had, for as sure as there is a God in heaven, if he ever does you any wrong, I shall kill him."

She looked at him in horror. He repeated his words. They cut the air like a dagger. The people round began to gape. A lady standing close to her tittered.

"Come away, Jim; come away," she whispered. He followed her doggedly, as she passed through the crowd. He felt glad at what he had said.

When they reached the Achilles Statue she turned round. There was pity in her eyes that became laughter on her lips. She shook her head at him. "You are foolish, Jim, utterly foolish; a bad-tempered boy, that is all. How can you say such horrible things? You don't know what you are talking about. You are simply jealous and unkind. Ah! I wish you would fall in love. Love makes people good, and what you said was wicked."

"I am sixteen," he answered, "and I know what I am about. Mother is no help to you. She doesn't understand how to look after you. I wish now that I was not going to Australia at all. I have a great mind to chuck the whole thing up. I would, if my articles hadn't been signed."

"Oh, don't be so serious, Jim. You are like one of the heroes of those silly melodramas mother used to be so fond of acting in. I am not going to quarrel with you. I have seen him, and oh! to see him is perfect happiness. We won't quarrel. I know you would never harm any-one I love, would you?"

"Not as long as you love him, I suppose," was the sullen answer.

"I shall love him for ever!" she cried.

"And he?"

"For ever, too!"

"He had better."

She shrank from him. Then she laughed and put her hand on his arm. He was merely a boy.

At the Marble Arch they hailed an omnibus, which left them close to their shabby home in the Euston Road. It was after five o'clock, and Sibyl had to lie

down for a couple of hours before acting. Jim insisted
that she should do so. He said that he would sooner
part with her when their mother was not present. She
would be sure to make a scene, and he detested scenes
of every kind.

In Sibyl's own room they parted. There was jealousy
in the lad's heart, and a fierce, murderous hatred of
the stranger who, as it seemed to him, had come between them. Yet, when her arms were flung round his
neck, and her fingers strayed through his hair, he
softened, and kissed her with real affection. There were
tears in his eyes as he went downstairs.

His mother was waiting for him below. She grumbled
at his unpunctuality, as he entered. He made no answer,
but sat down to his meagre meal. The flies buzzed round
the table, and crawled over the stained cloth. Through
the rumble of omnibuses, and the clatter of street-cabs,
he could hear the droning voice devouring each minute
that was left to him.

After some time, he thrust away his plate, and put
his head in his hands. He felt that he had a right to
know. It should have been told to him before, if it was
as he suspected. Leaden with fear, his mother watched
him. Words dropped mechanically from her lips. A
tattered lace handkerchief twitched in her fingers.
When the clock struck six, he got up, and went to the
door. Then he turned back, and looked at her. Their
eyes met. In hers he saw a wild appeal for mercy. It
enraged him.

"Mother, I have something to ask you," he said.
Her eyes wandered vaguely about the room. She made
no answer. "Tell me the truth. I have a right to know.
Were you married to my father?"

She heaved a deep sigh. It was a sigh of relief. The
terrible moment, the moment that night and day, for

weeks and months, she had dreaded, had come at last, and yet she felt no terror. Indeed in some measure it was a disappointment to her. The vulgar directness of the question called for a direct answer. The situation had not been gradually led up to. It was crude. It reminded her of a bad rehearsal.

"No," she answered, wondering at the harsh simplicity of life.

"My father was a scoundrel then!" cried the lad, clenching his fists.

She shook her head. "I knew he was not free. We loved each other very much. If he had lived, he would have made provision for us. Don't speak against him, my son. He was your father, and a gentleman. Indeed he was highly connected."

An oath broke from his lips. "I don't care for myself," he exclaimed, "but don't let Sibyl. . . . It is a gentleman, isn't it, who is in love with her, or says he is? Highly connected, too, I suppose."

For a moment a hideous sense of humiliation came over the woman. Her head drooped. She wiped her eyes with shaking hands. "Sibyl has a mother," she murmured; "I had none."

The lad was touched. He went towards her, and stooping down he kissed her. "I am sorry if I have pained you by asking about my father," he said, "but I could not help it. I must go now. Good-bye. Don't forget that you will have only one child now to look after, and believe me that if this man wrongs my sister, I will find out who he is, track him down, and kill him like a dog. I swear it."

The exaggerated folly of the threat, the passionate gesture that accompanied it, the mad melodramatic words, made life seem more vivid to her. She was familiar with the atmosphere. She breathed more freely, and for the first time for many months she really admired her son. She would have liked to have continued the scene on the same emotional scale, but he cut her short. Trunks had to be carried down, and mufflers looked for. The lodging-house drudge bustled in and out. There was the bargaining with the cabman. The moment was lost in vulgar details. It was with a renewed feeling of disappointment that she waved the tattered lace handkerchief from the window, as her son drove away. She was conscious that a great opportunity had been wasted. She consoled herself by telling Sibyl how desolate she felt her life would be, now that she had only one child to look after. She remembered the phrase. It had pleased her. Of the threat she said nothing. It was vividly and dramatically expressed. She felt that they would all laugh at it some day.

VI

"I SUPPOSE you have heard the news, Basil?" said Lord Henry that evening, as Hallward was shown into a little private room at the Bristol where dinner had been laid for three.

"No, Harry," answered the artist, giving his hat and coat to the bowing waiter. "What is it? Nothing about politics, I hope? They don't interest me. There is hardly a single person in the House of Commons worth painting; though many of them would be the better for a little whitewashing."

"Dorian Gray is engaged to be married," said Lord Henry, watching him as he spoke.

Hallward started, and then frowned. "Dorian engaged to be married!" he cried. "Impossible!"

"It is perfectly true."

"To whom?"

"To sóme little actress or other."

"I can't believe it. Dorian is far too sensible."

"Dorian is far too wise not to do foolish things now and then, my dear Basil."

"Marriage is hardly a thing that one can do now and then, Harry."

"Except in America," rejoined Lord Henry, languidly. "But I didn't say he was married. I said he was engaged to be married. There is a great difference. I have a distinct remembrance of being married, but I have no recollection at all of being engaged. I am inclined to think that I never was engaged."

"But think of Dorian's birth, and position, and wealth. It would be absurd for him to marry so much beneath him."

"If you want to make him marry this girl tell him that, Basil. He is sure to do it, then. Whenever a man does a thoroughly stupid thing, it is always from the noblest motives."

"I hope the girl is good, Harry. I don't want to see Dorian tied to some vile creature, who might degrade his nature and ruin his intellect."

"Oh, she is better than good—she is beautiful," murmured Lord Henry, sipping a glass of vermouth and orange-bitters. "Dorian says she is beautiful; and he is not often wrong about things of that kind. Your portrait of him has quickened his appreciation of the personal appearance of other people. It has had that excellent effect, amongst others. We are to see her to-night, if that boy doesn't forget his appointment."

"Are you serious?"

"Quite serious, Basil. I should be miserable if I thought I should ever be more serious than I am at the present moment."

"But do you approve of it, Harry?" asked the painter, walking up and down the room, and biting his lip. "You can't approve of it, possibly. It is some silly infatuation."

"I never approve, or disapprove, of anything now. It is an absurd attitude to take towards life. We are not sent into the world to air our moral prejudices. I never take any notice of what common people say, and I never interfere with what charming people do. If a personality fascinates me, whatever mode of expression that personality selects is absolutely delightful to me. Dorian Gray falls in love with a beautiful girl who acts Juliet, and proposes to marry her. Why not? If he wedded Messalina he would be none the less interesting. You know I am not a champion of marriage. The real drawback to marriage is that it makes one unselfish. And unselfish people are colourless. They lack individuality. Still, there are certain temperaments that marriage makes more complex. They retain their egotism, and add to it many other egos. They are forced to have more than one life. They become more highly organized, and to be highly organized is, I should fancy, the object of man's existence. Besides, every experience is of value, and, whatever one may say against marriage, it is certainly an experience. I hope that Dorian Gray will make this girl his wife, passionately adore her for six months, and then suddenly become fascinated by someone else. He would be a wonderful study."

"You don't mean a single word of all that, Harry; you know you don't. If Dorian Gray's life were spoiled, no one would be sorrier than yourself. You are much better than you pretend to be."

Lord Henry laughed. "The reason we all like to think so well of others is that we are all afraid for ourselves. The basis of optimism is sheer terror. We think that we are generous because we credit our neighbour with the possession of those virtues that are likely to be a benefit to us. We praise the banker that we may overdraw our account, and find good qualities in the highwayman in the hope that he may spare our pockets. I mean everything that I have said. I have the greatest contempt for optimism. As for a spoiled life, no life is spoiled but one whose growth is arrested. If you want to mar a nature, you have merely to reform it. As for marriage, of course that would be silly, but there are other and more interesting bonds between men and women. I will certainly encourage them. They have the charm of being fashionable. But here is Dorian himself. He will tell you more than I can."

"My dear Harry, my dear Basil, you must both congratulate me!" said the lad, throwing off his evening cape with its satin-lined wings, and shaking each of his friends by the hand in turn. "I have never been so happy. Of course it is sudden: all really delightful things are. And yet it seems to me to be the one thing I have been looking for all my life." He was flushed with excitement and pleasure, and looked extraordinarily handsome.

"I hope you will always be very happy, Dorian," said Hallward, "but I don't quite forgive you for not having let me know of your engagement. You let Harry know."

"And I don't forgive you for being late for dinner," broke in Lord Henry, putting his hand on the lad's shoulder, and smiling as he spoke. "Come, let us sit down and try what the new chef here is like, and then you will tell us how it all came about."

"There is really not much to tell," cried Dorian, as they took their seats at the small round table. "What happened was simply this. After I left you yesterday evening, Harry, I dressed, had some dinner at that little Italian restaurant in Rupert Street you introduced me

to, and went down at eight o'clock to the theatre. Sibyl
was playing Rosalind. Of course the scenery was dreadful, and the Orlando absurd. But Sibyl! You should
have seen her! When she came on in her boy's clothes
she was perfectly wonderful. She wore a moss-coloured
velvet jerkin with cinnamon sleeves, slim brown cross-
gartered hose, a dainty little green cap with a hawk's
feather caught in a jewel, and a hooded cloak lined with
dull red. She had never seemed to me more exquisite.
She had all the delicate grace of that Tanagra figurine
that you have in your studio, Basil. Her hair clustered
round her face like dark leaves round a pale rose. As
for her acting—well, you shall see her tonight. She is
simply a born artist. I sat in the dingy box absolutely
enthralled. I forgot that I was in London and in the
nineteenth century. I was away with my love in a forest
that no man had ever seen. After the performance was
over I went behind, and spoke to her. As we were sitting together, suddenly there came into her eyes a look
that I had never seen there before. My lips moved
toward hers. We kissed each other. I can't describe to
you what I felt at that moment. It seemed to me that all
my life had been narrowed to one perfect point of rose-
coloured joy. She trembled all over, and shook like a
white narcissus. Then she flung herself on her knees and
kissed my hands. I feel that I should not tell you all
this, but I can't help it. Of course our engagement is a
dead secret. She has not even told her own mother. I
don't know what my guardian will say. Lord Radley is
sure to be furious. I don't care. I shall be of age in less
than a year, and then I can do what I like. I have been
right, Basil, haven't I, to take my love out of poetry,
and to find my wife in Shakespeare's plays? Lips
that Shakespeare taught to speak have whispered their

secret in my ear. I have had the arms of Rosalind around me, and kissed Juliet on the mouth."

"Yes, Dorian, I suppose you were right," said Hallward, slowly.

"Have you seen her today?" asked Lord Henry.

Dorian Gray shook his head. "I left her in the forest of Arden, I shall find her in an orchard in Verona."

Lord Henry sipped his champagne in a meditative manner. "At what particular point did you mention the word marriage, Dorian? And what did she say in answer? Perhaps you forgot all about it."

"My dear Harry, I did not treat it as a business transaction, and I did not make any formal proposal. I told her that I loved her, and she said she was not worthy to be my wife. Not worthy! Why, the whole world is nothing to me compared with her."

"Women are wonderfully practical," murmured Lord Henry—"much more practical than we are. In situations of that kind we often forget to say anything about marriage, and they always remind us."

Hallward laid his hand upon his arm. "Don't, Harry. You have annoyed Dorian. He is not like other men. He would never bring misery upon anyone. His nature is too fine for that."

Lord Henry looked across the table. "Dorian is never annoyed with me," he answered. "I asked the question for the best reason possible, for the only reason, indeed, that excuses one for asking any question— simply curiosity. I have a theory that it is always the women who propose to us, and not we who propose to the women. Except, of course, in middle-class life. But then the middle classes are not modern."

Dorian Gray laughed, and tossed his head. "You are quite incorrigible, Harry; but I don't mind. It is impossible to be angry with you. When you see Sibyl Vane you will feel that the man who could wrong her would be a beast, a beast without a heart. I cannot understand how anyone can wish to shame the thing he loves. I love Sibyl Vane. I want to place her on a pedestal of gold, and to see the world worship the woman who is mine. What is marriage? An irrevocable vow. You mock at it for that. Ah! don't mock. It is an irrevocable vow that I want to take. Her trust makes me faithful, her belief makes me good. When I am with her, I regret all that you have taught me. I become different from what you have known me to be. I am changed, and the mere touch of Sibyl Vane's hand makes me forget you and all your wrong, fascinating, poisonous, delightful theories."

"And those are . . . ?" asked Lord Henry, helping himself to some salad.

"Oh, your theories about life, your theories about love, your theories about pleasure. All your theories, in fact, Harry."

"Pleasure is the only thing worth having a theory about," he answered, in his slow, melodious voice. "But I am afraid I cannot claim my theory as my own. It belongs to Nature, not to me. Pleasure is Nature's test, her sign of approval. When we are happy we are always good, but when we are good we are not always happy."

"Ah! but what do you mean by good?" cried Basil Hallward.

"Yes," echoed Dorian, leaning back in his chair, and looking at Lord Henry over the heavy clusters of purple-lipped irises that stood in the centre of the table, "what do you mean by good, Harry?"

"To be good is to be in harmony with one's self," he replied, touching the thin stem of his glass with his pale, fine-pointed fingers. "Discord is to be forced to be in harmony with others. One's own life—that is the important thing. As for the lives of one's neighbours, if one wishes to be a prig or a Puritan, one can flaunt one's moral views about them, but they are not one's concern. Besides, individualism has really the higher aim. Modern morality consists in accepting the standard of one's age. I consider that for any man of culture to accept the standard of his age is a form of the grossest immorality."

"But, surely, if one lives merely for one's self, Harry, one pays a terrible price for doing so?" suggested the painter.

"Yes, we are overcharged for everything nowadays. I should fancy that the real tragedy of the poor is that they can afford nothing but self-denial. Beautiful sins, like beautiful things, are the privilege of the rich."

"One has to pay in other ways but money."

"What sort of ways, Basil?"

"Oh! I should fancy in remorse, in suffering, in . . . well, in the consciousness of degradation."

Lord Henry shrugged his shoulders. "My dear fellow, mediæval art is charming, but mediæval emotions are out of date. One can use them in fiction, of course. But then the only things that one can use in fiction are the things that one has ceased to use in fact. Believe me, no civilized man ever regrets a pleasure, and no uncivilized man ever knows what a pleasure is."

"I know what pleasure is," cried Dorian Gray. "It is to adore someone."

"That is certainly better than being adored," he answered, toying with some fruits. "Being adored is a nuisance. Women treat us just as humanity treats its gods. They worship us, and are always bothering us to do something for them."

"I should have said that whatever they ask for they

had first given to us," murmured the lad, gravely. "They create love in our natures. They have a right to demand it back."

"That is quite true, Dorian," cried Hallward.

"Nothing is ever quite true," said Lord Henry.

"This is," interrupted Dorian. "You must admit, Harry, that women give to men the very gold of their lives."

"Possibly," he sighed, "but they invariably want it back in such very small change. That is the worry. Women, as some witty Frenchman once put it, inspire us with the desire to do masterpieces, and always prevent us from carrying them out."

"Harry, you are dreadful! I don't know why I like you so much."

"You will always like me, Dorian," he replied. "Will you have some coffee, you fellows?— Waiter, bring coffee, and *fine-champagne*, and some cigarettes. No; don't mind the cigarettes; I have some. Basil, I can't allow you to smoke cigars. You must have a cigarette. A cigarette is the perfect type of a perfect pleasure. It is exquisite, and it leaves one unsatisfied. What more can one want? Yes, Dorian, you will always be fond of me. I represent to you all the sins you have never had the courage to commit."

"What nonsense you talk, Harry!" cried the lad, taking a light from a fire-breathing silver dragon that the waiter had placed on the table. "Let us go down to the theatre. When Sibyl comes on the stage you will have a new ideal of life. She will represent something to you that you have never known."

"I have known everything," said Lord Henry, with a tired look in his eyes, "but I am always ready for a new emotion. I am afraid, however, that, for me at any rate, there is no such thing. Still, your wonderful girl may thrill me. I love acting. It is so much more real than life. Let us go. Dorian, you will come with me. I am so sorry, Basil, but there is only room for two in the brougham. You must follow us in a hansom."

They got up and put on their coats, sipping their coffee standing. The painter was silent and preoccupied. There was a gloom over him. He could not bear this marriage, and yet it seemed to him to be better than many other things that might have happened. After a few minutes, they all passed downstairs. He drove off by himself, as had been arranged, and watched the flashing lights of the little brougham in front of him. A strange sense of loss came over him. He felt that Dorian Gray would never again be to him all that he had been in the past. Life had come between them. . . . His eyes darkened, and the crowded, flaring streets became blurred to his eyes. When the cab drew up at the theatre, it seemed to him that he had grown years older.

VII

FOR some reason or other, the house was crowded that night, and the fat Jew manager who met them at the door was beaming from ear to ear with an oily, tremulous smile. He escorted them to their box with a sort of pompous humility, waving his fat jewelled hands, and talking at the top of his voice. Dorian Gray loathed him more than ever. He felt as if he had come to look for Miranda and had been met by Caliban. Lord Henry, upon the other hand, rather liked him. At least he declared he did, and insisted on shaking him by the hand, and assuring him that he was proud to meet a man who had discovered a real genius and gone bankrupt over a poet. Hallward amused himself with watching the faces in the pit. The heat was terribly oppressive, and the huge sunlight flamed like a monstrous dahlia with petals of yellow fire. The youths in the gallery had taken off their coats and waistcoats and hung them over the side. They talked to each other across the theatre, and shared their oranges with the tawdry girls who sat beside them. Some women were laughing in the pit. Their voices were horribly shrill and discordant. The sound of the popping of corks came from the bar.

"What a place to find one's divinity in!" said Lord Henry.

"Yes!" answered Dorian Gray. "It was here I found her, and she is divine beyond all living things. When she acts you will forget everything. These common, rough people, with their coarse faces and brutal gestures, become quite different when she is on the stage. They sit silently and watch her. They weep and laugh as she wills them to do. She makes them as responsive as a violin. She spiritualizes them, and one feels that they are of the same flesh and blood as oneself."

"The same flesh and blood as oneself! Oh, I hope not!" exclaimed Lord Henry, who was scanning the occupants of the gallery through his opera-glass.

"Don't pay any attention to him, Dorian," said the painter. "I understand what you mean, and I believe in this girl. Anyone you love must be marvellous, and any girl that has the effect you describe must be fine and noble. To spiritualize one's age—that is something worth doing. If this girl can give a soul to those who have lived without one, if she can create the sense of beauty in people whose lives have been sordid and

ugly, if she can strip them of their selfishness and lend
them tears for sorrows that are not their own, she is
worthy of all your adoration, worthy of the adoration of
the world. This marriage is quite right. I did not think
so at first, but I admit it now. The gods made Sibyl
Vane for you. Without her you would have been incomplete."

"Thanks, Basil," answered Dorian Gray, pressing his
hand. "I knew that you would understand me. Harry is
so cynical, he terrifies me. But here is the orchestra. It
is quite dreadful, but it only lasts for about five
minutes. Then the curtain rises, and you will see the
girl to whom I am going to give all my life, to whom
I have given everything that is good in me."

A quarter of an hour afterwards, amidst an extraordinary turmoil of applause, Sibyl Vane stepped on to
the stage. Yes, she was certainly lovely to look at—one
of the loveliest creatures, Lord Henry thought, that he
had ever seen. There was something of the fawn in her
shy grace and startled eyes. A faint blush, like the
shadow of a rose in a mirror of silver, came to her
cheeks as she glanced at the crowded, enthusiastic
house. She stepped back a few paces, and her lips
seemed to tremble. Basil Hallward leaped to his feet
and began to applaud. Motionless, and as one in a
dream, sat Dorian Gray, gazing at her. Lord Henry
peered through his glasses, murmuring, "Charming!
charming!"

The scene was the hall of Capulet's house, and
Romeo in his pilgrim's dress had entered with Mercutio
and his other friends. The band, such as it was, struck
up a few bars of music, and the dance began. Through
the crowd of ungainly, shabbily dressed actors, Sibyl
Vane moved like a creature from a finer world. Her

body swayed, while she danced, as a plant sways in the water. The curves of her throat were the curves of a white lily. Her hands seemed to be made of cool ivory.

Yet she was curiously listless. She showed no sign of joy when her eyes rested on Romeo. The few words she had to speak—

> "Good pilgrim, you do wrong your hand too much,
>   Which mannerly devotion shows in this;
> For saints have hands that pilgrims' hands do touch,
>   And palm to palm is holy palmers' kiss—"

with the brief dialogue that follows, were spoken in a thoroughly artificial manner. The voice was exquisite, but from the point of view of tone it was absolutely false. It was wrong in colour. It took away all the life from the verse. It made the passion unreal.

Dorian Gray grew pale as he watched her. He was puzzled and anxious. Neither of his friends dared to say anything to him. She seemed to them to be absolutely incompetent. They were horribly disappointed.

Yet they felt that the true test of any Juliet is the balcony scene of the second act. They waited for that. If she failed there, there was nothing in her.

She looked charming as she came out in the moonlight. That could not be denied. But the staginess of her acting was unbearable, and grew worse as she went on. Her gestures became absurdly artificial. She overemphasized everything that she had to say. The beautiful passage—

> "Thou knowest the mask of night is on my face,
>   Else would a maiden blush bepaint my cheek
> For that which thou hast heard me speak tonight—"

was declaimed with the painful precision of a schoolgirl who has been taught to recite by some second-rate professor of elocution. When she leaned over the balcony and came to those wonderful lines—

> "Although I joy in thee,
> I have no joy of this contract tonight;
> It is too rash, too unadvised, too sudden;
> Too like the lightning, which doth cease to be
> Ere one can say, 'It lightens.' Sweet, good night!
> This bud of love by summer's ripening breath
> May prove a beauteous flower when next we meet—"

she spoke the words as though they conveyed no meaning to her. It was not nervousness. Indeed, so far from being nervous, she was absolutely self-contained. It was simply bad art. She was a complete failure.

Even the common, uneducated audience of the pit and gallery lost their interest in the play. They got restless, and began to talk loudly and to whistle. The Jew manager, who was standing at the back of the dress-circle, stamped and swore with rage. The only person unmoved was the girl herself.

When the second act was over there came a storm of hisses, and Lord Henry got up from his chair and put on his coat. "She is quite beautiful, Dorian," he said, "but she can't act. Let us go."

"I am going to see the play through," answered the lad, in a hard, bitter voice. "I am awfully sorry that I have made you waste an evening, Harry. I apologize to you both."

"My dear Dorian, I should think Miss Vane was ill," interrupted Hallward. "We will come some other night."

"I wish she were ill," he rejoined. "But she seems to me to be simply callous and cold. She has entirely altered. Last night she was a great artist. This evening she is merely a commonplace, mediocre actress."

"Don't talk like that about anyone you love, Dorian. Love is a more wonderful thing than art."

"They are both simply forms of imitation," remarked Lord Henry. "But do let us go. Dorian, you must not stay here any longer. It is not good for one's morals to see bad acting. Besides, I don't suppose you will want your wife to act. So what does it matter if she plays Juliet like a wooden doll? She is very lovely, and if she knows as little about life as she does about acting, she will be a delightful experience. There are only two kinds of people who are really fascinating—people who know absolutely everything, and people who know absolutely nothing. Good heavens, my dear boy, don't look so tragic! The secret of remaining young is never to have an emotion that is unbecoming. Come to the club with Basil and myself. We will smoke cigarettes and drink to the beauty of Sibyl Vane. She is beautiful. What more can you want?"

"Go away, Harry," cried the lad. "I want to be alone. Basil, you must go. Ah! can't you see that my heart is breaking?" The hot tears came to his eyes. His lips trembled, and rushing to the back of the box, he leaned up against the wall, hiding his face in his hands.

"Let us go, Basil," said Lord Henry, with a strange tenderness in his voice; and the two young men passed out together.

A few moments afterwards the footlights flared up, and the curtain rose on the third act. Dorian Gray went back to his seat. He looked pale, and proud, and indifferent. The play dragged on, and seemed interminable. Half of the audience went out, tramping in heavy boots, and laughing. The whole thing was a fiasco. The last act was played to almost empty benches. The curtain went down on a titter, and some groans.

As soon as it was over, Dorian Gray rushed behind the scenes into the green-room. The girl was standing there alone, with a look of triumph on her face. Her eyes were lit with an exquisite fire. There was a radiance about her. Her parted lips were smiling over some secret of their own.

When he entered, she looked at him, and an expression of infinite joy came over her. "How badly I acted tonight, Dorian!" she cried.

"Horribly!" he answered, gazing at her in amazement —"horribly! It was dreadful. Are you ill? You have no idea what it was. You have no idea what I suffered."

The girl smiled. "Dorian," she answered, lingering over his name with long-drawn music in her voice, as though it were sweeter than honey to the red petals of her mouth—"Dorian, you should have understood. But you understand now, don't you?"

"Understand what?" he asked, angrily.

"Why I was so bad tonight. Why I shall always be bad. Why I shall never act well again."

He shrugged his shoulders. "You are ill, I suppose. When you are ill you shouldn't act. You make yourself ridiculous. My friends were bored. I was bored."

She seemed not to listen to him. She was transfigured with joy. An ecstasy of happiness dominated her.

"Dorian, Dorian," she cried, "before I knew you, acting was the one reality of my life. It was only in the theatre that I lived. I thought that it was all true. I was Rosalind one night, and Portia the other. The joy of Beatrice was my joy, and the sorrows of Cordelia were mine also. I believed in everything. The common people who acted with me seemed to me to be godlike. The painted scenes were my world. I knew nothing but shadows, and I thought them real. You came—oh, my beautiful love!—and you freed my soul from prison. You taught me what reality really is. Tonight, for the first time in my life, I saw through the hollowness, the sham, the silliness of the empty pageant in which I had always played. Tonight, for the first time, I became conscious that the Romeo was hideous, and old, and painted, that the moonlight in the orchard was false, that the scenery was vulgar, and that the words I had to speak were unreal, were not my words, were not what I wanted to say. You had brought me something higher, something of which all art is but a reflection. You had made me understand what love really is. My love! my love! Prince Charming! prince of life! I have grown sick of shadows. You are more to me than all art can ever be. What have I to do with the puppets of a play? When I came on tonight, I could not understand how it was that everything had gone from me. I thought that I was going to be wonderful. I found that I could do nothing. Suddenly it dawned on my soul what it all meant. The knowledge was exquisite to me. I heard them hissing, and I smiled. What could they know of love such as ours? Take me away, Dorian—take me away with you, where we can be quite alone. I hate the stage. I might mimic a passion that I do not feel, but I cannot mimic one that burns me like fire. Oh, Dorian, Dorian, you understand now what it signifies? Even if I could do it, it would be profanation for me to play at being in love. You have made me see that."

He flung himself down on the sofa, and turned away his face. "You have killed my love," he muttered.

She looked at him in wonder, and laughed. He made no answer. She came across to him, and with her little fingers stroked his hair. She knelt down and pressed his hands to her lips. He drew them away, and a shudder ran through him.

Then he leaped up, and went to the door. "Yes," he cried, "you have killed my love. You used to stir my imagination. Now you don't even stir my curiosity. You simply produce no effect. I loved you because you were marvellous, because you had genius and intellect, because you realized the dreams of great poets and gave shape and substance to the shadows of art. You have thrown it all away. You are shallow and stupid. My God! how mad I was to love you! What a fool I have been! You are nothing to me now. I will never see you again. I will never think of you. I will never mention your name. You don't know what you were to me, once. Why, once . . . Oh, I can't bear to think of it! I wish I had never laid eyes upon you! You have spoiled the romance of my life. How little you can know of love, if you say it mars your art! Without your art you are nothing. I would have made you famous, splendid, magnificent. The world would have worshipped you, and you would have borne my name. What are you now? A third-rate actress with a pretty face."

The girl grew white, and trembled. She clenched her hands together, and her voice seemed to catch in her throat. "You are not serious, Dorian?" she murmured. "You are acting."

"Acting! I leave that to you. You do it so well," he answered, bitterly.

She rose from her knees, and, with a piteous expression of pain in her face, came across the room to him. She put her hand upon his arm, and looked into his eyes. He thrust her back. "Don't touch me!" he cried.

A low moan broke from her, and she flung herself at his feet, and lay there like a trampled flower. "Dorian, Dorian, don't leave me!" she whispered. "I am so sorry I didn't act well. I was thinking of you all the time. But I will try—indeed, I will try. It came so suddenly across me, my love for you. I think I should never have known it if you had not kissed me—if we had not kissed each other. Kiss me again, my love. Don't go away from me. I couldn't bear it. Oh! don't go away from me. My brother. . . . No, never mind. He didn't mean it. He was in jest. . . . But you, oh! can't you forgive me for tonight? I will work so hard, and try to improve. Don't be cruel to me because I love you better than anything in the world. After all, it is only once that I have not pleased you. But you are quite right, Dorian. I should have shown myself more of an artist. It was foolish of me; and yet I couldn't help it. Oh, don't leave me, don't leave me." A fit of passionate sobbing choked her. She crouched on the floor like a wounded thing, and Dorian Gray, with his beautiful eyes, looked down at her, and his chiselled lips curled in exquisite disdain. There is always something ridiculous about the emotions of people whom one has ceased to love. Sibyl Vane seemed to him to be absurdly melodramatic. Her tears and sobs annoyed him.

"I am going," he said at last, in his calm, clear voice. "I don't wish to be unkind, but I can't see you again. You have disappointed me."

She wept silently, and made no answer, but crept nearer. Her little hands stretched blindly out, and appeared to be seeking for him. He turned on his heel, and left the room. In a few moments he was out of the theatre.

Where he went to he hardly knew. He remembered wandering through dimly lit streets, past gaunt black-shadowed archways and evil-looking houses. Women with hoarse voices and harsh laughter had called after him. Drunkards had reeled by cursing, and chattering to themselves like monstrous apes. He had seen grotesque children huddled upon doorsteps, and heard shrieks and oaths from gloomy courts.

As the dawn was just breaking he found himself close to Covent Garden. The darkness lifted, and, flushed with faint fires, the sky hollowed itself into a perfect pearl. Huge carts filled with nodding lilies rumbled slowly down the polished empty street. The air was heavy with the perfume of the flowers, and their beauty seemed to bring him an anodyne for his pain. He followed into the market, and watched the men unloading their wagons. A white-smocked carter offered him some cherries. He thanked him, wondered why he refused to accept any money for them, and began to eat them listlessly. They had been plucked at midnight, and the coldness of the moon had entered into them. A long line of boys carrying crates of striped tulips, and of yellow and red roses, defiled in front of him, threading their way through the huge jade-green piles of vegetables. Under the portico, with its grey sun-bleached pillars, loitered a troop of draggled bareheaded girls, waiting for the auction to be over. Others crowded round the swinging doors of the coffee-house in the piazza. The heavy cart-horses slipped and stamped upon the rough stones, shaking their bells and trappings. Some of the drivers were lying asleep on a pile of sacks. Iris-necked and pink-footed, the pigeons ran about picking up seeds.

After a little while, he hailed a hansom, and drove home. For a few moments he loitered upon the doorstep, looking round at the silent Square with its blank close-shuttered windows, and its staring blinds. The sky was pure opal now, and the roofs of the houses glistened like silver against it. From some chimney opposite a thin wreath of smoke was rising. It curled, a violet riband, through the nacre-coloured air.

In the huge gilt Venetian lantern, spoil of some Doge's barge, that hung from the ceiling of the great oak-panelled hall of entrance, lights were still burning from three flickering jets: thin blue petals of flame they seemed, rimmed with white fire. He turned them out, and, having thrown his hat and cape on the table,

passed through the library towards the door of his bedroom, a large octagonal chamber on the ground floor
that, in his new-born feeling for luxury, he had just had
decorated for himself, and hung with some curious
Renaissance tapestries that had been discovered stored
in a disused attic at Selby Royal. As he was turning
the handle of the door, his eye fell upon the portrait Basil
Hallward had painted of him. He started back as if
in surprise. Then he went on into his own room, looking
somewhat puzzled. After he had taken the buttonhole
out of his coat, he seemed to hesitate. Finally he came
back, went over to the picture, and examined it. In the
dim arrested light that struggled through the cream-
coloured silk blinds, the face appeared to him to be a
little changed. The expression looked different. One
would have said that there was a touch of cruelty in
the mouth. It was certainly strange.

He turned round, and, walking to the window, drew
up the blind. The bright dawn flooded the room, and
swept the fantastic shadows into dusky corners, where
they lay shuddering. But the strange expression that
he had noticed in the face of the portrait seemed to
linger there, to be more intensified even. The quivering,
ardent sunlight showed him the lines of cruelty round
the mouth as clearly as if he had been looking into a
mirror after he had done some dreadful thing.

He winced, and, taking up from the table an oval
glass framed in ivory Cupids, one of Lord Henry's many
presents to him, glanced hurriedly into its polished
depths. No line like that warped his red lips. What did
it mean?

He rubbed his eyes, and came close to the picture,
and examined it again. There were no signs of any
change when he looked into the actual painting, and yet
there was no doubt that the whole expression had

altered. It was not a mere fancy of his own. The thing
was horribly apparent.

He threw himself into a chair, and began to think.
Suddenly there flashed across his mind what he had said
in Basil Hallward's studio the day the picture had been
finished. Yes, he remembered it perfectly. He had
uttered a mad wish that he himself might remain
young, and the portrait grow old; that his own beauty
might be untarnished, and the face on the canvas bear
the burden of his passions and his sins; that the painted
image might be seared with the lines of suffering and
thought, and that he might keep all the delicate bloom
and loveliness of his then just conscious boyhood.
Surely his wish had not been fulfilled? Such things were
impossible. It seemed monstrous even to think of them.
And, yet, there was the picture before him, with the
touch of cruelty in the mouth.

Cruelty! Had he been cruel? It was the girl's fault,
not his. He had dreamed of her as a great artist, had
given his love to her because he had thought her great.
Then she had disappointed him. She had been shallow
and unworthy. And, yet, a feeling of infinite regret came
over him, as he thought of her lying at his feet sobbing
like a little child. He remembered with what callous-
ness he had watched her. Why had he been made like
that? Why had such a soul been given to him? But he
had suffered also. During the three terrible hours that
the play had lasted, he had lived centuries of pain, æon
upon æon of torture. His life was well worth hers. She
had marred him for a moment, if he had wounded her
for an age. Besides, women were better suited to bear
sorrow than men. They lived on their emotions. They
only thought of their emotions. When they took lovers,
it was merely to have someone with whom they could
have scenes. Lord Henry had told him that, and Lord

Henry knew what women were. Why should he trouble about Sibyl Vane? She was nothing to him now.

But the picture? What was he to say of that? It held the secret of his life, and told his story. It had taught him to love his own beauty. Would it teach him to loathe his own soul? Would he ever look at it again?

No; it was merely an illusion wrought on the troubled senses. The horrible night that he had passed had left phantoms behind it. Suddenly there had fallen upon his brain that tiny scarlet speck that makes men mad. The picture had not changed. It was folly to think so.

Yet it was watching him, with its beautiful marred face and its cruel smile. Its bright hair gleamed in the early sunlight. Its blue eyes met his own. A sense of infinite pity, not for himself, but for the painted image of himself, came over him. It had altered already, and would alter more. Its gold would wither into grey. Its red and white roses would die. For every sin that he committed, a stain would fleck and wreck its fairness. But he would not sin. The picture, changed or unchanged, would be to him the visible emblem of conscience. He would resist temptation. He would not see Lord Henry any more—would not, at any rate, listen to those subtle poisonous theories that in Basil Hallward's garden had first stirred within him the passion for impossible things. He would go back to Sibyl Vane, make her amends, marry her, try to love her again. Yes, it was his duty to do so. She must have suffered more than he had. Poor child! He had been selfish and cruel to her. The fascination that she had exercised over him would return. They would be happy together. His life with her would be beautiful and pure.

He got up from his chair, and drew a large screen right in front of the portrait, shuddering as he glanced at it. "How horrible!" he murmured to himself, and he

walked across to the window and opened it. When he
stepped out on to the grass, he drew a deep breath. The
fresh morning air seemed to drive away all his sombre
passions. He thought only of Sibyl. A faint echo of his
love came back to him. He repeated her name over and
over again. The birds that were singing in the dew-
drenched garden seemed to be telling the flowers about
her. .

VIII

IT WAS long past noon when he awoke. His valet had
crept several times on tiptoe into the room to see if
he was stirring, and had wondered what made his
young master sleep so late. Finally his bell sounded,
and Victor came in softly with a cup of tea, and a pile
of letters, on a small tray of old Sèvres china, and drew
back the olive-satin curtains, with their shimmering
blue lining, that hung in front of the three tall windows.

"Monsieur has well slept this morning," he said,
smiling.

"What o'clock is it, Victor?" asked Dorian Gray,
drowsily.

"One hour and a quarter, Monsieur."

How late it was! He sat up, and, having sipped some
tea, turned over his letters. One of them was from Lord
Henry, and had been brought by hand that morning. He
hesitated for a moment, and then put it aside. The
others he opened listlessly. They contained the usual
collection of cards, invitations to dinner, tickets for
private views, programmes of charity concerts, and the
like, that are showered on fashionable young men every
morning during the season. There was a rather heavy
bill, for a chased silver Louis-Quinze toilet-set, that he

had not yet had the courage to send on to his guardians, who were extremely old-fashioned people and did not realize that we live in an age when unnecessary things are our only necessities; and there were several very courteously worded communications from Jermyn Street moneylenders offering to advance any sum of money at a moment's notice and at the most reasonable rates of interest.

After about ten minutes he got up, and, throwing on an elaborate dressing gown of silk-embroidered cashmere wool, passed into the onyx-paved bathroom. The cool water refreshed him after his long sleep. He seemed to have forgotten all that he had gone through. A dim sense of having taken part in some strange tragedy came to him once or twice, but there was the unreality of a dream about it.

As soon as he was dressed, he went into the library and sat down to a light French breakfast, that had been laid out for him on a small round table close to the open window. It was an exquisite day. The warm air seemed laden with spices. A bee flew in, and buzzed round the blue-dragon bowl that, filled with sulphur-yellow roses, stood before him. He felt perfectly happy.

Suddenly his eye fell on the screen that he had placed in front of the portrait, and he started.

"Too cold for Monsieur?" asked his valet, putting an omelette on the table. "I shut the window?"

Dorian shook his head. "I am not cold," he murmured.

Was it all true? Had the portrait really changed? Or had it been simply his own imagination that had made him see a look of evil where there had been a look of joy? Surely a painted canvas could not alter? The thing was absurd. It would serve as a tale to tell Basil some day. It would make him smile.

And, yet, how vivid was his recollection of the whole thing! First in the dim twilight, and then in the bright dawn, he had seen the touch of cruelty round the warped lips. He almost dreaded his valet's leaving the room. He knew that when he was alone he would have to examine the portrait. He was afraid of certainty. When the coffee and cigarettes had been brought and the man turned to go, he felt a wild desire to tell him to remain. As the door was closing behind him he called him back. The man stood waiting for his orders. Dorian looked at him for a moment. "I am not at home to anyone, Victor," he said, with a sigh. The man bowed and retired.

Then he rose from the table, lit a cigarette and flung himself down on a luxuriously-cushioned couch that stood facing the screen. The screen was an old one, of gilt Spanish leather, stamped and wrought with a rather florid Louis-Quatorze pattern. He scanned it curiously, wondering if ever before it had concealed the secret of a man's life.

Should he move it aside, after all? Why not let it stay there? What was the use of knowing? If the thing was true, it was terrible. If it was not true, why trouble about it? But what if, by some fate or deadlier chance, eyes other than his spied behind, and saw the horrible change? What should he do if Basil Hallward came and asked to look at his own picture? Basil would be sure to do that. No, the thing had to be examined, and at once. Anything would be better than this dreadful state of doubt.

He got up, and locked both doors. At least he would be alone when he looked upon the mask of his shame. Then he drew the screen aside, and saw himself face to face. It was perfectly true. The portrait had altered.

As he often remembered afterwards, and always with

no small wonder, he found himself at first gazing at the portrait with a feeling of almost scientific interest. That such a change should have taken place was incredible to him. And yet it was a fact. Was there some subtle affinity between the chemical atoms, that shaped themselves into form and colour on the canvas, and the soul that was within him? Could it be that what that soul thought, they realized?—that what it dreamed, they made true? Or was there some other, more terrible reason? He shuddered, and felt afraid, and, going back to the couch, lay there, gazing at the picture in sickened horror.

One thing, however, he felt that it had done for him. It had made him conscious how unjust, how cruel, he had been to Sibyl Vane. It was not too late to make reparation for that. She could still be his wife. His unreal and selfish love would yield to some higher influence, would be transformed into some nobler passion, and the portrait that Basil Hallward had painted of him would be a guide to him through life, would be to him what holiness is to some, and conscience to others, and the fear of God to us all. There were opiates for remorse, drugs that could lull the moral sense to sleep. But here was a visible symbol of the degradation of sin. Here was an ever-present sign of the ruin men brought upon their souls.

Three o'clock struck, and four, and the half-hour rang its double chime, but Dorian Gray did not stir. He was trying to gather up the scarlet threads of life, and to weave them into a pattern; to find his way through the sanguine labyrinth of passion through which he was wandering. He did not know what to do, or what to think. Finally, he went over to the table and wrote a passionate letter to the girl he had loved, imploring her forgiveness, and accusing himself of madness. He covered page after page with wild words of sorrow, and wilder words of pain. There is a luxury in self-reproach. When we blame ourselves we feel that no one else has a right to blame us. It is the confession, not the priest, that gives us absolution. When Dorian had finished the letter, he felt that he had been forgiven.

Suddenly there came a knock to the door, and he heard Lord Henry's voice outside. "My dear boy, I must see you. Let me in at once. I can't bear your shutting yourself up like this."

He made no answer at first, but remained quite still. The knocking still continued, and grew louder. Yes, it was better to let Lord Henry in, and to explain to him the new life he was going to lead, to quarrel with him if it became necessary to quarrel, to part if parting was inevitable. He jumped up, drew the screen hastily across the picture, and unlocked the door.

"I am so sorry for it all, Dorian," said Lord Henry, as he entered. "But you must not think too much about it."

"Do you mean about Sibyl Vane?" asked the lad.

"Yes, of course," answered Lord Henry, sinking into a chair, and slowly pulling off his yellow gloves. "It is dreadful, from one point of view, but it was not your fault. Tell me, did you go behind and see her, after the play was over?"

"Yes."

"I felt sure you had. Did you make a scene with her?"

"I was brutal, Harry—perfectly brutal. But it is all right now. I am not sorry for anything that has happened. It has taught me to know myself better."

"Ah, Dorian, I am so glad you take it in that way! I was afraid I would find you plunged in remorse, and tearing that nice curly hair of yours."

"I have got through all that," said Dorian, shaking

his head, and smiling. "I am perfectly happy now. I know what conscience is, to begin with. It is not what you told me it was. It is the divinest thing in us. Don't sneer at it, Harry, any more—at least not before me. I want to be good. I can't bear the idea of my soul being hideous."

"A very charming artistic basis for ethics, Dorian! I congratulate you on it. But how are you going to begin?"

"By marrying Sibyl Vane."

"Marrying Sibyl Vane!" cried Lord Henry, standing up, and looking at him in perplexed amazement. "But, my dear Dorian—"

"Yes, Harry, I know what you are going to say. Something dreadful about marriage. Don't say it. Don't ever say things of that kind to me again. Two days ago I asked Sibyl to marry me. I am not going to break my word to her. She is to be my wife."

"Your wife! Dorian! . . . Didn't you get my letter? I wrote to you this morning, and sent the note down, by my own man."

"Your letter? Oh, yes, I remember. I have not read it yet, Harry. I was afraid there might be something in it that I wouldn't like. You cut life to pieces with your epigrams."

"You know nothing then?"

"What do you mean?"

Lord Henry walked across the room, and, sitting down by Dorian Gray, took both his hands in his own, and held them tightly. "Dorian," he said, "my letter—don't be frightened—was to tell you that Sibyl Vane is dead."

A cry of pain broke from the lad's lips, and he leaped to his feet, tearing his hands away from Lord Henry's grasp. "Dead! Sibyl dead! It is not true! It is a horrible lie! How dare you say it?"

"It is quite true, Dorian," said Lord Henry, gravely. "It is in all the morning papers. I wrote down to you to ask you not to see anyone till I came. There will have to be an inquest, of course, and you must not be mixed up in it. Things like that make a man fashionable in Paris. But in London people are so prejudiced. Here, one should never make one's début with a scandal. One should reserve that to give an interest to one's old age. I suppose they don't know your name at the theatre? If they don't, it is all right. Did anyone see you going round to her room? That is an important point."

Dorian did not answer for a few moments. He was dazed with horror. Finally he stammered, in a stifled voice, "Harry, did you say an inquest? What did you mean by that? Did Sibyl—? Oh, Harry, I can't bear it! But be quick. Tell me everything at once."

"I have no doubt it was not an accident, Dorian, though it must be put in that way to the public. It seems that as she was leaving the theatre with her mother, about half-past twelve or so, she said she had forgotten something upstairs. They waited some time for her, but she did not come down again. They ultimately found her lying dead on the floor of her dressing-room. She had swallowed something by mistake, some dreadful thing they use at theatres. I don't know what it was, but it had either prussic acid or white lead in it. I should fancy it was prussic acid, as she seems to have died instantaneously."

"Harry, Harry, it is terrible!" cried the lad.

"Yes; it is very tragic, of course, but you must not get yourself mixed up in it. I see by *The Standard* that she was seventeen. I should have thought she was almost younger than that. She looked such a child, and seemed to know so little about acting. Dorian, you mustn't let this thing get on your nerves. You must come and dine with me, and afterwards we will look in at the Opera. It is a Patti night, and everybody will be there. You can come to my sister's box. She has got some smart women with her."

"So I have murdered Sibyl Vane," said Dorian Gray, half to himself—"murdered her as surely as if I had cut her little throat with a knife. Yet the roses are not less lovely for all that. The birds sing just as happily in my garden. And tonight I am to dine with you, and then go on to the Opera, and sup somewhere, I suppose, afterwards. How extraordinarily dramatic life is! If I had read all this in a book, Harry, I think I would have wept over it. Somehow, now that it has happened actually, and to me, it seems far too wonderful for tears. Here is the first passionate love letter I have ever written in my life. Strange, that my first passionate love letter should have been addressed to a dead girl. Can they feel, I wonder, those white silent people we call the dead? Sibyl! Can she feel, or know, or listen? Oh, Harry, how I loved her once! It seems years ago to me now. She was everything to me. Then came that dreadful night—was it really only last night? —when she played so badly, and my heart almost broke. She explained it all to me. It was terribly pathetic. But I was not moved a bit. I thought her shallow. Suddenly something happened that made me afraid. I can't tell you what it was, but it was terrible. I said I would go back to her. I felt I had done wrong. And now she is dead. My God! my God! Harry, what shall I do? You don't know the danger I am in, and there is nothing to keep me straight. She would have done that for me. She had no right to kill herself. It was selfish of her."

"My dear Dorian," answered Lord Henry, taking a cigarette from his case, and producing a gold-latten matchbox, "the only way a woman can ever reform a man is by boring him so completely that he loses all possible interest in life. If you had married this girl you would have been wretched. Of course you would have treated her kindly. One can always be kind to people about whom one cares nothing. But she would have soon found out that you were absolutely indifferent to her. And when a woman finds that out about her husband, she either becomes dreadfully dowdy, or wears very smart bonnets that some other woman's husband has to pay for. I say nothing about the social mistake, which would have been abject, which, of course, I would not have allowed, but I assure you that in any case the whole thing would have been an absolute failure."

"I suppose it would," muttered the lad, walking up and down the room, and looking horribly pale. "But I thought it was my duty. It is not my fault that this terrible tragedy has prevented my doing what was right. I remember your saying once that there is a fatality about good resolutions—that they are always made too late. Mine certainly were."

"Good resolutions are useless attempts to interfere with scientific laws. Their origin is pure vanity. Their result is absolutely *nil*. They give us, now and then, some of those luxurious sterile emotions that have a certain charm for the weak. That is all that can be said for them. They are simply cheques that men draw on a bank where they have no account."

"Harry," cried Dorian Gray, coming over and sitting down beside him, "why is it that I cannot feel this tragedy as much as I want to? I don't think I am heartless. Do you?"

"You have done too many foolish things during the last fortnight to be entitled to give yourself that name, Dorian," answered Lord Henry, with his sweet, melancholy smile.

The lad frowned. "I don't like that explanation, Harry," he rejoined, "but I am glad you don't think I am heartless. I am nothing of the kind. I know I am not. And yet I must admit that this thing that has happened does not affect me as it should. It seems to me to be simply like a wonderful ending to a wonderful play. It has all the terrible beauty of a Greek tragedy, a tragedy in which I took a great part, but by which I have not been wounded."

"It is an interesting question," said Lord Henry, who found an exquisite pleasure in playing on the lad's unconscious egotism—"an extremely interesting question. I fancy that the true explanation is this. It often happens that the real tragedies of life occur in such an inartistic manner that they hurt us by their crude violence, their absolute incoherence, their absurd want of meaning, their entire lack of style. They affect us just as vulgarity affects us. They give us an impression of sheer brute force, and we revolt against that. Sometimes, however, a tragedy that possesses artistic elements of beauty crosses our lives. If these elements of beauty are real, the whole thing simply appeals to our sense of dramatic effect. Suddenly we find that we are no longer the actors, but the spectators of the play. Or rather we are both. We watch ourselves, and the mere wonder of the spectacle enthralls us. In the present case, what is it that has really happened? Someone has killed herself for love of you. I wish that I had ever had such an experience. It would have made me in love with love for the rest of my life. The people who have adored me—there have not been very many, but there have been some—have always insisted on living on, long after I had ceased to care for them, or they to care for me. They have become stout and tedious, and when I meet them they go in at once for reminiscences. That awful memory of woman! What a fearful thing it is! And what an utter intellectual stagnation it reveals! One should absorb the colour of life, but one should never remember its details. Details are always vulgar."

"I must sow poppies in my garden," sighed Dorian.

"There is no necessity," rejoined his companion. "Life has always poppies in her hands. Of course, now and then things linger. I once wore nothing but violets all through one season, as a form of artistic mourning for a romance that would not die. Ultimately, however, it did die. I forget what killed it. I think it was her proposing to sacrifice the whole world for me. That is always a dreadful moment. It fills one with the terror of eternity. Well—would you believe it?—a week ago, at Lady Hampshire's, I found myself seated at dinner next the lady in question, and she insisted on going over the whole thing again, and digging up the past, and raking up the future. I had buried my romance in a bed of asphodel. She dragged it out again, and assured me that I had spoiled her life. I am bound to state that she ate an enormous dinner, so I did not feel any anxiety. But what a lack of taste she showed! The one charm of the past is that it is the past. But women never know when the curtain has fallen. They always want a sixth act, and as soon as the interest of the play is entirely over they propose to continue it. If they were allowed their own way, every comedy would have a tragic ending, and every tragedy would culminate in a farce. They are charmingly artificial, but they have no sense of art. You are more fortunate than I am. I assure you, Dorian, that not one of the women I have known would have done for me what Sibyl Vane did for you. Ordinary women always console themselves. Some of them do it by going in for sentimental colours. Never trust a woman who wears mauve, whatever her age may be, or a woman over thirty-five who is fond of pink ribbons. It always means that they have a history. Others find a great consolation in suddenly discovering the good qualities of their husbands. They flaunt their conjugal felicity in one's face, as if it were the most fascinating of sins. Religion consoles some. Its mysteries have all the charm of a flirtation, a woman once told me; and I can quite understand it. Besides, nothing makes one so vain as being told that one is a sinner. Conscience makes egotists of us all. Yes; there is really no end to the consolations that women find in modern life. Indeed, I have not mentioned the most important one."

"What is that, Harry?" said the lad, listlessly.

"Oh, the obvious consolation. Taking someone else's admirer when one loses one's own. In good society that always whitewashes a woman. But really, Dorian, how different Sibyl Vane must have been from all the women one meets! There is something to me quite beautiful about her death. I am glad I am living in a century when such wonders happen. They make one believe in the reality of the things we all play with, such as romance, passion, and love."

"I was terribly cruel to her. You forget that."

"I am afraid that women appreciate cruelty, downright cruelty, more than anything else. They have wonderfully primitive instincts. We have emancipated them, but they remain slaves looking for their masters, all the same. They love being dominated. I am sure you were splendid. I have never seen you really and absolutely angry, but I can fancy how delightful you looked. And, after all, you said something to me the day before yesterday that seemed to me at the time to be merely fanciful, but that I see now was absolutely true, and it holds the key to everything."

"What was that, Harry?"

"You said to me that Sibyl Vane represented to you all the heroines of romance—that she was Desdemona one night, and Ophelia the other; that if she died as Juliet, she came to life as Imogen."

"She will never come to life again now," muttered the lad, burying his face in his hands.

"No, she will never come to life. She has played her last part. But you must think of that lonely death in the tawdry dressing-room simply as a strange lurid fragment from some Jacobean tragedy, as a wonderful scene from Webster, or Ford, or Cyril Tourneur. The girl never really lived, and so she has never really died. To you at least she was always a dream, a phantom that flitted through Shakespeare's plays and left them lovelier for its presence, a reed through which Shakespeare's music sounded richer and more full of joy. The moment she touched actual life, she marred it, and it marred her, and so she passed away. Mourn for Ophelia, if you like. Put ashes on your head because Cordelia was strangled. Cry out against Heaven because the daughter of Brabantio died. But don't waste your tears over Sibyl Vane. She was less real than they are."

There was a silence. The evening darkened in the room. Noiselessly, and with silver feet, the shadows crept in from the garden. The colours faded wearily out of things.

After some time Dorian Gray looked up. "You have explained me to myself, Harry," he murmured, with something of a sigh of relief. "I felt all that you have said, but somehow I was afraid of it, and I could not express it to myself. How well you know me! But we will not talk again of what has happened. It has been a marvellous experience. That is all. I wonder if life has still in store for me anything as marvellous."

"Life has everything in store for you, Dorian. There is nothing that you, with your extraordinary good looks, will not be able to do."

"But suppose, Harry, I became haggard, and old, and wrinkled? What then?"

"Ah, then," said Lord Henry, rising to go—"then, my dear Dorian, you would have to fight for your victories. As it is, they are brought to you. No, you must keep your good looks. We live in an age that reads too much to be wise, and that thinks too much to be beautiful. We cannot spare you. And now you had better dress, and drive down to the club. We are rather late, as it is."

"I think I shall join you at the Opera, Harry. I feel too tired to eat anything. What is the number of your sister's box?"

"Twenty-seven, I believe. It is on the grand tier. You will see her name on the door. But I am sorry you won't come and dine."

"I don't feel up to it," said Dorian, listlessly. "But I am awfully obliged to you for all that you have said to me. You are certainly my best friend. No one has ever understood me as you have."

"We are only at the beginning of our friendship, Dorian," answered Lord Henry, shaking him by the hand. "Good-bye. I shall see you before nine-thirty, I hope. Remember, Patti is singing."

As he closed the door behind him, Dorian Gray touched the bell, and in a few minutes Victor appeared with the lamps and drew the blinds down. He waited impatiently for him to go. The man seemed to take an interminable time over everything.

As soon as he had left, he rushed to the screen, and drew it back. No, there was no further change in the picture. It had received the news of Sibyl Vane's death before he had known of it himself. It was conscious of the events of life as they occurred. The vicious cruelty that marred the fine lines of the mouth had, no doubt, appeared at the very moment that the girl had drunk the poison, whatever it was. Or was it indifferent to results? Did it merely take cognizance of what passed within the soul? He wondered, and hoped that some day he would see the change taking place before his very eyes, shuddering as he hoped it.

Poor Sibyl! what a romance it had all been! She had often mimicked death on the stage. Then Death himself had touched her, and taken her with him. How had she played that dreadful last scene? Had she cursed him, as she died? No; she had died for love of him, and love would always be a sacrament to him now. She had atoned for everything, by the sacrifice she had made of her life. He would not think any more of what she had made him go through, on that horrible night at the theatre. When he thought of her, it would be as a wonderful tragic figure sent on to the world's stage to show the supreme reality of love. A wonderful tragic figure? Tears came to his eyes as he remembered her childlike look and winsome fanciful ways and shy tremulous grace. He brushed them away hastily, and looked again at the picture.

He felt that the time had really come for making his choice. Or had his choice already been made? Yes, life had decided that for him—life, and his own infinite curiosity about life. Eternal youth, infinite passion, pleasure subtle and secret, wild joys and wilder sins —he was to have all these things. The portrait was to bear the burden of his shame: that was all.

A feeling of pain crept over him as he thought of the desecration that was in store for the fair face on the canvas. Once, in boyish mockery of Narcissus, he had kissed, or feigned to kiss, those painted lips that now smiled so cruelly at him. Morning after morning he had sat before the portrait wondering at its beauty, almost enamoured of it, as it seemed to him at times. Was it to alter now with every mood to which he yielded? Was it to become a monstrous and loathsome thing, to be hidden away in a locked room, to be shut out from the sunlight that had so often touched to brighter gold the waving wonder of its hair? The pity of it! the pity of it!

For a moment he thought of praying that the horrible sympathy that existed between him and the picture might cease. It had changed in answer to a prayer; perhaps in answer to a prayer it might remain unchanged. And, yet, who, that knew anything about life, would surrender the chance of remaining always young, however fantastic that chance might be, or with what fateful consequences it might be fraught? Besides, was it really under his control? Had it indeed been prayer that had produced the substitution? Might there not be some curious scientific reason for it all? If thought could exercise its influence upon a living organism, might not thought exercise an influence upon dead and inorganic things? Nay, without thought or conscious desire, might not things external to ourselves vibrate in unison with our moods and passions, atom calling to atom in secret love or strange affinity? But the reason was of no importance. He would never again tempt by a prayer any terrible power. If the picture was to alter, it was to alter. That was all. Why inquire too closely into it?

For there would be a real pleasure in watching it. He would be able to follow his mind into its secret places. This portrait would be to him the most magical of mirrors. As it had revealed to him his own body, so it would reveal to him his own soul. And when winter came upon it, he would still be standing where spring trembles on the verge of summer. When the blood crept from its face, and left behind a pallid mask of chalk with leaden eyes, he would keep the glamour of boyhood. Not one blossom of his loveliness would ever fade. Not one pulse of his life would ever weaken. Like the gods of the Greeks, he would be strong, and fleet, and joyous. What did it matter what happened to the coloured image on the canvas? He would be safe. That was everything.

He drew the screen back into its former place in front of the picture, smiling as he did so, and passed into his bedroom, where his valet was already waiting for him. An hour later he was at the Opera, and Lord Henry was leaning over his chair.

IX

AS HE was sitting at breakfast next morning, Basil Hallward was shown into the room.

"I am so glad I have found you, Dorian," he said, gravely. "I called last night, and they told me you were at the Opera. Of course I knew that was impossible. But I wish you had left word where you had really gone to. I passed a dreadful evening, half afraid that one tragedy might be followed by another. I think you might have telegraphed for me when you heard of it first. I read of it quite by chance in a late edition of *The Globe,* that I picked up at the club. I came here at once, and was miserable at not finding you. I can't tell you how heartbroken I am about the whole thing. I know what you must suffer. But where were you? Did you go down and see the girl's mother? For a moment I thought of following you there. They gave the address in the paper. Somewhere in the Euston Road, isn't it? But I was afraid of intruding upon a sorrow that I could not lighten. Poor woman! What a state she must be in! And her only child, too! What did she say about it all?"

"My dear Basil, how do I know?" murmured Dorian Gray, sipping some pale-yellow wine from a delicate gold-beaded bubble of Venetian glass, and looking dreadfully bored. "I was at the Opera. You should have come on there. I met Lady Gwendolen, Harry's sister, for the first time. We were in her box. She is perfectly charming; and Patti sang divinely. Don't talk about horrid subjects. If one doesn't talk about a thing, it has never happened. It is simply expression, as Harry says, that gives reality to things. I may mention that she was not the woman's only child. There is a son, a charming fellow, I believe. But he is not on the stage. He is a sailor, or something. And now, tell me about yourself and what you are painting."

"You went to the Opera?" said Hallward, speaking very slowly, and with a strained touch of pain in his voice. "You went to the Opera while Sibyl Vane was lying dead in some sordid lodging? You can talk to me of other women being charming, and of Patti singing divinely, before the girl you loved has even the quiet of a grave to sleep in? Why, man, there are horrors in store for that little white body of hers!"

"Stop, Basil! I won't hear it!" cried Dorian leaping to his feet. "You must not tell me about things. What is done is done. What is past is past."

"You call yesterday the past?"

"What has the actual lapse of time got to do with it? It is only shallow people who require years to get rid of an emotion. A man who is master of himself can end a sorrow as easily as he can invent a pleasure. I don't want to be at the mercy of my emotions. I want to use them, to enjoy them, and to dominate them."

"Dorian, this is horrible! Something has changed you completely. You look exactly the same wonderful boy who, day after day, used to come down to my studio to sit for his picture. But you were simple, natural, and affectionate then. You were the most unspoiled creature in the whole world. Now, I don't know what has come over you. You talk as if you had no heart, no pity in you. It is all Harry's influence. I see that."

The lad flushed up, and, going to the window, looked out for a few moments on the green, flickering, sun-lashed garden. "I owe a great deal to Harry, Basil," he said, at last—"more than I owe to you. You only taught me to be vain."

"Well, I am punished for that, Dorian—or shall be some day."

"I don't know what you mean, Basil," he exclaimed, turning round. "I don't know what you want. What do you want?"

"I want the Dorian Gray I used to paint," said the artist, sadly.

"Basil," said the lad, going over to him, and putting his hand on his shoulder, "you have come too late.

Yesterday when I heard that Sibyl Vane had killed herself—"

"Killed herself! Good heavens! is there no doubt about that?" cried Hallward, looking up at him with an expression of horror.

"My dear Basil! Surely you don't think it was a vulgar accident? Of course she killed herself."

The elder man buried his face in his hands. "How fearful," he muttered, and a shudder ran through him.

"No," said Dorian Gray, "there is nothing fearful about it. It is one of the great romantic tragedies of the age. As a rule, people who act lead the most common-place lives. They are good husbands, or faithful wives, or something tedious. You know what I mean—middle-class virtue, and all that kind of thing. How different Sibyl was! She lived her finest tragedy. She was always a heroine. The last night she played—the night you saw her—she acted badly because she had known the reality of love. When she knew its unreality, she died, as Juliet might have died. She passed again into the sphere of art. There is something of the martyr about her. Her death has all the pathetic uselessness of martyrdom, all its wasted beauty. But, as I was saying, you must not think I have not suffered. If you had come in yesterday at a particular moment—about half-past five, perhaps, or a quarter to six—you would have found me in tears. Even Harry, who was here, who brought me the news, in fact, had no idea what I was going through. I suffered immensely. Then it passed away. I cannot repeat an emotion. No one can, except sentimentalists. And you are awfully unjust, Basil. You come down here to console me. That is charming of you. You find me consoled, and you are furious. How like a sympathetic person! You remind me of a story Harry told me about a certain philanthropist who spent twenty years of his life in trying to get some grievance redressed, or some unjust law altered—I forget exactly what it was. Finally he succeeded, and nothing could exceed his disappointment. He had absolutely nothing to do, almost died of ennui, and became a confirmed misanthrope. And besides, my dear old Basil, if you really want to console me, teach me rather to forget what has happened, or to see it from a proper artistic point of view. Was it not Gautier who used to write about *la consolation des arts?* I remember picking up a little vellum-covered book in your studio one day and chancing on that delightful phrase. Well, I am not like that young man you told me of when we were down at Marlow together, the young man who used to say that yellow satin could console one for all the miseries of life. I love beautiful things that one can touch and handle. Old brocades, green bronzes, lacquer-work, carved ivories, exquisite surroundings, luxury, pomp, there is much to be got from all these. But the artistic temperament that they create, or at any rate reveal, is still more to me. To become the spectator of one's own life, as Harry says, is to escape the suffering of life. I know you are surprised at my talking to you like this. You have not realized how I have developed. I was a schoolboy when you knew me. I am a man now. I have new passions, new thoughts, new ideas. I am different, but you must not like me less. I am changed, but you must always be my friend. Of course I am very fond of Harry. But I know that you are better than he is. You are not stronger—you are too much afraid of life—but you are better. And how happy we used to be together! Don't leave me, Basil, and don't quarrel with me. I am what I am. There is nothing more to be said."

The painter felt strangely moved. The lad was infinitely dear to him, and his personality had been the great turning-point in his art. He could not bear the idea of reproaching him any more. After all, his indifference was probably merely a mood that would pass away. There was so much in him that was good, so much in him that was noble.

"Well, Dorian," he said, at length, with a sad smile, "I won't speak to you again about this horrible thing, after today. I only trust your name won't be mentioned in connection with it. The inquest is to take place this afternoon. Have they summoned you?"

Dorian shook his head, and a look of annoyance passed over his face at the mention of the word "inquest." There was something so crude and vulgar about everything of the kind. "They don't know my name," he answered.

"But surely she did?"

"Only my Christian name, and that I am quite sure she never mentioned to anyone. She told me once that they were all rather curious to learn who I was, and that she invariably told them my name was Prince Charming. It was pretty of her. You must do me a drawing of Sibyl, Basil. I should like to have something more of her than the memory of a few kisses and some broken pathetic words."

"I will try and do something, Dorian, if it would please you. But you must come and sit to me yourself again. I can't get on without you."

"I can never sit to you again, Basil. It is impossible!" he exclaimed, starting back.

The painter stared at him. "My dear boy, what nonsense!" he cried. "Do you mean to say you don't like what I did for you? Where is it? Why have you pulled the screen in front of it? Let me look at it. It is the best thing I have ever done. Do take the screen away, Dorian. It is simply disgraceful of your servant hiding my work like that. I felt the room looked different as I came in."

"My servant has nothing to do with it, Basil. You don't imagine I let him arrange my room for me? He settles my flowers for me sometimes—that is all. No, I did it myself. The light was too strong on the portrait."

"Too strong! Surely not, my dear fellow? It is an admirable place for it. Let me see it." And Hallward walked towards the corner of the room.

A cry of terror broke from Dorian Gray's lips, and he rushed between the painter and the screen. "Basil," he said, looking very pale, "you must not look at it. I don't wish you to."

"Not look at my own work! you are not serious. Why shouldn't I look at it?" exclaimed Hallward, laughing.

"If you try to look at it, Basil, on my word of honour I will never speak to you again as long as I live. I am quite serious. I don't offer any explanation, and you are not to ask for any. But, remember, if you touch this screen, everything is over between us."

Hallward was thunderstruck. He looked at Dorian Gray in absolute amazement. He had never seen him like this before. The lad was actually pallid with rage. His hands were clenched, and the pupils of his eyes were like disks of blue fire. He was trembling all over.

"Dorian!"

"Don't speak!"

"But what is the matter? Of course I won't look at it if you don't want me to," he said, rather coldly, turning on his heel, and going over towards the window. "But, really, it seems rather absurd that I shouldn't see my own work, especially as I am going to exhibit it in Paris in the autumn. I shall probably have to give it another coat of varnish before that, so I must see it some day, and why not today?"

"To exhibit it! You want to exhibit it?" exclaimed Dorian Gray, a strange sense of terror creeping over him. Was the world going to be shown his secret? Were people to gape at the mystery of his life? That was impossible. Something—he did not know what—had to be done at once.

"Yes, I don't suppose you will object to that. Georges Petit is going to collect all my best pictures for a special exhibition in the Rue de Sèze, which will open the first week in October. The portrait will only be away a month. I should think you could easily spare it for that time. In fact, you are sure to be out of town. And if you keep it always behind a screen, you can't care much about it."

Dorian Gray passed his hand over his forehead. There were beads of perspiration there. He felt that he was on the brink of a horrible danger. "You told me a month ago that you would never exhibit it," he cried. "Why have you changed your mind? You people who go in for being consistent have just as many moods as others have. The only difference is that your moods are rather meaningless. You can't have forgotten that you assured me most solemnly that nothing in the world would induce you to send it to any exhibition. You told Harry exactly the same thing." He stopped suddenly, and a gleam of light came into his eyes. He remembered that Lord Henry had said to him once, half seriously and half in jest, "If you want to have a strange quarter of an hour, get Basil to tell you why he won't exhibit your picture. He told me why he wouldn't, and it was a revelation to me." Yes, perhaps, Basil, too, had his secret. He would ask him and try.

"Basil," he said, coming over quite close, and looking him straight in the face, "we have each of us a secret.

Let me know yours, and I shall tell you mine. What was your reason for refusing to exhibit my picture?"

The painter shuddered in spite of himself. "Dorian, if I told you, you might like me less than you do, and you would certainly laugh at me. I could not bear your doing either of those two things. If you wish me never to look at your picture again, I am content. I have always you to look at. If you wish the best work I have ever done to be hidden from the world, I am satisfied. Your friendship is dearer to me than any fame or reputation."

"No, Basil, you must tell me," insisted Dorian Gray. "I think I have a right to know." His feeling of terror had passed away, and curiosity had taken its place. He was determined to find out Basil Hallward's mystery.

"Let us sit down, Dorian," said the painter, looking troubled. "Let us sit down. And just answer me one question. Have you noticed in the picture something curious?—something that probably at first did not strike you, but that revealed itself to you suddenly?"

"Basil!" cried the lad, clutching the arms of his chair with trembling hands, and gazing at him with wild, startled eyes.

"I see you did. Don't speak. Wait till you hear what I have to say. Dorian, from the moment I met you, your personality had the most extraordinary influence over me. I was dominated, soul, brain, and power by you. You became to me the visible incarnation of that unseen ideal whose memory haunts us artists like an exquisite dream. I worshipped you. I grew jealous of everyone to whom you spoke. I wanted to have you all to myself. I was only happy when I was with you. When you were away from me you were still present

THE PICTURE OF DORIAN GRAY

in my art. . . . Of course I never let you know anything about this. It would have been impossible. You would not have understood it. I hardly understood it myself. I only knew that I had seen perfection face to face, and that the world had become wonderful to my eyes—too wonderful, perhaps, for in such mad worships there is peril, the peril of losing them, no less than the peril of keeping them. . . . Weeks and weeks went on, and I grew more and more absorbed in you. Then came a new development. I had drawn you as Paris in dainty armour, and as Adonis with huntsman's cloak and polished boar spear. Crowned with heavy lotus blossoms you had sat on the prow of Adrian's barge, gazing across the green turbid Nile. You had leant over the still pool of some Greek woodland, and seen in the water's silent silver the marvel of your own face. And it had all been what art should be, unconscious, ideal, and remote. One day, a fatal day I sometimes think, I determined to paint a wonderful portrait of you as you actually are, not in the costume of dead ages, but in your own dress and in your own time. Whether it was the realism of the method or the mere wonder of your own personality, thus directly presented to me without mist or veil, I cannot tell. But I know that as I worked at it, every flake and film of colour seemed to me to reveal my secret. I grew afraid that others would know of my idolatry. I felt, Dorian, that I had told too much, that I had put too much of myself into it. Then it was that I resolved never to allow the picture to be exhibited. You were a little annoyed; but then you did not realize all that it meant to me. Harry, to whom I talked about it, laughed at me. But I did not mind that. When the picture was finished, and I sat alone with it, I felt that I was right. . . . Well, after a few days the thing left my studio, and as soon as I had got rid of the intolerable fascination of its presence it seemed to me that I had been foolish in imagining that I had seen anything in it, more than that you were extremely good-looking and that I could paint. Even now I cannot help feeling that it is a mistake to think that the passion one feels in creation is ever really shown in the work one creates. Art is always more abstract than we fancy. Form and colour tell us of form and colour—that is all. It often seems to me that art conceals the artist far more completely than it ever reveals him. And so when I got this offer from Paris I determined to make your portrait the principal thing in my exhibition. It never occurred to me that you would refuse. I see now that you were right. The picture cannot be shown. You must not be angry with me, Dorian, for what I have told you. As I said to Harry, once, you are made to be worshipped."

Dorian Gray drew a long breath. The colour came back to his cheeks, and a smile played about his lips. The peril was over. He was safe for the time. Yet he could not help feeling infinite pity for the painter who had just made this strange confession to him, and wondered if he himself would ever be so dominated by the personality of a friend. Lord Henry had the charm of being very dangerous. But that was all. He was too clever and too cynical to be really fond of. Would there ever be someone who would fill him with a strange idolatry? Was that one of the things that life had in store?

"It is extraordinary to me, Dorian," said Hallward, "that you should have seen this in the portrait. Did you really see it?"

"I saw something in it," he answered, "something that seemed to me very curious."

"Well, you don't mind my looking at the thing now?"

Dorian shook his head. "You must not ask me that, Basil. I could not possibly let you stand in front of that picture."

"You will some day, surely?"

"Never."

"Well, perhaps you are right. And now good-bye, Dorian. You have been the one person in my life who has really influenced my art. Whatever I have done that is good, I owe to you. Ah! you don't know what it cost me to tell you all that I have told you."

"My dear Basil," said Dorian, "what have you told me? Simply that you felt that you admired me too much. That is not even a compliment."

"It was not intended as a compliment. It was a confession. Now that I have made it, something seems to have gone out of me. Perhaps one should never put one's worship into words."

"It was a disappointing confession."

"Why, what did you expect, Dorian? You didn't see anything else in the picture, did you? There was nothing else to see?"

"No; there was nothing else to see. Why do you ask? But you mustn't talk about worship. It is foolish. You and I are friends, Basil, and we must always remain so."

"You have got Harry," said the painter, sadly.

"Oh, Harry?" cried the lad, with a ripple of laughter. "Harry spends his days in saying what is incredible, and his evenings in doing what is improbable. Just the sort of life I would like to lead. But still I don't think I would go to Harry if I were in trouble. I would sooner go to you, Basil."

"You will sit to me again?"

"Impossible!"

"You spoil my life as an artist by refusing, Dorian.

No man came across two ideal things. Few come across one."

"I can't explain it to you, Basil, but I must never sit to you again. There is something fatal about a portrait. It has a life of its own. I will come and have tea with you. That will be just as pleasant."

"Pleasanter for you, I am afraid," murmured Hallward, regretfully. "And now good-bye. I am sorry you won't let me look at the picture once again. But that can't be helped. I quite understand what you feel about it."

As he left the room, Dorian Gray smiled to himself. Poor Basil! how little he knew of the true reason! And how strange it was that, instead of having been forced to reveal his own secret, he had succeeded, almost by chance, in wresting a secret from his friend! How much that strange confession explained to him! The painter's absurd fits of jealousy, his wild devotion, his extravagant panegyrics, his curious reticences—he understood them all now, and he felt sorry. There seemed to him to be something tragic in a friendship so coloured by romance.

He sighed, and touched the bell. The portrait must be hidden away at all costs. He could not run such a risk of discovery again. It had been mad of him to have allowed the thing to remain, even for an hour, in a room to which any of his friends had access.

X

WHEN his servant entered, he looked at him steadfastly, and wondered if he had thought of peering behind the screen. The man was quite impassive, and waited for his orders. Dorian lit a cigarette, and walked over to the glass and glanced into it. He could see the reflection of Victor's face perfectiy. It was like a placid mask of servility. There was nothing to be afraid of, there. Yet he thought it best to be on his guard.

Speaking very slowly, he told him to tell the housekeeper that he wanted to see her, and then to go to the frame-maker and ask him to send two of his men round at once. It seemed to him that as the man left the room his eyes wandered in the direction of the screen. Or was that merely his own fancy?

After a few moments, in her black silk dress with old-fashioned thread mittens on her wrinkled hands, Mrs. Leaf bustled into the library. He asked her for the key of the schoolroom.

"The old schoolroom, Mr. Dorian?" she exclaimed. "Why, it is full of dust. I must get it arranged, and put straight before you go into it. It is not fit for you to see, sir. It is not, indeed."

"I don't want it put straight, Leaf. I only want the key."

"Well, sir, you'll be covered with cobwebs if you go into it. Why, it hasn't been opened for nearly five years, not since his lordship died."

He winced at the mention of his grandfather. He had hateful memories of him. "That does not matter," he answered. "I simply want to see the place—that is all. Give me the key."

"And here is the key, sir," said the old lady, going over the contents of her bunch with tremulously uncertain hands. "Here is the key. I'll have it off the bunch in a moment. But you don't think of living up there, sir, and you so comfortable here?"

"No, no," he cried, petulantly. "Thank you, Leaf. That will do."

She lingered for a few moments, and was garrulous over some detail of the household. He sighed, and told her to manage things as she thought best. She left the room, wreathed in smiles.

As the door closed, Dorian put the key in his pocket, and looked round the room. His eye fell on a large purple satin coverlet heavily embroidered with gold, a splendid piece of late seventeenth-century Venetian work that his grandfather had found in a convent near Bologna. Yes, that would serve to wrap the dreadful thing in. It had perhaps served often as a pall for the dead. Now it was to hide something that had a corruption of its own, worse than the corruption of death itself—something that would breed horrors and yet would never die. What the worm was to the corpse, his sins would be to the painted image on the canvas. They would mar its beauty, and eat away its grace. They would defile it, and make it shameful. And yet the thing would still live on. It would be always alive.

He shuddered, and for a moment he regretted that he had not told Basil the true reason why he had wished to hide the picture away. Basil would have helped him to resist Lord Henry's influence, and the still more poisonous influences that came from his own temperament. The love that he bore him—for it was really love—had nothing in it that was not noble and intellectual. It was not that mere physical admiration of beauty that is born of the senses, and that dies when the senses tire. It was such love as Michelangelo had known, and Montaigne, and Winckelmann, and Shakespeare himself. Yes, Basil could have saved him. But it was too late now. The past could always be annihilated. Regret, denial, or forgetfulness could do that. But the future was inevitable. There were passions in him that would find their terrible outlet, dreams that would make the shadow of their evil real.

He took up from the couch the great purple-and-gold texture that covered it, and, holding it in his hands, passed behind the screen. Was the face on the canvas viler than before? It seemed to him that it was unchanged; and yet his loathing of it was intensified. Gold hair, blue eyes, and rose-red lips—they all were there. It was simply the expression that had altered. That was horrible in its cruelty. Compared to what he saw in it of censure or rebuke, how shallow Basil's reproaches about Sibyl Vane had been!—how shallow, and of what little account! His own soul was looking out at him from the canvas and calling him to judgment. A look of pain came across him, and he flung the rich pall over the picture. As he did so, a knock came to the door. He passed out as his servant entered.

"The persons are here, Monsieur."

He felt that the man must be got rid of at once. He must not be allowed to know where the picture was being taken to. There was something sly about him, and he had thoughtful, treacherous eyes. Sitting down at the writing-table, he scribbled a note to Lord Henry, asking him to send him round something to read, and reminding him that they were to meet at eight-fifteen that evening.

"Wait for an answer," he said, handing it to him, "and show the men in here."

In two or three minutes there was another knock, and Mr. Hubbard himself, the celebrated frame-maker of South Audley Street, came in with a somewhat rough-looking young assistant. Mr. Hubbard was a florid, red-whiskered little man, whose admiration for art was considerably tempered by the inveterate impecuniosity of most of the artists who dealt with him. As a rule, he never left his shop. He waited for people to come to him. But he always made an exception in favour of Dorian Gray. There was something about Dorian that charmed everybody. It was a pleasure even to see him.

"What can I do for you, Mr. Gray?" he said, rubbing his fat freckled hands. "I thought I would do myself the honour of coming round in person. I have just got a beauty of a frame, sir. Picked it up at a sale. Came from Fonthill, I believe. Admirably suited for a religious subject, Mr. Gray."

"I am so sorry you have given yourself the trouble of coming round, Mr. Hubbard. I shall certainly drop in and look at the frame—though I don't go in much at present for religious art—but today I only want a picture carried to the top of the house for me. It is rather heavy, so I thought I would ask you to lend me a couple of your men."

"No trouble at all, Mr. Gray. I am delighted to be of any service to you. Which is the work of art, sir?"

"This," replied Dorian, moving the screen back. "Can you move it, covering and all, just as it is? I don't want it to get scratched going upstairs."

"There will be no difficulty, sir," said the genial frame-maker, beginning, with the aid of his assistant, to unhook the picture from the long brass chains by which it was suspended. "And, now, where shall we carry it to, Mr. Gray?"

"I will show you the way, Mr. Hubbard, if you will kindly follow me. Or perhaps you had better go in front. I am afraid it is right at the top of the house. We will go up by the front staircase, as it is wider."

He held the door open for them, and they passed

out into the hall and began the ascent. The elaborate
character of the frame had made the picture extremely
bulky, and now and then, in spite of the obsequious
protests of Mr. Hubbard, who had the true tradesman's
spirited dislike of seeing a gentleman doing anything
useful, Dorian put his hand to it so as to help them.

"Something of a load to carry, sir," gasped the little
man, when they reached the top landing. And he
wiped his shiny forehead.

"I am afraid it is rather heavy," murmured Dorian,
as he unlocked the door that opened into the room that
was to keep for him the curious secret of his life and
hide his soul from the eyes of men.

He had not entered the place for more than four
years—not, indeed, since he had used it first as a play-
room when he was a child, and then as a study when
he grew somewhat older. It was a large, well-propor-
tioned room, which had been specially built by the
last Lord Kelso for the use of the little grandson
whom, for his strange likeness to his mother, and also
for other reasons, he had always hated and desired to
keep at a distance. It appeared to Dorian to have but
little changed. There was the huge Italian *cassone*, with
its fantastically painted panels and its tarnished gilt
mouldings, in which he had so often hidden himself as
a boy. There the satinwood bookcase filled with his
dog-eared schoolbooks. On the wall behind it was hanging the same ragged Flemish tapestry where a faded
king and queen were playing chess in a garden, while a
company of hawkers rode by, carrying hooded birds on
their gauntleted wrists. How well he remembered it
all! Every moment of his lonely childhood came back
to him as he looked round. He recalled the stainless
purity of his boyish life, and it seemed horrible to him
that it was here the fatal portrait was to be hidden

away. How little he had thought, in those dead days, of all that was in store for him!

But there was no other place in the house so secure from prying eyes as this. He had the key, and no one else could enter it. Beneath its purple pall, the face painted on the canvas could grow bestial, sodden, and unclean. What did it matter? No one could see it. He himself would not see it. Why should he watch the hideous corruption of his soul? He kept his youth—that was enough. And, besides, might not his nature grow finer, after all? There was no reason that the future should be so full of shame. Some love might come across his life, and purify him, and shield him from those sins that seemed to be already stirring in spirit and in flesh—those curious unpictured sins whose very mystery lent them their subtlety and their charm. Perhaps, some day, the cruel look would have passed away from the scarlet sensitive mouth, and he might show to the world Basil Hallward's masterpiece.

No, that was impossible. Hour by hour, and week by week, the thing upon the canvas was growing old. It might escape the hideousness of sin, but the hideousness of age was in store for it. The cheeks would become hollow or flaccid. Yellow crow's-feet would creep round the fading eyes and make them horrible. The hair would lose its brightness, the mouth would gape or droop, would be foolish or gross, as the mouths of old men are. There would be the wrinkled throat, the cold, blue-veined hands, the twisted body, that he remembered in the grandfather who had been so stern to him in his boyhood. The picture had to be concealed. There was no help for it.

"Bring it in, Mr. Hubbard, please," he said, wearily, turning round. "I am sorry I kept you so long. I was thinking of something else."

"Always glad to have a rest, Mr. Gray," answered the frame-maker, who was still gasping for breath. "Where shall we put it, sir?"

"Oh, anywhere. Here: this will do. I don't want to have it hung up. Just lean it against the wall. Thanks."

"Might one look at the work of art, sir?"

Dorian started. "It would not interest you, Mr. Hubbard," he said, keeping his eye on the man. He felt ready to leap upon him and fling him to the ground if he dared to lift the gorgeous hanging that concealed the secret of his life. "I shan't trouble you any more now. I am much obliged for your kindness in coming round."

"Not at all, not at all, Mr. Gray. Ever ready to do anything for you, sir." And Mr. Hubbard tramped downstairs, followed by the assistant, who glanced back at Dorian with a look of shy wonder in his rough, uncomely face. He had never seen anyone so marvellous.

When the sound of their footsteps had died away, Dorian locked the door, and put the key in his pocket. He felt safe now. No one would ever look upon the horrible thing. No eye but his would ever see his shame.

On reaching the library he found that it was just after five o'clock, and that the tea had been already brought up. On a little table of dark perfumed wood thickly incrusted with nacre, a present from Lady Radley, his guardian's wife, a pretty professional invalid, who had spent the preceding winter in Cairo, was lying a note from Lord Henry, and beside it was a book bound in yellow paper, the cover slightly torn and the edges soiled. A copy of the third edition of *The St. James's Gazette* had been placed on the tea tray. It was evident that Victor had returned. He wondered if he had met the men in the hall as they were leaving the house, and had wormed out of them what they had been doing. He would be sure to miss the picture—had no doubt missed it already, while he had been laying the tea-things. The screen had not been set back, and a blank space was visible on the wall. Perhaps some night he might find him creeping up-stairs and trying to force the door of the room. It was a horrible thing to have a spy in one's house. He had heard of rich men who had been blackmailed all their lives by some servant who had read a letter, or over-heard a conversation, or picked up a card with an address, or found beneath a pillow a withered flower or a shred of crumpled lace.

He sighed, and, having poured himself out some tea, opened Lord Henry's note. It was simply to say that he sent him round the evening paper, and a book that might interest him, and that he would be at the club at eight-fifteen. He opened *The St. James's* lan-guidly, and looked through it. A red pencil-mark on the fifth page caught his eye. It drew attention to the fol-lowing paragraph:—

"INQUEST ON AN ACTRESS.—An inquest was held this morning at the Bell Tavern, Hoxton Road, by Mr. Danby, the District Coroner, on the body of Sibyl Vane, a young actress recently engaged at the Royal Theatre, Holborn. A verdict of death by misadventure was returned. Considerable sympathy was expressed for the mother of the deceased, who was greatly af-fected during the giving of her own evidence, and that of Dr. Birrell, who had made the post-mortem ex-amination of the deceased."

He frowned, and, tearing the paper in two went across the room and flung the pieces away. How ugly it all was! And how horribly real ugliness made things! He felt a little annoyed with Lord Henry for having sent him the report. And it was certainly stupid of him to have marked it with red pencil. Victor might have read it. The man knew more than enough English for that.

Perhaps he had read it, and had begun to suspect something. And, yet, what did it matter? What had Dorian Gray to do with Sibyl Vane's death? There was nothing to fear. Dorian Gray had not killed her.

His eye fell on the yellow book that Lord Henry had sent him. What was it, he wondered. He went towards the little pearl-coloured octagonal stand, that had always looked to him like the work of some strange Egyptian bees that wrought in silver, and taking up the volume, flung himself into an arm-chair, and began to turn over the leaves. After a few minutes he became absorbed. It was the strangest book that he had ever read. It seemed to him that in exquisite raiment, and to the delicate sound of flutes, the sins of the world were passing in dumb show before him. Things that he had dimly dreamed of were suddenly made real to him. Things of which he had never dreamed were gradually revealed.

It was a novel without a plot, and with only one character, being indeed, simply a psychological study of a certain young Parisian, who spent his life trying to realize in the nineteenth century all the passions and modes of thought that belonged to every century except his own, and to sum up, as it were, in himself the various moods through which the world-spirit had ever passed, loving for their mere artificiality those renunciations that men have unwisely called virtue, as much as those natural rebellions that wise men still call sin. The style in which it was written was that curious jewelled style, vivid and obscure at once, full of argot and of archaisms, of technical expressions and of elaborate paraphrases, that characterizes the work of some of the finest artists of the French school of *Symbolistes*. There were in it metaphors as monstrous as orchids, and as subtle in colour. The life of the senses was described in the terms of mystical philosophy. One hardly knew at times whether one was reading the spiritual ecstasies of some mediæval saint or the morbid confessions of a modern sinner. It was a poisonous book. The heavy odour of incense seemed to cling about its pages and to trouble the brain. The mere cadence of the sentences, the subtle monotony of their music, so full as it was of complex refrains and movements elaborately repeated, produced in the mind of the lad, as he passed from chapter to chapter, a form of reverie, a malady of dreaming, that made him unconscious of the falling day and creeping shadows.

Cloudless, and pierced by one solitary star, a copper-green sky gleamed through the windows. He read on by its wan light till he could read no more. Then, after his valet had reminded him several times of the lateness of the hour, he got up, and, going into the next room, placed the book on the little Florentine table that always stood at his bedside, and began to dress for dinner.

It was almost nine o'clock before he reached the club, where he found Lord Henry sitting alone, in the morning-room, looking very much bored.

"I am so sorry, Harry," he cried, "but really it is entirely your fault. That book you sent me so fascinated me that I forgot how the time was going."

"Yes: I thought you would like it," replied his host, rising from his chair.

"I didn't say I liked it, Harry. I said it fascinated me. There is a great difference."

"Ah, you have discovered that?" murmured Lord Henry. And they passed into the dining-room.

XI

FOR years, Dorian Gray could not free himself from the influence of this book. Or perhaps it would be more accurate to say that he never sought to free himself from it. He procured from Paris no less than nine large-paper copies of the first edition, and had them bound in different colours, so that they might suit his various moods and the changing fancies of a nature over which he seemed, at times, to have almost entirely lost control. The hero, the wonderful young Parisian, in whom the romantic and the scientific temperaments were so strangely blended, became to him a kind of prefiguring type of himself. And, indeed, the whole book seemed to him to contain the story of his own life, written before he had lived it.

In one point he was more fortunate than the novel's fantastic hero. He never knew—never, indeed, had any cause to know—that somewhat grotesque dread of mirrors, and polished metal surfaces, and still water, which came upon the young Parisian so early in his life, and was occasioned by the sudden decay of a beauty that had once, apparently, been so remarkable. It was with an almost cruel joy—and perhaps in nearly every joy, as certainly in every pleasure, cruelty has its place—that he used to read the latter part of the book, with its really tragic, if somewhat overemphasized, account of the sorrow and despair of one who had himself lost what in others, and in the world, he had most dearly valued.

For the wonderful beauty that had so fascinated Basil Hallward, and many others besides him, seemed never to leave him. Even those who had heard the most evil things against him, and from time to time strange rumours about his mode of life crept through London and became the chatter of the clubs, could not believe anything to his dishonour when they saw him. He had always the look of one who had kept himself unspotted from the world. Men who talked grossly became silent when Dorian Gray entered the room. There was something in the purity of his face that rebuked them. His mere presence seemed to recall to them the memory of the innocence that they had tarnished. They wondered how one so charming and graceful as he was could have escaped the stain of an age that was at once sordid and sensual.

Often, on returning home from one of those mysterious and prolonged absences that gave rise to such strange conjecture among those who were his friends, or thought that they were so, he himself would creep upstairs to the locked room, open the door with the key that never left him now, and stand, with a mirror, in front of the portrait that Basil Hallward had painted of him, looking now at the evil and aging face on the canvas, and now at the fair young face that laughed back at him from the polished glass. The very sharpness of the contrast used to quicken his sense of pleasure. He grew more and more enamoured of his own beauty, more and more interested in the corruption of his own soul. He would examine with minute care, and sometimes with a monstrous and terrible delight, the hideous lines that seared the wrinkling forehead or crawled around the heavy sensual mouth, wondering sometimes which were the more horrible, the signs of sin or the signs of age. He would place his white hands beside the coarse bloated hands of the picture, and smile. He mocked the misshapen body and the failing limbs.

There were moments, indeed, at night, when, lying sleepless in his own delicately scented chamber, or in the sordid room of the little ill-famed tavern near the Docks, which, under an assumed name, and in disguise, it was his habit to frequent, he would think of the ruin he had brought upon his soul, with a pity that was all the more poignant because it was purely selfish. But moments such as these were rare. That curiosity about life which Lord Henry had first stirred in him, as they sat together in the garden of their friend, seemed to increase with gratification. The more he knew, the more he desired to know. He had mad hungers that grew more ravenous as he fed them.

Yet he was not really reckless, at any rate in his relations to society. Once or twice every month during the winter, and on each Wednesday evening while the season lasted, he would throw open to the world his beautiful house and have the most celebrated musicians of the day to charm his guests with the wonders of their art. His little dinners, in the settling of which Lord Henry always assisted him, were noted as much for the careful selection and placing of those invited, as for the exquisite taste shown in the decoration of the table, with its subtle symphonic arrangements of exotic flowers, and embroidered cloths, and antique plate of gold and silver. Indeed, there were many, especially among the very young men, who saw, or fancied that they saw, in Dorian Gray the true realization of a type of which they had often dreamed in Eton or Oxford days, a type that was to combine something of the real culture of the scholar with all the grace and distinction and perfect manner of a citizen of the world. To them he seemed to be of the company of those whom Dante describes as having sought to "make themselves perfect by the worship of beauty." Like Gautier, he was one for whom "the visible world existed."

And certainly, to him life itself was the first, the greatest, of the arts, and for it all the other arts seemed to be but a preparation. Fashion, by which what is really fantastic becomes for a moment universal, and dandyism, which, in its own way, is an attempt to assert the absolute modernity of beauty, had, of course their fascination for him. His mode of dressing, and the particular styles that from time to time he affected, had their marked influence on the young exquisites of the Mayfair balls and Pall Mall Club windows, who copied him in everything that he did, and tried to reproduce the accidental charm of his graceful, though to him only half-serious, fopperies.

For, while he was but too ready to accept the position that was almost immediately offered to him on his coming of age, and found, indeed, a subtle pleasure in the thought that he might really become to the London of his own day what to imperial Neronian Rome the author of the *Satyricon* once had been, yet in his inmost heart he desired to be something more than a mere *arbiter elegantiarum*, to be consulted on the wearing of a jewel, or the knotting of a necktie, or the conduct of a cane. He sought to elaborate some new scheme of life that would have its reasoned philosophy and its ordered principles, and find in the spiritualizing of the senses its highest realization.

The worship of the senses has often, and with much justice, been decried, men feeling a natural instinct of terror about passions and sensations that seem stronger than themselves, and that they are conscious of sharing with the less highly organized forms of existence. But it appeared to Dorian Gray that the true nature of the senses had never been understood, and that they had remained savage and animal merely because the world had sought to starve them into submission or to kill them by pain, instead of aiming at making them elements of a new spirituality, of which a fine instinct for beauty was to be the dominant characteristic. As he looked back upon man moving through history, he was haunted by a feeling of loss. So much had been surrendered! and to such little purpose! There had been mad wilful rejections, monstrous forms of self-torture and self-denial, whose origin was fear, and whose result was a degradation infinitely more terrible than that fancied degradation from which, in their ignorance, they had sought to escape, nature, in her wonderful irony, driving out the anchorite to feed with the wild animals of the desert and giving to the hermit the beasts of the field as his companions.

Yes: there was to be, as Lord Henry had prophesied, a new Hedonism that was to re-create life, and to save it from that harsh, uncomely Puritanism that is having, in our own day, its curious revival. It was to have its service of the intellect, certainly; yet, it was never to accept any theory or system that would involve the sacrifice of any mode of passionate experience. Its aim, indeed, was to be experience itself, and not the fruits of experience, sweet or bitter as they might be. Of the asceticism that deadens the senses, as of the vulgar profligacy that dulls them, it was to know nothing. But it was to teach man to concentrate himself upon the moments of a life that is itself but a moment.

There are few of us who have not sometimes wakened before dawn, either after one of those dreamless nights that make us almost enamoured of death, or one of those nights of horror and misshapen joy, when through the chambers of the brain sweep phantoms more terrible than reality itself, and instinct with that vivid life that lurks in all grotesques, and that lends to Gothic art its enduring vitality, this art being, one might fancy, especially the art of those whose minds have been troubled with the malady of reverie. Gradually white fingers creep through the curtains, and they appear to tremble. In black fantastic shapes, dumb shadows crawl into the corners of the room, and crouch there. Outside, there is the stirring of birds among the leaves, or the sound of men going forth to their work, or the sigh and sob of the wind coming down from the hills, and wandering round the silent house, as though it feared to wake the sleepers, and yet must needs call forth sleep from her purple cave. Veil after veil of thin dusky gauze is lifted, and by degrees the forms and colours of things are restored to them, and we watch the dawn remaking the world in its antique pattern. The wan mirrors get back their mimic life. The flameless tapers stand where we had left them, and beside them lies the half-cut book that we had been studying, or the wired flower that we had worn at the ball, or the letter that we had been afraid to read, or that we had read too often. Nothing seems to us changed. Out of the unreal shadows of the night comes back the real life that we had known. We have to resume it where we had left off and there steals over us a terrible sense of the necessity for the continuance of energy in the same wearisome round of stereotyped habits, or a wild longing, it may be, that our eyelids might open some morning upon a world that had been re-fashioned anew in the darkness for our pleasure, a world in which things would have fresh shapes and colours, and be changed, or have other secrets, a world in which the past would have little or no place, or survive, at any rate, in no conscious form of obligation or regret, the remembrance even of joy having its bitterness, and the memories of pleasure their pain.

It was the creation of such worlds as these that seemed to Dorian Gray to be the true object, or amongst the true objects, of life; and in his search for sensations that would be at once new and delightful, and possess that element of strangeness that is so essential to romance, he would often adopt certain modes of thought that he knew to be really alien to his nature, abandon himself to their subtle influences, and then, having, as it were, caught their colour and satisfied his intellectual curiosity, leave them with that curious indifference that is not incompatible with a real ardour of temperament, and that indeed, according to certain modern psychologists, is often a condition of it.

It was rumoured of him once that he was about to join the Roman Catholic communion; and certainly the Roman ritual had always a great attraction for him. The daily sacrifice, more awful really than all the sacrifices of the antique world, stirred him as much by its superb rejection of the evidence of the senses as by the primitive simplicity of its elements and the eternal pathos of the human tragedy that it sought to symbolize. He loved to kneel down on the cold marble pavement, and watch the priest, in his stiff flowered dalmatic, slowly and with white hands moving aside the veil of the tabernacle, or raising aloft the jewelled lantern-shaped monstrance with that pallid wafer that at times, one would fain think, is indeed the *"panis cælestis,"* the bread of angels, or, robed in the garments of the Passion of Christ, breaking the Host into the chalice, and smiting his breast for his sins. The fuming censers, that the grave boys, in their lace and scarlet, tossed into the air like great gilt flowers, had their subtle fascination for him. As he passed out, he used to look with wonder at the black confessionals, and long to sit in the dim shadow of one of them and listen to men and women whispering through the worn grating the true story of their lives.

But he never fell into the error of arresting his intellectual development by any formal acceptance of creed or system, or of mistaking, for a house in which to live, an inn that is but suitable for the sojourn of a night, or for a few hours of a night in which there are no stars and the moon is in travail. Mysticism, with its marvellous power of making common things strange to us, and the subtle antinomianism that always seems to accompany it, moved him for a season; and for a season he inclined to the materialistic doctrines of the *Darwinismus* movement in Germany, and found a curious pleasure in tracing the thoughts and passions of men to some pearly cell in the brain, or some white nerve in the body, delighting in the conception of the absolute dependence of the spirit on certain physical conditions, morbid or healthy, normal or diseased. Yet, as has been said of him before, no theory of life seemed to him to be of any importance compared with life itself. He felt keenly conscious of how barren all intellectual speculation is when separated from action and experiment. He knew that the senses, no less than the soul, have their spiritual mysteries to reveal.

And so he would now study perfumes, and the secrets of their manufacture, distilling heavily scented oils, and burning odorous gums from the East. He saw that there was no mood of the mind that had not its counterpart in the sensuous life, and set himself to discover their true relations, wondering what there was in frankincense that made one mystical, and in ambergris that stirred one's passions, and in violets that woke the memory of dead romances, and in musk that troubled the brain, and in champak that stained the imagination; and seeking often to elaborate a real psychology of perfumes, and to estimate the several influences of sweet-smelling roots, and scented pollen-laden flowers, of aromatic balms, and of dark and fragrant woods, of spikenard that sickens, of hovenia that makes men mad, and of aloes that are said to be able to expel melancholy from the soul.

At another time he devoted himself entirely to music, and in a long latticed room, with a vermilion-and-gold ceiling and walls of olive-green lacquer, he used to give curious concerts in which mad gypsies tore wild music from little zithers, or grave yellow-shawled Tunisians plucked at the strained strings of monstrous lutes, while grinning negroes beat monotonously upon copper drums, and, crouching upon scarlet mats, slim turbaned Indians blew through long pipes of reed or brass, and charmed, or feigned to charm, great hooded snakes and horrible horned adders. The harsh intervals and shrill discords of barbaric music stirred him at times when Schubert's grace, and Chopin's beautiful sorrows, and the mighty harmonies of Beethoven himself, fell unheeded on his ear. He collected together from all parts of the world the strangest instruments that could be found, either in the tombs of dead nations or among the few savage tribes that have survived contact with Western civilizations, and loved to touch and try them. He had the mysterious *juruparis* of the Rio Negro Indians, that women are not allowed to look at, and that even youths may not see till they have been subjected to fasting and scourging, and the earthen jars of the Peruvians that have the shrill cries of birds, and flutes of human bones such as Alfonso de Ovalle heard in Chili, and the sonorous green jaspers that are found near Cuzco and give forth a note of singular sweetness. He had painted gourds filled with pebbles that rattled when they were shaken; the long *clarin* of the Mexicans, into which the performer does not blow, but through which he inhales the air; the harsh *ture* of the Amazon tribes, that is sounded by the sentinels who sit all day long in high trees, and can be heard, it is said, at a distance of three leagues; the *teponaztli,* that has two vibrating tongues of wood, has her monsters, things of bestial shape and with an elastic gum obtained from the milky juice of plants; the *yotl* bells of the Aztecs, that are hung in clusters like grapes; and a huge cylindrical drum, covered with the skins of great serpents, like the one that Bernal Díaz saw when he went with Cortés into the Mexican temple, and of whose doleful sound he has left us so vivid a description. The fantastic character of these instruments fascinated him, and he felt a curious delight in the thought that art, like nature, has her monsters, things of bestial shape and with hideous voices. Yet, after some time, he wearied of them, and would sit in his box at the Opera, either alone or with Lord Henry, listening in rapt pleasure to *Tannhäuser,* and seeing in the prelude to that great work of art a presentation of the tragedy of his own soul.

On one occasion he took up the study of jewels, and appeared at a costume ball as Anne de Joyeuse, Admiral of France, in a dress covered with five hundred and sixty pearls. This taste enthralled him for years, and, indeed, may be said never to have left him. He would often spend a whole day settling and resettling in their cases the various stones that he had collected,

such as the olive-green chrysoberyl that turns red by
lamplight, the cymophane with its wirelike line of
silver, the pistachio-coloured peridot, rose-pink and
wine-yellow topazes, carbuncles of fiery scarlet with
tremulous four-rayed stars, flame-red cinnamon-stones,
orange and violet spinels, and amethysts with their
alternate layers of ruby and sapphire. He loved the
red gold of the sunstone, and the moonstone's pearly
whiteness, and the broken rainbow of the milky opal.
He procured from Amsterdam three emeralds of extraordinary size and richness of colour, and had a
turquoise *de la vieille roche* that was the envy of all
the connoisseurs.

He discovered wonderful stories, also, about jewels.
In Alphonso's *Clericalis disciplina* a serpent was mentioned with eyes of real jacinth, and in the romantic
history of Alexander, the Conqueror of Emathia was
said to have found in the vale of Jordan, snakes "with
collars of real emeralds growing on their backs." There
was a gem in the brain of the dragon, Philostratus
told us, and "by the exhibition of golden letters and a
scarlet robe" the monster could be thrown into a magical sleep, and slain. According to the great alchemist,
Pierre de Boniface, the diamond rendered a man invisible, and the agate of·India made him eloquent.
The cornelian appeased anger, and the hyacinth pro-
voked sleep, and the amethyst drove away the fumes of
wine. The garnet cast out demons, and the hydropicus
deprived the moon of her colour. The selenite waxed
and waned with the moon, and the meloceus, that dis-
covers thieves, could be affected only by the blood of
kids. Leonardus Camillus had seen a white stone taken
from the brain of a newly killed toad, that was a certain antidote against poison. The bezoar, that was
found in the heart of the Arabian deer, was a charm

that could cure the plague. In the nests of Arabian birds was the aspilates, that, according to Democritus, kept the wearer from any danger by fire.

The King of Ceylon rode through his city with a large ruby in his hand, at the ceremony of his coronation. The gates of the palace of John the Priest were "made of sardius, with the horn of the horned snake inwrought, so that no man might bring poison within." Over the gable were "two golden apples, in which were two carbuncles," so that the gold might shine by day, and the carbuncles by night. In Lodge's strange romance *A Margarite of America* it was stated that in the chamber of the queen one could behold "all the chaste ladies of the world, inchased out of silver, looking through fair mirrors of chrysolites, carbuncles, sapphires, and greene emeraults." Marco Polo had seen the inhabitants of Zipangu place rose-coloured pearls in the mouths of the dead. A sea monster had been enamoured of the pearl that the diver brought to King Perozes, and had slain the thief, and mourned for seven moons over its loss. When the Huns lured the king into the great pit, he flung it away—Procopius tells the story—nor was it ever found again, though the Emperor Anastasius offered five hundred-weight of gold pieces for it. The King of Malabar had shown to a certain Venetian a rosary of three hundred and four pearls, one for every god that he worshipped.

When the Duke de Valentinois, son of Alexander VI, visited Louis XII of France, his horse was loaded with gold leaves, according to Brantôme, and his cap had double rows of rubies that threw out a great light. Charles of England had ridden in stirrups hung with four hundred and twenty-one diamonds. Richard II had a coat, valued at thirty thousand marks, which was covered with balas rubies. Hall described Henry VIII, on his way to the Tower previous to his coronation, as wearing "a jacket of raised gold, the placard embroidered with diamonds and other rich stones, and a great bauderike about his neck of large balasses." The favourites of James I wore ear-rings of emeralds set in gold filigrane. Edward II gave to Piers Gaveston a suit of red-gold armour studded with jacinths, a collar of gold roses set with turquoise-stones, and a skull-cap *parsemé* with pearls. Henry II wore jewelled gloves reaching to the elbow, and had a hawk-glove sewn with twelve rubies and fifty-two great orients. The ducal hat of Charles the Rash, the last Duke of Burgundy of his race, was hung with pear-shaped pearls, and studded with sapphires.

How exquisite life had once been! How gorgeous in its pomp and decoration! Even to read of the luxury of the dead was wonderful.

Then he turned his attention to embroideries, and to the tapestries that performed the office of frescoes in the chill rooms of the Northern nations of Europe. As he investigated the subject—and he always had an extraordinary faculty of becoming absolutely absorbed for the moment in whatever he took up—he was almost saddened by the reflection of the ruin that time brought on beautiful and wonderful things. He, at any rate, had escapèd that. Summer followed summer, and the yellow jonquils bloomed and died many times, and nights of horror repeated the story of their shame, but he was unchanged. No winter marred his face or stained his flowerlike bloom. How different it was with material things! Where had they passed to? Where was the great crocus-coloured robe, on which the gods fought against the giants, that had been worked by brown girls for the pleasure of Athena? Where, the huge velarium that Nero had stretched across the Colosseum at Rome, that Titan sail of purple on which was represented the starry sky, and Apollo driving a chariot drawn by white gilt-reined steeds? He longed to see the curious table-napkins wrought for the Priest of the Sun, on which were displayed all the dainties and viands that could be wanted for a feast; the mortuary cloth of King Chilperic, with its three hundred golden bees; the fantastic robes that excited the indignation of the Bishop of Pontus, and were figured with "lions, panthers, bears, dogs, forests, rocks, hunters—all, in fact, that a painter can copy from nature"; and the coat that Charles of Orleans once wore, on the sleeves of which were embroidered the verses of a song beginning "*Madame, je suis tout joyeux,*" the musical accompaniment of the words being wrought in gold thread, and each note, of square shape in those days, formed with four pearls. He read of the room that was prepared at the palace at Reims for the use of Queen Joan of Burgundy, and was decorated with "thirteen hundred and twenty-one parrots, made in broidery, and blazoned with the king's arms, and five hundred and sixty-one butterflies, whose wings were similarly ornamented with the arms of the queen, the whole worked in gold." Catherine de' Medici had a mourning-bed made for her of black velvet powdered with crescents and suns. Its curtains were of damask, with leafy wreaths and garlands, figured upon a gold and silver ground, and fringed along the edges with broideries of pearls, and it stood in a room hung with rows of the queen's devices in cut black velvet upon cloth of silver. Louis XIV had gold embroidered caryatides fifteen feet high in his apartment. The state bed of Sobieski, King of Poland, was made of Smyrna gold brocade embroidered in turquoises with verses from the Koran. Its supports were of silver gilt, beautifully chased, and

profusely set with enamelled and jewelled medallions.
It had been taken from the Turkish camp before
Vienna, and the standard of Mohammed had stood
beneath the tremulous gilt of its canopy.

And so, for a whole year, he sought to accumulate
the most exquisite specimens that he could find of
textile and embroidered work, getting the dainty Delhi
muslins, finely wrought with gold-thread palmates, and
stitched over with iridescent beetles' wings; the Dacca
gauzes, that from their transparency are known in the
East as "woven air," and "running water," and "evening dew"; strange figured cloths from Java; elaborate
yellow Chinese hangings; books bound in tawny satins
or fair blue silks, and wrought with fleurs-de-lis, birds
and images; veils of *lacis* worked in Hungary point;
Sicilian brocades, and stiff Spanish velvets; Georgian
work with its gilt coins, and Japanese *Foukousas* with
their green-toned golds and their marvellously plum-
aged birds.

He had a special passion, also, for ecclesiastical
vestments, as indeed he had for everything connected
with the service of the Church. In the long cedar chests
that lined the west gallery of his house he had stored
away many rare and beautiful specimens of what is
really the raiment of the Bride of Christ, who must
wear purple and jewels and fine linen that she may
hide the pallid macerated body that is worn by the
suffering that she seeks for, and wounded by self-
inflicted pain. He possessed a gorgeous cope of crimson silk and gold-thread damask, figured with a repeating pattern of golden pomegranates set in six-petalled
formal blossoms, beyond which on either side was the
pine-apple device wrought in seed-pearls. The orphreys were divided into panels representing scenes from
the life of the Virgin, and the coronation of the Virgin

was figured in coloured silks upon the hood. This was
Italian work of the fifteenth century. Another cope was
of green velvet, embroidered with heart-shaped groups
of acanthus-leaves, from which spread long-stemmed
white blossoms, the details of which were picked out
with silver thread and coloured crystals. The morse
bore a seraph's head in gold-thread raised work. The
orphreys were woven in a diaper of red and gold silk,
and were starred with medallions of many saints and
martyrs, among whom was St. Sebastian. He had
chasubles, also, of amber-coloured silk, and blue silk
and gold brocade, and yellow silk damask and cloth of
gold, figured with representations of the Passion and
Crucifixion of Christ, and embroidered with lions and
peacocks and other emblems; dalmatics of white satin
and pink silk damask, decorated with tulips and dolphins and fleurs-de-lis; altar frontals of crimson velvet
and blue linen; and many corporals, chalice-veils, and
sudaria. In the mystic offices to which such things were
put, there was something that quickened his imagination.

For these treasures, and everything that he collected
in his lovely house, were to be to him means of forgetfulness, modes by which he could escape, for a season,
from the fear that seemed to him at times to be almost
too great to be borne. Upon the walls of the lonely
locked room where he had spent so much of his boyhood, he had hung with his own hands the terrible
portrait whose changing features showed him the real
degradation of his life, and in front of it had draped the
purple-and-gold pall as a curtain. For weeks he would
not go there, would forget the hideous painted thing,
and get back his light heart, his wonderful joyousness,
his passionate absorption in mere existence. Then, suddenly, some night he would creep out of the house,

go down to dreadful places near Blue Gate Fields, and stay there, day after day, until he was driven away. On his return he would sit in front of the picture, sometimes loathing it and himself, but filled, at other times, with that pride of individualism that is half the fascination of sin, and smiling, with secret pleasure, at the misshapen shadow that had to bear the burden that should have been his own.

After a few years he could not endure to be long out of England, and gave up the villa that he had shared at Trouville with Lord Henry, as well as the little white walled-in house at Algiers where they had more than once spent the winter. He hated to be separated from the picture that was such a part of his life, and was also afraid that during his absence someone might gain access to the room, in spite of the elaborate bars that he had caused to be placed upon the door.

He was quite conscious that this would tell them nothing. It was true that the portrait still preserved, under all the foulness and ugliness of the face, its marked likeness to himself; but what could they learn from that? He would laugh at anyone who tried to taunt him. He had not painted it. What was it to him how vile and full of shame it looked? Even if he told them, would they believe it?

Yet he was afraid. Sometimes when he was down at his great house in Nottinghamshire, entertaining the fashionable young men of his own rank who were his chief companions, and astounding the county by the wanton luxury and gorgeous splendour of his mode of life, he would suddenly leave his guests and rush back to town to see that the door had not been tampered with, and that the picture was still there. What if it should be stolen? The mere thought made him cold with horror. Surely the world would know his secret then. Perhaps the world already suspected it.

For, while he fascinated many, there were not a few who distrusted him. He was very nearly blackballed at a West End club of which his birth and social position fully entitled him to become a member, and it was said that on one occasion, when he was brought by a friend into the smoking-room of the Churchill, the Duke of Berwick and another gentleman got up in a marked manner and went out. Curious stories became current about him after he had passed his twenty-fifth year. It was rumoured that he had been seen brawling with foreign sailors in a low den in the distant parts of Whitechapel, and that he consorted with thieves and coiners and knew the mysteries of their trade. His extraordinary absences became notorious, and, when he used to reappear again in society, men would whisper to each other in corners, or pass him with a sneer, or look at him with cold searching eyes, as though they were determined to discover his secret.

Of such insolences and attempted slights he, of course, took no notice, and in the opinion of most people his frank debonair manner, his charming boyish smile, and the infinite grace of that wonderful youth that seemed never to leave him, were in themselves a sufficient answer to the calumnies, for so they termed them, that were circulated about him. It was remarked, however, that some of those who had been most intimate with him appeared, after a time, to shun him. Women who had wildly adored him, and for his sake had braved all social censure and set convention at defiance, were seen to grow pallid with shame or horror if Dorian Gray entered the room.

Yet these whispered scandals only increased in the eyes of many, his strange and dangerous charm. His great wealth was a certain element of security. Society, civilized society at least, is never very ready to believe anything to the detriment of those who are both rich and fascinating. It feels instinctively that manners are of more importance than morals, and, in its opinion, the highest respectability is of much less value than the possession of a good chef. And, after all, it is a very poor consolation to be told that the man who has given one a bad dinner, or poor wine, is irreproachable in his private life. Even the cardinal virtues cannot atone for half-cold entrées, as Lord Henry remarked once, in a discussion on the subject; and there is possibly a good deal to be said for his view. For the canons of good society are, or should be, the same as the canons of art. Form is absolutely essential to it. It should have the dignity of a ceremony, as well as its unreality, and should combine the insincere character of a romantic play with the wit and beauty that makes such plays delightful to us. Is insincerity such a terrible thing? I think not. It is merely a method by which we can multiply our personalities.

Such, at any rate, was Dorian Gray's opinion. He used to wonder at the shallow psychology of those who conceive the Ego in man as a thing simple, permanent, reliable, and of one essence. To him, man was a being with myriad lives and myriad sensations, a complex multiform creature that bore within itself strange legacies of thought and passion, and whose very flesh was tainted with the monstrous maladies of the dead. He loved to stroll through the gaunt cold picture-gallery of his country house and look at the various portraits of those whose blood flowed in his veins. Here was Philip Herbert, described by Francis Osborne, in his *Memoires on the Reigns of Queen Elizabeth and King James,* as one who was "caressed by the Court for his handsome face, which kept him not long company." Was it young Herbert's life that he sometimes led? Had some strange poisonous germ crept from body to body till it had reached his own? Was it some dim sense of that ruined grace that had made him so suddenly, and almost without cause, give utterance, in Basil Hallward's studio, to the mad prayer that had so changed his life? Here, in gold-embroidered red doublet, jewelled surcoat, and gilt-edged ruff and wrist-bands, stood Sir Anthony Sherard, with his silver-and-black armour piled at his feet. What had this man's legacy been? Had the lover of Giovanna of Naples bequeathed him some inheritance of sin and shame? Were his own actions merely the dreams that the dead man had not dared to realize? Here, from the fading canvas, smiled Lady Elizabeth Devereux, in her gauze hood, pearl stomacher, and pink slashed sleeves. A flower was in her right hand, and her left clasped an enamelled collar of white and damask roses. On a table by her side lay a mandolin and an apple. There were large green rosettes upon her little pointed shoes. He knew her life, and the strange stories that were told about her lovers. Had he something of her temperament in him? These oval heavy-lidded eyes seemed to look curiously at him. What of George Willoughby, with his powdered hair and fantastic patches? How evil he looked! The face was saturnine and swarthy, and the sensual lips seemed to be twisted with disdain. Delicate lace ruffles fell over the lean yellow hands that were so overladen with rings. He had been a macaroni of the eighteenth century, and the friend, in his youth, of Lord Ferrars. What of the second Lord Beckenham, the companion of the Prince Regent in his wildest days, and one of the witnesses at the secret marriage with Mrs. Fitzherbert? How proud and handsome he was, with his chestnut

curls and insolent pose! What passions had he bequeathed? The world had looked upon him as infamous. He had led the orgies at Carlton House. The
star of the Garter glittered upon his breast. Beside
him hung the portrait of his wife, a pallid, thin-lipped
woman in black. Her blood, also, stirred within him.
How curious it all seemed! And his mother with her
Lady Hamilton face, and her moist wine-dashed lips—
he knew what he had got from her. He had got from
her his beauty, and his passion for the beauty of others.
She laughed at him in her loose bacchante dress. There
were vine leaves in her hair. The purple spilled from
the cup she was holding. The carnations of the painting had withered, but the eyes were still wonderful in
their depth and brilliancy of colour. They seemed to
follow him wherever he went.

Yet one had ancestors in literature, as well as in one's
own race, nearer perhaps in type and temperament,
many of them, and certainly with an influence of which
one was more absolutely conscious. There were times
when it appeared to Dorian Gray that the whole of
history was merely the record of his own life, not as he
had lived it in act and circumstance, but as his imagination had created it for him, as it had been in his
brain and in his passions. He felt that he had known
them all, those strange terrible figures that had passed
across the stage of the world and made sin so marvellous and evil so full of subtlety. It seemed to him that
in some mysterious way their lives had been his own.

The hero of the wonderful novel that had so influenced his life had himself known this curious fancy.
In the seventh chapter he tells how, crowned with
laurel, lest lightning might strike him, he had sat, as
Tiberius, in a garden at Capri reading the shameful
books of Elephantis, while dwarfs and peacocks strutted

round him and the flute-player mocked the swinger of the censer; and, as Caligula, had caroused with the green-shirted jockeys in their stables, and supped in an ivory manger with a jewel-frontleted horse; and, as Domitian, had wandered through a corridor lined with marble mirrors, looking round with haggard eyes for the reflection of the dagger that was to end his days, and sick with that ennui, that terrible *tædium vitæ*, that comes on those to whom life denies nothing: and had peered through a clear emerald at the red shambles of the Circus, and then, in a litter of pearl and purple drawn by silver-shod mules, been carried through the Street of Pomegranates to a House of Gold, and heard men cry on Nero Cæsar as he passed by; and, as Elagabalus, had painted his face with colours, and plied the distaff among the women, and brought the Moon from Carthage, and given her in mystic marriage to the Sun.

Over and over again Dorian used to read this fantastic chapter, and the two chapters immediately following, in which, as in some curious tapestries or cunningly wrought enamels, were pictured the awful and beautiful forms of those whom vice and blood and weariness had made monstrous or mad: Filippo, Duke of Milan, who slew his wife, and painted her lips with a scarlet poison that her lover might suck death from the dead thing he fondled; Pietro Barbi, the Venetian, known as Paul the Second, who sought in his vanity to assume the title of Formosus, and whose tiara, valued at two hundred thousand florins, was bought at the price of a terrible sin; Gian Maria Visconti, who used hounds to chase living men, and whose murdered body was covered with roses by a harlot who had loved him; the Borgia on his white horse, with fratricide riding beside him, and his mantle stained with the blood of

Perotto; Pietro Riario, the young Cardinal Archbishop of Florence, child and minion of Sixtus IV, whose beauty was equalled only by his debauchery, and who received Leonora of Aragon in a pavilion of white and crimson silk, filled with nymphs and centaurs, and gilded a boy that he might serve at the feast as Ganymede or Hylas; Ezzelin, whose melancholy could be cured only by the spectacle of death, and who had a passion for red blood, as other men have for red wine—the son of the Fiend, as was reported, and one who had cheated his father at dice when gambling with him for his own soul: Giambattista Cibo, who in mockery took the name of Innocent, and into whose torpid veins the blood of three lads was infused by a Jewish doctor; Sigismondo Malatesta, the lover of Isotta, and the lord of Rimini, whose effigy was burned at Rome as the enemy of God and man, who strangled Polyssena with a napkin, and gave poison to Ginevra d'Este in a cup of emerald, and in honour of a shameful passion built a pagan church for Christian worship; Charles VI, who had so wildly adored his brother's wife that a leper had warned him of the insanity that was coming on him, and who, when his brain had sickened and grown strange, could only be soothed by Saracen cards painted with the images of love and death and madness; and, in his trimmed jerkin and jewelled cap and acanthus-like curls, Grifonetto Baglioni, who slew Astorre with his bride, and Simonetto with his page, and whose comeliness was such that, as he lay dying in the yellow piazza of Perugia, those who had hated him could not choose but weep, and Atalanta, who had cursed him, blessed him.

There was a horrible fascination in them all. He saw them at night, and they troubled his imagination in the day. The Renaissance knew of strange manners of poisoning—poisoning by a helmet and a lighted torch, by an embroidered glove and a jewelled fan, by a gilded pomander and by an amber chain. Dorian Gray had been poisoned by a book. There were moments when he looked on evil simply as a mode through which he could realize his conception of the beautiful.

XII

IT WAS on the ninth of November, the eve of his own thirty-eighth birthday as he often remembered afterwards.

He was walking home about eleven o'clock from Lord Henry's, where he had been dining, and was wrapped in heavy furs, as the night was cold and foggy. At the corner of Grosvenor Square and South Audley Street a man passed him in the mist, walking very fast, and with the collar of his grey ulster turned up. He had a bag in his hand. Dorian recognized him. It was Basil Hallward. A strange sense of fear, for which he could not account, came over him. He made no sign of recognition, and went on quickly, in the direction of his own house.

But Hallward had seen him. Dorian heard him first stopping on the pavement and then hurrying after him. In a few moments his hand was on his arm.

"Dorian! What an extraordinary piece of luck! I have been waiting for you in your library ever since nine o'clock. Finally I took pity on your tired servant, and told him to go to bed, as he let me out. I am off to Paris by the midnight train, and I particularly wanted to see you before I left. I thought it was you, or rather your fur coat, as you passed me. But I wasn't quite sure. Didn't you recognize me?"

"In this fog, my dear Basil? Why, I can't even recognize Grosvenor Square. I believe my house is somewhere about here, but I don't feel at all certain about it. I am sorry you are going away, as I have not seen you for ages. But I suppose you will be back soon?"

"No: I am going to be out of England for six months. I intend to take a studio in Paris, and shut myself up till I have finished a great picture I have in my head. However, it wasn't about myself I wanted to talk. Here we are at your door. Let me come in for a moment. I have something to say to you."

"I shall be charmed. But won't you miss your train?" said Dorian Gray, languidly, as he passed up the steps and opened the door with his latch-key.

The lamplight struggled out through the fog, and Hallward looked at his watch. "I have heaps of time," he answered. "The train doesn't go till twelve-fifteen, and it is only just eleven. In fact, I was on my way to the club to look for you, when I met you. You see, I shan't have any delay about luggage, as I have sent on my heavy things. All I have with me is in this bag, and I can easily get to Victoria in twenty minutes."

Dorian looked at him and smiled. "What a way for a fashionable painter to travel! A Gladstone bag, and an ulster! Come in, or the fog will get into the house. And mind you don't talk about anything serious. Nothing is serious nowadays. At least nothing should be."

Hallward shook his head, as he entered, and followed Dorian into the library. There was a bright wood fire blazing in the large open hearth. The lamps were lit, and an open Dutch silver spirit-case stood, with some siphons of soda-water and large cut-glass tumblers, on a little marqueterie table.

"You see your servant made me quite at home, Dorian. He gave me everything I wanted, including your best gold-tipped cigarettes. He is a most hospitable creature. I like him much better than the Frenchman you used to have. What has become of the Frenchman, by the bye?"

Dorian shrugged his shoulders. "I believe he married Lady Radley's maid, and has established her in Paris as an English dressmaker. *Anglomanie* is very fashionable over there now, I hear. It seems silly of the French, doesn't it? But—do you know?—he was not at all a bad servant. I never liked him, but I had nothing to complain about. One often imagines things that are quite absurd. He was really very devoted to me, and seemed quite sorry when he went away. Have another brandy-and-soda? Or would you like hock-and-selzer? I always take hock-and-selzer myself. There is sure to be some in the next room."

"Thanks, I won't have anything more," said the painter, taking his cap and coat off, and throwing them on the bag that he had placed in the corner. "And now, my dear fellow, I want to speak to you seriously. Don't frown like that. You make it so much more difficult for me."

"What is it all about?" cried Dorian, in his petulant way, flinging himself down on the sofa. "I hope it is not about myself. I am tired of myself tonight. I should like to be somebody else."

"It is about yourself," answered Hallward, in his grave, deep voice, "and I must say it to you. I shall only keep you half an hour."

Dorian sighed, and lit a cigarette. "Half an hour!" he murmured.

"It is not much to ask of you, Dorian, and it is entirely for your own sake that I am speaking. I think it right that you should know that the most dreadful things are being said against you in London."

"I don't wish to know anything about them. I love scandals about other people, but scandals about myself don't interest me. They have not got the charm of novelty."

"They must interest you, Dorian. Every gentleman is interested in his good name. You don't want people to talk of you as something vile and degraded. Of course you have your position, and your wealth, and all that kind of thing. But position and wealth are not everything. Mind you, I don't believe these rumours at all. At least, I can't believe them when I see you. Sin is a thing that writes itself across a man's face. It cannot be concealed. People talk sometimes of secret vices. There are no such things. If a wretched man has a vice, it shows itself in the lines of his mouth, the droop of his eyelids, the moulding of his hands even. Somebody—I won't mention his name, but you know him—came to me last year to have his portrait done. I had never seen him before, and had never heard anything about him at the time, though I have heard a good deal since. He offered an extravagant price. I refused him. There was something in the shape of his fingers that I hated. I know now that I was quite right in what I fancied about him. His life is dreadful. But you, Dorian, with your pure, bright, innocent face, and your marvellous untroubled youth—I can't believe anything against you. And yet I see you very seldom, and you never come down to the studio now, and when I am away from you, and I hear all these hideous things that people are whispering about you, I don't know what to say. Why is it, Dorian, that a man like the Duke of Berwick leaves the room of a club when you enter it? Why is it that so many gentlemen in London will neither go to your house nor invite

you to theirs? You used to be a friend of Lord Staveley.
I met him at dinner last week. Your name happened to
come up in conversation, in connection with the minia-
tures you have lent to the exhibition at the Dudley.
Staveley curled his lip, and said that you might have
the most artistic tastes, but that you were a man whom
no pure-minded girl should be allowed to know, and
whom no chaste woman should sit in the same room
with. I reminded him that I was a friend of yours, and
asked him what he meant. He told me. He told me right
out before everybody. It was horrible! Why is your
friendship so fatal to young men? There was that
wretched boy in the Guards who committed suicide.
You were his great friend. There was Sir Henry Ashton,
who had to leave England, with a tarnished name. You
and he were inseparable. What about Adrian Singleton,
and his dreadful end? What about Lord Kent's only
son, and his career? I met his father yesterday in St.
James's Street. He seemed broken with shame and
sorrow. What about the young Duke of Perth? What
sort of life has he got now? What gentleman would associate with him?"

"Stop, Basil. You are talking about things of which
you know nothing," said Dorian Gray, biting his lip,
and with a note of infinite contempt in his voice. "You
ask me why Berwick leaves a room when I enter it.
It is because I know everything about his life, not because he knows anything about mine. With such blood
as he has in his veins, how could his record be clean?
You ask me about Henry Ashton and young Perth. Did I
teach the one his vices, and the other his debauchery?
If Kent's silly son takes his wife from the streets, what
is that to me? If Adrian Singleton writes his friend's
name across a bill, am I his keeper? I know how people
chatter in England. The middle classes air their moral

prejudices over their gross dinner-tables, and whisper about what they call the profligacies of their betters in order to try and pretend that they are in smart society, and on intimate terms with the people they slander. In this country it is enough for a man to have distinction and brains for every common tongue to wag against him. And what sort of lives do these people, who pose as being moral, lead themselves? My dear fellow, you forget that we are in the native land of the hypocrite."

"Dorian," cried Hallward, "that is not the question. England is bad enough I know, and English society is all wrong. That is the reason why I want you to be fine. You have not been fine. One has a right to judge of a man by the effect he has over his friends. Yours seem to lose all sense of honour, of goodness, of purity. You have filled them with a madness for pleasure. They have gone down into the depths. You led them there. Yes, you led them there, and yet you can smile, as you are smiling now. And there is worse behind. I know you and Harry are inseparable. Surely for that reason, if for none other, you should not have made his sister's name a by-word."

"Take care, Basil. You go too far."

"I must speak, and you must listen. You shall listen. When you met Lady Gwendolen, not a breath of scandal had ever touched her. Is there a single decent woman in London now who would drive with her in the Park? Why, even her children are not allowed to live with her. Then there are other stories—stories that you have been seen creeping at dawn out of dreadful houses and slinking in disguise into the foulest dens in London. Are they true? Can they be true? When I first heard them, I laughed. I hear them now, and they make me shudder. What about your country house, and the life that is led there? Dorian, you don't know what is said about you. I won't tell you that I don't want to preach to you. I remember Harry saying once that every man who turned himself into an amateur curate for the moment always began by saying that, and then proceeded to break his word. I do want to preach to you. I want you to lead such a life as will make the world respect you. I want you to have a clean name and a fair record. I want you to get rid of the dreadful people you associate with. Don't shrug your shoulders like that. Don't be so indifferent. You have a wonderful influence. Let it be for good, not for evil. They say that you corrupt everyone with whom you become intimate, and that it is quite sufficient for you to enter a house, for shame of some kind to follow after. I don't know whether it is so or not. How should I know? But it is said of you. I am told things that it seems impossible to doubt. Lord Gloucester was one of my greatest friends at Oxford. He showed me a letter that his wife had written to him when she was dying alone in her villa at Mentone. Your name was implicated in the most terrible confession I ever read. I told him that it was absurd—that I knew you thoroughly, and that you were incapable of anything of the kind. Know you? I wonder do I know you? Before I could answer that, I should have to see your soul."

"To see my soul!" muttered Dorian Gray, starting up from the sofa and turning almost white from fear.

"Yes," answered Hallward, gravely, and with deeptoned sorrow in his voice—"to see your soul. But only God can do that."

A bitter laugh of mockery broke from the lips of the younger man. "You shall see it yourself, tonight!" he cried, seizing a lamp from the table. "Come: it is your own handiwork. Why shouldn't you look at it? You can tell the world all about it afterwards, if you choose.

Nobody would believe you. If they did believe you, they would like me all the better for it. I know the age better than you do, though you will prate about it so tediously. Come, I tell you. You have chattered enough about corruption. Now you shall look on it face to face."

There was the madness of pride in every word he uttered. He stamped his foot upon the ground in his boyish insolent manner. He felt a terrible joy at the thought that someone else was to share his secret, and that the man who had painted the portrait that was the origin of all his shame was to be burdened for the rest of his life with the hideous memory of what he had done.

"Yes," he continued, coming closer to him, and looking steadfastly into his stern eyes, "I shall show you my soul. You shall see the thing that you fancy only God can see."

Hallward started back. "This is blasphemy, Dorian!" he cried. "You must not say things like that. They are horrible, and they don't mean anything."

"You think so?" he laughed again.

"I know so. As for what I said to you tonight, I said it for your good. You know I have been always a staunch friend to you."

"Don't touch me. Finish what you have to say."

A twisted flash of pain shot across the painter's face. He paused for a moment, and a wild feeling of pity came over him. After all, what right had he to pry into the life of Dorian Gray? If he had done a tithe of what was rumoured about him, how much he must have suffered! Then he straightened himself up, and walked over to the fireplace, and stood there, looking at the burning logs with their frost-like ashes and their throbbing cores of flame.

"I am waiting, Basil," said the young man, in a hard, clear voice.

He turned round. "What I have to say is this," he cried. "You must give me some answer to these horrible charges that are made against you. If you tell me that they are absolutely untrue from beginning to end, I shall believe you. Deny them, Dorian, deny them! Can't you see what I am going through? My God! don't tell me that you are bad, and corrupt, and shameful."

Dorian Gray smiled. There was a curl of contempt in his lips. "Come upstairs, Basil," he said, quietly. "I keep a diary of my life from day to day, and it never leaves the room in which it is written. I shall show it to you if you come with me."

"I shall come with you, Dorian, if you wish it. I see I have missed my train. That makes no matter. I can go tomorrow. But don't ask me to read anything to-night. All I want is a plain answer to my question."

"That shall be given to you upstairs. I could not give it here. You will not have to read long."

XIII

HE PASSED out of the room, and began the ascent, Basil Hallward following close behind. They walked softly, as men do instinctively at night. The lamp cast fantastic shadows on the wall and staircase. A rising wind made some of the windows rattle.

When they reached the top landing, Dorian set the lamp down on the floor, and taking out the key turned it in the lock. "You insist on knowing, Basil?" he asked, in a low voice.

"Yes."

"I am delighted," he answered, smiling. Then he added, somewhat harshly; "You are the one man in the world who is entitled to know everything about me. You have had more to do with my life than you think": and, taking up the lamp, he opened the door and went in. A cold current of air passed them, and the light shot up for a moment in a flame of murky orange. He shuddered. "Shut the door behind you," he whispered, as he placed the lamp on the table.

Hallward glanced around him, with a puzzled expression. The room looked as if it had not been lived in for years. A faded Flemish tapestry, a curtained picture, an old Italian *cassone*, and an almost empty bookcase—that was all that it seemed to contain, besides a chair and a table. As Dorian Gray was lighting a half-burned candle that was standing on the mantelshelf, he saw that the whole place was covered with dust, and that the carpet was in holes. A mouse ran scuffling behind the wainscoting. There was a damp odour of mildew.

"So you think that it is only God who sees the soul, Basil? Draw that curtain back, and you will see mine."

The voice that spoke was cold and cruel. "You are mad, Dorian, or playing a part," muttered Hallward, frowning.

"You won't? Then I must do it myself," said the young man; and he tore the curtain from its rod, and flung it on the ground.

An exclamation of horror broke from the painter's lips as he saw in the dim light the hideous face on the canvas grinning at him. There was something in its expression that filled him with disgust and loathing. Good heavens! it was Dorian Gray's own face that he was looking at! The horror, whatever it was, had not yet entirely spoiled that marvellous beauty. There was still some gold in the thinning hair and some scarlet on

the sensual mouth. The sodden eyes had kept some
thing of the loveliness of their blue, the noble curves
had not yet completely passed away from chiselled nostrils and from plastic throat. Yes, it was Dorian himself.
But who had done it? He seemed to recognize his own
brush-work, and the frame was his own design. The idea
was monstrous, yet he felt afraid. He seized the lighted
candle, and held it to the picture. In the left-hand
corner was his own name, traced in long letters of
bright vermilion.

It was some foul parody, some infamous, ignoble
satire. He had never done that. Still, it was his own
picture. He knew it, and he felt as if his blood had
changed in a moment from fire to sluggish ice. His own
picture! What did it mean? Why had it altered? He
turned, and looked at Dorian Gray with the eyes of a
sick man. His mouth twitched, and his parched tongue
seemed unable to articulate. He passed his hand across
his forehead. It was dank with clammy sweat.

The young man was leaning against the mantelshelf,
watching him with that strange expression that one sees
on the faces of those who are absorbed in a play when
some great artist is acting. There was neither real
sorrow in it nor real joy. There was simply the passion
of the spectator, with perhaps a flicker of triumph in
his eyes. He had taken the flower out of his coat, and
was smelling it, or pretending to do so.

"What does this mean?" cried Hallward, at last. His
own voice sounded shrill and curious in his ears.

"Years ago, when I was a boy," said Dorian Gray,
crushing the flower in his hand, "you met me, flattered
me, and taught me to be vain of my good looks. One
day you introduced me to a friend of yours, who explained to me the wonder of youth, and you finished a
portrait of me that revealed to me the wonder of beauty.

In a mad moment, that, even now, I don't know whether I regret or not, I made a wish, perhaps you would call it a prayer. . . ."

"I remember it! Oh, how well I remember it! No! the thing is impossible. The room is damp. Mildew has got into the canvas. The paints I used had some wretched mineral poison in them. I tell you the thing is impossible."

"Ah, what is impossible?" murmured the young man, going over to the window, and leaning his forehead against the cold, mist-stained glass.

"You told me you had destroyed it."

"I was wrong. It has destroyed me."

"I don't believe it is my picture."

"Can't you see your ideal in it?" said Dorian, bitterly.

"My ideal, as you call it. . . ."

"As you called it."

"There was nothing evil in it, nothing shameful. You were to me such an ideal as I shall never meet again. This is the face of a satyr."

"It is the face of my soul."

"Christ! what a thing I must have worshipped! It has the eyes of a devil."

"Each of us has heaven and hell in him, Basil," cried Dorian, with a wild gesture of despair.

Hallward turned again to the portrait, and gazed at it. "My God! if it is true," he exclaimed, "and this is what you have done with your life, why, you must be worse even than those who talk against you fancy you to be!" He held the light up again to the canvas, and examined it. The surface seemed to be quite undisturbed, and as he had left it. It was from within, apparently, that the foulness and horror had come. Through some strange quickening of inner life the leprosies of sin were slowly eating the thing away. The rotting of a corpse in a watery grave was not so fearful.

His hand shook, and the candle fell from its socket on the floor, and lay there sputtering. He placed his foot on it and put it out. Then he flung himself into the rickety chair that was standing by the table and buried his face in his hands.

"Good God, Dorian, what a lesson! What an awful lesson!" There was no answer, but he could hear the young man sobbing at the window. "Pray, Dorian, pray," he murmured. "What is it that one was taught to say in one's boyhood? 'Lead us not into temptation. Forgive us our sins. Wash away our iniquities.' Let us say that together. The prayer of your pride has been answered. The prayer of your repentance will be answered also. I worshipped you too much. I am punished for it. You worshipped yourself too much. We are both punished."

Dorian Gray turned slowly around, and looked at him with tear-dimmed eyes. "It is too late, Basil," he faltered.

"It is never too late, Dorian. Let us kneel down and try if we cannot remember a prayer. Isn't there a verse somewhere, 'Though your sins be as scarlet, yet I will make them as white as snow'?"

"Those words mean nothing to me now."

"Hush! don't say that. You have done enough evil in your life. My God! Don't you see that accursed thing leering at us?"

Dorian Gray glanced at the picture, and suddenly an uncontrollable feeling of hatred for Basil Hallward came over him, as though it had been suggested to him by the image on the canvas, whispered into his ear by those grinning lips. The mad passions of a hunted animal stirred within him, and he loathed the man who was seated at the table, more than in his whole life he had ever loathed anything. He glanced wildly around. Something glimmered on the top of the painted chest that faced him. His eye fell on it. He knew what it was. It was a knife that he had brought up, some days before, to cut a piece of cord, and had forgotten to take away with him. He moved slowly towards it, passing Hallward as he did so. As soon as he got behind him, he seized it, and turned round. Hallward stirred in his chair as if he was going to rise. He rushed at him, and dug the knife into the great vein that is behind the ear, crushing the man's head down on the table, and stabbing again and again.

There was a stifled groan, and the horrible sound of someone choking with blood. Three times the outstretched arms shot up convulsively, waving grotesque stiff-fingered hands in the air. He stabbed him twice more, but the man did not move. Something began to trickle on the floor. He waited for a moment, still pressing the head down. Then he threw the knife on the table, and listened.

He could hear nothing, but the drip, drip on the threadbare carpet. He opened the door and went out on the landing. The house was absolutely quiet. No one was about. For a few seconds he stood bending over the balustrade, and peering down into the black seething well of darkness. Then he took out the key and returned to the room, locking himself in as he did so.

The thing was still seated in the chair, straining over the table with bowed head, and humped back, and long fantastic arms. Had it not been for the red jagged tear in the neck, and the clotted black pool that was slowly widening on the table, one would have said that the man was simply asleep.

How quickly it had all been done! He felt strangely

calm, and, walking over to the window, opened it, and stepped out on the balcony. The wind had blown the fog away, and the sky was like a monstrous peacock's tail, starred with myriads of golden eyes. He looked down, and saw the policeman going his rounds and flashing the long beam of his lantern on the doors of the silent houses. The crimson spot of a prowling hansom gleamed at the corner, and then vanished. A woman in a fluttering shawl was creeping slowly by the railings, staggering as she went. Now and then she stopped, and peered back. Once, she began to sing in a hoarse voice. The policeman strolled over and said something to her. She stumbled away, laughing. A bitter blast swept across the Square. The gas lamps flickered, and became blue, and the leafless trees shook their black iron branches to and fro. He shivered, and went back, closing the window behind him.

Having reached the door, he turned the key, and opened it. He did not even glance at the murdered man. He felt that the secret of the whole thing was not to realize the situation. The friend who had painted the fatal portrait to which all his misery had been due, had gone out of his life. That was enough.

Then he remembered the lamp. It was a rather curious one of Moorish workmanship, made of dull silver inlaid with arabesques of burnished steel, and studded with coarse turquoises. Perhaps it might be missed by his servant, and questions would be asked. He hesitated for a moment, then he turned back and took it from the table. He could not help seeing the dead thing. How still it was! How horribly white the long hands looked! It was like a dreadful wax image.

Having locked the door behind him, he crept quietly downstairs. The woodwork creaked, and seemed to cry out as if in pain. He stopped several times, and waited. No, everything was still. It was merely the sound of his own footsteps.

When he reached the library, he saw the bag and coat in the corner. They must be hidden away somewhere. He unlocked a secret press that was in the wainscoting, a press in which he kept his own curious disguises, and put them into it. He could easily burn them afterwards. Then he pulled out his watch. It was twenty minutes to two.

He sat down and began to think. Every year—every month, almost—men were strangled in England for what he had done. There had been a madness of murder in the air. Some red star had come too close to the earth. . . . And yet what evidence was there against him? Basil Hallward had left the house at eleven. No one had seen him come in again. Most of the servants were at Selby Royal. His valet had gone to bed. . . . Paris? Yes. It was to Paris that Basil had gone, and by the midnight train, as he had intended. With his curious reserved habits, it would be months before any suspicions would be aroused. Months! Everything could be destroyed long before then.

A sudden thought struck him. He put on his fur coat and hat, and went out into the hall. There he paused, hearing the slow, heavy tread of the policeman on the pavement outside, and seeing the flash of the bull's-eye reflected in the window. He waited, and held his breath.

After a few moments he drew back the latch, and slipped out, shutting the door very gently behind him. Then he began ringing the bell. In about five minutes his valet appeared, half dressed, and looking very drowsy.

"I am sorry to have had to wake you up, Francis,"

he said, stepping in; "but I had forgotten my latch-key. What time is it?"

"Ten minutes past two, sir," answered the man, looking at the clock and blinking.

"Ten minutes past two? How horribly late! You must wake me at nine tomorrow. I have some work to do."

"All right, sir."

"Did anyone call this evening?"

"Mr. Hallward, sir. He stayed here till eleven, and then he went away to catch his train."

"Oh! I am sorry I didn't see him. Did he leave any message?"

"No, sir, except that he would write to you from Paris, if he did not find you at the club."

"That will do, Francis. Don't forget to call me at nine tomorrow."

"No, sir."

The man shambled down the passage in his slippers.

Dorian Gray threw his hat and coat upon the table, and passed into the library. For a quarter of an hour he walked up and down the room biting his lip, and thinking. Then he took down the Blue book from one of the shelves, and began to turn over the leaves. "Alan Campbell, 152 Hertford Street, Mayfair." Yes; that was the man he wanted.

XIV

AT NINE o'clock the next morning his servant came in with a cup of chocolate on a tray, and opened the shutters. Dorian was sleeping quite peacefully, lying on his right side, with one hand underneath his cheek. He looked like a boy who had been tired out with play, or study.

The man had to touch him twice on the shoulder before he woke, and as he opened his eyes a faint smile passed across his lips, as though he had been lost in some delightful dream. Yet he had not dreamed at all. His night had been untroubled by any images of pleasure or of pain. But youth smiles without any reason. It is one of its chiefest charms.

He turned round, and, leaning upon his elbow, began to sip his chocolate. The mellow November sun came streaming into the room. The sky was bright, and there was a genial warmth in the air. It was almost like a morning in May.

Gradually the events of the preceding night crept with silent blood-stained feet into his brain and reconstructed themselves there with terrible distinctness. He winced at the memory of all that he had suffered, and for a moment the same curious feeling of loathing for Basil Hallward, that had made him kill him as he sat in the chair, came back to him, and he grew cold with passion. The dead man was still sitting there, too, and in the sunlight now. How horrible that was! Such hideous things were for the darkness, not for the day.

He felt that if he brooded on what he had gone through he would sicken or grow mad. There were sins whose fascination was more in the memory than in the doing of them, strange triumphs that gratified the pride more than the passions, and gave to the intellect a quickened sense of joy, greater than any joy they brought, or could ever bring, to the senses. But this was not one of them. It was a thing to be driven out of the mind, to be drugged with poppies, to be strangled lest it might strangle one itself.

When the half-hour struck, he passed his hand across

his forehead, and then got up hastily, and dressed himself with even more than his usual care, giving a good deal of attention to the choice of his necktie and scarf-pin, and changing his rings more than once. He spent a long time also over breakfast, tasting the various dishes, talking to his valet about some new liveries that he was thinking of getting made for the servants at Selby, and going through his correspondence. At some of the letters he smiled. Three of them bored him. One he read several times over, and then tore up with a slight look of annoyance in his face. "That awful thing, a woman's memory!" as Lord Henry had once said.

After he had drunk his cup of black coffee, he wiped his lips slowly with a napkin, motioned to his servant to wait, and going over to the table sat down and wrote two letters. One he put in his pocket, the other he handed to the valet.

"Take this round to 152 Hertford Street, Francis, and if Mr. Campbell is out of town, get his address."

As soon as he was alone, he lit a cigarette, and began sketching upon a piece of paper, drawing first flowers, and bits of architecture, and then human faces. Suddenly he remarked that every face that he drew seemed to have a fantastic likeness to Basil Hallward. He frowned, and, getting up, went over to the bookcase and took out a volume at hazard. He was determined that he would not think about what had happened until it became absolutely necessary that he should do so.

When he had stretched himself on the sofa, he looked at the title-page of the book. It was Gautier's *Emaux et Camées*, Charpentier's Japanese-paper edition, with the Jacquemart etching. The binding was of citron-green leather, with a design of gilt trellis-work and dotted pomegranates. It had been given to him by Adrian

Singleton. As he turned over the pages his eye fell on the poem about the hand of Lacenaire, the cold yellow hand *"du supplice encore mal lavée,"* with its downy red hairs and its *"doigts de faune."* He glanced at his own white taper fingers, shuddering slightly in spite of himself, and passed on, till he came to those lovely stanzas upon Venice:

> *Sur une gamme chromatique,*
> *Le sein de perles ruisselant,*
> *La Vénus de l'Adriatique*
> *Sort de l'eau son corps rose et blanc.*

> *Les dômes, sur l'azur des ondes*
> *Suivant la phrase au pur contour,*
> *S'enflent comme des gorges rondes*
> *Que soulève un soupir d'amour.*

> *L'esquif aborde et me dépose,*
> *Jetant son amarre au pilier,*
> *Devant une façade rose,*
> *Sur le marbre d'un escalier.*

How exquisite they were! As one read them, one seemed to be floating down the green waterways of the pink and pearl city, seated in a black gondola with silver prow and trailing curtains. The mere lines looked to him like those straight lines of turquoise-blue that follow one as one pushes out to the Lido. The sudden flashes of colour reminded him of the gleam of the opal-and-iris-throated birds that flutter round the tall honey-combed Campanile, or stalk, with such stately grace, through the dim, dust-stained arcades. Leaning back with half-closed eyes, he kept saying over and over to himself:—

> *Devant une façade rose,*
> *Sur le marbre d'un escalier.*

The whole of Venice was in those two lines. He remembered the autumn that he had passed there, and a wonderful love that had stirred him to mad, delightful follies. There was romance in every place. But Venice, like Oxford, had kept the background for romance, and, to the true romantic, background was everything, or almost everything. Basil had been with him part of the time, and had gone wild over Tintoretto. Poor Basil! what a horrible way for a man to die!

He sighed, and took up the volume again, and tried to forget. He read of the swallows that fly in and out of the little café at Smyrna where the Hadjis sit counting their amber beads and the turbaned merchants smoke their long tasselled pipes and talk gravely to each other; he read of the Obelisk in the Place de la Concorde that weeps tears of granite in its lonely sunless exile, and longs to be back by the hot lotus-covered Nile, where there are Sphinxes, and rose-red ibises, and white vultures with gilded claws, and crocodiles, with small beryl eyes, that crawl over the green steaming mud; he began to brood over those verses which, drawing music from kiss-stained marble, tell of that curious statue that Gautier compares to a contralto voice, the *"monstre charmant"* that couches in the porphyry-room of the Louvre. But after a time the book fell from his hand. He grew nervous, and a horrible fit of terror came over him. What if Alan Campbell should be out of England? Days would elapse before he could come back. Perhaps he might refuse to come. What could he do then? Every moment was of vital importance.

They had been great friends once, five years before—almost inseparable, indeed. Then the intimacy had come suddenly to an end. When they met in society now, it was only Dorian Gray who smiled; Alan Campbell never did.

He was an extremely clever young man, though he had no real appreciation of the visible arts, and whatever little sense of the beauty of poetry he possessed he had gained entirely from Dorian. His dominant intellectual passion was for science. At Cambridge he had spent a great deal of his time working in the Laboratory, and had taken a good class in the Natural Science Tripos of his year. Indeed, he was still devoted to the study of chemistry, and had a laboratory of his own, in which he used to shut himself up all day long, greatly to the annoyance of his mother, who had set her heart on his standing for Parliament and had a vague idea that a chemist was a person who made up prescriptions. He was an excellent musician, however, as well, and played both the violin and the piano better than most amateurs. In fact, it was music that had first brought him and Dorian Gray together—music and that indefinable attraction that Dorian seemed to be able to exercise whenever he wished, and indeed exercised often without being conscious of it. They had met at Lady Berkshire's the night that Rubinstein played there, and after that used to be always seen together at the Opera, and wherever good music was going on. For eighteen months their intimacy lasted. Campbell was always either at Selby Royal or in Grosvenor Square. To him, as to many others, Dorian Gray was the type of everything that is wonderful and fascinating in life. Whether or not a quarrel had taken place between them no one ever knew. But suddenly people remarked that they scarcely spoke when they met, and that Campbell seemed always to go away early from any party at which Dorian Gray was present. He had changed, too—was strangely melancholy at times, appeared almost to dislike hearing music, and would never himself play, giving as his excuse, when he was called upon, that he was so absorbed in science that he had no time left in which to practise. And this was certainly true. Every day he seemed to become more interested in biology, and his name appeared once or twice in some of the scientific reviews, in connection with certain curious experiments.

This was the man Dorian Gray was waiting for. Every second he kept glancing at the clock. As the minutes went by he became horribly agitated. At last he got up, and began to pace up and down the room, looking like a beautiful caged thing. He took long stealthy strides. His hands were curiously cold.

The suspense became unbearable. Time seemed to him to be crawling with feet of lead, while he by monstrous winds was being swept towards the jagged edge of some black cleft of precipice. He knew what was waiting for him there; saw it indeed, and, shuddering, crushed with dank hands his burning lids as though he would have robbed the very brain of sight, and driven the eyeballs back into their cave. It was useless. The brain had its own food on which it battened, and the imagination, made grotesque by terror, twisted and distorted as a living thing by pain, danced like some foul puppet on a stand, and grinned through moving masks. Then, suddenly, time stopped for him. Yes; that blind, slow-breathing thing crawled no more, and horrible thoughts, time being dead, raced nimbly on in front, and dragged a hideous future from its grave, and showed it to him. He stared at it. Its very horror made him stone.

At last the door opened, and his servant entered. He turned glazed eyes upon him.

"Mr. Campbell, sir," said the man.

A sigh of relief broke from his parched lips, and the colour came back to his cheeks.

"Ask him to come in at once, Francis." He felt that he was himself again. His mood of cowardice had passed away.

The man bowed, and retired. In a few moments Alan Campbell walked in, looking very stern and rather pale, his pallor being intensified by his coal-black hair and dark eyebrows.

"Alan! this is kind of you. I thank you for coming."

"I had intended never to enter your house again, Gray. But you said it was a matter of life and death." His voice was hard and cold. He spoke with slow deliberation. There was a look of contempt in the steady searching gaze that he turned on Dorian. He kept his hands in the pockets of his Astrakhan coat, and seemed not to have noticed the gesture with which he had been greeted.

"Yes; it is a matter of life and death, Alan, and to more than one person. Sit down."

Campbell took a chair by the table, and Dorian sat opposite to him. The two men's eyes met. In Dorian's there was infinite pity. He knew that what he was going to do was dreadful.

After a strained moment of silence, he leaned across and said, very quietly, but watching the effect of each word upon the face of him he had sent for, "Alan, in a locked room at the top of this house, a room to which nobody but myself has access, a dead man is seated at a table. He has been dead ten hours now. Don't stir, and don't look at me like that. Who the man is, why he died, how he died, are matters that do not concern you. What you have to do is this—"

"Stop, Gray. I don't want to know anything further. Whether what you have told me is true or not true, doesn't concern me. I entirely decline to be mixed up in your life. Keep your horrible secrets to yourself. They don't interest me any more."

"Alan, they will have to interest you. This one will have to interest you. I am awfully sorry for you, Alan. But I can't help myself. You are the one man who is able to save me. I am forced to bring you into the matter. I have no option. Alan, you are scientific. You know about chemistry, and things of that kind. You have made experiments. What you have got to do is to destroy the thing that is upstairs—to destroy it so that not a vestige of it will be left. Nobody saw this person come into the house. Indeed, at the present moment he is supposed to be in Paris. He will not be missed for months. When he is missed, there must be no trace of him found here. You, Alan, you must change him, and everything that belongs to him, into a handful of ashes that I may scatter in the air."

"You are mad, Dorian."

"Ah! I was waiting for you to call me Dorian."

"You are mad, I tell you—mad to imagine that I would raise a finger to help you, mad to make this monstrous confession. I will have nothing to do with this matter, whatever it is. Do you think I am going to peril my reputation for you? What is it to me what devil's work you are up to?"

"It was suicide, Alan."

"I am glad of that. But who drove him to it? You, I should fancy."

"Do you still refuse to do this for me?"

"Of course I refuse. I will have absolutely nothing to do with it. I don't care what shame comes on you. You deserve it all. I should not be sorry to see you disgraced, publicly disgraced. How dare you ask me, of all men in the world, to mix myself up in this horror?

I should have thought you knew more about people's characters. Your friend Lord Henry Wotton can't have taught you much about psychology, whatever else he has taught you. Nothing will induce me to stir a step to help you. You have come to the wrong man. Go to some of your friends. Don't come to me."

"Alan, it was murder. I killed him. You don't know what he had made me suffer. Whatever my life is, he had more to do with the making or the marring of it than poor Harry has had. He may not have intended it, the result was the same."

"Murder! Good God, Dorian, is that what you have come to? I shall not inform upon you. It is not my business. Besides, without my stirring in the matter, you are certain to be arrested. Nobody ever commits a crime without doing something stupid. But I will have nothing to do with it."

"You must have something to do with it. Wait, wait a moment; listen to me. Only listen, Alan. All I ask of you is to perform a certain scientific experiment. You go to hospitals and dead-houses, and the horrors that you do there don't affect you. If in some hideous dissecting-room or fetid laboratory you found this man lying on a leaden table with red gutters scooped out in it for the blood to flow through, you would simply look upon him as an admirable subject. You would not turn a hair. You would not believe that you were doing anything wrong. On the contrary, you would probably feel that you were benefiting the human race, or increasing the sum of knowledge in the world, or gratifying intellectual curiosity, or something of that kind. What I want you to do is merely what you have often done before. Indeed, to destroy a body must be far less horrible than what you are accustomed to work at. And, remember, it is the only piece of evidence against me. If it is discovered, I am lost; and it is sure to be discovered unless you help me."

"I have no desire to help you. You forget that. I am simply indifferent to the whole thing. It has nothing to do with me."

"Alan, I entreat you. Think of the position I am in. Just before you came I almost fainted with terror. You may know terror yourself some day. No! don't think of that. Look at the matter purely from the scientific point of view. You don't inquire where the dead things on which you experiment come from. Don't inquire now. I have told you too much as it is. But I beg of you to do this. We were friends once, Alan."

"Don't speak about those days, Dorian: they are dead."

"The dead linger sometimes. The man upstairs will not go away. He is sitting at the table with bowed head and outstretched arms. Alan! Alan! if you don't come to my assistance I am ruined. Why, they will hang me, Alan! Don't you understand? They will hang me for what I have done."

"There is no good in prolonging this scene. I absolutely refuse to do anything in the matter. It is insane of you to ask me."

"You refuse?"

"Yes."

"I entreat you, Alan."

"It is useless."

The same look of pity came into Dorian Gray's eyes. Then he stretched out his hand, took a piece of paper, and wrote something on it. He read it over twice, folded it carefully, and pushed it across the table. Having done this, he got up, and went over to the window.

Campbell looked at him in surprise, and then took up the paper, and opened it. As he read it, his face became ghastly pale, and he fell back in his chair. A horrible sense of sickness came over him. He felt as if his heart was beating itself to death in some empty hollow.

After two or three minutes of terrible silence, Dorian turned round, and came and stood behind him, putting his hand upon his shoulder.

"I am so sorry for you, Alan," he murmured, "but you leave me no alternative. I have a letter written already. Here it is. You see the address. If you don't help me, I must send it. If you don't help me, I will send it. You know what the result will be. But you are going to help me. It is impossible for you to refuse now. I tried to spare you. You will do me the justice to admit that. You were stern, harsh, offensive. You treated me as no man has ever dared to treat me—no living man, at any rate. I bore it all. Now it is for me to dictate terms."

Campbell buried his face in his hands, and a shudder passed through him.

"Yes, it is my turn to dictate terms, Alan. You know what they are. The thing is quite simple. Come, don't work yourself into this fever. The thing has to be done. Face it, and do it."

A groan broke from Campbell's lips, and he shivered all over. The ticking of the clock on the mantelpiece seemed to him to be dividing time into separate atoms of agony, each of which was too terrible to be borne. He felt as if an iron ring was being slowly tightened round his forehead, as if the disgrace with which he was threatened had already come upon him. The hand upon his shoulder weighed like a band of lead. It was intolerable. It seemed to crush him.

"Come, Alan, you must decide at once."

"I cannot do it," he said, mechanically, as though words could alter things.

"You must. You have no choice. Don't delay."

He hesitated a moment. "Is there a fire in the room upstairs?"

"Yes, there is a gas-fire with asbestos."

"I shall have to go home and get some things from the laboratory."

"No, Alan, you must not leave the house. Write out on a sheet of note-paper what you want, and my servant will take a cab and bring the things back to you."

Campbell scrawled a few lines, blotted them, and addressed an envelope to his assistant. Dorian took the note up and read it carefully. Then he rang the bell, and gave it to his valet, with orders to return as soon as possible, and to bring the things with him.

As the hall door shut, Campbell started nervously, and, having got up from the chair, went over to the chimney-piece. He was shivering with a kind of ague. For nearly twenty minutes, neither of the men spoke. A fly buzzed noisily about the room, and the ticking of the clock was like the beat of a hammer.

As the chime struck one, Campbell turned round, and, looking at Dorian Gray, saw that his eyes were filled with tears. There was something in the purity and refinement of that sad face that seemed to enrage him. "You are infamous, absolutely infamous!" he muttered.

"Hush, Alan: you have saved my life," said Dorian.

"Your life? Good heavens! what a life that is! You have gone from corruption to corruption, and you have culminated in crime. In doing what I am going to do, what you force me to do, it is not of your life that I am thinking."

"Ah, Alan," murmured Dorian, with a sigh, "I wish you had a thousandth part of the pity for me that I have for you." He turned away as he spoke, and stood looking out at the garden. Campbell made no answer.

After about ten minutes a knock came to the door, and the servant entered, carrying a large mahogany chest of chemicals, with a long coil of steel and platinum wire and two rather curiously shaped iron clamps.

"Shall I leave the things here, sir?" he asked Campbell.

"Yes," said Dorian. "And I am afraid, Francis, that I have another errand for you. What is the name of the man at Richmond who supplies Selby with orchids?"

"Harden, sir."

"Yes—Harden. You must go down to Richmond at once, see Harden personally, and tell him to send twice as many orchids as I ordered, and to have as few white ones as possible. In fact, I don't want any white ones. It is a lovely day, Francis, and Richmond is a very pretty place, otherwise I wouldn't bother you about it."

"No trouble, sir. At what time shall I be back?"

Dorian looked at Campbell. "How long will your experiment take, Alan?" he said, in a calm, indifferent voice. The presence of a third person in the room seemed to give him extraordinary courage.

Campbell frowned, and bit his lip. "It will take about five hours," he answered.

"It will be time enough, then, if you are back at half-past seven, Francis. Or stay: just leave my things out for dressing. You can have the evening to yourself. I am not dining at home, so I shall not want you."

"Thank you, sir," said the man, leaving the room.

"Now, Alan, there is not a moment to be lost. How heavy this chest is! I'll take it for you. You bring the other things." He spoke rapidly, and in an authoritative manner. Campbell felt dominated by him. They left the room together.

When they reached the top landing, Dorian took out the key and turned it in the lock. Then he stopped, and a troubled look came into his eyes. He shuddered. "I don't think I can go in, Alan," he murmured.

"It is nothing to me. I don't require you," said Campbell, coldly.

Dorian half opened the door. As he did so, he saw the face of his portrait leering in the sunlight. On the floor in front of it the torn curtain was lying. He remembered that the night before he had forgotten, for the first time in his life, to hide the fatal canvas, and was about to rush forward, when he drew back with a shudder.

What was that loathsome red dew that gleamed, wet and glistening, on one of the hands, as though the canvas had sweated blood? How horrible it was!—more horrible, it seemed to him for the moment, than the silent thing that he knew was stretched across the table, the thing whose grotesque misshapen shadow on the spotted carpet showed him that it had not stirred, but was still there, as he had left it.

He heaved a deep breath, opened the door a little wider, and with half-closed eyes and averted head walked quickly in, determined that he would not look even once upon the dead man. Then, stooping down, and taking up the gold-and-purple hanging, he flung it right over the picture.

There he stopped, feeling afraid to turn round, and his eyes fixed themselves on the intricacies of the pattern before him. He heard Campbell bringing in the heavy chest, and the irons, and the other things that he had required for his dreadful work. He began to wonder if he and Basil Hallward had ever met, and, if so, what they had thought of each other.

"Leave me now," said a stern voice behind him.

He turned and hurried out, just conscious that the dead man had been thrust back into the chair, and that Campbell was gazing into a glistening yellow face. As he was going downstairs he heard the key being turned in the lock.

It was long after seven when Campbell came back into the library. He was pale, but absolutely calm. "I have done what you asked me to do," he muttered. "And now, good-bye. Let us never see each other again."

"You have saved me from ruin, Alan. I cannot forget that," said Dorian, simply.

As soon as Campbell had left, he went upstairs. There was a horrible smell of nitric acid in the room. But the thing that had been sitting at the table was gone.

XV

THAT evening, at eight-thirty, exquisitely dressed, and wearing a large buttonhole of Parma violets, Dorian Gray was ushered into Lady Narborough's drawing-room by bowing servants. His forehead was throbbing with maddened nerves, and he felt wildly excited, but his manner as he bent over his hostess's hand was as easy and graceful as ever. Perhaps one never seems so much at one's ease as when one has to play a part. Certainly no one looking at Dorian Gray that night could have believed that he had passed through a tragedy as horrible as any tragedy of our age. Those finely shaped fingers could never have clutched a knife of sin, nor those smiling lips have cried out on God and goodness. He himself could not help wondering at the calm of his demeanour, and for a moment felt keenly the terrible pleasure of a double life.

It was a small party, got up rather in a hurry by Lady Narborough, who was a very clever woman, with what Lord Henry used to describe as the remains of really remarkable ugliness. She had proved an excellent wife to one of our most tedious ambassadors, and having buried her husband properly in a marble mausoleum, which she had herself designed, and married off her daughters to some rich, rather elderly men, she devoted herself now to the pleasures of French fiction, French cookery, and French *esprit* when she could get it.

Dorian was one of her especial favourites, and she always told him that she was extremely glad she had not met him in early life. "I know, my dear, I should have fallen madly in love with you," she used to say, "and thrown my bonnet right over the mills for your sake. It is most fortunate that you were not thought of at the time. As it was, our bonnets were so unbecoming, and the mills were so occupied in trying to raise the wind, that I never had even a flirtation with anybody. However, that was all Narborough's fault. He was dreadfully shortsighted, and there is no pleasure in taking in a husband who never sees anything."

Her guests this evening were rather tedious. The fact was, as she explained to Dorian, behind a very shabby fan, one of her married daughters had come up quite suddenly to stay with her, and, to make matters worse, had actually brought her husband with her. "I think it is most unkind of her, my dear," she whispered. "Of course I go and stay with them every summer after I come from Homburg, but then an old woman like me must have fresh air sometimes, and besides, I really wake them up. You don't know what an existence they lead down there. It is pure unadulterated country life. They get up early, because they have so much to do, and go to bed early because they have so little to think about. There has not been a scandal in the neighbourhood since the time of Queen Elizabeth, and consequently they all fall asleep after dinner. You shan't sit next either of them. You shall sit by me, and amuse me."

Dorian murmured a graceful compliment, and looked round the room. Yes, it was certainly a tedious party. Two of the people he had never seen before, and the others consisted of Ernest Harrowden, one of those middle-aged mediocrities so common in London clubs who have no enemies, but are thoroughly disliked by their friends; Lady Roxton, an overdressed woman of forty-seven, with a hooked nose, who was always trying to get herself compromised, but was so peculiarly plain that to her great disappointment no one would ever believe anything against her; Mrs. Erlynne, a pushing nobody, with a delightful lisp, and Venetian-red hair; Lady Alice Chapman, his hostess's daughter, a dowdy dull girl, with one of those characteristic British faces, that, once seen are never remembered; and her husband, a red-cheeked, white-whiskered creature who, like so many of his class, was under the impression that inordinate joviality can atone for an entire lack of ideas.

He was rather sorry he had come, till Lady Narborough, looking at the great ormolu gilt clock that sprawled in gaudy curves on the mauve-draped mantel-shelf, exclaimed: "How horrid of Henry Wotton to be so late! I sent round to him this morning on chance, and he promised faithfully not to disappoint me."

It was some consolation that Harry was to be there, and when the door opened and he heard his slow musical voice lending charm to some insincere apology, he ceased to feel bored.

But at dinner he could not eat anything. Plate after plate went away untasted. Lady Narborough kept scolding him for what she called "an insult to poor Adolphe, who invented the menu specially for you," and now and then Lord Henry looked across at him, wondering at his silence and abstracted manner. From time to time the butler filled his glass with champagne. He drank eagerly, and his thirst seemed to increase.

"Dorian," said Lord Henry, at last, as the *chaudfroid* was being handed round, "what is the matter with you tonight? You are quite out of sorts."

"I believe he is in love," cried Lady Narborough, "and that he is afraid to tell me for fear I should be jealous. He is quite right. I certainly should."

"Dear Lady Narborough," murmured Dorian, smiling, "I have not been in love for a whole week—not, in fact, since Madame de Ferrol left town."

"How you men can fall in love with that woman!" exclaimed the old lady. "I really cannot understand it."

"It is simply because she remembers you when you were a little girl, Lady Narborough," said Lord Henry. "She is the one link between us and your short frocks."

"She does not remember my short frocks at all, Lord Henry. But I remember her very well at Vienna thirty years ago, and how *décolletée* she was then."

"She is still *décolletée*," he answered, taking an olive in his long fingers; "and when she is in a very smart gown she looks like an *édition de luxe* of a bad French novel. She is really wonderful, and full of surprises. Her capacity for family affection is extraordinary. When her third husband died, her hair turned quite gold from grief."

"How can you, Harry!" cried Dorian.

"It is a most romantic explanation," laughed the hostess. "But her third husband, Lord Henry! You don't mean to say Ferrol is the fourth?"

"Certainly, Lady Narborough."

"I don't believe a word of it."

"Well, ask Mr. Gray. He is one of her most intimate friends."

"Is it true, Mr. Gray?"

"She assures me so, Lady Narborough," said Dorian. "I asked her whether, like Marguerite de Navarre, she had their hearts embalmed and hung at her girdle. She told me she didn't, because none of them had had any hearts at all."

"Four husbands! Upon my word that is *trop de zéle.*"

"*Trop d'audace,* I tell her," said Dorian.

"Oh! she is audacious enough for anything, my dear. And what is Ferrol like? I don't know him."

"The husbands of very beautiful women belong to the criminal classes," said Lord Henry, sipping his wine.

Lady Narborough hit him with her fan. "Lord Henry, I am not at all surprised that the world says that you are extremely wicked."

"But what world says that?" asked Lord Henry, elevating his eyebrows. "It can only be the next world. This world and I are on excellent terms."

"Everybody I know says you are very wicked," cried the old lady, shaking her head.

Lord Henry looked serious for some moments. "It is perfectly monstrous," he said, at last, "the way people go about nowadays saying things against one behind one's back that are absolutely and entirely true."

"Isn't he incorrigible?" cried Dorian, leaning forward in his chair.

"I hope so," said his hostess, laughing. "But really if you all worship Madame de Ferrol in this ridiculous way, I shall have to marry again so as to be in the fashion."

"You will never marry again, Lady Narborough," broke in Lord Henry. "You were far too happy. When a woman marries again it is because she detested her first husband. When a man marries again, it is because he adored his first wife. Women try their luck; men risk theirs."

"Narborough wasn't perfect," cried the old lady.

"If he had been, you would not have loved him, my dear lady," was the rejoinder. "Women love us for our defects. If we have enough of them they will forgive us everything, even our intellects. You will never ask me to dinner again, after saying this, I am afraid, Lady Narborough; but it is quite true."

"Of course it is true, Lord Henry. If we women did not love you for your defects, where would you all be? Not one of you would ever be married. You would be a set of unfortunate bachelors. Not, however, that that would alter you much. Nowadays all the married men live like bachelors, and all the bachelors like married men."

"*Fin de siècle*," murmured Lord Henry.

"*Fin du globe*," answered his hostess.

"I wish it were *fin du globe*," said Dorian, with a sigh. "Life is a great disappointment."

"Ah, my dear," cried Lady Narborough, putting on her gloves, "don't tell me that you have exhausted life.

When a man says that one knows that life has exhausted him. Lord Henry is very wicked, and I sometimes wish that I had been; but you are made to be good—you look so good. I must find you a nice wife. Lord Henry, don't you think that Mr. Gray should get married?"

"I am always telling him so, Lady Narborough," said Lord Henry, with a bow.

"Well, we must look out for a suitable match for him. I shall go through Debrett carefully tonight, and draw out a list of all the eligible young ladies."

"With their ages, Lady Narborough?" asked Dorian.

"Of course, with their ages, slightly edited. But nothing must be done in a hurry. I want it to be what *The Morning Post* calls a suitable alliance, and I want you both to be happy."

"What nonsense people talk about happy marriages!" exclaimed Lord Henry. "A man can be happy with any woman, as long as he does not love her."

"Ah! what a cynic you are!" cried the old lady, pushing back her chair, and nodding to Lady Ruxton. "You must come and dine with me soon again. You are really an admirable tonic, much better than what Sir Andrew prescribes for me. You must tell me what people you would like to meet, though. I want it to be a delightful gathering."

"I like men who have a future, and women who have a past," he answered. "Or do you think that would make it a petticoat party?"

"I fear so," she said, laughing, as she stood up. "A thousand pardons, my dear Lady Ruxton," she added, "I didn't see you hadn't finished your cigarette."

"Never mind, Lady Narborough. I smoke a great deal too much. I am going to limit myself, for the future."

"Pray don't, Lady Ruxton," said Lord Henry. "Moderation is a fatal thing. Enough is as bad as a meal. More than enough is as good as a feast."

Lady Ruxton glanced at him curiously. "You must come and explain that to me some afternoon, Lord Henry. It sounds a fascinating theory," she murmured, as she swept out of the room.

"Now, mind you don't stay too long over your politics and scandal," cried Lady Narborough from the door. "If you do, we are sure to squabble upstairs."

The men laughed, and Mr. Chapman got up solemnly from the foot of the table and came up to the top. Dorian Gray changed his seat, and went and sat by Lord Henry. Mr. Chapman began to talk in a loud voice about the situation in the House of Commons. He guffawed at his adversaries. The word *doctrinaire*—word full of terror to the British mind—reappeared from time to time between his explosions. An alliterative prefix served as an ornament of oratory. He hoisted the Union Jack on the pinnacles of thought. The inherited stupidity of the race—sound English common sense he jovially termed it—was shown to be the proper bulwark for society.

A smile curved Lord Henry's lips, and he turned round and looked at Dorian.

"Are you better, my dear fellow?" he asked. "You seemed rather out of sorts at dinner."

"I am quite well, Harry. I am tired. That is all."

"You were charming last night. The little Duchess is quite devoted to you. She tells me she is going down to Selby."

"She has promised to come on the twentieth."

"Is Monmouth to be there too?"

"Oh, yes, Harry."

"He bores me dreadfully, almost as much as he bores

her. She is very clever, too clever for a woman. She lacks the indefinable charm of weakness. It is the feet of clay that makes the gold of the image precious. Her feet are very pretty, but they are not feet of clay. White porcelain feet, if you like. They have been through the fire, and what fire does not destroy, it hardens. She has had experiences."

"How long has she been married?" asked Dorian.

"An eternity, she tells me. I believe, according to the peerage, it is ten years, but ten years with Monmouth must have been like eternity, with time thrown in. Who else is coming?"

"Oh, the Willoughbys, Lord Rugby and his wife, our hostess, Geoffrey Clouston, the usual set. I have asked Lord Grotrian."

"I like him," said Lord Henry. "A great many people don't, but I find him charming. He atones for being occasionally somewhat overdressed, by being always absolutely overeducated. He is a very modern type."

"I don't know if he will be able to come, Harry. He may have to go to Monte Carlo with his father."

"Ah! what a nuisance people's people are! Try and make him come. By the way, Dorian, you ran off very early last night. You left before eleven. What did you do afterwards? Did you go straight home?"

Dorian glanced at him hurriedly, and frowned. "No, Harry," he said at last, "I did not get home till nearly three."

"Did you go to the club?"

"Yes," he answered. Then he bit his lip. "No, I don't mean that. I didn't go to the club. I walked about. I forget what I did. . . . How inquisitive you are, Harry! You always want to know what one has been doing. I always want to forget what I have been doing. I came in at half-past two, if you wish to know the exact time.

I had left my latch-key at home, and my servant had to let me in. If you want any corroborative evidence on the subject you can ask him."

Lord Henry shrugged his shoulders. "My dear fellow, as if I cared! Let us go up to the drawing-room. No sherry, thank you, Mr. Chapman. Something has happened to you, Dorian. Tell me what it is. You are not yourself tonight."

"Don't mind me, Harry. I am irritable, and out of temper. I shall come round and see you tomorrow, or next day. Make my excuses to Lady Narborough. I shan't go upstairs. I shall go home. I must go home."

"All right, Dorian. I dare say I shall see you tomorrow at teatime. The Duchess is coming."

"I will try to be there, Harry," he said, leaving the room. As he drove back to his own house he was conscious that the sense of terror he thought he had strangled had come back to him. Lord Henry's casual questioning had made him lose his nerve for the moment, and he wanted his nerve still. Things that were dangerous had to be destroyed. He winced. He hated the idea of even touching them.

Yet it had to be done. He realized that, and when he had locked the door of his library, he opened the secret press into which he had thrust Basil Hallward's coat and bag. A huge fire was blazing. He piled another log on it. The smell of the singeing clothes and burning leather was horrible. It took him three-quarters of an hour to consume everything. At the end he felt faint and sick, and having lit some Algerian pastilles in a pierced copper brazier, he bathed his hands and forehead with a cool musk-scented vinegar.

Suddenly he started. His eyes grew strangely bright and he gnawed nervously at his underlip. Between two of the windows stood a large Florentine cabinet, made out of ebony, and inlaid with ivory and blue lapis. He watched it as though it were a thing that could fascinate and make afraid, as though it held something that he longed for and yet almost loathed. His breath quickened. A mad craving came over him. He lit a cigarette and then threw it away. His eyelids drooped till the long fringed lashes almost touched his cheek. But he still watched the cabinet. At last he got up from the sofa on which he had been lying, went over to it, and, having unlocked it, touched some hidden spring. A triangular drawer passed slowly out. His fingers moved instinctively towards it, dipped in, and closed on something. It was a small Chinese box of black and gold-dust lacquer, elaborately wrought, the sides patterned with curved waves, and the silken cords hung with round crystals and tasselled in plaited metal threads. He opened it. Inside was a green paste waxy in lustre, the odour curiously heavy and persistent.

He hesitated for some moments, with a strangely immobile smile upon his face. Then shivering, though the atmosphere of the room was terribly hot, he drew himself up, and glanced at the clock. It was twenty minutes to twelve. He put the box back, shutting the cabinet doors as he did so, and went into his bedroom.

As midnight was striking bronze blows upon the dusky air, Dorian Gray, dressed commonly, and with a muffler wrapped round his throat, crept quietly out of his house. In Bond Street he found a hansom with a good horse. He hailed it, and in a low voice gave the driver an address.

The man shook his head. "It is too far for me," he muttered.

"Here is a sovereign for you," said Dorian. "You shall have another if you drive fast."

"All right, sir," answered the man, "you will be there

in an hour," and after his fare had got in he turned his horse round, and drove rapidly towards the river.

XVI

A COLD rain began to fall, and the blurred street lamps looked ghastly in the dripping mist. The public-houses were just closing, and dim men and women were clustering in broken groups round their doors. From some of the bars came the sound of horrible laughter. In others, drunkards brawled and screamed.

Lying back in the hansom, with his hat pulled over his forehead, Dorian Gray watched with listless eyes the sordid shame of the great city, and now and then he repeated to himself the words that Lord Henry had said to him on the first day they had met, "To cure the soul by means of the senses, and the senses by means of the soul." Yes, that was the secret. He had often tried it, and would try it again now. There were opium dens, where one could buy oblivion, dens of horror where the memory of old sins could be destroyed by the madness of sins that were new.

The moon hung low in the sky like a yellow skull. From time to time a huge misshapen cloud stretched a long arm across and hid it. The gas lamps grew fewer, and the streets more narrow and gloomy. Once the man lost his way, and had to drive back half a mile. A steam rose from the horse as it splashed up the puddles. The side-windows of the hansom were clogged with a grey-flannel mist.

"To cure the soul by means of the senses, and the senses by means of the soul!" How the words rang in his ears! His soul, certainly, was sick to death. Was it true that the senses could cure it? Innocent blood had been spilt. What could atone for that? Ah! for that there was no atonement; but though forgiveness was impossible, forgetfulness was possible still, and he was determined to forget, to stamp the thing out, to crush it as one would crush the adder that had stung one. Indeed, what right had Basil to have spoken to him as he had done? Who had made him a judge over others? He had said things that were dreadful, horrible, not to be endured.

On and on plodded the hansom, going slower, it seemed to him, at each step. He thrust up the trap, and called to the man to drive faster. The hideous hunger for opium began to gnaw at him. His throat burned, and his delicate hands twitched nervously together. He struck at the horse madly with his stick. The driver laughed, and whipped up. He laughed in answer, and the man was silent.

The way seemed interminable, and the streets like the black web of some sprawling spider. The monotony became unbearable, and, as the mist thickened, he felt afraid.

Then they passed by lonely brickfields. The fog was lighter here, and he could see the strange bottle-shaped kilns with their orange fan-like tongues of fire. A dog barked as they went by, and far away in the darkness some wandering seagull screamed. The horse stumbled in a rut, then swerved aside, and broke into a gallop.

After some time they left the clay road, and rattled again over rough-paven streets. Most of the windows were dark, but now and then fantastic shadows were silhouetted against some lamp-lit blind. He watched them curiously. They moved like monstrous marionettes, and made gestures like live things. He hated them. A dull rage was in his heart. As they turned a corner a woman yelled something at them from an open door, and two men ran after the hansom for about a hundred yards. The driver beat at them with his whip.

It is said that passion makes one think in a circle. Certainly with hideous iteration the bitten lips of Dorian Gray shaped and reshaped those subtle words that dealt with soul and sense, till he had found in them the full expression, as it were, of his mood, and justified, by intellectual approval, passions that without such justification would still have dominated his temper. From cell to cell of his brain crept the one thought; and the wild desire to live, most terrible of all man's appetites, quickened into force each trembling nerve and fibre. Ugliness that had once been hateful to him because it made things real, became dear to him now for that very reason. Ugliness was the one reality. The coarse brawl, the loathsome den, the crude violence of disordered life, the very vileness of thief and outcast, were more vivid, in their intense actuality of impression, than all the gracious shapes of art, the dreamy shadows of song. They were what he needed for forgetfulness. In three days he would be free.

Suddenly the man drew up with a jerk at the top of a dark lane. Over the low roofs and jagged chimney-stacks of the houses rose the black masts of ships. Wreaths of white mist clung like ghostly sails to the yards.

"Somewhere about here, sir, ain't it?" he asked huskily through the trap.

Dorian started, and peered round. "This will do," he answered, and, having got out hastily, and given the driver the extra fare he had promised him, he walked

quickly in the direction of the quay. Here and there a
lantern gleamed at the stern of some huge merchant-
man. The light shook and splintered in the puddles.
A red glare came from an outward-bound steamer that
was coaling. The slimy pavement looked like a wet
mackintosh.

He hurried on towards the left, glancing back now
and then to see if he was being followed. In about seven
or eight minutes he reached a small shabby house, that
was wedged in between two gaunt factories. In one of
the top windows stood a lamp. He stopped, and gave a
peculiar knock.

After a little time he heard steps in the passage,
and the chain being unhooked. The door opened
quietly, and he went in without saying a word to the
squat misshapen figure that flattened itself into the
shadow as he passed. At the end of the hall hung a
tattered green curtain that swayed and shook in the
gusty wind which had followed him in from the street.
He dragged it aside, and entered a long, low room
which looked as if it had once been a third-rate dancing-
saloon. Shrill flaring gas jets, dulled and distorted in the
fly-blown mirrors that faced them, were ranged round
the walls. Greasy reflectors of ribbed tin backed them,
making quivering disks of light. The floor was covered
with ochre-coloured sawdust, trampled here and there
into mud, and stained with rings of spilt liquor. Some
Malays were crouching by a little charcoal stove playing with bone counters, and showing their white teeth
as they chattered. In one corner with his head buried in
his arms, a sailor sprawled over a table, and by the
tawdrily painted bar that ran across one complete side
stood two haggard women mocking an old man who
was brushing the sleeves of his coat with an expression
of disgust. "He thinks he's got red ants on him," laughed

one of them, as Dorian passed by. The man looked at her in terror, and began to whimper.

At the end of the room there was a little staircase, leading to a darkened chamber. As Dorian hurried up its three rickety steps, the heavy odour of opium met him. He heaved a deep breath, and his nostrils quivered with pleasure. When he entered, a young man with smooth yellow hair, who was bending over a lamp lighting a long thin pipe, looked up at him, and nodded in a hesitating manner.

"You here, Adrian?" muttered Dorian.

"Where else should I be?" he answered, listlessly. "None of the chaps will speak to me now."

"I thought you had left England."

"Darlington is not going to do anything. My brother paid the bill at last. George doesn't speak to me either. . . . I don't care," he added, with a sigh. "As long as one has this stuff, one doesn't want friends. I think I have had too many friends."

Dorian winced, and looked round at the grotesque things that lay in such fantastic postures on the ragged mattresses. The twisted limbs, the gaping mouths, the staring lustreless eyes, fascinated him. He knew in what strange heavens they were suffering, and what dull hells were teaching them the secret of some new joy. They were better off than he was. He was prisoned in thought. Memory, like a horrible malady, was eating his soul away. From time to time he seemed to see the eyes of Basil Hallward looking at him. Yet he felt he could not stay. The presence of Adrian Singleton troubled him. He wanted to be where no one would know who he was. He wanted to escape from himself.

"I am going on to the other place," he said, after a pause.

"On the wharf?"

"Yes."

"That mad-cat is sure to be there. They won't have her in this place now."

Dorian shrugged his shoulders. "I am sick of women who love one. Women who hate one are much more interesting. Besides, the stuff is better."

"Much the same."

"I like it better. Come and have something to drink. I must have something."

"I don't want anything," murmured the young man.

"Never mind."

Adrian Singleton rose up wearily, and followed Dorian to the bar. A half-caste, in a ragged turban and a shabby ulster, grinned a hideous greeting as he thrust a bottle of brandy and two tumblers in front of them. The women sidled up, and began to chatter. Dorian turned his back on them, and said something in a low voice to Adrian Singleton.

A crooked smile, like a Malay crease, writhed across the face of one of the women. "We are very proud tonight," she sneered.

"For God's sake don't talk to me," cried Dorian, stamping his foot on the ground. "What do you want? Money? Here it is. Don't ever talk to me again."

Two red sparks flashed for a moment in the woman's sodden eyes, then flickered out, and left them dull and glazed. She tossed her head, and raked the coins off the counter with greedy fingers. Her companion watched her enviously.

"It's no use," sighed Adrian Singleton. "I don't care to go back. What does it matter? I am quite happy here."

"You will write to me if you want anything, won't you?" said Dorian, after a pause.

"Perhaps."

"Good night, then."

"Good night," answered the young man, passing up the steps, and wiping his parched mouth with a handkerchief.

Dorian walked to the door with a look of pain in his face. As he drew the curtain aside a hideous laugh broke from the painted lips of the woman who had taken the money. "There goes the devil's bargain!" she hiccoughed, in a hoarse voice.

"Curse you," he answered, "don't call me that."

She snapped her fingers. "Prince Charming is what you like to be called, ain't it?" she yelled after him.

The drowsy sailor leapt to his feet as she spoke, and looked wildly round. The sound of the shutting of the hall door fell on his ear. He rushed out as if in pursuit.

Dorian Gray hurried along the quay through the drizzling rain. His meeting with Adrian Singleton had strangely moved him, and he wondered if the ruin of that young life was really to be laid at his door, as Basil Hallward had said to him with such infamy of insult. He bit his lip, and for a few seconds his eyes grew sad. Yet, after all, what did it matter to him? One's days were too brief to take the burden of another's errors on one's shoulders. Each man lived his own life, and paid his own price for living it. The only pity was one had to pay so often for a single fault. One had to pay over and over again, indeed. In her dealings with man Destiny never closed her accounts.

There are moments, psychologists tell us, when the passion for sin, or for what the world calls sin, so dominates a nature, that every fibre of the body, as every cell of the brain, seems to be instinct with fearful impulses. Men and women at such moments lose the freedom of their will. They move to their terrible end as automatons move. Choice is taken from them, and conscience is either killed, or, if it lives at all, lives but to give rebellion its fascination, and disobedience its charm. For all sins, as theologians weary not of reminding us, are sins of disobedience. When that high spirit, that morning star of evil, fell from heaven, it was as a rebel that he fell.

Callous, concentrated on evil, with stained mind, and soul hungry for rebellion, Dorian Gray hastened on, quickening his step as he went, but as he darted aside into a dim archway, that had served him often as a short cut to the ill-famed place where he was going, he felt himself suddenly seized from behind, and before he had time to defend himself he was thrust back against the wall, with a brutal hand round his throat.

He struggled madly for life, and by a terrible effort wrenched the tightening fingers away. In a second he heard the click of a revolver, and saw the gleam of a polished barrel pointing straight at his head, and the dusky form of a short thick-set man facing him.

"What do you want?" he gasped.

"Keep quiet," said the man. "If you stir, I shoot you."

"You are mad. What have I done to you?"

"You wrecked the life of Sibyl Vane," was the answer, "and Sibyl Vane was my sister. She killed herself. I know it. Her death is at your door. I swore I would kill you in return. For years I have sought you. I had no clue, no trace. The two people who could have described you were dead. I knew nothing of you but the pet name she used to call you. I heard it tonight by chance. Make your peace with God, for tonight you are going to die."

Dorian Gray grew sick with fear. "I never knew her," he stammered. "I never heard of her. You are mad."

"You had better confess your sin, for as sure as I am James Vane, you are going to die." There was a horrible moment. Dorian did not know what to say or do. "Down on your knees!" growled the man. "I give you one minute to make your peace—no more. I go on board tonight for India, and I must do my job first. One minute. That's all."

Dorian's arms fell to his side. Paralyzed with terror, he did not know what to do. Suddenly a wild hope flashed across his brain. "Stop," he cried. "How long ago is it since your sister died? Quick, tell me!"

"Eighteen years," said the man. "Why do you ask me? What do years matter?"

"Eighteen years," laughed Dorian Gray, with a touch of triumph in his voice. "Eighteen years! Set me under the lamp and look at my face."

James Vane hesitated for a moment, not understanding what was meant. Then he seized Dorian Gray and dragged him from the archway.

Dim and wavering as was the windblown light, yet it served to show him the hideous error, as it seemed, into which he had fallen, for the face of the man he had sought to kill had all the bloom of boyhood, all the unstained purity of youth. He seemed little more than a lad of twenty summers, hardly older, if older indeed at all, than his sister had been when they had parted so many years ago. It was obvious that this was not the man who had destroyed her life.

He loosened his hold and reeled back. "My God! my God!" he cried, "and I would have murdered you!"

Dorian Gray drew a long breath. "You have been on the brink of committing a terrible crime, my man," he said, looking at him sternly. "Let this be a warning to you not to take vengeance into your own hands."

"Forgive me, sir," muttered James Vane. "I was deceived. A chance word I heard in that damned den set me on the wrong track."

"You had better go home, and put that pistol away, or you may get into trouble," said Dorian, turning on his heel, and going slowly down the street.

James Vane stood on the pavement in horror. He was trembling from head to foot. After a little while a black shadow that had been creeping along the dripping wall, moved out into the light and came close to him with stealthy footsteps. He felt a hand laid on his arm and looked round with a start. It was one of the women who had been drinking at the bar.

"Why didn't you kill him?" she hissed out, putting her haggard face quite close to his. "I knew you were following him when you rushed out from Daly's. You fool! You should have killed him. He has lots of money, and he's as bad as bad."

"He is not the man I am looking for," he answered, "and I want no man's money. I want a man's life. The man whose life I want must be nearly forty now. This one is little more than a boy. Thank God, I have not got his blood upon my hands."

The woman gave a bitter laugh. "Little more than a boy!" she sneered. "Why, man, it's nigh on eighteen years since Prince Charming made me what I am."

"You lie!" cried James Vane.

She raised her hand up to heaven. "Before God I am telling the truth," she cried.

"Before God?"

"Strike me dumb if it ain't so. He is the worst one that comes here. They say he has sold himself to the devil for a pretty face. It's nigh on eighteen years since I met him. He hasn't changed much since then. I have though," she added, with a sickly leer.

"You swear this?"

"I swear it," came in hoarse echo from her flat mouth. "But don't give me away to him," she whined; "I am afraid of him. Let me have some money for my night's lodging."

He broke from her with an oath, and rushed to the corner of the street, but Dorian Gray had disappeared. When he looked back, the woman had vanished also.

XVII

A WEEK later Dorian Gray was sitting in the conservatory at Selby Royal talking to the pretty Duchess of Monmouth, who with her husband, a jaded-looking man of sixty, was amongst his guests. It was teatime, and the mellow light of the huge lace-covered lamp that stood on the table lit up the delicate china and hammered silver of the service at which the Duchess was presiding. Her white hands were moving daintily among the cups, and her full red lips were smiling at something that Dorian had whispered to her. Lord Henry was lying back in a silk-draped wicker chair looking at them. On a peach-coloured divan sat Lady Narborough pretending to listen to the Duke's description of the last Brazilian beetle that he had added to his collection. Three young men in elaborate smoking-suits were handing tea-cakes to some of the women. The house party consisted of twelve people, and there were more expected to arrive on the next day.

"What are you two talking about?" said Lord Henry, strolling over to the table, and putting his cup down. "I hope Dorian has told you about my plan for rechristening everything, Gladys. It is a delightful idea."

"But I don't want to be rechristened, Harry," rejoined the Duchess, looking up at him with her wonderful eyes. "I am quite satisfied with my own name, and I am sure Mr. Gray should be satisfied with his."

"My dear Gladys, I would not alter either name for the world. They are both perfect. I was thinking chiefly of flowers. Yesterday I cut an orchid, for my button-hole. It was a marvellous spotted thing, as effective as the seven deadly sins. In a thoughtless moment I asked one of the gardeners what it was called. He told me it was a fine specimen of *Robinsoniana,* or something dreadful of that kind. It is a sad truth, but we have lost the faculty of giving lovely names to things. Names are everything. I never quarrel with actions. My one quarrel is with words. That is the reason I hate vulgar realism in literature. The man who could call a spade a spade should be compelled to use one. It is the only thing he is fit for."

"Then what should we call you, Harry?" she asked.

"His name is Prince Paradox," said Dorian.

"I recognize him in a flash," exclaimed the Duchess.

"I won't hear of it," laughed Lord Henry, sinking into a chair. "From a label there is no escape! I refuse the title."

"Royalties may not abdicate," fell as a warning from pretty lips.

"You wish me to defend my throne, then?"

"Yes."

"I give the truths of tomorrow."

"I prefer the mistakes of today," she answered.

"You disarm me, Gladys," he cried, catching the wilfulness of her mood.

"Of your shield, Harry: not of your spear."

"I never tilt against beauty," he said, with a wave of his hand.

"That is your error, Harry, believe me. You value beauty far too much."

"How can you say that? I admit that I think that it is better to be beautiful than to be good. But on the other hand no one is more ready than I am to acknowledge that it is better to be good than to be ugly."

"Ugliness is one of the seven deadly sins, then?" cried the Duchess. "What becomes of your simile about the orchid?"

"Ugliness is one of the seven deadly virtues, Gladys. You, as a good Tory, must not underrate them. Beer, the Bible, and the seven deadly virtues have made our England what she is."

"You don't like your country, then?" she asked.

"I live in it."

"That you may censure it the better."

"Would you have me take the verdict of Europe on it?" he enquired.

"What do they say of us?"

"That Tartuffe has emigrated to England and opened a shop."

"Is that yours, Harry?"

"I give it to you."

"I could not use it. It is too true."

"You need not be afraid. Our countrymen never recognize a description."

"They are practical."

"They are more cunning than practical. When they make up their ledger, they balance stupidity by wealth, and vice by hypocrisy."

"Still, we have done great things."

"Great things have been thrust on us, Gladys."

"We have carried their burden."

"Only as far as the Stock Exchange."

She shook her head. "I believe in the race," she cried.

"It represents the survival of the pushing."

"It has development."

"Decay fascinates me more."

"What of art?" she asked.

"It is a malady."

"Love?"

"An illusion."

"Religion?"

"The fashionable substitute for belief."

"You are a sceptic."

"Never! Scepticism is the beginning of faith."

"What are you?"

"To define is to limit."

"Give me a clue."

"Threads snap. You would lose your way in the labyrinth."

"You bewilder me. Let us talk of someone else."

"Our host is a delightful topic. Years ago he was christened Prince Charming."

"Ah! don't remind me of that," cried Dorian Gray.

"Our host is rather horrid this evening," answered the Duchess, colouring. "I believe he thinks that Monmouth married me on purely scientific principles as the best specimen he could find of a modern butterfly."

"Well, I hope he won't stick pins into you, Duchess," laughed Dorian.

"Oh! my maid does that already, Mr. Gray, when she is annoyed with me."

"And what does she get annoyed with you about, Duchess?"

"For the most trivial things, Mr. Gray, I assure you. Usually because I come in at ten minutes to nine and tell her that I must be dressed by half-past eight."

"How unreasonable of her! You should give her warning."

"I daren't, Mr. Gray. Why, she invents hats for me. You remember the one I wore at Lady Hilstone's garden party? You don't, but it is nice of you to pretend that you do. Well, she made it out of nothing. All good hats are made out of nothing."

"Like all good reputations, Gladys," interrupted Lord Henry. "Every effect that one produces gives one an enemy. To be popular one must be a mediocrity."

"Not with women," said the Duchess, shaking her head; "and women rule the world. I assure you we can't bear mediocrities. We women, as someone says, love with our ears, just as you men love with your eyes, if you ever love at all."

"It seems to me that we never do anything else," murmured Dorian.

"Ah! then, you never really love, Mr. Gray," answered the Duchess, with mock sadness.

"My dear Gladys!" cried Lord Henry. "How can you say that? Romance lives by repetition, and repetition converts an appetite into an art. Besides, each time that one loves is the only time one has ever loved. Difference of object does not alter singleness of passion. It merely intensifies it. We can have in life but one great experience at best, and the secret of life is to reproduce that experience as often as possible."

"Even when one has been wounded by it, Harry?" asked the Duchess, after a pause.

"Especially when one has been wounded by it," answered Lord Henry.

The Duchess turned and looked at Dorian Gray with a curious expression in her eyes. "What do you say to that, Mr. Gray?" she enquired.

Dorian hesitated for a moment. Then he threw his head back and laughed. "I always agree with Harry, Duchess."

"Even when he is wrong?"

"Harry is never wrong, Duchess."

"And does his philosophy make you happy?"

"I have never searched for happiness. Who wants happiness? I have searched for pleasure."

"And found it, Mr. Gray?"

"Often. Too often."

The Duchess sighed. "I am searching for peace," she said, "and if I don't go and dress, I shall have none this evening."

"Let me get you some orchids, Duchess," cried Dorian, starting to his feet, and walking down the conservatory.

"You are flirting disgracefully with him," said Lord Henry to his cousin. "You had better take care. He is very fascinating."

"If he were not, there would be no battle."

"Greek meets Greek, then?"

"I am on the side of the Trojans. They fought for a woman."

"They were defeated."

"There are worse things than capture," she answered.

"You gallop with a loose rein."

"Pace gives life," was the ripost.

"I shall write it in my diary tonight."

"What?"

"That a burnt child loves the fire."

"I am not even singed. My wings are untouched."

"You use them for everything, except flight."

"Courage has passed from men to women. It is a new experience for us."

"You have a rival."

"Who?"

He laughed. "Lady Narborough," he whispered. "She perfectly adores him."

"You fill me with apprehension. The appeal to Antiquity is fatal to us who are romanticists."

"Romanticists! You have all the methods of science."

"Men have educated us."

"But not explained you."

"Describe us as a sex," was her challenge.

"Sphinxes without secrets."

She looked at him, smiling. "How long Mr. Gray is!" she said. "Let us go and help him. I have not yet told him the colour of my frock."

"Ah! you must suit your frock to his flowers, Gladys."

"That would be a premature surrender."

"Romantic art begins with its climax."

"I must keep an opportunity for retreat."

"In the Parthian manner?"

"They found safety in the desert. I could not do that."

"Women are not always allowed a choice," he answered, but hardly had he finished the sentence before from the far end of the conservatory came a stifled groan, followed by the dull sound of a heavy fall. Everybody started up. The Duchess stood motionless in horror. And with fear in his eyes Lord Henry rushed through the flapping palms, to find Dorian Gray lying face downwards on the tiled floor in a death-like swoon.

He was carried at once into the blue drawing-room, and laid upon one of the sofas. After a short time he came to himself, and looked round with a dazed expression.

"What has happened?" he asked. "Oh! I remember. Am I safe here, Harry?" He began to tremble.

"My dear Dorian," answered Lord Henry, "you merely fainted. That was all. You must have overtired yourself. You had better not come down to dinner. I will take your place."

"No, I will come down," he said, struggling to his feet. "I would rather come down. I must not be alone."

He went to his room and dressed. There was a wild recklessness of gaiety in his manner as he sat at table, but now and then a thrill of terror ran through him when he remembered that, pressed against the window of the conservatory, like a white handkerchief, he had seen the face of James Vane watching him.

XVIII

THE next day he did not leave the house, and, indeed, spent most of the time in his own room, sick with a wild terror of dying, and yet indifferent to life itself. The consciousness of being hunted, snared, tracked down, had begun to dominate him. If the tapestry did but tremble in the wind, he shook. The dead leaves that were blown against the leaded panes seemed to him like his own wasted resolutions and wild regrets. When he closed his eyes, he saw again the sailor's face peering through the mist-stained glass, and horror seemed once more to lay its hand upon his heart.

But perhaps it had been only his fancy that had called vengeance out of the night, and set the hideous shapes of punishment before him. Actual life was chaos, but there was something terribly logical in the imagination. It was the imagination that·set remorse to dog the feet of sin. It was the imagination that made each crime bear its misshapen brood. In the common world of fact the wicked were not punished, nor the good rewarded. Success was given to the strong, failure thrust upon the weak. That was all. Besides, had any stranger been prowling round the house he would have been seen by the servants or the keepers. Had any footmarks been found on the flower-beds, the gardeners would have reported it. Yes, it had been merely fancy. Sibyl Vane's brother had not come back to kill him. He had sailed away in his ship to founder in some winter sea. From him, at any rate, he was safe. Why, the man did not know who he was, could not know who he was. The mask of youth had saved him.

And yet if it had been merely an illusion, how terrible it was to think that conscience could raise such fearful phantoms, and give them visible form, and make them move before one! What sort of life would his be if, day and night, shadows of his crime were to peer at him from silent corners, to mock him from secret places, to whisper in his ear as he sat at the feast, to wake him with icy fingers as he lay asleep! As the thought crept through his brain, he grew pale with terror, and the air seemed to him to have become suddenly colder. Oh! in what a wild hour of madness he had killed his friend! How ghastly the mere memory of the scene! He saw it all again. Each hideous detail came back to him with added horror. Out of the black cave of time, terrible and swathed in scarlet, rose the image of his sin. When Lord Henry came in at six o'clock, he found him crying as one whose heart will break.

It was not till the third day that he ventured to go out. There was something in the clear, pine-scented air of that winter morning that seemed to bring him back his joyousness and his ardour for life. But it was not merely the physical conditions of environment that had caused the change. His own nature had revolted against the excess of anguish that had sought to maim and mar the perfection of its calm. With subtle and finely wrought temperaments it is always so. Their strong passions must either bruise or bend. They either slay the man, or themselves die. Shallow sorrows and shal-

low loves live on. The loves and sorrows that are great
are destroyed by their own plenitude. Besides, he had
convinced himself that he had been the victim of a
terror-stricken imagination, and looked back now on
his fears with something of pity and not a little of
contempt.

After breakfast he walked with the Duchess for an
hour in the garden, and then drove across the park to
join the shooting party. The crisp frost lay like salt
upon the grass. The sky was an inverted cup of blue
metal. A thin film of ice bordered the flat reed-grown
lake.

At the corner of the pine wood he caught sight of
Sir Geoffrey Clouston, the Duchess's brother, jerking
two spent cartridges out of his gun. He jumped from
the cart, and having told the groom to take the mare
home, made his way towards his guest through the
withered bracken and rough undergrowth.

"Have you had good sport, Geoffrey?" he asked.

"Not very good, Dorian. I think most of the birds
have gone to the open. I dare say it will be better after
lunch, when we get to new ground."

Dorian strolled along by his side. The keen aromatic
air, the brown and red lights that glimmered in the
wood, the hoarse cries of the beaters ringing out from
time to time, and the sharp snaps of the guns that followed, fascinated him, and filled him with a sense of
delightful freedom. He was dominated by the carelessness of happiness, by the high indifference of joy.

Suddenly from a lumpy tussock of old grass, some
twenty yards in front of them, with black-tipped ears
erect, and long hinder limbs throwing it forward, started
a hare. It bolted for a thicket of alders. Sir Geoffrey
put his gun to his shoulder, but there was something in
the animal's grace of movement that strangely charmed

Dorian Gray, and he cried out at once, "Don't shoot it, Geoffrey. Let it live."

"What nonsense, Dorian!" laughed his companion, and as the hare bounded into the thicket he fired. There were two cries heard, the cry of a hare in pain, which is dreadful, the cry of a man in agony, which is worse.

"Good heavens! I have hit a beater!" exclaimed Sir Geoffrey. "What an ass the man was to get in front of the guns! Stop shooting there!" he called out at the top of his voice. "A man is hurt."

The head-keeper came running up with a stick in his hand.

"Where, sir? Where is he?" he shouted. At the same time the firing ceased along the line.

"Here," answered Sir Geoffrey, angrily, hurrying towards the thicket. "Why on earth don't you keep your men back? Spoiled my shooting for the day."

Dorian watched them as they plunged into the alder-clump, brushing the lithe, swinging branches aside. In a few moments they emerged, dragging a body after them into the sunlight. He turned away in horror. It seemed to him that misfortune followed wherever he went. He heard Sir Geoffrey ask if the man was really dead, and the affirmative answer of the keeper. The wood seemed to him to have become suddenly alive with faces. There was the trampling of myriad feet, and the low buzz of voices. A great copper-breasted pheasant came beating through the boughs overhead.

After a few moments, that were to him, in his perturbed state, like endless hours of pain, he felt a hand laid on his shoulder. He started, and looked round.

"Dorian," said Lord Henry, "I had better tell them that the shooting is stopped for today. It would not look well to go on."

"I wish it were stopped for ever, Harry," he an-

swered, bitterly. "The whole thing is hideous and cruel.
Is the man . . . ?"

He could not finish the sentence.

"I am afraid so," rejoined Lord Henry. "He got the
whole charge of shot in his chest. He must have died
almost instantaneously. Come; let us go home."

They walked side by side in the direction of the
avenue for nearly fifty yards without speaking. Then
Dorian looked at Lord Henry, and said, with a heavy
sigh, "It is a bad omen, Harry, a very bad omen."

"What is?" asked Lord Henry. "Oh! this accident, I
suppose. My dear fellow, it can't be helped. It was the
man's own fault. Why did he get in front of the guns?
Besides, it is nothing to us. It is rather awkward for
Geoffrey, of course. It does not do to pepper beaters.
It makes people think that one is a wild shot. And
Geoffrey is not; he shoots very straight. But there is
no use talking about·the matter."

Dorian shook his head. "It is a bad omen, Harry. I
feel as if something horrible were going to happen to
some of us. To myself, perhaps," he added, passing
his hand over his eyes, with a gesture of pain.

The elder man laughed. "The only horrible thing in
the world is ennui, Dorian. That is the one sin for
which there is no forgiveness. But we are not likely to
suffer from it, unless these fellows keep chattering about
this thing at dinner. I must tell them that the subject
is to be tabooed. As for omens, there is no such thing
as an omen. Destiny does not send us heralds. She
is too wise or too cruel for that. Besides, what on
earth could happen to you, Dorian? You have everything in the world that a man can want. There is no
one who would not be delighted to change places with
you."

"There is no one with whom I would not change

places, Harry. Don't laugh like that. I am telling you the truth. The wretched peasant who has just died is better off than I am. I have no terror of death. It is the coming of death that terrifies me. Its monstrous wings seem to wheel in the leaden air around me. Good heavens! don't you see a man moving behind the trees there, watching me, waiting for me?"

Lord Henry looked in the direction in which the trembling gloved hand was pointing. "Yes," he said, smiling, "I see the gardener waiting for you. I suppose he wants to ask you what flowers you wish to have on the table tonight. How absurdly nervous you are, my dear fellow! You must come and see my doctor, when we get back to town."

Dorian heaved a sigh of relief as he saw the gardener approaching. The man touched his hat, glanced for a moment at Lord Henry in a hesitating manner, and then produced a letter, which he handed to his master. "Her Grace told me to wait for an answer," he murmured.

Dorian put the letter into his pocket. "Tell her Grace that I am coming in," he said, coldly. The man turned round, and went rapidly in the direction of the house.

"How fond women are of doing dangerous things!" laughed Lord Henry. "It is one of the qualities in them that I admire most. A woman will flirt with anybody in the world as long as other people are looking on."

"How fond you are of saying dangerous things, Harry! In the present instance you are quite astray. I like the Duchess very much, but I don't love her."

"And the Duchess loves you very much, but she likes you less, so you are excellently matched."

"You are talking scandal, Harry, and there is never any basis for scandal."

"The basis of every scandal is an immoral certainty," said Lord Henry, lighting a cigarette.

"You would sacrifice anybody, Harry, for the sake of an epigram."

"The world goes to the altar of its own accord," was the answer.

"I wish I could love," cried Dorian Gray, with a deep note of pathos in his voice. "But I seem to have lost the passion, and forgotten the desire. I am too much concentrated on myself. My own personality has become a burden to me. I want to escape, to go away, to forget. It was silly of me to come down here at all. I think I shall send a wire to Harvey to have the yacht got ready. On a yacht one is safe."

"Safe from what, Dorian? You are in some trouble. Why not tell me what it is? You know I would help you."

"I can't tell you, Harry," he answered, sadly. "And I dare say it is only a fancy of mine. This unfortunate accident has upset me. I have a horrible presentiment that something of the kind may happen to me."

"What nonsense!"

"I hope it is, but I can't help feeling it. Ah! here is the Duchess, looking like Artemis in a tailor-made gown. You see we have come back, Duchess."

"I have heard all about it, Mr. Gray," she answered. "Poor Geoffrey is terribly upset. And it seems that you asked him not to shoot the hare. How curious!"

"Yes, it was very curious. I don't know what made me say it. Some whim, I suppose. It looked the loveliest of little live things. But I am sorry they told you about the man. It is a hideous subject."

"It is an annoying subject," broke in Lord Henry. "It has no psychological value at all. Now if Geoffrey had done the thing on purpose, how interesting he would be! I should like to know someone who had committed a real murder."

"How horrid of you, Harry!" cried the Duchess. "Isn't it, Mr. Gray? Harry, Mr. Gray is ill again. He is going to faint."

Dorian drew himself up with an effort, and smiled. "It is nothing, Duchess," he murmured; "my nerves are dreadfully out of order. That is all. I am afraid I walked too far this morning. I didn't hear what Harry said. Was it very bad? You must tell me some other time. I think I must go and lie down. You will excuse me, won't you?"

They had reached the great flight of steps that led from the conservatory onto the terrace. As the glass door closed behind Dorian, Lord Henry turned and looked at the Duchess with his slumberous eyes. "Are you very much in love with him?" he asked.

She did not answer for some time, but stood gazing at the landscape. "I wish I knew," she said at last.

He shook his head. "Knowledge would be fatal. It is the uncertainty that charms one. A mist makes things wonderful."

"One may lose one's way."

"All ways end at the same point, my dear Gladys."

"What is that?"

"Disillusion."

"It was my début in life," she sighed.

"It came to you crowned."

"I am tired of strawberry leaves."

"They become you."

"Only in public."

"You would miss them," said Lord Henry.

"I will not part with a petal."

"Monmouth has ears."

"Old age is dull of hearing."

"Has he never been jealous?"

"I wish he had been."

He glanced about as if in search of something. "What are you looking for?" she enquired.

"The button from your foil," he answered. "You have dropped it."

She laughed. "I have still the mask."

"It makes your eyes lovelier," was his reply.

She laughed again. Her teeth showed like white seeds in a scarlet fruit.

Upstairs, in his own room, Dorian Gray was lying on a sofa, with terror in every tingling fibre of his body. Life had suddenly become too hideous a burden for him to bear. The dreadful death of the unlucky beater, shot in the thicket like a wild animal, had seemed to him to prefigure death for himself also. He had nearly swooned at what Lord Henry had said in a chance mood of cynical jesting.

At five o'clock he rang his bell for his servant, and gave him orders to pack his things for the night-express to town, and to have the brougham at the door by eight-thirty. He was determined not to sleep another night at Selby Royal. It was an ill-omened place. Death walked there in the sunlight. The grass of the forest had been spotted with blood.

Then he wrote a note to Lord Henry, telling him that he was going up to town to consult his doctor, and asking him to entertain his guests in his absence. As he was putting it into the envelope, a knock came to the door, and his valet informed him that the head-keeper wished to see him. He frowned, and bit his lip. "Send him in," he muttered, after some moments' hesitation.

As soon as the man entered Dorian pulled his cheque-book out of a drawer, and spread it out before him.

"I suppose you have come about the unfortunate

accident of this morning, Thornton?" he said, taking up a pen.

"Yes, sir," answered the gamekeeper.

"Was the poor fellow married? Had he any people dependent on him?" asked Dorian, looking bored. "If so, I should not like them to be left in want, and will send them any sum of money you may think necessary."

"We don't know who he is, sir. That is what I took the liberty of coming to you about."

"Don't know who he is?" said Dorian, listlessly. "What do you mean? Wasn't he one of your men?"

"No, sir. Never saw him before. Seems like a sailor, sir."

The pen dropped from Dorian Gray's hand, and he felt as if his heart had suddenly stopped beating. "A sailor?" he cried out. "Did you say a sailor?"

"Yes, sir. He looks as if he had been a sort of sailor; tattooed on both arms, and that kind of thing."

"Was there anything found on him?" said Dorian, leaning forward and looking at the man with startled eyes. "Anything that would tell his name?"

"Some money, sir—not much, and a six-shooter. There was no name of any kind. A decent-looking man, sir, but rough-like. A sort of sailor we think."

Dorian started to his feet. A terrible hope fluttered past him. He clutched at it madly. "Where is the body?" he exclaimed. "Quick! I must see it at once."

"It is in an empty stable in the Home Farm, sir. The folk don't like to have that sort of thing in their houses. They say a corpse brings bad luck."

"The Home Farm! Go there at once and meet me. Tell one of the grooms to bring my horse round. No. Never mind. I'll go to the stables myself. It will save time."

In less than a quarter of an hour Dorian Gray was galloping down the long avenue as hard as he could go. The trees seemed to sweep past him in spectral procession, and wild shadows to fling themselves across his path. Once the mare swerved at a white gate-post and nearly threw him. He lashed her across the neck with his crop. She cleft the dusky air like an arrow. The stones flew from her hoofs.

At last he reached the Home Farm. Two men were loitering in the yard. He leapt from the saddle and threw the reins to one of them. In the farthest stable a light was glimmering. Something seemed to tell him that the body was there, and he hurried to the door, and put his hand upon the latch.

There he paused for a moment, feeling that he was on the brink of a discovery that would either make or mar his life. Then he thrust the door open, and entered.

On a heap of sacking in the far corner was lying the dead body of a man dressed in a coarse shirt and a pair of blue trousers. A spotted handkerchief had been placed over the face. A coarse candle, stuck in a bottle, sputtered beside it.

Dorian Gray shuddered. He felt that his could not be the hand to take the handkerchief away, and called out to one of the farm servants to come to him.

"Take that thing off the face. I wish to see it," he said, clutching at the doorpost for support.

When the farm servant had done so, he stepped forward. A cry of joy broke from his lips. The man who had been shot in the thicket was James Vane.

He stood there for some minutes looking at the dead body. As he rode home, his eyes were full of tears, for he knew he was safe.

XIX

"THERE is no use your telling me that you are going to be good," cried Lord Henry, dipping his white fingers into a red copper bowl filled with rose-water. "You are quite perfect. Pray, don't change."

Dorian Gray shook his head. "No, Harry, I have done too many dreadful things in my life. I am not going to do any more. I began my good actions yesterday."

"Where were you yesterday?"

"In the country, Harry. I was staying at a little inn by myself."

"My dear boy," said Lord Henry, smiling, "anybody can be good 'in the country. There are no temptations there. That is the reason why people who live out of town are so absolutely uncivilized. Civilization is not by any means an easy thing to attain to. There are only two ways by which man can reach it. One is by being cultured, the other by being corrupt. Country people have no opportunity of being either, so they stagnate."

"Culture and corruption," echoed Dorian. "I have known something of both. It seems terrible to me now that they should ever be found together. For I have a new ideal, Harry. I am going to alter. I think I have altered."

"You have not yet told me what your good action was. Or did you say you had done more than one?" asked his companion, as he spilt into his plate a little crimson pyramid of seeded strawberries, and through a perforated shell-shaped spoon snowed white sugar upon them.

"I can tell you, Harry. It is not a story I could tell to anyone else. I spared somebody. It sounds vain, but you understand what I mean. She was quite beautiful and wonderfully like Sibyl Vane. I think it was that which first attracted me to her. You remember Sibyl, don't you? How long ago that seems! Well, Hetty was not one of our own class, of course. She was simply a girl in a village. But I really loved her. I am quite sure that I loved her. All during this wonderful May that we have been having, I used to run down and see her two or three times a week. Yesterday she met me in a little orchard. The apple-blossoms kept tumbling down on her hair, and she was laughing. We were to have gone away together this morning at dawn. Suddenly I determined to leave her as flower-like as I had found her."

"I should think the novelty of the emotion must have given you a thrill of real pleasure, Dorian," interrupted Lord Henry. "But I can finish your idyll for you. You gave her good advice, and broke her heart. That was the beginning of your reformation."

"Harry, you are horrible! You mustn't say these dreadful things. Hetty's heart is not broken. Of course she cried, and all that. But there is no disgrace upon her. She can live, like Perdita, in her garden of mint and marigold."

"And weep over a faithless Florizel," said Lord Henry, laughing, as he leant back in his chair. "My dear Dorian, you have the most curiously boyish moods. Do you think this girl will ever be really contented now with anyone of her own rank? I suppose she will be married some day to a rough carter or a grinning ploughman. Well, the fact of having met you, and loved you, will teach her to despise her husband, and she will be wretched. From a moral point of view, I cannot say that I think much of your great renunciation. Even as a beginning, it is poor. Besides, how do you know that Hetty isn't floating at the present moment in some star-lit millpond, with lovely water-lilies round her, like Ophelia?"

"I can't bear this, Harry! You mock at everything, and then suggest the most serious tragedies. I am sorry I told you now. I don't care what you say to me. I know I was right in acting as I did. Poor Hetty! As I rode past the farm this morning, I saw her white face at the window, like a spray of jasmine. Don't let us talk about it any more, and don't try to persuade me that the first good action I have done for years, the first little bit of self-sacrifice I have ever known, is really a sort of sin. I want to be better. I am going to be better. Tell me something about yourself. What is going on in town? I have not been to the club for days."

"The people are still discussing poor Basil's disappearance."

"I should have thought they had got tired of that by this time," said Dorian, pouring himself out some wine, and frowning slightly.

"My dear boy, they have only been talking about it for six weeks, and the British public are really not equal to the mental strain of having more than one topic every three months. They have been very fortunate lately, however. They have had my own divorce-case, and Alan Campbell's suicide. Now they have got the mysterious disappearance of an artist. Scotland Yard still insists that the man in the grey ulster who left for Paris by the midnight train on the ninth of November was poor Basil, and the French police declare that Basil never arrived in Paris at all. I suppose in about a fortnight we shall be told that he has been seen in San Francisco. It is an odd thing, but everyone who disappears is said to be seen at San Francisco. It must be a delightful city, and possess all the attractions of the next world."

"What do you think has happened to Basil?" asked Dorian, holding up his Burgundy against the light, and wondering how it was that he could discuss the matter so calmly.

"I have not the slightest idea. If Basil chooses to hide himself, it is no business of mine. If he is dead, I don't want to think about him. Death is the only thing that ever terrifies me. I hate it."

"Why?" said the younger man, wearily.

"Because," said Lord Henry, passing beneath his nostrils the gilt trellis of an open vinaigrette box, "one can survive everything nowadays except that. Death and vulgarity are the only two facts in the nineteenth century that one cannot explain away. Let us have our coffee in the music-room, Dorian. You must play Chopin to me. The man with whom my wife ran away played Chopin exquisitely. Poor Victoria! I was very fond of her. The house is rather lonely without her. Of course married life is merely a habit, a bad habit. But then one regrets the loss even of one's worst habits. Perhaps one regrets them the most. They are such an essential part of one's personality."

Dorian said nothing, but rose from the table, and, passing into the next room, sat down to the piano and let his fingers stray across the white and black ivory of the keys. After the coffee had been brought in, he stopped, and, looking over at Lord Henry, said, "Harry, did it ever occur to you that Basil was murdered?"

Lord Henry yawned. "Basil was very popular, and always wore a Waterbury watch. Why should he have been murdered? He was not clever enough to have enemies. Of course he had a wonderful genius for painting. But a man can paint like Velásquez and yet be as dull as possible. Basil was really rather dull. He only interested me once, and that was when he told me, years ago, that he had a wild adoration for you, and that you were the dominant motive of his art."

"I was very fond of Basil," said Dorian, with a note of sadness in his voice. "But don't people say that he was murdered?"

"Oh, some of the papers do. It does not seem to me to be at all probable. I know there are dreadful places in Paris, but Basil was not the sort of man to have gone to them. He had no curiosity. It was his chief defect."

"What would you say, Harry, if I told you that I had murdered Basil?" said the younger man. He watched him intently after he had spoken.

"I would say, my dear fellow, that you were posing for a character that doesn't suit you. All crime is vulgar, just as all vulgarity is crime. It is not in you, Dorian, to commit a murder. I am sorry if I hurt your vanity by saying so, but I assure you it is true. Crime belongs exclusively to the lower orders. I don't blame them in the smallest degree. I should fancy that crime was to them what art is to us, simply a method of procuring extraordinary sensations."

"A method of procuring sensations? Do you think, then, that a man who has once committed a murder could possibly do the same crime again? Don't tell me that."

"Oh! anything becomes a pleasure if one does it too often," cried Lord Henry, laughing. "That is one of the most important secrets of life. I should fancy, however, that murder is always a mistake. One should never do anything that one cannot talk about after dinner. But let us pass from poor Basil. I wish I could believe that he had come to such a really romantic end as you suggest; but I can't. I dare say he fell into the Seine off an omnibus, and that the conductor hushed up the scandal. Yes, I should fancy that was his end. I see him lying now on his back under those dull-green waters with the heavy barges floating over him, and long weeds catching in his hair. Do you know, I don't think he would have done much more good work. During the last ten years his painting had gone off very much."

Dorian heaved a sigh, and Lord Henry strolled across the room and began to stroke the head of a curious Java parrot, a large grey-plumaged bird, with pink crest and tail, that was balancing itself upon a bamboo perch. As his pointed fingers touched it, it dropped the white scurf of crinkled lids over black glass-like eyes, and began to sway backwards and forwards.

"Yes," he continued, turning round, and taking his handkerchief out of his pocket; "his painting had quite gone off. It seemed to me to have lost something. It had lost an ideal. When you and he ceased to be great friends, he ceased to be a great artist. What was it separated you? I suppose he bored you. If so, he never forgave you. It's a habit bores have. By the way, what has become of that wonderful portrait he did of you? I don't think I have ever seen it since he finished it. Oh! I remember your telling me years ago that you had sent it down to Selby, and that it had got mislaid or stolen on the way. You never got it back? What a pity! It was really a masterpiece. I remember I wanted to buy it. I wish I had now. It belonged to Basil's best period. Since then, his work was that curious mixture of bad painting and good intentions that always entitles a man to be called a representative British artist. Did you advertise for it? You should."

"I forget," said Dorian. "I suppose I did. But I never really liked it. I am sorry I sat for it. The memory of the thing is hateful to me. Why do you talk of it? It used to remind me of those curious lines in some play —*Hamlet*, I think—how do they run?—

'Like the painting of a sorrow,
  A face without a heart.'

Yes, that is what it was like."

Lord Henry laughed. "If a man treats life artistically, his brain is his heart," he answered, sinking into an arm-chair.

Dorian Gray shook his head, and struck some soft chords on the piano. "'Like the painting of a sorrow,'" he repeated, "'a face without a heart.'"

The elder man lay back and looked at him with half-closed eyes. "By the way, Dorian," he said, after a pause, "'what does it profit a man if he gain the whole world and lose'—how does the quotation run?—'his own soul?'"

The music jarred and Dorian Gray started, and stared at his friend. "Why do you ask me that, Harry?"

"My dear fellow," said Lord Henry, elevating his eyebrows in surprise, "I asked you because I thought you might be able to give me an answer. That is all. I was going through the Park last Sunday, and close by the Marble Arch there stood a little crowd of shabby-looking people listening to some vulgar street-preacher. As I passed by, I heard the man yelling out that question to his audience. It struck me as being rather dramatic. London is very rich in curious effects of that kind. A wet Sunday, an uncouth Christian in a mack-intosh, a ring of sickly white faces under a broken roof of dripping umbrellas, and a wonderful phrase flung into the air by shrill, hysterical lips—it was really very good in its way, quite a suggestion. I thought of telling the prophet that art had a soul, but that man had not. I am afraid, however, he would not have understood me."

"Don't, Harry. The soul is a terrible reality. It can be bought, and sold, and bartered away. It can be poisoned, or made perfect. There is a soul in each one of us. I know it."

"Do you feel quite sure of that, Dorian?"

"Quite sure."

"Ah! then it must be an illusion. The things one feels absolutely certain about are never true. That is the fatality of faith, and the lesson of romance. How grave you are! Don't be so serious. What have you or I to do with the superstitions of our age? No, we have given up our belief in the soul. Play me something. Play me a nocturne, Dorian, and, as you play, tell me, in a low voice, how you have kept your youth. You must have some secret. I am only ten years older than you are, and I am wrinkled, and worn, and yellow. You are really wonderful, Dorian. You have never looked more charming than you do tonight. You remind me of the day I saw you first. You were rather cheeky, very shy, and absolutely extraordinary. You have changed, of course, but not in appearance. I wish you would tell me your secret. To get back my youth I would do anything in the world, except take exercise, get up early, or be respectable. Youth! There is nothing like it. It's absurd to talk of the ignorance of youth. The only people to whose opinions I listen now with any respect are people much younger than myself. They seem in front of me. Life has revealed to them her latest wonder. As for the aged, I always contradict the aged. I do it on principle. If you ask them their opinion on something that happened yesterday, they solemnly give you the opinions current in 1820, when people wore high stocks, believed in everything, and knew absolutely nothing. How lovely that thing you are playing is! I wonder did Chopin write it at Majorca, with the sea weeping round the villa, and the salt spray dashing against the panes? It is marvellously romantic. What a blessing it is that there is one art left to us that is not imitative! Don't stop. I want music tonight. It seems to me that you are the young Apollo, and that I am Marsyas listening to you. I have sorrows, Dorian, of my own, that even you know nothing of. The tragedy of old age is not that one is old, but that one is young. I am amazed sometimes at my own sincerity. Ah, Dorian, how happy you are! What an exquisite life you have had! You have drunk deeply of everything. You have crushed the grapes against your palate. Nothing has been hidden from you. And it has all been to you no more than the sound of music. It has not marred you. You are still the same."

"I am not the same, Harry."

"Yes, you are the same. I wonder what the rest of your life will be. Don't spoil it by renunciations. At present you are a perfect type. Don't make yourself incomplete. You are quite flawless now. You need not shake your head: you know you are. Besides, Dorian, don't deceive yourself. Life is not governed by will or intention. Life is a question of nerves, and fibres, and slowly built-up cells in which thought hides itself and passion has its dreams. You may fancy yourself safe, and think yourself strong. But a chance tone of colour in a room or a morning sky, a particular perfume that you had once loved and that brings subtle memories with it, a line from a forgotten poem that you had come across again, a cadence from a piece of music that you had ceased to play—I tell you, Dorian, that it is on things like these that our lives depend. Browning writes about that somewhere; but our own senses will imagine them for us. There are moments when the odour of *lilas blanc* passes suddenly across me, and I have to live the strangest month of my life over again. I wish I could change places with you, Dorian. The world has cried out against us both, but it has always worshipped you. It always will worship you. You are the type of what the age is searching for, and what it is afraid it has found. I am so glad that you have never done anything, never carved a statue, or painted a picture, or produced anything outside of yourself! Life has been your art. You have set yourself to music. Your days are your sonnets."

Dorian rose up from the piano, and passed his hand through his hair. "Yes, life has been exquisite," he murmured, "but I am not going to have the same life, Harry. And you must not say these extravagant things to me. You don't know everything about me. I think that if you did, even you would turn from me. You laugh. Don't laugh."

"Why have you stopped playing, Dorian? Go back and give me the nocturne over again. Look at that great honey-coloured moon that hangs in the dusky air. She is waiting for you to charm her, and if you play she will come closer to the earth. You won't? Let us go to the club, then. It has been a charming evening, and we must end it charmingly. There is someone at White's who wants immensely to know you—young Lord Poole, Bournemouth's eldest son. He has already copied your neckties, and has begged me to introduce him to you. He is quite delightful, and rather reminds me of you."

"I hope not," said Dorian, with a sad look in his eyes. "But I am tired tonight, Harry. I shan't go to the club. It is nearly eleven, and I want to go to bed early."

"Do stay. You have never played so well as tonight. There was something in your touch that was wonderful. It had more expression than I had ever heard from it before."

"It is because I am going to be good," he answered, smiling. "I am a little changed already."

"You cannot change to me, Dorian," said Lord Henry. "You and I will always be friends."

"Yet you poisoned me with a book once. I should not forgive that. Harry, promise me that you will never lend that book to anyone. It does harm."

"My dear boy, you are really beginning to moralize. You will soon be going about like the converted, and the revivalist, warning people against all the sins of which you have grown tired. You are much too delightful to do that. Besides, it is no use. You and I are what we are, and will be what we will be. As for being poisoned by a book, there is no such thing as that. Art has no influence upon action. It annihilates the desire to act. It is superbly sterile. The books that the world calls immoral are books that show the world its own shame. That is all. But we won't discuss literature. Come round tomorrow. I am going to ride at eleven. We might go together, and I will take you to lunch afterwards with Lady Branksome. She is a charming woman, and wants to consult you about some tapestries she is thinking of buying. Mind you come. Or shall we lunch with our little Duchess? She says she never sees you now. Perhaps you are tired of Gladys? I thought you would be. Her clever tongue gets on one's nerves. Well, in any case, be here at eleven."

"Must I really come, Harry?"

"Certainly. The Park is quite lovely now. I don't think there have been such lilacs since the year I met you."

"Very well. I shall be here at eleven," said Dorian. "Good night, Harry." As he reached the door he hesitated for a moment, as if he had something more to say. Then he sighed and went out.

XX

IT WAS a lovely night, so warm that he threw his coat over his arm, and did not even put his silk scarf round his throat. As he strolled home, smoking his cigarette, two young men in evening dress passed him. He heard one of them whisper to the other, "That is Dorian Gray." He remembered how pleased he used to be when he was pointed out, or stared at, or talked about. He was tired of hearing his own name now. Half the charm of the little village where he had been so often lately was that no one knew who he was. He had often told the girl whom he had lured to love him that he was poor, and she had believed him. He had told her once that he was wicked, and she had laughed at him, and answered that wicked people were always very old and very ugly. What a laugh she had!—just like a thrush singing. And how pretty she had been in her cotton dresses and her large hats! She knew nothing, but she had everything that he had lost.

When he reached home, he found his servant waiting up for him. He sent him to bed, and threw himself down on the sofa in the library, and began to think over some of the things that Lord Henry had said to him.

Was it really true that one could never change? He felt a wild longing for the unstained purity of his boyhood—his rose-white boyhood, as Lord Henry had once called it. He knew that he had tarnished himself, filled his mind with corruption and given horror to his fancy; that he had been an evil influence to others and had experienced a terrible joy in being so; and that of the lives that had crossed his own it had been the fairest and the most full of promise that he had brought to shame. But was it all irretrievable? Was there no hope for him?

Ah! in what a monstrous moment of pride and passion he had prayed that the portrait should bear the burden of his days, and he keep the unsullied splendour of eternal youth! All his failure had been due to that. Better for him that each sin of his life had brought its sure, swift penalty along with it. There was purification in punishment. Not "Forgive us our sins," but "Smite us for our iniquities" should be the prayer of man to a most just God.

The curiously carved mirror that Lord Henry had given to him, so many years ago now, was standing on the table, and the white-limbed Cupids laughed round it as of old. He took it up, as he had done on that night of horror, when he had first noted the change in the fatal picture, and with wild tear-dimmed eyes looked into its polished shield. Once, someone who had terribly loved him, had written to him a mad letter, ending with these idolatrous words: "The world is changed because you are made of ivory and gold. The curves of your lips rewrite history." The phrases came back to his memory, and he repeated them over and over to himself. Then he loathed his own beauty, and flinging the mirror on the floor crushed it into silver splinters beneath his heel. It was his beauty that had ruined him, his beauty and the youth that he had prayed for. But for those two things, his life might have been free from stain. His beauty had been to him but a mask, his youth but a mockery. What was youth at best? A green, an unripe time, a time of shallow moods, and sickly thoughts. Why had he worn its livery? Youth had spoiled him.

It was better not to think of the past. Nothing could alter that. It was of himself, and of his own future, that he had to think. James Vane was hidden in a name-less grave in Selby churchyard. Alan Campbell had shot himself one night in his laboratory, but had not revealed the secret that he had been forced to know. The excitement, such as it was, over Basil Hallward's disappearance would soon pass away. It was already waning. He was perfectly safe there. Nor, indeed, was it the death of Basil Hallward that weighed most upon his mind. It was the living death of his own soul that troubled him. Basil had painted the portrait that had marred his life. He could not forgive him that. It was the portrait that had done everything. Basil had said things to him that were unbearable, and that he had yet borne with patience. The murder had been simply the madness of a moment. As for Alan Campbell, his suicide had been his own act. He had chosen to do it. It was nothing to him.

A new life! That was what he wanted. That was what he was waiting for. Surely he had begun it already. He had spared one innocent thing, at any rate. He would never again tempt innocence. He would be good.

As he thought of Hetty Merton, he began to wonder if the portrait in the locked room had changed. Surely it was not still so horrible as it had been? Perhaps if his life became pure, he would be able to expel every sign of evil passion from the face. Perhaps the signs of evil had already gone away. He would go and look.

He took the lamp from the table and crept upstairs. As he unbarred the door, a smile of joy flitted across his strangely young-looking face and lingered for a moment about his lips. Yes, he would be good, and the hideous thing that he had hidden away would no longer be a terror to him. He felt as if the load had been lifted from him already.

He went in quietly, locking the door behind him, as was his custom, and dragged the purple hanging from the portrait. A cry of pain and indignation broke from him. He could see no change, save that in the eyes there was a look of cunning, and in the mouth the curved wrinkle of the hypocrite. The thing was still loathsome—more loathsome, if possible, than before—and the scarlet dew that spotted the hand seemed brighter, and more like blood newly spilt. Then he trembled. Had it been merely vanity that had made him do his one good deed? Or the desire for a new sensation, as Lord Henry had hinted, with his mocking laugh? Or that passion to act a part that sometimes makes us do things finer than we are ourselves? Or, perhaps, all these? And why was the red stain larger than it had been? It seemed to have crept like a horrible disease over the wrinkled fingers. There was blood on the painted feet, as though the thing had dripped—blood even on the hand that had not held the knife. Confess? Did it mean that he was to confess? To give himself up, and be put to death? He laughed. He felt that the idea was monstrous. Besides, even if he did confess, who would believe him? There was no trace of the murdered man anywhere. Everything belonging to him had been destroyed. He himself had burned what had been below-stairs. The world would simply say that he was mad. They would shut him up if he persisted in his story. . . . Yet it was his duty to confess, to suffer public shame, and to make public atonement. There was a God who called upon men to tell their sins to earth as well as to heaven. Nothing that he could do would cleanse him till he had told his own sin. His sin? He shrugged his shoulders. The death of Basil Hallward seemed very little to him. He was thinking of Hetty Merton. For it was an unjust mirror, this mirror of his soul that he was looking at. Vanity? Curiosity? Hypocrisy? Had there been nothing more in his renunciation than that? There had been something more. At least he thought so. But who could tell? . . . No. There had been nothing more. Through vanity he had spared her. In hypocrisy he had worn the mask of goodness. For curiosity's sake he had tried the denial of self. He recognized that now.

But this murder—was it to dog him all his life? Was he always to be burdened by his past? Was he really to confess? Never. There was only one bit of evidence left against him. The picture itself—that was evidence. He would destroy it. Why had he kept it so long? Once it had given him pleasure to watch it changing and growing old. Of late he had felt no such pleasure. It had kept him awake at night. When he had been away, he had been filled with terror lest other eyes should look upon it. It had brought melancholy across his passions. Its mere memory had marred many moments of joy. It had been like conscience to him. Yes, it had been conscience. He would destroy it.

He looked round, and saw the knife that had stabbed Basil Hallward. He had cleaned it many times, till there was no stain left upon it. It was bright, and glistened. As it had killed the painter, so it would kill the painter's work, and all that that meant. It would kill the past, and when that was dead he would be free. It would kill this monstrous soul-life, and without its hideous warnings, he would be at peace. He seized the thing, and stabbed the picture with it.

There was a cry heard, and a crash. The cry was so horrible in its agony that the frightened servants woke, and crept out of their rooms. Two gentlemen, who were passing in the Square below, stopped, and looked up at the great house. They walked on till they met a policeman, and brought him back. The man rang the bell several times, but there was no answer. Except for a light in one of the top windows, the house was all dark. After a time, he went away, and stood in an adjoining portico and watched.

"Whose house is that, constable?" asked the elder of the two gentlemen.

"Mr. Dorian Gray's, sir," answered the policeman.

They looked at each other, as they walked away, and sneered. One of them was Sir Henry Ashton's uncle.

Inside, in the servants' part of the house, the half-clad domestics were talking in low whispers to each other. Old Mrs. Leaf was crying, and wringing her hands. Francis was as pale as death.

After about a quarter of an hour, he got the coachman and one of the footmen and crept upstairs. They knocked, but there was no reply. They called out. Everything was still. Finally, after vainly trying to force the door, they got on the roof, and dropped down on to the balcony. The windows yielded easily: their bolts were old.

When they entered, they found hanging upon the wall a splendid portrait of their master as they had last seen him, in all the wonder of his exquisite youth and beauty. Lying on the floor was a dead man, in evening dress, with a knife in his heart. He was withered, wrinkled, and loathsome of visage. It was not till they had examined the rings that they recognized who it was.

Salomé

A Tragedy in One Act

The Persons of the Play

HEROD ANTIPAS, Tetrarch of Judæa
JOKANAAN, the Prophet
THE YOUNG SYRIAN, Captain of the Guard
TIGELLINUS, a Young Roman
A CAPPADOCIAN
A NUBIAN
FIRST SOLDIER
SECOND SOLDIER
THE PAGE OF HERODIAS
JEWS, NAZARENES, ETC.
A SLAVE
NAAMAN, the Executioner
HERODIAS, Wife of the Tetrarch
SALOMÉ, Daughter of Herodias
THE SLAVES OF SALOMÉ

Scene. A great terrace in the Palace of HEROD, set above the banqueting-hall. Some soldiers are leaning over the balcony. To the right there is a gigantic stair-case, to the left, at the back, an old cistern surrounded by a wall of green bronze. The moon is shining very brightly.

THE YOUNG SYRIAN. How beautiful is the Princess Salomé tonight!

THE PAGE OF HERODIAS. Look at the moon. How strange the moon seems! She is like a woman rising from a tomb. She is like a dead woman. One might fancy she was looking for dead things.

THE YOUNG SYRIAN. She has a strange look. She is like a little princess who wears a yellow veil, and whose feet are of silver. She is like a princess who has little white doves for feet. One might fancy she was dancing.

THE PAGE OF HERODIAS. She is like a woman who is dead. She moves very slowly.

(*Noise in the banqueting-hall.*)

FIRST SOLDIER. What an uproar! Who are those wild beasts howling?

SECOND SOLDIER. The Jews. They are always like that. They are disputing about their religion.

FIRST SOLDIER. Why do they dispute about their religion?

SECOND SOLDIER. I cannot tell. They are always doing it. The Pharisees, for instance, say that there are angels, and the Sadducees declare that angels do not exist.

FIRST SOLDIER. I think it is ridiculous to dispute about such things.

THE YOUNG SYRIAN. How beautiful is the Princess Salomé tonight!

THE PAGE OF HERODIAS. You are always looking at her. You look at her too much. It is dangerous to look at people in such fashion. Something terrible may happen.

THE YOUNG SYRIAN. She is very beautiful tonight.

FIRST SOLDIER. The Tetrarch has a sombre aspect.

SECOND SOLDIER. Yes; he has a sombre aspect.

FIRST SOLDIER. He is looking at something.

SECOND SOLDIER. He is looking at someone.

FIRST SOLDIER. At whom is he looking?

SECOND SOLDIER. I cannot tell.

THE YOUNG SYRIAN. How pale the Princess is! Never have I seen her so pale. She is like the shadow of a white rose in a mirror of silver.

THE PAGE OF HERODIAS. You must not look at her. You look too much at her.

FIRST SOLDIER. Herodias has filled the cup of the Tetrarch.

THE CAPPADOCIAN. Is that the Queen Herodias, she who wears a black mitre sewed with pearls, and whose hair is powdered with blue dust?

FIRST SOLDIER. Yes; that is Herodias, the Tetrarch's wife.

SECOND SOLDIER. The Tetrarch is very fond of wine. He has wine of three sorts. One which is brought from the Island of Samothrace, and is purple like the cloak of Cæsar.

THE CAPPADOCIAN. I have never seen Cæsar.

SECOND SOLDIER. Another that comes from a town called Cyprus, and is as yellow as gold.

THE CAPPADOCIAN. I love gold.

SECOND SOLDIER. And the third is a wine of Sicily. That wine is as red as blood.

THE NUBIAN. The gods of my country are very fond. Twice in the year we sacrifice to them young men and maidens; fifty young men and a hundred maidens. But I am afraid that we never give them quite enough, for they are very harsh to us.

THE CAPPADOCIAN. In my country there are no gods left. The Romans have driven them out. There are some who say that they have hidden themselves in the mountains, but I do not believe it. Three nights I have been on the mountains seeking them everywhere. I did not find them. And at last I called them by their names, and they did not come. I think they are dead.

FIRST SOLDIER. The Jews worship a God that one cannot see.

THE CAPPADOCIAN. I cannot understand that.

FIRST SOLDIER. In fact, they only believe in things that one cannot see.

THE CAPPADOCIAN. That seems to me altogether ridiculous.

THE VOICE OF JOKANAAN. After me shall come another mightier than I. I am not worthy so much as to unloose the latchet of his shoes. When he cometh, the solitary places shall be glad. They shall blossom like the rose. The eyes of the blind shall see the day, and the ears of the deaf shall be opened. The suckling child shall put his hand upon the dragon's lair, he shall lead the lions by their manes.

SECOND SOLDIER. Make him be silent. He is always saying ridiculous things.

FIRST SOLDIER. No, no. He is a holy man. He is very gentle, too. Every day, when I give him to eat he thanks me.

THE CAPPADOCIAN. Who is he?

FIRST SOLDIER. A prophet.

THE CAPPADOCIAN. What is his name?

FIRST SOLDIER. Jokanaan.

THE CAPPADOCIAN. Whence comes he?

FIRST SOLDIER. From the desert where he fed on locusts and wild honey. He was clothed in camel's hair, and round his loins he had a leathern belt. He was very terrible to look upon. A great multitude used to follow him. He even had disciples.

THE CAPPADOCIAN. What is he talking of?

FIRST SOLDIER. We can never tell. Sometimes he says things that affright one, but it is impossible to understand what he says.

THE CAPPADOCIAN. May one see him?

FIRST SOLDIER. No. The Tetrarch has forbidden it.

THE YOUNG SYRIAN. The Princess has hidden her face behind her fan! Her little white hands are fluttering like doves that fly to their dovecots. They are like white butterflies. They are just like white butterflies.

THE PAGE OF HERODIAS. What is that to you? Why do you look at her? You must not look at her. . . . Something terrible may happen.

THE CAPPADOCIAN (*Pointing to the cistern*). What a strange prison!

SECOND SOLDIER. It is an old cistern.

THE CAPPADOCIAN. An old cistern! That must be a poisonous place in which to dwell!

SECOND SOLDIER. Oh no! For instance, the Tetrarch's brother, his elder brother, the first husband of Herodias the Queen, was imprisoned there for twelve years. It did not kill him. At the end of the twelve years he had to be strangled.

THE CAPPADOCIAN. Strangled? Who dared to do that?

SECOND SOLDIER (*Pointing to the Executioner, a huge Negro*). That man yonder, Naaman.

THE CAPPADOCIAN. He was not afraid?

SECOND SOLDIER. Oh no! The Tetrarch sent him the ring.

THE CAPPADOCIAN. What ring?

SECOND SOLDIER. The death-ring. So he was not afraid.

THE CAPPADOCIAN. Yet it is a terrible thing to strangle a king.

FIRST SOLDIER. Why? Kings have but one neck, like other folk.

THE CAPPADOCIAN. I think it terrible.

THE YOUNG SYRIAN. The Princess is getting up! She is leaving the table! She looks very troubled. Ah, she is coming this way. Yes, she is coming towards us. How pale she is! Never have I seen her so pale.

THE PAGE OF HERODIAS. I pray you not to look at her.

THE YOUNG SYRIAN. She is like a dove that has strayed. . . . She is like a narcissus trembling in the wind. . . . She is like a silver flower.

(*Enter* SALOMÉ.)

SALOMÉ. I will not stay. I cannot stay. Why does the Tetrarch look at me all the while with his mole's eyes under his shaking eyelids? It is strange that the husband of my mother looks at me like that. I know not what it means. Of a truth I know it too well.

THE YOUNG SYRIAN. You have left the feast, Princess?

SALOMÉ. How sweet is the air here! I can breathe here! Within there are Jews from Jerusalem who are tearing each other in pieces over their foolish ceremonies, and barbarians who drink and drink, and spill their wine on the pavement, and Greeks from Smyrna with painted eyes and painted cheeks, and frizzed hair curled in columns, and Egyptians silent and subtle, with long nails of jade and russet cloaks, and Romans brutal and coarse, with their uncouth jargon. Ah! how I loathe the Romans! They are rough and common, and they give themselves the airs of noble lords.

THE YOUNG SYRIAN. Will you be seated, Princess?

THE PAGE OF HERODIAS. Why do you speak to her? Oh! something terrible will happen. Why do you look at her?

SALOMÉ. How good to see the moon! She is like a little piece of money, a little silver flower. She is cold and chaste. I am sure she is a virgin. Yes, she is a virgin. She has never defiled herself. She has never abandoned herself to men, like the other goddesses.

THE VOICE OF JOKANAAN. Behold! the Lord hath come. The son of man is at hand. The centaurs have hidden themselves in the rivers, and the nymphs have left the rivers, and are lying beneath the leaves of the forest.

SALOMÉ. Who was that who cried out?

SECOND SOLDIER. The prophet, Princess.

SALOMÉ. Ah, the prophet! He of whom the Tetrarch is afraid?

SECOND SOLDIER. We know nothing of that, Princess. It was the prophet Jokanaan who cried out.

THE YOUNG SYRIAN. Is it your pleasure that I bid them bring your litter, Princess? The night is fair in the garden.

SALOMÉ. He says terrible things about my mother, does he not?

SECOND SOLDIER. We never understand what he says, Princess.

SALOMÉ. Yes; he says terrible things about her.

(*Enter a slave.*)

THE SLAVE. Princess, the Tetrarch prays you to return to the feast.

THE YOUNG SYRIAN. Pardon me, Princess, but if you return not some misfortune may happen.

SALOMÉ. Is he an old man, this prophet?

THE YOUNG SYRIAN. Princess, it were better to return. Suffer me to lead you in.

SALOMÉ. This prophet . . . is he an old man?

FIRST SOLDIER. No, Princess, he is quite young.

SECOND SOLDIER. One cannot be sure. There are those who say he is Elias.

SALOMÉ. Who is Elias?

SECOND SOLDIER. A prophet of this country in bygone days, Princess.

THE SLAVE. What answer may I give the Tetrarch from the Princess?

THE VOICE OF JOKANAAN. Rejoice not, O land of Palestine, because the rod of him who smote thee is broken. For from the seed of the serpent shall come a basilisk, and that which is born of it shall devour the birds.

SALOMÉ. What a strange voice! I would speak with him.

FIRST SOLDIER. I fear it may not be, Princess. The Tetrarch does not suffer anyone to speak with him. He has even forbidden the high priest to speak with him.

SALOMÉ. I desire to speak with him.

FIRST SOLDIER. It is impossible, Princess.

SALOMÉ. I will speak with him.

THE YOUNG SYRIAN. Would it not be better to return to the banquet?

SALOMÉ. Bring forth this prophet. (*Exit the slave.*)

FIRST SOLDIER. We dare not, Princess.

SALOMÉ (*Approaching the cistern and looking down into it*). How black it is, down there! It must be terrible to be in so black a hole! It is like a tomb. . . . (*To the soldiers.*) Did you not hear me? Bring out the prophet. I would look on him.

SECOND SOLDIER. Princess, I beg you do not require this of us.

SALOMÉ. You are making me wait upon your pleasure.

FIRST SOLDIER. Princess, our lives belong to you, but we cannot do what you have asked of us. And indeed, it is not of us that you should ask this thing.

SALOMÉ (*Looking at the young Syrian*). Ah!

THE PAGE OF HERODIAS. Oh! what is going to happen? I am sure that something terrible will happen.

SALOMÉ (*Going up to the young Syrian*). Thou wilt do this thing for me, wilt thou not, Narraboth? Thou wilt do this thing for me. I have ever been kind towards thee. Thou wilt do it for me. I would but look at him, this strange prophet. Men have talked so much of him. Often I have heard the Tetrarch talk of him. I think he is afraid of him, the Tetrarch. Art thou, even thou, also afraid of him, Narraboth?

THE YOUNG SYRIAN. I fear him not, Princess; there is no man I fear. But the Tetrarch has formally forbidden that any man should raise the cover of this well.

SALOMÉ. Thou wilt do this thing for me, Narraboth, and tomorrow when I pass in my litter beneath the gate-way of the idol-sellers I will let fall for thee a little flower, a little green flower.

THE YOUNG SYRIAN. Princess, I cannot, I cannot.

SALOMÉ (Smiling). Thou wilt do this thing for me, Narraboth. Thou knowest that thou wilt do this thing for me. And on the morrow when I shall pass in my litter by the bridge of the idol-buyers, I will look at thee through the muslin veils, I will look at thee, Narraboth, it may be I will smile at thee. Look at me, Narraboth, look at me. Ah! thou knowest that thou wilt do what I ask of thee. Thou knowest it. . . . I know that thou wilt do this thing.

THE YOUNG SYRIAN (Signing to the third soldier). Let the prophet come forth. . . . The Princess Salomé desires to see him.

SALOMÉ. Ah!

THE PAGE OF HERODIAS. Oh! How strange the moon looks. Like the hand of a dead woman who is seeking to cover herself with a shroud.

THE YOUNG SYRIAN. She has a strange aspect! She is like a little princess, whose eyes are eyes of amber. Through the clouds of muslin she is smiling like a little princess.

(*The prophet comes out of the cistern.* SALOMÉ *looks at him and steps slowly back.*)

JOKANAAN. Where is he whose cup of abominations is now full? Where is he, who in a robe of silver shall one day die in the face of all the people? Bid him come forth, that he may hear the voice of him who hath cried in the waste places and in the houses of kings.

SALOMÉ. Of whom is he speaking?

THE YOUNG SYRIAN. No one can tell, Princess.

JOKANAAN. Where is she who saw the images of men painted on the walls, even the images of the Chaldeans painted with colours, and gave herself up unto the lust of her eyes, and sent ambassadors into the land of Chaldæa?

SALOMÉ. It is of my mother that he is speaking.

THE YOUNG SYRIAN. Oh, no, Princess.

SALOMÉ. Yes; it is of my mother that he is speaking.

JOKANAAN. Where is she who gave herself unto the Captains of Assyria, who have baldricks on their loins, and crowns of many colours on their heads? Where is she who hath given herself to the young men of the Egyptians, who are clothed in fine linen and hyacinth, whose shields are of gold, whose helmets are of silver, whose bodies are mighty? Go, bid her rise up from the bed of her abominations, from the bed of her incestuousness, that she may hear the words of him who prepareth the way of the Lord, that she may repent her of her iniquities. Though she will not repent, but will stick fast in her abominations; go, bid her come, for the fan of the Lord is in His hand.

SALOMÉ. Ah, but he is terrible, he is terrible!

THE YOUNG SYRIAN. Do not stay here, Princess, I beseech you.

SALOMÉ. It is his eyes above all that are terrible.

They are like black holes burned by torches in a tapestry of Tyre. They are like the black caverns of Egypt in which the dragons make their lairs. They are like black lakes troubled by fantastic moons. . . . Do you think he will speak again?

THE YOUNG SYRIAN. Do not stay here, Princess. I pray you do not stay here.

SALOMÉ. How wasted he is! He is like a thin ivory statue. He is like an image of silver. I am sure he is chaste as the moon is. He is like a moonbeam, like a shaft of silver. I would look closer at him. I must look at him closer.

THE YOUNG SYRIAN. Princess! Princess!

JOKANAAN. Who is this woman who is looking at me? I will not have her look at me. Wherefore doth she look at me with her golden eyes, under her gilded eyelids. I know not who she is. I do not desire to know who she is. Bid her begone. It is not to her that I would speak.

SALOMÉ. I am Salomé, daughter of Herodias, Princess of Judæa.

JOKANAAN. Back! daughter of Babylon! Come not near the chosen of the Lord. Thy mother hath filled the earth with the wine of her iniquities, and the cry of her sinning hath come up even to the ears of God.

SALOMÉ. Speak again, Jokanaan. Thy voice is as music to mine ear.

THE YOUNG SYRIAN. Princess! Princess! Princess!

SALOMÉ. Speak again! Speak again, Jokanaan, and tell me what I must do.

JOKANAAN. Daughter of Sodom, come not near me! But cover thy face with a veil, and scatter ashes upon thine head, and get thee to the desert and seek out the Son of Man.

SALOMÉ. Who is he, the Son of Man? Is he as beautiful as thou art, Jokanaan?

JOKANAAN. Get thee behind me! I hear in the palace the beating of the wings of the angel of death.

THE YOUNG SYRIAN. Princess, I beseech thee to go within.

JOKANAAN. Angel of the Lord God, what dost thou here with thy sword? Whom seekest thou in this palace? The day of him who shall die in a robe of silver has not yet come.

SALOMÉ. Jokanaan!

JOKANAAN. Who speaketh?

SALOMÉ. I am amorous of thy body, Jokanaan! Thy body is white like the lilies of a field that the mower hath never mowed. Thy body is white like the snows that lie on the mountains of Judæa, and come down into the valleys. The roses in the garden of the Queen of Arabia are not so white as thy body. Neither the roses of the garden of the Queen of Arabia, the garden of spices of the Queen of Arabia, nor the feet of the dawn when they light on the leaves, nor the breast of the moon when she lies on the breast of the sea. . . . There is nothing in the world so white as thy body. Suffer me to touch thy body.

JOKANAAN. Back! daughter of Babylon! By woman came evil into the world. Speak not to me. I will not listen to thee. I listen but to the voice of the Lord God.

SALOMÉ. Thy body is hideous. It is like the body of a leper. It is like a plastered wall where vipers have crawled; like a plastered wall where the scorpions have made their nest. It is like a whitened sepulchre full of loathsome things. It is horrible, thy body is horrible. It is thy hair that I am enamoured of, Jokanaan. Thy hair is like clusters of grapes, like the clusters of black grapes that hang from the vine-trees of Edom in the land of the Edomites. Thy hair is like the cedars of Lebanon, like the great cedars of Lebanon that give their shade to the lions and to the robbers who would hide them by day. The long black nights, when the moon hides her face, when the stars are afraid, are not so black as thy hair. The silence that dwells in the forest is not so black. There is nothing in the world that is so black as thy hair. . . . Suffer me to touch thy hair.

JOKANAAN. Back, daughter of Sodom! Touch me not. Profane not the temple of the Lord God.

SALOMÉ. Thy hair is horrible. It is covered with mire and dust. It is like a knot of serpents coiled round thy neck. I love not thy hair. . . . It is thy mouth that I desire, Jokanaan. Thy mouth is like a band of scarlet on a tower of ivory. It is like a pomegranate cut in twain with a knife of ivory. The pomegranate flowers that blossom in the gardens of Tyre, and are redder than roses, are not so red. The red blasts of trumpets that herald the approach of kings, and make afraid the enemy, are not so red. Thy mouth is redder than the feet of the doves who inhabit the temples and are fed by the priests. It is redder than the feet of him who cometh from a forest where he hath slain a lion, and seen gilded tigers. Thy mouth is like a branch of coral that fishers have found in the twilight of the sea, the coral that they keep for the kings! . . . It is like the vermilion that the Moabites find in the mines of Moab, the vermilion that the kings take from them. It is like the bow of the King of the Persians, that is painted with vermilion, and is tipped with coral. There is nothing in the world so red as thy mouth. . . . Suffer me to kiss thy mouth.

JOKANAAN. Never! daughter of Babylon! Daughter of Sodom! Never.

SALOMÉ. I will kiss thy mouth, Jokanaan. I will kiss thy mouth.

THE YOUNG SYRIAN. Princess, Princess, thou who art like a garden of myrrh, thou who art the dove of all doves, look not at this man, look not at him! Do not speak such words to him. I cannot endure it. . . . Princess, do not speak these things.

SALOMÉ. I will kiss thy mouth, Jokanaan.

THE YOUNG SYRIAN. Ah! (*He kills himself and falls between* SALOMÉ *and* JOKANAAN.)

THE PAGE OF HERODIAS. The young Syrian has slain himself! The young captain has slain himself! He has slain himself who was my friend! I gave him a little box of perfumes and ear-rings wrought in silver, and now he has killed himself! Ah, did he not say that some misfortune would happen? I too said it, and it has come to pass. Well I knew that the moon was seeking a dead thing, but I knew not that it was he whom she sought. Ah! why did I not hide him from the moon? If I had hidden him in a cavern she would not have seen him.

FIRST SOLDIER. Princess, the young captain has just slain himself.

SALOMÉ. Suffer me to kiss thy mouth, Jokanaan.

JOKANAAN. Art thou not afraid, daughter of Herodias? Did I not tell thee that I had heard in the palace the beatings of the wings of the angel of death, and hath he not come, the angel of death?

SALOMÉ. Suffer me to kiss thy mouth.

JOKANAAN. Daughter of adultery, there is but one who can save thee, it is He of whom I spake. Go seek Him. He is in a boat on the sea of Galilee, and He talketh with His disciples. Kneel down on the shore of the sea, and call unto Him by His name. When He cometh to thee (and to all who call on Him He cometh), bow thyself at His feet and ask of Him the remissions of thy sins.

SALOMÉ. Suffer me to kiss thy mouth.

JOKANAAN. Cursed be thou! daughter of an incestuous mother, be thou accursed!

SALOMÉ. I will kiss thy mouth, Jokanaan.

JOKANAAN. I will not look at thee, thou art accursed, Salomé, thou art accursed. (*He goes down into the cistern.*)

SALOMÉ. I will kiss thy mouth, Jokanaan; I will kiss thy mouth.

FIRST SOLDIER. We must bear away the body to another place. The Tetrarch does not care to see dead bodies, save the bodies of those whom he himself has slain.

THE PAGE OF HERODIAS. He was my brother, and nearer to me than a brother. I gave him a little box full of perfumes, and a ring of agate that he wore always on his hand. In the evening we were wont to walk by the river, and among the almond trees, and he used to tell me of the things of his country. He spake ever very low. The sound of his voice was like the sound of the flute, of one who playeth upon the flute. Also he had much joy to gaze at himself in the river. I used to reproach him for that.

SECOND SOLDIER. You are right; we must hide the body. The Tetrarch must not see it.

FIRST SOLDIER. The Tetrarch will not come to this place. He never comes on the terrace. He is too much afraid of the prophet.

(*Enter* HEROD, HERODIAS, *and all the Court.*)

HEROD. Where is Salomé? Where is the Princess? Why did she not return to the banquet as I commanded her? Ah! there she is!

HERODIAS. You must not look at her! You are always looking at her!

HEROD. The moon has a strange look tonight. Has she not a strange look? She is like a mad woman who is seeking everywhere for lovers. She is naked too. She is quite naked. The clouds are seeking to clothe her nakedness, but she will not let them. She shows herself naked in the sky. She reels through the clouds like a drunken woman. . . . I am sure she is looking for lovers. Does she not reel like a drunken woman? She is like a mad woman, is she not?

HERODIAS. No; the moon is like the moon, that is all. Let us go within. . . . We have nothing to do here.

HEROD. I will stay here! Manasseh, lay carpets there. Light torches, bring forth the ivory table, and the tables of jasper. The air here is sweet. I will drink more wine with my guests. We must show all honours to the ambassadors of Cæsar.

HERODIAS. It is not because of them that you remain.

HEROD. Yes; the air is very sweet. Come, Herodias, our guests await us. Ah! I have slipped! I have slipped in blood! It is an ill omen. Wherefore is there blood here? . . . and this body, what does this body here? Think you I am like the King of Egypt, who gives no feast to his guests but that he shows them a corpse? Whose is it? I will not look on it.

FIRST SOLDIER. It is our captain, sire. He is the young Syrian whom you made captain of the guard but three days gone.

HEROD. I issued no order that he should be slain.

SECOND SOLDIER. He slew himself, sire.

HEROD. For what reason? I had made him captain of my guard.

SECOND SOLDIER. We do not know, sire. But with his own hand he slew himself.

HEROD. That seems strange to me. I had thought it

was but the Roman philosophers who slew themselves. Is it not true, Tigellinus, that the philosophers at Rome slay themselves?

TIGELLINUS. There be some who slay themselves, sire. They are the Stoics. The Stoics are people of no cultivation. They are ridiculous people. I myself regard them as being perfectly ridiculous.

HEROD. I also. It is ridiculous to kill oneself.

TIGELLINUS. Everybody at Rome laughs at them. The Emperor has written a satire against them. It is recited everywhere.

HEROD. Ah! he has written a satire against them? Cæsar is wonderful. He can do everything. . . . It is strange that the young Syrian has slain himself. I am sorry he has slain himself. I am very sorry; for he was fair to look upon. He was even very fair. He had very languorous eyes. I remember that I saw that he looked languorously at Salomé. Truly, I thought he looked too much at her.

HERODIAS. There are others who look too much at her.

HEROD. His father was a king. I drove him from his kingdom. And of his mother, who was a queen, you made a slave—Herodias. So he was here as my guest, as it were, and for that reason I made him my captain. I am sorry he is dead. Ho! why have you left the body here? I will not look at it—away with it! (*They take away the body.*) It is cold here. There is a wind blowing. Is there not a wind blowing?

HERODIAS. No; there is no wind.

HEROD. I tell you there is a wind that blows. . . . And I hear in the air something that is like the beating of wings, like the beating of vast wings. Do you not hear it?

HERODIAS. I hear nothing.

HEROD. I hear it no longer. But I heard it. It was the blowing of the wind. It has passed away. But no, I hear it again. Do you not hear it? It is just like the beating of wings.

HERODIAS. I tell you there is nothing. You are ill. Let us go within.

HEROD. I am not ill. It is your daughter who is sick to death. Never have I seen her so pale.

HERODIAS. I have told you not to look at her.

HEROD. Pour me forth wine. (*Wine is brought.*) Salomé, come drink a little wine with me. I have here a wine that is exquisite. Cæsar himself sent it me. Dip into it thy little red lips, that I may drain the cup.

SALOMÉ. I am not thirsty, Tetrarch.

HEROD. You hear how she answers me, this daughter of yours?

HERODIAS. She does right. Why are you always gazing at her?

HEROD. Bring me ripe fruits. (*Fruits are brought.*) Salomé, come and eat fruits with me. I love to see in a fruit the mark of thy little teeth. Bite but a little of this fruit that I may eat what is left.

SALOMÉ. I am not hungry, Tetrarch.

HEROD (*To* HERODIAS). You see how you have brought up this daughter of yours.

HERODIAS. My daughter and I come of a royal race. As for thee, thy father was a camel driver! He was a thief and a robber to boot!

HEROD. Thou liest!

HERODIAS. Thou knowest well that it is true.

HEROD. Salomé, come and sit next to me. I will give thee the throne of thy mother.

SALOMÉ. I am not tired, Tetrarch.

HERODIAS. You see in what regard she holds you.

HEROD. Bring me—what is it that I desire? I forget. Ah! ah! I remember.

THE VOICE OF JOKANAAN. Behold the time is come! That which I foretold has come to pass. The day that I spoke of is at hand.

HERODIAS. Bid him be silent. I will not listen to his voice. This man is for ever hurling insults against me.

HEROD. He has said nothing against you. Besides, he is a very great prophet.

HERODIAS. I do not believe in prophets. Can a man tell what will come to pass? No man knows it. Also he is for ever insulting me. But I think you are afraid of him. . . . I know well that you are afraid of him.

HEROD. I am not afraid of him. I am afraid of no man.

HERODIAS. I tell you, you are afraid of him. If you are not afraid of him why do you not deliver him to the Jews who for these six months past have been clamouring for him?

A JEW. Truly, my lord, it were better to deliver him into our hands.

HEROD. Enough on this subject. I have already given you my answer. I will not deliver him into your hands. He is a holy man. He is a man who has seen God.

A JEW. That cannot be. There is no man who hath seen God since the prophet Elias. He is the last man who saw God face to face. In these days God doth not show Himself. God hideth Himself. Therefore great evils have come upon the land.

ANOTHER JEW. Verily, no man knoweth if Elias the prophet did indeed see God. Peradventure it was but the shadow of God that he saw.

A THIRD JEW. God is at no time hidden. He showeth

Himself at all times and in all places. God is in what is evil even as He is in what is good.

A FOURTH JEW. Thou shouldst not say that. It is a very dangerous doctrine. It is a doctrine that cometh from Alexandria, where men teach the philosophy of the Greeks. And the Greeks are Gentiles: They are not even circumcised.

A FIFTH JEW. No one can tell how God worketh. His ways are very dark. It may be that the things which we call evil are good, and that the things which we call good are evil. There is no knowledge of anything. We can but bow our heads to His will, for God is very strong. He breaketh in pieces the strong together with the weak, for He regardeth not any man.

FIRST JEW. Thou speaketh truly. Verily God is terrible; He breaketh in pieces the strong and the weak as a man breaks corn in a mortar. But as for man, he hath never seen God. No man hath seen God since the prophet Elias.

HERODIAS. Make them be silent. They weary me.

HEROD. But I have heard it said that Jokanaan is in very truth your prophet Elias.

THE JEW. That cannot be. It is more than three hundred years since the days of the prophet Elias.

HEROD. There be some who say that this man is Elias the prophet.

A NAZARENE. I am sure that he is Elias the prophet.

THE JEW. Nay, but he is not Elias the prophet.

THE VOICE OF JOKANAAN. Behold the day is at hand, the day of the Lord, and I hear upon the mountains the feet of Him who shall be the Saviour of the world.

HEROD. What does that mean? The Saviour of the world?

TIGELLINUS. It is a title that Cæsar adopts.

HEROD. But Cæsar is not coming into Judæa. Only yesterday I received letters from Rome. They contained nothing concerning this matter. And you, Tigellinus, who were at Rome during the winter, you heard nothing concerning this matter, did you?

TIGELLINUS. Sire, I heard nothing concerning the matter. I was explaining the title. It is one of Cæsar's titles.

HEROD. But Cæsar cannot come. He is too gouty. They say that his feet are like the feet of an elephant. Also there are reasons of State. He who leaves Rome loses Rome. He will not come. Howbeit, Cæsar is lord, he will come if such be his pleasure. Nevertheless, I think he will not come.

FIRST NAZARENE. It was not concerning Cæsar that the prophet spake these words, sire.

HEROD. How?—it was not concerning Cæsar?

FIRST NAZARENE. No, my lord.

HEROD. —Concerning whom then did he speak?

FIRST NAZARENE. Concerning Messias who has come.

A JEW. Messias hath not come.

FIRST NAZARENE. He hath come, and everywhere He worketh miracles.

HERODIAS. Ho! ho! miracles! I do not believe in miracles. I have seen too many. (*To the Page.*) My fan.

FIRST NAZARENE. This Man worketh true miracles. Thus, at a marriage which took place in a little town of Galilee, a town of some importance, He changed water into wine. Certain persons who were present related it to me. Also He healed two lepers that were seated before the Gate of Capernaum simply by touching them.

SECOND NAZARENE. Nay, it was blind men that He healed at Capernaum.

FIRST NAZARENE. Nay; they were lepers. But He

hath healed blind people also, and He was seen on a mountain talking with angels.

A Sadducee. Angels do not exist.

A Pharisee. Angels exist, but I do not believe that this Man has talked with them.

First Nazarene. He was seen by a great multitude of people talking with angels.

Herodias. How these men weary me! They are ridiculous! (*To the Page.*) Well! my fan! (*The Page gives her the fan.*) You have a dreamer's look; you must not dream. It is only sick people who dream. (*She strikes the Page with her fan.*)

Second Nazarene. There is also the miracle of the daughter of Jairus.

First Nazarene. Yea, that is sure. No man can gainsay it.

Herodias. These men are mad. They have looked too long on the moon. Command them to be silent.

Herod. What is this miracle of the daughter of Jairus?

First Nazarene. The daughter of Jairus was dead. This Man raised her from the dead.

Herod. How! He raises people from the dead?

First Nazarene. Yea, sire, He raiseth the dead.

Herod. I do not wish Him to do that. I forbid Him to do that. I suffer no man to raise the dead. This Man must be found and told that I forbid Him to raise the dead. Where is this Man at present?

Second Nazarene. He is in every place, my lord, but it is hard to find Him.

First Nazarene. It is said that He is now in Samaria.

A Jew. It is easy to see that this is not Messias, if He is in Samaria. It is not to the Samaritans that Messias shall come. The Samaritans are accursed. They bring no offerings to the Temple.

SECOND NAZARENE. He left Samaria a few days since. I think that at the present moment He is in the neighbourhood of Jerusalem.

FIRST NAZARENE. No; He is not there. I have just come from Jerusalem. For two months they have had no tidings of Him.

HEROD. No matter! But let them find Him, and tell Him, thus saith Herod the King, "I will not suffer Thee to raise the dead!" To change water into wine, to heal the lepers and the blind. . . . He may do these things if He will. I say nothing against these things. In truth I hold it a kindly deed to heal a leper. But no man shall raise the dead. It would be terrible if the dead came back.

THE VOICE OF JOKANAAN. Ah! the wanton one! The harlot! Ah! the daughter of Babylon with her golden eyes and her gilded eyelids! Thus saith the Lord God, Let there come up against her a multitude of men. Let the people take stones and stone her. . . .

HERODIAS. Command him to be silent.

THE VOICE OF JOKANAAN. Let the captains of the hosts pierce her with their swords, let them crush her beneath their shields.

HERODIAS. Nay, but it is infamous.

THE VOICE OF JOKANAAN. It is thus that I will wipe out all wickedness from the earth, and that all women shall learn not to imitate her abominations.

HERODIAS. You hear what he says against me? You suffer him to revile her who is your wife?

HEROD. He did not speak your name.

HERODIAS. What does that matter? You know well that it is I whom he seeks to revile. And I am your wife, am I not?

HEROD. Of a truth, dear and noble Herodias, you are

my wife, and before that you were the wife of my
brother

HERODIAS. It was thou didst snatch me from his arms.

HEROD. Of a truth I was stronger than he was. . . .
But let us not talk of that matter. I do not desire to talk
of it. It is the cause of the terrible words that the
prophet has spoken. Peradventure on account of it a
misfortune will come. Let us not speak of this matter.
Noble Herodias, we are not mindful of our guests. Fill
thou my cup, my well-beloved. Ho! fill with wine the
great goblets of silver, and the great goblets of glass.
I will drink to Cæsar. There are Romans here, we must
drink to Cæsar.

ALL. Cæsar! Cæsar!

HEROD. Do you not see your daughter, how pale
she is?

HERODIAS. What is that to you if she be pale or not?

HEROD. Never have I seen her so pale.

HERODIAS. You must not look at her.

THE VOICE OF JOKANAAN. In that day the sun shall
become black like sackcloth of hair, and the moon shall
become like blood, and the stars of the heaven shall fall
upon the earth like unripe figs that fall from the fig tree,
and the kings of the earth shall be afraid.

HERODIAS. Ah! Ah! I should like to see that day of
which he speaks, when the moon shall become like
blood, and when the stars shall fall upon the earth like
unripe figs. This prophet talks like a drunken man . . .
but I cannot suffer the sound of his voice. I hate his
voice. Command him to be silent.

HEROD. I will not. I cannot understand what it is
that he saith, but it may be an omen.

HERODIAS. I do not believe in omens. He speaks like
a drunken man.

HEROD. It may be he is drunk with the wine of God.

HERODIAS. What wine is that, the wine of God? From what vineyards is it gathered? In what winepress may one find it?

HEROD (*From this point he looks all the while at* SALOMÉ). Tigellinus, when you were at Rome of late, did the Emperor speak with you on the subject of . . .?

TIGELLINUS. On what subject, my Lord?

HEROD. On what subject? Ah! I asked you a question, did I not? I have forgotten what I would have asked you.

HERODIAS. You are looking again at my daughter. You must not look at her. I have already said so.

HEROD. You say nothing else.

HERODIAS. I say it again.

HEROD. And that restoration of the Temple about which they have talked so much, will anything be done? They say the veil of the Sanctuary has disappeared, do they not?

HERODIAS. It was thyself didst steal it. Thou speakest at random and without wit. I will not stay here. Let us go within.

HEROD. Dance for me, Salomé.

HERODIAS. I will not have her dance.

SALOMÉ. I have no desire to dance, Tetrarch.

HEROD. Salomé, daughter of Herodias, dance for me.

HERODIAS. Peace! let her alone.

HEROD. I command thee to dance, Salomé.

SALOMÉ. I will not dance, Tetrarch.

HERODIAS. (*Laughing*). You see how she obeys you.

HEROD. What is it to me whether she dance or not? It is naught to me. Tonight I am happy, I am exceeding happy. Never have I been so happy.

FIRST SOLDIER. The Tetrarch has a sombre look. Has he not a sombre look?

Second Soldier. Yes, he has a sombre look.

Herod. Wherefore should I not be happy? Cæsar, who is lord of the world, Cæsar, who is lord of all things, loves me well. He has just sent me most precious gifts. Also he has promised me to summon to Rome the King of Cappadocia, who is my enemy. It may be that at Rome he will crucify him, for he is able to do all things that he has a mind to. Verily, Cæsar is lord. Therefore I do well to be happy. There is nothing in the world that can mar my happiness.

The Voice of Jokanaan. He shall be seated on this throne. He shall be clothed in scarlet and purple. In his hand he shall bear a golden cup full of his blasphemies. And the angel of the Lord shall smite him. He shall be eaten of worms.

Herodias. You hear what he says about you. He says that you will be eaten of worms.

Herod. It is not of me that he speaks. He speaks never against me. It is of the King of Cappadocia that he speaks; the King of Cappadocia who is mine enemy. It is he who shall be eaten of worms. It is not I. Never has he spoken word against me, this prophet, save that I sinned in taking to wife the wife of my brother. It may be he is right. For, of a truth, you are sterile.

Herodias. I am sterile, I? You say that, you that are ever looking at my daughter, you that would have her dance for your pleasure? You speak as a fool. I have borne a child. You have gotten no child, no, not on one of your slaves. It is you who are sterile, not I.

Herod. Peace, woman! I say that you are sterile. You have borne me no child, and the prophet says that our marriage is not a true marriage. He says that it is a marriage of incest, a marriage that will bring evils. . . . I fear he is right; I am sure that he is right. I would be happy at this. Of a truth, I am happy. There is nothing I lack.

HERODIAS. I am glad you are of so fair a humour tonight. It is not your custom. But it is late. Let us go within. Do not forget that we hunt at sunrise. All honours must be shown to Cæsar's ambassadors, must they not?

SECOND SOLDIER. The Tetrarch has a sombre look.

FIRST SOLDIER. Yes, he has a sombre look.

HEROD. Salomé, Salomé, dance for me. I pray thee dance for me. I am sad tonight. Yes; I am passing sad tonight. When I came hither I slipped in blood, which is an evil omen; also I heard in the air a beating of wings, a beating of giant wings. I cannot tell what they mean. . . . I am sad tonight. Therefore dance for me. Dance for me, Salomé, I beseech thee. If thou dancest for me thou mayest ask of me what thou wilt, and I will give it thee, even unto the half of my kingdom.

SALOMÉ (*Rising*). Will you indeed give me whatsoever I shall ask of thee, Tetrarch?

HERODIAS. Do not dance, my daughter.

HEROD. Whatsoever thou shalt ask of me, even unto the half of my kingdom.

SALOMÉ. You swear it, Tetrarch?

HEROD. I swear it, Salomé.

HERODIAS. Do not dance, my daughter.

SALOMÉ. By what will you swear this thing, Tetrarch?

HEROD. By my life, by my crown, by my gods. Whatsoever thou shalt desire I will give it thee, even to the half of my kingdom, if thou wilt but dance for me. O Salomé, Salomé, dance for me!

SALOMÉ. You have sworn an oath, Tetrarch.

HEROD. I have sworn an oath.

HERODIAS. My daughter, do not dance.

HEROD. Even to the half of my kingdom. Thou wilt be passing fair as a queen, Salomé, if it please thee to ask for the half of my kingdom. Will she not be fair as a queen? Ah! it is cold here! There is an icy wind, and I hear . . . wherefore do I hear in the air this beating of wings? Ah! one might fancy a huge black bird that hovers over the terrace. Why can I not see it, this bird? The beat of its wings is terrible. The breath of the wind of its wings is terrible. It is a chill wind. Nay, but it is not cold, it is hot. I am choking. Pour water on my hands. Give me snow to eat. Loosen my mantle. Quick! quick! loosen my mantle. Nay, but leave it. It is my garland that hurts me, my garland of roses. The flowers are like fire. They have burned my forehead. (*He tears the wreath from his head and throws it on the table.*) Ah! I can breathe now. How red those petals are! They are like stains of blood on the cloth. That does not matter. It is not wise to find symbols in everything that one sees. It makes life too full of terrors. It were better to say that stains of blood are as lovely as rose petals. It were better far to say that. . . . But we will not speak of this. Now I am happy. I am passing happy. Have I not the right to be happy? Your daughter is going to dance for me. Wilt thou not dance for me, Salomé? Thou hast promised to dance for me.

HERODIAS. I will not have her dance.

SALOMÉ. I will dance for you, Tetrarch.

HEROD. You hear what your daughter says. She is going to dance for me. Thou doest well to dance for me, Salomé. And when thou hast danced for me, forget not to ask of me whatsoever thou hast a mind to ask. Whatsoever thou shalt desire I will give it thee, even to the half of my kingdom. I have sworn it, have I not?

SALOMÉ. Thou hast sworn it, Tetrarch.

HEROD. And I have never broken my word. I am

not of those who break their oaths. I know not how to
lie. I am the slave of my word, and my word is the word
of a king. The King of Cappadocia had ever a lying
tongue, but he is no true king. He is a coward. Also he
owes me money that he will not repay. He has even
insulted my ambassadors. He has spoken words that
were wounding. But Cæsar will crucify him when he
comes to Rome. I know that Cæsar will crucify him.
And if he crucify him not, yet will he die, being eaten of
worms. The prophet has prophesied it. Well! wherefore dost thou tarry, Salomé?

SALOMÉ. I am waiting until my slaves bring perfumes
to me and the seven veils, and take from off my feet my
sandals. (*Slaves bring perfumes and the seven veils, and
take off the sandals of* SALOMÉ.)

HEROD. Ah, thou art to dance with naked feet. 'Tis
well! 'Tis well. Thy little feet will be like white doves.
They will be like little white flowers that dance upon the
trees. . . . No, no, she is going to dance on blood.
There is blood spilt on the ground. She must not dance
on blood. It were an evil omen.

HERODIAS. What is it to thee if she dance on blood?
Thou hast waded deep enough in it. . . .

HEROD. What is it to me? Ah! look at the moon!
She has become red. She has become red as blood.
Ah! the prophet prophesied truly. He prophesied that
the moon would become as blood. Did he not prophesy
it? All of ye heard him prophesying it. And now the
moon has become as blood. Do ye not see it?

HERODIAS. Oh, yes, I see it well, and the stars are
falling like unripe figs, are they not? and the sun is becoming black like sackcloth of hair, and the kings of the
earth are afraid. That at least one can see. The prophet
is justified of his words in that at least, for truly the
kings of the earth are afraid. . . . Let us go within. You

are sick. They will say at Rome that you are mad. Let us go within, I tell you.

THE VOICE OF JOKANAAN. Who is this who cometh from Edom, who is this who cometh from Bozra, whose raiment is dyed with purple, who shineth in the beauty of his garments, who walketh mighty in his greatness? Wherefore is thy raiment stained with scarlet?

HERODIAS. Let us go within. The voice of that man maddens me. I will not have my daughter dance while he is continually crying out. I will not have her dance while you look at her in this fashion. In a word, I will not have her dance.

HEROD. Do not rise, my wife, my queen, it will avail thee nothing. I will not go within till she hath danced. Dance, Salomé, dance for me.

HERODIAS. Do not dance, my daughter.

SALOMÉ. I am ready, Tetrarch.

(SALOMÉ *dances the dance of the seven veils.*)

HEROD. Ah! wonderful! wonderful! You see that she has danced for me, your daughter. Come near, Salomé, come near, that I may give thee thy fee. Ah! I pay a royal price to those who dance for my pleasure. I will pay thee royally. I will give thee whatsoever thy soul desireth. What wouldst thou have? Speak.

SALOMÉ (*Kneeling*). I would that they presently bring me in a silver charger. . . .

HEROD (*Laughing.*) In a silver charger? Surely yes, in a silver charger. She is charming, is she not? What is it thou wouldst have in a silver charger, O sweet and fair Salomé, thou art fairer than all the daughters of Judæa? What wouldst thou have them bring thee in a silver charger? Tell me. Whatsoever it may be, thou shalt receive it. My treasures belong to thee. What is it that thou wouldst have, Salomé?

SALOMÉ (*Rising*). The head of Jokanaan.

HERODIAS. Ah! that is well said, my daughter.

HEROD. No, no!

HERODIAS. That is well said, my daughter.

HEROD. No, no, Salomé. It is not that thou desirest. Do not listen to thy mother's voice. She is ever giving thee evil counsel. Do not heed her.

SALOMÉ. It is not my mother's voice that I heed. It is for mine own pleasure that I ask the head of Jokanaan in a silver charger. You have sworn an oath, Herod. Forget not that you have sworn an oath.

HEROD. I know it. I have sworn an oath by my gods. I know it well. But I pray thee, Salomé, ask of me something else. Ask of me the half of my kingdom, and I will give it thee. But ask not of me what thy lips have asked.

SALOMÉ. I ask of you the head of Jokanaan.

HEROD. No, no, I will not give it thee.

SALOMÉ. You have sworn an oath, Herod.

HERODIAS. Yes, you have sworn an oath. Everybody heard you. You swore it before everybody.

HEROD. Peace, woman! It is not to you I speak.

HERODIAS. My daughter has done well to ask the head of Jokanaan. He has covered me with insults. He has said unspeakable things against me. One can see that she loves her mother well. Do not yield, my daughter. He has sworn an oath, he has sworn an oath.

HEROD. Peace! Speak not to me! . . . Salomé, I pray thee be not stubborn. I have ever been kind toward thee. I have ever loved thee. . . . It may be that I have loved thee too much. Therefore ask not this thing of me. This is a terrible thing, an awful thing to ask of me. Surely, I think thou art jesting. The head of a man that is cut from his body is ill to look upon, is it not? It is not meet that the eyes of a virgin should look upon such a thing. What pleasure couldst thou have in it? There is no pleasure that thou couldst have in it. No, no, it is not that thou desirest. Hearken to me. I have an emerald, a great emerald, thou canst see that which passeth afar off. Cæsar himself carries such an emerald when he goes to the circus. But my emerald is the larger. I know well that it is the larger. It is the largest emerald in the whole world. Thou wilt take that, wilt thou not? Ask it of me and I will give it thee.

SALOMÉ. I demand the head of Jokanaan.

HEROD. Thou art not listening. Thou art not listening. Suffer me to speak, Salomé.

SALOMÉ. The head of Jokanaan.

HEROD. No, no, thou wouldst not have that. Thou sayest that but to trouble me, because I have looked at thee and ceased not this night. It is true, I have looked at thee and ceased not this night. Thy beauty has troubled me. Thy beauty has grievously troubled me, and I have looked at thee over-much. Nay, but I will look at thee no more. One should not look at anything. Neither at things, nor at people should one look. Only in mirrors is it well to look, for mirrors do but show us masks. Oh! oh! bring wine! I thirst. . . . Salomé, Salomé, let us be as friends. Bethink thee. . . . Ah! what would I say? What was't? Ah! I remember it! . . . Salomé—nay but come nearer to me; I fear thou wilt not hear my words—Salomé, thou knowest my white peacocks, my beautiful white peacocks, that walk in the garden between the myrtles and the tall cypress trees. Their beaks are gilded with gold and the grains that they eat are smeared with gold, and their feet are stained with purple. When they cry out the rain comes, and the moon shows herself in the heavens when they spread their tails. Two by two they walk between the cypress trees and the black myrtles, and each has a slave to tend it. Sometimes they fly across the trees, and

anon they crouch in the grass, and round the pools of
the water. There are not in all the world birds so wonderful. I know that Cæsar himself has no birds so fair
as my birds. I will give thee fifty of my peacocks. They
will follow thee whithersoever thou goest, and in the
midst of them thou wilt be like unto the moon in the
midst of a great white cloud. . . . I will give them to
thee all. I have but a hundred, and in the whole world
there is no king who has peacocks like unto my peacocks. But I will give them all to thee. Only thou must
loose me from my oath, and must not ask of me that
which thy lips have asked of me. (*He empties the cup
of wine.*)

SALOMÉ. Give me the head of Jokanaan.

HERODIAS. Well said, my daughter! As for you, you
are ridiculous with your peacocks.

HEROD. Ah! thou art not listening to me. Be calm.
As for me, am I not calm? I am altogether calm. Listen.
I have jewels hidden in this place—jewels that thy
mother even has never seen; jewels that are marvellous
to look at. I have a collar of pearls, set in four rows.
They are like unto moons chained with rays of silver.
They are even as half a hundred moons caught in a
golden net. On the ivory breast of a queen they have
rested. Thou shalt be as fair as a queen when thou
wearest them. I have amethysts of two kinds, one that
is black like wine, and one that is red like wine that
one has coloured with water. I have topazes, yellow
as are the eyes of tigers, and topazes that are pink
as the eyes of a wood pigeon, and green topazes that
are as the eyes of cats. I have opals that burn always,
with a flame that is cold as ice, opals that make sad
men's minds, and are afraid of the shadows. I have
onyxes like the eyeballs of a dead woman. I have moon
stones that change when the moon changes, and are

wan when they see the sun. I have sapphires big like eggs, and as blue as blue flowers. The sea wanders within them and the moon comes never to trouble the blue of their waves. I have chrysolites and beryls and chrysoprases and rubies. I have sardonyx and hyacinth stones, and stones of chalcedony, and I will give them all unto thee, all, and other things will I add to them. The King of the Indies has but even now sent me four fans fashioned from the feathers of parrots, and the King of Numidia a garment of ostrich feathers. I have a crystal, into which it is not lawful for a woman to look, nor may young men behold it until they have been beaten with rods. In a coffer of nacre I have three wondrous turquoises. He who wears them on his forehead can imagine things which are not, and he who carries them in his hand can turn the fruitful woman into a woman that is barren. These are great treasures above all price. But this is not all. In an ebony coffer I have two cups, amber, that are like apples of pure gold. If an enemy pour poison into these cups they become like apples of silver. In a coffer incrusted with amber I have sandals incrusted with glass. I have mantles that have been brought from the land of the Seres, and bracelets decked about with carbuncles and with jade that come from the city of Euphrates. . . . What desirest thou more than this, Salomé! Tell me the thing that thou desirest, and I will give it thee. All that thou askest I will give thee, save one thing only. I will give thee all that is mine, save only the head of one man. I will give thee the mantle of the high priest. I will give thee the veil of the Sanctuary.

THE JEWS. Oh! oh!

SALOMÉ. Give me the head of Jokanaan.

HEROD. (*Sinking back in his seat*). Let her be given what she asks! Of a truth she is her mother's child!

(*The first Soldier approaches.* HERODIAS *draws from the hand of the Tetrarch the ring of death, and gives it to the Soldier, who straightway bears it to the Executioner. The Executioner looks scared.*) Who has taken my ring? There was a ring on my right hand. Who has drunk my wine? There was wine in my cup. It was full of wine. Someone has drunk it! Oh! surely some evil will befall someone. (*The Executioner goes down into the cistern.*) Ah! Wherefore did I give my oath? Hereafter let no king swear an oath. If he keep it not, it is terrible, and if he keep it, it is terrible also.

HERODIAS. My daughter has done well.

HEROD. I am sure that some misfortune will happen.

SALOMÉ (*She leans over the cistern and listens*). There is no sound. I hear nothing. Why does he not cry out, this man? Ah! if any man sought to kill me, I would cry out, I would struggle, I would not suffer. . . . Strike, strike, Naaman, strike, I tell you. . . . No, I hear nothing. There is a silence, a terrible silence. Ah! something has fallen upon the ground. I heard something fall. He is afraid, this slave. He is a coward, this slave! Let soldiers be sent. (*She sees the Page of* HERODIAS *and addresses him.*) Come thither, thou wert the friend of him who is dead, wert thou not? Well, I tell thee, there are not dead men enough. Go to the soldiers and bid them go down and bring me the thing I ask, the thing the Tetrarch has promised me, the thing that is mine. (*The Page recoils. She turns to the soldiers.*) Hither, ye soldiers. Get ye down into this cistern and bring me the head of this man. Tetrarch, Tetrarch, command your soldiers that they bring me the head of Jokanaan.

(*A huge black arm, the arm of the Executioner, comes forth from the cistern, bearing on a silver shield the head of* JOKANAAN. SALOMÉ *seizes it.* HEROD *hides his*

face with his cloak. HERODIAS *smiles and fans herself.*
The Nazarenes fall on their knees and begin to pray.)

Ah! thou wouldst not suffer me to kiss thy mouth,
Jokanaan. Well, I will kiss it now. I will bite it with
my teeth as one bites a ripe fruit. Yes, I will kiss thy
mouth, Jokanaan. I said it; did I not say it? I said it.
Ah! I will kiss it now. . . . But, wherefore dost thou
not look at me, Jokanaan? Thine eyes that were so terrible, so full of rage and scorn, are shut now. Wherefore are they shut? Open thine eyes! Lift up thine eyelids, Jokanaan! Wherefore dost thou not look at me?
Art thou afraid of me, Jokanaan, that thou wilt not
look at me? . . . And thy tongue, that was like a red
snake darting poison, it moves no more, it speaks no
words, Jokanaan, that scarlet viper that spat its venom
upon me. It is strange, is it not? How is it that the red
viper stirs no longer? . . . Thou wouldst have none
of me, Jokanaan. Thou rejectedst me. Thou didst speak
evil words against me. Thou didst bear thyself toward
me as to a harlot, as to a woman that is a wanton, to
me, Salomé, daughter of Herodias, Princess of Judæa!
Well, I still live, but thou art dead, and thy head belongs to me. I can do with it what I will. I can throw it
to the dogs and to the birds of the air. That which the
dogs leave, the birds of the air shall devour. . . . Ah,
Jokanaan, thou wert the man that I loved alone among
men. All other men were hateful to me. But thou wert
beautiful! Thy body was a column of ivory set upon
feet of silver. It was a garden full of doves and lilies
of silver. It was a tower of silver decked with shields of
ivory. There was nothing in the world so white as thy
body. There was nothing in the world so black as thy
hair. In the whole world there was nothing so red as
thy mouth. Thy voice was a censer that scattered
strange perfumes, and when I looked on thee I heard a

strange music. Ah! wherefore didst thou not look at me,
Jokanaan? With the cloak of thine hands and with the
cloak of thy blasphemies thou didst hide thy face. Thou
didst put upon thine eyes the covering of him who
would see his God. Well, thou hast seen thy God,
Jokanaan, but me, me, thou didst never see. If thou
hadst seen me thou hadst loved me. I saw thee, and I
loved thee. Oh, how I loved thee! I love thee yet,
Jokanaan, I love only thee. . . . I am athirst for thy
beauty; I am hungry for thy body; and neither wine nor
apples can appease my desire. What shall I do now,
Jokanaan? Neither the floods nor the great waters can
quench my passion. I was a princess, and thou didst
scorn me. I was a virgin, and thou didst take my vir-
ginity from me. I was chaste, and thou didst fill my
veins with fire. . . . Ah! ah! wherefore didst thou not
look at me? If thou hadst looked at me thou hadst
loved me. Well I know that thou wouldst have loved
me, and the mystery of love is greater than the mystery
of death.

HEROD. She is monstrous, thy daughter, I tell thee she
is monstrous. In truth, what she has done is a great
crime. I am sure that it is. A crime against some unknown God.

HERODIAS. I am well pleased with my daughter. She
has done well. And I would stay here now.

HEROD (*Rising*). Ah! There speaks my brother's wife!
Come! I will not stay in this place. Come, I tell thee.
Surely some terrible thing will befall. Manasseh, Is-
sadar, Zias, put out the torches. I will not look at things,
I will not suffer things to look at me. Put out the torches!
Hide the moon! Hide the stars! Let us hide ourselves in
our palace, Herodias. I begin to be afraid.

(*The slaves put out the torches. The stars disappear:
A great cloud crosses the moon and conceals it com-*

pletely. The stage becomes quite dark. The Tetrarch begins to climb the staircase.)

THE VOICE OF SALOMÉ. Ah! I have kissed thy mouth, Jokanaan, I have kissed thy mouth. There was a bitter taste on my lips. Was it the taste of blood? . . . Nay; but perchance it was the taste of love. . . . They say that love hath a bitter taste. . . . But what matter? what matter? I have kissed thy mouth.

HEROD (*Turning round and seeing* SALOMÉ). Kill that woman!

(*The soldiers rush forward and crush beneath their shields* SALOMÉ, *daughter of* HERODIAS, *Princess of Judæa.*)

CURTAIN

The Importance
of Being Earnest

The Persons of the Play

JOHN WORTHING, J.P.
ALGERNON MONCRIEFF
REV. CANON CHASUBLE, D.D.
MERRIMAN, Butler
LANE, Manservant
LADY BRACKNELL
HON. GWENDOLEN FAIRFAX
CECILY CARDEW
MISS PRISM, Governess

The Scenes of the Play

ACT   I *Algernon Moncrieff's Flat*
          in Half-Moon Street, W.
ACT II *The Garden at the Manor House, Woolton.*
ACT III *Drawing-Room at the Manor House, Woolton.*

First Act

Scene. Morning-room in ALGERNON's flat in Half-Moon Street. The room is luxuriously and artistically furnished. The sound of a piano is heard in the adjoining room.

(LANE is arranging afternoon tea on the table, and after the music has ceased, Algernon enters.)

ALGERNON. Did you hear what I was playing, Lane?

LANE. I didn't think it polite to listen, sir.

ALGERNON. I'm sorry for that, for your sake. I don't play accurately—anyone can play accurately—but I play with wonderful expression. As far as the piano is concerned, sentiment is my forte. I keep science for life.

LANE. Yes, sir.

ALGERNON. And, speaking of the science of life, have you got the cucumber sandwiches cut for Lady Bracknell?

LANE. Yes, sir. (*Hands them on a salver.*)

ALGERNON. (*Inspects them, takes two, and sits down on the sofa.*) Oh! . . . by the way, Lane, I see from your book that on Thursday night, when Lord Shoreman and Mr. Worthing were dining with me, eight bottles of champagne are entered as having been consumed.

LANE. Yes, sir; eight bottles and a pint.

ALGERNON. Why is it that at a bachelor's establishment the servants invariably drink the champagne? I ask merely for information.

LANE. I attribute it to the superior quality of the wine, sir. I have often observed that in married households the champagne is rarely of a first-rate brand.

ALGERNON. Good Heavens! Is marriage so demoralizing as that?

LANE. I believe it *is* a very pleasant state, sir. I have had very little experience of it myself up to the present. I have only been married once. That was in consequence of a misunderstanding between myself and a young person.

ALGERNON. (*Languidly.*) I don't know that I am much interested in your family life, Lane.

LANE. No, sir; it is not a very interesting subject. I never think of it myself.

ALGERNON. Very natural, I am sure. That will do, Lane, thank you.

LANE. Thank you, sir. (LANE *goes out.*)

ALGERNON. Lane's views on marriage seem somewhat lax. Really, if the lower orders don't set us a good example, what on earth is the use of them? They seem, as a class, to have absolutely no sense of moral responsibility.

(*Enter* LANE.)

LANE. Mr. Ernest Worthing.

(*Enter* JACK.) (LANE *goes out.*)

ALGERNON. How are you, my dear Ernest? What brings you up to town?

JACK. Oh, pleasure, pleasure! What else should bring one anywhere? Eating as usual, I see, Algy!

ALGERNON. (*Stiffly.*) I believe it is customary in good society to take some slight refreshment at five o'clock. Where have you been since last Thursday?

JACK. (*Sitting down on the sofa.*) In the country.

ALGERNON. What on earth do you do there?

JACK. (*Pulling off his gloves.*) When one is in town one amuses oneself. When one is in the country one amuses other people. It is excessively boring.

ALGERNON. And who are the people you amuse?

JACK. (*Airily.*) Oh, neighbours, neighbours.

ALGERNON. Got nice neighbours in your part of Shropshire?

JACK. Perfectly horrid! Never speak to one of them.

ALGERNON. How immensely you must amuse them! (*Goes over and takes sandwich.*) By the way, Shropshire is your county, is it not?

JACK. Eh? Shropshire? Yes, of course. Hallo! Why all these cups? Why cucumber sandwiches? Why such reckless extravagance in one so young? Who is coming to tea?

ALGERNON. Oh! merely Aunt Augusta and Gwendolen.

JACK. How perfectly delightful!

ALGERNON. Yes, that is all very well; but I am afraid Aunt Augusta won't quite approve of your being here.

JACK. May I ask why?

ALGERNON. My dear fellow, the way you flirt with Gwendolen is perfectly disgraceful. It is almost as bad as the way Gwendolen flirts with you.

JACK. I am in love with Gwendolen. I have come up to town expressly to propose to her.

ALGERNON. I thought you had come up for pleasure? . . . I call that business.

JACK. How utterly unromantic you are!

ALGERNON. I really don't see anything romantic in proposing. It is very romantic to be in love. But there is nothing romantic about a definite proposal. Why, one may be accepted. One usually is, I believe. Then the excitement is all over. The very essence of romance is uncertainty. If ever I get married, I'll certainly try to forget the fact.

JACK. I have no doubt about that, dear Algy. The Divorce Court was specially invented for people whose memories are so curiously constituted.

ALGERNON. Oh! there is no use speculating on that subject. Divorces are made in Heaven— (JACK *puts out his hand to take a sandwich.* ALGERNON *at once inter-*

feres.) Please don't touch the cucumber sandwiches. They are ordered specially for Aunt Augusta. (*Takes one and eats it.*)

JACK. Well, you have been eating them all the time.

ALGERNON. That is quite a different matter. She is my aunt. (*Takes plate from below.*) Have some bread and butter. The bread and butter is for Gwendolen. Gwendolen is devoted to bread and butter.

JACK. (*Advancing to table and helping himself.*) And very good bread and butter it is too.

ALGERNON. Well, my dear fellow, you need not eat as if you were going to eat it all. You behave as if you were married to her already. You are not married to her already, and I don't think you ever will be.

JACK. Why on earth do you say that?

ALGERNON. Well, in the first place girls never marry the men they flirt with. Girls don't think it right.

JACK. Oh, that is nonsense!

ALGERNON. It isn't. It is a great truth. It accounts for the extraordinary number of bachelors that one sees all over the place. In the second place, I don't give my consent.

JACK. Your consent!

ALGERNON. My dear fellow, Gwendolen is my first cousin. And before I allow you to marry her, you will have to clear up the whole question of Cecily. (*Rings bell.*)

JACK. Cecily! What on earth do you mean? What do you mean, Algy, by Cecily? I don't know anyone of the name of Cecily.

(*Enter* LANE.)

ALGERNON. Bring me that cigarette case Mr. Worthing left in the smoking-room the last time he dined here.

LANE. Yes, sir.   (LANE *goes out.*)

JACK. Do you mean to say you have had my cigarette case all this time? I wish to goodness you had let me know. I have been writing frantic letters to Scotland Yard about it. I was very nearly offering a large reward.

ALGERNON. Well, I wish you would offer one. I happen to be more than usually hard up.

JACK. There is no good offering a large reward now that the thing is found.

(*Enter* LANE *with the cigarette case on a salver.* ALGERNON *takes it at once.* LANE *goes out.*)

ALGERNON. I think that is rather mean of you, Ernest, I must say. (*Opens case and examines it.*) However, it makes no matter, for, now that I look at the inscription inside, I find that the thing isn't yours after all.

JACK. Of course it's mine. (*Moving to him.*) You have seen me with it a hundred times, and you have no right whatsoever to read what is written inside. It is a very ungentlemanly thing to read a private cigarette case.

ALGERNON. Oh! it is absurd to have a hard-and-fast rule about what one should read and what one shouldn't. More than half of modern culture depends on what one shouldn't read.

JACK. I am quite aware of the fact, and I don't propose to discuss modern culture. It isn't the sort of thing one should talk of in private. I simply want my cigarette case back.

ALGERNON. Yes; but this isn't your cigarette case. This cigarette case is a present from someone of the name of Cecily, and you said you didn't know anyone of that name.

JACK. Well, if you want to know, Cecily happens to be my aunt.

ALGERNON. Your aunt!

JACK. Yes. Charming old lady she is, too. Lives at Tunbridge Wells. Just give it back to me, Algy.

ALGERNON. (*Retreating to back of sofa.*) But why does she call herself Cecily if she is your aunt and lives at Tunbridge Wells? (*Reading.*) "From little Cecily with her fondest love."

JACK. (*Moving to sofa and kneeling upon it.*) My dear fellow, what on earth is there in that? Some aunts are tall, some aunts are not tall. That is a matter that surely an aunt may be allowed to decide for herself. You seem to think that every aunt should be exactly like your aunt! That is absurd! For Heaven's sake give me back my cigarette case. (*Follows* ALGERNON *round the room.*)

ALGERNON. Yes. But why does your aunt call you her uncle? "From little Cecily, with her fondest love to her dear Uncle Jack." There is no objection, I admit, to an aunt being a small aunt, but why an aunt, no matter what her size may be, should call her own nephew her uncle, I can't quite make out. Besides, your name isn't Jack at all; it is Ernest.

JACK. It isn't Ernest; it's Jack.

ALGERNON. You have always told me it was Ernest. I have introduced you to everyone as Ernest. You answer to the name of Ernest. You look as if your name was Ernest. You are the most earnest looking person I ever saw in my life. It is perfectly absurd your saying that your name isn't Ernest. It's on your cards. Here is one of them. (*Taking it from case.*) "Mr. Ernest Worthing, B. 4, The Albany." I'll keep this as a proof that your name is Ernest if ever you attempt to deny it to me, or to Gwendolen, or to anyone else. (*Puts the card in his pocket.*)

JACK. Well, my name is Ernest in town and Jack in

the country, and the cigarette case was given to me in the country.

ALGERNON. Yes, but that does not account for the fact that your small Aunt Cecily, who lives at Tunbridge Wells, calls you her dear uncle. Come, old boy, you had much better have the thing out at once.

JACK. My dear Algy, you talk exactly as if you were a dentist. It is very vulgar to talk like a dentist when one isn't a dentist. It produces a false impression.

ALGERNON. Well, that is exactly what dentists always do. Now, go on! Tell me the whole thing. I may mention that I have always suspected you of being a confirmed and secret Bunburyist; and I am quite sure of it now.

JACK. Bunburyist? What on earth do you mean by a Bunburyist?

ALGERNON. I'll reveal to you the meaning of that incomparable expression as soon as you are kind enough to inform me why you are Ernest in town and Jack in the country.

JACK. Well, produce my cigarette case first.

ALGERNON. Here it is. (*Hands cigarette case.*) Now produce your explanation, and pray make it improbable. (*Sits on sofa.*)

JACK. My dear fellow, there is nothing improbable about my explanation at all. In fact it's perfectly ordinary. Old Mr. Thomas Cardew, who adopted me when I was a little boy, made me in his will guardian to his granddaughter, Miss Cecily Cardew. Cecily, who addresses me as her uncle from motives of respect that you could not possibly appreciate, lives at my place in the country under the charge of her admirable governess, Miss Prism.

ALGERNON. Where is that place in the country, by the way?

JACK. That is nothing to you, dear boy. You are not going to be invited. . . . I may tell you candidly that the place is not in Shropshire.

ALGERNON. I suspected that, my dear fellow! I have Bunburyed all over Shropshire on two separate occasions. Now, go on. Why are you Ernest in town and Jack in the country?

JACK. My dear Algy, I don't know whether you will be able to understand my real motives. You are hardly serious enough. When one is placed in the position of guardian, one has to adopt a very high moral tone on all subjects. It's one's duty to do so. And as a high moral tone can hardly be said to conduce very much to either one's health or one's happiness, in order to get up to town I have always pretended to have a younger brother of the name of Ernest, who lives in the Albany, and gets into the most dreadful scrapes. That, my dear Algy, is the whole truth pure and simple.

ALGERNON. The truth is rarely pure and never simple. Modern life would be very tedious if it were either, and modern literature a complete impossibility!

JACK. That wouldn't be at all a bad thing.

ALGERNON. Literary criticism is not your forte, my dear fellow. Don't try it. You should leave that to people who haven't been at a University. They do it so well in the daily papers. What you really are is a Bunburyist. I was quite right in saying you were a Bunburyist. You are one of the most advanced Bunburyists I know.

JACK. What on earth do you mean?

ALGERNON. You have invented a very useful young brother called Ernest, in order that you may be able to come up to town as often as you like. I have invented an invaluable permanent invalid called Bunbury, in order that I may be able to go down into the country whenever I choose. Bunbury is perfectly invaluable. If it wasn't for Bunbury's extraordinary bad health, for instance, I wouldn't be able to dine with you at Willis's tonight, for I have been really engaged to Aunt Augusta for more than a week.

JACK. I haven't asked you to dine with me anywhere tonight.

ALGERNON. I know. You are absurdly careless about sending out invitations. It is very foolish of you. Nothing annoys people so much as not receiving invitations.

JACK. You had much better dine with your Aunt Augusta.

ALGERNON. I haven't the smallest intention of doing anything of the kind. To begin with, I dined there on Monday, and once a week is quite enough to dine with one's own relations. In the second place, whenever I do dine there I am always treated as a member of the family, and sent down with either no woman at all, or two. In the third place, I know perfectly well whom she will place me next to, tonight. She will place me next Mary Farquhar, who always flirts with her own husband across the dinner-table. That is not very pleasant. Indeed, it is not even decent . . . and that sort of thing is enormously on the increase. The amount of women in London who flirt with their own husbands is perfectly scandalous. It looks so bad. It is simply washing one's clean linen in public. Besides, now that I know you to be a confirmed Bunburyist, I naturally want to talk to you about Bunburying. I want to tell you the rules.

JACK. I'm not a Bunburyist at all. If Gwendolen accepts me, I am going to kill my brother, indeed I think I'll kill him in any case. Cecily is a little too much interested in him. It is rather a bore. So I am going to get rid of Ernest. And I strongly advise you to do the same with Mr. . . . with your invalid friend who has the absurd name.

ALGERNON. Nothing will induce me to part with Bunbury, and if you ever get married, which seems to me extremely problematic, you will be very glad to know Bunbury. A man who marries without knowing Bunbury has a very tedious time of it.

JACK. That is nonsense. If I marry a charming girl like Gwendolen, and she is the only girl I ever saw in my life that I would marry, I certainly won't want to know Bunbury.

ALGERNON. Then your wife will. You don't seem to realize, that in married life three is company and two is none.

JACK. (*Sententiously.*) That, my dear young friend, is the theory that the corrupt French Drama has been propounding for the last fifty years.

ALGERNON. Yes; and that the happy English home has proved in half the time.

JACK. For heaven's sake, don't try to be cynical. It's perfectly easy to be cynical.

ALGERNON. My dear fellow, it isn't easy to be anything nowadays. There's such a lot of beastly competition about. (*The sound of an electric bell is heard.*) Ah! that must be Aunt Augusta. Only relatives, or creditors, ever ring in that Wagnerian manner. Now, if I get her out of the way for ten minutes, so that you can have an opportunity for proposing to Gwendolen, may I dine with you tonight at Willis's?

JACK. I suppose so, if you want to.

ALGERNON. Yes, but you must be serious about it. I hate people who are not serious about meals. It is so shallow of them.

(*Enter* LANE.)

LANE. Lady Bracknell and Miss Fairfax.

(ALGERNON *goes forward to meet them. Enter* LADY BRACKNELL *and* GWENDOLEN.)

LADY BRACKNELL. Good afternoon, dear Algernon, I hope you are behaving very well.

ALGERNON. I'm feeling very well, Aunt Augusta.

LADY BRACKNELL. That's not quite the same thing. In fact the two things rarely go together. (*Sees* JACK *and bows to him with icy coldness.*)

ALGERNON. (*To* GWENDOLEN.) Dear me, you are smart!

GWENDOLEN. I am always smart! Aren't I, Mr. Worthing?

JACK. You're quite perfect, Miss Fairfax.

GWENDOLEN. Oh! I hope I am not that. It would leave no room for developments, and I intend to develop in many directions. (GWENDOLEN *and* JACK *sit down together in the corner.*)

LADY BRACKNELL. I'm sorry if we are a little late, Algernon, but I was obliged to call on dear Lady Harbury. I hadn't been there since her poor husband's death. I never saw a woman so altered; she looks quite twenty years younger. And now I'll have a cup of tea, and one of those nice cucumber sandwiches you promised me.

ALGERNON. Certainly, Aunt Augusta. (*Goes over to tea-table.*)

LADY BRACKNELL. Won't you come and sit here, Gwendolen?

GWENDOLEN. Thanks, Mamma, I'm quite comfortable where I am.

ALGERNON. (*Picking up empty plate in horror.*) Good heavens! Lane! Why are there no cucumber sandwiches? I ordered them specially.

LANE. (*Gravely.*) There were no cucumbers in the market this morning, sir. I went down twice.

ALGERNON. No cucumbers!

LANE. No, sir. Not even for ready money.

ALGERNON. That will do, Lane, thank you.

LANE. Thank you, sir.

ALGERNON. I am greatly distressed, Aunt Augusta, about there being no cucumbers, not even for ready money.

LADY BRACKNELL. It really makes no matter, Algernon. I had some crumpets with Lady Harbury, who seems to me to be living entirely for pleasure now.

ALGERNON. I hear her hair has turned quite gold from grief.

LADY BRACKNELL. It certainly has changed its colour. From what cause I, of course, cannot say. (ALGERNON *crosses and hands tea.*) Thank you. I've quite a treat for you tonight, Algernon. I am going to send you down with Mary Farquhar. She is such a nice woman, and so attentive to her husband. It's delightful to watch them.

ALGERNON. I am afraid, Aunt Augusta, I shall have to give up the pleasure of dining with you tonight after all.

LADY BRACKNELL. (*Frowning.*) I hope not, Algernon. It would put my table completely out. Your uncle would have to dine upstairs. Fortunately he is accustomed to that.

ALGERNON. It is a great bore, and, I need hardly say, a terrible disappointment to me, but the fact is I have just had a telegram to say that my poor friend Bunbury is very ill again. (*Exchanges glances with* JACK.) They seem to think I should be with him.

LADY BRACKNELL. It is very strange. This Mr. Bunbury seems to suffer from curiously bad health.

ALGERNON. Yes; poor Bunbury is a dreadful invalid.

LADY BRACKNELL. Well, I must say, Algernon, that

I think it is high time that Mr. Bunbury made up his mind whether he was going to live or to die. This shilly-shallying with the question is absurd. Nor do I in any way approve of the modern sympathy with invalids. I consider it morbid. Illness of any kind is hardly a thing to be encouraged in others. Health is the primary duty of life. I am always telling that to your poor uncle, but he never seems to take much notice . . . as far as any improvement in his ailments goes. I should be obliged if you would ask Mr. Bunbury, from me, to be kind enough not to have a relapse on Saturday, for I rely on you to arrange my music for me. It is my last reception, and one wants something that will encourage conversation, particularly at the end of the season when everyone has practically said whatever they had to say, which, in most cases, was probably not much.

ALGERNON. I'll speak to Bunbury, Aunt Augusta, if he is still conscious, and I think I can promise you he'll be all right by Saturday. Of course the music is a great difficulty. You see, if one plays good music, people don't listen, and if one plays bad music, people don't talk. But I'll run over the programme I've drawn out, if you will kindly come into the next room for a moment.

LADY BRACKNELL. Thank you, Algernon. It is very thoughtful of you. (*Rising, and following* ALGERNON.) I'm sure the programme will be delightful, after a few expurgations. French songs I cannot possibly allow. People always seem to think that they are improper, and either look shocked, which is vulgar, or laugh, which is worse. But German sounds a thoroughly respectable language, and indeed, I believe is so. Gwendolen, you will accompany me.

GWENDOLEN. Certainly, Mamma.

(LADY BRACKNELL *and* ALGERNON *go into the music-room,* GWENDOLEN *remains behind.*)

JACK. Charming day it has been, Miss Fairfax.

GWENDOLEN. Pray don't talk to me about the weather, Mr. Worthing. Whenever people talk to me about the weather, I always feel quite certain that they mean something else. And that makes me so nervous.

JACK. I do mean something else.

GWENDOLEN. I thought so. In fact, I am never wrong.

JACK. And I would like to be allowed to take advantage of Lady Bracknell's temporary absence. . . .

GWENDOLEN. I would certainly advise you to do so. Mamma has a way of coming back suddenly into a room that I have often had to speak to her about.

JACK. (*Nervously.*) Miss Fairfax, ever since I met you I have admired you more than any girl . . . I have ever met since . . . I met you.

GWENDOLEN. Yes, I am quite aware of the fact. And I often wish that in public, at any rate, you had been more demonstrative. For me you have always had an irresistible fascination. Even before I met you I was far from indifferent to you. (JACK *looks at her in amazement.*) We live, as I hope you know, Mr. Worthing, in an age of ideals. The fact is constantly mentioned in the more expensive monthly magazines, and has reached the provincial pulpits I am told: and my ideal has always been to love someone of the name of Ernest. There is something in that name that inspires absolute confidence. The moment Algernon first mentioned to me that he had a friend called Ernest, I knew I was destined to love you.

JACK. You really love me, Gwendolen?

GWENDOLEN. Passionately!

JACK. Darling! You don't know how happy you've made me.

GWENDOLEN. My own Ernest!

JACK. But you don't really mean to say that you couldn't love me if my name wasn't Ernest?

GWENDOLEN. But your name is Ernest.

JACK. Yes, I know it is. But supposing it was something else? Do you mean to say you couldn't love me then?

GWENDOLEN. (*Glibly.*) Ah! that is clearly a metaphysical speculation, and like most metaphysical speculations has very little reference at all to the actual facts of real life, as we know them.

JACK. Personally, darling, to speak quite candidly, I don't much care about the name of Ernest . . . I don't think the name suits me at all.

GWENDOLEN. It suits you perfectly. It is a divine name. It has a music of its own. It produces vibrations.

JACK. Well, really, Gwendolen, I must say that I think there are lots of other much nicer names. I think Jack, for instance, a charming name.

GWENDOLEN. Jack? . . . No, there is very little music in the name Jack, if any at all, indeed. It does not thrill. It produces absolutely no vibrations. . . . I have known several Jacks, and they all, without exception, were more than usually plain. Besides, Jack is a notorious domesticity for John! And I pity any woman who is married to a man called John. She would probably never be allowed to know the entrancing pleasure of a single moment's solitude. The only really safe name is Ernest.

JACK. Gwendolen, I must get christened at once—I mean we must get married at once. There is no time to be lost.

GWENDOLEN. Married, Mr. Worthing?

JACK. (*Astounded.*) Well . . . surely. You know that I love you, and you led me to believe, Miss Fairfax, that you were not absolutely indifferent to me.

GWENDOLEN. I adore you. But you haven't proposed to me yet. Nothing has been said at all about marriage. The subject has not even been touched on.

JACK. Well . . . may I propose to you now?

GWENDOLEN. I think it would be an admirable opportunity. And to spare you any possible disappointment, Mr. Worthing, I think it only fair to tell you quite frankly beforehand that I am fully determined to accept you.

JACK. Gwendolen!

GWENDOLEN. Yes, Mr. Worthing, what have you got to say to me?

JACK. You know what I have got to say to you.

GWENDOLEN. Yes, but you don't say it.

JACK. Gwendolen, will you marry me? (*Goes on his knees.*)

GWENDOLEN. Of course I will, darling. How long you have been about it! I am afraid you have had very little experience in how to propose.

JACK. My own one, I have never loved anyone in the world but you.

GWENDOLEN. Yes, but men often propose for practice. I know my brother Gerald does. All my girl-friends tell me so. What wonderfully blue eyes you have, Ernest! They are quite, quite blue. I hope you will always look at me just like that, especially when there are other people present.

(*Enter* LADY BRACKNELL.)

LADY BRACKNELL. Mr. Worthing! Rise, sir, from this semi-recumbent posture. It is most indecorous.

GWENDOLEN. Mamma! (*He tries to rise; she restrains*

him.) I must beg you to retire. This is no place for you. Besides, Mr. Worthing has not quite finished yet.

LADY BRACKNELL. Finished what, may I ask?

GWENDOLEN. I am engaged to Mr. Worthing, Mamma. (*They rise together.*)

LADY BRACKNELL. Pardon me, you are not engaged to anyone. When you do become engaged to someone, I, or your father, should his health permit him, will inform you of the fact. An engagement should come on a young girl as a surprise, pleasant or unpleasant, as the case may be. It is hardly a matter that she could be allowed to arrange for herself. . . . And now I have a few questions to put to you, Mr. Worthing. While I am making these inquiries, you, Gwendolen, will wait for me below in the carriage.

GWENDOLEN. (*Reproachfully.*) Mamma!

LADY BRACKNELL. In the carriage, Gwendolen! (GWENDOLEN *goes to the door. She and* JACK *blow kisses to each other behind* LADY BRACKNELL'S *back.* LADY BRACKNELL *looks vaguely about as if she could not understand what the noise was. Finally turns round.*) Gwendolen, the carriage!

GWENDOLEN. Yes, Mamma. (*Goes out, looking back at* JACK.)

LADY BRACKNELL. (*Sitting down.*) You can take a seat, Mr. Worthing.

(*Looks in her pocket for note-book and pencil.*)

JACK. Thank you, Lady Bracknell, I prefer standing.

LADY BRACKNELL. (*Pencil and note-book in hand.*) I feel bound to tell you that you are not down on my list of eligible young men, although I have the same list as the dear Duchess of Bolton has. We work together, in fact. However, I am quite ready to enter your name, should your answers be what a really affectionate mother requires. Do you smoke?

JACK. Well, yes, I must admit I smoke.

LADY BRACKNELL. I am glad to hear it. A man should always have an occupation of some kind. There are far too many idle men in London as it is. How old are you?

JACK. Twenty-nine.

LADY BRACKNELL. A very good age to be married at. I have always been of opinion that a man who desires to get married should know either everything or nothing. Which do you know?

JACK. (*After some hesitation.*) I know nothing, Lady Bracknell.

LADY BRACKNELL. I am pleased to hear it. I do not approve of anything that tampers with natural ignorance. Ignorance is like a delicate exotic fruit; touch it and the bloom is gone. The whole theory of modern education is radically unsound. Fortunately in England, at any rate, education produces no effect whatsoever. If it did, it would prove a serious danger to the upper classes, and probably lead to acts of violence in Grosvenor Square. What is your income?

JACK. Between seven and eight thousand a year.

LADY BRACKNELL. (*Makes a note in her book.*) In land, or in *investments*?

JACK. In investments, chiefly.

LADY BRACKNELL. That is satisfactory. What between the duties expected of one during one's lifetime, and the duties exacted from one after one's death, land has ceased to be either a profit or a pleasure. It gives one position, and prevents one from keeping it up. That's all that can be said about land.

JACK. I have a country house with some land, of course, attached to it, about fifteen hundred acres, I believe; but I don't depend on that for my real income.

In fact, as far as I can make out, the poachers are the only people who make anything out of it.

LADY BRACKNELL. A country house! How many bed-rooms? Well, that point can be cleared up afterwards. You have a town house, I hope? A girl with a simple, unspoiled nature, like Gwendolen, could hardly be expected to reside in the country.

JACK. Well, I own a house in Belgrave Square, but it is let by the year to Lady Bloxham. Of course, I can get it back whenever I like, at six months' notice.

LADY BRACKNELL. Lady Bloxham? I don't know her.

JACK. Oh, she goes about very little. She is a lady considerably advanced in years.

LADY BRACKNELL. Ah, nowadays that is no guarantee of respectability of character. What number in Belgrave Square?

JACK. 149.

LADY BRACKNELL. (*Shaking her head.*) The unfashionable side. I thought there was something. However, that could easily be altered.

JACK. Do you mean the fashion, or the side?

LADY BRACKNELL. (*Sternly.*) Both, if necessary, I presume. What are your politics?

JACK. Well, I am afraid I really have none. I am a Liberal Unionist.

LADY BRACKNELL. Oh, they count as Tories. They dine with us. Or come in the evening, at any rate. Now to minor matters. Are your parents living?

JACK. I have lost both my parents.

LADY BRACKNELL. Both? . . . That seems like carelessness. Who was your father? He was evidently a man of some wealth. Was he born in what the Radical papers call the purple of commerce, or did he rise from the ranks of aristocracy?

JACK. I am afraid I really don't know. The fact is, Lady Bracknell, I said I had lost my parents. It would be nearer the truth to say that my parents seem to have lost me. . . . I don't actually know who I am by birth. I was . . . well, I was found.

LADY BRACKNELL. Found!

JACK. The late Mr. Thomas Cardew, an old gentleman of a very charitable and kindly disposition, found me, and gave me the name of Worthing, because he happened to have a first-class ticket for Worthing in his pocket at the time. Worthing is a place in Sussex. It is a seaside resort.

LADY BRACKNELL. Where did the charitable gentleman who had a first-class ticket for this seaside resort find you?

JACK. (*Gravely.*) In a handbag.

LADY BRACKNELL. A handbag?

JACK. (*Very seriously.*) Yes, Lady Bracknell. I was in a handbag—a somewhat large, black leather handbag, with handles to it—an ordinary handbag, in fact.

LADY BRACKNELL. In what locality did this Mr. James, or Thomas, Cardew come across this ordinary handbag?

JACK. In the cloakroom at Victoria Station. It was given to him in mistake for his own.

LADY BRACKNELL. The cloakroom at Victoria Station?

JACK. Yes. The Brighton line.

LADY BRACKNELL. The line is immaterial. Mr. Worthing, I confess I feel somewhat bewildered by what you have just told me. To be born, or at any rate, bred in a handbag, whether it had handles or not, seems to me to display a contempt for the ordinary decencies of family life that remind one of the worst excesses of the French Revolution. And I presume you know what that unfortunate movement led to? As for the particular locality in which the handbag was found, a cloakroom at a railway station might serve to conceal a social indiscretion—has probably, indeed, been used for that purpose before now—but it could hardly be regarded as an assured basis for a recognized position in good society.

JACK. May I ask you then what you would advise me to do? I need hardly say I would do anything in the world to ensure Gwendolen's happiness.

LADY BRACKNELL. I would strongly advise you, Mr. Worthing, to try and acquire some relations as soon as possible, and to make a definite effort to produce at any rate one parent, of either sex, before the season is quite over.

JACK. Well, I don't see how I could possibly manage to do that. I can produce the handbag at any moment. It is in my dressing-room at home. I really think that should satisfy you, Lady Bracknell.

LADY BRACKNELL. Me, sir! What has it to do with me? You can hardly imagine that I and Lord Bracknell would dream of allowing our only daughter—a girl brought up with the utmost care—to marry into a cloakroom, and form an alliance with a parcel? Good morning, Mr. Worthing!

(LADY BRACKNELL *sweeps out in majestic indignation.*)

JACK. Good morning! (ALGERNON, *from the other room, strikes up the* Wedding March. JACK *looks perfectly furious, and goes to the door.*) For goodness' sake don't play that ghastly tune, Algy! How idiotic you are!

(*The music stops, and* ALGERNON *enters cheerily.*)

ALGERNON. Didn't it go off all right, old boy? You

don't mean to say Gwendolen refused you? I know it is a way she has. She is always refusing people. I think it is most ill-natured of her.

JACK. Oh, Gwendolen is as right as a trivet. As far as she is concerned, we are engaged. Her mother is perfectly unbearable. Never met such a gorgon . . . I don't really know what a gorgon is like, but I am quite sure that Lady Bracknell is one. In any case, she is a monster, without being a myth, which is rather unfair . . . I beg your pardon, Algy, I suppose I shouldn't talk about your own aunt in that way before you.

ALGERNON. My dear boy, I love hearing my relations abused. It is the only thing that makes me put up with them at all. Relations are simply a tedious pack of people who haven't got the remotest knowledge of how to live, nor the smallest instinct about when to die.

JACK. Oh, that is nonsense!

ALGERNON. It isn't!

JACK. Well, I won't argue about the matter. You always want to argue about things.

ALGERNON. That is exactly what things were originally made for.

JACK. Upon my word, if I thought that, I'd shoot myself. . . . (*A pause.*) You don't think there is any chance of Gwendolen becoming like her mother in about a hundred and fifty years, do you, Algy?

ALGERNON. All women become like their mothers. That is their tragedy. No man does. That's his.

JACK. Is that clever?

ALGERNON. It is perfectly phrased! and quite as true as any observation in civilized life should be.

JACK. I am sick to death of cleverness. Everybody is clever nowadays. You can't go anywhere without meeting clever people. The thing has become an absolute public nuisance. I wish to goodness we had a few fools left.

ALGERNON. We have.

JACK. I should extremely like to meet them. What do they talk about?

ALGERNON. The fools! Oh! about the clever people, of course.

JACK. What fools!

ALGERNON. By the way, did you tell Gwendolen the truth about your being Ernest in town, and Jack in the country?

JACK. (*In a very patronizing manner.*) My dear fellow, the truth isn't quite the sort of thing one tells to a nice sweet refined girl. What extraordinary ideas you have about the way to behave to a woman!

ALGERNON. The only way to behave to a woman is to make love to her, if she is pretty, and to someone else if she is plain.

JACK. Oh, that is nonsense.

ALGERNON. What about your brother? What about the profligate Ernest?

JACK. Oh, before the end of the week I shall have got rid of him. I'll say he died in Paris of apoplexy. Lots of people die of apoplexy, quite suddenly, don't they?

ALGERNON. Yes, but it's hereditary, my dear fellow. It's a sort of thing that runs in families. You had much better say a severe chill.

JACK. You are sure a severe chill isn't hereditary, or anything of that kind?

ALGERNON. Of course it isn't!

JACK. Very well, then. My poor brother Ernest is carried off suddenly in Paris, by a severe chill. That gets rid of him.

ALGERNON. But I thought you said that . . . Miss

Cardew was a little too much interested in your poor brother Ernest? Won't she feel his loss a good deal?

JACK. Oh, that is all right. Cecily is not a silly romantic girl, I am glad to say. She has got a capital appetite, goes long walks, and pays no attention at all to her lessons.

ALGERNON. I would rather like to see Cecily.

JACK. I will take very good care you never do. She is excessively pretty, and she is only just eighteen.

ALGERNON. Have you told Gwendolen yet that you have an excessively pretty ward who is only just eighteen?

JACK. Oh! one doesn't blurt these things out to people. Cecily and Gwendolen are perfectly certain to be extremely great friends. I'll bet you anything you like that half an hour after they have met, they will be calling each other sister.

ALGERNON. Women only do that when they have called each other a lot of other things first. Now, my dear boy, if we want to get a good table at Willis's, we really must go and dress. Do you know it is nearly seven?

JACK. (*Irritably.*) Oh! it always is nearly seven.

ALGERNON. Well, I'm hungry.

JACK. I never knew you when you weren't. . . .

ALGERNON. What shall we do after dinner? Go to the theatre?

JACK. Oh no! I loathe listening.

ALGERNON. Well, let us go to the club?

JACK. Oh, no! I hate talking.

ALGERNON. Well, we might trot round to the Empire at ten?

JACK. Oh no! I can't bear looking at things. It is so silly.

ALGERNON. Well, what shall we do?

JACK. Nothing!

ALGERNON. It is awfully hard work doing nothing. However, I don't mind hard work where there is no definite object of any kind.

(*Enter* LANE.)

LANE. Miss Fairfax.

(*Enter* GWENDOLEN. LANE *goes out.*)

ALGERNON. Gwendolen, upon my word!

GWENDOLEN. Algy, kindly turn your back. I have something very particular to say to Mr. Worthing.

ALGERNON. Really, Gwendolen, I don't think I can allow this at all.

GWENDOLEN. Algy, you always adopt a strictly immoral attitude towards life. You are not quite old enough to do that. (ALGERNON *retires to the fireplace.*)

JACK. My own darling!

GWENDOLEN. Ernest, we may never be married. From the expression on Mamma's face I fear we never shall. Few parents nowadays pay any regard to what their children say to them. The old-fashioned respect for the young is fast dying out. Whatever influence I ever had over Mamma, I lost at the age of three. But although she may prevent us from becoming man and wife, and I may marry someone else, and marry often, nothing that she can possibly do can alter my eternal devotion to you.

JACK. Dear Gwendolen!

GWENDOLEN. The story of your romantic origin, as related to me by Mamma, with unpleasing comments, has naturally stirred the deeper fibres of my nature. Your Christian name has an irresistible fascination. The simplicity of your character makes you exquisitely incomprehensible to me. Your town address at the Albany I have. What is your address in the country?

JACK. The Manor House, Woolton, Hertfordshire.

(ALGERNON, *who has been carefully listening, smiles to himself, and writes the address on his shirt-cuff. Then picks up the Railway Guide.*)

GWENDOLEN. There is a good postal service, I suppose? It may be necessary to do something desperate. That of course will require serious consideration. I will communicate with you daily.

JACK. My own one!

GWENDOLEN. How long do you remain in town?

JACK. Till Monday.

GWENDOLEN. Good! Algy, you may turn round now.

ALGERNON. Thanks, I've turned round already.

GWENDOLEN. You may also ring the bell.

JACK. You will let me see you to your carriage, my own darling?

GWENDOLEN. Certainly.

JACK. (*To* LANE, *who now enters.*) I will see Miss Fairfax out.

LANE. Yes, sir. (JACK *and* GWENDOLEN *go off.*)

(LANE *presents several letters on a salver to* ALGERNON. *It is to be surmised that they are bills, as* ALGERNON *after looking at the envelopes, tears them up.*)

ALGERNON. A glass of sherry, Lane.

LANE. Yes, sir.

ALGERNON. Tomorrow, Lane, I'm going Bunburying.

LANE. Yes, sir.

ALGERNON. I shall probably not be back till Monday. You can put up my dress clothes, my smoking jacket, and all the Bunbury suits. . . .

LANE. Yes, sir. (*Handing sherry.*)

ALGERNON. I hope tomorrow will be a fine day, Lane.

LANE. It never is, sir.

ALGERNON. Lane, you're a perfect pessimist.

LANE. I do my best to give satisfaction, sir.

(*Enter* JACK. LANE *goes off.*)

JACK. There's a sensible, intellectual girl! The only girl I ever cared for in my life. (ALGERNON *is laughing immoderately.*) What on earth are you so amused at?

ALGERNON. Oh, I'm a little anxious about poor Bunbury, that is all.

JACK. If you don't take care, your friend Bunbury will get you into a serious scrape some day.

ALGERNON. I love scrapes. They are the only things that are never serious.

JACK. Oh, that's nonsense, Algy. You never talk anything but nonsense.

ALGERNON. Nobody ever does.

(JACK *looks indignantly at him, and leaves the room.* ALGERNON *lights a cigarette, reads his shirt-cuff, and smiles.*)

ACT-DROP.

Second Act·

Scene. Garden at the Manor House. A flight of grey stone steps leads up to the house. The garden, an old-fashioned one, full of roses. Time of year, July. Basket chairs, and a table covered with books, are set under a large yew tree.

(MISS PRISM discovered seated at the table. CECILY is at the back watering flowers.)

MISS PRISM. (*Calling.*) Cecily, Cecily! Surely such a utilitarian occupation as the watering of flowers is rather Moulton's duty than yours? Especially at a moment when intellectual pleasures await you. Your German grammar is on the table. Pray open it ·at page fifteen. We will repeat yesterday's lesson.

CECILY. (*Coming over very slowly.*) But I don't like German. It isn't at all a becoming language. I know perfectly well that I look quite plain after my German lesson.

MISS PRISM. Child, you know how anxious your guardian is that you should improve yourself in every way. He laid particular stress on your German, as he was leaving for town yesterday. Indeed, he always lays stress on your German when he is leaving for town.

CECILY. Dear Uncle Jack is so very serious! Sometimes he is so serious that I think he cannot be quite well.

MISS PRISM. (*Drawing herself up.*) Your guardian enjoys the best of health, and his gravity of demeanour is especially to be commended in one so comparatively young as he is. I know no one who has a higher sense of duty and responsibility.

CECILY. I suppose that is why he often looks a little bored when we three are together.

MISS PRISM. Cecily! I am surprised at you. Mr. Worthing has many troubles in his life. Idle merriment and triviality would be out of place in his conversation. You must remember his constant anxiety about that unfortunate young man his brother.

CECILY. I wish Uncle Jack would allow that unfortunate young man, his brother, to come down here sometimes. We might have a good influence over him, Miss Prism. I am sure you certainly would. You know German, and Geology, and things of that kind influence a man very much. (CECILY *begins to write in her diary.*)

MISS PRISM. (*Shaking her head.*) I do not think that even I could produce any effect on a character that according to his own brother's admission is irretrievably weak and vacillating. Indeed I am not sure that I would desire to reclaim him. I am not in favour of this modern mania for turning bad people into good people at a moment's notice. As a man sows so let him reap. You must put away your diary, Cecily. I really don't see why you should keep a diary at all.

CECILY. I keep a diary in order to enter the wonderful secrets of my life. If I didn't write them down I should probably forget all about them.

MISS PRISM. Memory, my dear Cecily, is the diary that we all carry about with us.

CECILY. Yes, but it usually chronicles the things that have never happened, and couldn't possibly have happened. I believe that memory is responsible for nearly all the three-volume novels that Mudie sends us.

MISS PRISM. Do not speak slightingly of the three-volume novel, Cecily. I wrote one myself in earlier days.

CECILY. Did you really, Miss Prism? How wonderfully clever you are! I hope it did not end happily? I don't like novels that end happily. They depress me so much.

MISS PRISM. The good ended happily, and the bad unhappily. That is what fiction means.

CECILY. I suppose so. But it seems very unfair. And was your novel ever published?

MISS PRISM. Alas! no. The manuscript unfortunately was abandoned. I use the word in the sense of lost or mislaid. To your work, child, these speculations are profitless.

CECILY. (*Smiling.*) But I see dear Dr. Chasuble coming up through the garden.

MISS PRISM. (*Rising and advancing.*) Dr. Chasuble! This is indeed a pleasure.

(*Enter* CANON CHASUBLE.)

CHASUBLE. And how are we this morning? Miss Prism, you are, I trust, well?

CECILY. Miss Prism has just been complaining of a slight headache. I think it would do her so much good to have a short stroll with you in the Park, Dr. Chasuble.

MISS PRISM. Cecily, I have not mentioned anything about a headache.

CECILY. No, dear Miss Prism, I know that, but I felt instinctively that you had a headache. Indeed I was thinking about that, and not about my German lesson, when the Rector came in.

CHASUBLE. I hope, Cecily, you are not inattentive.

CECILY. Oh, I am afraid I am.

CHASUBLE. That is strange. Were I fortunate enough to be Miss Prism's pupil, I would hang upon her lips. (MISS PRISM *glares*.) I spoke metaphorically.—My metaphor was drawn from bees. Ahem! Mr. Worthing, I suppose, has not returned from town yet?

MISS PRISM. We do not expect him till Monday afternoon.

CHASUBLE. Ah yes, he usually likes to spend his Sunday in London. He is not one of those whose sole aim is enjoyment, as, by all accounts, that unfortunate young man his brother seems to be. But I must not disturb Egeria and her pupil any longer.

MISS PRISM. Egeria? My name is Lætitia, Doctor.

CHASUBLE. (*Bowing*.) A classical allusion merely, drawn from the pagan authors. I shall see you both no doubt at Evensong?

MISS PRISM. I think, dear Doctor, I will have a stroll with you. I find I have a headache after all, and a walk might do it good.

CHASUBLE. With pleasure, Miss Prism, with pleasure. We might go as far as the schools and back.

MISS PRISM. That would be delightful. Cecily, you will read your Political Economy in my absence. The chapter on the Fall of the Rupee you may omit. It is somewhat too sensational. Even these metallic problems have their melodramatic side.

(*Goes down the garden with* DR. CHASUBLE.)

CECILY. (*Picks up books and throws them back on table.*) Horrid Political Economy! Horrid Geography! Horrid, horrid German!

(*Enter* MERRIMAN *with a card on a salver.*)

MERRIMAN. Mr. Ernest Worthing has just driven over from the station. He has brought his luggage with him.

CECILY. (*Takes the card and reads it.*) "Mr. Ernest Worthing, B. 4 The Albany, W." Uncle Jack's brother! Did you tell him Mr. Worthing was in town?

MERRIMAN. Yes, Miss. He seemed very much disappointed. I mentioned that you and Miss Prism were in the garden. He said he was anxious to speak to you privately for a moment.

CECILY. Ask Mr. Ernest Worthing to come here. I suppose you had better talk to the housekeeper about a room for him.

MERRIMAN. Yes, Miss.   (MERRIMAN *goes off.*)

CECILY. I have never met any really wicked person before. I feel rather frightened. I am so afraid he will look just like everyone else.

(*Enter* ALGERNON, *very gay and debonair.*)
He does!

ALGERNON. (*Raising his hat.*) You are my little cousin Cecily, I'm sure.

CECILY. You are under some strange mistake. I am

not little. In fact, I believe I am more than usually tall for my age. (ALGERNON *is rather taken aback.*) But I am your cousin Cecily. You, I see from your card, are Uncle Jack's brother, my cousin Ernest, my wicked cousin Ernest.

ALGERNON. Oh! I am not really wicked at all, cousin Cecily. You mustn't think that I am wicked.

CECILY. If you are not, then you have certainly been deceiving us all in a very inexcusable manner. I hope you have not been leading a double life, pretending to be wicked and being really good all the time. That would be hypocrisy.

ALGERNON. (*Looks at her in amazement.*) Oh! Of course I have been rather reckless.

CECILY. I am glad to hear it.

ALGERNON. In fact, now you mention the subject, I have been very bad in my own small way.

CECILY. I don't think you should be so proud of that, though I am sure it must have been very pleasant.

ALGERNON. It is much pleasanter being here with you.

CECILY. I can't understand how you are here at all. Uncle Jack won't be back till Monday afternoon.

ALGERNON. That is a great disappointment. I am obliged to go up by the first train on Monday morning. I have a business appointment that I am anxious . . . to miss.

CECILY. Couldn't you miss it anywhere but in London?

ALGERNON. No; the appointment is in London.

CECILY. Well, I know, of course, how important it is not to keep a business engagement, if one wants to retain any sense of the beauty of life, but still I think you had better wait till Uncle Jack arrives. I know he wants to speak to you about your emigrating.

ALGERNON. About my what?

CECILY. Your emigrating. He has gone up to buy your outfit.

ALGERNON. I certainly wouldn't let Jack buy my outfit. He has no taste in neckties at all.

CECILY. I don't think you will require neckties. Uncle Jack is sending you to Australia.

ALGERNON. Australia? I'd sooner die.

CECILY. Well, he said at dinner on Wednesday night, that you would have to choose between this world, the next world, and Australia.

ALGERNON. Oh, well! The accounts I have received of Australia and the next world are not particularly encouraging. This world is good enough for me, cousin Cecily.

CECILY. Yes, but are you good enough for it?

ALGERNON. I'm afraid I'm not that. That is why I want you to reform me. You might make that your mission, if you don't mind, cousin Cecily.

CECILY. I'm afraid I've no time, this afternoon.

ALGERNON. Well, would you mind my reforming myself this afternoon?

CECILY. It is rather quixotic of you. But I think you should try.

ALGERNON. I will. I feel better already.

CECILY. You are looking a little worse.

ALGERNON. That is because I am hungry.

CECILY. How thoughtless of me. I should have remembered that when one is going to lead an entirely new life, one requires regular and wholesome meals. Won't you come in?

ALGERNON. Thank you. Might I have a button-hole first? I never have any appetite unless I have a button-hole first.

CECILY. A Maréchal Niel? (*Picks up scissors.*)

ALGERNON. No, I'd sooner have a pink rose.

CECILY. Why? (*Cuts a flower.*)

ALGERNON. Because you are like a pink rose, cousin Cecily.

CECILY. I don't think it can be right for you to talk to me like that. Miss Prism never says such things to me.

ALGERNON. Then Miss Prism is a short-sighted old lady. (CECILY *puts the rose in his button-hole.*) You are the prettiest girl I ever saw.

CECILY. Miss Prism says that all good looks are a snare.

ALGERNON. They are a snare that every sensible man would like to be caught in.

CECILY. Oh! I don't think I would care to catch a sensible man. I shouldn't know what to talk to him about.

(*They pass into the house.* MISS PRISM *and* DR. CHASUBLE *return.*)

MISS PRISM. You are too much alone, dear Dr. Chasuble. You should get married. A misanthrope I can understand—a womanthrope, never!

CHASUBLE. (*With a scholar's shudder.*) Believe me, I do not deserve so neologistic a phrase. The precept as well as the practice of the Primitive Church was distinctly against matrimony.

MISS PRISM. (*Sententiously.*) That is obviously the reason why the Primitive Church has not lasted up to the present day. And you do not seem to realize, dear Doctor, that by persistently remaining single, a man converts himself into a permanent public temptation. Men should be more careful; this very celibacy leads weaker vessels astray.

CHASUBLE. But is a man not equally attractive when married?

MISS PRISM. No married man is ever attractive except to his wife.

CHASUBLE. And often, I've been told, not even to her.

MISS PRISM. That depends on the intellectual sympathies of the woman. Maturity can always be depended on. Ripeness can be trusted. Young women are green. (DR. CHASUBLE *starts*.) I spoke horticulturally. My metaphor was drawn from fruits. But where is Cecily?

CHASUBLE. Perhaps she followed us to the schools.

(*Enter* JACK *slowly from the back of the garden. He is dressed in the deepest mourning, with crape hatband and black gloves.*)

MISS PRISM. Mr. Worthing!

CHASUBLE. Mr. Worthing?

MISS PRISM. This is indeed a surprise. We did not look for you till Monday afternoon.

JACK. (*Shakes* MISS PRISM'S *hand in a tragic manner.*) I have returned sooner than I expected. Dr. Chasuble, I hope you are well?

CHASUBLE. Dear Mr. Worthing, I trust this garb of woe does not betoken some terrible calamity?

JACK. My brother.

MISS PRISM. More shameful debts and extravagance?

CHASUBLE. Still leading his life of pleasure?

JACK. (*Shaking his head.*) Dead!

CHASUBLE. Your brother Ernest dead?

JACK. Quite dead.

MISS PRISM. What a lesson for him! I trust he will profit by it.

CHASUBLE. Mr. Worthing, I offer you my sincere condolence. You have at least the consolation of knowing that you were always the most generous and forgiving of brothers.

JACK. Poor Ernest! He had many faults, but it is a sad, sad blow.

CHASUBLE. Very sad indeed. Were you with him at the end?

JACK. No. He died abroad; in Paris, in fact. I had a telegram last night from the manager of the Grand Hotel.

CHASUBLE. Was the cause of death mentioned?

JACK. A severe chill, it seems.

MISS PRISM. As a man sows, so shall he reap.

CHASUBLE. (*Raising his hand.*) Charity, dear Miss Prism, charity! None of us are perfect. I myself am peculiarly susceptible to draughts. Will the interment take place here?

JACK. No. He seemed to have expressed a desire to be buried in Paris.

CHASUBLE. In Paris! (*Shakes his head.*) I fear that hardly points to any very serious state of mind at the last. You would no doubt wish me to make some slight allusion to this tragic domestic affliction next Sunday. (JACK *presses his hand convulsively.*) My sermon on the meaning of the manna in the wilderness can be adapted to almost any occasion, joyful, or, as in the present case, distressing. (*All sigh.*) I have preached it at harvest celebrations, christenings, confirmations, on days of humiliation and festal days. The last time I delivered it was in the Cathedral, as a charity sermon on behalf of the Society for the Prevention of Discontent among the Upper Orders. The Bishop, who was present, was much struck by some of the analogies I drew.

JACK. Ah! that reminds me, you mentioned christenings, I think, Dr. Chasuble? I suppose you know how to christen all right? (DR. CHASUBLE *looks astounded.*)

I mean, of course, you are continually christening, aren't you?

MISS PRISM. It is, I regret to say, one of the Rector's most constant duties in this parish. I have often spoken to the poorer classes on the subject. But they don't seem to know what thrift is.

CHASUBLE. But is there any particular infant in whom you are interested, Mr. Worthing? Your brother was, I believe, unmarried, was he not?

JACK. Oh, yes.

MISS PRISM. (*Bitterly.*) People who live entirely for pleasure usually are.

JACK. But it is not for any child, dear Doctor. I am very fond of children. No! the fact is, I would like to be christened myself, this afternoon, if you have nothing better to do.

CHASUBLE. But surely, Mr. Worthing, you have been christened already?

JACK. I don't remember anything about it.

CHASUBLE. But have you any grave doubts on the subject?

JACK. I certainly intend to have. Of course I don't know if the thing would bother you in any way, or if you think I am a little too old now.

CHASUBLE. Not at all. The sprinkling, and, indeed, the immersion of adults is a perfectly canonical practice.

JACK. Immersion!

CHASUBLE. You need have no apprehensions. Sprinkling is all that is necessary, or indeed I think advisable. Our weather is so changeable. At what hour would you wish the ceremony performed?

JACK. Oh, I might trot round about five if that would suit you.

CHASUBLE. Perfectly, perfectly! In fact I have two

similar ceremonies to perform at that time. A case of twins that occurred recently in one of the outlying cottages on your own estate. Poor Jenkins the carter, a most hard-working man.

JACK. Oh! I don't see much fun in being christened along with other babies. It would be childish. Would half-past five do?

CHASUBLE. Admirably! Admirably! (*Takes out watch.*) And now, dear Mr. Worthing, I will not intrude any longer into a house of sorrow. I would merely beg you not to be too much bowed down by grief. What seems to us bitter trials are often blessings in disguise.

MISS PRISM. This seems to me a blessing of an extremely obvious kind.

(*Enter* CECILY *from the house.*)

CECILY. Uncle Jack! Oh, I am pleased to see you back. But what horrid clothes you have got on! Do go and change them.

MISS PRISM. Cecily!

CHASUBLE. My child! my child! (CECILY *goes towards* JACK; *he kisses her brow in a melancholy manner.*)

CECILY. What is the matter, Uncle Jack? Do look happy! You look as if you had toothache, and I have got such a surprise for you. Who do you think is in the dining-room? Your brother!

JACK. Who?

CECILY. Your brother Ernest. He arrived about half an hour ago.

JACK. What nonsense! I haven't got a brother!

CECILY. Oh, don't say that. However badly he may have behaved to you in the past he is still your brother. You couldn't be so heartless as to disown him. I'll tell him to come out. And you will shake hands with him, won't you, Uncle Jack? (*Runs back into the house.*)

CHASUBLE. These are very joyful tidings.

MISS PRISM. After we had all been resigned to his loss, his sudden return seems to me peculiarly distressing.

JACK. My brother is in the dining-room? I don't know what it all means. I think it is perfectly absurd.

(*Enter* ALGERNON *and* CECILY *hand in hand. They come slowly up to* JACK.)

JACK. Good heavens! (*Motions* ALGERNON *away.*)

ALGERNON. Brother John, I have come down from town to tell you that I am very sorry for all the trouble I have given you, and that I intend to lead a better life in the future. (JACK *glares at him and does not take his hand.*)

CECILY. Uncle Jack, you are not going to refuse your own brother's hand?

JACK. Nothing will induce me to take his hand. I think his coming down here disgraceful. He knows perfectly well why.

CECILY. Uncle Jack, do be nice. There is some good in everyone. Ernest has just been telling me about his poor invalid friend Mr. Bunbury whom he goes to visit so often. And surely there must be much good in one who is kind to an invalid, and leaves the pleasures of London to sit by a bed of pain.

JACK. Oh! he has been talking about Bunbury, has he?

CECILY. Yes, he has told me all about poor Mr. Bunbury, and his terrible state of health.

JACK. Bunbury! Well, I won't have him talk to you about Bunbury or about anything else. It is enough to drive one perfectly frantic.

ALGERNON. Of course I admit that the faults were all on my side. But I must say that I think that Brother John's coldness to me is peculiarly painful. I expected a more enthusiastic welcome, especially considering it is the first time I have come here.

CECILY. Uncle Jack, if you don't shake hands with Ernest, I will never forgive you.

JACK. Never forgive me?

CECILY. Never, never, never!

JACK. Well, this is the last time I shall ever do it. (*Shakes hands with* ALGERNON *and glares.*)

CHASUBLE. It's pleasant, is it not, to see so perfect a reconciliation? I think we might leave the two brothers together.

MISS PRISM. Cecily, you will come with us.

CECILY. Certainly, Miss Prism. My little task of reconciliation is over.

CHASUBLE. You have done a beautiful action today, dear child.

MISS PRISM. We must not be premature in our judgments.

CECILY. I feel very happy. (*They all go off.*)

JACK. You young scoundrel, Algy, you must get out of this place as soon as possible. I don't allow any Bunburying here.

(*Enter* MERRIMAN.)

MERRIMAN. I have put Mr. Ernest's things in the room next to yours, sir. I suppose that is all right?

JACK. What?

MERRIMAN. Mr. Ernest's luggage, sir. I have unpacked it and put it in the room next to your own.

JACK. His luggage?

MERRIMAN. Yes, sir. Three portmanteaus, a dressing-case, two hat boxes, and a large luncheon-basket.

ALGERNON. I am afraid I can't stay more than a week this time.

JACK. Merriman, order the dog-cart at once. Mr. Ernest has been suddenly called back to town.

MERRIMAN. Yes, sir. (*Goes back into the house.*)

ALGERNON. What a fearful liar you are, Jack. I have not been called back to town at all.

JACK. Yes, you have.

ALGERNON. I haven't heard anyone call me.

JACK. Your duty as a gentleman calls you back.

ALGERNON. My duty as a gentleman has never interfered with my pleasures in the smallest degree.

JACK. I can quite understand that.

ALGERNON. Well, Cecily is a darling.

JACK. You are not to talk of Miss Cardew like that. I don't like it.

ALGERNON. Well, I don't like your clothes. You look perfectly ridiculous in them. Why on earth don't you go up and change? It is perfectly childish to be in deep mourning for a man who is actually staying for a whole week with you in your house as a guest. I call it grotesque.

JACK. You are certainly not staying with me for a whole week as a guest or anything else. You have got to leave . . . by the four-five train.

ALGERNON. I certainly won't leave you so long as you are in mourning. It would be most unfriendly. If I were in mourning you would stay with me, I suppose. I should think it very unkind if you didn't.

JACK. Well, will you go if I change my clothes?

ALGERNON. Yes, if you are not too long. I never saw anybody take so long to dress, and with such little result.

JACK. Well, at any rate, that is better than being always overdressed as you are.

ALGERNON. If I am occasionally a little overdressed, I make up for it by being always immensely over-educated.

JACK. Your vanity is ridiculous, your conduct an outrage, and your presence in my garden utterly absurd. However, you have got to catch the four-five, and I hope you will have a pleasant journey back to town. This Bunburying, as you call it, has not been a great success for you.   (*Goes into the house.*)

ALGERNON. I think it has been a great success. I'm in love with Cecily, and that is everything.

(*Enter* CECILY *at the back of the garden. She picks up the can and begins to water the flowers.*)

But I must see her before I go, and make arrangements for another Bunbury. Ah, there she is.

CECILY. Oh, I merely came back to water the roses. I thought you were with Uncle Jack.

ALGERNON. He's gone to order the dog-cart for me.

CECILY. Oh, is he going to take you for a nice drive?

ALGERNON. He's going to send me away.

CECILY. Then have we got to part?

ALGERNON. I am afraid so. It's very painful parting.

CECILY. It is always painful to part from people whom one has known for a very brief space of time. The absence of old friends one can endure with equanimity. But even a momentary separation from anyone to whom one has just been introduced is almost unbearable.

ALGERNON. Thank you.

(*Enter* MERRIMAN.)

MERRIMAN. The dog-cart is at the door, sir. (ALGERNON *looks appealingly at* CECILY.)

CECILY. It can wait, Merriman . . . for . . . five minutes.

MERRIMAN. Yes, Miss.   (*Exit* MERRIMAN.)

ALGERNON. I hope, Cecily, I shall not offend you if I state quite frankly and openly that you seem to me to be in every way the visible personification of absolute perfection.

CECILY. I think your frankness does you great credit, Ernest. If you will allow me I will copy your remarks into my diary. (*Goes over to table and begins writing in diary.*)

ALGERNON. Do you really keep a diary? I'd give anything to look at it. May I?

CECILY. Oh no. (*Puts her hand over it.*) You see, it is simply a very young girl's record of her own thoughts and impressions, and consequently meant for publication. When it appears in volume form I hope you will order a copy. But pray, Ernest, don't stop. I delight in taking down from dictation. I have reached "absolute perfection." You can go on. I am quite ready for more.

ALGERNON. (*Somewhat taken aback.*) Ahem! Ahem!

CECILY. Oh, don't cough, Ernest. When one is dictating one should speak fluently and not cough. Besides, I don't know how to spell a cough.

(*Writes as* ALGERNON *speaks.*)

ALGERNON. (*Speaking very rapidly.*) Cecily, ever since I first looked upon your wonderful and incomparable beauty, I have dared to love you wildly, passionately, devotedly, hopelessly.

CECILY. I don't think that you should tell me that you love me wildly, passionately, devotedly, hopelessly. Hopelessly doesn't seem to make much sense, does it?

ALGERNON. Cecily!

(*Enter* MERRIMAN.)

MERRIMAN. The dog-cart is waiting, sir.

ALGERNON. Tell it to come round next week, at the same hour.

MERRIMAN. (*Looks at* CECILY, *who makes no sign.*) Yes, sir.   (MERRIMAN *retires.*)

CECILY. Uncle Jack would be very much annoyed if he knew you were staying on till next week, at the same hour.

ALGERNON. Oh, I don't care about Jack. I don't care for anybody in the whole world but you. I love you, Cecily. You will marry me, won't you?

CECILY. You silly boy! Of course. Why, we have been engaged for the last three months.

ALGERNON. For the last three months?

CECILY. Yes, it will be exactly three months on Thursday.

ALGERNON. But how did we become engaged?

CECILY. Well, ever since dear Uncle Jack first confessed to us that he had a younger brother who was very wicked and bad, you of course have formed the chief topic of conversation between myself and Miss Prism. And of course a man who is much talked about is always very attractive. One feels there must be something in him after all. I daresay it was foolish of me, but I fell in love with you, Ernest.

ALGERNON. Darling! And when was the engagement actually settled?

CECILY. On the 14th of February last. Worn out by your entire ignorance of my existence, I determined to end the matter one way or the other, and after a long struggle with myself I accepted you under this dear old tree here. The next day I bought this little ring in your name, and this is the little bangle with the true lovers' knot I promised you always to wear.

ALGERNON. Did I give you this? It's very pretty, isn't it?

CECILY. Yes, you've wonderfully good taste, Ernest. It's the excuse I've always given for your leading such a bad life. And this is the box in which I keep all your dear letters. (*Kneels at table, opens box, and produces letters tied up with blue ribbon.*)

ALGERNON. My letters! But my own sweet Cecily, I have never written you any letters.

CECILY. You need hardly remind me of that, Ernest. I remember only too well that I was forced to write your letters for you. I always wrote three times a week, and sometimes oftener.

ALGERNON. Oh, do let me read them, Cecily?

CECILY. Oh, I couldn't possibly. They would make you far too conceited. (*Replaces box.*) The three you wrote me after I had broken off the engagement are so beautiful, and so badly spelled, that even now I can hardly read them without crying a little.

ALGERNON. But was our engagement ever broken off?

CECILY. Of course it was. On the 22nd of last March. You can see the entry if you like. (*Shows diary.*) "To-day I broke off my engagement with Ernest. I feel it is better to do so. The weather still continues charming."

ALGERNON. But why on earth did you break it off? What had I done? I had done nothing at all. Cecily, I am very much hurt indeed to hear you broke it off. Particularly when the weather was so charming.

CECILY. It would hardly have been a really serious engagement if it hadn't been broken off at least once. But I forgave you before the week was out.

ALGERNON. (*Crossing to her, and kneeling.*) What a perfect angel you are, Cecily.

CECILY. You dear romantic boy. (*He kisses her, she puts her fingers through his hair.*) I hope your hair curls naturally, does it?

ALGERNON. Yes, darling, with a little help from others.

CECILY. I am so glad.

ALGERNON. You'll never break off our engagement again, Cecily?

CECILY. I don't think I could break it off now that I have actually met you. Besides, of course, there is the question of your name.

ALGERNON. Yes, of course. (*Nervously.*)

CECILY. You must not laugh at me, darling, but it had always been a girlish dream of mine to love someone whose name was Ernest. (ALGERNON *rises*, CECILY *also.*) There is something in that name that seems to inspire absolute confidence. I pity any poor married woman whose husband is not called Ernest.

ALGERNON. But, my dear child, do you mean to say you could not love me if I had some other name?

CECILY. But what name?

ALGERNON. Oh, any name you like—Algernon—for instance. . . .

CECILY. But I don't like the name of Algernon.

ALGERNON. Well, my own dear, sweet, loving little darling, I really can't see why you should object to the name of Algernon. It is not at all a bad name. In fact, it is rather an aristocratic name. Half of the chaps who get into the Bankruptcy Court are called Algernon. But seriously, Cecily . . . (*Moving to her*) . . . if my name was Algy, couldn't you love me?

CECILY. (*Rising.*) I might respect you, Ernest, I might admire your character, but I fear that I should not be able to give you my undivided attention.

ALGERNON. Ahem! Cecily! (*Picking up hat.*) Your Rector here is, I suppose, thoroughly experienced in the practice of all the rites and ceremonials of the Church?

CECILY. Oh, yes. Dr. Chasuble is a most learned man. He has never written a single book, so you can imagine how much he knows.

ALGERNON. I must see him at once on a most important christening—I mean on most important business.

CECILY. Oh!

ALGERNON. I shan't be away more than half an hour.

CECILY. Considering that we have been engaged since February the 14th, and that I only met you to-day for the first time, I think it is rather hard that you should leave me for so long a period as half an hour. Couldn't you make it twenty minutes?

ALGERNON. I'll be back in no time.

(*Kisses her and rushes down the garden.*)

CECILY. What an impetuous boy he is! I like his hair so much. I must enter his proposal in my diary.

(*Enter* MERRIMAN.)

MERRIMAN. A Miss Fairfax has just called to see Mr. Worthing. On very important business Miss Fairfax states.

CECILY. Isn't Mr. Worthing in his library?

MERRIMAN. Mr. Worthing went over in the direction of the Rectory some time ago.

CECILY. Pray ask the lady to come out here; Mr. Worthing is sure to be back soon. And you can bring tea.

MERRIMAN. Yes, Miss. (*Goes out.*)

CECILY. Miss Fairfax! I suppose one of the many good elderly women who are associated with Uncle Jack in some of his philanthropic work in London. I don't quite like women who are interested in philanthropic work. I think it is so forward of them.

(*Enter* MERRIMAN.)

MERRIMAN. Miss Fairfax.

(*Enter* GWENDOLEN.) (*Exit* MERRIMAN.)

CECILY. (*Advancing to meet her.*) Pray let me introduce myself to you. My name is Cecily Cardew.

GWENDOLEN. Cecily Cardew? (*Moving to her and shaking hands.*) What a very sweet name! Something tells me that we are going to be great friends. I like you already more than I can say. My first impressions of people are never wrong.

CECILY. How nice of you to like me so much after we have known each other such a comparatively short time. Pray sit down.

GWENDOLEN. (*Still standing up.*) I may call you Cecily, may I not?

CECILY. With pleasure!

GWENDOLEN. And you will always call me Gwendolen, won't you?

CECILY. If you wish.

GWENDOLEN. Then that is all quite settled, is it not?

CECILY. I hope so. (*A pause. They both sit down together.*)

GWENDOLEN. Perhaps this might be a favourable opportunity for my mentioning who I am. My father is Lord Bracknell. You have never heard of Papa, I suppose?

CECILY. I don't think so.

GWENDOLEN. Outside the family circle, Papa, I am glad to say, is entirely unknown. I think that is quite as it should be. The home seems to me to be the proper sphere for the man. And certainly once a man begins to neglect his domestic duties he becomes painfully effeminate, does he not? And I don't like that. It makes men so very attractive. Cecily, Mamma, whose views on education are remarkably strict, has brought me up to be extremely short-sighted; it is part of her system; so do you mind my looking at you through my glasses?

CECILY. Oh! not at all, Gwendolen. I am very fond of being looked at.

GWENDOLEN. (*After examining* CECILY *carefully through a lorgnette.*) You are here on a short visit I suppose.

CECILY. Oh no! I live here.

GWENDOLEN. (*Severely.*) Really? Your mother, no

doubt, or some female relative of advanced years, resides here also?

CECILY. Oh no! I have no mother, nor, in fact, any relations.

GWENDOLEN. Indeed?

CECILY. My dear guardian, with the assistance of Miss Prism, has the arduous task of looking after me.

GWENDOLEN. Your guardian?

CECILY. Yes, I am Mr. Worthing's ward.

GWENDOLEN. Oh! It is strange he never mentioned to me that he had a ward. How secretive of him! He grows more interesting hourly. I am not sure, however, that the news inspires me with feelings of unmixed delight. (*Rising and going to her.*) I am very fond of you, Cecily; I have liked you ever since I met you! But I am bound to state that now that I know that you are Mr. Worthing's ward, I cannot help expressing a wish you were—well just a little older than you seem to be—and not quite so very alluring in appearance. In fact, if I may speak candidly—

CECILY. Pray do! I think that whenever one has anything unpleasant to say, one should always be quite candid.

GWENDOLEN. Well, to speak with perfect candour, Cecily, I wish that you were fully forty-two, and more than usually plain for your age. Ernest has a strong upright nature. He is the very soul of truth and honour. Disloyalty would be as impossible to him as deception. But even men of the noblest possible moral character are extremely susceptible to the influence of the physical charms of others. Modern, no less than ancient history, supplies us with many most painful examples of what I refer to. If it were not so, indeed, history would be quite unreadable.

CECILY. I beg your pardon, Gwendolen, did you say Ernest?

GWENDOLEN. Yes.

CECILY. Oh, but it is not Mr. Ernest Worthing who is my guardian. It is his brother—his elder brother.

GWENDOLEN. (*Sitting down again.*) Ernest never mentioned to me that he had a brother.

CECILY. I am sorry to say they have not been on good terms for a long time.

GWENDOLEN. Ah! that accounts for it. And now that I think of it I have never heard any man mention his brother. The subject seems distasteful to most men. Cecily, you have lifted a load from my mind. I was growing almost anxious. It would have been terrible if any cloud had come across a friendship like ours, would it not? Of course you are quite, quite sure that it is not Mr. Ernest Worthing who is your guardian?

CECILY. Quite sure. (*A pause.*) In fact, I am going to be his.

GWENDOLEN. (*Enquiringly.*) I beg your pardon?

CECILY. (*Rather shy and confidingly.*) Dearest Gwendolen, there is no reason why I should make a secret of it to you. Our little county newspaper is sure to chronicle the fact next week. Mr. Ernest Worthing and I are engaged to be married.

GWENDOLEN. (*Quite politely, rising.*) My darling Cecily, I think there must be some slight error. Mr. Ernest Worthing is engaged to me. The announcement will appear in the *Morning Post* on Saturday at the latest.

CECILY. (*Very politely, rising.*) I am afraid you must be under some misconception. Ernest proposed to me exactly ten minutes ago. (*Shows diary.*)

GWENDOLEN. (*Examines diary through her lorgnette carefully.*) It is certainly very curious, for he asked me to be his wife yesterday afternoon at 5:30. If you would care to verify the incident, pray do so. (*Produces diary of her own.*) I never travel without my diary. One should always have something sensational to read in the train. I am so sorry, dear Cecily, if it is any disappointment to you, but I am afraid *I* have the prior claim.

CECILY. It would distress me more than I can tell you, dear Gwendolen, if it caused you any mental or physical anguish, but I feel bound to point out that since Ernest proposed to you he clearly has changed his mind.

GWENDOLEN. (*Meditatively.*) If the poor fellow has been entrapped into any foolish promise I shall consider it my duty to rescue him at once, and with a firm hand.

CECILY. (*Thoughtfully and sadly.*) Whatever unfortunate entanglement my dear boy may have got into, I will never reproach him with it after we are married.

GWENDOLEN. Do you allude to me, Miss Cardew, as an entanglement? You are presumptuous. On an occasion of this kind it becomes more than a moral duty to speak one's mind. It becomes a pleasure.

CECILY. Do you suggest, Miss Fairfax, that I entrapped Ernest into an engagement? How dare you? This is no time for wearing the shallow mask of manners. When I see a spade I call it a spade.

GWENDOLEN. (*Satirically.*) I am glad to say that I have never seen a spade. It is obvious that our social spheres have been widely different.

(*Enter* MERRIMAN, *followed by the footman. He carries a salver, table cloth, and plate stand.* CECILY *is about to retort. The presence of the servants exercises a restraining influence, under which both girls chafe.*)

MERRIMAN. Shall I lay tea here as usual, Miss?

CECILY. (*Sternly, in a calm voice.*) Yes, as usual. (MERRIMAN *begins to clear table and lay cloth. A long pause.* CECILY *and* GWENDOLEN *glare at each other.*)

GWENDOLEN. Are there many interesting walks in the vicinity, Miss Cardew?

CECILY. Oh! yes! a great many. From the top of one of the hills quite close one can see five counties.

GWENDOLEN. Five counties! I don't think I should like that. I hate crowds.

CECILY. (*Sweetly.*) I suppose that is why you live in town? (GWENDOLEN *bites her lip, and beats her foot nervously with her parasol.*)

GWENDOLEN. (*Looking round.*) Quite a well-kept garden this is, Miss Cardew.

CECILY. So glad you like it, Miss Fairfax.

GWENDOLEN. I had no idea there were any flowers in the country.

CECILY. Oh, flowers are as common here, Miss Fairfax, as people are in London.

GWENDOLEN. Personally I cannot understand how anybody manages to exist in the country, if anybody who is anybody does. The country always bores me to death.

CECILY. Ah! This is what the newspapers call agricultural depression, is it not? I believe the aristocracy are suffering very much from it just at present. It is almost an epidemic amongst them, I have been told. May I offer you some tea, Miss Fairfax?

GWENDOLEN. (*With elaborate politeness.*) Thank you. (*Aside.*) Detestable girl! But I require tea!

CECILY. (*Sweetly.*) Sugar?

GWENDOLEN. (*Superciliously.*) No, thank you. Sugar is not fashionable any more. (CECILY *looks angrily at her, takes up the tongs and puts four lumps of sugar into the cup.*)

CECILY. (*Severely.*) Cake or bread and butter?

GWENDOLEN. (*In a bored manner.*) Bread and butter, please. Cake is rarely seen at the best houses nowadays.

CECILY. (*Cuts a very large slice of cake, and puts it on the tray.*) Hand that to Miss Fairfax.

(MERRIMAN *does so, and goes out with footman.* GWENDOLEN *drinks the tea and makes a grimace. Puts down cup at once, reaches out her hand to the bread and butter, looks at it, and finds it is cake. Rises in indignation.*)

GWENDOLEN. You have filled my tea with lumps of sugar, and though I asked most distinctly for bread and butter, you have given me cake. I am known for the gentleness of my disposition, and the extraordinary sweetness of my nature, but I warn you, Miss Cardew, you may go too far.

CECILY. (*Rising.*) To save my poor, innocent, trusting boy from the machinations of any other girl there are no lengths to which I would not go.

GWENDOLEN. From the moment I saw you I distrusted you. I felt that you were false and deceitful. I am never deceived in such matters. My first impressions of people are invariably right.

CECILY. It seems to me, Miss Fairfax, that I am trespassing on your valuable time. No doubt you have many other calls of a similar character to make in the neighbourhood.

(*Enter* JACK.)

GWENDOLEN. (*Catching sight of him.*) Ernest! My own Ernest!

JACK. Gwendolen! Darling! (*Offers to kiss her.*)

GWENDOLEN. (*Drawing back.*) A moment! May I ask if you are engaged to be married to this young lady? (*Points to* CECILY.)

JACK. (*Laughing.*) To dear little Cecily! Of course not! What could have put such an idea into your pretty little head?

GWENDOLEN. Thank you. You may! (*Offers her cheek.*)

CECILY. (*Very sweetly.*) I knew there must be some misunderstanding, Miss Fairfax. The gentleman whose arm is at present round your waist is my dear guardian, Mr. John Worthing.

GWENDOLEN. I beg your pardon?

CECILY. This is Uncle Jack.

GWENDOLEN. (*Receding.*) Jack! Oh!

(*Enter* ALGERNON.)

CECILY. Here is Ernest.

ALGERNON. (*Goes straight over to* CECILY *without noticing anyone else.*) My own love! (*Offers to kiss her.*)

CECILY. (*Drawing back.*) A moment, Ernest! May I ask you—are you engaged to be married to this young lady?

ALGERNON. (*Looking round.*) To what young lady? Good heavens! Gwendolen!

CECILY. Yes! to good heavens, Gwendolen, I mean to Gwendolen.

ALGERNON. (*Laughing.*) Of course not! What could have put such an idea into your pretty little head?

CECILY. Thank you. (*Presenting her cheek to be kissed.*) You may. (ALGERNON *kisses her.*)

GWENDOLEN. I felt there was some slight error, Miss Cardew. The gentleman who is how embracing you is my cousin, Mr. Algernon Moncrieff.

CECILY. (*Breaking away from* ALGERNON.) Algernon Moncrieff! Oh! (*The two girls move towards each other and put their arms round each other's waists as if for protection.*)

CECILY. Are you called Algernon?

ALGERNON. I cannot deny it.

CECILY. Oh!

GWENDOLEN. Is your name really John?

JACK. (*Standing rather proudly.*) I could deny it if I liked. I could deny anything if I liked. But my name certainly is John. It has been John for years.

CECILY. (*To* GWENDOLEN.) A gross deception has been practised on both of us.

GWENDOLEN. My poor wounded Cecily!

CECILY. My sweet wronged Gwendolen!

GWENDOLEN. (*Slowly and seriously.*) You will call me sister, will you not? (*They embrace.* JACK *and* ALGERNON *groan and walk up and down.*)

CECILY. (*Rather brightly.*) There is just one question I would like to be allowed to ask my guardian.

GWENDOLEN. An admirable idea! Mr. Worthing, there is just one question I would like to be permitted to put to you. Where is your brother Ernest? We are both engaged to be married to your brother Ernest, so it is a matter of some importance to us to know where your brother Ernest is at present.

JACK. (*Slowly and hesitatingly.*) Gwendolen—Cecily —it is very painful for me to be forced to speak the truth. It is the first time in my life that I have ever been reduced to such a painful position, and I am really quite inexperienced in doing anything of the kind. However I will tell you quite frankly that I have no brother Ernest. I have no brother at all. I never had a brother in my life, and I certainly have not the smallest intention of ever having one in the future.

CECILY. (*Surprised.*) No brother at all?

JACK. (*Cheerily.*) None!

GWENDOLEN. (*Severely.*) Had you never a brother of any kind?

JACK. (*Pleasantly.*) Never. Not even of any kind.

GWENDOLEN. I am afraid it is quite clear, Cecily, that neither of us is engaged to be married to anyone.

CECILY. It is not a very pleasant position for a young girl suddenly to find herself in. Is it?

GWENDOLEN. Let us go into the house. They will hardly venture to come after us there.

CECILY. No, men are so cowardly, aren't they?

(*They retire into the house with scornful looks.*)

JACK. This ghastly state of things is what you call Bunburying, I suppose?

ALGERNON. Yes, and a perfectly wonderful Bunbury it is. The most wonderful Bunbury I have ever had in my life.

JACK. Well, you've no right whatsoever to Bunbury here.

ALGERNON. That is absurd. One has a right to Bunbury anywhere one chooses. Every serious Bunburyist knows that.

JACK. Serious Bunburyist! Good heavens!

ALGERNON. Well, one must be serious about something, if one wants to have any amusement in life. I happen to be serious about Bunburying. What on earth you are serious about I haven't got the remotest idea. About everything, I should fancy. You have such an absolutely trivial nature.

JACK. Well, the only small satisfaction I have in the whole of this wretched business is that your friend Bunbury is quite exploded. You won't be able to run down to the country quite so often as you used to do, dear Algy. And a very good thing too.

ALGERNON. Your brother is a little off colour, isn't he, dear Jack? You won't be able to disappear to London quite so frequently as your wicked custom was. And not a bad thing either.

JACK. As for your conduct towards Miss Cardew, I must say that your taking in a sweet, simple, innocent girl like that is quite inexcusable. To say nothing of the fact that she is my ward.

ALGERNON. I can see no possible defence at all for your deceiving a brilliant, clever, thoroughly experienced young lady like Miss Fairfax. To say nothing of the fact that she is my cousin.

JACK. I wanted to be engaged to Gwendolen, that is all. I love her.

ALGERNON. Well, I simply wanted to be engaged to Cecily. I adore her.

JACK. There is certainly no chance of your marrying Miss Cardew.

ALGERNON. I don't think there is much likelihood, Jack, of you and Miss Fairfax being united.

JACK. Well, that is no business of yours.

ALGERNON. If it was my business, I wouldn't talk about it. (*Begins to eat muffins.*) It is very vulgar to talk about one's business. Only people like stockbrokers do that, and then merely at dinner parties.

JACK. How you can sit there, calmly eating muffins when we are in this horrible trouble, I can't make out. You seem to me to be perfectly heartless.

ALGERNON. Well, I can't eat muffins in an agitated manner. The butter would probably get on my cuffs. One should always eat muffins quite calmly. It is the only way to eat them.

JACK. I say it's perfectly heartless your eating muffins at all, under the circumstances.

ALGERNON. When I am in trouble, eating is the only thing that consoles me. Indeed, when I am in really great trouble, as anyone who knows me intimately will tell you, I refuse everything except food and drink. At the present moment I am eating muffins because I am unhappy. Besides, I am particularly fond of muffins. (*Rising.*)

JACK. (*Rising.*) Well, that is no reason why you should eat them all in that greedy way. (*Takes muffins from* ALGERNON.)

ALGERNON. (*Offering tea-cake.*) I wish you would have tea-cake instead. I don't like tea-cake.

JACK. Good heavens! I suppose a man may eat his own muffins in his own garden.

ALGERNON. But you have just said it was perfectly heartless to eat muffins.

JACK. I said it was perfectly heartless of you, under the circumstances. That is a very different thing.

ALGERNON. That may be. But the muffins are the same. (*He seizes the muffin-dish from* JACK.)

JACK. Algy, I wish to goodness you would go.

ALGERNON. You can't possibly ask me to go without having some dinner. It's absurd. I never go without my dinner. No one ever does, except vegetarians and people like that. Besides I have just made arrangements with Dr. Chasuble to be christened at a quarter to six under the name of Ernest.

JACK. My dear fellow, the sooner you give up that nonsense the better. I made arrangements this morning with Dr. Chasuble to be christened myself at 5:30, and I naturally will take the name of Ernest. Gwendolen would wish it. We can't both be christened Ernest. It's absurd. Besides, I have a perfect right to be christened if I like. There is no evidence at all that I ever have been christened by anybody. I should think it extremely probable I never was, and so does Dr. Chasuble. It is entirely different in your case. You have been christened already.

ALGERNON. Yes, but I have not been christened for years.

JACK. Yes, but you have been christened. That is the important thing.

ALGERNON. Quite so. So I know my constitution can stand it. If you are not quite sure about your ever having been christened, I must say I think it rather dangerous your venturing on it now. It might make you very unwell. You can hardly have forgotten that some-one very closely connected with you was very nearly carried off this week in Paris by a severe chill.

JACK. Yes, but you said yourself that a severe chill was not hereditary.

ALGERNON. It usen't to be, I know—but I daresay it is now. Science is always making wonderful improve-ments in things.

JACK. (*Picking up the muffin-dish.*) Oh, that is non-sense; you are always talking nonsense.

ALGERNON. Jack, you are at the muffins again! I wish you wouldn't. There are only two left. (*Takes them.*) I told you I was particularly fond of muffins.

JACK. But I hate tea-cake.

ALGERNON. Why on earth then do you allow tea-cake to be served up for your guests? What ideas you have of hospitality!

JACK. Algernon! I have already told you to go. I don't want you here. Why don't you go!

ALGERNON. I haven't quite finished my tea yet! and there is still one muffin left. (JACK *groans, and sinks into a chair,* ALGERNON *still continues eating.*)

ACT-DROP.

Third Act

Scene. Morning-room at the Manor House.

(GWENDOLEN and CECILY are at the window, looking out into the garden.)

GWENDOLEN. The fact that they did not follow us at once into the house, as anyone else would have done, seems to me to show that they have some sense of shame left.

CECILY. They have been eating muffins. That looks like repentance.

GWENDOLEN. (*After a pause.*) They don't seem to notice us at all. Couldn't you cough?

CECILY. But I haven't got a cough.

GWENDOLEN. They're looking at us. What effrontery!

CECILY. They're approaching. That's very forward of them.

GWENDOLEN. Let us preserve a dignified silence.

CECILY. Certainly. It's the only thing to do now.

(*Enter* JACK *followed by* ALGERNON. *They whistle some dreadful popular air from a British opera.*)

GWENDOLEN. This dignified silence seems to produce an unpleasant effect.

CECILY. A most distasteful one.

GWENDOLEN. But we will not be the first to speak.

CECILY. Certainly not.

GWENDOLEN. Mr. Worthing, I have something very particular to ask you. Much depends on your reply.

CECILY. Gwendolen, your common sense is invaluable. Mr. Moncrieff, kindly answer me the following question. Why did you pretend to be my guardian's brother?

ALGERNON. In order that I might have an opportunity of meeting you.

CECILY. (*To* GWENDOLEN.) That certainly seems a satisfactory explanation, does it not?

GWENDOLEN. Yes, dear, if you can believe him.

CECILY. I don't. But that does not affect the wonderful beauty of his answer.

GWENDOLEN. True. In matters of grave importance, style, not sincerity is the vital thing. Mr. Worthing, what explanation can you offer to me for pretending to have a brother? Was it in order that you might have an opportunity of coming up to town to see me as often as possible?

JACK. Can you doubt it, Miss Fairfax?

GWENDOLEN. I have the gravest doubts upon the subject. But I intend to crush them. This is not the moment for German scepticism. (*Moving to* CECILY.) Their explanations appear to be quite satisfactory, especially Mr. Worthing's. That seems to me to have the stamp of truth upon it.

CECILY. I am more than content with what Mr. Moncrieff said. His voice alone inspires one with absolute credulity.

GWENDOLEN. Then you think we should forgive them?

CECILY. Yes. I mean no.

GWENDOLEN. True! I had forgotten. There are principles at stake that one cannot surrender. Which of us should tell them? The task is not a pleasant one.

CECILY. Could we not both speak at the same time?

GWENDOLEN. An excellent idea! I nearly always speak at the same time as other people. Will you take the time from me?

CECILY. Certainly. (GWENDOLEN *beats time with uplifted finger.*)

GWENDOLEN AND CECILY. (*Speaking together.*) Your Christian names are still an insuperable barrier. That is all!

JACK AND ALGERNON. (*Speaking together.*) Our Christian names! Is that all? But we are going to be christened this afternoon.

GWENDOLEN. (*To* JACK.) For my sake you are prepared to do this terrible thing?

JACK. I am.

CECILY. (*To* ALGERNON.) To please me you are ready to face this fearful ordeal?

ALGERNON. I am!

GWENDOLEN. How absurd to talk of the equality of the sexes! Where questions of self-sacrifice are concerned, men are infinitely beyond us.

JACK. We are. (*Clasps hands with* ALGERNON.)

CECILY. They have moments of physical courage of which we women know absolutely nothing.

GWENDOLEN. (*To* JACK.) Darling!

ALGERNON. (*To* CECILY.) Darling. (*They fall into each other's arms.*)

(*Enter* MERRIMAN. *When he enters he coughs loudly, seeing the situation.*)

MERRIMAN. Ahem! Ahem! Lady Bracknell!

JACK. Good heavens!

(*Enter* LADY BRACKNELL. *The couples separate in alarm. Exit* MERRIMAN.)

LADY BRACKNELL. Gwendolen! What does this mean?

GWENDOLEN. Merely that I am engaged to be married to Mr. Worthing, Mamma.

LADY BRACKNELL. Come here. Sit down. Sit down immediately. Hesitation of any kind is a sign of mental decay in the young, of physical weakness in the old. (*Turns to* JACK.) Apprised, sir, of my daughter's sudden flight by her trusty maid, whose confidence I purchased by means of a small coin, I followed her at once by a luggage train. Her unhappy father is, I am glad to say, under the impression that she is attending a more than usually lengthy lecture by the . University Extension Scheme on the influence of a permanent income on thought. I do not propose to undeceive him. Indeed I have never undeceived him on any question. I would consider it wrong. But of course, you will clearly understand that all communication between yourself and my daughter must cease immediately from this moment. On this point, as indeed on all points, I am firm.

JACK. I am engaged to be married to Gwendolen, Lady Bracknell!

LADY BRACKNELL. You are nothing of the kind, sir. And now, as regards Algernon! . . . Algernon!

ALGERNON. Yes, Aunt Augusta.

LADY BRACKNELL. May I ask if it is in this house that your invalid friend Mr. Bunbury resides?

ALGERNON. (*Stammering.*) Oh! No! Bunbury doesn't live here. Bunbury is somewhere else at present. In fact, Bunbury is dead.

LADY BRACKNELL. Dead! When did Mr. Bunbury die? His death must have been extremely sudden.

ALGERNON. (*Airily.*) Oh! I killed Bunbury this afternoon. I mean poor Bunbury died this afternoon.

LADY BRACKNELL. What did he die of?

ALGERNON. Bunbury? Oh, he was quite exploded.

LADY BRACKNELL. Exploded! Was he the victim of a revolutionary outrage? I was not aware that Mr. Bunbury was interested in social legislation. If so, he is well punished for his morbidity.

ALGERNON. My dear Aunt Augusta, I mean he was found out! The doctors found out that Bunbury could not live, that is what I mean—so Bunbury died.

LADY BRACKNELL. He seems to have had great confidence in the opinion of his physicians. I am glad, however, that he made up his mind at the last to some definite course of action, and acted under proper medical advice. And now that we have finally got rid of this Mr. Bunbury, may I ask, Mr. Worthing, who is that young person whose hand my nephew Algernon is now holding in what seems to me a peculiarly unnecessary manner?

JACK. That lady is Miss Cecily Cardew, my ward. (LADY BRACKNELL *bows coldly to* CECILY.)

ALGERNON. I am engaged to be married to Cecily, Aunt Augusta.

LADY BRACKNELL. I beg your pardon?

CECILY. Mr. Moncrieff and I are engaged to be married, Lady Bracknell.

LADY BRACKNELL. (*With a shiver, crossing to the sofa and sitting down.*) I do not know whether there is anything peculiarly exciting in the air of this particular part of Hertfordshire, but the number of engagements that go on seems to me considerably above the proper average that statistics have laid down for our guidance. I think some preliminary enquiry on my part would not be out of place. Mr. Worthing, is Miss Cardew at all connected with any of the larger railway stations in London? I merely desire information. Until yesterday I had no idea that there were any families or persons whose origin was a Terminus. (JACK *looks perfectly furious, but restrains himself.*)

JACK. (*In a clear, cold voice.*) Miss Cardew is the granddaughter of the late Mr. Thomas Cardew of 149, Belgrave Square, S.W.; Gervase Park, Dorking, Surrey; and the Sporran, Fifeshire, N.B.

LADY BRACKNELL. That sounds not unsatisfactory. Three addresses always inspire confidence, even in tradesmen. But what proof have I of their authenticity?

JACK. I have carefully preserved the Court Guides of the period. They are open to your inspection, Lady Bracknell.

LADY BRACKNELL. (*Grimly.*) I have known strange errors in that publication.

JACK. Miss Cardew's family solicitors are Messrs. Markby, Markby, and Markby.

LADY BRACKNELL. Markby, Markby, and Markby? A firm of the very highest position in their profession. Indeed I am told that one of the Mr. Markbys is occasionally to be seen at dinner parties. So far I am satisfied.

JACK. (*Very irritably.*) How extremely kind of you, Lady Bracknell! I have also in my possession, you will be pleased to hear, certificates of Miss Cardew's birth, baptism, whooping cough, registration, vaccination, confirmation, and the measles; both the German and the English variety.

LADY BRACKNELL. Ah! A life crowded with incident, I see; though perhaps somewhat too exciting for a young girl. I am not myself in favour of premature experiences. (*Rises, looks at her watch.*) Gwendolen! the time approaches for our departure. We have not a moment to lose. As a matter of form, Mr. Worthing, I had better ask you if Miss Cardew has any little fortune?

JACK. Oh! about a hundred and thirty thousand pounds in the Funds. That is all. Good-bye, Lady Bracknell. So pleased to have seen you.

LADY BRACKNELL. (*Sitting down again.*) A moment, Mr. Worthing. A hundred and thirty thousand pounds! And in the Funds! Miss Cardew seems to me a most attractive young lady, now that I look at her. Few girls of the present day have any really solid qualities, any of the qualities that last, and improve with time. We live, I regret to say, in an age of surfaces. (*To* CECILY.)

Come over here, dear. (CECILY *goes across*.) Pretty child! your dress is sadly simple, and your hair seems almost as nature might have left it. But we can soon alter all that. A thoroughly experienced French maid produces a really marvellous result in a very brief space of time. I remember recommending one to young Lady Lancing, and after three months her own husband did not know her.

JACK. (*Aside*.) And after six months nobody knew her.

LADY BRACKNELL. (*Glares at* JACK *for a few moments. Then bends, with a practised smile, to* CECILY.) Kindly turn round, sweet child. (CECILY *turns completely round*.) No, the side view is what I want. (CECILY *presents her profile*.) Yes, quite as I expected. There are distinct social possibilities in your profile. The two weak points in our age are its want of principle and its want of profile. The chin a little higher, dear. Style largely depends on the way the chin is worn. They are worn very high, just at present. Algernon!

ALGERNON. Yes, Aunt Augusta!

LADY BRACKNELL. There are distinct social possibilities in Miss Cardew's profile.

ALGERNON. Cecily is the sweetest, dearest, prettiest girl in the whole world. And I don't care twopence about social possibilities.

LADY BRACKNELL. Never speak disrespectfully of Society, Algernon. Only people who can't get into it do that. (*To* CECILY.) Dear child, of course you know that Algernon has nothing but his debts to depend upon. But I do not approve of mercenary marriages. When I married Lord Bracknell I had no fortune of any kind. But I never dreamed for a moment of allowing that to stand in my way. Well, I suppose I must give my consent.

ALGERNON. Thank you, Aunt Augusta.

LADY BRACKNELL. Cecily, you may kiss me!

CECILY. (*Kisses her.*) Thank you, Lady Bracknell.

LADY BRACKNELL. You may also address me as Aunt Augusta for the future.

CECILY. Thank you, Aunt Augusta.

LADY BRACKNELL. The marriage, I think, had better take place quite soon.

ALGERNON. Thank you, Aunt Augusta.

CECILY. Thank you, Aunt Augusta.

LADY BRACKNELL. To speak frankly, I am not in favour of long engagements. They give people the opportunity of finding out each other's character before marriage, which I think is never advisable.

JACK. I beg your pardon for interrupting you, Lady Bracknell, but this engagement is quite out of the question. I am Miss Cardew's guardian, and she cannot marry without my consent until she comes of age. That consent I absolutely decline to give.

LADY BRACKNELL. Upon what grounds may I ask? Algernon is an extremely, I may almost say an ostentatiously, eligible young man. He has nothing, but he looks everything. What more can one desire?

JACK. It pains me very much to have to speak frankly to you, Lady Bracknell, about your nephew, but the fact is that I do not approve at all of his moral character. I suspect him of being untruthful. (ALGERNON *and* CECILY *look at him in indignant amazement.*)

LADY BRACKNELL. Untruthful! My nephew Algernon? Impossible! He is an Oxonian.

JACK. I fear there can be no possible doubt about the matter. This afternoon, during my temporary absence in London on an important question of romance, he obtained admission to my house by means of the false pretence of being my brother. Under an assumed name he drank, I've just been informed by my butler, an entire pint bottle of my Perrier-Jouet, Brut, '89; a wine I was specially reserving for myself. Continuing his disgraceful deception, he succeeded in the course of the afternoon in alienating the affections of my only ward. He subsequently stayed to tea, and devoured every single muffin. And what makes his conduct all the more heartless is, that he was perfectly well aware from the first that I have no brother, that I never had a brother, and that I don't intend to have a brother, not even of any kind. I distinctly told him so myself yesterday afternoon.

LADY BRACKNELL. Ahem! Mr. Worthing, after careful consideration I have decided entirely to overlook my nephew's conduct to you.

JACK. That is very generous of you, Lady Bracknell. My own decision, however, is unalterable. I decline to give my consent.

LADY BRACKNELL. (*To* CECILY.) Come here, sweet child. (CECILY *goes over.*) How old are you, dear?

CECILY. Well, I am really only eighteen, but I always admit to twenty when I go to evening parties.

LADY BRACKNELL. You are perfectly right in making some slight alteration. Indeed, no woman should ever be quite accurate about her age. It looks so calculating. . . . (*In a meditative manner.*) Eighteen, but admitting to twenty at evening parties. Well, it will not be very long before you are of age and free from the restraints of tutelage. So I don't think your guardian's consent is, after all, a matter of any importance.

JACK. Pray excuse me, Lady Bracknell, for interrupting you again, but it is only fair to tell you that according to the terms of her grandfather's will Miss Cardew does not come legally of age till she is thirty-five.

LADY BRACKNELL. That does not seem to me to be a grave objection. Thirty-five is a very attractive age. London society is full of women of the very highest birth who have, of their own free choice, remained thirty-five for years. Lady Dumbleton is an instance in point. To my own knowledge she has been thirty-five ever since she arrived at the age of forty, which was many years ago now. I see no reason why our dear Cecily should not be even still more attractive at the age you mention than she is at present. There will be a large accumulation of property.

CECILY. Algy, could you wait for me till I was thirty-five?

ALGERNON. Of course I could, Cecily. You know I could.

CECILY. Yes, I felt it instinctively, but I couldn't wait all that time. I hate waiting even five minutes for anybody. It always makes me rather cross. I am not punctual myself, I know, but I do like punctuality in others, and waiting, even to be married, is quite out of the question.

ALGERNON. Then what is to be done, Cecily?

CECILY. I don't know, Mr. Moncrieff.

LADY BRACKNELL. My dear Mr. Worthing, as Miss Cardew states positively that she cannot wait till she is thirty-five—a remark which I am bound to say seems to me to show a somewhat impatient nature—I would beg of you to reconsider your decision.

JACK. But my dear Lady Bracknell, the matter is entirely in your own hands. The moment you consent to my marriage with Gwendolen, I will most gladly allow your nephew to form an alliance with my ward.

LADY BRACKNELL. (*Rising and drawing herself up.*) You must be quite aware that what you propose is out of the question.

JACK. Then a passionate celibacy is all that any of us can look forward to.

LADY BRACKNELL. That is not the destiny I propose for Gwendolen. Algernon, of course, can choose for himself. (*Pulls out her watch.*) Come, dear; (GWENDOLEN *rises*) we have already missed five, if not six, trains. To miss any more might expose us to comment on the platform.

(*Enter* DR. CHASUBLE.)

CHASUBLE. Everything is quite ready for the christenings.

LADY BRACKNELL. The christenings, sir! Is not that somewhat premature?

CHASUBLE. (*Looking rather puzzled, and pointing to* JACK *and* ALGERNON.) Both these gentlemen have expressed a desire for immediate baptism.

LADY BRACKNELL. At their age? The idea is grotesque and irreligious! Algernon, I forbid you to be baptized. I will not hear of such excesses. Lord Bracknell would be highly displeased if he learned that that was the way in which you wasted your time and money.

CHASUBLE. Am I to understand then that there are to be no christenings at all this afternoon?

JACK. I don't think that, as things are now, it would be of much practical value to either of us, Dr. Chasuble.

CHASUBLE. I am grieved to hear such sentiments from you, Mr. Worthing. They savour of the heretical views of the Anabaptists, views that I have completely refuted in four of my unpublished sermons. However, as your present mood seems to be one peculiarly secular, I will return to the church at once. Indeed, I have just been informed by the pew-opener that for the last hour and a half Miss Prism has been waiting for me in the vestry.

LADY BRACKNELL. (*Starting.*) Miss Prism! Did I hear you mention a Miss Prism?

CHASUBLE. Yes, Lady Bracknell. I am on my way to join her.

LADY BRACKNELL. Pray allow me to detain you for a moment. This matter may prove to be one of vital importance to Lord Bracknell and myself. Is this Miss Prism a female of repellent aspect, remotely connected with education?

CHASUBLE. (*Somewhat indignantly.*) She is the most cultivated of ladies, and the very picture of respectability.

LADY BRACKNELL. It is obviously the same person. May I ask what position she holds in your household?

CHASUBLE. (*Severely.*) I am a celibate, madam.

JACK. (*Interposing.*) Miss Prism, Lady Bracknell, has been for the last three years Miss Cardew's esteemed governess and valued companion.

LADY BRACKNELL. In spite of what I hear of her, I must see her at once. Let her be sent for.

CHASUBLE. (*Looking off.*) She approaches; she is nigh.

(*Enter* MISS PRISM *hurriedly.*)

MISS PRISM. I was told you expected me in the vestry, dear Canon. I have been waiting for you there for an hour and three quarters. (*Catches sight of* LADY BRACKNELL *who has fixed her with a stony glare.* MISS PRISM *grows pale and quails. She looks anxiously round as if desirous to escape.*)

LADY BRACKNELL. (*In a severe, judicial voice.*) Prism! (MISS PRISM *bows her head in shame.*) Come here, Prism! (MISS PRISM *approaches in a humble manner.*) Prism! Where is that baby? (*General consternation. The* CANON *starts back in horror.* ALGERNON *and* JACK *pretend to be anxious to shield* CECILY *and* GWENDOLEN *from hearing the details of a terrible public scandal.*) Twenty-eight years ago, Prism, you left Lord

Bracknell's house, Number 104, Upper Grosvenor Street, in charge of a perambulator that contained a baby, of the male sex. You never returned. A few weeks later, through the elaborate investigations of the Metropolitan police, the perambulator was discovered at midnight, standing by itself in a remote corner of Bayswater. It contained the manuscript of a three-volume novel of more than usually revolting sentimentality. (MISS PRISM *starts in involuntary indignation.*) But the baby was not there! (*Everyone looks at* MISS PRISM.) Prism! Where is that baby? (*A pause.*)

MISS PRISM. Lady Bracknell, I admit with shame that I do not know. I only wish I did. The plain facts of the case are these. On the morning of the day you mention, a day that is for ever branded on my memory, I prepared as usual to take the baby out in its perambulator. I had also with me a somewhat old, but capacious handbag, in which I had intended to place the manuscript of a work of fiction that I had written during my few unoccupied hours. In a moment of mental abstraction, for which I never can forgive myself, I deposited the manuscript in the bassinette, and placed the baby in the handbag.

JACK. (*Who has been listening attentively.*) But where did you deposit the handbag?

MISS PRISM. Do not ask me, Mr. Worthing.

JACK. Miss Prism, this is a matter of no small importance to me. I insist on knowing where you deposited the handbag that contained that infant.

MISS PRISM. I left it in the cloakroom of one of the larger railway stations in London.

JACK. What railway station?

MISS PRISM. (*Quite crushed.*) Victoria. The Brighton line. (*Sinks into a chair.*)

JACK. I must retire to my room for a moment. Gwendolen, wait here for me.

GWENDOLEN. If you are not too long, I will wait here for you all my life. (*Exit* JACK *in great excitement.*)

CHASUBLE. What do you think this means, Lady Bracknell?

LADY BRACKNELL. I dare not even suspect, Dr. Chasuble. I need hardly tell you that in families of high position strange coincidences are not supposed to occur. They are hardly considered the thing.

(*Noises heard overhead as if someone was throwing trunks about. Everyone looks up.*)

CECILY. Uncle Jack seems strangely agitated.

CHASUBLE. Your guardian has a very emotional nature.

LADY BRACKNELL. This noise is extremely unpleasant. It sounds as if he was having an argument. I dislike arguments of any kind. They are always vulgar, and often convincing.

CHASUBLE. (*Looking up.*) It has stopped now. (*The noise is redoubled.*)

LADY BRACKNELL. I wish he would arrive at some conclusion.

GWENDOLEN. This suspense is terrible. I hope it will last.

(*Enter* JACK *with a handbag of black leather in his hand.*)

JACK. (*Rushing over to* MISS PRISM.) Is this the handbag, Miss Prism? Examine it carefully before you speak. The happiness of more than one life depends on your answer.

MISS PRISM. (*Calmly.*) It seems to be mine. Yes, here is the injury it received through the upsetting of a Gower Street omnibus in younger and happier days.

Here is the stain on the lining caused by the explosion of a temperance beverage, an incident that occurred at Leamington. And here, on the lock, are my initials. I had forgotten that in an extravagant mood I had had them placed there. The bag is undoubtedly mine. I am delighted to have it so unexpectedly restored to me. It has been a great inconvenience being without it all these years.

Jack. (*In a pathetic voice.*) Miss Prism, more is restored to you than this handbag. I was the baby you placed in it.

Miss Prism. (*Amazed.*) You?

Jack. (*Embracing her.*) Yes . . . mother!

Miss Prism. (*Recoiling in indignant astonishment.*) Mr. Worthing! I am unmarried!

Jack. Unmarried! I do not deny that is a serious blow. But after all, who has the right to cast a stone against one who has suffered? Cannot repentance wipe out an act of folly? Why should there be one law for men, and another for women? Mother, I forgive you. (*Tries to embrace her again.*)

Miss Prism. (*Still more indignant.*) Mr. Worthing, there is some error. (*Pointing to* Lady Bracknell.) There is the lady who can tell you who you really are.

Jack. (*After a pause.*) Lady Bracknell, I hate to seem inquisitive, but would you kindly inform me who I am?

Lady Bracknell. I am afraid that the news I have to give you will not altogether please you. You are the son of my poor sister, Mrs. Moncrieff, and consequently Algernon's elder brother.

Jack. Algy's elder brother! Then I have a brother after all. I knew I had a brother! I always said I had a brother! Cecily,—how could you have ever doubted that I had a brother? (*Seizes hold of* Algernon.) Dr.

Chasuble, my unfortunate brother. Miss Prism, my unfortunate brother. Gwendolen, my unfortunate brother. Algy, you young scoundrel, you will have to treat me with more respect in the future. You have never behaved to me like a brother in all your life.

ALGERNON. Well, not till today, old boy, I admit. I did my best, however, though I was out of practice. (*Shakes hands.*)

GWENDOLEN. (*To* JACK.) My own! But what own are you? What is your Christian name, now that you have become someone else?

JACK. Good heavens! . . . I had quite forgotten that point. Your decision on the subject of my name is irrevocable, I suppose?

GWENDOLEN. I never change, except in my affections.

CECILY. What a noble nature you have, Gwendolen!

JACK. Then the question had better be cleared up at once. Aunt Augusta, a moment. At the time when Miss Prism left me in the handbag, had I been christened already?

LADY BRACKNELL. Every luxury that money could buy, including christening, had been lavished on you by your fond and doting parents.

JACK. Then I was christened! That is settled. Now, what name was I given? Let me know the worst.

LADY BRACKNELL. Being the eldest son you were naturally christened after your father.

JACK. (*Irritably.*) Yes, but what was my father's Christian name?

LADY BRACKNELL. (*Meditatively.*) I cannot at the present moment recall what the General's Christian name was. But I have no doubt he had one. He was eccentric, I admit. But only in later years. And that was the result of the Indian climate, and marriage, and indigestion, and other things of that kind.

JACK. Algy! Can't you recollect what our father's Christian name was?

ALGERNON. My dear boy, we were never even on speaking terms. He died before I was a year old.

JACK. His name would appear in the Army Lists of the period, I suppose, Aunt Augusta?

LADY BRACKNELL. The General was essentially a man of peace, except in his domestic life. But I have no doubt his name would appear in any military directory.

JACK. The Army Lists of the last forty years are here. These delightful records should have been my constant study. (*Rushes to bookcase and tears the books out.*) M. Generals . . . Mallam, Maxbohm, Magley, what ghastly names they have—Markby, Migsby, Mobbs, Moncrieff! Lieutenant 1840, Captain, Lieutenant-Colonel, Colonel, General 1869, Christian names, Ernest John. (*Puts book very quietly down and speaks quite calmly.*) I always told you, Gwendolen, my name was Ernest, didn't I? Well, it is Ernest after all. I mean it naturally is Ernest.

LADY BRACKNELL. Yes, I remember now that the General was called Ernest. I knew I had some particular reason for disliking the name.

GWENDOLEN. Ernest! My own Ernest! I felt from the first that you could have no other name!

JACK. Gwendolen, it is a terrible thing for a man to find out suddenly that all his life he has been speaking nothing but the truth. Can you forgive me?

GWENDOLEN. I can. For I feel that you are sure to change.

JACK. My own one!

CHASUBLE. (*To* MISS PRISM.) Lætitia! (*Embraces her.*)

MISS PRISM. (*Enthusiastically.*) Frederick! At last!

ALGERNON. Cecily! (*Embraces her.*) At last!

JACK. Gwendolen! (*Embraces her.*) At last!

LADY BRACKNELL. My nephew, you seem to be displaying signs of triviality.

JACK. On the contrary, Aunt Augusta, I've now realized for the first time in my life the vital Importance of Being Earnest.

CURTAIN.

De Profundis

MY PLACE would be between Gilles de Retz
and the Marquis de Sade. I daresay it is best
so. I have no desire to complain. One of the many
lessons that one learns in prison is, that things are what
they are and will be what they will be. Nor have I any
doubt that the leper of mediævalism and the author of
Justine will prove better company than Sandford and
Merton. . . .

All this took place in the early part of November
of the year before last. A great river of life flows between me and a date so distant. Hardly, if at all, can
you see across so wide a waste. But to me it seems to
have occurred, I will not say yesterday, but today.
Suffering is one very long moment. We cannot divide it
by seasons. We can only record its moods, and chronicle
their return. With us time itself does not progress. It
revolves. It seems to circle round one centre of pain.
The paralyzing immobility of a life every circumstance
of which is regulated after an unchangeable pattern,
so that we eat and drink and lie down and pray, or
kneel at least for prayer, according to the inflexible
laws of an iron formula: this immobile quality, that
makes each dreadful day in the very minutest detail
like its brother, seems to communicate itself to those
external forces, the very essence of whose existence is
ceaseless change. Of seed-time or harvest, of the reapers

508

bending over the corn, or the grape gatherers threading through the vines, of the grass in the orchard made
white with broken blossoms or strewn with fallen
fruit: of these we know nothing, and can know nothing.

For us there is only one season, the season of sorrow.
The very sun and moon seem taken from us. Outside,
the day may be blue and gold, but the light that creeps
down through the thickly muffled glass of the small
iron-barred window beneath which one sits is grey and
niggard. It is always twilight in one's cell, as it is always
twilight in one's heart. And in the sphere of thought,
no less than in the sphere of time, motion is no more.
The thing that you personally, have long ago forgotten,
or can easily forget, is happening to me now, and will
happen to me again tomorrow. Remember this, and
you will be able to understand a little of why I am
writing, and in this manner writing. . . .

A week later, I am transferred here. Three more
months go over and my mother dies. No one knew how
deeply I loved and honoured her. Her death was terrible to me; but I, once a lord of language, have no
words in which to express my anguish and my shame.
Never even in the most perfect days of my development
as an artist could I have found words fit to bear so
august a burden; or to move with sufficient stateliness
of music through the purple pageant of my incom-
municable woe. She and my father had bequeathed me
a name they had made noble and honoured, not merely
in literature, art, archæology, and science, but in the
public history of my own country, in its evolution as
a nation. I had disgraced that name eternally. I had
made it a low byword among low people. I had dragged
it through the very mire. I had given it to brutes that
they might make it brutal, and to fools that they might
turn it into a synonym for folly. What I suffered then,

and still suffer, is not for pen to write or paper to record. My wife, always kind and gentle to me, rather than that I should hear the news from indifferent lips, travelled, ill as she was, all the way from Genoa to England to break to me herself the tidings of so irreparable, so irredeemable, a loss. Messages of sympathy reached me from all who had still affection for me. Even people who had not known me personally, hearing that a new sorrow had broken into my life, wrote to ask that some expression of their condolence should be conveyed to me. . . .

Three months go over. The calendar of my daily conduct and labour that hangs on the outside of my cell door, with my name and sentence written upon it, tells me that it is May. . . .

Prosperity, pleasure, and success, may be rough of grain and common in fibre, but sorrow is the most sensitive of all created things. There is nothing that stirs in the whole world of thought to which sorrow does not vibrate in terrible and exquisite pulsation. The thin beaten-out leaf of tremulous gold that chronicles the direction of forces the eye cannot see is in comparison coarse. It is a wound that bleeds when any hand but that of love touches it, and even then must bleed again, though not in pain.

Where there is sorrow there is holy ground. Some day people will realize what that means. They will know nothing of life till they do. —— and natures like his can realize it. When I was brought down from my prison to the Court of Bankruptcy, between two policemen, —— waited in the long dreary corridor that, before the whole crowd, whom an action so sweet and simple hushed into silence, he might gravely raise his hat to me, as, handcuffed and with bowed head, I passed him by. Men have gone to heaven for smaller things than

that. It was in this spirit, and with this mode of love,
that the saints knelt down to wash the feet of the poor,
or stooped to kiss the leper on the cheek. I have never
said one single word to him about what he did. I do not
know to the present moment whether he is aware that
I was even conscious of his action. It is not a thing for
which one can render formal thanks in formal words.
I store it in the treasure-house of my heart. I keep it
there as a secret debt that I am glad to think I can
never possibly repay. It is embalmed and kept sweet
by the myrrh and cassia of many tears. When wisdom
has been profitless to me, philosophy barren, and the
proverbs and phrases of those who have sought to give
me consolation as dust and ashes in my mouth, the
memory of that little, lovely, silent act of love has un-
sealed for me all the wells of pity: made the desert
blossom like a rose, and brought me out of the bitterness of lonely exile into harmony with the wounded,
broken, and great heart of the world. When people are
able to understand, not merely how beautiful ——'s
action was, but why it meant so much to me, and
always will mean so much, then, perhaps, they will
realize how and in what spirit they should approach
me. . . .

The first volume of Poems that in the very springtide
of his manhood a young man sends forth to the world
should be like a blossom or flower of spring, like the
white thorn in the meadow at Magdalen or the cowslips
in the Cumnor fields. It should not be burdened by
the weight of a terrible and revolting tragedy; a terrible
revolting scandal. If I had allowed my name to serve
as herald to such a book, it would have been a grave
artistic error; it would have brought a wrong atmosphere round the whole work and in modern art

atmosphere counts for so much. Modern life is complex and relative; those are its two distinguishing notes; to render the first we require atmosphere with its subtlety of nuances, of suggestion, of strange perspectives; as for the second we require background. That is why sculpture has ceased to be a representative art and why music is a representative art and why literature is, and has been and always will remain the supreme representative art. . . .

Every twelve weeks R—— writes to me a little budget of literary news. Nothing can be more charming than his letters, in their wit, their clever concentrated criticism, their light touch: they are real letters, they are like a person talking to one; they have the quality of a French *causerie intime:* and in his delicate mode of deference to me, appealing at one time to my judgment, at another to my sense of humour, at another to my instinct for beauty or to my culture, and reminding me in a hundred subtle ways that once I was to many arbiter of style in art; the supreme arbiter to some; he shows how he has the tact of love as well as the tact of literature. His letters have been the messengers between me and that beautiful unreal world of art where once I was King, and would have remained King indeed, had I not let myself be lured into the imperfect world of coarse uncompleted passion, of appetite without distinction, desire without limit, and formless greed. Yet when all is said, surely —— might have been able to understand or conceive, at any rate that on the ordinary grounds of mere psychological curiosity it would have been more interesting to me to hear from —— than to learn that Alfred Austin was trying to bring out a volume of poems; that George Street was writing dramatic criticism for the *Daily*

Chronicle; or that by one who cannot speak a panegyric without stammering, Mrs. Meynell had been pronounced to be the new sibyl of style. . . .

Other miserable men when they are thrown into prison, if they are robbed of the beauty of the world are at least safe in some measure from the world's most deadly slings, most awful arrows. They can hide in the darkness of their cells and of their very disgrace make a mode of sanctuary. The world having had its will goes its way, and they are left to suffer undisturbed. With me it has been different. Sorrow after sorrow has come beating at the prison doors in search of me; they have opened the gates wide and let them in. Hardly if at all have my friends been suffered to see me. But my enemies have had full access to me always; twice in my public appearances in the Bankruptcy Court; twice again in my public transferences from one prison to another have I been shown under conditions of unspeakable humiliation to the gaze and mockery of men. The messenger of Death has brought me his tidings and gone his way; and in entire solitude and isolated from all that could give me comfort or suggest relief I have had to bear the intolerable burden of misery and remorse, which the memory of my mother placed upon me and places on me still. Hardly has that wound been dulled, not healed, by time, when violent and bitter and harsh letters come to me from solicitors. I am at once taunted and threatened with poverty. That I can bear. I can school myself to worse than that; but my two children are taken from me by legal procedure. That is, and always will remain to me a source of infinite distress, of infinite pain, of grief without end or limit. That the law should decide and take upon itself to decide that I am one unfit; to be with my own children is something quite horrible to me. The disgrace of prison is as nothing compared with it. I envy the other men who tread the yard along with me. I am sure that their children wait for them, look for their coming, will be sweet to them.

The poor are wiser, more charitable, more kind, more sensitive than we are. In their eyes prison is a tragedy in a man's life, a misfortune, a casualty, something that calls for sympathy in others. They speak of one who is in prison as of one who is "in trouble" simply. It is the phrase they always use, and the expression has the perfect wisdom of love in it. With people of our own rank it is different. With us, prison makes a man a pariah. I, and such as I am, have hardly any right to air and sun. Our presence taints the pleasures of others. We are unwelcome when we reappear. To revisit the glimpses of the moon is not for us. Our very children are taken away. Those lovely links with humanity are broken. We are doomed to be solitary, while our sons still live. We are denied the one thing that might heal us and keep us, that might bring balm to the bruised heart, and peace to the soul in pain. . . .

I must say to myself that I ruined myself, and that nobody great or small can be ruined except by his own hand. I am quite ready to say so. I am trying to say so, though they may not think it at the present moment. This pitiless indictment I bring without pity against myself. Terrible as was what the world did to me, what I did to myself was far more terrible still.

I was a man who stood in symbolic relations to the art and culture of my age. I had realized this for myself at the very dawn of my manhood, and had forced my age to realize it afterwards. Few men hold such a position in their own lifetime, and have it so acknowledged.

It is usually discerned, if discerned at all, by the historian, or the critic, long after both the man and his age have passed away. With me it was different. I felt it myself, and made others feel it. Byron was a symbolic figure, but his relations were to the passion of his age and its weariness of passion. Mine were to something more noble, more permanent, of more vital issue, of larger scope.

The gods had given me almost everything. I had genius, a distinguished name, high social position, brilliancy, intellectual daring; I made art a philosophy and philosophy an art: I altered the minds of men and the colours of things: there was nothing I said or did that did not make people wonder. I took the drama, the most objective form known to art, and made it as personal a mode of expression as the lyric or sonnet; at the same time I widened its range and enriched its characterization. Drama, novel, poem in prose, poem in rhyme, subtle or fantastic dialogue, whatever I touched, I made beautiful in a new mode of beauty: to truth itself I gave what is false no less than what is true as its rightful province, and showed that the false and the true are merely forms of intellectual existence. I treated art as the supreme reality and life as a mere mode of fiction. I awoke the imagination of my century so that it created myth and legend around me. I summed up all systems in a phrase and all existence in an epigram. Along with these things I had things that were different. But I let myself be lured into long spells of senseless and sensual ease. I amused myself with being a *flâneur*, a dandy, a man of fashion. I surrounded myself with the smaller natures and the meaner minds. I became the spendthrift of my own genius, and to waste an eternal youth gave me a curious joy. Tired of being on the heights, I deliberately went to the depths in the search for new sensation. What the paradox was to me in the sphere of thought, perversity became to me in the sphere of passion. Desire, at the end, was a malady, or a madness, or both. I grew careless of the lives of others. I took pleasure where it pleased me, and passed on. I forgot that every little action of the common day makes or unmakes character, and that therefore what one has done in the secret chamber one has some day to cry aloud on the housetops. I ceased to be lord over myself. I was no longer the captain of my soul, and did not know it. I allowed pleasure to dominate me. I ended in horrible disgrace. There is only one thing for me now, absolute humility.

I have lain in prison for nearly two years. Out of my nature has come wild despair; an abandonment to grief that was piteous even to look at; terrible and impotent rage; bitterness and scorn; anguish that wept aloud; misery that could find no voice; sorrow that was dumb. I have passed through every possible mood of suffering. Better than Wordsworth himself I know what Wordsworth meant when he said—

> Suffering is permanent, obscure, and dark,
> And has the nature of infinity.

But while there were times when I rejoiced in the idea that my sufferings were to be endless, I could not bear them to be without meaning. Now I find hidden somewhere away in my nature something that tells me that nothing in the whole world is meaningless, and suffering least of all. That something hidden away in my nature, like a treasure in a field, is Humility.

It is the last thing left in me, and the best: the ultimate discovery at which I have arrived, the starting-point for a fresh development. It has come to me right out of myself, so I know that it has come at the proper time. It could not have come before, nor later. Had anyone told me of it, I would have rejected it. Had it been brought to me, I would have refused it. As I found it, I want to keep it. I must do so. It is the one thing that has in it the elements of life, of a new life, a *Vita Nuova* for me. Of all things it is the strangest; one cannot give it away and another may not give it to one. One cannot acquire it except by surrendering everything that one has. It is only when one has lost all things, that one knows that one possesses it.

Now I have realized that it is in me, I see quite clearly what I ought to do; in fact, must do. And when I use such a phrase as that, I need not say that I am not alluding to any external sanction or command. I admit none. I am far more of an individualist than I ever was. Nothing seems to me of the smallest value except what one gets out of oneself. My nature is seeking a fresh mode of self-realization. That is all I am concerned with. And the first thing that I have got to do is to free myself from any possible bitterness of feeling against the world.

I am completely penniless, and absolutely homeless. Yet there are worse things in the world than that. I am quite candid when I say that rather than go out from this prison with bitterness in my heart against the world, I would gladly and readily beg my bread from door to door. If I got nothing from the house of the rich I would get something at the house of the poor. Those who have much are often greedy; those who have little always share. I would not a bit mind sleeping in the cool grass in summer, and when winter came on sheltering myself by the warm close-thatched rick, or under the penthouse of a great barn, provided I had love in my heart. The external things of life seem to me now of no importance at all. You can see to what intensity of individualism I have arrived—or am ar-riving rather, for the journey is long, and "where I walk there are thorns."

Of course I know that to ask alms on the highway is not to be my lot, and that if ever I lie in the cool grass at night-time it will be to write sonnets to the moon. When I go out of prison, R—— will be waiting for me on the other side of the big iron-studded gate, and he is the symbol, not merely of his own affection, but of the affection of many others besides. I believe I am to have enough to live on for about eighteen months at any rate, so that if I may not write beautiful books, I may at least read beautiful books; and what joy can be greater? After that, I hope to be able to re-create my creative faculty.

But were things different: had I not a friend left in the world; were there not a single house open to me in pity; had I to accept the wallet and ragged cloak of sheer penury: as long as I am free from all resentment, hardness, and scorn, I would be able to face the life with much more calm and confidence than I would were my body in purple and fine linen, and the soul within me sick with hate.

And I really shall have no difficulty. When you really want love you will find it waiting for you.

I need not say that my task does not end there. It would be comparatively easy if it did. There is much more before me. I have hills far steeper to climb, valleys much darker to pass through. And I have to get it all out of myself. Neither religion, morality, nor reason can help me at all.

Morality does not help me. I am a born antinomian. I am one of those who are made for exceptions, not for laws. But while I see that there is nothing wrong in what one does, I see that there is something wrong in what one becomes. It is well to have learned that.

Religion does not help me. The faith that others give to what is unseen, I give to what one can touch, and look at. My gods dwell in temples made with hands; and within the circle of actual experience is my creed made perfect and complete: too complete, it may be, for like many or all of those who have placed their heaven in this earth, I have found in it not merely the beauty of heaven, but the horror of hell also. When I think about religion at all, I feel as if I would like to found an order for those who *cannot* believe: the Confraternity of the Fatherless[1] one might call it, where on an altar, on which no taper burned, a priest, in whose heart peace had no dwelling, might celebrate with unblessed bread and a chalice empty of wine. Everything to be true must become a religion. And agnosticism should have its ritual no less than faith. It has sown its martyrs, it should reap its saints, and praise God daily for having hidden Himself from man. But whether it be faith or agnosticism, it must be nothing external to me. Its symbols must be of my own creating. Only that is spiritual which makes its own form. If I may not find its secret within myself, I shall never find it: if I have not got it already, it will never come to me.

Reason does not help me. It tells me that the laws under which I am convicted are wrong and unjust laws, and the system under which I have suffered a wrong and unjust system. But, somehow, I have got to

---

[1] In the early editions the word read *Faithless*. Wilde's writing, usually so clear, was sometimes cramped in the MSS. of *De Profundis*. I read it, however, *Faithless* until someone pointed out to me that from the context it must be *Fatherless*; an expert on handwriting has decided in favour of the new reading. (Note by Robert Ross in standard edition.)

make both of these things just and right to me. And exactly as in art one is only concerned with what a particular thing is at a particular moment to oneself, so it is also in the ethical evolution of one's character. I have got to make everything that has happened to me good for me. The plank bed, the loathsome food, the hard ropes shredded into oakum till one's finger-tips grow dull with pain, the menial offices with which each day begins and finishes, the harsh orders that routine seems to necessitate, the dreadful dress that makes sorrow grotesque to look at, the silence, the solitude, the shame—each and all of these things I have to transform into a spiritual experience. There is not a single degradation of the body which I must not try and make into a spiritualizing of the soul.

I want to get to the point when I shall be able to say quite simply, and without affectation, that the two great turning-points in my life were when my father sent me to Oxford, and when society sent me to prison. I will not say that prison is the best thing that could have happened to me; for that phrase would savour of too great bitterness towards myself. I would sooner say, or hear it said of me, that I was so typical a child of my age, that in my perversity, and for that perversity's sake, I turned the good things of my life to evil, and the evil things of my life to good.

What is said, however, by myself or by others, matters little. The important thing, the thing that lies before me, the thing that I have to do, if the brief remainder of my days is not to be maimed, marred, and incomplete, is to absorb into my nature all that has been done to me, to make it part of me, to accept it without complaint, fear, or reluctance. The supreme vice is shallowness. Whatever is realized is right.

When first I was put into prison some people advised

me to try and forget who I was. It was ruinous advice.
It is only by realizing what I am that I have found
comfort of any kind. Now I am advised by others to
try on my release to forget that I have ever been in a
prison at all. I know that would be equally fatal. It
would mean that I would always be haunted by an intolerable sense of disgrace, and that those things that
are meant for me as much as for anybody else—the
beauty of the sun and moon, the pageant of the seasons, the music of daybreak and the silence of great
nights, the rain falling through the leaves, or the dew
creeping over the grass and making it silver—would
all be tainted for me, and lose their healing power and
their power of communicating joy. To regret one's own
experiences is to arrest one's own development. To
deny one's own experiences is to put a lie into the lips
of one's own life. It is no less than a denial of the soul.

For just as the body absorbs things of all kinds,
things common and unclean no less than those that the
priest or a vision has cleansed, and converts them into
swiftness or strength, into the play of beautiful muscles
and the moulding of fair flesh, into the curves and
colours of the hair, the lips, the eye; so the soul in its
turn has its nutritive functions also, and can transform
into noble moods of thought and passions of high import what in itself is base, cruel, and degrading; nay,
more, may find in these its most august modes of assertion, and can often reveal itself most perfectly through
what was intended to desecrate or destroy.

The fact of my having been the common prisoner of
a common gaol I must frankly accept, and, curious as
it may seem, one of the things I shall have to teach
myself is not to be ashamed of it. I must accept it as
a punishment, and if one is ashamed of having been
punished, one might just as well never have been

punished at all. Of course there are many things of which I was convicted that I had not done, but then there are many things of which I was convicted that I had done, and a still greater number of things in my life for which I was never indicted at all. And as the gods are strange, and punish us for what is good and humane in us as much as for what is evil and perverse, I must accept the fact that one is punished for the good as well as for the evil that one does. I have no doubt that it is quite right one should be. It helps one, or should help one, to realize both, and not to be too conceited about either. And if I then am not ashamed of my punishment, as I hope not to be, I shall be able to think, and walk, and live with freedom.

Many men on their release carry their prison about with them into the air, and hide it as a secret disgrace in their hearts, and at length, like poor poisoned things, creep into some hole and die. It is wretched that they should have to do so, and it is wrong, terribly wrong, of society that it should force them to do so. Society takes upon itself the right to inflict appalling punishment on the individual, but it also has the supreme vice of shallowness, and fails to realize what it has done. When the man's punishment is over, it leaves him to himself; that is to say, it abandons him at the very moment when its highest duty towards him begins. It is really ashamed of its own actions, and shuns those whom it has punished, as people shun a creditor whose debt they cannot pay, or one on whom they have inflicted an irreparable, an irredeemable wrong. I can claim on my side that if I realize what I have suffered, society should realize what it has inflicted on me; and that there should be no bitterness or hate on either side.

Of course I know that from one point of view things will be made different for me than for others; must indeed, by the very nature of the case, be made so. The poor thieves and outcasts who are imprisoned here with me are in many respects more fortunate than I am. The little way in grey city or green field that saw their sin is small; to find those who know nothing of what they have done they need go no further than a bird might fly between the twilight at dawn and dawn itself: but for me the world is shrivelled to a handsbreadth, and everywhere I turn my name is written on the rocks in lead. For I have come, not from obscurity into the momentary notoriety of crime, but from a sort of eternity of fame to a sort of eternity of infamy, and sometimes seem to myself to have shown, if indeed it required showing, that between the famous and the infamous there is but one step, if as much as one.

Still, in the very fact that people will recognize me wherever I go, and know all about my life, as far as its follies go, I can discern something good for me. It will force on me the necessity of again asserting myself as an artist, and as soon as I possibly can. If I can produce only one beautiful work of art I shall be able to rob malice of its venom, and cowardice of its sneer, and to pluck out the tongue of scorn by the roots.

And if life be, as it surely is, a problem to me, I am no less a problem to life. People must adopt some attitude towards me, and so pass judgment both on themselves and me. I need not say I am not talking of particular individuals. The only people I would care to be with now are artists and people who have suffered: those who know what beauty is, and those who know what sorrow is: nobody else interests me. Nor am I making any demands on life. In all that I have said I am simply concerned with my own mental attitude towards life as a whole; and I feel that not to be ashamed of having been punished is one of the first points I must attain

to, for the sake of my own perfection, and because I am
so imperfect.

Then I must learn how to be happy. Once I knew
it, or thought I knew it, by instinct. It was always
springtime once in my heart. My temperament was
akin to joy. I filled my life to the very brim with pleasure, as one might fill a cup to the very brim with
wine. Now I am approaching life from a completely
new standpoint, and even to conceive happiness is often
extremely difficult for me. I remember during my first
term at Oxford reading in Pater's *Renaissance*—that
book which has had such strange influence over my
life—how Dante places low in the Inferno those who
wilfully live in sadness; and going to the college library
and turning to the passage in the *Divine Comedy*
where beneath the dreary marsh lie those who were
"sullen in the sweet air," saying for ever and ever
through their sighs—

> *"Tristi fummo*
> *Nell aer dolce che dal sol s'allegra."*

I knew the Church condemned *accidia*, but the whole
idea seemed to me quite fantastic, just the sort of sin,
I fancied, a priest who knew nothing about real life
would invent. Nor could I understand how Dante, who
says that "sorrow remarries us to God," could have
been so harsh to those who were enamoured of melancholy, if any such there really were. I had no idea that
some day this would become to me one of the greatest
temptations of my life.

While I was in Wandsworth prison I longed to die.
It was my one desire. When after two months in the in-
firmary I was transferred here, and found myself growing gradually better in physical health, I was filled with
rage. I determined to commit suicide on the very day
on which I left prison. After a time that evil mood

passed away, and I made up my mind to live, but to wear gloom as a king wears purple; never to smile again; to turn whatever house I entered into a house of mourning: to make my friends walk slowly in sadness with me: to teach them that melancholy is the true secret of life: to maim them with an alien sorrow: to mar them with my own pain. Now I feel quite differently. I see it would be both ungrateful and unkind of me to pull so long a face that when my friends came to see me they would have to make their faces still longer in order to show their sympathy; or, if I desired to entertain them, to invite them to sit down silently to bitter herbs and funeral baked meats. I must learn how to be cheerful and happy.

The last two occasions on which I was allowed to see my friends here, I tried to be as cheerful as possible, and to show my cheerfulness, in order to make them some slight return for their trouble in coming all the way from town to see me. It is only a slight return, I know, but it is the one, I feel certain, that pleases them most. I saw R—— for an hour on Saturday week, and I tried to give the fullest possible expression of the delight I really felt at our meeting. And that, in the views and ideas I am here shaping for myself, I am quite right is shown to me by the fact that now for the first time since my imprisonment I have a real desire for life.

There is before me so much to do that I would regard it as a terrible tragedy if I died before I was allowed to complete at any rate a little of it. I see new developments in art and life, each one of which is a fresh mode of perfection. I long to live so that I can explore what is no less than a new world to me. Do you want to know what this new world is? I think you can guess what it is. It is the world in which I have been living. Sorrow, then, and all that it teaches one, is my new world.

I used to live entirely for pleasure. I shunned suffering and sorrow of every kind. I hated both. I resolved to ignore them as far as possible: to treat them, that is to say, as modes of imperfection. They were not part of my scheme of life. They had no place in my philosophy. My mother, who knew life as a whole, used often to quote to me Goethe's lines—written by Carlyle in a book he had given her years ago, and translated by him, I fancy, also:—

> Who never ate his bread in sorrow,
>   Who never spent the midnight hours
> Weeping and waiting for the morrow,—
>   He knows you not, ye heavenly powers.

They were the lines which that noble Queen of Prussia, whom Napoleon treated with such coarse brutality, used to quote in her humiliation and exile; they were the lines my mother often quoted in the troubles of her later life. I absolutely declined to accept or admit the enormous truth hidden in them. I could not understand it. I remember quite well how I used to tell her that I did not want to eat my bread in sorrow, or to pass any night weeping and watching for a more bitter dawn.

I had no idea that it was one of the special things that the Fates had in store for me: that for a whole year of my life, indeed, I was to do little else. But so has my portion been meted out to me; and during the last few months I have, after terrible difficulties and struggles, been able to comprehend some of the lessons hidden in the heart of pain. Clergymen and people who use phrases without wisdom sometimes talk of suffering as a mystery. It is really a revelation. One discerns things one never discerned before. One approaches the whole of history from a different stand-point. What one had felt dimly, through instinct, about art, is intellectually and emotionally realized with perfect clearness of vision and absolute intensity of apprehension.

I now see that sorrow, being the supreme emotion of which man is capable, is at once the type and test of all great art. What the artist is always looking for is the mode of existence in which soul and body are one and indivisible: in which the outward is expressive of the inward: in which form reveals. Of such modes of existence there are not a few: youth and the arts preoccupied with youth may serve as a model for us at one moment: at another we may like to think that in its subtlety and sensitiveness of impression, its suggestion of a spirit dwelling in external things and making its raiment of earth and air, of mist and city alike, and in its morbid sympathy of its moods, and tones, and colours, modern landscape art is realizing for us pictorially what was realized in such plastic perfection by the Greeks. Music, in which all subject is absorbed in expression and cannot be separated from it, is a complex example, and a flower or a child a simple example, of what I mean; but sorrow is the ultimate type both in life and art.

Behind joy and laughter there may be a temperament, coarse, hard, and callous. But behind sorrow there is always sorrow. Pain, unlike pleasure, wears no mask. Truth in art is not any correspondence between the essential idea and the accidental existence; it is not the resemblance of shape to shadow, or of the form mirrored in the crystal to the form itself; it is no echo coming from a hollow hill, any more than it is a silver well of water in the valley that shows the moon to the moon and Narcissus to Narcissus. Truth in art is the unity of a thing with itself: the outward rendered expressive of the inward: the soul made incarnate: the body instinct with spirit. For this reason there is no truth comparable to sorrow. There are times when sorrow seems to me to be the only truth. Other things may be illusions of the eye or the appetite, made to blind the one and cloy the other, but out of sorrow have the worlds been built, and at the birth of a child or a star there is pain.

More than this, there is about sorrow an intense, an extraordinary reality. I have said of myself that I was one who stood in symbolic relations to the art and culture of my age. There is not a single wretched man in this wretched place along with me who does not stand in symbolic relation to the very secret of life. For the secret of life is suffering. It is what is hidden behind everything. When we begin to live, what is sweet is so sweet to us, and what is bitter is so bitter, that we inevitably direct all our desires towards pleasures, and seek not merely for a "month or twain to feed on honeycomb," but for all our years to taste no other food, ignorant all the while that we may really be starving the soul.

I remember talking once on this subject to one of the most beautiful personalities I have ever known: a woman, whose sympathy and noble kindness to me, both before and since the tragedy of my imprisonment, have been beyond power and description; one who has really assisted me, though she does not know it, to bear the burden of my troubles more than anyone else in the whole world has, and all through the mere fact of her existence, through her being what she is—partly an ideal and partly an influence: a suggestion of what one might become as well as a real help towards becoming it; a soul that renders the common air sweet, and makes what is spiritual seem as simple and natural as sunlight or the sea: one for whom beauty and sorrow walk hand in hand, and have the same message. On the occasion of which I am thinking I recall distinctly how I said to her that there was enough suffering in one narrow London lane to show that God did not love man, and that wherever there was any sorrow, though but that of a child in some little garden weeping over a fault that it had or had not committed, the whole face of creation was completely marred. I was entirely wrong. She told me so, but I could not believe her. I was not in the sphere in which such belief was to be attained to. Now it seems to me that love of some kind is the only possible explanation of the extraordinary amount of suffering that there is in the world. I cannot conceive of any other explanation. I am convinced that there is no other, and that if the world has indeed, as I have said, been built of sorrow, it has been built by the hands of love, because in no other way could the soul of man, for whom the world was made, reach the full stature of its perfection. Pleasure for the beautiful body, but pain for the beautiful soul.

When I say that I am convinced of these things I speak with too much pride. Far off, like a perfect pearl, one can see the city of God. It is so wonderful that it seems as if a child could reach it in a summer's day. And so a child could. But with me and such as me it is different. One can realize a thing in a single moment, but one loses it in the long hours that follow with leaden feet. It is so difficult to keep "heights that the soul is competent to gain." We think in eternity, but we move slowly through time; and how slowly time goes with us who lie in prison I need not tell again, nor of the weariness and despair that creep back into one's cell, and into the cell of one's heart, with such strange insistence that one has, as it were, to garnish and sweep one's house for their coming, as for an unwelcome guest, or a bitter master, or a slave whose slave it is one's chance or choice to be.

And, though at present my friends may find it a hard thing to believe, it is true none the less, that for them living in freedom and idleness and comfort it is more easy to learn the lessons of humility than it is for me, who begin the day by going down on my knees and washing the floor of my cell. For prison life with its endless privations and restrictions makes one rebellious. The most terrible thing about it is not that it breaks one's heart—hearts are made to be broken— but that it turns one's heart to stone. One sometimes feels that it is only with a front of brass and a lip of scorn that one can get through the day at all. And he who is in a state of rebellion cannot receive grace, to use the phrase of which the Church is so fond—so rightly fond, I dare say—for in life as in art the mood of rebellion closes up the channels of the soul, and shuts out the airs of heaven. Yet I must learn these lessons here if I am to learn them anywhere, and must be filled with joy if my feet are on the right road and my face set towards "the gate which is called beautiful," though I may fall many times in the mire and often in the mist go astray.

This New Life, as through my love of Dante I like sometimes to call it, is of course no new life at all, but simply the continuance by means of development and evolution, of my former life. I remember when I was at Oxford saying to one of my friends as we were strolling round Magdalen's narrow bird-haunted walks one morning in the year before I took my degree, that I wanted to eat of the fruit of all the trees in the garden of the world, and that I was going out into the world with that passion in my soul. And so, indeed, I went out, and so I lived. My only mistake was that I confined myself so exclusively to the trees of what seemed to me the sunlit side of the garden, and shunned the other side for its shadow and its gloom. Failure, disgrace, poverty, sorrow, despair, suffering, tears even, the broken words that come from lips in pain, remorse that makes one walk on thorns, conscience that condemns, self-abasement that punishes, the misery that puts ashes on its head, the anguish that chooses sackcloth for its raiment and into its own drink puts gall:— all these were things of which I was afraid. And as I had determined to know nothing of them, I was forced to taste each of them in turn, to feed on them, to have for a season, indeed, no other food at all.

I don't regret for a single moment having lived for pleasure. I did it to the full, as one should do everything that one does. There was no pleasure I did not experience. I threw the pearl of my soul into a cup of wine. I went down the primrose path to the sound of flutes. I lived on honeycomb. But to have continued the same life would have been wrong because it would have been limiting. I had to pass on. The other half of the garden had its secrets for me also. Of course all this is foreshadowed and prefigured in my books. Some of it is in *The Happy Prince*, some of it in *The Young King*, notably in the passage where the bishop says to the kneeling boy, "Is not He who made misery wiser than thou art?" a phrase which when I wrote it seemed to me little more than a phrase; a great deal of it is hidden away in the note of doom that like a purple thread runs through the texture of *Dorian Gray*; in *The Critic as Artist* it is set forth in many colours; in *The Soul of Man* it is written down, and in letters too easy to read; it is one of the refrains whose recurring *motifs* make *Salomé* so like a piece of music and bind it together as a ballad; in the prose poem of the man who from the bronze of the image of the "Pleasure that liveth for a moment" has to make the image of the "Sorrow that abideth for ever" it is incarnate. It could not have been otherwise. At every single moment of one's life one is what one is going to be no less than what one has been. Art is a symbol, because man is a symbol.

It is, if I can fully attain to it, the ultimate realization of the artistic life. For the artistic life is simply self-development. Humility in the artist is his frank acceptance of all experiences, just as love in the artist is simply the sense of beauty that reveals to the world its body and its soul. In *Marius the Epicurean* Pater seeks to reconcile the artistic life with the life of religion, in the deep, sweet, and austere sense of the word. But Marius is little more than a spectator: an ideal spectator indeed, and one to whom it is given "to contemplate the spectacle of life with appropriate emotions," which Wordsworth defines as the poet's true aim; yet a spectator merely, and perhaps a little too much occupied with the comeliness of the benches of the sanctuary to notice that it is the sanctuary of sorrow that he is gazing at.

I see a far more intimate and immediate connexion between the true life of Christ and the true life of the artist; and I take a keen pleasure in the reflection that long before sorrow had made my days her own and bound me to her wheel I had written in *The Soul of Man* that he who would lead a Christ-like life must be entirely and absolutely himself, and had taken as my types not merely the shepherd on the hillside and the prisoner in his cell, but also the painter to whom the world is a pageant and the poet for whom the world is a song. I remember saying once to André Gide, as we sat together in some Paris café, that while metaphysics had but little real interest for me, and morality absolutely none, there was nothing that either Plato or Christ had said that could not be transferred immediately into the sphere of art and there find its complete fulfilment.

Nor is it merely that we can discern in Christ that close union of personality with perfection which forms the real distinction between the classical and romantic movement in life, but the very basis of His nature was the same as that of the nature of the artist—an intense and flamelike imagination. He realized in the entire sphere of human relations that imaginative sympathy which in the sphere of art is the sole secret of creation. He understood the leprosy of the leper, the darkness of the blind, the fierce misery of those who live for pleasure, the strange poverty of the rich. Someone wrote to me in trouble, "When you are not on your pedestal you are not interesting." How remote was the writer from what Matthew Arnold calls "the Secret of Jesus." Either would have taught him that whatever happens to another happens to oneself, and if you want an inscription to read at dawn and at night-time, and for pleasure or for pain, write up on the walls of your house in letters for the sun to gild and the moon to silver, "Whatever happens to oneself happens to another."

Christ's place indeed is with the poets. His whole conception of Humanity sprang right out of the imagination and can only be realized by it. What God was to the pantheist, man was to Him. He was the first to conceive the divided races as a unity. Before His time there had been gods and men, and, feeling through the mysticism of sympathy that in Himself each had been

made incarnate, He calls Himself the Son of the one
or the Son of the other, according to His mood. More
than anyone else in history He wakes in us that temper
of wonder to which romance always appeals. There is
still something to me almost incredible in the idea of a
young Galilean peasant imagining that He could bear
on His own shoulders the burden of the entire world:
all that had already been done and suffered, and all
that was yet to be done and suffered: the sins of Nero,
of Cæsar Borgia, of Alexander VI, and of him who was
Emperor of Rome and Priest of the Sun: the sufferings
of those whose names are legion and whose dwelling
is among the tombs: oppressed nationalities, factory
children, thieves, people in prison, outcasts, those who
are dumb under oppression and whose silence is heard
only of God; and not merely imagining this but actually
achieving it, so that at the present moment all who come
in contact with His personality, even though they may
neither bow to His altar nor kneel before His priest, in
some way find that the ugliness of their sin is taken
away and the beauty of their sorrow revealed to them.

I had said of Christ that He ranks with the poets.
That is true. Shelley and Sophocles are of His company.
But His entire life also is the most wonderful of poems.
For "pity and terror" there is nothing in the entire
cycle of Greek tragedy to touch it. The absolute purity
of the Protagonist raises the entire scheme to a height
of romantic art from which the sufferings of Thebes and
Pelops' line are by their very horror excluded, and
shows how wrong Aristotle was when he said in his
treatise on the drama that it would be impossible to bear
the spectacle of one blameless in pain. Nor in Æschylus
nor Dante, those stern masters of tenderness, in Shakespeare, the most purely human of all the great artists,
in the whole of Celtic myth and legend, where the

loveliness of the world is shown through a mist of tears, and the life of a man is no more than the life of a flower, is there anything that, for sheer simplicity of pathos wedded and made one with sublimity of tragic effect, can be said to equal or even approach the last act of Christ's Passion. The little supper with His companions, one of whom has already sold Him for a price; the anguish in the quiet moonlit garden; the false friend coming close to Him so as to betray Him with a kiss; the friend who still believed in Him, and on whom as on a rock He had hoped to build a house of refuge for Man, denying Him as the bird cried to the dawn; His own utter loneliness, His submission, His acceptance of everything; and along with it all such scenes as the high priest of orthodoxy rending his raiment in wrath, and the magistrate of civil justice calling for water in the vain hope of cleansing himself of that stain of innocent blood that makes him the scarlet figure of history; the coronation ceremony of sorrow, one of the most wonderful things in the whole of recorded time; the crucifixion of the Innocent One before the eyes of His mother and of the disciple whom He loved; the soldiers gambling and throwing dice for His clothes; the terrible death by which He gave the world its most eternal symbol; and His final burial in the tomb of the rich man, His body swathed in Egyptian linen with costly spices and perfumes as though He had been a king's son. When one contemplates all this from the point of view of art alone one cannot but be grateful that the supreme office of the Church should be the playing of the tragedy without the shedding of blood: the mystical presentation, by means of dialogue and costume and gesture even, of the Passion of her Lord; and it is always a source of pleasure and awe to me to remember that the ultimate survival of the Greek chorus, lost elsewhere to art, is to be found in the servitor answering the priest at Mass.

Yet the whole life of Christ—so entirely may sorrow and beauty be made one in their meaning and mani-festation—is really an idyll, though it ends with the veil of the temple being rent, and the darkness coming over the face of the earth, and the stone rolled to the door of the sepulchre. One always thinks of Him as a young bridegroom with His companions, as indeed He somewhere describes Himself; as a shepherd straying through a valley with His sheep in search of green meadow or cool stream; as a singer trying to build out of the music the walls of the City of God; or as a lover for whose love the whole world was too small. His miracles seem to me to be as exquisite as the coming of spring, and quite as natural. I see no difficulty at all in believing that such was the charm of His personality that His mere presence could bring peace to souls in anguish, and that those who touched His garments or His hands forgot their pain; or that as He passed by on the highway of life people who had seen nothing of life's mystery saw it clearly, and others who had been deaf to every voice but that of pleasure heard for the first time the voice of love and found it as "musical as Apollo's lute"; or that evil passions fled at His approach, and men whose dull unimaginative lives had been but a mode of death rose as it were from the grave when He called them; or that when He taught on the hillside the multitude forgot their hunger and thirst and the cares of this world, and that to His friends who listened to Him as He sat at meat the coarse food seemed delicate, and the water had the taste of good wine, and the whole house became full of the odour and sweetness of nard.

Renan in his *Vie de Jésus*—that gracious fifth gospel, the gospel according to St. Thomas, one might call it

—says somewhere that Christ's great achievement was that He had made Himself as much loved after His death as He had been during His lifetime. And certainly, if His place is among the poets, He is the leader of all the lovers. He saw that love was the first secret of the world for which the wise men had been looking, and that it was only through love that one could approach either the heart of the leper or the feet of God.

And above all, Christ is the most supreme of individualists. Humility, like the artistic acceptance of all experiences, is merely a mode of manifestation. It is man's soul that Christ is always looking for. He calls it "God's Kingdom," and finds it in everyone. He compares it to little things, to a tiny seed, to a handful of leaven, to a pearl. That is because one realizes one's soul only by getting rid of all alien passions, all acquired culture, and all external possessions, be they good or evil.

I bore up against everything with some stubbornness of will and much rebellion of nature, till I had absolutely nothing left in the world but one thing. I had lost my name, my position, my happiness, my freedom, my wealth. I was a prisoner and a pauper. But I still had my children left. Suddenly they were taken away from me by the law. It was a blow so appalling that I did not know what to do, so I flung myself on my knees, and bowed my head, and wept, and said, "The body of a child is as the body of the Lord: I am not worthy of either." That moment seemed to save me. I saw then that the only thing for me was to accept everything. Since then—curious as it will no doubt sound—I have been happier. It was of course my soul in its ultimate essence that I had reached. In many ways I had been its enemy, but I found it waiting for me as a friend. When one comes in contact with the soul it makes one simple as a child, as Christ said one should be.

It is tragic how few people ever "possess their souls" before they die. "Nothing is more rare in any man," says Emerson, "than an act of his own." It is quite true. Most people are other people. Their thoughts are some-one else's opinions, their lives a mimicry, their passions a quotation. Christ was not merely the supreme in-dividualist, but He was the first individualist in history. People have tried to make Him out an ordinary philanthropist, or ranked Him as an altruist with the unscientific and sentimental. But He was really neither one nor the other. Pity He has, of course, for the poor, for those who are shut up in prisons, for the lowly, for the wretched; but He has far more pity for the rich, for the hard hedonists, for those who waste their free-dom in becoming slaves to things, for those who wear soft raiment and live in king's houses. Riches and pleasure seemed to Him to be really greater tragedies than poverty or sorrow. And as for altruism, who knew better than He that it is vocation not volition that deter-mines us, and that one cannot gather grapes of thorns or figs from thistles?

To live for others as a definite self-conscious aim was not His creed. It was not the basis of His creed. When He says, "Forgive your enemies," it is not for the sake of the enemy, but for one's own sake that He says so, and because love is more beautiful than hate. In His own entreaty to the young man, "Sell all that thou hast and give to the poor," it is not of the state of the poor that He is thinking, but of the soul of the young man, the soul that wealth was marring. In His view of life He is one with the artist who knows that by the inevitable law of self-perfection, the poet must sing, and the sculptor think in bronze, and the painter make the world a mirror for his moods, as surely and as certainly as the hawthorn must blossom in spring, and the corn turn to gold at harvest-time, and the moon in her ordered wanderings change from shield to sickle, and from sickle to shield.

But while Christ did not say to men, "Live for others," He pointed out that there was no difference at all between the lives of others and one's own life. By this means He gave to man an extended, a Titan personality. Since His coming the history of each separate individual is, or can be made, the history of the world. Of course, culture has intensified the personality of man. Art has made us myriad-minded. Those who have the artistic temperament go into exile with Dante and learn how salt is the bread of others, and how steep their stairs; they catch for a moment the serenity and calm of Goethe, and yet know but too well that Baudelaire cried to God:

> *O Seigneur, donnez-moi la force et le courage*
> *De contempler mon corps et mon cœur sans dégoût.*

Out of Shakespeare's sonnets they draw, to their own hurt it may be, the secret of his love and make it their own; they look with new eyes on modern life, because they have listened to one of Chopin's nocturnes, or handled Greek things, or read the story of the passion of some dead man for some dead woman whose hair was like threads of fine gold, and whose mouth was as a pomegranate. But the sympathy of the artistic temperament is necessarily with what has found expression. In words or in colours, in music or in marble, behind the painted masks of an Æschylean play, or through some Sicilian shepherd's pierced and jointed reeds, the Man and His message must have been revealed.

To the artist, expression is the only mode under

which he can conceive life at all. To him what is dumb
is dead. But to Christ it was not so. With a width and
wonder of imagination that fills one almost with awe, He
took the entire world of the inarticulate, the voiceless
world of pain, as His kingdom, and made of Himself its
external mouthpiece. Those of whom I have spoken,
who are dumb under oppression and "whose silence
is heard only of God," He chose as His brothers. He
sought to become eyes to the blind, ears to the deaf,
and a cry in the lips of those whose tongues had been
tied. His desire was to be to the myriads who had found
no utterance a very trumpet through which they might
call to heaven. And feeling, with the artistic nature of
one to whom suffering and sorrow were modes through
which he could realize His conception of the beautiful,
that an idea is of no value till it becomes incarnate and
is made an image, He made of Himself the image of
the Man of Sorrows, and as such has fascinated and
dominated art as no Greek god ever succeeded in doing.

For the Greek gods, in spite of the white and red
of their fair fleet limbs, were not really what they
appeared to be. The curved brow of Apollo was like
the sun's disc over a hill at dawn, and his feet were as
the wings of the morning, but he himself had been cruel
to Marsyas and had made Niobe childless. In the steel
shields of Athena's eyes there had been no pity for
Arachne; the pomp and peacocks of Hera were all that
was really noble about her: and the Father of the Gods
himself had been too fond of the daughters of men.
The two most deeply suggestive figures of Greek
mythology were, for religion, Demeter, an earth goddess, not one of the Olympians, and for art, Dionysus,
the son of a mortal woman to whom the moment of his
birth had proved also the moment of her death.

But life itself from its lowliest and most humble

sphere produced one far more marvellous than the mother of Proserpina or the son of Semele. Out of the Carpenter's shop at Nazareth had come a personality infinitely greater than any made by myth and legend, and one, strangely enough, destined to reveal to the world the mystical meaning of wine and the real beauties of the lilies of the field as none, either on Cithæron or at Enna, had ever done.

The song of Isaiah, "He is despised and rejected of men, a man of sorrows and acquainted with grief: and we hid as it were our faces from him," had seemed to Him to prefigure Himself, and in Him the prophecy was fulfilled. We must not be afraid of such a phrase. Every single work of art is the fulfilment of a prophecy: for every work of art is the conversion of an idea into an image. Every single human being should be the fulfilment of a prophecy: for every human being should be the realization of some ideal, either in the mind of God or in the mind of man. Christ found the type and fixed it, and the dream of a Virgilian poet either at Jerusalem or at Babylon, became in the long progress of the centuries incarnate in Him for whom the world was "waiting." "His visage was so marred more than any man, and his form was more than the sons of men," are among the signs noted by Isaiah as distinguishing the new ideal, and as soon as art understood what was meant it opened like a flower at the presence of One in whom truth in art was set forth as it had never been before. For is not truth in art, as I have said, "that in which the outward is expressive of the inward; in which the soul is made flesh and the body instinct with spirit in which form reveals."

To me one of the things in history the most to be regretted, is that the Christ's own renaissance which has produced the Cathedral at Chartres, the Arthurian cycle of legends, the life of St. Francis of Assisi, the art of Giotto, and Dante's *Divine Comedy*, was not allowed to develop on its own lines, but was interrupted and spoiled by the dreary classical Renaissance that gave us Petrarch, and Raphael's frescoes, and Palladian architecture, and formal French tragedy, and St. Paul's Cathedral, and Pope's poetry, and everything that is made from without and by dead rules, and does not spring from within through some spirit informing it. But wherever there is a romantic movement in art there somehow, and under some form, is Christ, or the soul of Christ. He is in *Romeo and Juliet*, in the *Winter's Tale*, in Provençal poetry, in the *Ancient Mariner*, in *La Belle Dame sans Merci*, and in Chatterton's *Ballad of Charity*.

We owe to him the most diverse things and people. Hugo's *Les Misérables*, Baudelaire's *Fleurs du Mal*, the note of pity in Russian novels, Verlaine and Verlaine's poems, the stained glass and tapestries and the Quattrocento work of Burne-Jones and Morris, belong to him no less than the tower of Giotto, Lancelot and Guinevere, Tannhäuser, the troubled romantic marbles of Michelangelo, pointed architecture, and the love of children and flowers—for both of which, indeed, in classical art there was but little place, hardly enough for them to grow or play in, but which, from the twelfth century down to our own day, have been continually making their appearances in art, under various modes and at various times, coming fitfully and wilfully, as children, as flowers, are apt to do: spring always seeming to one as if the flowers had been in hiding, and only came out into the sun because they were afraid that grown-up people would grow tired of looking for them and give up the search; and the life of a child being no more than an April day on which there is both rain and sun for the narcissus.

It is the imaginative quality of Christ's own nature that makes Him this palpitating centre of romance. The strange figures of poetic drama and ballad are made by the imagination of others, but out of His own imagination entirely did Jesus of Nazareth create Himself. The cry of Isaiah had really no more to do with His coming than the song of the nightingale has to do with the rising of the moon—no more, though perhaps no less. He was the denial as well as the affirmation of prophecy. For every expectation that He fulfilled there was another that He destroyed. "In all beauty," says Bacon, "there is some strangeness of proportion," and of those who are born of the spirit—of those, that is to say, who like Himself are dynamic forces—Christ says that they are like the wind that "bloweth where it listeth, and no man can tell whence it cometh and whither it goeth." That is why He is so fascinating to artists. He has all the colour elements of life: mystery, strangeness, pathos, suggestion, ecstasy, love. He appeals to the temper of wonder, and creates that mood in which alone He can be understood.

And to me it is a joy to remember that if He is "of imagination all compact," the world itself is of the same substance. I said in *Dorian Gray* that the great sins of the world take place in the brain: but it is in the brain that everything takes place. We know now that we do not see with the eyes or hear with the ears. They are really channels for the transmission, adequate or inadequate, of sense impressions. It is in the brain that the poppy is red, that the apple is odorous, that the skylark sings.

Of late I have been studying with diligence the

four prose poems about Christ. At Christmas I managed to get hold of a Greek Testament, and every morning, after I had cleaned my cell and polished my tins, I read a little of the Gospels, a dozen verses taken by chance anywhere. It is a delightful way of opening the day. Everyone, even in a turbulent, ill-disciplined life, should do the same. Endless repetition, in and out of season, has spoiled for us the freshness, the naïveté, the simple romantic charm of the Gospels. We hear them read far too often and far too badly, and all repetition is anti-spiritual. When one returns to the Greek, it is like going into a garden of lilies out of some narrow and dark house.

And to me, the pleasure is doubled by the reflection that it is extremely probable that we have the actual terms, the *ipsissima verba*, used by Christ. It was always supposed that Christ talked in Aramaic. Even Renan thought so. But now we know that the Galilean peasants, like the Irish peasants of our own day, were bilingual, and that Greek was the ordinary language of intercourse all over Palestine, as indeed all over the Eastern world. I never liked the idea that we knew of Christ's own words only through a translation of a translation. It is a delight to me to think that as far as His conversation was concerned, Charmides might have listened to Him, and Socrates reasoned with Him, and Plato understood Him: That He really said ἐγώ εἰμι ὁ ποιμὴν ὁ καλός, that when He thought of the lilies of the field and how they neither toil nor spin, His absolute expression was καταμάθετε τὰ κρίνα τοῦ ἀγροῦ πῶς αὐξάνει· οὐ κοπιᾷ οὐδὲ νήθει, and that His last word when He cried out "my life has been completed, has reached its fulfilment, has been perfected," was exactly as St. John tells us it was: τετέλεσται—no more.

While in reading the Gospels—particularly that of St. John himself, or whatever early Gnostic took his name and mantle—I see the continual assertion of the imagination as the basis of all spiritual and material life, I see also that to Christ imagination was simply a form of love, and that to Him love was lord in the fullest meaning of the phrase. Some six weeks ago I was allowed by the doctor to have white bread to eat instead of the coarse black or brown bread of ordinary prison fare. It is a great delicacy. It will sound strange that dry bread could possibly be a delicacy to anyone. To me it is so much so that at the close of each meal I carefully eat whatever crumbs may be left on my tin plate, or have fallen on the rough towel that one uses as a cloth so as not to soil one's table; and I do so not from hunger—I get now quite sufficient food—but simply in order that nothing should be wasted of what is given to me. So one should look on love.

Christ, like all fascinating personalities, had the power of not merely saying beautiful things Himself, but of making other people say beautiful things to Him; and I love the story St. Mark tells us about the Greek woman, who, when as a trial of her faith He said to her that He could not give her the bread of the children of Israel, answered Him that the little dogs—(κυνάρια, "little dogs" it should be rendered)—who are under the table eat of the crumbs that the children let fall. Most people live for love and admiration. But it is by love and admiration that we should live. If any love is shown us we should recognize that we are quite unworthy of it. Nobody is worthy to be loved. The fact that God loves man shows us that in the divine order of ideal things it is written that eternal love is to be given to what is eternally unworthy. Or if that phrase seems to be a bitter one to bear, let us say that everyone is worthy of love, except him who thinks that he is. Love is a sacrament that should be taken kneeling, and *Domine, non sum dignus* should be on the lips and in the hearts of those who receive it.

If ever I write again, in the sense of producing artistic work, there are just two subjects on which and through which I desire to express myself: one is "Christ as the precursor of the romantic movement in life": the other is "The artistic life considered in its relation to conduct." The first is, of course, intensely fascinating, for I see in Christ not merely the essentials of the supreme romantic type, but all the accidents, the wilfulnesses even, of the romantic temperament also. He was the first person who ever said to people that they should live "flower-like lives." He fixed the phrase. He took children as the type of what people should try to become. He held them up as examples to their elders, which I myself have always thought the chief use of children, if what is perfect should have a use. Dante describes the soul of a man as coming from the hand of God "weeping and laughing like a little child," and Christ also saw that the soul of each one should be *a guisa di fanciulla che piangendo e ridendo pargoleggia.* He felt that life was changeful, fluid, active, and that to allow it to be stereotyped into any form was death. He saw that people should not be too serious over material, common interests: that to be unpractical was to be a great thing: that one should not bother too much over affairs. The birds didn't, why should man? He is charming when He says, "Take no thought for the morrow; is not the soul more than meat? is not the body more than raiment?" A Greek might have used the latter phrase. It is full of Greek feeling. But only Christ could have said both, and so summed up life perfectly for us.

His morality is all sympathy, just what morality should be. If the only thing that He ever said had been, "Her sins are forgiven her because she loved much," it would have been worth while dying to have said it. His justice is all poetical justice, exactly what justice should be. The beggar goes to heaven because he has been unhappy. I cannot conceive a better reason for his being sent there. The people who work for an hour in the vineyard in the cool of the evening receive just as much reward as, those who have toiled there all day long in the hot sun. Why shouldn't they? Probably no one deserved anything. Or perhaps they were a different kind of people. Christ had no patience with the dull lifeless mechanical systems that treat people as if they were things, and so treat everybody alike: for Him there were no laws: there were exceptions merely, as if anybody, or anything, for that matter, was like aught else in the world!

That which is the very keynote of romantic art was to Him the proper basis of natural life. He saw no other basis. And when they brought Him one taken in the very act of sin and showed Him her sentence written in the law, and asked Him what was to be done, He wrote with His finger on the ground as though He did not hear them, and finally, when they pressed Him again, looked up and said, "Let him of you who has never sinned be the first to throw the stone at her." It was worth while living to have said that.

Like all poetical natures He loved ignorant people. He knew that in the soul of one who is ignorant there is always room for a great idea. But He could not stand stupid people, especially those who are made stupid by education: people who are full of opinions not one of which they even understand, a peculiarly modern type, summed up by Christ when He describes it as the type of one who has the key of knowledge, cannot use it himself, and does not allow other people to use it, though it may be made to open the gate of God's Kingdom. His chief war was against the Philistines. That is the war every child of light has to wage. Philistinism was the note of the age and community in which he lived. In their heavy inaccessibility to ideas, their dull respectability, their tedious orthodoxy, their worship of vulgar success, their entire preoccupation with the gross materialistic side of life, and their ridiculous estimate of themselves and their importance, the Jews of Jerusalem in Christ's day were the exact counterpart of the British Philistine of our own. Christ mocked at the "whited sepulchre" of respectability, and fixed that phrase for ever. He treated worldly success as a thing absolutely to be despised. He saw nothing in it at all. He looked on wealth as an encumbrance to a man. He would not hear of life being sacrificed to any system of thought or morals. He pointed out that forms and ceremonies were made for man, not man for forms and ceremonies. He took Sabbatarianism as a type of the things that should be set at nought. The cold philanthropies, the ostentatious public charities, the tedious formalisms so dear to the middle-class mind, He exposed with utter and relentless scorn. To us, what is termed orthodoxy is merely a facile unintelligent acquiescence; but to them, and in their hands, it was a terrible and paralyzing tyranny. Christ swept it aside. He showed that the spirit alone was of value. He took a keen pleasure in pointing out to them that though they were always reading the law and the prophets, they had not really the smallest idea of what either of them meant. In opposition to their tithing of each separate day into the fixed routine of prescribed duties, as they tithe mint and rue, He preached the enormous importance of living completely for the moment.

Those whom He saved from their sins are saved simply for beautiful moments in their lives. Mary Magdalen, when she sees Christ, breaks the rich vase of alabaster that one of her seven lovers had given her, and spills the odorous spices over His tired dusty feet, and for that one moment's sake sits for ever with Ruth and Beatrice in the tresses of the snow-white rose of Paradise. All that Christ says to us by the way of a little warning is that every moment should be beautiful, that the soul should always be ready for the coming of the bridegroom, always waiting for the voice of the lover, Philistinism being simply that side of man's nature that is not illumined by the imagination. He sees all the lovely influences of life as modes of light: the imagination itself is the world of light. The world is made by it, and yet the world cannot understand it: that is because the imagination is simply a manifestation of love, and it is love and the capacity for it that distinguishes one human being from another.

But it is when He deals with a sinner that Christ is most romantic, in the sense of most real. The world had always loved the saint as being the nearest possible approach to the perfection of God. Christ, through some divine instinct in Him, seems to have always loved the sinner as being the nearest possible approach to the perfection of man. His primary desire was not to reform people, any more than His primary desire was to relieve suffering. To turn an interesting thief into a tedious honest man was not His aim. He would have thought little of the Prisoners' Aid Society and other modern movements of the kind. The conversion of a publican into a Pharisee would not have seemed to Him a great achievement. But in a manner not yet

understood of the world He regarded sin and suffering
as being in themselves beautiful holy things and modes
of perfection.

It seems a very dangerous idea. It is—all great ideas
are dangerous. That it was Christ's creed admits of
no doubt. That it is the true creed I don't doubt myself.

Of course the sinner must repent. But why? Simply
because otherwise he would be unable to realize what
he had done. The moment of repentance is the moment
of initiation. More than that: it is the means by which
one alters one's past. The Greeks thought that impossible. They often say in their Gnomic aphorisms, "Even
the Gods cannot alter the past." Christ showed that
the commonest sinner could do it, that it was the one
thing he could do. Christ, had He been asked, would
have said—I feel quite certain about it—that the
moment the prodigal son fell on his knees and wept, he
made his having wasted his substance with harlots,
his swine-herding and hungering for the husks they
ate, beautiful and holy moments in his life. It is difficult for most people to grasp the idea. I dare say one
has to go to prison to understand it. If so, it may be
worth while going to prison.

There is something so unique about Christ. Of
course just as there are false dawns before the dawn
itself, and winter days so full of sudden sunlight that
they will cheat the wise crocus into squandering its
gold before its time, and make some foolish bird call
to its mate to build on barren boughs, so there were
Christians before Christ. For that we should be grateful. The unfortunate thing is that there have been none
since. I make one exception, St. Francis of Assisi. But
then God had given him at his birth the soul of a
poet, as he himself when quite young had in mystical

marriage taken poverty as his bride: and with the soul of a poet and the body of a beggar he found the way to perfection not difficult. He understood Christ, and so he became like him. We do not require the *Liber Conformitatum* to teach us that the life of St. Francis was the true *Imitatio Christi*, a poem compared to which the book of that name is merely prose.

Indeed, that is the charm about Christ, when all is said: He is just like a work of art. He does not really teach one anything, but by being brought into His presence one becomes something. And everybody is predestined to His presence. Once at least in his life each man walks with Christ to Emmaus.

As regards the other subject, "the relation of the artistic life to conduct," it will no doubt seem strange to you that I should select it. People point to Reading Gaol and say, "That is where the artistic life leads a man." Well, it might lead to worse places. The more mechanical people to whom life is a shrewd speculation depending on a careful calculation of ways and means, always know where they are going, and go there. They start with the ideal desire of being the parish beadle, and in whatever sphere they are placed they succeed in being the parish beadle and no more. A man whose desire is to be something separate from himself, to be a member of Parliament, or a successful grocer, or a prominent solicitor, or a judge, or something equally tedious, invariably succeeds in being what he wants to be. That is his punishment. Those who want a mask have to wear it.

But with the dynamic forces of life, and those in whom those dynamic forces become incarnate, it is different. People whose desire is solely for self-realization never know where they are going. They can't know. In one sense of the word it is of course necessary, as the

Greek oracle said, to know oneself: that is the first achievement of knowledge. But to recognize that the soul of a man is unknowable, is the ultimate achievement of wisdom. The final mystery is oneself. When one has weighed the sun in the balance, and measured the steps of the moon, and mapped out the seven heavens star by star, there still remains oneself. Who can calculate the orbit of his own soul? When the son went out to look for his father's asses, he did not know that a man of God was waiting for him with the very chrism of coronation, and that his own soul was already the soul of a king.

I hope to live long enough and to produce work of such a character that I shall be able at the end of my days to say, "Yes! this is just where the artistic life leads a man!" Two of the most perfect lives I have come across in my own experience are the lives of Verlaine and of Prince Kropotkin: both of them men who have passed years in prison: the first, the one Christian poet since Dante; the other, a man with a soul of that beautiful white Christ which seems coming out of Russia. And for the last seven or eight months, in spite of a succession of great troubles reaching me from the outside world almost without intermission, I have been placed in direct contact with a new spirit working in this prison through man and things, that has helped me beyond any possibility of expression in words: so that while for the first year of my imprisonment I did nothing else, and can remember doing nothing else, but wring my hands in impotent despair, and say, "What an ending, what an appalling ending!" now I try to say to myself, and sometimes when I am not torturing myself do really and sincerely say, "What a beginning, what a wonderful beginning!" It may really be so. It may become so. If it does I shall owe much to this new personality that has altered every man's life in this place.

You may realize it when I say that had I been released last May, as I tried to be, I would have left this place loathing it and every official in it with a bitterness of hatred that would have poisoned my life. I have had a year longer of imprisonment, but humanity has been in the prison along with us all, and now when I go out I shall always remember great kindnesses that I have received here from almost everybody, and on the day of my release I shall give many thanks to many people, and ask to be remembered by them in turn.

The prison style is absolutely and entirely wrong. I would give anything to be able to alter it when I go out. I intend to try. But there is nothing in the world so wrong but that the spirit of humanity, which is the spirit of love, the spirit of the Christ who is not in churches, may make it, if not right, at least possible to be borne without too much bitterness of heart.

I know also that much is waiting for me outside that is very delightful, from what St. Francis of Assisi calls "my brother the wind, and my sister the rain," lovely things both of them, down to the shop-windows and sunsets of great cities. If I made a list of all that still remains to me, I don't know where I should stop; for, indeed, God made the world just as much for me as for anyone else. Perhaps I may go out with something that I had not got before. I need not tell you that to me reformations in morals are as meaningless and vulgar as Reformations in theology. But while to propose to be a better man is a piece of unscientific cant, to have become a deeper man is the privilege of those who have suffered. And such I think I have become.

If after I am free a friend of mine gave a feast, and did not invite me to it, I should not mind a bit. I can be perfectly happy by myself. With freedom, flowers, books, and the moon, who could not be perfectly happy? Besides, feasts are not for me any more. I have given too many to care about them. That side of life is over for me, very fortunately, I dare say. But if after I am free a friend of mine had a sorrow and refused to allow me to share it, I should feel it most bitterly. If he shut the doors of the house of mourning against me, I would come back again and again and beg to be admitted, so that I might share in what I was entitled to share in. If he thought me unworthy, unfit to weep with him, I should feel it as the most poignant humiliation, as the most terrible mode in which disgrace could be inflicted on me. But that could not be. I have a right to share in sorrow, and he who can look at the loveliness of the world and share its sorrow, and realize something of the wonder of both, is in immediate contact with divine things, and has got as near to God's secret as anyone can get.

Perhaps there may come into my art also, no less than into my life, a still deeper note, one of greater unity of passion, and directness of impulse. Not width but intensity is the true aim of modern art. We are no longer in art concerned with the type. It is with the exception that we have to do. I cannot put my sufferings into any form they took, I need hardly say. Art only begins where imitation ends, but something must come into my work, of fuller memory of words perhaps, of richer cadences, of more curious effects, of simpler architectural order, of some æsthetic quality at any rate.

When Marsyas was "torn from the scabbard of his limbs"—*della vagina della membra sue*, to use one of Dante's most terrible Tacitean phrases—he had no more song, the Greek said. Apollo had been victor. The lyre had vanquished the reed. But perhaps the Greeks were mistaken. I hear in much modern art the cry of Marsyas. It is bitter in Baudelaire, sweet and plaintive in Lamartine, mystic in Verlaine. It is in the deferred resolutions of Chopin's music. It is in the discontent that haunts Burne-Jones's women. Even Matthew Arnold, whose song of Callicles tells of "the triumph of the sweet persuasive lyre," and the "famous final victory," in such a clear note of lyrical beauty, has not a little of it; in the troubled undertone of doubt and distress that haunts his verses, neither Goethe nor Wordsworth could help him, though he followed each in turn, and when he seeks to mourn for *Thyrsis* or to sing of the *Scholar Gipsy*, it is the reed that he has to take for the rendering of his strain. But whether or not the Phrygian Faun was silent, I cannot be. Expression is as necessary to me as leaf and blossoms are to the black branches of the trees that show themselves above the prison walls and are so restless in the wind. Between my art and the world there is now a wide gulf, but between art and myself there is none. I hope at least that there is none.

To each of us different fates are meted out. My lot has been one of public infamy, of long imprisonment, of misery, of ruin, of disgrace, but I am not worthy of it —not yet, at any rate. I remember that I used to say that I thought I could bear a real tragedy if it came to me with purple pall and a mask of noble sorrow, but that the dreadful thing about modernity was that it put tragedy into the raiment of comedy, so that the great realities seemed commonplace or grotesque or lacking in style. It is quite true about modernity. It has probably always been true about actual life. It is said that all martyrdoms seemed mean to the looker on. The nineteenth century is no exception to the rule.

Everything about my tragedy has been hideous, mean, repellent, lacking in style; our very dress makes us grotesque. We are the zanies of sorrow. We are clowns whose hearts are broken. We are specially designed to appeal to the sense of humour. On November 13th, 1895, I was brought down here from London. From two o'clock till half-past two on that day I had to stand on the centre platform of Clapham Junction in convict dress, and handcuffed, for the world to look at. I had been taken out of the hospital ward without a moment's notice being given to me. Of all possible objects I was the most grotesque. When people saw me they laughed. Each train as it came up swelled the audience. Nothing could exceed their amusement. That was, of course, before they knew who I was. As soon as they had been informed they laughed still more. For half an hour I stood there in the grey November rain surrounded by a jeering mob.

For a year after that was done to me I wept every day at the same hour and for the same space of time. That is not such a tragic thing as possibly it sounds to you. To those who are in prison tears are a part of every day's experience. A day in prison on which one does not weep is a day on which one's heart is hard, not a day on which one's heart is happy.

Well, now I am really beginning to feel more regret for the people who laughed than for myself. Of course when they saw me I was not on my pedestal, I was in the pillory. But it is a very unimaginative nature that only cares for people on their pedestals. A pedestal may be a very unreal thing. A pillory is a terrific reality. They should have known also how to interpret sorrow better. I have said that behind sorrow there is always sorrow. It were wiser still to say that behind sorrow there is always a soul. And to mock at a soul in pain is a dreadful thing. In the strangely simple economy of the world people only get what they give, and to those who have not enough imagination to penetrate the mere outward of things, and feel pity, what pity can be given save that of scorn?

I write this account of the mode of my being transferred here simply that it should be realized how hard it has been for me to get anything out of my punishment but bitterness and despair. I have, however, to do it, and now and then I have moments of submission and acceptance. All the spring may be hidden in the single bud, and the low ground-nest of the lark may hold the joy that is to herald the feet of many rose-red dawns. So perhaps whatever beauty of life still remains to me is contained in some moment of surrender, abasement, and humiliation. I can, at any rate, merely proceed on the lines of my own development, and, accepting all that has happened to me, make myself worthy of it.

People used to say of me that I was too individualistic. I must be far more of an individualist than ever I was. I must get far more out of myself than ever I got, and ask for less of the world than ever I asked. Indeed, my ruin came not from too great individualism of life, but from too little. The one disgraceful, unpardonable, and to all time contemptible action of my life was to allow myself to appeal to society for help and protection. To have made such an appeal would have been from the individualist point of view bad enough, but what excuse can there ever be put forward for having made it? Of course once I had put into motion the forces of society, society turned on me and said, "Have you been living all this time in defiance of my laws, and do you now appeal to those laws for protection? You shall have those laws exercised to the

full. You shall abide by what you have appealed to."
The result is I am in gaol. Certainly no man ever fell
so ignobly, and by such ignoble instruments, as I did.
I say in *Dorian Gray* somewhere that "A man cannot
be too careful in the choice of his enemies." I little
thought that it was by a pariah I was to be made a
pariah myself.

The Philistine element in life is not the failure to
understand art. Charming people such as fishermen,
shepherds, ploughboys, peasants and the like, know
nothing about art, and are the very salt of the earth.
He is the Philistine who upholds and aids the heavy,
cumbrous, blind, mechanical forces of society, and who
does not recognize dynamic force when he meets it
either in a man or a movement.

People thought it dreadful of me to have entertained
at dinner the evil things of life, and to have found
pleasure in their company. But then, from the point of
view through which I, as an artist in life, approach
them they were delightfully suggestive and stimulating.
It was like feasting with panthers; the danger was half
the excitement. I used to feel as a snake-charmer must
feel when he lures the cobra to stir from the painted
cloth or reed basket that holds it and makes it spread
its hood at his bidding and sway to and fro in the air
as a plant sways restfully in a stream. They were to
me the brightest of gilded snakes, their poison was part
of their perfection. I did not know that when they
were to strike at me it was to be at another's piping
and at another's pay. I don't feel at all ashamed at having known them, they were intensely interesting; what
I do feel ashamed of is the horrible Philistine atmosphere into which I was brought. My business as an artist
was with Ariel, I set myself to wrestle with Caliban.
Instead of making beautiful coloured musical things

such as *Salomé* and *The Florentine Tragedy* and *La
Sainte Courtisane* I forced myself to send long lawyer's
letters and was constrained to appeal to the very things
against which I had always protested. Clibborn and
Atkins were wonderful in their infamous war against
life. To entertain them was an astounding adventure;
Dumas *père*, Cellini, Goya, Edgar Allan Poe, or Baudelaire would have done just the same. What is loathsome to me is the memory of interminable visits paid
by me to the solicitor H——, when in the ghastly
glare of a bleak room I would sit with a serious face
telling serious lies to a bald man till I really groaned
and yawned with ennui. There is where I found myself,
right in the centre of Philistia, away from everything
that was beautiful or brilliant or wonderful or daring.
I had come forward as the champion of respectability
in conduct, of puritanism in life, and of morality in
art. *Voilà où menent les mauvais chemins* . . . but
I can think with gratitude of those who by kindness
without stint, devotion without limit, cheerfulness and
joy in giving have lightened my black burden for me,
have visited me again and again, have written to me
beautiful and sympathetic letters, have managed my
affairs for me, arranged my future life, and stood by me
in the teeth of obloquy, taunt and open sneer, or insult
even. I owe everything to them. The very books in my
cell are paid for by —— out of his pocket-money;
from the same source are to come clothes for me when
I am released. I am not ashamed of taking a thing that
is given in love and affection; I am proud of it. Yes, I
think of my friends, such as More Adey, R——, Robert
Sherard, Frank Harris, Arthur Clifton, and what
they have been to me, in giving me help, affection, and
sympathy. I think of every single person who has been
kind to me in my prison life down to the warder who

gives me a "Good morning" and a "Good night" (not one of his prescribed duties) down to the common policemen who, in their homely, rough way strove to comfort me on my journeys to and fro from the Bankruptcy Court under conditions of terrible mental distress—down to the poor thief who recognizing me as we tramped round the yard at Wandsworth, whispered to me in the hoarse prison voice men get from long and compulsory silence: "I am sorry for you; it is harder for the likes of you than it is for the likes of us."

A great friend of mine—a friend of ten years' standing—came to see me some time ago, and told me that he did not believe a single word of what was said against me, and wished me to know that he considered me quite innocent, and the victim of a hideous plot. I burst into tears at what he said, and told him that while there was much amongst the definite charges that was quite untrue and transferred to me by revolting malice, still that my life had been full of perverse pleasures, and that unless he accepted that as a fact about me and realized it to the full I could not possibly be friends with him any more, or ever be in his company. It was a terrible shock to him, but we are friends, and I have not got his friendship on false pretences. I have said to you to speak the truth is a painful thing. To be forced to tell lies is much worse.

I remember that as I was sitting in the Dock on the occasion of my last trial listening to Lockwood's appalling denunciation of me—like a thing out of Tacitus, like a passage in Dante, like one of Savonarola's indictments of the Popes of Rome—and being sickened with horror at what I heard. Suddenly it occurred to me, *How splendid it would be, if I was saying all this about myself.* I saw then at once that what is said of a man is nothing. The point is, who says it. A man's very highest moment is, I have no doubt at all, when he kneels in the dust, and beats his breast, and tells all the sins of his life.

Emotional forces, as I say somewhere in *Intentions*, are as limited in extent and duration as the forces of physical energy. The little cup that is made to hold so much can hold so much and no more, though all the purple vats of Burgundy be filled with wine to the brim, and the treaders stand knee-deep in the gathered grapes of the stony vineyards of Spain. There is no error more common than that of thinking that those who are the causes or occasions of great tragedies share in the feelings suitable to the tragic mood: no error more fatal than expecting it of them. The martyr in his "shirt of flame" may be looking on the face of God, but to him who is piling the faggots or loosening the logs for the blast the whole scene is no more than the slaying of an ox is to the butcher, or the felling of a tree to the charcoal burner in the forest, or the fall of a flower to one who is mowing down the grass with a scythe. Great passions are for the great of soul, and great events can be seen only by those who are on a level with them. We think we can have our emotions for nothing. We cannot. Even the finest and the most self-sacrificing emotions have to be paid for. Strangely enough, that is what makes them fine. The intellectual and emotional life of ordinary people is a very contemptible affair. Just as they borrow their ideas from a sort of circulating library of thought—the *Zeitgeist* of an age that has no soul and send them back soiled at the end of each week—so they always try to get their emotions on credit, or refuse to pay the bill when it comes in. We must pass out of that conception of life; as soon as we have to pay for an emotion we shall know its quality and be the better for such knowledge.

Remember that the sentimentalist is always a cynic at heart. Indeed sentimentality is merely the Bank-holiday of cynicism. And delightful as cynicism is from its intellectual side, now that it has left the tub for the club, it never can be more than the perfect philosophy for a man who has no soul. It has its social value; and to an artist all modes of expression are interesting, but in itself it is a poor affair, for to the true cynic nothing is ever revealed.

I know of nothing in all drama more incomparable from the point of view of art, nothing more suggestive in its subtlety of observation, than Shakespeare's drawing of Rosencrantz and Guildenstern. They are Hamlet's college friends. They have been his companions. They bring with them memories of pleasant days together. At the moment when they come across him in the play he is staggering under the weight of a burden intolerable to one of his temperament. The dead have come armed out of the grave to impose on him a mission at once too great and too mean for him. He is a dreamer, and he is called upon to act. He has the nature of the poet, and he is asked to grapple with the common complexity of cause and effect, with life in its practical realization, of which he knows nothing, not with life in its ideal essence, of which he knows so much. He has no conception of what to do, and his folly is to feign folly. Brutus used madness as a cloak to conceal the sword of his purpose, the dagger of his will, but the Hamlet madness is a mere mask for the hiding of weakness. In the making of fancies and jests he sees a chance of delay. He keeps playing with action as an artist plays with a theory. He makes himself the spy of his proper actions and listening to his own words knows them to be but "words, words, words."

Instead of trying to be the hero of his own history, he seeks to be the spectator of his own tragedy. He disbelieves in everything including himself, and yet his doubt helps him not, as it comes not from scepticism but from a divided will.

Of all this Guildenstern and Rosencrantz realize nothing. They bow and smirk and smile, and what the one says the other echoes with sickliest intonation. When, at last, by means of the play within the play, and the puppets in their dalliance, Hamlet "catches the conscience" of the King, and drives the wretched man in terror from his throne, Guildenstern and Rosencrantz see no more in his conduct than a rather painful breach of Court etiquette. That is as far as they can attain to in "the contemplation of the spectacle of life with appropriate emotions." They are close to his very secret and know nothing of it. Nor would there be any use in telling them. They are the little cups that can hold so much and no more. Towards the close it is suggested that, caught in a cunning spring set for another, they have met, or may meet, with a violent and sudden death. But a tragic ending of this kind, though touched by Hamlet's humour with something of the surprise and justice of comedy, is really not for such as they. They never die. Horatio, who in order to "report Hamlet and his cause aright to the unsatisfied,"

> Absents him from felicity a while,
> And in this harsh world draws his breath in pain,

dies, though not before an audience and leaves no brother. But Guildenstern and Rosencrantz are as immortal as Angelo and Tartuffe, and should rank with them. They are what modern life has contributed to the antique ideal of friendship. He who writes a new *De Amicitia* must find a niche for them, and praise them in Tusculan prose. They are types fixed for all time. To censure them would show "a lack of appreciation." They are merely out of their sphere: that is all. In sublimity of soul there is no contagion. High thoughts and high emotions are by their very existence isolated.

I am to be released, if all goes well with me, towards the end of May, and hope to go at once to some little seaside village abroad with R——— and M———.

The sea, as Euripides says in one of his plays about Iphigeneia, washes away the stains and wounds of the world.

I hope to be at least a month with my friends, and to gain peace and balance, and a less troubled heart, and a sweeter mood; and then if I feel able I shall arrange through R——— to go to some quiet foreign town like Bruges whose grey houses and green canals and cool still ways had a charm for me years ago. I have a strange longing for the great simple primeval things, such as the sea, to me no less of a mother than the Earth. It seems to me that we all look at Nature too much, and live with her too little. I discern great sanity in the Greek attitude. They never chattered about sunsets, or discussed whether the shadows on the grass were really mauve or not. But they saw that the sea was for the swimmer, and the sand for the feet of the runner. They loved the trees for the shadow that they cast, and the forest for its silence at noon. The vineyard-dresser wreathed his hair with ivy that he might keep off the rays of the sun as he stooped over the young shoots, and for the artist and the athlete, the two types that Greece gave us, they plaited with garlands the leaves of the bitter laurel and of the wild parsley, which else had been of no service to men.

We call ours a utilitarian age, and we do not know the uses of any single thing. We have forgotten that water can cleanse, and fire purify, and that the Earth is mother to us all. As a consequence our art is of the moon and plays with shadows, while Greek art is of the sun and deals directly with things. I feel sure that in elemental forces there is purification, and I want to go back to them and live in their presence.

It is not for nothing or to no purpose that in my life-long cult of literature I have made myself

> Miser of sound and syllable, no less
> Than Midas of his coinage.

I must not be afraid of the past; if people tell me that it is irrevocable I shall not believe them; the past, the present, and the future are one moment in the sight of God, in whose sight we should try to live. Time and space, succession and extension, are merely accidental conditions of thought, the imagination can transcend them and move in a free sphere of ideal existences. Things also are in their essence of what we choose to make them; a thing *is* according to the mode in which we look at it. "Where others," says Blake, "see but the dawn coming over the hill, I see the sons of God shouting for joy." What seemed to the world and to myself my future I lost when I allowed myself to be taunted into taking action against Queensberry; I dare-say I lost it really long before that. What lies before me is my past. I have got to make myself look on that with different eyes, to make God look on it with dif-ferent eyes. This I cannot do by ignoring it, or slight-ing it, or praising it, or denying it; it is only to be done by accepting it as an inevitable part of the evolution of my life and character: by bowing my head to every-thing I have suffered. How far I am away from the true temper of soul, this letter in its changing uncer-tain moods, its scorn and bitterness, its aspirations and its failure to realize those aspirations, shows quite clearly; but do not forget in what a terrible school I am sitting at my task, and incomplete, imperfect as I am, my friends have still much to gain. They came to me to learn the pleasure of life and the pleasure of art. Perhaps I am chosen to teach them something more wonderful, the meaning of sorrow and its beauty.

Of course to one so modern as I am, *"enfant de mon siècle,"* merely to look at the world will be always lovely. I tremble with pleasure when I think that on the very day of my leaving prison both the laburnum and the lilac will be blooming in the gardens, and that I shall see the wind stir into restless beauty the swaying gold of the one, and make the other toss the pale purple of its plumes so that all the air shall be Arabia for me. Linnæus fell on his knees and wept for joy when he saw for the first time the long heath of some English upland made yellow with the tawny aromatic blossoms of the common furze; and I know that for me, to whom flowers are part of desire, there are tears waiting in the petals of some rose. It has always been so with me from my boyhood. There is not a single colour hidden away in the chalice of a flower, or the curve of a shell, to which, by some subtle sympathy with the very soul of things, my nature does not answer. Like Gautier, I have always been one of those *"pour qui le monde visible existe."*

Still, I am conscious now that behind all this beauty, satisfying though it may be, there is some spirit hidden of which the painted forms and shapes are but modes of manifestation, and it is with this spirit that I desire to become in harmony. I have grown tired of the articulate utterances of men and things. The Mystical in Art, the Mystical in Life, the Mystical in Nature—this is what I am looking for. It is absolutely necessary for me to find it somewhere.

All trials are trials for one's life, just as all sentences are sentences of death; and three times have I been tried. The first time I left the box to be arrested, the second time to be led back to the house of detention, the third time to pass into a prison for two years. Society, as we have constituted it, will have no place for me, has none to offer; but Nature, whose sweet rains fall on unjust and just alike, will have clefts in the rocks where I may hide, and secret valleys in whose silence I may weep undisturbed. She will hang the night with stars so that I may walk abroad in the darkness without stumbling, and send the wind over my footprints so that none may track me to my hurt: she will cleanse me in great waters, and with bitter herbs make me whole.

Poems, Poems in Prose, and a Fairy Tale

Hélas!

To drift with every passion till my soul
Is a stringed lute on which all winds can play,
Is it for this that I have given away
Mine ancient wisdom, and austere control?—
Methinks my life is a twice-written scroll
Scrawled over on some boyish holiday
With idle songs for pipe and virelay
Which do but mar the secret of the whole.
Surely there was a time I might have trod
The sunlit heights, and from life's dissonance
Struck one clear chord to reach the ears of God;
Is that time dead? lo! with a little rod
I did but touch the honey of romance—
And must I lose a soul's inheritance?

FROM *Ave Imperatrix*

For not in quiet English fields
    Are these, our brothers, laid to rest,
Where we might deck their broken shields
    With all the flowers the dead love best.

For some are by the Delhi walls,
    And many in the Afghan land,

And many where the Ganges falls
   Through seven mouths of shifting sand.

And some in Russian waters lie,
   And others in the seas which are
The portals to the East, or by
   The wind-swept heights of Trafalgar.

And thou whose wounds are never healed,
   Whose weary race is never won,
O Cromwell's England! must thou yield
   For every inch of ground a son?

Requiescat

Tread lightly, she is near
   Under the snow,
Speak gently, she can hear
   The daisies grow.

All her bright golden hair
   Tarnished with rust,
She that was young and fair
   Fallen to dust.

Lily-like, white as snow,
   She hardly knew
She was a woman, so
   Sweetly she grew.

Coffin-board, heavy stone,
   Lie on her breast,
I vex my heart alone
   She is at rest.

Peace, peace, she cannot hear
Lyre or sonnet,
All my life's buried here,
Heap earth upon it.

Avignon

FROM *The Burden of Itys*

The heron passes homeward to the mere,
The blue mist creeps among the shivering trees,
Gold world by world the silent stars appear,
And like a blossom blown before the breeze,
A white moon drifts across the shimmering sky,
Mute arbitress of all thy sad, thy rapturous threnody.

FROM *Charmides*

On the green bank he lay, and let one hand
Dip in the cool dark eddies listlessly,
And soon the breath of morning came and fanned
His hot flushed cheeks, or lifted wantonly
The tangled curls from off his forehead, while
He on the running water gazed with strange and secret
smile.

And soon the shepherd in rough woollen cloak
With his long crook undid the wattled cotes,
And from the stack a thin blue wreath of smoke
Curled through the air across the ripening oats,
And on the hill the yellow house-dog bayed
As through the crisp and rustling fern the heavy
cattle strayed.

And when the light-foot mower went a-field
  Across the meadows laced with threaded dew,
And the sheep bleated on the misty weald,
  And from its nest the waking corn-crake flew,
Some woodmen saw him lying by the stream
And marvelled much that any lad so beautiful could
    seem . . .

*

"Deeper than ever falls the fishers' line
  Already a huge Triton blows his horn,
And weaves a garland from the crystalline
  And drifting ocean-tendrils to adorn
The emerald pillars of our bridal bed,
For sphered in foaming silver, and with coral-crowned
    head,

We two will sit upon a throne of pearl,
  And a blue wave will be our canopy,
And at our feet the water-snakes will curl
  In all their amethystine panoply
Of diamonded mail, and we will mark
The mullets swimming by the mast of some storm-
    foundered bark,

Vermilion-finned with eyes of bossy gold
  Like flakes of crimson light, and the great deep
His glassy-portaled chamber will unfold,
  And we will see the painted dolphins sleep
Cradled by murmuring halcyons on the rocks
Where Proteus in quaint suit of green pastures his
    monstrous flocks.

And tremulous opal-hued anemones
  Will wave their purple fringes where we tread

Upon the mirrored floor, and argosies
  Of fishes flecked with tawny scales will thread
The drifting cordage of the shattered wreck,
And honey-coloured amber beads our twining limbs
    will deck."

*

For as a gardener turning back his head
  To catch the last notes of the linnet, mows
With careless scythe too near some flower bed,
  And cuts the thorny pillar of the rose,
And with the flower's loosened loveliness
Strews the brown mould, or as some shepherd lad in
    wantonness

Driving his little flock along the mead
  Treads down two daffodils which side by side
Have lured the lady-bird with yellow brede
  And made the gaudy moth forget its pride,
Treads down their brimming golden chalices
Under light feet which were not made for such rude
    ravages,

Or as a schoolboy tired of his book
  Flings himself down upon the reedy grass
And plucks two water-lilies from the brook,
  And for a time forgets the hour glass,
Then wearies of their sweets, and goes his way,
And lets the hot sun kill them, even so these lovers lay.

The Sphinx

To Marcel Schwob
In friendship and admiration

In a dim corner of my room for longer than my fancy
thinks
A beautiful and silent Sphinx has watched me through
the shifting gloom.

Inviolate and immobile she does not rise, she does not
stir,
For silver moons are naught to her and naught to her
the suns that reel.

Red follows grey across the air, the waves of moonlight ebb and flow,
But with the dawn she does not go and in the night-
time she is there.

Dawn follows Dawn and Nights grow old, and all the
while this curious cat
Lies couching on the Chinese mat with eyes of satin
rimmed with gold.

Upon the mat she lies and leers and on the tawny throat
of her
Flutters the soft and silky fur or ripples to her pointed
ears.

Come forth, my lovely seneschal! so somnolent, so
statuesque!
Come forth you exquisite grotesque! half woman and
half animal!

Come forth my lovely languorous Sphinx! and put your
    head upon my knee!
And let me stroke your throat and see your body spotted
    like the Lynx!

And let me touch those curving claws of yellow ivory
    and grasp
The tail that like a monstrous Asp coils round your
    heavy velvet paws!

*

A thousand weary centuries are thine while I have
    hardly seen
Some twenty summers cast their green for Autumn's
    gaudy liveries.

But you can read the Hieroglyphs on the great sand-
    stone obelisks,
And you have talked with Basilisks, and you have
    looked on Hippogriffs.

O tell me, were you standing by when Isis to Osiris
    knelt?
And did you watch the Egyptian melt her union for
    Antony,

And drink the jewel-drunken wine, and bend her head
    in mimic awe
To see the huge proconsul draw the salted tunny from
    the brine?

And did you mark the Cyprian kiss white Adon on his
    catafalque?
And did you follow Amenalk, the God of Heliopolis?

And did you talk with Thoth, and did you hear the
    moon-horned Io weep?
And know the painted kings who sleep beneath the
    wedge-shaped Pyramid?

*

Lift up your large black satin eyes which are like
    cushions where one sinks!
Fawn at my feet, fantastic Sphinx! and sing me all
    your memories!

Sing to me of the Jewish maid who wandered with the
    Holy Child,
And how you led them through the wild, and how they
    slept beneath your shade.

Sing to me of that odorous green eve when crouching
    by the marge
You heard from Adrian's gilded barge the laughter of
    Antinöus,

And lapped the stream and fed your drouth and
    watched with hot and hungry stare
The ivory body of that rare young slave with his pome-
    granate mouth!

Sing to me of the Labyrinth in which the two-formed
    bull was stalled!
Sing to me of the night you crawled across the temple's
    granite plinth,

When through the purple corridors the screaming
    scarlet Ibis flew

In terror, and a horrid dew dripped from the moaning
    Mandragores,

And the great torpid crocodile within the tank shed
    slimy tears,
And tare the jewels from his ears and staggered back
    into the Nile,

And the priests cursed you with shrill psalms as in
    your claws you seized the snake,
And crept away with it to slake your passion by the
    shuddering palms.

*

Who were your lovers? who were they who wrestled
    for you in the dust?
Which was the vessel of your Lust? What Leman had
    you, every day?

Did giant Lizards come and crouch before you on the
    reedy banks?
Did Gryphons with great metal flanks leap on you in
    your trampled couch?

Did monstrous hippopotami come sidling toward you
    in the mist?
Did gilt-scaled dragons writhe and twist with passion
    as you passed them by?

And from the brick-built Lycian tomb what horrible
    Chimera came
With fearful heads and fearful flame to breed new
    wonders from your womb?

Or had you shameful secret quests and did you harry
    to your home
Some Nereid coiled in amber foam with curious rock-
    crystal breasts?

Or did you treading through the froth call to the brown
    Sidonian
For tidings of Leviathan, Leviathan or Behemoth?

Or did you when the sun was set climb up the cactus-
    covered slope
To meet your swarthy Ethiop whose body was of
    polished jet?

Or did you while the earthen skiffs dropped down the
    grey Nilotic flats
At twilight, and the flickering bats flew round the
    temple's triple glyphs,

Steal to the border of the bar and swim across the
    silent lake
And slink into the vault and make the Pyramid your
    lúpanar,

Till from each black sarcophagus rose up the painted
    swathéd dead?
Or did you lure unto your bed the ivory-horned Tra-
    gelaphos?

Or did you love the god of flies who plagued the He-
    brew and was splashed
With wine unto the waist? or Pasht, who had green
    beryls for her eyes?

Or that young god, the Tyrian, who was more amorous
    than the dove
Of Ashtaroth? or did you love the god of the Assyrian

Whose wings, like strange transparent talc, rose high
    above his hawk-faced head,
Painted with silver and with red and ribbed with rods
    of Oreichalch?

Or did huge Apis from his car leap down and lay before
    your feet
Big blossoms of the honey-sweet and honey-coloured
    nenuphar?

*

How subtle-secret is your smile! Did you love none
    then? Nay, I know
Great Ammon was your bedfellow! He lay with you
    beside the Nile!

The river-horses in the slime trumpeted when they saw
    him come
Odorous with Syrian galbanum and smeared with
    spikenard and with thyme.

He came along the river bank like some tall galley
    argent-sailed,
He strode across the waters, mailed in beauty, and the
    waters sank.

He strode across the desert sand: he reached the valley
    where you lay:
He waited till the dawn of day: then touched your
    black breasts with his hand.

You kissed his mouth with mouth of flame: you made
the hornéd god your own:
You stood behind him on his throne: you called him
by his secret name.

You whispered monstrous oracles into the caverns of
his ears:
With blood of goats and blood of steers you taught him
monstrous miracles.

White Ammon was your bedfellow! Your chamber was
the steaming Nile!
And with your curved archaic smile you watched his
passion come and go.
*

With Syrian oils his brows were bright: and wide-
spread as a tent at noon
His marble limbs made pale the moon and lent the
day a larger light.

His long hair was nine cubits' span and coloured like
that yellow gem
Which hidden in their garments' hem the merchants
bring from Kurdistan.

His face was as the must that lies upon a vat of new-
made wine:
The seas could not insapphirine the perfect azure of
his eyes.

His thick soft throat was white as milk and threaded
with thin veins of blue:
And curious pearls like frozen dew were broidered on
his flowing silk.
*

On pearl and porphyry pedestalled he was too bright
    to look upon:
For on his ivory breast there shone the wondrous ocean-
    emerald,

That mystic moonlit jewel which some diver of the
    Colchian caves
Had found beneath the blackening waves and carried
    to the Colchian witch.

Before his gilded galiot ran naked vine-wreathed
    corybants,
And lines of swaying elephants knelt down to draw
    his chariot.

And lines of swarthy Nubians bare up his litter as he
    rode
Down the great granite-paven road between the nod-
    ding peacock fans.

The merchants brought him steatite from Sidon in
    their painted ships:
The meanest cup that touched his lips was fashioned
    from a chrysolite.

The merchants brought him cedar chests of rich ap-
    parel bound with cords:
His train was borne by Memphian lords: young kings
    were glad to be his guests.

Ten hundred shaven priests did bow to Ammon's altar
    day and night,
Ten hundred lamps did wave their light through Am-
    mon's carven house—and now

Foul snake and speckled adder with their young ones
    crawl from stone to stone
For ruined is the house and prone the great rose-marble
    monolith!

Wild ass or trotting jackal comes and couches in the
    mouldering gates:
Wild satyrs call unto their mates across the fallen
    fluted drums.

And on the summit of the pile the blue-faced ape of
    Horus sits
And gibbers while the fig-tree splits the pillars of the
    peristyle.

*

The god is scattered here and there: deep hidden in the
    windy sand
I saw his giant granite hand still clenched in impotent
    despair.

And many a wandering caravan of stately negroes
    silken-shawled,
Crossing the desert halts appalled before the neck
    that none can span.

And many a bearded Bedouin draws back his yellow-
    striped burnous
To gaze upon the Titan thews of him who was thy
    paladin.

*

Go, seek his fragments on the moor and wash them in
    the evening dew,

And from their pieces make anew thy mutilated para-
    mour!

Go, seek them where they lie alone and from their
    broken pieces make
Thy bruiséd bedfellow! And wake mad passion in the
    senseless stone!

Charm his dull ear with Syrian hymns! he loved your
    body! oh, be kind,
Pour spikenard on his hair, and wind soft rolls of linen
    round his limbs.

Wind round his head the figured coins! stain with red
    fruits those pallid lips!
Weave purple for his shrunken hips! and purple for
    his barren loins!

*

Away to Egypt! Have no fear. Only one God has ever
    died.
Only one God has let His side be wounded by a sol-
    dier's spear.

But these, thy lovers, are not dead. Still by the hundred-
    cubit gate
Dog-faced Anubis sits in state with lotus-lilies for thy
    head.

Still from his chair of porphyry gaunt Memnon strains
    his lidless eyes
Across the empty land, and cries each yellow morning
    unto thee.

And Nilus with his broken horn lies in his black and
    oozy bed,
And till thy coming will not spread his waters on the
    withering corn.

Your lovers are not dead, I know. They will rise up
    and hear your voice
And clash their cymbals and rejoice and run to kiss
    your mouth! And so,

Set wings upon your argosies! Set horses to your ebon
    car!
Back to your Nile! Or if you are grown sick of dead
    divinities

Follow some roving lion's spoor across the copper-
    coloured plain,
Reach out and hale him by the mane and bid him be
    your paramour!

Couch by his side upon the grass and set your white
    teeth in his throat
And when you hear his dying note lash your long
    flanks of polished brass,

And take a tiger for your mate, whose amber sides are
    flecked with black,
And ride upon his gilded back in triumph through the
    Theban gate,

And toy with him in amorous jests, and when he turns,
    and snarls, and gnaws,
O smite him with your jasper claws! and bruise him with
    your agate breasts!

Why are you tarrying? Get hence! I weary of your
    sullen ways,
I weary of your steadfast gaze, your somnolent magnif-
    icence.

Your horrible and heavy breath makes the light flicker
    in the lamp,
And on my brow I feel the damp and dreadful dews
    of night and death.

Your eyes are like fantastic moons that shiver in some
    stagnant lake,
Your tongue is like a scarlet snake that dances to fan-
    tastic tunes,

Your pulse makes poisonous melodies, and your black
    throat is like the hole
Left by some torch or burning coal on Saracenic
    tapestries.

Away! The sulphur-coloured stars are hurrying through
    the Western gate!
Away! Or it may be too late to climb their silent silver
    cars!

See, the dawn shivers round the grey gilt-dialled
    towers, and the rain
Streams down each diamonded pane and blurs with
    tears the wannish day.

What snake-tressed fury fresh from Hell, with uncouth
    gestures and unclean,
Stole from the poppy-drowsy queen and led you to a
    student's cell?

What songless tongueless ghost of sin crept through the
    curtains of the night,
And saw my taper burning bright, and knocked, and
    bade you enter in?

Are there not others more accursed, whiter with lep-
    rosies than I?
Are Abana and Pharphar dry that you come here to
    slake your thirst?

Get hence, you loathsome mystery! Hideous animal,
    get hence!
You wake in me each bestial sense, you make me what
    I would not be.

You make my creed a barren sham, you wake foul
    dreams of sensual life,
And Atys with his blood-stained knife were better
    than the thing I am.

False Sphinx! False Sphinx! By reedy Styx old Charon,
    leaning on his oar,
Waits for my coin. Go thou before, and leave me with
    my crucifix,

Whose pallid burden, sick with pain, watches the world
    with wearied eyes,
And weeps for every soul that dies, and weeps for
    every soul in vain.

Symphony in Yellow

An omnibus across the bridge
　　Crawls like a yellow butterfly,
　　And, here and there, a passer-by
Shows like a little restless midge.

Big barges full of yellow hay
　　Are moored against the shadowy wharf,
　　And, like a yellow silken scarf,
The thick fog hangs along the quay.

The yellow leaves begin to fade
　　And flutter from the Temple elms,
　　And at my feet the pale green Thames
Lies like a rod of rippled jade.

The Harlot's House

We caught the tread of dancing feet,
We loitered down the moonlit street,
And stopped beneath the Harlot's House.
Inside, above the din and fray,
We heard the loud musicians play
The *Treues Liebes Herz* of Strauss.

Like strange mechanical grotesques,
Making fantastic arabesques,
The shadows raced across the blind.
We watched the ghostly dancers spin,
To sound of horn and violin,
Like black leaves wheeling in the wind.

   Like wire-pulled Automatons,
   Slim silhouetted skeletons
Went sidling through the slow quadrille,
   Then took each other by the hand,
   And danced a stately saraband;
Their laughter echoed thin and shrill.

   Sometimes a clock-work puppet pressed
   A phantom lover to her breast,
Sometimes they seemed to try and sing.
   Sometimes a horrible Marionette
   Came out and smoked its cigarette
Upon the steps like a live thing.

   Then turning to my love I said,
   "The dead are dancing with the dead,
The dust is whirling with the dust."
   But she, she heard the violin,
   And left my side and entered in:
Love passed into the House of Lust.

   Then suddenly the tune went false,
   The dancers wearied of the waltz,
The shadows ceased to wheel and whirl,
   And down the long and silent street,
   The dawn with silver-sandalled feet,
Crept like a frightened girl.

The Ballad of Reading Gaol

In memoriam C.T.W.
sometime trooper of the Royal Horse Guards
obiit H.M. prison, Reading, Berkshire, July 7, 1896

I

He did not wear his scarlet coat,
    For blood and wine are red,
And blood and wine were on his hands
    When they found him with the dead,
The poor dead woman whom he loved,
    And murdered in her bed.

He walked amongst the Trial Men
    In a suit of shabby grey;
A cricket cap was on his head,
    And his step seemed light and gay;
But I never saw a man who looked
    So wistfully at the day.

I never saw a man who looked
    With such a wistful eye
Upon that little tent of blue
    Which prisoners call the sky,
And at every drifting cloud that went
    With sails of silver by.

I walked, with other souls in pain,
    Within another ring,
And was wondering if the man had done
    A great or little thing,
When a voice behind me whispered low,
    "That fellow's got to swing."

Dear Christ! the very prison walls
  Suddenly seemed to reel,
And the sky above my head became
  Like a casque of scorching steel;
And, though I was a soul in pain,
  My pain I could not feel.

I only knew what hunted thought
  Quickened his step, and why
He looked upon the garish day
  With such a wistful eye;
The man had killed the thing he loved,
  And so he had to die.

*

Yet each man kills the thing he loves,
  By each let this be heard,
Some do it with a bitter look,
  Some with a flattering word,
The coward does it with a kiss,
  The brave man with a sword!

Some kill their love when they are young,
  And some when they are old;
Some strangle with the hands of Lust,
  Some with the hands of Gold:
The kindest use a knife, because
  The dead so soon grow cold.

Some love too little, some too long,
  Some sell, and others buy;
Some do the deed with many tears,
  And some without a sigh:
For each man kills the thing he loves,
  Yet each man does not die.

He does not die a death of shame
   On a day of dark disgrace,
Nor have a noose about his neck,
   Nor a cloth upon his face,
Nor drop feet foremost through the floor
   Into an empty space.

He does not sit with silent men
   Who watch him night and day;
Who watch him when he tries to weep,
   And when he tries to pray;
Who watch him lest himself should rob
   The prison of its prey.

He does not wake at dawn to see
   Dread figures throng his room,
The shivering Chaplain robed in white,
   The Sheriff stern with gloom,
And the Governor all in shiny black,
   With the yellow face of Doom.

He does not rise in piteous haste
   To put on convict-clothes,
While some coarse-mouthed Doctor
   gloats, and notes
Each new and nerve-twitched pose,
Fingering a watch whose little ticks
   Are like horrible hammer-blows.

He does not feel that sickening thirst
   That sands one's throat, before
The hangman with his gardener's gloves
   Comes through the padded door,
And binds one with three leathern thongs,
   That the throat may thirst no more.

He does not bend his head to hear
   The Burial Office read,
Nor, while the anguish of his soul
   Tells him he is not dead,
Cross his own coffin, as he moves
   Into the hideous shed.

He does not stare upon the air
   Through a little roof of glass:
He does not pray with lips of clay
   For his agony to pass;
Nor feel upon his shuddering cheek
   The kiss of Caiaphas.

II

Six weeks the guardsman walked the yard
   In the suit of shabby grey:
His cricket cap was on his head,
   And his step seemed light and gay,
But I never saw a man who looked
   So wistfully at the day.

I never saw a man who looked
   With such a wistful eye
Upon that little tent of blue
   Which prisoners call the sky,
And at every wandering cloud that trailed
   Its ravelled fleeces by.

He did not wring his hands, as do
   Those witless men who dare
To try to rear the changeling Hope
   In the cave of black Despair:

He only looked upon the sun,
   And drank the morning air.

He did not wring his hands nor weep,
   Nor did he peek or pine,
But he drank the air as though it held
   Some healthful anodyne;
With open mouth he drank the sun
   As though it had been wine!

And I and all the souls in pain,
   Who tramped the other ring,
Forgot if we ourselves had done
   A great or little thing,
And watched with gaze of dull amaze
   The man who had to swing.

For strange it was to see him pass
   With a step so light and gay,
And strange it was to see him look
   So wistfully at the day,
And strange it was to think that he
   Had such a debt to pay.

*

For oak and elm have pleasant leaves
   That in the spring-time shoot:
But grim to see is the gallows-tree,
   With its adder-bitten root,
And, green or dry, a man must die
   Before it bears its fruit!

The loftiest place is that seat of grace
   For which all worldlings try:

But who would stand in hempen band
    Upon a scaffold high,
And through a murderer's collar take
    His last look at the sky?

It is sweet to dance to violins
    When Love and Life are fair:
To dance to flutes, to dance to lutes
    Is delicate and rare:
But it is not sweet with nimble feet
    To dance upon the air!

So with curious eye and sick surmise
    We watched him day by day,
And wondered if each one of us
    Would end the self-same way,
For none can tell to what red Hell
    His sightless soul may stray.

At last the dead man walked no more
    Amongst the Trial Men,
And I knew that he was standing up
    In the black dock's dreadful pen,
And that never would I see his face
    For weal or woe again.

Like two doomed ships that pass in storm
    We had crossed each other's way:
But we made no sign, we said no word,
    We had no word to say;
For we did not meet in the holy night,
    But in the shameful day.

A prison wall was round us both,
    Two outcast men we were:

The world had thrust us from its heart,
  And God from out His care:
And the iron gin that waits for Sin
  Had caught us in its snare.

III

In Debtors' Yard the stones are hard,
  And the dripping wall is high,
So it was there he took his air
  Beneath the leaden sky,
And by each side a warder walked,
  For fear the man might die.

Or else he sat with those who watched
  His anguish night and day;
Who watched him when he rose to weep,
  And when he crouched to pray;
Who watched him lest himself should rob
  Their scaffold of its prey.

The Governor was strong upon
  The Regulations Act:
The Doctor said that Death was but
  A scientific fact:
And twice a day the Chaplain called,
  And left a little tract.

And twice a day he smoked his pipe,
  And drank his quart of beer:
His soul was resolute, and held
  No hiding-place for fear;
He often said that he was glad
  The hangman's day was near.

But why he said so strange a thing
   No warder dared to ask:
For he to whom a watcher's doom
   Is given as his task,
Must set a lock upon his lips
   And make his face a mask.

Or else he might be moved, and try
   To comfort or console:
And what should Human Pity do
   Pent up in Murderer's Hole?
What word of grace in such a place
   Could help a brother's soul?

With slouch and swing around the ring
   We trod the Fools' Parade!
We did not care: we knew we were
   The Devil's Own Brigade:
And shaven head and feet of lead
   Make a merry masquerade.

We tore the tarry rope to shreds
   With blunt and bleeding nails;
We rubbed the doors, and scrubbed the floors,
   And cleaned the shining rails:
And, rank by rank, we soaped the plank,
   And clattered with the pails.

We sewed the sacks, we broke the stones,
   We turned the dusty drill:
We banged the tins, and bawled the hymns,
   And sweated on the mill:
But in the heart of every man
   Terror was lying still.

So still it lay that every day
   Crawled like a weed-clogged wave:
And we forgot the bitter lot
   That waits for fool and knave,
Till once, as we tramped in from work,
   We passed an open grave.

With yawning mouth the yellow hole
   Gaped for a living thing;
The very mud cried out for blood
   To the thirsty asphalt ring;
And we knew that ere one dawn grew fair
   Some prisoner had to swing.

Right in we went, with soul intent
   On Death and Dread and Doom:
The hangman, with his little bag,
   Went shuffling through the gloom:
And I trembled as I groped my way
   Into my numbered tomb.

*

That night the empty corridors
   Were full of forms of Fear,
And up and down the iron town
   Stole feet we could not hear,
And through the bars that hide the stars
   White faces seemed to peer.

He lay as one who lies and dreams
   In a pleasant meadow-land,
The watchers watched him as he slept,
   And could not understand
How one could sleep so sweet a sleep
   With a hangman close at hand.

But there is no sleep when men must weep
  Who never yet have wept:
So we—the fool, the fraud, the knave—
  That endless vigil kept,
And through each brain on hands of pain
  Another's terror crept.

Alas! it is a fearful thing
  To feel another's guilt!
For, right, within, the Sword of Sin
  Pierced to its poisoned hilt,
And as molten lead were the tears we shed
  For the blood we had not spilt.

The warders with their shoes of felt
  Crept by each padlocked door,
And peeped and saw, with eyes of awe,
  Grey figures on the floor,
And wondered why men knelt to pray
  Who never prayed before.

All through the night we knelt and prayed,
  Mad mourners of a corse!
The troubled plumes of midnight shook
  The plumes upon a hearse:
The bitter wine upon a sponge
  Was the savour of Remorse.

*

The grey cock crew, the red cock crew,
  But never came the day:
And crooked shapes of Terror crouched,
  In the corners where we lay:
And each evil sprite that walks by night
  Before us seemed to play.

They glided past, they glided fast,
  Like travellers through a mist:
They mocked the moon in a rigadoon
  Of delicate turn and twist,
And with formal pace and loathsome grace
  The phantoms kept their tryst.

With mop and mow, we saw them go,
  Slim shadows hand in hand:
About, about, in ghostly rout
  They trod a saraband:
And the damned grotesques made arabesque
  Like the wind upon the sand!

With the pirouettes of marionettes,
  They tripped on pointed tread:
But with flutes of Fear they filled the ear,
  As their grisly masque they led,
And loud they sang, and long they sang,
  For they sang to wake the dead.

"Oho!" they cried. "The world is wide,
  But fettered limbs go lame!
And once, or twice, to throw the dice
  Is a gentlemanly game,
But he does not win who plays with Sin
  In the secret House of Shame."

No things of air these antics were,
  That frolicked with such glee:
To men whose lives were held in gyves,
  And whose feet might not go free,
Ah! wounds of Christ! they were living things,
  Most terrible to see.

Around, around, they waltzed and wound;
  Some wheeled in smirking pairs;
With the mincing step of a demirep
  Some sidled up the stairs;
And with subtle sneer, and fawning leer,
  Each helped us at our prayers.

The morning wind began to moan,
  But still the night went on:
Though its giant loom the web of gloom
  Crept till each thread was spun:
And, as we prayed, we grew afraid
  Of the Justice of the Sun.

The moaning wind went wandering round
  The weeping prison-wall:
Till like a wheel of turning steel
  We felt the minutes crawl:
O moaning wind! what had we done
  To have such a seneschal?

At last I saw the shadowed bars,
  Like a lattice wrought in lead,
Move right across the whitewashed wall
  That faced my three-plank bed,
And I knew that somewhere in the world
  God's dreadful dawn was red.

At six o'clock we cleaned our cells,
  At seven all was still,
But the sough and swing of a mighty wing
  The prison seemed to fill,
For the Lord of Death with icy breath
  Had entered in to kill.

He did not pass in purple pomp,
  Nor ride a moon-white steed.
Three yards of cord and a sliding board
  Are all the gallows' need:
So with rope of shame the Herald came
  To do the secret deed.

We were as men who through a fen
  Of filthy darkness grope:
We did not dare to breathe a prayer,
  Or to give our anguish scope:
Something was dead in each of us,
  And what was dead was Hope.

For Man's grim Justice goes its way,
  And will not swerve aside:
It slays the weak, it slays the strong,
  It has a deadly stride:
With iron heel it slays the strong,
  The monstrous parricide!

We waited for the stroke of eight:
  Each tongue was thick with thirst:
For the stroke of eight is the stroke of Fate
  That makes a man accursed,
And Fate will use a running noose
  For the best man and the worst.

We had no other thing to do,
  Save to wait for the sign to come:
So, like things of stone in a valley lone,
  Quiet we sat and dumb:
But each man's heart beat thick and quick,
  Like a madman on a drum!

With sudden shock the prison-clock
  Smote on the shivering air,
And from all the gaol rose up a wail
  Of impotent despair,
Like the sound that frightened marshes hear
  From some leper in his lair.

And as one sees most fearful things
  In the crystal of a dream,
We saw the greasy hempen rope
  Hooked to the blackened beam,
And heard the prayer the hangman's snare
  Strangled into a scream.

And all the woe that moved him so
  That he gave that bitter cry,
And the wild regrets, and the bloody sweats,
  None knew so well as I:
For he who lives more lives than one
  More deaths than one must die.

IV

There is no chapel on the day
  On which they hang a man:
The Chaplain's heart is far too sick,
  Or his face is far too wan,
Or there is that written in his eyes
  Which none should look upon.

So they kept us close till nigh on noon,
  And then they rang the bell,
And the warders with their jingling keys
  Opened each listening cell,

And down the iron stair we tramped,
  Each from his separate Hell.

Out into God's sweet air we went,
  But not in wonted way,
For this man's face was white with fear,
  And that man's face was grey,
And I never saw sad men who looked
  So wistfully at the day.

I never saw sad men who looked
  With such a wistful eye
Upon that little tent of blue
  We prisoners called the sky,
And at every happy cloud that passed
  In such strange freedom by.

But there were those amongst us all
  Who walked with downcast head,
And knew that, had each got his due,
  They should have died instead:
He had but killed a thing that lived,
  Whilst they had killed the dead.

For he who sins a second time
  Wakes a dead soul to pain,
And draws it from its spotted shroud,
  And makes it bleed again,
And makes it bleed great gouts of blood,
  And makes it bleed in vain!

*

Like ape or clown, in monstrous garb
  With crooked arrows starred,

Silently we went round and round
  The slippery asphalt yard;
Silently we went round and round,
  And no man spoke a word.

Silently we went round and round,
  And through each hollow mind
The Memory of dreadful things
  Rushed like a dreadful wind,
And Horror stalked before each man,
  And Terror crept behind.

*

The warders strutted up and down,
  And watched their herd of brutes,
Their uniforms were spick and span,
  And they wore their Sunday suits,
But we knew the work they had been at
  By the quicklime on their boots.

For where a grave had opened wide,
  There was no grave at all:
Only a stretch of mud and sand
  By the hideous prison-wall,
And a little heap of burning lime,
  That the man should have his pall.

For he has a pall, this wretched man,
  Such as few men can claim:
Deep down below a prison-yard,
  Naked for greater shame,
He lies, with fetters on each foot,
  Wrapt in a sheet of flame!

And all the while the burning lime
    Eats flesh and bone away,
It eats the brittle bone by night,
    And the soft flesh by day,
It eats the flesh and bone by turns,
    But it eats the heart alway.

*

For three long years they will not sow
    Or root or seedling there:
For three long years the unblessed spot
    Will sterile be and bare,
And look upon the wondering sky
    With unreproachful stare.

They think a murderer's heart would taint
    Each simple seed they sow.
It is not true! God's kindly earth
    Is kindlier than men know,
And the red rose would but blow more red,
    The white rose whiter blow.

Out of his mouth a red, red rose!
    Out of his heart a white!
For who can say by what strange way,
    Christ brings His will to light,
Since the barren staff the pilgrim bore
    Bloomed in the great Pope's sight?

But neither milk-white rose nor red
    May bloom in prison-air;
The shard, the pebble, and the flint,
    Are what they give us there:
For flowers have been known to heal
    A common man's despair.

So never will wine-red rose or white,
  Petal by petal, fall
On that stretch of mud and sand that lies
  By the hideous prison-wall,
To tell the men who tramp the yard
  That God's Son died for all.

*

Yet though the hideous prison-wall
  Still hems him round and round,
And a spirit may not walk by night
  That is with fetters bound,
And a spirit may but weep that lies
  In such unholy ground,

He is at peace—this wretched man—
  At peace, or will be soon:
There is no thing to make him mad,
  Nor does Terror walk at noon,
For the lampless Earth in which he lies
  Has neither Sun nor Moon.

They hanged him as a beast is hanged:
  They did not even toll
A requiem that might have brought
  Rest to his startled soul,
But hurriedly they took him out,
  And hid him in a hole.

The warders stripped him of his clothes,
  And gave him to the flies:
They mocked the swollen purple throat,
  And the stark and staring eyes:
And with laughter loud they heaped the shrou
  In which the convict lies.

The Chaplain would not kneel to pray
  By his dishonoured grave:
Nor mark it with that blessed Cross
  That Christ for sinners gave,
Because the man was one of those
  Whom Christ came down to save.

Yet all is well; he has but passed
  To Life's appointed bourne:
And alien tears will fill for him
  Pity's long-broken urn,
For his mourners will be outcast men,
  And outcasts always mourn.

V

I know not whether Laws be right,
  Or whether Laws be wrong;
All that we know who lie in gaol
  Is that the wall is strong;
And that each day is like a year,
  A year whose days are long.

But this I know, that every Law
  That men have made for Man,
Since first Man took his brother's life,
  And the sad world began,
But straws the wheat and saves the chaff
  With a most evil fan.

This too I know—and wise it were
  If each could know the same—
That every prison that men build
  Is built with bricks of shame,

And bound with bars lest Christ should see
  How men their brothers maim.

With bars they blur the gracious moon,
  And blind the goodly sun:
And they do well to hide their Hell,
  For in it things are done
That Son of God nor son of Man
  Ever should look upon!

       *

The vilest deeds like poison weeds,
  Bloom well in prison-air;
It is only what is good in Man
  That wastes and withers there:
Pale Anguish keeps the heavy gate,
  And the Warder is Despair.

For they starve the little frightened child
  Till it weeps both night and day:
And they scourge the weak, and flog the fool,
  And gibe the old and grey,
And some grow mad, and all grow bad,
  And none a word may say.

Each narrow cell in which we dwell
  Is a foul and dark latrine,
And the fetid breath of living Death
  Chokes up each grated screen,
And all, but Lust, is turned to dust
  In humanity's machine.

The brackish water that we drink
  Creeps with a loathsome slime,

And the bitter bread they weigh in scales
  Is full of chalk and lime,
And Sleep will not lie down, but walks
  Wild-eyed, and cries to Time.

*

But though lean Hunger and green Thirst
  Like asp with adder fight,
We have little care of prison fare,
  For what chills and kills outright
Is that every stone one lifts by day
  Becomes one's heart by night.

With midnight always in one's heart,
  And twilight in one's cell,
We turn the crank, or tear the rope,
  Each in his separate Hell,
And the silence is more awful far
  Than the sound of a brazen bell.

And never a human voice comes near
  To speak a gentle word:
And the eye that watches through the door
  Is pitiless and hard:
And by all forgot, we rot and rot,
  With soul and body marred.

And thus we rust Life's iron chain
  Degraded and alone:
And some men curse, and some men weep,
  And some men make no moan:
But God's eternal Laws are kind
  And break the heart of stone.

And every human heart that breaks,
    In prison-cell or yard,
Is as that broken box that gave
    Its treasure to the Lord,
And filled the unclean leper's house
    With the scent of costliest nard.

Ah! happy they whose hearts can break
    And peace of pardon win!
How else may man make straight his plan
    And cleanse his soul from Sin!
How else but through a broken heart
    May Lord Christ enter in?

*

And he of the swollen purple throat,
    And the stark and staring eyes,
Waits for the holy hands that took
    The thief to Paradise;
And a broken and a contrite heart
    The Lord will not despise.

The man in red who reads the Law
    Gave him three weeks of life,
Three little weeks in which to heal
    His soul of his soul's strife,
And cleanse from every blot of blood
    The hand that held the knife.

And with tears of blood he cleansed the hand,
    The hand that held the steel:
For only blood can wipe out blood,
    And only tears can heal:
And the crimson stain that was of Cain
    Became Christ's snow-white seal.

VI

In Reading gaol by Reading town
  There is a pit of shame,
And in it lies a wretched man
  Eaten by teeth of flame,
In a burning winding-sheet he lies,
  And his grave has got no name.

And there, till Christ call forth the dead,
  In silence let him lie:
No need to waste the foolish tear,
  Or heave the windy sigh:
The man had killed the thing he loved,
  And so he had to die.

And all men kill the thing they love,
  By all let this be heard,
Some do it with a bitter look,
  Some with a flattering word,
The coward does it with a kiss,
  The brave man with a sword!

The Doer of Good

IT WAS night-time and He was alone.

And He saw afar-off the walls of a round city and went towards the city.

And when He came near He heard within the city the tread of the feet of joy, and the laughter of the mouth of gladness and the loud noise of many lutes. And He knocked at the gate and certain of the gate-keepers opened to Him.

And He beheld a house that was of marble and had fair pillars of marble before it. The pillars were hung with garlands, and within and without there were torches of cedar. And He entered the house.

And when He had passed through the hall of chalcedony and the hall of jasper, and reached the long hall of feasting, He saw lying on a couch of sea-purple one whose hair was crowned with red roses and whose lips were red with wine.

And He went behind him and touched him on the shoulder and said to him, "Why do you live like this?"

And the young man turned round and recognized Him, and made answer and said, "But I was a leper once, and you healed me. How else should I live?"

And He passed out of the house and went again into the street.

And after a little while He saw one whose face and raiment were painted and whose feet were shod with pearls. And behind her came, slowly as a hunter, a young man who wore a cloak of two colours. Now the face of the woman was as the fair face of an idol, and the eyes of the young man were bright with lust.

And He followed swiftly and touched the hand of the young man and said to him, "Why do you look at this woman and in such wise?"

And the young man turned round and recognized Him and said, "But I was blind once, and you gave me sight. At what else should I look?"

And He ran forward and touched the painted raiment of the woman and said to her, "Is there no other way in which to walk save the way of sin?"

And the woman turned round and recognized Him, and laughed and said, "But you forgave me my sins, and the way is a pleasant way."

And He passed out of the city.

And when He had passed out of the city He saw seated by the roadside a young man who was weeping.

And He went towards him and touched the long locks of his hair and said to him, "Why are you weeping?"

And the young man looked up and recognized Him and made answer, "But I was dead once and you raised me from the dead. What else should I do but weep?"

The Disciple

When Narcissus died the pool of his pleasure changed from a cup of sweet waters into a cup of salt tears, and the Oreads came weeping through the woodland that they might sing to the pool and give it comfort.

And when they saw that the pool had changed from a cup of sweet waters into a cup of salt tears, they loosened the green tresses of their hair and cried to the pool and said, "We do not wonder that you should mourn in this manner for Narcissus, so beautiful was he."

"But was Narcissus beautiful?" said the pool.

"Who should know better than you?" answered the Oreads. "Us did he ever pass by, but you he sought for, and would lie on your banks and look down at you, and in the mirror of your waters he would mirror his own beauty."

And the pool answered, "But I loved Narcissus because, as he lay on my banks and looked down at me, in the mirror of his eyes I saw ever my own beauty mirrored."

FROM *L'Envoi*

But I think that the best likeness to the quality of this young poet's work I ever saw was in the landscape by the Loire. We were staying once, he and I, at Amboise, that little village with its grey slate roofs and steep streets and gaunt, grim gateway, where the quiet cottages nestle like white pigeons into the sombre clefts of the great bastioned rock, and the stately Renaissance houses stand silent and apart— very desolate now, but with some memory of the old days still lingering about the delicately twisted pillars, and the carved doorways, with their grotesque animals, and laughing masks, and quaint heraldic devices, all reminding one of a people who could not think life real till they had made it fantastic. And above the village, and beyond the bend of the river, we used to go in the afternoon, and sketch from one of the big barges that bring the wine in autumn and the wood in winter down to the sea, or lie in the long grass and make plans *pour la gloire, et pour ennuyer les philistins,* or wander along the low, sedgy banks, "matching our reeds in sportive rivalry," as comrades used in the old Sicilian days; and the land was an ordinary land enough, and bare, too, when one thought of Italy, and how the oleanders were robing the hillsides by Genoa in scarlet, and the cyclamen filling with its purple every valley from Florence to Rome; for there was not much real beauty, perhaps, in it, only long, white dusty roads and straight rows of formal poplars; but now and then, some little breaking gleam of broken light would lend to the grey field and the silent barn a secret and a mystery that were hardly their own, would transfigure for one exquisite moment the peasants passing down through the vineyard, or the shepherd watching on the hill, would tip the willows with silver and touch the river into gold; and the wonder of the effect, with the strange simplicity of the material, always seemed to me to be a little like the quality of these the verses of my friend.

—Wilde, introduction to Rennell Rodd, *Rose Leaf and Apple Leaf* (Philadelphia: J.M. Stoddard & Co., 1882).

The Selfish Giant

EVERY afternoon, as they were coming from school, the children used to go and play in the Giant's garden.

It was a large lovely garden, with soft green grass. Here and there over the grass stood beautiful flowers like stars, and there were twelve peach trees that in the springtime broke out into delicate blossoms of pink and pearl, and in the autumn bore rich fruit. The birds sat on the trees and sang so sweetly that the children used to stop their games in order to listen to them. "How happy we are here!" they cried to each other.

One day the Giant came back. He had been to visit his friend the Cornish ogre, and had stayed with him for seven years. After the seven years were over he had said all that he had to say, for his conversation was limited, and he determined to return to his own castle. When he arrived he saw the children playing in the garden.

"What are you doing there?" he cried in a very gruff voice, and the children ran away.

"My own garden is my own garden," said the Giant; "anyone can understand that, and I will allow nobody to play in it but myself." So he built a high wall all around it, and put up a notice-board.

TRESPASSERS
WILL BE
PROSECUTED

He was a very selfish Giant.

The poor children had now nowhere to play. They

tried to play on the road, but the road was very dusty and full of hard stones, and they did not like it. They used to wander round the high wall when their lessons were over, and talk about the beautiful garden inside. "How happy we were there," they said to each other.

Then the Spring came, and all over the country there were little blossoms and little birds. Only in the garden of the Selfish Giant it was still winter. The birds did not care to sing in it as there were no children, and the trees forgot to blossom. Once a beautiful flower put its head out from the grass, but when it saw the notice-board it was so sorry for the children that it slipped back into the ground again, and went off to sleep. The only people who were pleased were the Snow and the Frost. "Spring has forgotten this garden," they cried, "so we will live here all the year round." The Snow covered up the grass with her great white cloak, and the Frost painted all the trees silver. Then they invited the North Wind to stay with them, and he came. He was wrapped in furs, and he roared all day about the garden, and blew the chimney-pots down. "This is a delightful spot," he said, "we must ask the Hail on a visit." So the Hail came. Every day for three hours he rattled on the roof of the castle till he broke most of the slates, and then he ran round and round the garden as fast as he could go. He was dressed in grey, and his breath was like ice.

"I cannot understand why the Spring is so late in coming," said the Selfish Giant, as he sat at the window and looked out at his cold white garden; "I hope there will be a change in the weather."

But the Spring never came, nor the Summer. The Autumn gave golden fruit to every garden, but to the Giant's garden she gave none. "He is too selfish," she said. So it was always winter there, and the North

Wind, and the Hail, and the Frost, and the Snow danced about through the trees.

One morning the Giant was lying awake in bed when he heard some lovely music. It sounded so sweet to his ears that he thought it must be the King's musicians passing by. It was really only a little linnet singing outside his window, but it was so long since he had heard a bird sing in his garden that it seemed to him to be the most beautiful music in the world. Then the Hail stopped dancing over his head, and the North Wind ceased roaring, and a delicious perfume came to him through the open casement. "I believe the Spring has come at last," said the Giant; and he jumped out of bed and looked out.

What did he see?

He saw a most wonderful sight. Through a little hole in the wall the children had crept in, and they were sitting in the branches of the trees. In every tree that he could see there was a little child. And the trees were so glad to have the children back again that they had covered themselves with blossoms, and were waving their arms gently above the children's heads. The birds were flying about and twittering with delight, and the flowers were looking up through the green grass and laughing. It was a lovely scene, only in one corner it was still winter. It was the farthest corner of the garden, and in it was standing a little boy. He was so small that he could not reach up to the branches of the tree, and he was wandering all round it, crying bitterly. The poor tree was still quite covered with frost and snow, and the North Wind was blowing and roaring above it. "Climb up! little boy," said the Tree, and it bent its branches down as low as it could; but the boy was too tiny.

And the Giant's heart melted as he looked out. "How selfish I have been!" he said; "now I know why the Spring would not come here. I will put that poor little boy on the top of the tree, and then I will knock down the wall, and my garden shall be the children's playground for ever and ever." He was really very sorry for what he had done.

So he crept downstairs and opened the front door quite softly, and went out into the garden. But when the children saw him they were so frightened that they all ran away, and the garden became winter again. Only the little boy did not run, for his eyes were so full of tears that he did not see the Giant coming. And the Giant stole up behind him and took him gently in his hand, and put him up into the tree. And the tree broke at once into blossom, and the birds came and sang on it, and the little boy stretched out his two arms and flung them round the Giant's neck, and kissed him. And the other children, when they saw that the Giant was not wicked any longer, came running back, and with them came the Spring. "It is your garden now, little children," said the Giant, and he took a great axe and knocked down the wall. And when the people were going to market at twelve o'clock they found the Giant playing with the children in the most beautiful garden they had ever seen.

All day long they played, and in the evening they came to the Giant to bid him good-bye.

"But where is your little companion?" he said; "the boy I put into the tree." The Giant loved him the best because he had kissed him.

"We don't know," answered the children; "he has gone away."

"You must tell him to be sure and come here to-morrow," said the Giant. But the children said that they did not know where he lived, and had never seen him before; and the Giant felt very sad.

Every afternoon, when school was over, the children came and played with the Giant. But the little boy whom the Giant loved was never seen again. The Giant was very kind to all the children, yet he longed for his first little friend, and often spoke of him. "How I would like to see him!" he used to say.

Years went over, and the Giant grew very old and feeble. He could not play about any more, so he sat in a huge arm-chair, and watched the children at their games, and admired his garden. "I have many beautiful flowers," he said; "but the children are the most beautiful flowers of all."

One winter morning he looked out of his window as he was dressing. He did not hate the Winter now, for he knew that it was merely the Spring asleep, and that the flowers were resting.

Suddenly he rubbed his eyes in wonder, and looked and looked. It certainly was a marvellous sight. In the farthest corner of the garden was a tree quite covered with lovely white blossoms. Its branches were all golden, and silver fruit hung down from them, and underneath it stood the little boy he had loved.

Downstairs ran the Giant in great joy, and out into the garden. He hastened across the grass, and came near to the child. And when he came quite close his face grew red with anger, and he said, "Who hath dared to wound thee?" For on the palms of the child's hands were the prints of two nails, and the prints of two nails were on the little feet.

"Who hath dared to wound thee?" cried the Giant; "tell me, that I may take my big sword and slay him."

"Nay!" answered the child; "but these are the wounds of Love."

"Who art thou?" said the Giant, and a strange awe fell on him, and he knelt before the little child.

And the child smiled on the Giant, and said to him, "You let me play once in your garden, today you shall come with me to my garden, which is Paradise."

And when the children ran in that afternoon, they found the Giant lying dead under the tree, all covered with white blossoms.

Reviews

FROM *A Bevy of Poets*

This spring the little singers are out before the little sparrows and have already begun chirruping. Here are four volumes already, and who knows how many more will be given to us before the laburnums blossom? The best-bound volume must of course have precedence. It is called *Echoes of Memory* by Atherton Furlong, and is cased in creamy vellum and tied with ribbons of yellow silk. Mr. Furlong's charm is the unsullied sweetness of his simplicity. Indeed, we can strongly recommend to the School-Board the *Lines on the Old Town Pump* as eminently suitable for recitation by children. Such a verse, for instance, as:

> I hear the little children say
> (For the tale will never die)
> How the old pump flowed both night and day
> When the brooks and the wells ran dry,

has all the ring of Macaulay in it, and is a form of poetry which cannot possibly harm anybody, even if translated into French. Any inaccurate ideas of the laws of nature which the children might get from the passage in question could easily be corrected afterwards by a lecture on Hydrostatics. The poem, however, which gives us most pleasure is the one called *The Dear Old Knocker on the Door*. It is appropriately illustrated by

Mr. Tristram Ellis. We quote the concluding verses
of the first and last stanzas:

> Blithe voices then so dear
>   Send up their shouts once more,
> Then sounds again on mem'ry's ear
>   The dear old knocker on the door.
>
> .   .   .
>
> When mem'ry turns the key
> Where time has placed my score,
> Encased 'mid treasured thoughts must be
> The dear old knocker on the door.

The cynic may mock at the subject of these verses,
but we do not. Why not an ode on a knocker? Does
not Victor Hugo's tragedy of Lucrèce Borgia turn on
the defacement of a doorplate? Mr. Furlong must not
be discouraged. Perhaps he will write poetry some day.
If he does we would earnestly appeal to him to give
up calling a cock "proud chanticleer". . . .

—Pall Mall Gazette, March 27, 1885.

FROM Pleasing and Prattling

On the whole, there is a great deal to be said for
our ordinary English novelists. They have all some story
to tell, and most of them tell it in an interesting manner.
Where they fail is in concentration of style. Their
characters are far too eloquent and talk themselves to
tatters. What we want is a little more reality and a
little less rhetoric. We are most grateful to them that
they have not as yet accepted any frigid formula, nor
stereotyped themselves into a school, but we wish that
they would talk less and think more. They lead us
through a barren desert of verbiage to a mirage that
they call life; we wander aimlessly through a very

wilderness of words in search of one touch of nature. However, one should not be too severe on English novels: they are the only relaxation of the intellectually unemployed.

—*Ibid.*, August 4, 1886.

FROM A *"Jolly"* Art Critic

There is a healthy bank-holiday atmosphere about this book which is extremely pleasant. Mr. Quilter is entirely free from affectation of any kind. He rollicks through art with the recklessness of the tourist and describes its beauties with the enthusiasm of the auctioneer. To many, no doubt, he will seem to be somewhat blatant and bumptious, but we prefer to regard him as being simply British. Mr. Quilter is the apostle of the middle classes, and we are glad to welcome his gospel. . . .

As for his *Sententiae*, they differ very widely in character and subject. Some of them are ethical, such as "Humility may be carried too far"; some literary, as "For one Froude there are a thousand Mrs. Markhams"; and some scientific, as "Objects which are near display more detail than those which are further off." Some, again, breathe a fine spirit of optimism, as "Picturesqueness is the birthright of the bargee"; others are jubilant, as "Paint firm and be jolly"; and many are purely autobiographical, such as No. 97, "Few of us understand what it is that we mean by Art."

—*Ibid.*, November 18, 1886.

FROM A Cheap Edition of a Great Man

No doubt there are many people who will be deeply
interested to know that Rossetti was once chased round
the garden by an infuriated zebu he was trying to exhibit to Mr. Whistler, or that he had a great affection
for a dog called "Dizzy," or that "sloshy" was one of
his favourite words of contempt, or that Mr. Gosse
thought him very like Chaucer in appearance or that
he had "an absolute disqualification" for whist-playing,
or that he was very fond of quoting the *Bab Ballads,* or
that he once said that if he could live by poetry he
would see painting d——d! For our part, however, we
cannot help expressing our regret that such a shallow
and superficial biography as this should ever have
been published. It is but a sorry task to rip the twisted
ravel from the worn garment of life and to turn the
grout in a drained cup. Better, after all, that we knew
a painter only through his vision and a poet through
his song, than that the image of a great man should be
marred and made mean for us by the clumsy geniality
of good intentions.

—*Ibid.,* April 18, 1887.

FROM The Poets' Corner, III

Such a pseudonym for a poet as "Glenessa" reminds
us of the good old days of the Della Cruscans, but it
would not be fair to attribute Glenessa's poetry to any
known school of literature, either past or present. What-

ever qualities it possesses are entirely its own. Glenessa's most ambitious work, and the one that gives the title to his book, is a poetic drama about the Garden of Eden. The subject is undoubtedly interesting, but the execution can hardly be said to be quite worthy of it. Devils, on account of their inherent wickedness, may be excused for singing—

> Then we'll rally—rally—rally—
> Yes, we'll rally—rally O!

but such scenes as—

Enter ADAM.

ADAM (*excitedly*): Eve, where art thou?
EVE (*surprised*):   Oh!
ADAM (*in astonishment*): Eve! My God, she's there
   Beside that fatal tree;
or—

Enter ADAM and EVE.

EVE (*in astonishment*): Well, is not this surprising?
ADAM (*distractedly*): It is—

seem to belong rather to the sphere of comedy than to that of serious verse. Poor Glenessa! the gods have not made him poetical, and we hope he will abandon his wooing of the muse. He is fitted, not for better, but for other things.

—*Ibid.*, May 30, 1887.

FROM *The Poets' Corner*, V

The Chronicle of Mites is a mock-heroic poem about the inhabitants of a decaying cheese who speculate about the origin of their species and hold learned discussions upon the meaning of evolution and the Gospel according to Darwin. This cheese-epic is a rather unsavoury production and the style is at times so monstrous and so realistic that the author should be called the Gorgon-Zola of literature.

—*Ibid.*, February 15, 1888.

Twelve Formerly Unpublished Letters

To HIS MOTHER

Wednesday. [Spring, 1875.]
Milan. Albergo della Francia.

So busy travelling and sight seeing for last five days that I have had no time to write.

Diary. Left Florence with much regret on Saturday night—passed through the Appenines beautiful Alpine scenery—train runs on side of mountains—half way up—above us pine forests and crags—below us the valley—villages and swollen rivers—supper at Bologna—about 5.30 in the morning came near Venice—immediately on leaving the mts. a broad flat table land—(there are no hills in Italy—mountains or flat plain) cultivated like a rich garden—within four miles of Venice a complete change—a bleak bog—exactly like bog of Allen only flatter—crossed a big lagune on a bridge and arrived at Venice 7.30—seized on immediately by gondoliers and embarked with our luggage into a *black* hearselike barge—such as King Arthur was taken away in after the fatal battle—finally through long narrow canals we arrived at our Hotel, which was

finally through long narrow ways &
we arrived at our Hotel.
which was in the great Piazza
S. Marco. the only place in
Venice. except the Realto anyone
walks in. plan of it

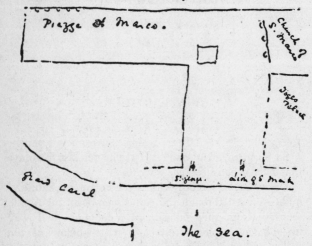

The Church of S. Marco is most
gorgeous — a splendid Byzantine
church: covered with gilding &
mosaics, moods and art.
The floor of inlaid marbles, of colours
and design indescribable. & through
the sinking of the Piles undulates
in big sweeping waves.

in the great Piazza St Marco—the only place in Venice except the Rialto anyone walks in—plan of it

The Church of S. Marco is most gorgeous—a splendid Byzantine church—covered with gilding and mosaics, inside and out. The floor of inlaid marbles, of colour and design indescribable, and through the sinking of the piles undulates in big sweeping waves—splendid gates of bronze—everything glorious—next to it the Doges Palace—which is beyond praise—inside the giant council chambers—the walls painted with frescoes by Titian of the great battles of the Venetians—the ceiling crossed by gilded beams and rich in gilded carving—rooms fit for the noble looking grave senators whose pictures are on the walls by Titian and Tintoretto.

Council Room of the celebrated "Three"—black marble and gold—two dismal passages lead from it across the "Ponte dei Sospiri"—in size and colour and dignity the rooms are beyond description—and the view from the window across the sea wonderful—beneath all this greatness are the most dismal dungeons and torture rooms—most terrible.

Here we spent the morning—afterwards took a gondola and visited some of the islands off Venice—on one an Armenian monastery where Byron used to live—went to another S. [at?] Lido a favourite place on Sunday and had oysters and shrimps—returned home in the flood of a great sunset. Venice is a city just risen from the sea—a long line of crowded churches and palaces—everywhere white or gilded domes and tall campanili—no *opening* in the whole city except at the Piazza S. Marco—a great pink sunset with a long line of purple thunderclouds behind the city. After dinner went to the Theatre and saw a good circus. Luckily a wonderful moon—we landed from our gondola coming from the Theatre at the Lion of St. Mark. The scene was so romantic that [it?] seemed to be an artistic scene from an opera. We sat on the base of the Pillar —on one side of us the Doges Palace on the other the Kings Palace—behind us the campanile—the water steps crowded with black gondolas—and a great flood of light coming right up to us across the water—every moment a black silent gondola would glide across this great stream of light and be lost in the darkness.

Milan. Thursday.

I believe you left me last looking at the moon from the Piazza St. Marco. With difficulty we tore ourselves away to the Hotel— Next morning we went up the grand canal in a gondola. Great palaces on each side with huge steps leading down to the water—and all round big posts to moor the gondolas to, coloured with the arms of the family—wonderful colour everywhere —windows hung with striped yellow awnings—domes and churches of white marble, campanili of red brick —great gondolas filled with fruit and vegetables going to the Rialto where the market is. Stopped to see the Picture gallery which as usual was in a suppressed monastery—Titian and Tintoretto in great force—Titian's Assumption certainly the best picture in Italy— went to a lot of Churches all however in extravagant "baroque" style, very rich in worked metal and polished marble and mosaic but as a rule inartistic. In the picture gallery beside the Titians there are two great pictures—one a beautiful Madonna by Bellini, the other a picture of Dives and Lazarus of Bonifazio containing the only *lovely* womans face I have seen in Italy.

Spent the day in gondolas and markets—and the evening a great band and promenade of all the swells of Venice in the Piazza S. Marco. Every women nearly, over thirty powdered the front of their hair—most wore veils but I see that bonnets are now made with very high crowns and two wreaths, one under the diadem and one round the crown. After marriage the Italian women degenerate awfully—but the boys and girls are beautiful—amongst married women the general type are "Titiens" and an ugly sallow likeness of "Isabelli Bettini" (*sic*).

In the morning breakfasted on board the **P. & O.** steamer Baroda. I was asked by the Doctor a young Dublin fellow called Fraser. Left for Padua at 12 o'c. Believe me Venice in beauty of architecture and colour is beyond description. It is the meeting place of the Byzantine and Italian Art—a city belonging to the *East* as much as to the West.

Arrived at Padua at 2 o'c. In the middle of a rich vineyard stands the Baptistery, the great work of Giotto—the walls covered entirely with frescoes by him—one wall the life of Mary the other the life of Christ—the ceiling blue with gold stars and medallion pictures—the W. wall a great picture of Heaven and Hell siggested to him by Dante who weary of trudging up the steep *stairs*, as he says, of the *Scali*gieri when in exile at Verona came to stay at Padua with Giotto in a house still to be seen there. Of the beauty and purity of sentiment, the clear transparent colour, bright as the day it was painted on, and the harmony of the whole building I am unable to tell you. He is the first of all painters—we stayed over an hour at the Baptistery filled with wonder and reverence and above all love for the scenes he has painted.

Padua is a quaint town with good colonnades along each street—a university like a barracks—one charming Church (S. Anastasia) and a lot of bad ones and the best Restaurant in Italy—where we dined. Arrived at

Milan in a shower of rain—went in the evening to the
theatre and saw a good Ballet.

This morning the Cathedral—outside most elaborate
in pinnacles and statues awfully out of proportion with
rest of the building. Inside most impressive through its
huge size and giant pillars supporting the roof—some
good old stained glass and a lot of hideous modern
windows. These moderns don't see that the use of a
window in a church is to show a beautiful massing together and blending of colour—a good old window has
the rich pattern of a Turkey carpet—the figures are
quite subordinate and only serve to show the sentiment of the designer—the modern frescoe style of
window has suâ naturâ to compete with painting and
of course looks monstrous and theatrical.

The Cathedral is an awful failure—outside the design
is monstrous and inartistic—the over elaborated details
stuck high up where no one can see them—everything
is vile in it. It is however imposing and gigantic as a
failure—through its great size and elaborate execution.

From Padua I forgot to tell you we went to Verona
at 6 o'c.—and in the old Roman Amphitheatre (as perfect inside as it was in the old Roman times) saw the
play of Hamlet performed—and certainly indifferently
—but you can imagine how romantic it was to sit in
the old Amphitheatre on a lovely moonlight night. In
the morning went to see the tombs of the Scaligieri—
good examples of rich florid Gothic work and iron work
—a good market place filled with the most gigantic
umbrellas I ever saw—like young palm trees—under
which sat the fruit sellers. Of our arrival in Milan I
have told you—yesterday (Thursday) went first to
the Ambrosian Library where we saw some great
M.S.S. and two very good Palimpsests—and a Bible
with Irish glosses of 6th or 7th cent. which has been

collated by Todd and Whiteley Stokes and others—
a good collection of pictures besides, particularly a set
of drawings and sketches in chalk by Raffaelle—much
more interesting I think than his pictures—good Hol-
beins and Albrecht Durers—

Then to the picture gallery—some good Correggios
and Peruginos—the gem of the whole collection a
lovely Madonna of Bernardino standing among a lot
of trellised roses that Morris and Rossetti would love—
another of his we saw in the Library with background
of lilies.

Milan is a second Paris—wonderful arcades and
galleries—all the town white stone and gilding. Dined
excellently at the Biffi Restaurant and had some good
wine of Asti—like good cider and sweet champagne. In
the evening went to see a New Opera "Dolores" by a
young maestro called Auberi (?)—a good imitation
of Bellini in some parts, some pretty rondos—but its
general character was inharmonious shouting. However
the frantic enthusiasm of the People knew no bounds—
every five minutes a terrible furore and yelling of
Bravos from every part of the house—followed by a
frantic rush of all the actors for the composer—who was
posted at the side scenes ready to rush out at the
slightest symptom of approval—A weak looking creature who placed his grimy hand on a shady looking
shirt to show his emotion, fell on the Prima Donna's
neck in ecstasy and blew kisses to us all. He came out
no less than nineteen times—and finally three crowns
were brought out, one of which a green laurel one with
green ribbons was clapped on his head, and as his head
was very narrow it rested partly on a very large angular
nose and partly on his grimy shirt collar. Such an absurd scene as the whole thing was I never saw. The
Opera except in two places is devoid of merit. The

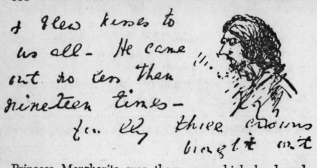

& flew kisses to us all — He came out so ten then nineteen times — few [illegible] three crowns bought mt

Princess Margharita was there—very high bred and pale.

I write this at Arona on the Lago Maggiore—a beautiful spot—Mahaffy and young Goulding I left at Milan and they will go on to Genoa. As I had no money I was obliged to leave them and feel very lonely. We have had a delightful tour. Tonight at 12 o'c. the diligence starts—we go over the Simplon Pass till near Lausanne. 18 hours en diligence—tomorrow night (Saturday) I get to Lausanne.

Yours
Oscar

[Slip enclosed in above letter.]

If there is no money at Paris for me I will not know what to do—but I feel sure there will be the genial £5.

yours ever
Oscar O'F Wilde

To MR. A.S. BENSON

[No place. No date. 1876-78?]

My dear Benson,

I don't at all agree with you about the decorative value of Morris' wall papers. They seem to me often deficient in real beauty of colour: this may be due as you say to his workmen, but Art admits of no excuses of that kind: then as regards the design, he is far more successful with those designs which are meant for textures which hang in folds, than for those which have to be seen flat on a stretched material: a fact which may be due to the origin of many of his patterns, but which is a fact still. Setting aside however a point on which we were sure for obvious reasons to disagree, I am surprised to find we are at such variance on the question of the value of pure colour on the walls of a room. No one I think would paint a room in distemper entirely, for the ceiling and the upper part of the wall distemper is excellent, for the lower part (as for the woodwork) one uses oil paint which has the great advantage of being cleanable—if there is such a word—nor are the colours one gets in distemper and oils necessarily spoiled by the introduction of silk embroidery or oil pictures.

These things depend entirely on the scheme of colour one selects for the room, and on one's own knowledge of colour harmonies. I have for instance a dining room done in different shades of white, with white curtains embroidered in yellow silk, the effect is absolutely delightful, and the room is beautiful. I have seen far more rooms spoiled by wall papers than by anything else, when everything is covered with a design the room is restless and the eye disturbed. A good picture is always improved by being hung on a coloured surface that suits it or by being placed in surroundings which are harmonious to it, but the delicacy of line in an etching for instance is often spoiled by the broad, if not coarse, pattern on a block printed wall paper—my eye requires in a room a resting place of pure colour, and I prefer to keep design for more delicate materials than papers, for embroidery for instance—paper in itself is not a lovely material and the only papers which I ever use now are the Japanese gold ones, they are exceedingly decorative, and no English paper can compete with them either for beauty or for practical wear, with these and with colour in oil and distemper a lovely house can be made. Some day if you do us the pleasure of calling I will show you a little room with blue ceiling and frieze (distemper) yellow (oil) walls, and white woodwork and fittings, which is joyous and exquisite, the only piece of design being the Morris blue and white curtains, and a white and yellow silk coverlet. I hope, and in my lectures always try and bring it about, that people will study the value of pure colour more than they do, the ugly ceilings of modern houses are often due to the excessive use of wall papers, and I do not think Morris himself sets the exaggerated value on wall papers which you do, anybody with a real artistic sense must see the value and repose of pure colour, and even taking the matter in a practical light wall papers collect dirt and dust to a great extent and cannot be cleaned. They are economical and often pretty and charming but they are not the final word of art in decoration by any means. I hope they will be used much less frequently than they are, and that Morris will devote his time, as I think he is doing, to textile fabrics, their dyes and their designs, and not so much to a form of wall decoration which has its value of course, but whose value has been over estimated, and whose use is often misunderstood. I saw Frank* at Oxford, there was a charming performance and lovely costumes. He seemed very pleased at it and so was I.

> Believe, very truly yours,
> Oscar Wilde

How can you see Socialism in the Earthly Paradise? If it is there it is an accident not a quality—there is a great difference.

To MRS. ALFRED HUNT**

St. Stephens Club, Westminster [May 20, 1880.]

Dear Mrs Hunt,

I shall be *very glad* to come on Sunday evening— How *could* you be too shy to ask me on Tuesday? I should have been delighted to stay—I always enjoy my evenings with you all so much: but you really must not write me such charming letters or I shall be coming a great deal too often—I count it a very great privilege indeed to know anyone whose art I have always loved and admired so much as Mr Hunt (Though he *has* this terrible passion for barricades and revolutions!) and it is very nice of you to think of me as a friend— indeed I shall like to be one.

> Believe me
> Very sincerely Yrs
> Oscar Wilde

---

* [Frank Benson, actor and producer. Ed.]
** [She was the wife of "Watercolour" Hunt, and mother of Violet Hunt, novelist and gossip. Ed.]

To MRS. ALFRED HUNT

Tite Street, Chelsea, 25th Aug. [1880.]

Dear Mrs Hunt—

It was so good of you to take the trouble of sending me such a long account from [of your?] little village— I have been hoping to go every week—but have had so many engagements that it has been out of my power —which, believe me, is no small disappointment—I should like so much to be with you all—and now I am trying to settle a new House—where Mr Miles and I are going to live—the address is *horrid* but the House very pretty—it is much nearer you than my old House, so I hope we shall often, if you let me, have "dishes of tea" at one another [another's?] houses—I have broken a promise shamefully to Miss Violet about a poem I promised to send her—my only excuse is that now-a-days the selection of colours and furniture has quite taken the place of the cares of conscience of the middle ages, and usually involve quite as much remorse— however I send her one I have just published—I hope she will see some beauty in it—and that your wonderful husbands [husband's?] wonderful radicalism will be appeased by my first attempt at political prophecy (which occurs in the last verse—) if she will send me a little line to say what she thinks of it it will give me such pleasure—I hope she has been writing herself —after all, the Muses are as often to be met with in our English fields as they ever were by Castaly, or Helicon—though I have always in my heart thought that the simultaneous appears of *nine* (*unmarried*) sisters at one time must have been a little embarassing.

Please remember me *most* kindly to yr husband, and all yours, and Believe

Yrs truly,
Oscar Wilde

[Printed copy of "Ave Imperatrix" enclosed. Ed.]

To MRS. ALFRED HUNT

Keats House, Tite St. [*February 17, 1881.*]

Dear Mrs Hunt,

Thank you so much for your kind invitation but I am in the "lions' den" on both days: Sunday I dine to meet Mr Lowell, a poet, statesman, and—an American in one! a sort of three headed Cerberus of civilization who barks when he is baited and is often mistaken for a lion, at a distance.—

And on Wednesday the 2nd. I have a long standing engagement to dine with Sir Charles Dilke—a lion who has clipped his radical claws and only roars through the medium of a Quarterly Review now—a harmless way of roaring. So I cannot come to you— which *makes me very sad*: I ought, like Sir Boyle Roche's bird, to be able to be in two places at once— but in that case I shd. *always* be at Tor Villas—I hope to see you all soon again.

Oscar Wilde

To MISS VIOLET HUNT

Keats House, Tite Street, Chelsea. [*July 22, 1881.*]

Dear Miss Violet Hunt,

I thank you very much for your kind letter, and am infintely delighted that you have thought my poems beautiful—in an age like this, when Slander, and Ridicule, and Envy walk quite unashamed among us, and when any attempt to produce serious beautiful work is greeted with a very Tornado of lies and evil-speaking, it is a wonderful joy, a wonderful spur for ambition and work, to receive any such encouragement and appreciation as your letter brought me, and I thank you for it again and again—,

The poem I like best is the "Burden of Styx" [Itys?] and next to that the Garden of Eros—they are the most lyrical—and I would sooner have any power or quality of "Song" writing than be the greatest sonnet writer since Petrarch.

I go to the Thanes this afternoon with Mr Burne Jones but will hope to see you when I return—

You have made me very happy.

Believe me

Ever sincerely yours

Oscar Wilde

To COLONEL MORSE

S. Louis. [Spring, 1882.]

Dear Colonel Morse,

Will you kindly go to a good costumier (theatrical) for me and get them to make, (you will not mention my name) two coats—to wear at matinees and perhaps in evening—they shd. be beautiful—tight velvet doublets with large flowered sleeves—and little ruffs —[Drawing] of cambric coming up under collar—I send you design and measurements—they should be ready at *Chicago* on Saty for matinée there—at any rate the black one—any good costumier wd. know what I want—sort of Francis Ist dress: only knee breeches instead of long hose also get me two pair grey silk stockings to suit grey mouse-coloured velvet, the sleeves are to be flowered—if not velvet then plush— stamped with large pattern—they will excite a great sensation—I leave the matter to you—they were dreadfully disappointed at Cincinnati at my not wearing knee breeches.

Yrs truly

Oscar Wilde

[Written in pencil. Ed.]

To NORMAN [Forbes-Robertson?]

[No address. No date. 1885-86.]

Dear Norman.

Thanks for your congratulations: yes. come to-morrow, the baby is wonderful—it has a bridge to its nose! which the nurse says is a proof of genius! It also has a superb voice—which it freely exercises: its style is essentially Wagnerian. Constance is doing capitally and is in excellent spirits. I was delighted to get yr. telegram—you must get married *at once!*

Yrs

Oscar

To MRS. ALFRED HUNT

16 Tite Street, Chelsea [*August 29, 1887.*]

Dear Mrs Hunt,

I have been asked by Cassell to reconstruct the Ladies World, and am anxious to make it the recognised organ through which women of culture and position will express their views, and to which they will contribute.

I hope you will allow me to add your name to my list, and that you will send me either a short story, or a short article.

Would you do me an article on "Some Old Fashion Books"—that could be illustrated. I dont know if there are any Fashion Books earlier than this century, or the end of the last—but I know you have written on such things.

I do not know if Miss Violet cares for prose-writing but I hope she will send me a short poem at any rate. A sonnet on Whitby, with an illustration of one of Mr Hunt's pictures would be delightful.

Believe

Ever Yrs

Oscar Wilde.

To DAVID NUTT

16 Tite Street, Chelsea, S.W. [1888.]

Dear Mr Nutt,

I will try and arrange with Miss Terry—it certainly would be charming to hear her read the Happy Prince.

I find I have forgotten the Century Guild Hobby Horse. Will you kindly send them a copy for review—at 28 Southampton Street, Strand, W.C. The Irish Times I suppose has got its copy? Also wd. it not be well to have a *card* for the booksellers to hang up in their shops. It may show Crane's Frontispiece as well as the title etc. of the book. And is not time for a few advertisements. "Punch" and the "World" are capital papers to advertise in—*once*. Mr Pater has written me a wonderful letter about my prose, so I am in high spirits.

Yours faithfully
Oscar Wilde

To OSCAR BROWNING

16 Tite Street, Chelsea, S.W. [Late 1880's?]

My dear O.B.

I am so disappointed, but I must put off my visit to Cambridge—one of our little boys is not at all well, and my wife who is very nervous has begged me not to leave town. You are so fond of children that I am sure you will understand how one feels about things of this kind, and I think it would be rather horrid of me to go away—I hope you will let me know when you come to town, I want you and Bobbie at dinner.

Ever yrs
Oscar

To MRS. BERNARD-BEERE

16 Tite St., S.W. [Undated.]

My dear Bernie,

Of course: we must fly to Australia: I could not let you go alone.

I have written to Cartwright—a bald genius who is dear Dot's agent—to ask him if it can be arranged. They have also "Mrs Tanqueray," in which I long to see you.

I have also asked Cartwright if Dot is coming over— or I suppose I should say coming up from Australia— I believe that absurdly shaped country lies right underneath the floor of one's coal cellar.

Why rusticate in this reckless way? You are wanted in town—"Once upon a Time" was dreadful—since the appearance of Tree in pyjamas—there has been the greatest sympathy for Mrs Tree. It throws a lurid light on the difficulties of their married life.

Who is the fortunate mortal who has the honour of entertaining you? I dislike him more than I can tell you.

Ever yours
Oscar

Other Letters

To MRS. BERNARD-BEERE

Kansas City, Missouri [*April* 17, 1882.]

My dear Bernie,

I have lectured to the Mormons—the Opera House at Salt Lake City is an enormous affair about the size of Covent Garden, and holds with ease 14 families. They sit like this

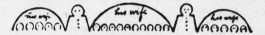

and are very, very ugly. The President, a nice old man, sat with 5 wives in the stage box. I visited him in the afternoon and saw a charming daughter of his.

I have also lectured at Leadville, the great mining city in the Rocky Mountains. We took a whole day to get up to it on a narrow gauge railway 14,000 feet in height. My audience was entirely miners; their make-up excellent; red shirts and blond beards, the whole of the first three rows being filled by McKee Rankins of every colour and dimension. I spoke to them of the early Florentines, and they slept as though no crime had ever stained the ravines of their mountain home. I described to them the picture of Botticelli and the name, which

645

seemed to them like a new drink, roused them from their dreams, but when I told them in my boyish eloquence of the "secret of Botticelli" the strong men wept like children. Their sympathy touched me and I approached modern art and had almost won them over to a real reverence for what is beautiful when unluckily I described one of Jimmy Whistler's "nocturnes in blue and gold." Then they leaped to their feet and in their grand simple way swore that such things should not be. Some of the younger ones pulled their revolvers out and left hurriedly to see if Jimmy was "prowling about the saloons" or "wrastling a hash" at any eating shop. Had he been there I fear he would have been killed, their feeling was so bitter. Their enthusiasm satisfied me and I ended my lecture there. Then I found the Governor of the State waiting in a bullock *waggon* to bring me down the great silver mine of the world, the "Matchless." So off we drove, the miners carrying torches before us till we came to the shaft and were shot down in buckets (I of course true to my principle being graceful even in a bucket) and down in the great gallery of the mine, the walls and ceilings glittering metal ore, was spread a banquet for us.

The amazement of the miners when they saw that art and appetite could go hand in hand knew no bounds; when I lit a long cigar they cheered till the silver fell in dust from the roof on our plates; and when I quaffed a cocktail without flinching, they unanimously pronounced me in their grand simple way "a bully boy with no glass eye,"—artless and spontaneous praise which touched me more than the pompous panygyrics of literary critics ever did or could. Then I had to open a new vein, or lode, which with a silver drill I brilliantly performed, amidst unanimous applause. The silver drill was presented to me and the lode named "The Oscar." I had hoped that in their simple, grand way they would have offered me shares in "The Oscar," but in their artless untutored fashion they did not. Only the silver drill remains as a memory of my night at Leadville.

I have had a delightful time all through California and Colorado and am now returning home—twice as affected as ever, my dear Bernie. Please remember me to dear Dot, to Regie and all our mutual friends including Monty Morris, who won't write to me or even criticise me.

Good bye, Your sincere friend

—Martin Birnbaum, *Oscar Wilde, Fragments and Memories* (London: Elkin Mathews, 1920).

To LORD ALFRED DOUGLAS

[Torquay, 189?]

My Own Boy,

Your sonnet is quite lovely, and it is a marvel that those rose-red lips of yours should have been made no less for music of song than for madness of kisses. Your slim gilt soul walks between passion and poetry. I know Hyacinthus, whom Apollo loved so madly, was you, in Greek days.

Why are you alone in London, and when do you go to Salisbury? Do go there to cool your hands in the grey twilight of Gothic things, and come here whenever you like. It is a lovely place—it only lacks you; but go to Salisbury first.

Always, with undying love,

—Read in Court as evidence. This version taken from: Boris Brasol, *Oscar Wilde* (London: Williams and Norgate, 1938).

To WARDER MARTIN

[Reading Gaol, 1896-97.]

Please find out for me the name of A.2.II. Also, the names of the children who are in for the rabbits, and the amount of the fine.

Can I pay this and get them out? If so I will get them out to-morrow. Please, dear friend, do this for me. I must get them out.

Think what a thing for me it would be to be able to help three little children. I would be delighted beyond words: if I can do this by paying the fine tell the children that they are to be released tomorrow by a friend, and ask them to be happy and not to tell anyone.

—Frank Harris, *Oscar Wilde, His Life and Confessions* (New York, 1918, published by the author).

To ROBERT ROSS

Hotel de la Plage, Berneval-sur-Mer
[May 28, 1897.]

My dear Robbie,

This is my first day alone, and of course a very unhappy one. I begin to realise my terrible position of isolation, and I have been rebellious and bitter of heart all day. Is it not sad? I thought I was accepting everything so well and so simply, and I have had moods of rage passing over my nature, like gusts of bitter wind or storm spoiling the sweet corn or blasting the young shoots.

I found a little chapel, full of the most fantastic saints

—so ugly and Gothic and painted quite gaudily—
some of them with smiles curved to a *rictus* almost, like
primitive things—that they all seemed to me to be
idols. I laughed with amusement when I saw them.
Fortunately there was a lovely crucifix in a side chapel
—not a Jansenist one, but with wide-stretched arms
of gold. I was pleased at that, and wandered then
by the cliffs where I fell asleep on the warm coarse
brown sea-grass. I had hardly any sleep last night.
[Douglas's] letter was in the room, and foolishly I had
read it again and left it by my bedside. My dream was
that my mother was speaking to me with some stern-
ness, and that she was in trouble. I quite see that whenever I am in danger she will in some way warn me. . . .

For yourself, dear Robbie, I am haunted by the idea
that many of those who love you will think and do
think it selfish of me to allow you and wish you to be
with me from time to time. But still they might see
the difference between your going about with me in
my days of gilded infamy—my Neronian hours—rich,
profligate, cynical, materialistic—and your coming to
comfort me, a lonely, dishonoured man, in disgrace
and obscurity and poverty. How lacking in imagination
they are! If I were rich again and sought to repeat my
former life I don't think you would care very much
to be with me—I think you would regret what I was
doing: but now, dear Robbie, you come with the heart
of Christ; and you help me intellectually as no one else
can or ever could do—you are helping me to save my
soul alive—not in the theological sense, but in the
plain meaning of the words: for my soul was really
dead in the slough of coarse pleasures: my life was
unworthy of an artist: you can heal me and help me—
no other friend have I now in this beautiful world. I
want no other. Yet I am distressed to think that I shall

be looked on as careless of your own welfare and indifferent to your own good. You are made to help me. I weep with sorrow when I think how much I need help, but I weep with joy when I think I have you to give it to me.

I do hope to do some work in these six weeks, that when you come I shall be able to read you something. I know you love me, but I want to have your respect, your sincere admiration, or rather, for that is a word of ill omen, your sincere appreciation of my effort to recreate my artistic life. But if I have to think that I am harming you, all pleasure in your society will be tainted for me. With you, at any rate, I want to be free of any sense of guilt—the sense of spoiling another's life. Dear Robbie, I couldn't spoil your life by accepting the sweet companionship you offer me from time to time. It is not for nothing that I named you in prison St Robert of Phillimore. Love can canonise people. The saints are those who have been the most loved.

I made only one mistake in prison in things that I wrote of you or to you in my book—my poem should have run, "When I came out of prison *you* met me with garments, with spices, with wise counsel. You met me with Love." Not others did it, but you. I really laugh when I think how true in detail the lines are.

8.30. I have just received your telegram. A man bearded, no doubt, for purposes of disguise, dashed up on a bicycle, brandishing a blue telegram. I knew it was from you. Well, I am really pleased, and look forward to the paper. I do think it will help. I now think I shall write my prison article for the *Chronicle*. It is interested in prison-reform, and the thing would not look like an advertisement. Let me have your opinion.— I intend to write to Massingham. Reading between the lines of your telegram I seem to discern that you are pleased. The telegram was much needed. They had offered me serpent for dinner! A serpent cut up, in an umber-green sauce! I explained that I was not a *mangeur de serpents* and have converted the *patron*. No serpent is now to be served to any guest. He grew quite hot over it. What a good thing it is that I am an experienced Ichthyologist!

I am very tired—and the rain is coming down. You will be glad to hear that I have not been planting *cacao* in plantain swamps, and that "Lloyd" is not sitting on the Verandah, nor is "Fanny" looking after the "labour-boys," and that of "Belle" I know nothing. So now dear Colvin—(what an awful pen), I mean dear Robbie, good night:

with all love and affection
Yours

—*After Reading, Letters of Oscar Wilde to Robert Ross* (London: C.W. Beaumont, 1921).

To WILLIAM ROTHENSTEIN

From M. Sebastian Melmoth
Hotel de la Plage.
Berneval-sur-Mer, Dieppe.
Wednesday [June 9, 1897.]

My dear good Friend,

I cannot tell you how pleased I was to get your kind and affectionate letter yesterday, and I look forward with real delight to the prospect of seeing you, though it be only for a day. I am going to Dieppe to breakfast with the Stannards, who have been most kind to me, and I will send you a telegram from there. I so hope you can come tomorrow by the daily boat, so that you and your friend can dine and sleep here. There is no one in this little inn but myself, but it is most comfortable, and the chef, there is a real chef—is an artist of great distinction; he walks in the evening by the sea to get ideas for the next day. Is it not sweet of him? I have taken a chalet for the whole season for £32, so I shall be able I hope to work again, and write plays or something. I know, dear Will, you will be pleased to know that I have not come out of prison an embittered or disappointed man. On the contrary. In many ways I have gained much. I am not really ashamed of having been in prison: I often was in more shameful places: but I *am* really ashamed of having led a life unworthy of an artist. I don't say that Messalina is a better companion than Sporus, or that the one is all right and the other all wrong: I know simply that a life of definite and studied materialism, and philosophy of appetite and cynicism, and a cult of sensual and senseless ease, are bad things for an artist: they narrow the imagination, and dull the more delicate sensibilities. I was all wrong, my dear boy, in my life. I was not getting the best out of me. *Now*, I think that with good health, and the friendship of a few good, simple nice fellows like yourself, and a quiet mode of living, with isolation for thought, and freedom from the endless hunger for pleasures that wreck the body and imprison the soul,—well, I think I may do things yet, that you all may like. Of course I have lost much, but still, my dear Will, when I reckon up all that is *left* to me, the sun and the sea of this beautiful world; its dawns dim with gold and its nights hung with silver; many books, and all flowers, and a few good friends; and a brain and body to which health and power are not denied—really I am *rich* when I count up what I still have: and as for money, my money did me horrible harm. It wrecked me. I hope just to have enough to enable me to live simply and write well. So remember that you will find me in many respects very happy—and of course by your sweetness in coming to see me, you will bring me happiness along with you.

As for the silent songs on stone, I am charmed at the prospect of having society of yours. It is awfully good of you to think of it. I have had many sweet presents, but none I shall value more than yours.

You ask me if you can bring me anything from London. Well, the salt soft air kills my cigarettes, and I have no box in which to keep them. If you are in a millionaire condition and could bring me a box for keeping cigarettes in, it would be a great boon. In Dieppe there is nothing between a trunk and a *bonbonnière*. I do hope to see you tomorrow. (Thursday) for dinner and sleep. If not, well Friday morning. I am up now at 8 oc. regularly!

I hope you never forget that *but for me* you would not be *Will* Rothenstein: *Artist*. You would be simply *William* Rothenstein, *R.A.* It is one of the most important facts in the history of art.

I look forward greatly to seeing Strangman. His translating *Lady Windermere* is delightful.

Your sincere and grateful friend,

—*Sixteen Letters From Oscar Wilde*, edited by John Rothenstein (New York: Coward-McCann, Inc., 1930; London: Faber & Faber, 1930).

Anecdotes and Sayings

FROM *Letter to Joaquin Miller*

Who are these scribes who, passing with purposeless alacrity from the *Police News* to the Parthenon, and from crime to criticism, sway with such serene incapacity the office which they so lately swept?

How to Make Enemies

On one occasion . . . he gravely offended a couple of conscientious and artistic actors who were sustaining two of the roles in *The Three Musketeers* by comprehensively summing up the performance as "Athos, Pathos, and Bathos."

—Leonard Cresswell Ingleby, *Oscar Wilde; Some Reminiscences* (London: T. Werner Laurie, Ltd., n.d.).

The Agriculturists

(A journalist named Cottsford Dick used one of Wilde's epigrams in his column. When they next met. . . .)

"You and I ought to call ourselves the agriculturists," said Wilde.

"Why?" asked Cottsford Dick.

"Because while I *mot*, you reap."

—*Ibid.*

Pater's Lecture

Once he (i.e. Pater) lectured to a select company at the Literary Institute in Albemarle Street, and when the audience were retreating, he whispered, turning to Wilde—

"I hope you heard me, Mr. Wilde?"

"We overheard you."

"Really, Mr. Wilde! You have a phrase for everything."

—Thomas Wright, *The Life of Walter Pater*, 2 vols. (New York: G.P. Putnam's Sons, 1907).

The French Bonnet

He said that he once saw in a French journal under a drawing of a bonnet the words: "With this style the mouth is worn slightly open."

—*Ibid.*

Children

He was one of the first to advocate the making of not only homes but also schools beautiful, so beautiful that the punishment for undutiful children should be that they should be debarred from going to school the following day. He wanted to see children allowed to use their hands more, and said: "Give a child something to make, and he will be perfectly happy."

—*Ibid.*

Wilde's Talk

How like was his talk to the play of a sunlit fountain! It rose in the air constantly changing its shape, but always with the hues of the rainbow on it, and almost before you could realize the outline of this jet or of that, it had vanished and another sparkled where it had been, so that you could hardly remember even the moment afterwards, what exactly it was that had enchanted you. Like all talk, it is completely unreproducible, for gesture and voice had no small part in it, and, essentially so, his own glee in what he said.

—E.F. Benson, *As We Were, a Victorian Peep Show* (New York: Longmans, Green and Co., 1930).

Mr. Wilde's Athletics

. . . he would find himself at some week-end house party of athletic tendencies, and agreeable occupations for Sunday afternoon were being discussed at lunch. Everybody wanted to be out of doors, and to play some game. There was golf, there was tennis, there were boats on the river for those who could row, and water in the river for those who could swim. When asked what he would like to do, he sighed:

"I am afraid I play no outdoor games at all, except dominoes," he said; "I have sometimes played dominoes outside French cafés."

—*Ibid.*

Mr. Wilde and the Atlantic Ocean

"I am not exactly pleased with the Atlantic, it is not
so majestic as I expected."

—Holbrook Jackson, *The Eighteen
Nineties* (London: Grant Richards, 1913).

Mr. Wilde and Niagara Falls

"I was disappointed with Niagara. Most people must
be disappointed with Niagara. Every American bride
is taken there, and the sight of the stupendous water-
fall must be one of the earliest if not the keenest dis-
appointments in American married life."

—*Ibid.*

Mr. Wilde and Mr. Whistler

"I wish I had said that," he remarked once, approving
of one of Whistler's witticisms.
"You will, Oscar; you will."

—*Ibid.*

Mr. Whistler Again

"Oscar has the courage of the opinions . . . of
others."

—*Ibid.*

Mr. Wilde's Dominion

"The man who can dominate a London dinner-table can dominate the world."

—*Ibid.*

Principles

"It is personalities, not principles, that move the age."

—*Ibid.*

Oscar in San Francisco

"Is not this something new to you, Mr. Wilde? I suppose you have never before met a lady reporter?"

"No," he replied smilingly, "I have not; we don't have them in our country."

Glancing round the room a pile of newspapers attracted my notice, and naturally suggested the next question. "Are you pleased at the newspaper reports of yourself, and the reporters' interviews?" Evidently this had struck a rich vein, for he looked up with·a peculiar and hearty smile; but, evidently remembering that his questioner was of the same genus as the subject spoken about, he seemed to restrain himself, but replied, with a laugh: "Frankly, then, I read them all; and not only here but all over America, I have been quite amused at the struggle each of the gentlemen has had to write what I did not say; but I have the utmost sympathy with the writers of the articles which strive to be what is called here in the United States 'funny,' their hard work has been so apparent."

From this on the conversation was quite easy, and Mr. Wilde displayed a fund of shrewd common sense hardly to be expected from an art-enthusiast and a poet.

—Mary Watson, *People I Have Met* (San Francisco: Francis, Valentine & Co., Printers, 1890).

In New York

It was at Delmonico's, shortly after he told our local Customs that he had nothing to declare but genius, that I first met him. He was dressed like a mountebank. Without, at the entrance, a crowd had collected. In the restaurant people stood up and stared. Wilde was beautifully unmoved. He was talking, at first about nothing whatever, which is always an interesting topic, then about *Vera*, a play of his for which a local manager had offered him an advance, five thousand dollars I think, "mere starvation wages," as he put it, and he went on to say that the manager wanted him to make certain changes in it. He paused and added: "But who am I to tamper with a masterpiece?"—a jest which afterwards he was too generous to hoard.

—Edgar Saltus, *Oscar Wilde* (Chicago: Brothers of the Book, 1917).

Tight Money

Someone else entered and Hope asked what was new in the City. "Money is very tight," came the reply. "Ah, yes," Wilde cut in. "And of a tightness that has been felt even in Tite Street. Believe me, I passed the forenoon at the British Museum looking at a gold piece in a case."

—*Ibid.*

The Beggar

Afterwards we drove to Chelsea. It was a vile night, bleak and bitter. On alighting, a man came up to me. He wore a short jacket which he opened. From neck to waist he was bare. I gave him a shilling. Then came the rebuke. With entire simplicity Wilde took off his overcoat and put it about the man.

But the simplicity seemed to me too Hugoesque and I said: "Why didn't you ask him in to dinner?"

Wilde gestured. "Dinner is not a feast, it is a ceremony."

—*Ibid.*

Simple Tastes

I put a bold face on it. "Come to my shop," I said, "and have dinner with me. Though," I added, "I don't know what I can give you."

"Oh, anything," Wilde replied. "Anything, no matter what. I have the simplest tastes. I am always satisfied with the best."

—*Ibid.*

Wilde's Influence

The man who was afterwards branded as a corrupter of youth exerted on me, as a young man, an influence altogether beneficial. If he had taught me nothing but the great value and happiness of life, I should still owe him an unpayable debt, for my disposition tended to that *taedium vitae* which makes existence pure misery. . . .

The example of his purity of life in such a city as Paris, of his absolute decency of language, of his conversation, in which never an improper suggestion intruded, the loftier ideals that he pursued, the elegance and refinement which endowed him, would have compelled even the most perverse and dissolute to some restraint. The companionship of Oscar Wilde, in the days in which I lived in his intimacy, would have made a gentleman, at least outwardly, of a man of bad morals and unclean tongue.

—Robert Harborough Sherard, *Oscar Wilde* (London: The Hermes Press, 1902, privately printed).

Paris in 1891

During the same year we frequently met in Paris, where he had now begun to be counted, and seriously, amongst European celebrities. In December he was much fêted in the best houses, and leading *littérateurs* and artists crowded to his hotel. The Princess of Monaco, sending him her portrait at that time, wrote upon it: *"Au vrai Art—à Oscar Wilde."*

—*Ibid.*

London in 1894

It was at Christmas that I met him last, before the catastrophe of 1895, and my impression was altogether a painful one. He was not the friend I had known and admired for so many years. I dined with him at Tite Street: for once there was no pleasure, but distress rather, in the occasion. He looked bloated. His face seemed to have lost its spiritual beauty, and was oozing with material prosperity. And his conversation also was not agreeable. I concluded that too much good living and too great success had momentarily affected him both morally and physically.

—*Ibid.*

Between Trials

On leaving the prison after his bail had been accepted, he had driven to an hotel. It was late in the evening. Two rooms were engaged for him and dinner was ordered. Just as he sat down to table, the manager roughly entered the room and said, "You are Oscar Wilde, I believe." Then he added, "You must leave the house at once."

From this hotel he drove to another in a distant part of London, where he was not known or recognized. He had sunk down exhausted on the bed of the room he had engaged when the landlord appeared. He had been followed from his last refuge by a band of men, prize-fighters, and had been denounced in the hall below. The landlord expressed regret, but insisted on his leaving. "The men say they will sack the house and raise the street if you stay here a moment longer."

At last, long past midnight, Willy Wilde, in his mother's house in Oakley Street, heard a feeble rap at the front door. Opening it, he saw his brother, who, white as death, reeled forward into the passage. "Give me shelter, Willy," he cried. "Let me lie on the floor, or I shall die in the streets."

—*Ibid.*

Before the Verdict

I had thought that I should never see him again. But as that dreadful Saturday dragged on, the impulse grew stronger and stronger within me to go to him, so as to be with him at the end. In the afternoon then, meeting Ernest Dowson, I asked him to accompany me to the Old Bailey. We drove there, and as we alighted in front of the court-house, a shout arose from the rabble that thronged the street, "Here are some more aristocrats! Here are some more of them!"

I said to Dowson, as we passed through the doorway which leads into the little yard between the court-house and Newgate, "That shout explains that much of the popular execration of our friend proceeds from class hatred. He represents the aristocrat, poor fellow, to them, and they are exulting in the downfall of an aristocrat."

—*Ibid.*

After the Verdict

Warders touched my poor friend on the shoulder. He shuddered and gave one wild look round the Court. Then he turned and lumbered forward to the head of the stairs which led to the bottomless pit. He was swept down and disappeared.

As I staggered down the steps to leave the court-house, I dimly heard the cries of exultation which those crowding down with me were uttering. But this fiendish joy in the ruin of a life was to be impressed upon me still more vividly. For when the verdict and the sentence on "the aristocrat" reached the rabble in Old Bailey, men and women joined hands and danced an ungainly farandole, flung up the London mud in *feu de joie*, and the hideous faces were distorted with savage triumph. . . .

That evening I went to see (Alphonse) Daudet. He said, "This is a fine country. I admire a country where justice is administered as it is here, as is shown by today's verdict and sentence."

—*Ibid.*

A Prison Experience

He was fond of relating an incident of a dramatic nature connected with his stay in Reading. One day, whilst tramping his round in the prison-yard at exercise, he heard the man behind him say, "A strange place in which to meet Lord Henry." He turned round at the first opportunity and recognized in the speaker, an old tramp, to whom a year or two previously, during a country walk, he had given a half-crown. It was not explained how the old beggar had acquired his knowledge of *The Picture of Dorian Gray*.

—*Ibid.*

A Luncheon

His wife was quite unsympathetic towards him. This will give you an idea of her. Oscar was always the essence of charm and good nature, and would never do anything to disappoint her. One day, when I was with them at Tite Street, she asked him if he would come in for lunch on the following day, as some old Dublin friends (a clergyman among them) were coming to see her and very much wanted to meet him.

Oscar, to whom this sort of thing was the reverse of attractive, said: "All right, my dear, if Bobbie can come as well." Of course she asked me, though I knew she didn't want to, and it was then and there arranged. We found his wife's friends the typical provincial sort, full of their own local news and nothing much else. Oscar talked during lunch as I never heard him talk before— divinely. Had the company included the Queen and all the Royal Family, he couldn't have surpassed himself. Humour, tale, epigram, flowed from his lips, and his listeners sat spellbound under the influence. Suddenly in the midst of one of his most entrancing stories—his audience with wide eyes and parted mouths, their food untasted—his wife broke in: "Oh, Oscar, *did* you re-member to call for Cyril's boots?"

> —Robert Ross, in Hesketh Pearson, *Modern Men and Mummers* (New York: Harcourt, Brace & Co., 1922; London: Allen & Unwin, 1921).

Mr. and Mrs. Oscar Wilde

Mrs. Wilde was a pretty young woman of the inno-cent Kate Greenaway type. They seemed very happy together, though it was impossible not to predict suffering for a woman so simple and domestic mated with a mind so searching and so perverse and a character so self-indulgent. It was hard to see where two such different natures could find a meeting place, particularly as poor Mrs. Wilde was entirely devoid of humour and evangelically religious. So sweet and pretty and good, how came she by her outrageously intellectual husband, to whose destructive wit little was sacred and all things comedy? When one thinks that Mrs. Wilde's chief interest after her children was —missionaries, and her bosom friend that Lady Sandhurst who was one of the pillars of British church work. . . !

"Missionaries, my dear!" I remember Wilde once saying at a dinner party, "Don't you realize that missionaries are the divinely provided food for destitute and underfed cannibals? Whenever they are on the brink of starvation, Heaven, in its infinite mercy, sends them a nice plump missionary."

To which Mrs. Wilde could only pathetically exclaim: "Oh, Oscar! you cannot surely be in earnest. You can only be joking."

—Richard Le Gallienne, *The Romantic Nineties*
(New York: Doubleday, Page and Co., 1925).

Oscar and the Tax-Gatherer

One day, as he stood outside his Tite Street door, preparing to insert his latchkey, a little humble man came up, saying that he had called about the taxes.

"Taxes!" said Wilde, looking down at him from his lordly height. "Why should I pay taxes?"

"But sir," said the little man, "you are the householder, are you not? . . . You live here—you sleep here?"

"Ah, yes!" said Wilde, with utter solemnity, "but then, you see—I sleep so badly."

—*Ibid.*

Oscar and the Beggar

On another occasion, as he walked in the Haymarket, a beggar came up and asked for alms. He had, he said, no work to do and no bread to eat.

"Work!" said Wilde. "Why should you want to work? And bread? Why should you eat bread?"

Then, after an elaborate pause, he continued, putting his hand good-naturedly on the tatterdemalion's shoulder:

"Now, if you had come to me and said that you had work to do, but you couldn't dream of working, and that you had bread to eat, but couldn't think of eating bread—I would have given you half-a-crown."—Another pause—"As it is, I give you two shillings."

—*Ibid.*

Death of Mr. Wilde's Publisher

His *Intentions* were published in London by Osgood, McIlvaine & Co., a new firm who made a point in all their advertisements of the fact that all their books were "published simultaneously in London and New York." That was their "slogan," as the advertising men put it. Well, one morning I happened to meet Wilde in Piccadilly. After our first greetings, he assumed an air of deep grief: "Did you see in the papers, this morning," he said, "that Osgood is dead?" He paused for a moment, his manner deepening in solemnity, and continued: "Poor Osgood! He is a great loss to us! However," he added, as with consolatory cheerfulness, "I suppose they will bury him simultaneously in London and New York!"

—*Ibid.*

Mr. Tree's Hamlet

Of course, Wilde was there, and went behind to see Tree, who, all excitement, perspiration, and grease paint, eagerly asked, "Well, Oscar, what do you think of my Hamlet?" Wilde assumed his gravest, most pontifical air, and, spacing out his words with long pauses of even more than his usual deliberation, as though he was almost too impressed to speak at all, he said: "My dear Tree—I think—your Hamlet . . . your—Hamlet—my dear Tree . . . I think—your Hamlet." —Tree, meanwhile, hanging expectant on each slow-dropping word, nervous and keyed up as most actors are on a first night, anxiously filling the pauses with "Yes, yes, my dear Oscar . . ." while Wilde continued to keep him on tenterhooks with further preliminary ejaculations of "My dear Tree" and "I think your Hamlet." At last, when he could hold the suspended compliment no longer, Wilde ended with: "My dear Tree—I—think—your Hamlet . . . is . . . funny . . . without—being vulgar."

—*Ibid.*

Richard—or Oscar?

". . . Our friend Richard is very beautiful, isn't he? Wasn't it you who told me that Swinburne described him to you as 'Shelley with a chin'? I don't agree. Swinburne might just as well have described himself as 'Shelley without a chin.' No, it is the Angel Gabriel in Rossetti's National Gallery painting of the Annunciation of which Richard reminds me. The hair, worn long and fanning out into a wonderful halo around the head, always reminds me of Rossetti's angel. However, my story is that an American woman, in that terribly crude way that Americans have, asked Richard, 'Why do you wear your hair so long, Mr. Le Gallienne?' Richard is sometimes brilliant as well as always beautiful, but

on this occasion he could think of nothing less banal
and foolish to say than 'Perhaps, dear lady, for advertisement.' 'But you, Mr. Le Gallienne, you who
have such genius!' Richard blushed and bowed and
smiled until the lady added cruelly—'for advertisement!'"

Wilde was quite right in saying I had heard the
story before. It had been told me as happening to himself in America. . . .

—Coulson Kernahan, *In Good Company*
(London: John Lane, 1917).

Wilde's Talk

I had heard him talked about at Stéphane Mallarmé's
house, where he was described as a brilliant conversationalist, and I expressed a wish to know him, little
hoping that I should ever do so. A happy chance, or
rather a friend, gave me the opportunity, and to him
I made known my desire. Wilde was invited to dinner.
It was at a restaurant. We were a party of four, but
three of us were content to listen. Wilde did not converse—he told tales. During the whole meal he hardly
stopped. He spoke in a slow, musical tone, and his very
voice was wonderful. He knew French almost perfectly, but pretended, now and then, to hesitate a little
for a word to which he wanted to call our attention.
He had scarcely any accent, at least only when it
pleased him to affect when it might give a somewhat
new or strange appearance to a word—for instance, he
used purposely to pronounce *scepticisme* as skepticism.

—André Gide, *Oscar Wilde, a Study*, translated
by Stuart Mason (Christopher Sclater Milland) (Oxford: The Holywell Press, 1905).

The Two Worlds

. . . as soon as we were alone again he would begin,
"Well, what have you been doing since yesterday?"
Now, as at that time my life was passing uneventfully
enough, the telling of what I had been doing was of no
interest. So, to humour him, I began recounting some
trifling incidents, and noticed while I was speaking that
Wilde's face was growing gloomy.

"You really did that?" he said.

"Yes," I answered.

"And you are speaking the truth?"

"Yes."

"Then why repeat it? You must see that it is not of
the slightest importance. You must understand that
there are two worlds—the one exists and is never talked
about; it is called the real world because there is no
need to talk about it in order to see it. The other is the
world of Art; one must talk about that, because otherwise it would not exist."

—*Ibid.*

Inviting Tragedy

Wilde's lyrical adoration was fast becoming a
frenzied madness. A fatality led him on; he could not
and would not withdraw himself from it. He seemed to
devote all his zeal and all his worth to over-rating his
destiny, and over-reaching himself. "*My* special duty,"
he used to say, "is to plunge madly into amusement."
He used to make a point of searching for pleasure as
one faces an appointed duty. Nietzsche surprised me

less, on a later occasion, because I had heard Wilde say, "No, not happiness! Certainly not happiness! Pleasure. One must always set one's heart upon the most tragic."

—*Ibid.*

The Great Drama

"Would you like to know the great drama of my life? It is that I have put my genius into my life—I have put only my talent into my works."

—*Ibid.*

At Berneval

"Here everyone is most good to me—the Curé especially. I am so fond of the little church, and would you believe it, it is called Notre Dame de Liesse. Now, is that not charming? And now I know that I can never leave Berneval, because only this morning the Curé offered me a perpetual seat in the choir-stalls.

"And the Custom-house men, poor fellows, are so bored here with nothing to do, that I asked them if they had not anything to read, and now I am giving them all the elder Dumas' novels. So I must stay here, you see. And the children, oh, the children, they adore me. On the day of the Queen's Jubilee I gave a grand fête and a big dinner, when I had forty children from the school, all of them, and the schoolmaster, to celebrate it. Is not that absolutely charming? You know that I admire the Queen very much. I always have her portrait with me."

—*Ibid.*

Books in Prison

"I thought, at first, that what would please me most would be Greek literature, so I asked for Sophocles, but I could not get a relish for it. Then I thought of the Fathers of the Church, but I found them equally uninteresting. And suddenly I thought of Dante. Oh! Dante. I read Dante every day, in Italian, and all through, but neither the *Purgatorio* nor the *Paradiso* seemed written for me. It was his *Inferno* above all that I read; how could I help liking it? Cannot you guess? Hell, we were in it—Hell, that was prison!"

—*Ibid.*

Pity

I went into prison with a heart of stone, thinking only of my own pleasure, but now my heart is utterly broken—pity has entered into my heart. I have learned now that pity is the greatest and most beautiful thing in the world. And that is why I cannot bear ill-will towards those who caused my suffering and those who condemned me; no, nor to anyone, because without them I should not have known all that. Douglas writes me terrible letters. He says he does not understand me, that he does not understand that I do not wish everyone ill, and that everyone has been horrid to me. No, he does not understand me any more. But I keep on telling him that in every letter: we cannot follow the same road. He has his, and it is beautiful—I have mine. His is that of Alcibiades; mine is now that of St. Francis of Assisi.

—*Ibid.*

Fame

A friend of mine is the son of a clergyman, and, chancing one day to take home some books of Wilde's, left them lying on the table. His father saw them and thus concluded the inevitable lecture which followed: "That, my son, is a name which not even the *angels* can pronounce without a blush."

—K.F. Callaghan, "The Literature of Oscar Wilde," *The Caian, The Magazine of Gonville and Caius College,* Lent Term, 1911, printed at the University Press for subscribers only.

Inexperience

If you were wise you would learn life only by inexperience. That is what makes it always unexpected and delightful. Never to realize—that is the true ideal.

—Laurence Housman, *Echo de Paris* (New York: D. Appleton and Co., 1924).

America

When I was in America, I did not dare to tell America the truth; but I saw it clearly even then—that the discovery of America was the beginning of the death of Art. But not yet; no, not yet! Whistler left America in order to remain an artist, and Mr. Sargent to become one, I believe. . . .

—*Ibid.*

Scots

A Scotsman? That explains everything. For a man
to be both a genius and a Scotsman is the very stage for
tragedy. . . .

. . . your Scotsman believes only in success. How can
a man, who regards success as the goal of life, be a
true artist? God saved the genius of Robert Burns to
poetry by driving him through drink to failure. . . .

To fail and to die young is the only hope for a
Scotsman who wishes to remain an artist. . . .

Because Carlyle was a Scotsman, he would not take
for his hero the man whose life ended in failure: he
could not bring himself to face the débâcle of Waterloo,
the enduring ignominy and defeat of St. Helena.

—*Ibid.*

Between the Trials

He seemed so unhappy with his family at this time
that we asked him to stay with us, feeling that he
would be more at ease with friends than with relatives.
Before he came, we called together all the servants,
parlour-maid, housemaid, cook, kitchen-maid and our
old nurse, Mrs. Field, who acted as my maid. We told
them what was coming, offering them a month's wages
if they wished to leave at once. For the affair was now
such a scandal as had rarely been known. Little else
was talked of in London; the papers were full of it;
America, Germany, all the Continent joined in the con-
troversy, the foreigners saying, "This is how you behave to your poets," while the Americans said, "This

is how your poets behave." Each servant in turn refused to leave. They appeared proud to wait on "poor
Mr. Wilde," to whom indeed they had been devoted
ever since he had started coming to the house. We sent
the coachman away for a holiday, as we feared he
might talk in public-houses. The others promised to
keep the secret.

Then I went to fetch Oscar. He accepted with joy.
And he came back with me in the little pill-box
brougham. When we arrived I showed him his rooms,
the nursery floor, which was almost a flat in itself, two
big rooms, one small one, and a bathroom. My little
boy was in the country at the time.

I asked him if he would like me to take away the
toys in the room. "Please leave them," he said. So, in
the presence of a rocking-horse, golliwogs, a blue and
white nursery dado with rabbits and other animals on
it, the most serious and tragic matters were discussed.
The poet leant his elbow on the American cloth of the
nursery table, and talked over the coming trial with his
solicitor.

While all our friends as well as the whole public
were discussing Oscar, no one had any idea that he was
under our roof.

He made certain rules in order to avoid any em-
barrassment for us. He never left the nursery floor till
six o'clock. He had breakfast, luncheon, and tea up
there, and received all his loyal friends there. He never
would discuss his troubles before me; such exaggerated
delicacy seems today almost incredible. But every day
at six he would come down dressed for dinner, and talk
to me for a couple of hours in the drawing-room. As
always he was most carefully dressed, there was a
flower in his button-hole, and he had received his

usual daily visit from the old hairdresser who shaved
him and waved his hair. His ambition was always to
look like a Roman bust.

—Ada Leverson, *Letters to the Sphinx from
Oscar Wilde, with Some Reminiscences of the
Author* (London: Duckworth, 1930).

Anne of Cleves

I have told you, a chance turn in talk might evoke
some flight of fancy. The mention of Elizabeth has
brought one back to my memory, for he was fascinated
by the days of the Tudors. Someone was speaking of
the beauty of Holbein's portrait of Anne of Cleves,
whose ugliness had overwhelmed Henry VIII. "You
believe she was really ugly?" he (Wilde) questioned.
"No, my dear boy, she was exquisite as we see her in
the Louvre; but in the escort, sent to bring her to
England, travelled also a beautiful young nobleman
of whom she became passionately enamoured and, on
the ship, they became lovers . . . what could be
done? Discovery meant death. So she stained her
face, and put uncouth clothes upon her body, till she
seemed the monster Henry thought her. Years passed,
and one day, when the king went hawking, he heard a
woman singing in an orchard close, and, rising in his
stirrups to see who, with lovely voice, had entranced
him, he beheld Anne of Cleves, young and beautiful,
singing in the arms of her lover."

—Jean Paul Raymond* and Charles Ricketts, *Oscar Wilde
Recollections* (Bloomsbury: The Nonesuch Press, 1932).

---

* [Jean Paul Raymond is a pseudonym used by Ricketts. Ed.]

The Prison Chaplain

When in Reading Gaol he told me that the warders
in the dock had been gentle and kind, but the visit
of the chaplain in his first prison began with these
words:

"Mr. Wilde, did you have morning prayers in your
house?"

"I am sorry . . . I fear not."

"You see where you are now!"

—Ibid.

Kindliness

I remember Oscar once saying of a famous actress
who, after a life of tragic experience, had married a
fool: "She thought that, because he was stupid, he
would be kindly when, of course, kindliness requires
imagination and intellect."

—Ibid.

Wilde's Manner

Kindliness and the desire to please gave charm to
his face, which had aged prematurely, and graciousness
to a certain ceremoniousness in address, which may
possibly have reflected the elaborate courtesy of Ruskin,
or shall we say Disraeli, whose manner, I have been
told by elderly contemporaries, showed a great resemblance to that of Wilde. Disraeli, you will realize, continued the Brummel tradition which belonged to the
eighteenth century. Kindliness and an irrepressible in-

ward gaiety discounted those calculated affectations
which many mistook for arrogance and vanity. An irrepressible peal of laughter would preface an exaggerated aphorism, and a wave of the hand discount
the literal significance of some sallies which seemed
forced or stilted when repeated or printed.

—*Ibid.*

"Walk down Piccadilly, with a poppy or a lily"

This trivial incident he once told me may be at the
root of "Walking down the Strand with a lily in his
hand." Wilde had gone to Covent Garden to purchase
some Jersey lilies to give to Mrs. Langtry and was waiting for a hansom when a street arab, fascinated by the
orange flowers, exclaimed, "How rich you are!"

Jimmy Whistler

"Ah, Whistler! Yes, wonderful, of course, but, how
he fears beauty! He puts a blot, a mere stain like a
petal, a butterfly upon a sheet of paper and dares not
touch it, lest its charm be lost. His portraits remind
me of the painter in Balzac's *Chef-d'oeuvre inconnu*,
labouring his canvas for years and when he draws the
curtain to show the masterpiece, lo, there is nothing."
Wilde paused and smiled. "Then Jimmy explains things
in the newspapers. Art should always remain mysterious. Artists, like Gods, must never leave their
pedestals."

—*Ibid.*

Privacy

(From an interview in Reading Gaol.)

He exclaimed laughingly, "Both my dear friends would wish me to retire to a monastery . . . why not La Trappe? . . . or worse still, to some dim country place in England: I believe it was Twyford. They speak of Venice later with its silence and dead waterways. No, I have had enough silence!"

"But, Oscar," I murmured, "is not Venice, with its beauty and stillness, the very place for work and privacy? There you could see your friends if. . . ."

"No!" he exclaimed. "Privacy! work! my dear Ricketts. I wish to look at life, not to become a monument for tourists! The French have produced *Salomé* during my stay here and it was reviewed in the English press. France understands the value of an artist for what he is, not for what he may have done. Privacy! I have had two years of it . . . save for that other self —the man I once was. . . ."

—*Ibid.*

Purple Patches

Modern English criticism holds up to ridicule the "purple patches" in his prose, incidentally the phrase "purple patches" was his invention. Even today his popularity here is half-hearted, his countrymen never having forgiven him the cruelty of his sentence and tragic death.

—*Ibid.*

At the End

In the last days of his illness he smiled, saying to Ross, his devoted friend, "When the last trumpet sounds and we are couched in our porphyry tombs, I will turn and say 'Robbie, Robbie, let us pretend we do not hear!'" Or again, but the comedy of this is tragic, "I fear I am dying as I have lived, beyond my means!"

—Ibid.

Oscar and the Literary Warder

Later he spoke of his prison experiences, of the horrors of the first few months, and how by degrees he became reconciled to his situation. He seemed to have lost none of his old wit and gaiety. He told how, although talking was strictly forbidden, one of his warders would exchange a remark with him now and then. He had a great respect for Oscar as a literary man, and he did not intend to miss such a chance of improving himself. He could only get in a few words at a time.

"Excuse me, sir; but Charles Dickens, sir, would he be considered a great writer now, sir?" To which Oscar replied: "Oh yes; a great writer, indeed; you see he is no longer alive." "Yes, I understand, sir. Being dead he would be a great writer, sir."

Another time he asked about John Strange Winter. "Would you tell me what you think of him, sir?" "A charming person," says Oscar, "but a lady, you know, not a man. Not a great stylist, perhaps, but a good, simple story-teller." "Thank you, sir, I did not know he was a lady, sir."

And a third time: "Excuse me, sir, but Marie

Corelli, would she be considered a great writer, sir?"

"This was more than I could bear," continued Oscar, "and putting my hand on his shoulder I said: 'Now don't think I've anything against her *moral* character, but from the way she writes she *ought to be here.*'" "You say so, sir, you say so," said the warden, surprised, but respectful.

—William Rothenstein, *Men and Memories*
(New York: Coward-McCann, Inc., 1931;
London: Faber & Faber, 1931), Vol. I.

Life Imitating Art

"When I was a boy my two favourite characters were Lucien de Rubempré and Julien Sorel. Lucien hanged himself, Julien died on the scaffold, and I died in prison."

—Vincent O'Sullivan, *Aspects of Wilde*
(New York: Henry Holt & Co., 1936).

The World's Attitude to Wilde

The most ignorant and brutal attacks on Wilde came from America. The French, among whom he chose to live out his final years, dealt with him according to their temperament, just as the English did. They allowed him to live as he liked, but they tolerated his presence rather than welcomed it. They did absolutely nothing to make his burden easier. His presence was often resented in public places. Some places he was insolently forbidden to enter. I heard that Catulle Mendés, finding Wilde at some huge banquet of a hundred or more, made a great fuss, squalled that he was insulted, and left the room. Now and then a poisonous little paragraph about Wilde would appear in the French papers.

—*Ibid.*

Why Nero Persecuted Christians

"You know, Nero was obliged to do something. They were making him ridiculous. What he thought was: 'Here everything was going on very well, when one day two incredible creatures arrived from somewhere in the provinces. They are called Peter and Paul, or some unheard-of names like that. Since they are here, life in Rome has become impossible. They collect crowds and block the traffic with their miracles. It is really intolerable. I, the Emperor, have no peace. When I get up in the morning and look out of the window, the first thing I see is a miracle going on in the back garden.'"

—*Ibid.*

France and England

"I was thinking in bed this morning that the great superiority of France over England is that in France every bourgeois wants to be an artist, whereas in England every artist wants to be a bourgeois."

—*Ibid.*

Max Beerbohm

"The gods bestowed on Max the gift of perpetual old age."

—*Ibid.*

SAYINGS

FROM A Woman of No Importance

Children begin by loving their parents; after a time they judge them; rarely, if ever, do they forgive them.

*

The youth of America is their oldest tradition. It has been going on now for three hundred years. To hear them talk one would imagine they were in their first childhood. As far as civilization goes they are in their second.

*

The English country gentleman galloping after a fox—the unspeakable in full pursuit of the uneatable.

*

A bad man is the sort of man who admires innocence.

*

Women as a sex are Sphinxes without secrets.

After a good dinner one could forgive anybody, even one's own relations.

*

Simple pleasures are the last refuge of the complex.

*

Duty is what one expects from others—it is not what one does oneself.

*

Memory in a woman is the beginning of dowdiness.

*

When a man says he has exhausted life one always knows life has exhausted him.

*

Women have a much better time than men in this world; there are far more things forbidden them.

*

Life is a *mauvais quart d'heure* made up of exquisite moments.

FROM *An Ideal Husband*

Nothing is so dangerous as being too modern; one is apt to grow old-fashioned quite suddenly.

*

Philanthropy is the refuge of people who wish to annoy their fellow-creatures.

*

There is only one real tragedy in a woman's life. The fact that her past is always her lover, and her future invariably her husband.

*

In modern life nothing produces such an effect as a good platitude. It makes the whole world kin.

*

The only thing to do with good advice is to pass it on.

*

To love oneself is the beginning of a lifelong romance.

Being educated puts one almost on a level with the commercial classes.

FROM *Lady Windermere's Fan*

I can resist everything except temptation.

＊

Nowadays to be intelligible is to be found out.

＊

A cynic is a man who knows the price of everything, and the value of nothing.

＊

The world is packed with good women. To know them is a middle-class education.

＊

We are all in the gutter, but some of us are looking at the stars.

＊

Nothing looks so like innocence as an indiscretion.

＊

Nature's gentlemen are the worst type of gentlemen.

FROM *The Soul of Man under Socialism*

There are three kinds of despots. There is the despot who tyrannizes over the body. There is the despot who tyrannizes over the soul. There is the despot who tyrannizes over the soul and body alike. The first is called the Prince. The second is called the Pope. The third is called the People.

*

Selfishness is not living as one wishes to live. It is asking other people to live as one wishes to live.

*

In America the President reigns for four years, and Journalism governs for ever and ever.

*

One who is an emperor or king may stoop down and pick up a brush for a painter, but when the democracy stoops down it is merely to throw mud.

*

There is only one class in the community that thinks more about money than the rich, and that is the poor. The poor can think of nothing else. That is the misery of being poor.

As for begging, it is safer to beg than to take, but it is finer to take than to beg.

*

Art should never try to be popular. The public should try to make itself artistic.

ACKNOWLEDGMENTS

I wish to thank my friend, Larry Powell, for his kindness in opening the William Andrews Clark Memorial Library of the University of California to my investigations. I am indebted to Mr. Archer and the other members of the staff for their help in finding the books and MSS. I wanted.

Thanks are due to Mr. Vyvyan Holland, the Administrator of the Estate of Oscar Wilde, for giving his consent to include the twelve hitherto unpublished Wilde letters and others previously published and also to Dr. Powell and the Clark Memorial Library for making them available.

Acknowledgment is due to the following who have kindly granted permission to use excerpts from the books listed:

Harcourt, Brace and Company, Inc., New York, and George Allen & Unwin, London: *Modern Men and Mummers* by Hesketh Pearson.

Doubleday, Doran & Company, Inc., New York: *The Romantic Nineties* by Richard Le Gallienne. Copyright 1925 by Doubleday, Doran & Company, Inc.

The Holywell Press, Oxford: *Oscar Wilde, A Study* by André Gide.

Richard Steele & Son, London: *Echo de Paris* by Laurence Housman.

The Nonesuch Press, London and New York: *Oscar Wilde Recollections* by Jean Paul Raymond and Charles Ricketts.

Coward-McCann, Inc., New York, and Faber and Faber, London: *Men and Memories*, Vol. I, by William Rothenstein.

Francis-Valentine Co., San Francisco: *People I Have Met* by Mary Watson.

Henry Holt and Company, New York, and Constable and Company, London: *Aspects of Wilde* by Vincent O'Sullivan.

John Rothenstein and Faber and Faber, London: *Sixteen Letters from Oscar Wilde* edited by John Rothenstein.

T. Werner Laurie, Ltd., London: *Oscar Wilde: Some Reminiscences* by Leonard Cresswell Ingleby.

G. P. Putnam's Sons, New York: *The Life of Walter Pater* by Thomas Wright.

Longmans, Green and Co., New York: *As We Were: A Victorian Peep Show* by E. F. Benson.

Jonathan Cape, Ltd., London: *The Eighteen Nineties* by Holbrook Jackson.

John Lane, The Bodley Head Ltd., London: *In Good Company* by Coulson Kernahan.

Special acknowledgment is made to Mr. Vyvyan Holland, holder of the copyright in *De Profundis,* and to G. P. Putnam's Sons, New York, for permission to include that work.

POETS OF THE ENGLISH LANGUAGE
Edited by W.H. Auden and Norman Holmes Pearson.
MEDIEVAL AND RENAISSANCE POETS.   015.490 8
ELIZABETHAN AND JACOBEAN POETS.   015.050 1
RESTORATION AND AUGUSTAN POETS.   015.051 X
ROMANTIC POETS.   015.052 8
VICTORIAN AND EDWARDIAN POETS.   015.053 6

HENRY JAMES
Edited by Morton Dauwen Zabel. Revised by Lyall H. Powers.
015.055 2

ROMAN READER
Edited by Basil Davenport.   015.056 0

CERVANTES
Translated and edited by Samuel Putnam.   015.057 9

MELVILLE
Edited by Jay Leyda.   015.058 7

GIBBON
Edited by Dero A. Saunders.   015.060 9

RENAISSANCE READER
Edited by James Bruce Ross and Mary Martin McLaughlin.   015.061 7

THE GREEK HISTORIANS
Edited by M. I. Finley.   015.065 X

STEPHEN CRANE
Edited by Joseph Katz.   015.068 4

NORTH AMERICAN INDIAN READER
Edited by Frederick W. Turner III.   015.077 3

WALT WHITMAN
Edited by Mark Van Doren. Revised edition.   015.078 1

THOMAS JEFFERSON
Edited by Merrill D. Peterson.   015.080 3

CHAUCER
Edited and translated by Theodore Morrison. Revised edition.
015.081 1

MACHIAVELLI
Edited by Peter Bondanella and Mark Musa.   015.092 7

Oscar Wilde

SELECTED PLAYS
*(Salome, A Woman of No Importance,
An Ideal Husband,
The Importance of Being Earnest,
Lady Windermere's Fan)*

George Bernard Shaw

ANDROCLES AND THE LION

THE APPLE CART

THE DOCTOR'S DILEMMA

HEARTBREAK HOUSE

MAJOR BARBARA

MAN AND SUPERMAN

PLAYS UNPLEASANT
*(Widowers' Houses, The Philanderer,
Mrs Warren's Profession)*

PYGMALION

SAINT JOAN

SELECTED ONE-ACT PLAYS
*(The Shewing-up of Blanco Posnet,
How He Lied to Her Husband, O'Flaherty V.C.,
The Inca of Perusalem, Annajanska,
Village Wooing, The Dark Lady of the Sonnets,
Overruled, Great Catherine,
Augustus Does His Bit, The Six of Calais)*

Arthur Miller

THE CRUCIBLE

DEATH OF A SALESMAN

A VIEW FROM THE BRIDGE

Charles Dickens

GREAT EXPECTATIONS
Edited by Angus Calder

Great Expectations (first published in 1860–61) is one of the most mature and serious of Dickens's novels. As Angus Calder points out in his introduction, it resembles a detective story—but in the sense in which *Oedipus Rex* also resembles one. From the first shock of the early pages, when Pip encounters the convict Magwitch, the mystery grips our attention, and its psychological and moral truth holds up until the end. For, in discovering the secret of his "great expectations," Pip also begins to discover the truth about himself.

HARD TIMES
Edited by David Craig

Hard Times, which has never achieved the popularity and seldom the recognition of Dickens's other novels, is his withering portrait of a Lancashire mill-town in the 1840s. In the persons of Gradgrind and Bounderby he powerfully stigmatized the prevalent philosophy of Utilitarianism which, whether in school or factory, allowed human beings to be caged in a dreary scenery of brick terraces and foul chimneys, to be enslaved by machines, and reduced to numbers.

"It has a kind of perfection as a work of art that we don't associate with Dickens. . . .The prose is that of one of the greatest masters of English, and the dialogue—very much a test in such an undertaking—is consummate; beautifully natural in its stylization"—F. R. Leavis in *The Great Tradition.*

PENGUIN CLASSICS

The Penguin Classics, first and most varied series of world masterpieces in soft covers, began in 1946 with E. V. Rieu's now famous translation of *The Odyssey*. Since then, the series has maintained the unqualified respect of scholars and teachers throughout the English-speaking world. Today, it includes over three hundred volumes, and more are added each year. Its purpose is to render the great writings of all ages and civilizations into vivid, living English that captures both the spirit and the content of the original. Each volume begins with an introductory essay, and most contain notes, maps, glossaries, or other material to help the reader appreciate the work fully.

A sampling of Penguin Classics titles follows:

THE ORESTEIAN TRILOGY, Aeschylus
COUSIN BETTE, Honoré de Balzac
THE CANTERBURY TALES, Geoffrey Chaucer
THE BROTHERS KARAMAZOV (2 vols.),
Fyodor Dostoyevsky
MADAME BOVARY, Gustave Flaubert
DEAD SOULS, Nikolai Gogol
HEDDA GABLER AND OTHER PLAYS, Henrik Ibsen
THUS SPAKE ZARATHUSTRA, Friedrich Nietzsche
THE LAST DAYS OF SOCRATES, Plato
THE EPIC OF GILGAMESH
THE THEBAN PLAYS, Sophocles
SCARLET AND BLACK, Stendhal
ANNA KARENIN, Leo Tolstoy
FATHERS AND SONS, Ivan Turgenev
GERMINAL, Emile Zola